THE NEW MIND TRAVELERS

BOOK TWO

IN THE

SPACE EXPLORATION

FICTION SERIES

Published in Australia by
Optimistic Publishing
PO Box 1190, Kangaroo Flat Vic. 3555, Australia
phillipboas@netspace.net.au
www.phillboas.com.au

First published in Australia 2022

National Library of Australia Cataloguing in Publication entry

A catalogue record for this book is available from the National Library of Australia

ISBN: 978-0-6489420-3-0 (paperback)
ISBN: 978-0-6489420-4-7 (epub)

Cover layout and design by SusansArt
Book layout and design Sophie White

Printed by Ingram Spark

A Utopian Speculative Science Fiction Novel

THE NEW MIND TRAVELERS

BOOK TWO
IN THE SPACE
EXPLORATION
FICTION SERIES

Phill Boas

TO MY WIFE,
MADELEINE
AND DOG, KAYLA

PART 3

DEVELOPMENT OF THE NEW MIND TRAVELERS

Earth, Zed, the Human Telepaths

CHAPTER 1

Zed Returns Home

The gentle cool of the air conditioning greeted me as I entered my apartment building. I lived in an entirely new area of Greater Canberra, and being summer the cool of the building was a relief after the early-afternoon heat. I considered for a moment making a simultaneity jump into my apartment, but realized building security would probably have a seizure if I disappeared off its monitoring unit. So I stepped onto the elevator platform, murmured my apartment number and code, and in seconds I was smoothly transported to my door, which opened to my instruction, and I stepped inside, leaving the security system feeling calm.

It was only eight weeks to Christmas 2097, I had been away just over a year, and as I stood inside the front entrance, my mind reached for the memory of that first day around a year ago. I had been another person then. Still Zed Eko but in truth nothing in any substantial way like the Zed Eko standing here now. I had learned that I had abilities greater than my imagination could have given credence the last time I stood here. And I wondered what I would be like in another year.

The debrief with the crew had gone well, even better than I had expected, and Miyuki was now on board for a change in the debriefing process for all crews and wanted me to make that my first task on my return from what she had acknowledged was a well-deserved leave.

The decision had been made that the final meetings of the Global Assembly – 20 individuals representing interests from across the world, presently selecting the one area in which the world would seek Olarian assistance – would take place in four weeks' time. So far the process had taken six months, and the extent of dissent and disharmony had seriously disturbed everyone except a few members of the group.

Originally the Olarians had been scheduled to leave OlarCret in six weeks' time, and Miyuki had agreed to send a probe with the details of the request for assistance. However, since they had built the *Energystreamer* and brought her back with us that would no longer be necessary. The *Energystreamer*'s journey had been made possible because Tanzin had taken Olaria, Jald and his eldest son, Esan, now 320 years old, on several detailed simulations of the entire journey, and finally all were confident the three of them and Esan's brother could navigate the *Energystreamer* through the journey. This unlikely reality was possible because, without fully understanding the maths, calculus, physics and geometry involved, the Olarians were able to absorb and recall at very high speed the calculations and models Tanzin had used to create and manage the track between Earth and OlarCret. In order not to disrupt Tanzin's return, Esan and not Jald was on board, along with, as was common with the Olarians, three other men and four women.

So I was free to enjoy my six weeks' leave. I was, however, not certain how much of that time would be truly restful. I dumped my kit on the bedroom floor, stripped and took myself through my return ritual. I took all the clothes from my kit and dumped everything in the Total Cleaning System in my small but efficient laundry unit, thinking as I did so I could do the cleaning much more quickly and efficiently using the Olarian process. However, I switched the unit on and returned to my bedroom. I unpacked everything else, put the kitbag away and stepped into my shower where I luxuriated for nearly five minutes, confident that not a drop of water would be wasted or lost. After that, I dressed in comfortable civvies and sat down in my favorite lounge chair with a specially brewed coffee and allowed my holo unit to give me a fully filtered summary of the year's messages. There were fewer than a dozen actually requiring my attention.

The unit had summarized and prioritized them and, 20 minutes later, I was free. Now my time might have been my own except the fake holo address I had established for my meeting with Kiyoshi-san was claiming my attention. I knew it was likely Kiyoshi-san, the head of one of the largest and most powerful Yakuza enterprises in Japan, would be claiming his favor. I would be obliged to fulfill his request so long as it involved no activities of which I disapproved.

My offer to do him a favor had been incurred at the time Januti had a problem that required engagement. Januti Ito was the first of the seven other human telepaths I was to meet, 28 years old, and while she held two postgraduate degrees, she was presently managing an upmarket nightclub. On my first visit to her apartment I had an extraordinary and intense sense of connection to her, not unlike my experience with Olaria, but our meeting had ended with my imagining she might not be pleased to see me again. Kiyoshi-san had given me the help I requested when the situation had been just a little tricky.

It was early afternoon in Australia and in Japan. I decided now was probably a good time for me to honor my commitment. I sought out Januti and confirmed that she was well and safe in her apartment. I then sought out Kiyoshi-san in his Eyrie, and, without being visible, I sat in his visitor chair and spoke.

Kiyoshi-san, greetings. You cannot see me and I would appreciate your making no attempt to activate your security systems. This conversation is taking place telepathically and so my part of it is not being recorded by either your sound or visual recording devices. I would appreciate your simply thinking what you want me to know. That will ensure no record of our discussion will exist. Do you understand?

Kyoshi-san replied, remembering the extraordinary events that had taken place when he had first experienced me.

Yes.

He was thinking and not speaking, which simplified our engagement.

Okay, please explain your need for my assistance.

My great-granddaughter is five years old. A rival clan, presently attempting to negotiate a very valuable building contract, captured her and her mother 10 days ago. Their leader threatens to return them to me one finger at a time if, by close of business tomorrow, I do not agree to withdraw from this contract. Frankly, I don't care enough about this contract to even hesitate to withdraw, however, this man has no honor and absolutely is not trustworthy. He has reason to hate me and would, in all likelihood, savagely torture both my great-granddaughter and her mother, record it on a holo, and send it to me simply as an act of vengeance even if I agree to his terms. Normally I would be able to manage this on my own, however, I have too large a stake in the outcome and no room for error. So I most humbly request you to intercede on their behalf and release them and discourage this man from again threatening such disgusting behavior toward my family.

I studied Kiyoshi-san's thinking. It was true he would never permit such a barbaric act to be undertaken in his organization.

Kiyoshi-san, I need some indication of the likely location of either your great-granddaughter or her captor.

I immediately saw the picture in his mind of his enemy and probable location, and although the leader and Kiyoshi-san's family were not there, it was not a complicated process to locate them using the thoughts of the 'soldiers' at that location. I asked Kiyoshi-san to please wait while I left him briefly. Within moments I located the girl and her mother in a room with two goons standing guard. I shifted to be invisibly in the room and listened in to their thoughts, not a pleasant experience. I froze the goons. A single energy strand wrapped neatly around anything, encased with dark matter, acted as a kind of holding process for just about anything alive, and it did not hamper breathing. Then, holding the leader of this Yakuza syndicate immobile, I spoke to him.

I bring you a message from Kiyoshi-san.

The expression on his face was a delight: amazement, confusion then anger then rage at his growing awareness that he was immobilized, then fear. He tried to open his mouth to speak but could not. I decided to do this simply and directly.

Be silent! Make no attempt to speak. Listen with great care to what I am about to tell you. Remember it, for your existence and the existence of those close to you will in future depend upon it. This is the one and only message you will receive from Kiyoshi-san. I plan to remove the little girl and her mother in a moment and take them out of your reach. You will never, ever again make any move to capture or harm any member of Kiyoshi-san's family. Are you very clear about this instruction or do you need a demonstration of Kiyoshi-san's ability to carry out irreparable damage to you and your organization?

I watched as he processed the message. His plan was to make no move until he was free, and if the girl and her mother were taken from his grasp, he intended to kill several members of Kiyoshi-san's immediate family as soon as they were outside their protected compounds. I watched as he planned his revenge; it was horrible and repulsive. Not only did it turn my stomach, it marked him as a dangerous and viciously insensitive human being. So I made a decision.

It is clear you are a man without honor, however, you also have a family.

I watched as he thought of his immediate family, then I had him imagine the houses and apartments in which they were staying burn to ashes, killing every last one. In his mind he was screaming 'No'. I removed the images.

No harm has yet come to your family, however if you again think of retribution for the removal of this child and her mother from your prison, do not imagine you will not have a real live demonstration of how prepared we are to play tit-plus for tat. Is that clear enough for you?

This time I knew he had been impacted, that he got the message, and more than anything else wanted an end to this affray he had begun with Kiyoshi-san. He was deeply puzzled at the power that Kiyoshi-san appeared to have invoked and was deeply afraid of it.

I led the girl and her mother to the door, and once outside I freed the Yakuza group. I was now pretty certain there would be no further retributive acts. Without revealing myself I led the startled mother and daughter to the street, watched while they picked up a homing cab and began their journey home. I returned briefly to Kiyoshi-san's office.

Please contact your granddaughter.

A moment later, with a huge smile on his face, he thanked me for keeping my promise. He wanted to confront me to thank me properly, but I had no intention of ever being seen by him, so I bade him farewell, indicating that I did not imagine we would meet again and respectfully thanking him for his part in our transaction. Then I left. At this point I did not imagine our paths would cross again.

I returned to my apartment. It was time to move on.

CHAPTER 2

First Real Connection with the Others

I decided my next step was to begin connection with the other human telepaths. It was not that I lacked the confidence to do this; it was the sense of complexity that surrounded us that gave me pause. They were not looking for others like themselves, as the original Olarians had been; I was the only one looking for the others. I suspected they did not even know of the existence of one another. We each had busy lives that we were living in ordinary circumstances; on the surface there was no obvious reason for us to unite and I felt there needed to be. We had not been raised into a co-operative society; if any of us were, for any reason, seriously destructive, all of us could be in a lot of trouble. But there was only one way to find out for sure. So I began with the most known.

Hello, Januti! It's me, Zed. I'd like to visit with you. Is that okay?

I wondered for a moment what I would have said or done if she had replied 'No'. Given where I imagined we had left off, that was definitely on the list of possible reactions. I was, in fact, quite nervous about her.

However, she didn't, and in a moment I was inside the front door of her apartment. I was aware I was preferring traveling using simultaneity than any regular forms of transport and realized I needed to think carefully about this. I certainly could not use this mode for most of my everyday duties at SFC. But at this moment I needed to be not seen by the security cameras, which were everywhere.

Januti emerged from her bedroom and stared at me.

You might imagine I am becoming familiar with you simply appearing somewhere in my apartment.

She had spoken telepathically and I could feel the undertone of gentle amusement, sadness and warmth.

I searched in her mind and received a significant surprise. She would have been truly delighted if I had turned up naked in her bed and made love with her. I felt confused; I had been imagining she was seriously annoyed with my interference in her life. Turns out I was entirely wrong and Olaria had been entirely right.

I smiled at her in appreciation of her beauty and her honesty and she smiled back at me as she realized I would have enjoyed making love with her. For a moment she too was taken aback with the honesty of what had just happened between us but was certainly pleased. Both of us were aware of the charge that seemed to exist between us.

Can we put that thought aside just for a moment, Januti? I think we need to talk.

She looked at me not just with recognition but with something else.

I saw you when the Sunstreamer *returned from OlarCret and realized you were the crew psych and then I realized why you had been away and then I realized you had visited me while you were on OlarCret and then I realized what that had to mean and it nearly blew all my fuses. Then I actually began to understand how you had protected me from Jenko and somehow from the Yakuza; that's true, isn't it?*

I acknowledged it was true. She was persistent.

So tell me how you did that please.

This was not the direction I had been hoping to take this conversation, however, I recognized she had a right to know and she was being very insistent and she had not really been able to assimilate what I had told her when I was here last. So I slowly thought through the events that had occurred since I met her; I could feel her mind following me. She looked at me with large eyes and a touch of incredulity.

My god, you're like a bundle of superheroes all rolled into one, aren't you?

I was uncomfortable with the words and the tone. She knew immediately, had read my mood and looked at me a little puzzled.

Why would you be surprised? I have never known someone to look after me with such determination. It's flattering, disconcerting and very endearing at the same time. Why would you do that for me? We are not lovers, we are not related, you have no obligation toward me. But, and this is a first, I want you intimately and personally more than any man I have ever met, and that is in addition to the fact that you are a small dynamo of almost inexplicable power.

Januti, there are only eight of us on this planet.

Januti was surprised, puzzled and then curious.

So, I said, *although I do not yet know all of you I have a feeling of connection, some sort of responsibility, some deep concerns and some high hopes. Perhaps because I have seen a society that works? The Olarians are genetically like us and they have a totally co-operative culture. I think I am desperately wanting the eight of us to be like them and a part of me fears that I may not be able to help us to become like them yet I feel obliged to really try.*

She looked at me, following my thoughts and feelings very carefully.

Wow! You are having a daughter with Olaria! Fifteen hundred years old and she is indeed beautiful.

She was reading me well and then she followed my thoughts, picking up the images, and then she began to follow the story or at least fragments of it.

Zed, please stop. I am getting freaked out here. All the thoughts about us having babies with each other and with the Olarians...

It had been a mistake to let my mind wander while she was following me, yet in truth this was going to happen over and over again.

What if I don't want to? she asked.

Januti, you will never, ever, be obliged to engage with anything about which you are not totally comfortable. I'd like you to trust me on this.

And surprisingly, I could feel suddenly that she did. She was absolutely trusting me. She moved toward me saying, *I need a hug, please.*

She knew it was okay and I could feel her strength and absolute trust; it was a feeling I knew with Olaria, and Januti was surrendering herself to me with that same very seductive complete faith. I held her and the depth and intensity of our contact disturbed and surprised me. But it pleased and re-assured me too. What was going on between us was a kind of bonding that I had only ever felt with Olaria but now recognized was a result of certainty about feelings free of doubts – unconditional trust – and I knew I would always feel safe and confident with her. It was an unusual and deeply satisfying experience. Feeling safe enough to be open and honest with a woman was a still novel experience for me but a deeply satisfying one.

Oh my god, is this what it is like when you really love somebody? Or will I feel like this with other people like us?

I looked at her and imagined what it must have been like for Jard with Leiti, Olaria's parents and two of the original Olarian telepaths.

I think so, Januti. It is how I felt when I was with Olaria and I have never felt like this with anyone else until now so I can't tell you for certain. I hope so. I can and will show you Olarians, who love one another like this and who have learned to take care of each other emotionally and sexually and in other simple ways that make this kind of experience their normal, not the kind you and I have known in our lives.

Can I expect to feel this way with the other six of us?

The question was so obviously a right question and I had to say, *I truly don't know. Perhaps. It feels unlikely but not impossible. Right now I need to get some help. Can you feel the two Olarians, Esan and Serra – they have been with us during this entire conversation just at the edge of your mind?*

Januti frowned at me.

Among telepaths like ourselves, you can always be present with one another, any time, through intimacy, problem sorting, anything, and it is never hurtful or intrusive in an oppressive or destructive way. And you can always ask to be alone, and for periods of time anyone will let you have that. However, privacy becomes anathema, almost the most destructive feeling you will come to know!

She stepped away from me but stayed connected and smiled in acknowledgement that she could hold that link, then she let herself become aware of Esan and Serra. She found herself seeking out their feelings and thoughts and knew they were very close to each other, that they were sometimes lovers, were not in any lasting relationship, yet they were incredibly warm and close and trusting, and she knew they were aware how she was feeling and she slowly let go her looking to say hello and express her pleasure at meeting them even when they were so far away.

A conversation began about their roles and where they were and the couple took her on a trip through the *Energystreamer* and introduced the other Olarian crew. The warmth, openness and clarity of each connection slowly had the effect of grounding her and she thanked them and was able to slide her mind back to me.

Zed, I just love this. You know that I am feeling love and desire for you; I have never felt such trust and safety with a man before. And I can sense your connection. I know you feel all right about this but do not need to act on it like I normally would. I get that we have some stuff to do that is going to stretch my mind and my emotions and for whatever reason that seems to be okay. So, now, what next? I think I am becoming infected with your desire for the eight of us and—Oh fuck!

She had seen me thinking my way through what I needed to do over the coming days, trying to find a right way to proceed.

Januti, you just met Space Fleet Command, Raille and Jess, the other six of you telepaths, Olaria and Rozari, and you can now begin to see the kind of juggle I am attempting to manage. It is not overwhelming, but taking one step at a time is hard.

Zed, stop, please. She sat down. *I don't even know these people!*

Januti, slide your attention out of my mind. Focus on me on the outside, here in this room. I absolutely do not want to push you away, but my problems and issues are not yours although I am delighted to have someone with whom to share them, just a bit.

She smiled, and I felt her withdraw her attention; she was getting the idea. She was still with me but not all through me.

That feels better, she said. *How can I help? What part can I play?*

As yet she did not know how to contact the others and I thought that was probably a good thing in the circumstances and I felt her acknowledgment.

I need to leave you, Januti, but over the coming days you will be able to contact me by just letting your mind find me. It will get easier, and I think it would be good if you were to think about how the eight of us on this planet might be able to get together. I am going to rest for a few hours, then I am going to visit the others. If you scan my mind you will see the others.

I waited, thinking about each of them and feeling her following me, giving her a more complete picture.

I will be free in a few days. I would like us to stay in touch and for you to consider how we might come together. Any ideas would be welcome. In the meantime, I would like you to let the Energystreamer *crew show you some holos on the history of the Original Olarians and on the intimate relationships they explore and they will show you any other stuff you want to see. It would also be helpful if you kept practicing your telekinetic abilities.*

Let me show you, she said.

And in the next instant she had levitated every piece of furniture in the room and placed it back down again. She was delighted with herself and smiled happily at me.

I can't tell you how safe these abilities have made me feel for the first time in my life.

Then she got up from her chair, came toward me and held me warmly and reassuringly. It was a mutual hug but it was also much more than that and it was with a deep feeling of reluctance I said goodbye. I knew we had a powerful connection, one I hoped would not be repeated with all the women in our group, and left for my apartment. I felt her stay with me until I arrived, made sure she knew where I was, and then she left me and for just a moment I felt abandoned.

One of the *Energystreamer* crew slid into my mind.

Zed, Olaria thought Januti would be your soulmate, which is probably why you were first drawn to her.

And I knew he was right about that!

I decided I would visit each of the others and settle my concerns about our collective security and begin to organize what was promising to be a very full life.

◘

My next call was to Natalya. She knew immediately when I slid into her mind and she asked out loud, in Russian, 'How do you do that?'

So I decided to play her game. *How do you know what I am doing?*

It's as though I have just thought of something except I know it is not me thinking, so I sort of think/feel your presence. Are you going to visit?

Will you be pleased to see me?

It was not a coy request. I wanted to get some sense of what she was willing to say to me.

Of course, and now at least I know who you are. I saw the news broadcast of your return from OlarCret. I know you visited me while you were ostensibly on OlarCret. I have been thinking about our meeting and I have been practicing with more clarity and intent with my clients. It is time for you to begin to explain to me my part in this.

I made the jump to her apartment where she was writing in her study. However, before anything else I shut down the listen and watch security system in her apartment so we could not be observed. I used the same process I had used with Januti's apartment.

Hello Natalya, it is a pleasure to see you again. I had very little opportunity on my last visit. I could only be away from OlarCret for a short time. Tell me what you have learned about your abilities since then, please.

She looked at me. *I think, Zed, that it is you who needs to be doing the telling. I feel a bit like a child when I think about you.*

There was an edge to her enquiry. She was trying very hard to get a read on my thinking and my emotional state but had not fully grasped the process she needed to make this conscious. It was also not difficult to recognize that she was annoyed and disturbed by this. It was, after all, her primary means of ensuring her safety with the men who were her livelihood, some of them potentially very dangerous.

Natalya, please think about the various ways you have been exploring your telepathic abilities since we were briefly together. Once I understand what you have already found, I promise to take it further with you.

She had used it ingeniously to gain useful information about her clientele and as a result had made some changes; there were some clients she would no longer see. However, she knew she had made herself more vulnerable in doing this and I felt some responsibility for her increased risk. However, she did also know more about her telepathic and telekinetic abilities and felt somewhat more secure as a result.

Natalya, you have more power than you can imagine, however, you are also more vulnerable and you need more information and we need to unlock some more of your abilities. However, I need to know that you are aware that the more you know, the more you can do the more endangered you will be and you could increase the risk for the rest of us.

Natalya stopped her intense scanning of me and frowned. *Please speak more frankly to me, Zed.*

Natalya, you and I are not the only telepathic humans.

I watched her register the information, then the leap of curiosity and desire to know of and connect to the others.

Natalya, there are in total, so far as I can presently ascertain, eight of us on this planet. If our existence became known our lives – all our lives – might well be put in jeopardy. We are extraordinarily fortunate to have at this time the Olarian telepaths at hand, however, I am not sure even they could help us if we were known. So I am being more than a little paranoid and cautious as I make contact with each of you. And yes, we will need to meet and learn about one another. And each of you will need help to develop your capabilities. And yes, the Olarians know us all and are for the moment able to keep an eye on us, because at this point in time I really cannot be certain I am fully able to do that.

She looked at me, totally focused. *What am I potentially able to do that I do not know about?*

I truly do not have a complete answer to that, however, we are not entirely alone. I would like to introduce you to the Olarians who are presently visiting us aboard their spacecraft the Energystreamer. *Are you up for that?*

She looked into my mind, seeking hidden meanings and complexities, but could find nothing. *Are you blocking me?*

No, Natalya, but as yet you do not have the discrimination you need to get what you want. I would really encourage you to trust that I am looking after your interests as best I can until I can help you be as safe as possible by yourself. But, the truth is, I am hoping that the eight of us on Earth will get together, somehow, and be able to sort out what we need in order to be out of harm's way.

She nodded thoughtfully. *I can feel your sincerity, Zed, and I do trust you. So thank you. Yes, I would love to meet the Olarians, but how will you do this?*

Simultaneity. You have this ability as yet undeveloped. For now, I will transport you aboard their vessel. However, before I can do that safely, we must make certain that no-one will contact you here while we are away, that no-one can get into your apartment and that your holo communicator will safely dispose of incoming calls. Can you do that or would you like me to assist you? You should know that before we began I shut down and adjusted the listening and watching devices that are part of your security system.

She immediately realized that there were aspects of my request about which she was uncertain.

So I said to her, *Natalya, I will seal off your apartment from access by anyone while we are away. I suggest you follow what I am doing. It can be easily one of your ways to take care of yourself. However, you need to ensure that my doing this does not put your operation here at any risk.*

She understood. We set up her apartment for security and inaccessibility and I contacted the Olarians and asked if they were okay about my bringing Natalya aboard to meet everyone. I did not need to explain where she was at. Without hesitation they agreed.

Natalya, please keep a firm hold on my hand.

She did, and I made the jump to the flight deck of *Energystreamer* using the same process I had used with Raille on OlarCret.

Natalya was made of stern stuff. The jump to *Energystreamer* must have been as amazing as my first experience of simultaneity but she just smiled with delight when she found herself on board with me.

Oh my god, she said, *now this is a really useful maneuver. It could easily save my life.*

And that, I was to learn, was typical of Natalya: every experience seen as an opportunity to improve the quality of her life. She turned to the crew with a smile that would melt any heart and within minutes we could all see why she was so successful. She was extraordinarily sensitive to the people and the world around her. They smiled into her mind and gently reminded her that all of us knew how she was thinking and feeling and that her ability to take care of herself was something about which we were all genuinely pleased. For just a moment she was nonplussed, and I realized she felt exposed, then as she assimilated the fact there were no hostiles here at all, that she was genuinely among warm and caring people, she relaxed, chuckled and looked at me.

Zed, tell me I am really not dreaming, that this is not just a mind trick.

I smiled at her willing honesty, and turned to Serra. *Perhaps you could show Natalya where we are?*

A moment later the Earth was clear on the *Energystreamer*'s equivalent of a holo screen. Serra slowly expanded the image until the detail of the surface below was in sharp focus and Natalya shook her head slowly, her soft, long blonde hair swinging around her shoulders. Her features were classically beautiful and her smile was truly dazzling and I knew this woman could bewitch men if she chose and I don't know why I was surprised. Which brought her attention fully onto me and for the first time a frown appeared on her face.

What?

She knew I was seeing her but I had deliberately closed off that thought, put it out of range of her as yet limited vision, and I realized that she would soon want me to cease doing that with her. It was a very strange feeling and I guessed she might indeed be very powerful. I was a little surprised because I could feel her attraction to me and I was not used to finding beautiful women deeply attracted to me; Olaria had been the first and I was fairly certain Januti would be the second.

We looked over the ship and she asked some interesting questions as she clearly understood that the Olarians were not a technological culture and was genuinely curious about how they had constructed the *Energystreamer* and then she was asking me, *Will I ever be able to do what these amazing people have done?*

And I answered her without hesitation, *Yes.*

Thank you, Zed.

With that, her hand, still holding mine, tightened, and she sent a shiver of warm trusting care through my body and I knew she had learned more than I had at first thought and I smiled, inside and out. In one of those rare flashes of insight I realized one of the essential differences between men and women: no ordinary heterosexual man, no matter how closely connected we were, would have done the thing she just did to me. More important I would not have naturally done that to Olaria, about whom I felt similarly. The Olarian crew looked at me and then at one another and Esan spoke.

Zed, you have grown up on a world dominated by men and by the way men cast reality and usually also relationships. The men in your world, those who wield power, are materialists in essence. Your women appear, in spite of their struggle for equality, to have succeeded in a male-made world. On OlarCret, we have developed a world where feminine, masculine or shared reality frames – what you call models or maps of the world – can and often are used at different times for different purposes. So women are more likely to act with warmth to someone who excites their desire and admiration! On OlarCret a man might also do this to another man or a woman. On Earth we have noticed women will also do it to other women.

What you notice with Olaria and just now with Natalya is essentially a woman taking control of how things will be done and managing you using her way of shaping reality. You will probably find, because you are open to essentially non-material things, Natalya or Januti can help you manage many aspects of your existence from which you do not choose to shut them out. And, surprisingly, among humans, we have noticed the distinction between emotional warmth and sexual intent are poorly sorted. So you would not hold Raille's hand even when you are feeling warm and caring toward him because of the high probability your warmth would contain some of the intimate feeling you primarily reserve for your relationship with a woman.

I became still, reviewing the consequences of his words and felt again a shift inside me, in my reality, in my grasp of the way things were. I could feel the shifting of frames that held, so tentatively, what I thought I knew. Then I was back, but not without leaving a new marker to which I knew I must shortly return.

In the end we spent only 30 minutes aboard the *Energystreamer,* with the crew also letting both of us know that one of them was keeping an eye on Natalya so I could know instantly if anything was wrong. The Olarians were, I realized again, incredibly committed to the eight of us and wanted to ensure, to the best of their ability, that we reached a point where we were able to hold our own in our society. And underneath I could feel the fierce determination to try to be with us so totally that we would create with them a new generation of ourselves, Olarian and human telekinetic telepaths.

However, I also knew they would not overstep a boundary that we all understood. I had knowingly and willingly breached this fragile boundary with the conception of Rozari and the children with the other seven Olarian women, and in truth all of us wanted to feel comfortable about moving on, and Natalya heard, felt, the message and looked at me, first in astonishment and then with increasing awareness as she filled the picture out from the thinking in which it was inevitable we were all engaged.

She turned to me. *Zed, I need you to be uncompromisingly honest with me about the fragments of understanding I think I have just picked up.*

Natalya, you have my word.

I spoke to Esan.

As soon as she is ready, will you replay the Jard and Leiti history for her and the other experiences we discussed?

He never hesitated. *Yes.*

With that we said our farewells and returned to Natalya's apartment.

Oh my god, Zed, what have you got me into? Am I supposed to become an incubator for the Olarians or something?

I felt a sadness slip over me. My experience with Olaria was so rich and satisfying, my thoughts about my daughter so rich and promising, I did not want Natalya or any of the women to feel they were obligated in any way. I knew that was a pipe-dream, but I was determined that, if and when the time came, they would be truly comfortable and as wholesomely delighted as was Olaria, or, should it happen that they decided they did not desire this way, they would feel genuinely comfortable and undisturbed by their decision.

Natalya was following me very carefully.

All right, I get you, but Zed, I need to know you will never, ever, deceive me about what is actually going on.

Natalya, I know that someday soon you will be more powerful and self-assured than you are now and that you will know more of what this might be about. In the meantime I give you my word I will never deceive you either directly or by what I have come to call sleight of mind, so if you ever want to know something, you ask and I will allow you in until you can do that for yourself. Do you understand and do you believe me?

She looked at me for a long moment; she thought and felt her way through our connection, and while she was exploring she let me know that she was going to want more of me than I currently seemed willing to share and I told her that would be all right.

All right, Zed, I'm with you, and I am happy for you to take me on the next stage of my journey.

I have to leave you shortly, Natalya, reluctantly I must say. However, I have some things to ask of you and to show you. First, when you are ready and have several hours free, ask one of the Olarian crew to replay for you the history of the original Olarian telepaths, of Jard and Leiti. That will take two to three hours. Then I would like you to allow them to take you on a deeply intimate/sensual journey that is a part of every Olarian's education and that all of our crew took while we were on OlarCret. I want you to understand a little more of the world into which you are slipping.

Finally, before I go today, I want to fully activate your telekinetic capabilities. Can we start that now and are you okay with all this?

Natalya looked into me with all the intensity she possessed, and that was no small thing. She stayed there for maybe 30 seconds before she turned to me.

Will you let me kiss you properly before we begin?

I was not caught totally off guard; I knew how she managed her clientele.

If, Natalya, you also allow me in those moments of passion and intimacy that you have in mind to share some of my message with you.

She smiled, confident of her skills, and we kissed.

I say we kissed, but this was no ordinary kiss; this was molten passion and desire and intense connection from her and I knew I should slide back just a little, nevertheless it was deliciously satisfying. So that she could know that doing one of her brilliantly successful numbers on me was repeatable, I turned the energy around and filled her with a warm, safe feeling of being cared for, taking the passion out of the interaction. It was one of those tricky moments that can only partly be conveyed in words. However, when it was over she realized this was not a pattern she could use with me to get her way and I could feel the slightly sad but acknowledging pout. I knew she had never before failed to get her way with a man. She was almost angry and a little bewildered; she relied on this ability.

I said, *Natalya, you are a very seductive and powerful and uncompromising person, but I should not be your challenge. Just allow me to help you find the power you have inside.*

She slowly let me go, her heart pumping and the smile in her eyes indescribable, but I knew she had a canniness that needed to be brought under more control. It was tied to too many negative experiences to serve her well. She settled on the other end of the sofa and we spent the next two hours getting new telekinetic and some new telepathic pieces to practice.

Natalya, it is nearly time for me to go.

I felt her disappointment.

If you want to talk to me, then think my name and seek me out. I will hear you. But please be careful. Our lives are invisible to all but the Olarians and the others like us. Soon I will be able to introduce you to the others but you need to allow me to meet each and then connect you. I need you to trust me absolutely if we are to be all right. Please tell me you understand?

I watched as she thought this through and then knew she would be all right.

One of the Olarians said, *She is okay, Zed.*

Natalya smiled at us in her mind and I said goodbye, not before being given a genuine loving hug. And I could feel how I would be okay with this women in times to come but, although I believed we would not be partners, I knew until she chose a partner for herself, it could be a relationship that would have its challenges.

Natalya

I was expecting him and I was not disappointed. But his call set me on edge. He was older and vastly more powerful than anything I had ever imagined, and compared to the apparatchiks and the political power people who were my clients he was simply in another league. I was being drawn to him and yet I barely knew him. He was clean – not just physically but emotionally and intellectually. Everything with him was dead straight and that was an entirely new experience. He was 38 – 10 years older than me – but most of my clients were at least 10, 20 or 30 years older than me. They were, in a way, easier to manage. So there he was.

I think some inner awareness had had me looking for someone like him all my life but I could feel that we did not have the kind of connection that would allow us to have an intimate relationship and I was more than a little disappointed, and I knew immediately that he knew.

He was definitely more than I had expected. I would have been delighted to have him as a client but knew he would never fit that category. I had tests for my men and he simply flashed past all the markers no matter what I was concerned about. Within a few minutes of trying to manage him I realized that was never going to happen yet I felt absolutely safe and comfortable with him and that was in itself amazing, a lifetime first.

I wanted to know him and I wanted him to know me, and that was another first. Zed was no target, he was the main game, yet some deep intuition simply told me I was going to be unable to outmaneuver him or con him in any way, so in some deep part of my being I felt, for the first time, ever, a deep sense of relief, of peace and, more surprisingly, safety. I hoped the other men from whom I would probably, I realized, need to choose were like this.

I had always imagined that somewhere among the rich and powerful there would be somebody just for me. I had never imagined it would be another psychic like me, yet I knew that this lean, gentle yet fiercely determined psychotherapist, stronger than any human being anyone had ever seen and able to make the entire universe his home by the exercise of his mind, was not the one; I could feel he was taken. He was deliciously complex, a joy, a treasure I did not intend to let slip away, and he was looking into my mind and seeing me think about him and was enjoying me yet knowing we were not quite the right fit. I was feeling things I had not imagined in a life of sensual pleasure-seeking; one, however, always constrained by economics and safety. I had not imagined I would ever be left feeling inadequate, but here I was, and I intended to make sure that changed. I am a fast learner. I knew if there were other men anything like him I would find a mate.

Then I became aware that he was watching and listening to me think about myself and him and instead of anger and frustration, which would have been my fallback position, I was relieved and deeply glad. I could not resist throwing my arms around his neck and kissing him with more passion and special energy than I was wont to do. And he was ready for me and returned that warmth several times over. A part of me was sad – I knew he was not mine, would not become mine – but I wanted him close, a genuine friend, not like the other girls who worked with the rich in the luxurious apartments around me. A friend I would have to be willing to share.

When he brought my telekinetic power into my consciousness I felt stronger and safer than I had ever felt, unbelievably so. The way he gently but inexorably took control of my mind and led me to pathways of power that would become mine was just delicious. He never overwhelmed me, never tried to take me over, but if he had asked I think I would have willingly let myself be taken over for his purposes. But he remained respectful and sometimes as he showed me things and led me to new connections I wished he would just become my master and I would have been his willing slave yet he never challenged my integrity in any way. It was some ride but I could feel his restraint.

So when he said goodbye for now, I was energized to meet the other men in our group. I realized that I would probably need to choose one as a partner, that I could never be deeply connected to a non-telepathic man. A part of me felt trapped and angry that this had been – was being – taken out of my control. It was to be several days before the full set of consequence would seep in and I would realize just how all-consuming this new reality was already becoming.

Zed

As I arrived back home and felt Natalya leave me, I realized Olaria had almost certainly felt her potential but also that she had not expected Natalya was meant to be with me. I was reasonably sure she had recognized this; it had more to do with Natalya's energy than any connection between us. The connection with Januti had been immediate and a deep, strong heartfelt pull from somewhere way down inside; I had missed her immediately I left her. With Natalya the pull was power and intensity but not deeply romantic. She was going to be a challenge and I was okay with that.

As I moved through my apartment I suddenly became aware something was wrong – very wrong! I raised a strong energy shield around myself, sat quietly in my special chair and let my mind move slowly over every section of my home. Then I got it. Someone had been able to access my apartment, and that should have been well-nigh impossible. It was protected by a complex electronic awareness system, and that was apart from my little psychic warning net. Then my warning system identified it – in the ceiling, carefully and artfully concealed in the metal edge of a light fitting, was a very sophisticated holo recorder. After a few minutes' careful examination I realized it had been there for some time but had only been activated while I was away.

I sat very still and let my mind trace its energy link. A woman sitting in what appeared to be a rapid transit vehicle was watching and listening to the device. I remained seated and still, and I slid into her mind. She was my security operative! But what was she doing with a watch-and-listen device in my apartment? Her name was Melanie Jasset and I realized almost at once that she was indeed on official duty, responsible for my safety!

Oh no, I thought, *this level of observation is definitely not going to happen*. I reduced her consciousness almost to sleep, ensuring she would be unaware of any change in sights or sounds for several minutes. Then, with no further manipulation, I walked out the door, took the fast rider to the street, walked to her vehicle and let myself in the passenger side door before releasing her attention.

She nearly leapt out of the car and was reaching for her weapon when she felt my hand restrain her with enough force that she could not move.

'Melanie, you know I'm Dr Zed Eko. I know you are the duty officer of my security team – a piece of information Dr Khan apparently neglected to give me when I took this job. Would you please explain to me exactly what you are doing?'

'Bloody hell, Zed, Julian tried to warn me about you. How did you get down here without my seeing you?'

'You were apparently taking a short nap. Look back over your recording.'

She did. No more reassured, she asked, 'How is that possible?'

'Well, Melanie, you were not alert, clearly. But more to the point I need you to remove the device and give me your assurance there will be no repeat of such an intrusion into my life. I will take this matter up with Julian Kared and Dr Khan. I do not believe I need a security detail, certainly not one as easily outmaneuvered as you have been. And most certainly not one that plans to spy on me without my permission and without my knowledge. So please go and retrieve your device now and assure me you will not try anything so inappropriate again.'

But she sat semi-frozen.

I was angry. I should have been more careful. I could easily have been seen making a jump into or out of the apartment. I quickly scanned her recording to ensure it had not captured anything it should not have. Fortunately, it had not been activated until just before I had sat down in my chair today. I breathed a sigh of relief.

She did not know what to do.

I, on the other hand, did. I flipped open my holo communicator and initialised my direct channel to Miyuki. She responded immediately.

'Zed? I thought you were on leave.'

'Dr Khan, I am currently in the vehicle of a Melanie Jasset who it turns out is a member of my security team! I think you must have forgotten to warn me that she would be following me and that she would bug my apartment? I understand our senior staff security protocols, but I was not aware she had authority to install watch-and-listen devices in my apartment without my consent?'

I waited a second, monitoring Melanie and Miyuki. Miyuki knew she had not given Security authority to bug my apartment and that Security Director Kared, who felt some concern about me, had obviously exceeded his authority. And then I realized, exceeded his authority before he officially knew I had been promoted!

'Put her on please, Zed.'

I tilted the communicator in Melanie's direction and raised an eyebrow in query.

'Dr Khan, this is Agent Melanie Jasset. I have only been following the instruction of my head of department with respect to Dr Eko's security.'

'Agent Jasset, please immediately remove the device from Dr Eko's apartment, relieve yourself of your security shift with Dr Eko, report to Security Director Kared and ensure that you and he are in my office immediately following the arrival of your shuttle to Moon Base One. Is that quite clear?'

'Yes Ma'am.'

'Zed, my apologies. I am certain you can look after yourself while you are on leave. I will have security stand down for the six weeks unless you request them to be reinstated. They will resume duty when you return to duty and you and I will discuss this incident and the future needs of your security then. Please enjoy your leave and be assured I will manage this on your behalf.'

I could see the ironic smile on her lips. She knew my ability to take care of myself was well beyond the capabilities of a junior agent and was surprised at Julian Kared's apparent poor judgment around this.

Melanie was flustered. I reassured her she was not in trouble, that she should relax and go remove the bug, which she did and then left, still apologizing. I took particular note of her method of accessing my apartment. A very 'cute' device enabled the security system to be confused for a fraction of a second, enough to allow a second element of the device to bypass the locking and warning elements and voila, the door was open and she could walk inside! I would hold the images until I met and became acquainted with Ajit, my next contact. He would, I felt sure, be able to take the image of the device and its actions and know how to protect us against it.

However, I had been warned. I would pay a great deal more attention to the security issues surrounding me from now on.

Although I was not feeling emotionally or intellectually overwhelmed, I was conscious that I had taken on an ever increasing workload at a time I would have liked to take a break from the world and allow the events of the past year to fully catch up with me. Certainly this was not going to happen anytime soon, but the notion sat quietly in the back of my mind and for the third time I did a serious reconnaissance over every area of my apartment and the adjacent spaces.

That done, I created an energy barrier that would not permit any smart electronics to confuse it and allow the service lines into the apartment to be the only entry and exit spaces. Then I checked those. Finally I checked the audio and video access points and realized I could not wholly control them without disturbing the operation of my life. So I made a mental note to monitor more closely and realized my life had indeed taken a major jump in complexity. My apartment was no longer the secure haven I had imagined.

At every entry point I set a simple energy warning system using the pattern I had seen the Olarians use to allow them to know about the movement of stock; if anyone did bypass the locking devices on the door or windows I would have a clear image of their activities and now they would find themselves unable to move into the apartment through the energy barriers at the windows and door. Finally I felt secure. While not becoming paranoid I clearly needed to be a great deal more careful. And I needed to establish what Julian Kared was up to and why.

However, for now I had more pressing concerns. I decided to take the remainder of the evening off, sleep in until midday, give myself a serious physical workout and begin the next step of my journey in the early afternoon.

CHAPTER 3

Meeting More of My Eight

It was early afternoon when I left my apartment and so arrived in Mumbai at 9am to see Ajit Patel. Our 31-year-old Indian computer and holo programmer was wide awake and busy. I had had no chance to study him and I decided to connect with him in his apartment. He was a swarthier version of me, more directly handsome, lightly built, younger and apparently unaware of his telepathic abilities. I decided on a more carefully managed approach on this occasion and simply connected to his holo communicator. He answered immediately and looked at me intensely.

'Yes, how can I help you?'

The voice was clear and almost free of local accent.

'I have a pressing need to meet with you. I am presently in Mumbai, outside your apartment complex; is now a convenient time?'

There was a pause while he scanned me very carefully.

'I know you, don't I?'

I watched him think through the images of the *Sunstreamer*'s return; yes, he knew who I was.

'You've seen me on the news channels. Can I come up?'

I knew he was going to say yes; his curiosity was high and his intuition was likewise good. But he genuinely had no idea about his abilities and I wondered what strategy I would choose when we were together. As he greeted me I spoke to him telepathically so he could see my lips were not moving. He frowned. Then before he could speak I checked his apartment and de-powered all the listening and watching devices and sealed it from sound or sight from watchers or listeners anywhere. My level of caution was now extremely high and I was hypersensitive to dangers about which I had previously been careless.

'My god, you're telepathic.'

As are you, Ajit.

'No!'

Yes. Tell me you have never wondered about some of the things you know.

He continued to stare at me.

If I was telepathic, I would know, wouldn't I?

I did not learn I was telepathic until I reached OlarCret. You know you are different from all the members of your family except your parents who never speak of their fears for you, do they?

Not a sound would have been recorded by his home security system as he stood there, shaking his head. I watched him reflect on his parents' behavior. He had always known they were afraid for him but never understood why. He had always been exceptional at almost everything he did and then he began to make some of the connections. He sat, looking at me intensely, and then he said, without making a sound, *Of course! Why did I never see it before?*

And in a flash he was in my mind.

Gently, Ajit!

Sorry. Oh wow, tell me what I need to know.

I saw the speed of his connection. He must have made millions of connections in the time it took me to see how bright he really was. It was like watching a spacecraft launch into outer space. Barely a blur from zero to near light speed. It was a delight to watch. But...

Ajit, STOP.

He came to a halt, looking at me, frowning. *What aren't you telling me?*

Ajit, this is just a beginning. Telepathy is just the start. Please allow me to slow you down just a little. There are hazards, which your parents recognized, and they are still there for us.

I watched him reflect on what I had just said and realized he was entirely capable of thinking that through.

I get it, Zed, but I need more information.

You do, Ajit, but if you are not careful you will put me and the others in serious danger.

I had his attention and he was studying me carefully.

How many of us are there?

There are eight human telepaths including you and me.

He was leaping from one awareness to another.

Yes. And I need you to recognize what will be the consequence for you and some of the rest of us if you do not manage your excitement and your explorations. Please reassure me that you really understand the danger you could put yourself and others in by careless exposure. Imagine what various authorities would like to do with you and your abilities. Now, so you are clear that you have only just begun to explore, stay with me while I show you that you are also seriously telekinetic.

His eyebrows went up.

Watch. And I pointed to the table on the other side of the room, a solid teak dining table. I lifted it off the ground, turned it around 360 degrees and replaced it.

Ajit's jaw dropped. *I can do that?*

That and a whole lot more. Now watch the small side table. As I focus on it you will briefly see colored lights dancing around it.

I had helped him look in what I thought of as the Olarian way. He got it immediately.

Yes.

Okay, now focus on the table with me and think how you would like it to rise just a little off the floor.

I remained tightly linked with his mind and as he focused I helped him use the part of his mind he had so far never explored. It took maybe 10 seconds and he had the basics. And then as with the telepathy his mind began to pick up speed and I could see him making connections as fast as I had done when I first experienced the power.

Slowly! Get control of the speed of your learning. As you focus on the table there is no exertion required. You are using energy that is present in the world around you.

His learning rate was astonishing and within the hour he had the basics of energy management and he was tired.

Zed, this is amazing, you are amazing. I get the drift. Tell me how to make sure I do not risk any of us. I don't need to know about the others yet but I do want to learn how to control and manage all this.

Ajit, I want you to meet one of the Olarian couples who are managing Energystreamer. *They will be available to help if you should find yourself in any kind of difficulty, but please, only if absolutely necessary.*

He was looking at me and I could see that he was slowly grasping the boundaries. He nodded. I asked Esan and Serra to join us. Ajit followed my request and smiled as the two appeared in his apartment.

Can I do that?

Yes.

Each of them said, *Once you have mastered the basics you will be able to make small simultaneity jumps. Zed will help you.*

And then a new round of introductions and connections and the Olarians left, reassuring Ajit that in an emergency they would be available to help. Ajit sat down and I knew he wanted to know if I could do that, so I shifted to be in another chair. He was overloaded, hungry to learn and now rapidly grasping the significance of all that had gone on for him in the past hours.

The Olarians had assured Ajit they would make the holos of Olarian history and the other recordings available for him to view in his apartment but requested him to first switch off his watch and listening devices. He checked them and found them all off and turned to me.

Yes, Ajit, I turned everything off before I entered and adjusted the time record. You will need to do the same whenever you are home and are going to undertake anything that could be seen as odd. Also, SFC seems to have found a way to bypass security devices. I am going to leave you with the images from my apartment. Would you look at them and find us a way to protect ourselves against them?

Yes

He got it immediately and thought carefully through the implications. We discussed each of the systems and ways he could be secure and not give himself away. It was a long and quite complicated discussion and I realized I had never thought consciously or clearly about the amount of monitoring that went on in our world.

I spent several hours with him and there was no doubt he was a competent and speedy learner. Serra and Esan took him off my hands when they realized I was outrageously tired. They promised to look after him and for the first time I was ready to leave my post and his learning to them and I said goodbye to Ajit.

He thanked me and I could feel the solidity of him and felt considerably reassured. I liked him, had done almost immediately I met him, and could feel that he reciprocated. I said goodbye and made the jump to my apartment and before going to sleep I asked the Olarians to please have someone watch Ajit until I could be with him tomorrow.

Definitely, Serra said, confirming she was on it.

I filled the tub and soaked until I had thought my way through the issue of our security, formulated some plans, checked in with Januti longer than I really needed to and was ready to sleep. It was going to take me a week or two to cover the group before I could try to figure out our next step. Suddenly I was aware that all 16 of the Olarians presently on Earth were with me. It felt seriously reassuring. I asked them if any of them had any ideas.

Several of them chimed in almost together.

Zed, we have all been watching you and, although quite unnecessarily, watching over you, and the truth is we all believe your task is very complicated and none of us could see you doing anything more constructive than we have seen you do so far. Also, and please do not take this in a not constructive way, but all four of the women who have traveled to Earth are willing to bear children to any of the four of you, however, we realize that the culture gap is much greater than we realized and if no connection is possible during this trip everyone is more than happy to wait until it feels right to all of you. We know how tricky the first steps were for our Original Eight.

None of the men feel it would be appropriate for any of your four telepathic women to bear children to any of us until they have born children to each of you. We are certain of this. It is almost coded into your basic makeup. I know that for you this is very far out in the scheme of things but we wanted you to know what we have been thinking and discussing while you have been properly absorbed in your tasks. We were not fully aware of the listening and watching devices we saw you observe in your apartment but can now assure you we have identified the patterns involved and are carefully checking each of the others. If we identify any that we believe need to be temporarily disabled, our inclination is to disable them first and then tell you about them. Would this be the best procedure?

I thought for a moment. *Yes please. If you would let me know as soon as that is done, unless I am asleep I will follow each of them up. Thank you.*

Please be confident we will give you any help you seek if it is in our power. Now we all hope you will have a restful sleep. Goodnight.

The goodnights slid through my mind from each of them. Within seconds I was deeply asleep.

CHAPTER 4

And the Rest

My next visit was to Peter in Tavistock. For this I had to leave home around four in the morning. When I arrived he was running a group therapy session and I watched. He was not aware of me until his session finished and then he felt a disquiet he was unable to shake off. That was me trying to be with him, but he could not quite truly feel or hear me. He headed for his apartment, still feeling disquiet, and then suddenly, with just the slightest help, he broke through.

'Who are you? Where exactly are you?'

Hi Peter, I'm Zed. We have not yet met properly, but it is time we did. Are you okay about meeting in your apartment?

'Yes, but who are you, and how am I hearing you in my head?'

Peter was an outstanding therapist but without insight into his telepathic abilities. He had always been able to understand what people were thinking and feeling but without any awareness of how much additional help he had when he did this. His journey through and into therapy had been so easy he had never had to struggle to understand therapeutic models or people or what was going on between people and had difficulty understanding why others were not the same!

He was obsessed with his work, but in his daily life was without the insightful awareness he brought to his work. Interestingly, as I watched him work, I knew he was seeking understanding about himself as he helped the members of his group. His parents, like mine, had clearly discouraged his social networking for fear of his abilities being discovered. So now he was looking for himself. Of course, like me at that stage, he did not really know what it was he wanted to find: friends, other people like him with whom he could connect...

I debated the best way to connect with him.

'Do I know you? Oh, of course.'

He was actually seeing me but somehow not realizing what that meant.

Dr Zed Eko. What psychotherapist has not heard of you, would not recognize you especially after your return from OlarCret and your appointment to the head of SFC Psych Unit? Now it seems I am about to know some things I would not even have dreamed... You're telepathic, no wonder you're so amazing.

I shifted into his apartment.

Well, Peter, everyone in this room is telepathic. Do you notice that neither of us is speaking out loud?

He had a wonderful look of amazement mixed with a confused delight. Finally he became still and very thoughtful.

You mean it? My god, you do. Oh no, that's not possible. I would know.

Really?

He stopped talking and in his mind began to reflect, then slowly, ever so slowly, he began to nod.

Oh lord, and all these years... how did I not know?

I looked at where the thought was taking him and thought, directly into his mind, *Think about it. Think about your parents and how hard they fought to keep you focused on being normal. Why do you suppose they thought they needed to do that? It seems we all had the same problems with fearful parents. The Olarians never have that problem because their parents expect them to be – knew they would be – telepathic and telekinetic. They don't have our blocked fears and blindness and they don't have emotional constipation to deal with.*

Never wondered how come you are so much more competent and sure about what is going on in your groups? Wonder no more. Peter, it's time. I fear you must step out of your particular closet. You are one of eight human telekinetic telepaths. So the two of us are one quarter of this world's population. Four women and four men. Now do you feel ready to cast off your parents' fog and explore the light?

He was silent for several moments, digesting what he clearly knew was true.

My god, I've been cheating all this time. How am I going to tell my friends and colleagues?

I paused for a brief moment. He had genuinely caught me on the hop, so in a tone of utter disbelief I asked, *Are you really that naive? Please think about what the consequences for your life might be if you were so monumentally stupid as to seriously consider such a lethal act?*

I could see within a moment or two he got it and I felt my anxiety settle and I relaxed.

Now, will you please be serious?

The range of emotions that chased themselves around his mind nearly bewildered me until I recognized the depth of his true British conservatism.

Peter, you need to stop sliding back to your roots when you think about yourself now. You are nothing, nothing remotely like the man you were thinking yourself to be before I contacted you just a few moments ago. This is not going to be easy for either of us.

He was frighteningly upper-middle class British conservative and he was getting only bits of the reality I needed him to grasp. I drew breath and regrouped.

Peter, please sit still and tell me how you imagine you will be able to explain this.

With that I levitated his chair and, holding him firmly in it, gently twirled him around the room then carefully placed him back exactly as he had been.

If I had all the time in the world I would do this more slowly. However, you have been brought up in one of the most controlled and conservative environments in the free world. Protected more than most of us from understanding who you really are. However, you at least chose the right profession to increase the likelihood that you will grasp what is involved.

Over the next hour, as I talked with him, helped him open up his mind and find the channels that were simply waiting for someone to help him open, we slowly began to make a genuine connection. I found myself liking him and enjoying his incredible conservatism and sense of propriety.

He had a pleasant face, sandy-brown hair just a little untidy that he often threw back off his face with a gesture of his head. He was a light to medium build, in good health, worked out regularly at the gym, ran every day and was a consummate fencer and, surprisingly, a knife fighter, and the walls of his personal study/office were covered with the most extraordinary collection of fighting and throwing knives from around the world and over many centuries. It also took only a moment for Peter, as he watched me scan his knife collection, to realize why he was probably so expert. He looked at me enquiringly. From my chair I lifted a wicked-looking throwing knife off the wall, brought it into my hand then threw it exactly back into its rest on the wall. He nodded understandingly.

Wow, just as well my colleagues do not know!

It was, however, Peter's frames of mind that were limiting him. So, as I engaged gently with each of his skill sets, these opened up, so he came to see the kind of explorations he needed to make. I introduced him to the Olarians and the ways he needed to explore his powers, and made absolutely certain he understood the potential disaster he could cause were he to reveal any part of his abilities to anyone outside the seven of us and the Olarians.

I know you are still somewhat in shock but you need to remember that you may well also hold the lives of the other seven of us in your hands.

I could see him chewing that over.

That, of course, works both ways, he said.

Yes, it does. Before I leave you, we need to open some of the channels in your brain that have been closed off for most of your life.

It was a real pleasure as we explored entering other minds, following without making himself known, and learning to let himself find the lights. I thanked whatever power was looking after me that I had watched Leiti show Jard about the lights – they together with Olaria's introduction had been the trigger to me seeing the bands of energy and to being able to let them go and return to my normal vision. Peter got them first go and in no time his mind was opening up at the same phenomenal rate I had seen with the others. It was the telekinetic abilities that most focused his attention and which he chose to explore most seriously, but by the time three hours had passed he was hurtling up the learning curve and I knew that I need have no fears for him. I was beginning to realize he was incredibly determined, steely strong but not stubborn.

So I said, *I need to leave you shortly. First I would like to introduce you to some people who are absolutely trustworthy and who already know about you – the Olarians on* Energystreamer.

I took him on the journey through *Energystreamer*, had him meet everyone and agree to see the Living Library holos and history of the early Olarian telepaths and the other things I thought they all needed to share. Before I left him I ensured that the Olarian crew still had the resources to keep an eye on him, that *Energystreamer* was not yet ready to return to OlarCret, and that he knew what things he needed to practice. Then I said goodbye for the moment.

I was left with Darcy, Donna and Ai Shen. Next step was to meet Darcy. I arrived outside the door of his apartment. Inside I could see Darcy and two attractive young women. I quickly realized they were students and that Darcy had had a brief fling with one of them and was not particularly interested in continuing it and was not emotionally connected to the other. I scanned him and learned that the lesson would be over in about 10 minutes and he was looking forward to some alone time. When the two young women had left, I connected to his holocom. He looked at me curiously.

'Yes.'

'Would you care to let me in?'

Out of curiosity and little else he opened the door. Stopped, looked at me, tried in the very basic way he had developed to find out what I wanted, was unsuccessful, looked puzzled but asked, 'What can I do for you?'

It was a request in French.

I replied telepathically, *You could take up a very significant opportunity to cease being bored with your life.*

'Wait a minute, I've seen you. Yes, you're Dr Zed Eko. You are the SFC psych who just returned from OlarCret. What have you got to do with me?'

Are you going to invite me in?

'Of course. Please do come in.'

He was gentle and friendly and bored, and I was offering him some novelty.

Darcy, do not speak to me out loud again please. At least for a little while.

And I saw his jaw drop and a look of guilt and uncertainty in his emotional response.

Darcy, I am no threat to you, and you do, I'm sorry to say, need me.

Darcy looked at me and tried to get clear what I wanted.

I thought it was time we met. You are extraordinarily adept at languages. Perhaps you are less clear that the reason is because you hear what people are thinking in their head so you do not immediately need to understand their spoken language. You have learned to use this to make a living, but you are finding it a little boring, although it does provide you with a stream of attractive women with whom to have a relationship, usually a brief one. And before you ask how I would know, I am watching you think about the last few you had including Marietta who just left you.

For a moment he reflected on my comments but was nowhere near ready to acknowledge any of this.

I silently asked two of the Olarians if they would join us and within seconds they were in the room with us. Darcy came to a halt and before he could ask I introduced him.

Darcy, on my left is Esan the navigator on the Energystreamer *presently in orbit above us and beside him is Serra, their equivalent of our biomed. I am going to get you to travel with them to* Energystreamer *to meet the other Olarian crew and see the ship and then we will come back here. Is that okay with you?*

Yes!

He looked more than a little bemused.

When we returned to his home alone, he was still shaking his head and looking... stunned, so he and I sat down to talk. He was a genuinely decent man and more than anything else a deeply frustrated one. He had talents he did not know about and he was seriously bored with his life. We began a detailed exploration of the unexplored areas of his brain, which again lasted for a little over three hours.

I told him everything I could in the time we were together and obtained an assurance of his discretion. I put him in touch with the Olarian holos to listen and watch some of the important things I had shared with the others and promised to be back to him soon. During the time we had together we had opened some of his telepathic and telekinetic channels and he was ecstatic, deeply satisfied and absolutely bursting to explore everything around him.

I watched him practice each of the pieces of his telepathy and the beginning journey of his telekinesis. As with the others, watching him learn was a real joy. His brown hair was short and his beard trimmed neatly. Green eyes locked at me, the windows to a penetrating intelligence that I found reassuring. He was the most curious individual I had met. His mind opened to every challenge and kept working until he had reached the edges of the element he was exploring. He was a little shorter than me and dapper. I liked him and I could see why women were drawn to him. He was alight with curiosity. I had him test his ability to contact me when I left him to play and returned home. I knew he was safe. He had spent several minutes testing his apartment for sound and visual recording devices and was clear on his need to not be caught out.

◘

The next visit was to Donna at her apartment on the Upper East Side in New York. A very nice apartment. Donna's parents had money and as their only child she had been indulged; nevertheless, she had her feet planted firmly on the ground. She had several really smart and interesting friends with whom I had watched her interact. She felt just a little uncomfortable with them, mostly because she was unaware how attuned she was to their lies, deceits and inconsistencies, and yet she clung to them like a lifeline.

After a qualification in child care she had begun a medical degree out of a mixture of curiosity and boredom and had quickly found the limitations of the medical models she was required to understand, realizing they would be seriously constraining. So she had gone exploring both the literature and the unusual and alternative medical models available around the world.

Finally, she settled for an eclectic set of intervention models that worked well for her and eventually built her a high-quality reputation. Wanting more excitement, she had applied for and got an appointment to the SFC biomedical unit and I would undoubtedly have met her sooner or later, but now was to be the time. It was Donna who Olaria had missed when she found the others. Donna had been off-world on a mission and did not return until Olaria had left.

She was nearly six feet tall, had shoulder-length softly waved dark hair and a smooth, lightly tanned complexion, a generous mouth in a heart-shaped face and a laugh that, like the Olarians', filtered liltingly through you, leaving behind a residue of warmth and bubbles.

Knowing it was an evening where she had no outing planned, I sat on the floor outside her door and waited for her to come home from work. I already knew she had had no intimate relationships for over a year; the last one, without knowing why or how, she had telepathically recognized as a somewhat secretly violent piece of work and had ditched after their first date, not allowing him even to return to her apartment. The experience had been so frightening she had decided she could live without it, especially as he had been a crew member on her last tour of duty and she was uncertain how she was going to deal with him in her work context. Although she had been able to keep him at arm's length, the experience had disturbed her feeling of competence and safety with men.

Most of this I had obtained while she was sitting quietly on her journey home. I was getting quite expert at knowing which questions would take people through memories I could watch. The truth of it was, I did enjoy learning about them.

Now she was confronted with me, sitting on the cold marble floor outside her apartment. However, I sent her a warm, loving, gentle vibe, something she could relate to, and she just looked at me with a mixture of fear and curiosity.

'Okay Mr Front Door Sitter, what exactly can I do for you?' The tone was not hostile but her anxiety was high in spite of my gentle warming connection. She made no move to touch her electronic door lock or even move closer. She was thinking of using her security alarm, the one she had picked up after her last failed attempt at a male relationship.

'Donna, you probably do know me,' I said as I stood.

She stifled a gasp. 'Oh yes I do. You're the new head of Psych Services!

Dr Zed Eko. I saw you disembarking from *Sunstreamer* when she returned from OlarCret not so long ago.'

'Yes, Donna. Now, are you going to shelve your fears about men long enough to invite me into your home?'

She was well dressed but conservatively. She was an attractive woman, and she was not used to being surprised, but I could see she was enjoying this little sally and, because of the help I was giving her, she was feeling safe enough to enjoy the moment. I knew she was now more comfortable than afraid and I decided it was time to act.

'Donna, I need to speak with you, urgently. Please invite me in.'

At this point manners and common sense took over.

'I'm sorry, I tend to be very cautious with men since my last boyfriend. Please come in, Zed. I imagine if they were willing to take you to OlarCret and make you head of Psych Services, it's probably safe for me to invite you in.'

Before we moved inside I searched for and found the audio and visual security devices and their backup units and Donna's panic alarm. Checked that they were all disconnected and there were no other tricky devices and made sure I had properly managed them and the corridor cameras. I laughed warmly directly into her mind and followed her in. Her apartment was a model of good taste and comfort.

'So, Dr Eko, why is it so urgent that an internationally known member of SFC wants to speak to an insignificant biomed who he could easily have required to come to see him at work?'

'Please sit.'

She did.

'What I am about to tell you will be quite difficult for you to believe, so I am going to call in some help. You are aware that at this time there is an Olarian space vehicle called *Energystreamer* in Earth orbit?'

She nodded.

'You do know that the Olarians are both telepathic and telekinetic?'

'Of course, yes.'

'I would like you to meet their navigator, Esan, and his partner, the *Energystreamer*'s version of a biomed, Serra. Are you okay with that?'

She nodded, eyebrows raised. The two appeared in the room standing beside my chair. I stood as did she, and I made the introductions totally telepathically with no sound in the room. She greeted them with courtesy and with less surprise than I would have expected.

Can I get you something to drink?

It was an automated response from Donna who then recognized the strangeness of the request but still raised her eyebrows to follow up the query.

Thank you, no, they answered almost in unison.

Serra continued, *We are here because Zed asked us to visit and we do not want you to feel obliged in any way to treat us like visitors. Zed has an extraordinarily difficult task, which he is in the process of managing and we are delighted to help him. I apologize for the inference, but you are one of his tasks and he was happy for you to know that he hoped we could assist him, something we are more than willing to do because* – she looked at me and I nodded – *you are one of us.*

Donna frowned. *An Olarian?*

Serra chuckled. *No, sorry about the language confusion. You are both telepathic and telekinetic like us and like Zed. Your abilities have been very deeply hidden from you by your very loving but fearful parents so you have never, it appears, even had an inkling of your abilities. Your friends and their children, on the other hand, although they have no conscious awareness, all instinctively know and so trust you absolutely, do they not?*

Donna sat and stared in a bewildered fashion at the three of us.

It's true, Donna, I said. *I do not have a great deal of time at the moment and I desperately need you to understand and be willing to explore with me. I believed meeting these two might help.*

The conversation had been entirely telepathic; she had not opened her mouth to speak the entire time. She was silent, reviewing times with her parents and her studies and finally she looked up, nodded gently and smiled.

Are you telling me that I am capable of knowing what people are thinking and feeling and that I am more than capable of taking care of myself if I am physically threatened?

All of us nodded at her and it was almost as if we could see her stand and shake off a wrinkled skin and appear even taller, stronger... freed. It was an astonishing transformation. The smile on her face was something to behold.

We'llll. She drawled the word, strung it out with inflections. *Please, teach me!*

The Olarians turned and smiled at me.

I don't think you will be needing us any further? Serra said.

I believe you are right and thank you so much.

They both did something I had never seen them do before – they gently held Donna and kissed her cheek, let her know she would soon be able to speak with them whenever she needed, assured her she would be very welcome and would soon meet the others, then left.

It was as if a wall had been removed from her mind. Moreover, she looked like an entirely different person. All semblance of shyness and fear had vanished. The transformation was complete. For the next few hours we worked at opening her channels and capabilities. She just got it every time. No sooner was one piece open and operational than she was on to the next. I had no idea what her limits might be but we were not going to reach them today or any time soon. I was absolutely delighted and so was she.

Before I left she had visited *Energystreamer*, met the crew and agreed to work with the Living Library and watch the holos and the experiences she needed to ensure she was connected to a new frame that I wanted to be part of our new group's understanding. Before I left I carefully took her through the practicalities of the eight of us and the need to be carefully aware as she explored her new world of possibilities.

I also showed her the security devices in her apartment and how I had disabled them. Then she and I had a complicated discussion about what things needed never be seen or heard by those devices. She fully understood and we discussed the practicalities of managing them, then spent some time discussing SFC and our roles in it. Finally we decided we would manage our work relationship carefully so we did not make a faux pas that would give us away and she was delighted and excited.

For the first time, perhaps since my early childhood, Zed, I feel free. I know now I can be safe and you should beware – I could so easily fall in love with you. I feel as though you have allowed me to reclaim life. I feel fantastic and please do not concern yourself, I will be very careful.

Donna, you know you can reach me anytime you need. I will be back as soon as I can arrange my time. Today has been just such a delight. I'm sure you know that.

She came across the room and took me in her arms and just held me tightly to her. I could feel the joy and delight and love and a pantheon of wonderful emotions tumbling over one another. Then she kissed me gently and we said goodbye for now.

◘

My final visit was to Ai Shen. Her apartment was also high quality, in one of the more elegant parts of downtown Shanghai from which most of her clientele were drawn. I felt the need to be even more circumspect in China, especially with regards to being seen or identified. So before leaving my apartment I reached out for Ai as she was walking from her veterinary clinic toward her personal transport unit. When she stepped into her transport, I spoke to her.

Ai Shen, this is Zed Eko. Do you recognize me?

She turned very slowly and examined the rear seat of her light-blue transport unit. Then she looked left and right then straight ahead and without speaking out loud she answered me.

Why here, Zed?

I think it would be fair to say she caught me off guard. *You were expecting me?*

I felt you talking to Januti and Natalya. I have sort of known about them for more than a year. So I sort of knew about you when you made contact with Natalya but I was not really clear who you were until the Sunstreamer *returned and I felt you when you stepped off and one of the Olarians spoke to you. I couldn't reach either of you but I knew you were there. And now I have to say I am absolutely ecstatic you have found me and are talking to me. It has been very lonely. I do not trust anybody close to me, so it is most heart-warming to hear you. Can we meet?*

I will be in your apartment when you arrive home. Have a speedy trip.

You will be in my apartment, did you say?

Yes, Ai, if that is all right with you.

Oh yes, definitely. Don't go away, will you?

She punched in the automated codes that would take her directly home without a moment's pause and when she opened the door and came inside she nearly bowled me over with the enthusiasm of her welcome. Totally out of character for everything I had been able to find out about her. I held her for a moment at arm's length to look at her. *Good Lord,* I thought, *another beautiful young woman. Why are they all so attractive? Seven very attractive people.*

Seven? she said. *You really should not exclude yourself. Show me the others.*

I was looking into a pair of beautiful, clear dark-brown eyes, bewitching, strong and demanding. I smiled, and one by one I showed her.

Oh yes, she said, and I could see she was pleased. *I've only actually seen Natalya and she is so beautiful. I wondered about the others. You would like a drink?*

I smiled. She was the last of my group and she was definitely okay. *Yes please. Coffee?*

Of course.

Before she moved away I explained to her that I had disabled the security devices in her apartment and we had a brief discussion about them. She immediately understood and followed my process for disabling them. It was necessarily complex because the time period during which they were disabled had to look as though it was in fact normal but with no disturbing activity.

Then she was gone into her small but very well equipped kitchen. It was hard for me to think clearly about the eight of us but the other seven felt so good I felt like giving myself a hug and I wanted to be with Olaria. I tried reaching her by thinking my way through the star route but for the moment I was completely unable to make any contact with OlarCret, unless of course I made a simultaneity jump. Okay, but not right now. Then Januti came into my mind.

Please, share with me.

I felt the jolt. Knew she was... where I needed her to be and promised her I would join her as soon as I could. I felt her warmth and her smile across the thousands of miles that separated us.

Ai returned with two deliciously brewed coffees in exquisite china and sat down so she could be close and opposite to me, wanting to look at me, and I could feel the warmth and satisfaction and genuine delight at knowing who and what I was. She had removed her working clothes and wore a loose soft sweater and her skin looked soft and like alabaster. Looking at her nearly took my breath away. She had done something and then I picked it up – she had changed her emotional space. It was a transformation I had never consciously witnessed before but as soon as I saw what she had done I was entranced and could see the value of the clever use of subtle altered perceptual cues she was manipulating.

Shapeshifting, I thought. *You want me to see you as beautiful?*

Of course, she replied. *Why would I not? I have waited for a moment like this for more than a decade, sometimes not believing it would ever happen. This is like a miracle, a gift beyond measure. You are like a gift beyond measure. I cannot remember being this happy since I was a small child.*

I looked at her in wonder, thinking how fortunate we were to be such an attractive, interesting group of people, given the things we needed to do in order to survive. And, I thought, how useful to see the transformation she had wrought; it was just a few degrees short of shapeshifting. Assuming the shift could be detected by holo scanners, with a little bit of adjustment it might enable us to become invisible when we met in public and I was instantly relieved at one tricky dilemma that might now be resolved; I realized I had actually seen Olaria make such a move and smiled to myself, surprised I had not consciously noticed it.

I knew Ai was following my thoughts but was unable to see beyond into the details.

Please, tell me. You know I can't reach into you any further, but I want to know everything.

Ai, right now we do not have the time for me to tell you everything. What I am doing is having everyone meet the Olarians on Energystreamer *and get some basic information on the original Olarian telepaths with whom we have certain qualities in common, learn a little about their erotic, sensual behaviors and proclivities, and generally ensure that we are all on the same page before we actually get together, which I hope to be able to arrange shortly.*

I again spent a little over three hours with her and opened up some of her kinesthetic channels and showed her how to expand her telepathic range and depth. Knowing she now had a great deal to do, I gave her a hug and said goodbye. If she hadn't been bubbling with enthusiasm to spend some more time with the Olarians, see the holos and try out some of her new skills, I think she would have nailed me to the chair.

CHAPTER 5

Januti & Zed

I made the jump to my apartment, showered, changed and then made the jump to Januti. She was waiting for me, had been following me. I looked carefully at her. She was naturally beautiful, but now she was breathtaking, and I realized she had been watching Ai and had absorbed the knowledge necessary to enhance herself. She was dressed in what at first looked like a soft, blue kimono and nothing else; it fell in gentle folds over her body and showed her shape to perfection. Then I realized it was an Olarian garment – pure energy. I felt my body respond to her instinctively. She moved across the space between us and almost melted into me. She smelled delicious and I just surrendered to her clear and unequivocal desire.

The next hour simply disappeared and then we must have fallen asleep. My next memory was waking early in the morning in a tangle of arms and legs with Januti kissing me softly and my entire being feeling at peace with the world, an experience I would not have believed possible at this point. I don't know exactly what shred of consciousness drew me to hold her and just whisper softly to her. Somewhere inside I knew there was so much to do. She knew immediately.

Shall I make us some coffee?

I didn't need to respond and we sat in her lounge room sipping coffee and began to talk.

There's something I think of as indescribable about two telepaths sharing their lives, especially when they are young, as we were, at least in Olarian terms. We just talked, silently, until there came a moment and we were silent. We had been sprawled on her sofa, talking, silently, my hands softly stroking her body, holding her breasts and feeling her while she with the smallest amount of activity was managing to keep me hard as stone. This was a level of pleasure and intimacy I could not remember apart from my experiences on OlarCret. I was deeply enjoying our contact and our learning about each other when I realized we had an audience of more than a dozen others silently enjoying us.

I think I must have been acclimatized to the loss of privacy on OlarCret, but Januti was not. She became aware at about the same moment I did.

Oh my god!

Her embarrassment was huge but I held her, softly whispering comforting words and gently reminding her who we were already becoming. Several minutes passed as I held her, talked to her and let the others gently, warmly reassure her they were being loving, caring, respectful and kind. Slowly the reality of our new lives began to sink in. The Olarians were full of pleasure for us and the others who had been able to be with us were careful and respectful and gentle. Maybe 10 minutes passed with Januti holding me tightly, her arms around me, her head on my shoulder, embarrassment slowly seeping away.

This is our life now, isn't it? she murmured, and I nodded. She was beginning to settle down, nodding and responding to the warmth and delight and the safe honesty of it. We held each other tightly and her heart slowed as understanding flooded in. We both knew our lives were being determined for us, outside our control; yet even to me it felt extraordinarily new.

I did not want to leave her, however, there were things I knew must be done and I could not easily ignore them. I said I would see her that night and I kissed her, lingering for one more moment, then I made the jump to my apartment. So far as the building security cameras were aware, I had spent the night at home. I changed and went for a run, meeting Raille at our cafe when I was done. He talked enthusiastically about his new life with Jess and I felt truly delighted for him. I told him about a new girlfriend, but no details yet. He smiled. I saw immediately he was guessing she was telepathic, and I just smiled back. He knew that asking, at this point, was probably not wise and we reverted to some discussions about the future. When we parted it was with the subtext, 'to be continued'.

My mind was now occupied with arranging to bring the eight of us together, problem being, firstly, we were spread all over the globe. Several of us had jobs from which we could not simply disappear, and it was probably important we not be seen together as a group – perhaps ever, if that could be avoided. We lived in a society where holo and satellite scanners with the very able assistance of their almost unimaginably complex and elegant software could reveal pretty much where everyone was for anyone who had the right clearances and wanted to know.

So I decided that for our first meeting I had to be sure that each of the others could make the small simultaneity jump necessary to reach *Energystreamer*. As a precaution, I asked Esan if the Olarians were willing to help each of us to actually make the jump. Because of the time difference it took me 24 hours to check with each of them. Then, before we could each make a jump with our Olarian partner, we had to co-ordinate a whole mess of personal commitments and obligations. This took nearly two days and almost scrambled my brain. However, we did get organized and the Olarian crew were delighted for us to use their meeting space and their extra sleeping accommodation and were also more than pleased to feed us. Okay, logistics were now partly under control!

I needed us to meet. We all needed to meet. We had lots to do personally and operationally. How the hell should we begin? I know I spent more than one night trying to bring myself to take the next step.

If our little network was to come to life, it pretty much had to be me taking the initiative at the start. I spent some constructive time making certain we were not under surveillance. This was not like being on OlarCret and I felt it was not right for me to make any unnecessary use of the Olarians, it felt too one-sided. I knew they did not feel this way, but I had to live with myself first. So I stretched out my mind and said 'Hello' to Januti, making sure she was awake.

She was. I told her what I wanted to do. I wanted a brief first meeting in which all of us were involved. I wanted a telepathic connection between me and the other seven. I wanted it not to be *my* pipe dream. She was delighted and I could feel the deep emotional connection again and a mutual pull for us to be together; it still surprised me and I was not yet able to fully trust it. However, I was nearly overloaded and unable to be with her right now and she got that and was okay with it.

It was 10pm in Canberra when I contacted the other seven simultaneously and that meant everyone was awake; some were working but everyone was able to find a private space. I began by asking everyone to make a brief statement about how they were feeling about their newfound capabilities and whether they felt ready to meet together.

Esan and Serra joined us, an entirely Olarian thing to do but disconcerting to several of the group. I spent some time helping the group become familiar with the open lack of privacy to which they were now card-carrying members. That discussion took place with the Olarians listening in a semi-puzzled way to the group and their anxieties and me slowly refocusing their perspective.

Privacy dies hard and our little group had been very private for years and knew they needed the invisibility of privacy from the non-telepathic world. So some repetition of our basic messages about openness was needed before it could settle down and the Olarians were genuinely comfortable about being part of our discussions. They too needed acclimatizing to us and our difficulties.

Look everyone, I am uncomfortable about our separateness at this early stage of our development and feel a strong sense of urgency about us coming together for three days soon. All we now need is for everyone to find a three-day period when you can be away from your home and work and not be noticed.

Essentially you will need to be known to be going somewhere that is ill-defined so no-one can expect you and on the way to which you can disappear without holo evidence. It needs to be from a place where one of the Energystreamer *crew can meet you out of sight and make a jump to* Energystreamer. *Please remember, you need to be going to a place where you could be expected not to be taking calls.*

It was Ajit, our programmer, computer and electronics wizard, who came up with a solution that appeared safe and workable for the planning part of this exercise. His suggestion was simple enough: *If each of you mark on your diaries all the days in the next 14 during which you could be away for three together, I can access your diaries through the nets without being visible, figure out the timing and then let everyone know telepathically what the dates will be.*

Then, each of you need only make arrangements with the people around you and your Olarian Energystreamer *crew member. This will permit them to follow you until you reach a point where it will be totally safe for them to pick you up and take you aboard.*

And that was what we did and it worked and I hoped it would be the one and only time we would need to have so elaborate and difficult a plan in order to meet.

CHAPTER 6

The First Telekinetic Telepathic Group Meet

We arrived on *Energystreamer* over several hours. The crew, who had met us all separately, knew everyone. I knew everyone. The others were all meeting face to face for the first time. It was a meeting I thought would be remembered. We were the only current living group of human telekinetic telepaths and all of us were wondering now if we were actually 'human'.

The Olarians came initially into the meeting room to welcome us and say hello face to face before leaving us to sort ourselves out. It's hard to describe how eight telepathic novices connect. I watched and listened. At first everyone was talking out loud but the babble and the fact that everyone was kind of listening in on everyone made for a seriously confusing experience. So within minutes the conversations were more one to one and silent and the group began to explore itself. I suggested we sit, and people stopped talking and sat.

Everyone was listening in to one another and they were finding that a little confusing when I broke in.

I think, I said out loud and telepathically, *we need a little time to adjust to the best ways for us to be together. I know our hosts are with us, so it might be useful if we listened in to them for a few moments to get a sense of how they manage all the overlaps. It is no different to when everyone speaks out loud. So it is like in any social gathering. The difference is the additional scanning that is going on to assess meaning and intention. Also, it takes a moment when it is new to access the appropriate prior memories that are influencing the idea. At first this will slow you down, until it becomes a familiar pattern. All of you will by now realize it is way faster than any of us are currently processing information.*

I promise you, that will change. It has already changed for me. In addition, all of us are used to privacy; we now need to get used to an absence of privacy. Forever. Once we've got that the rest will, I think, fall into place. That's how it has worked for me, and remember, please, I have had a year to adjust.

I paused and could feel the pastiche, everyone behaving in their unique ways, yet all the ingredients were here, but they were being explored and used simultaneously and I could feel the interest and surprise but also the connectedness from our hosts. The eight Olarians who were with the decision-making group with Miyuki were at present on board *Energystreamer* and I felt them join us and they too were taking some delight in seeing the beginnings of a new telepathic community. When I listened in to them it sounded and felt more like family.

Somehow that felt right. However, for the seven newly discovered human telepaths this was a great deal more than disturbing. A shift from more or less absolute privacy to absolutely no privacy, at all, ever again – that was really hard to absorb and unsurprisingly most of them did not as yet actually get it.

I looked at us, almost total strangers, pulled from around the world into an alien spaceship and buzzing with warmth and connectedness, and I found myself missing Olaria. I felt a twinge of sadness and I drew myself into our last journey to Tall Trees Valley. I felt her there and knew that she had been telling me this was an end to an important aspect of what I think of as our love affair. I realized I had known this when she took me on the most intimate journey of my life. I knew she had intended it as a parting gift and an unspoken shove to move me on to a new life on Earth.

I also knew that it was not that she wanted me to feel less intimately connected to her or reduce my sense of being her partner in our daughter, it's just she had been clearer than I that I needed to move on; there was no possessiveness in it. She was surrounded by family and people who loved and cared for her, and I realized everyone I had met on OlarCret had such supportive connections without obligations and without end. In that moment I finally realized that she had known our intimate relationship must end if I was to adjust to and become part of the next piece of my life on Earth. And I was here, now, in the middle of it. Well... the beginning of it, actually.

I had begun to become a part of that network of connection on OlarCret and I had to make that process be a part of what we were going to have to do here on Earth. Her gift had been a connector and an ending of a piece of our relationship. She had known, better than I, that I needed to be connected to the waiting members of my new family! I slid the slightly self-pitying edge of emotion out of my mind and I felt Esan whisper, quietly and with warmth.

Grandmother will never cease to love you, Zed, any more than she will cease to love me. But you need to take what I know she gave you willingly and honestly and use it here to create your new intimacies and build a proper life here. She will always be there for you, even when she takes another lover, and I think that won't be for many years. Like all of us she will connect Rozari to her eight and you will also be part of that and so connected to all of us forever. That will also be true for your other children: four boys and three girls.

I had a family on OlarCret, I had already created that, and I think that reality had not yet sunk in.

He was of course right. And as I looked around I thanked him, I felt a shared warmth and he slid out.

I regrouped and focused on our little group. And then, for just an instant I realized, I felt, 'good heavens', I really did have a new family, and a warmth and delight filled me. I felt Esan touch it and smile with real pleasure before I let it go for now. I had been holding the group at bay but now I let go and allowed them in. Soon I would be unable to do this; they would have unlimited access to me. And I was not surprised to hear myself saying to them, *You need to get used to the idea that a lack of privacy is not damaging. The Olarians have all been raised in a society where doing no harm and mutual care-taking are the norm. We have not. So when any of us think unpleasant or negative thoughts about someone else, we can all know... depends on who is listening in at the time. Importantly, we did not have decades from our earliest memories to learn the values we need.*

There is no room in this process for someone to say they do not want you listening in. It will be so completely habitual and inevitable that we all will need to work on our values and social skills. But the really biggest thing: every connection feels all right when it is done with love and you know you never have to be defensive about it. Conflict, feeling or holding different ideas need have no negative valence, no destructive harm in it, and that makes it so much easier to learn and change.

So, for example I know that the erotic likes and preferences and desires that have been sparked over these last 10 minutes for everyone are known to everyone. So the usual social norms from which we operate can slowly be put to rest. Let me remind you of the history of the original Olarian telepaths and their need to raise children and build a telepathic community. Unlike them we did not set out to find each other. I set out to find each of you.

As each of you also know I found all four of our female members deeply attractive, as, all of you now know, did every man here, and interestingly the opposite was also true for every woman in our group. However, sex, coupling, children and our community are all issues about which we are going to have to talk – a lot. And yes, the issue of having or creating children with the Olarians is also an issue.

However, as some of you partially know already, the Olarians can hold their age stationary at any age. That age is usually around 38 but it can be older or younger as they wish. There are still some of the children of the Originals alive on OlarCret and they are as healthy at 3000 as they were at 38 or so when they stabilized their age and some of them still occasionally have a child.

I have had my age stabilized at 38 for some months only. I am also able to perform the process for you, but each of you needs to think this through and want to do it. At this point most of you have years to make up your mind, so you do not need to rush into a decision, however, it is now an option.

The group went very silent and I watched and listened as they thought through the issue. It seemed they were actually thinking about it for the first time as being connected to them.

You will all see that we have some extraordinary issues to consider and decisions to make. The Olarians have developed processes for maintaining optimal health; we are going to need to learn and incorporate these into our lives.

I waited while they thought this through sufficiently to allow me to move on.

At this point in time it seems to me extremely important to keep our existence a secret known only to the eight of us and the Olarians. I think we need a serious discussion about this and genuine consensus. If our current and latent abilities were known we would be, potentially, in a very difficult situation. Not necessarily at physical risk but our lives would be instantly changed and not, I believe, for the better.

I should also let you know that my friend Raille and his partner, Jessiqana, from a powerful Cretian family, also know that I am telepathic and telekinetic. I believe I have nothing to fear from them and they know nothing about the seven of you. Raille and Jessiqana pretty much know this about me because I ferried them using simultaneity to and from Cretia over several months. At first I thought they might believe the Olarians were doing it through me, however, it was far too frequent for them to be fooled for long. However, I repeat, they do not know about you and I do trust them implicitly.

There is no reason they should ever come to know you unless circumstances should change in some unexpected fashion. You should all know that I will protect them with whatever capability I possess. I feel closer to them than any other human person, and Raille has been my only friend for a very long time.

On OlarCret I was really only finding out about myself. I had no perspective on the future and I did not know you. However, I did know of your existence through Olaria and had met Januti and Natalya briefly. If any of us feel the need to bring a non-telepathic friend into our world this will necessarily be all right, however, it would be helpful if we were able to talk about it in advance if that is possible. And we will necessarily have to feel okay about it and manage whatever consequences it will have on our future.

The group was watching and listening to me very attentively then, one by one, they acknowledged that they understood my feelings, respected them and realized we would need to discuss such an event, probably when it was about to happen or when it had simply happened. After some considerable conversation about it, this remained our agreed position.

Another very large issue is the business of our development – the building of each of our abilities both telepathically and telekinetically. Also it is important to establish the extent of simultaneity capability in each of us.

There was a rush of questions. I answered them initially by saying, *While I was on OlarCret I found that I can make simultaneity jumps across the cosmos. I can, and do, regularly visit Olaria and my daughter Rozari on OlarCret. Has anyone ever felt they may be able to make such a jump?*

I knew immediately that no-one did but Natalya and Januti thought they would like to work on that. Some of the others wanted to know how they would know and I asked them to put that on hold for a few moments. Then I outlined the capability range that I believed all of them could develop and I knew they had seen some of this in the Living Library replays and more importantly that this was only what we presently knew. We knew from the Olarians that we possessed other areas in our brains that were still inactive and the function of which was unknown to either ourselves or the Olarians.

There is a lot to explore and our environment is not all that conducive to sites we could use to experiment. However, I have a more pressing issue I would like to talk over with you. It has to do with how our situation differs significantly from the Olarians'. It is different because of our culture and our situation here. It is about truth, honesty, privacy, relationships and integrity.

None of us can lie to one another, we cannot behave with duplicity, we really cannot express emotions that are not genuinely ones we are feeling without all of us knowing. These are all things we can experience with other people but not among ourselves. We need to manage this reality, which is quite different from the reality of ordinary non-telepathic people: the people who, up until now, we have believed ourselves to be.

I thought about the reality that we were all together for the first time. They knew, basically, what we needed to do. I don't know why it felt important, but for some reason becoming couples seemed to be something important we needed to do! On the surface, this may appear ridiculous, however, I was unable to let it go and I became aware I was not alone. I wondered why I was thinking about the importance of us becoming couples, why all eight of us were also fixed on that as our first priority. I could not see why it seemed to be so pressing except it did feel as though it was.

While I was able to drag myself back to our present, I could not shift the sense of urgency around coupling. Then, eerily and disturbingly, I suddenly became aware that we were not driving this necessity! If I knew, they must also know, so I decided simply to move on.

I was aware there were several intimate and other relationships between members of the group and non-telepaths, yet a moment's checking found me staring wide-eyed at a piece of information to which I clearly had been paying no attention. All, and I mean every one of the relationships that had existed for any of the members of our small group, had been terminated by the members of the group before they made the jump to be here today! I simply shook my head and thought, as my mother would have said, 'bless my cotton picking socks!', then I simply let it go.

What is or has been a truth for someone, sometime, does not have to be our truth going forward. Please tell me everyone gets it. This is a structure, a belief, that will permit us to not be trapped in our own or another person's past.

The idea of live and let live probably should be more like the Olarians' system. I believe we shouldn't tolerate interpersonal violence, or emotional or physical abuse, or hostile emotions. I also believe, having watched how our crew on OlarCret had to engage with our individual foibles, that this is going to take some serious work to which we need to have 100 percent commitment.

Does everyone get it? And do you agree? And are you ready to have an initial conversation about ourselves and all this messy stuff? I say all this knowing that we appear to represent an interesting cross-section of the culture groups of our world.

It was difficult to describe the emotional complexity generated by my dump. I had thought I was simply expressing how I saw our initial task. There was a babble of conversation then the group settled down and for more than 30 minutes chewed over the issues I had raised.

We had agreed to spend three days together this first time. They decided we should learn about ourselves first as individuals and then about our different abilities. We all knew there was an artificiality about it, but our situation really did not allow us a lot of choice if we were going to make it. I didn't think it mattered where we began just so long as there was some sort of order to it.

I stopped. I knew how critical this simple idea really was. I felt the need for complete understanding and agreement. To my deep satisfaction, after many explorations around the group, I knew they had got it. Finally my churning neurotic anxiety settled and I felt safe to move on.

CHAPTER 7

The Group Journey on Energystreamer Begins

As I looked around I realized we had no familiar ways of being together. Then it occurred to me that I had never actually knowingly used my telepathic abilities to fully explore another person. The only real intimate relationships I had had on OlarCret had been with Olaria, which had been close but still not as intimate as it could have been had I been more focused. After that my explorations had been far more superficial with the seven women who would bear our children! So as I looked around at our group I thought, *I will only ever know you if you choose to share the history of your life with me! If I define the degree of intimacy I believe we actually need! Somehow.*

Januti and I had shared a little of our history, but as I thought about it, not deeply. What's more, I was thinking of that intimate knowledge as private! Not something I would feel free to exchange! I could just see it: 'Now Januti, take me on the sexual experience with your last partner or your first time!' Would it ever be something I could or would ask about? And, if it wasn't, why not? What was the significance of secrecy here? Given how this experience worked, she would only need to remember and I would have an almost exact replay of how it was for her. How would that be for me? And if I replayed my experiences for her, my early disasters or my later successes with Olaria... it felt like cheating, yet Olaria and I had shared more and others had been there with us. Real, deep knowledge could be had by simply being there when it was occurring. I had had that experience. But going there on recall...

When you have lived for more than a thousand years, how much of your experience could another person explore? Then I became aware the room was silent and the seven of them were following my thinking and I could see the nods and frowns, the eyebrows pulled down, eyes cast questioningly to one side, and as I watched each of them, the feelings of concern, of uncertainty and confusion begin to slide in and overtake everything else. It was as though I was finally beginning to grasp some actual understanding of the issue, one I had not considered once during the entire year! Yet I vividly remembered one or two of the deeply intimate experiences I had watched and felt when Olaria and I visited some other couple making love or replayed their stored memories from the Living Library.

I let my consciousness reach out to Esan and Serra, both of whom I thought I knew more fully than the rest of the *Energystreamer* crew, but came to a full stop. Esan was saying to me, *How could it be otherwise, Zed? I never gave it a thought and I think Mother probably didn't either. In fact, I believe none of us may have. When we meet someone new, with whom we have decided we might like to explore an intimate relationship, we have developed a pattern for learning about each other.*

He stopped and I knew he already understood I had seen the pattern and I was shaking my head. Olaria and I had sat and lain together for hours while I had relived much of my life for her, and she had asked questions that had led me to think through, feel through, so much of my life including my childhood and my sexual failures. She had done the same for me, taken me through innumerable important events of her life. But I remembered how I had baulked at her taking me through the intimate experiences of her sexual and relational life with her other partners and her birthing experiences. I knew her more fully than any human being I had ever met. I realized as I replayed the year on OlarCret, she had let me understand her life in ways so intimate, so... almost embarrassingly transparent, that I had not given even a moment's objective thought to the process I had been experiencing. How could I have been so thick, so insensitive?

I looked at us. I could feel the anxiety, the confusion, the distress, the uncertainty, the expanding awareness of what it actually meant to be telepathic in the way we were. Intimacy was always fully available if we wished to choose it. Why had I stopped short of it with the seven mothers of my children yet to be born? It was a human, not an Olarian, thing. The seven of my human cohort were following me with a strong feeling of heightened anxiety and concern. Then I realized, like everything else, it really was up to me! Oh how embarrassing, how... I could not even find the descriptive words. My strongest realization, one I was still able to prevent them hearing, was my embarrassment at actually doing it.

So, looking at each of them in turn, I asked: *Do you actually understand what it means for us to be telepathic, for example, in understanding each other's sexual experiences, likes and dislikes? And understand I am choosing sexual experiences because they are the most intimate and extreme I know to choose.*

Allowing someone else to fully experience what your build-up to orgasm feels like, what you like and do not enjoy? Realise, you do not have to say anything, you just have to remember it. Realise too, the reason the Olarians have their children follow deeply sexual, sensuous intimate relationships pretty early in their lives is, I believe, to help them understand what sharing intimacy is about, how it works and what it feels like. After that, pretty much everything a person experiences is easier to share.

It's why I wanted each of you to watch the Olarian sexual relationship tapes. When you have experienced the extreme intimacy physical and emotional of another, you are, freed, in a sense, from embarrassment and so are likely to be able to be better connected to one another.

And so the scene was set. We needed to know one another and with only another half hour's discussion we had complete, if uncomfortable, agreement about what we would do and how we would do it. We would each sit quietly and think through our lives, stopping at any event we believed was significant or which one of the others of us wanted to understand better. And so began the strangest two days of my life. Each of us explored our personal development and our history in extraordinarily intimate detail. We stayed on board *Energystreamer*. When the two days were up and the last tale told, Natalya spoke to the group.

That was the most excruciating, yet satisfying, experience of my entire life. I feel overwhelmed. I am surprised. I am tired yet stimulated, excited, and a word that is strange even to say out loud – cleansed. Immediately I knew she was not alone. All of us felt that way. *We cannot be Olarians, none of us grew up in their world with their experiences as children, so we must somehow give ourselves permission to fail when we hit a bump, as we inevitably will. However, we do need, I think, to be willing to accept this truth.*

And to that she received 100 percent agreement and commitment.

I want us to pair up. I know exactly who goes with whom and I am certain you also know, and she was right.

She and Peter: she pointed out to him that he had been pretty much unable to take his eyes off her since she arrived and both had been totally absorbed with one another's journeys. She wanted Ai Shen to confirm that Ajit was her partner and that she had been as absorbed with him as had he been with her. No argument there. Donna, who had initially been uncomfortable with Darcy, had, during his journey through his life, connected to him and felt him join with her as she lived out her life story. Their initial discomfort had entirely vanished by the end of their stories and they were already sitting together.

They all looked at me, but it was Ai Shen who opened the engagement with me.

Zed, we all know how deeply entwined you and Januti are, but I feel that I need to ask how you will be able to manage the relationship with Januti and the relationship with Olaria who we know has been your partner on OlarCret and with whom you have a daughter, Rozari.

The question was fair enough and deserved an appropriate answer.

Olaria ended our sexual relationship with my complete agreement and understanding. She did it in an Olarian way and it was a decision with which I was entirely satisfied. We both knew, she better than me, that I could not build an intimate relational life back here if we did not end the sexual part of our relationship. I was sad to lose her but I know she will be more than well cared for on OlarCret. It was something we had both anticipated and it was something she wanted. I was pleased that we had agreed that I would play an active role in the life of our daughter, Rozari.

It was at this point that Esan rejoined our conversation.

Zed, I hope you will not think I am overstepping a boundary here. But, he hesitated, *but... I need to say some things to you. Olaria is surrounded by people who love her dearly. She knew this situation was going to arise for you. The last journey she took you on, that was very intimate and special. She has done that journey only three times in 1500 years. Once was with my grandfather, once when she was very young, around 120 years old, with her first real true love. You met them both. Now you. She knew you had to commit yourself to one of the human telepaths and she knew how hard that was going to be.*

Because she truly admires you and loves you, she gave you the most intimate journey an Olarian can give. It is a gift not everyone can give. Usually, but not always, it is a woman's gift. It has been called, and this is just my best translation, the Gift of Everlasting Intimacy. She knows you are basically a one-woman man and that she could never be that woman for you. She knows that when you make your decision to be Januti's partner you will cease to be her lover and that will be totally okay for both of you, and Rozari will be the point of contact for you and her and Januti.

With her final loving gift to you, she guaranteed first that you would never need to be alone again and that you would be able, when you were ready, to share that gift with your human partner, but only when you are ready. With that gift you became a part of her forever and free to move on with your life.

He focused on the human group.

You do realize, don't you, that she met six of you on her visit? She did not find you, Donna, as you were off-world at that time.

Each of them were acknowledging what he had said.

The room on the *Energystreamer* was absolutely quiet and still. There were almost no ship's sounds, unlike *Sunstreamer*, just the barely audible flow of the uniquely Olarian/human-constructed air purifiers.

Finally I looked at Januti.

You heard what Esan has said. This is one of those moments when I feel myself to be cosmically minute and insignificant because I knew without awareness when I left Olaria to make the jump back to my apartment on Earth what she had done. That she was saying goodbye to a piece of our brief time together.

I didn't want to acknowledge it; I was not ready to feel abandoned and I did not really understand that she was not abandoning me. I realize now as I recall that morning clear as it was when I was there, as you can see, she was happily opening a door to a piece of my life for which I was completely unprepared but for which I was entirely responsible. It was inevitable. How could I have been so thick and so naive? So unprepared?

CHAPTER 8

Rozari Intervenes!

I stopped and was deeply silent and in that moment I was suddenly in contact with Olaria across the intergalactic space, pure audio simultaneity, and she spoke silently to me.

Zed, I had a hunch your simultaneity had more than we had yet seen. Do not hold us here too long but know that Esan does know. Rozari is beautiful. I know she sends her love for you as do I, thank you.

And my awareness was back on *Energystreamer.*

Everyone was looking at me with stunned expressions. But it was Esan who put it into words.

You did it, didn't you? Your mind made the simultaneous jump – for a few seconds, you were home with her?

I nodded to him.

That is a step she and Jald could not make when they were traveling and now you and apparently only you can open that door! You are amazing and I am delighted. This means that when you wish it and are ready, you will be able to make new journeys we can as yet not conceive.

The silence hung like a lazy smoke cloud in the room making its own unique shapes, and slowly, ever so slowly, time and space returned to the room and everyone was looking at me!

Januti was watching me, the expression on her face one of wry irony; she was gently shaking her head, her soft black hair swinging around her shoulders.

You are a genuine five-star puzzle, and I am the one who must ask why a man more capable than anyone alive of extending reality in ways barely conceivable would choose me as his woman?

At which point I burst out laughing.

I feel like a human drone, being piloted from somewhere distant, beyond my ability to conceive or even comprehend and under remote control, yet still, apparently, required to make my own decisions about things over which I appear to have no control and which I obviously do not understand. And, the truth is, Januti, you and I need to find some place from which we can move on!

She looked at me. She had been deeply attracted to me from the moment she had stopped being anxious about me. When she had realized what I had done for her, for no conceivable reason she could understand, she had taken a leap of faith of which she had not even been aware. There had not been, since that moment, any sense that she would belong with anyone else. She looked deeply into me, studied me while the group watched and knew, absolutely, she had been right.

I have never really wanted a man before. Never felt there was someone out there for me until the day you stepped into my life. I have studied you, I know how deeply Olaria is in you. Tell me if you believe you will be willing to explore that same depth with me.

I wept, silently and deeply. I could feel her through my being, in my bones, and I watched as she used Ai Shen's shapeshifting trick to make herself more completely mine, surrendering her all to have me be her partner on this world. And, right now, in this moment, I surrendered to an inexplicable inevitability. My entire body was vibrating with energy. Silently, one sub-atomic particle at a time, my body/mind was reconstituting itself. I had no conscious part in this process; I felt as if something inside me had been set in motion the moment I had reached across the galaxy to speak with Olaria. Now, something inside me was shifting. Time seemed to stand still. Then with no appreciable change in anything, I felt as though I had just reclaimed myself. I don't even know what that means. But now finally I knew I could move on and I smiled at and into Januti.

I hope you will have me, was all I could say, and there was a gigantic sense of relief and she was sitting on my lap, her hands gently holding my face and we were kissing although the whole group was staring intently at us and the Olarian crew were watching. I was so deeply connected into her I felt utterly at peace, one of the few times in my life. Then, when she let me go and slipped into the seat beside me, I felt whole and, finally, peacefully connected. I knew it was the moment to move on.

I know you have all seen the story of the first Olarian telepaths, so you know they made a clear decision to have children with their partner and then each couple had a child with each other, thus spreading the gene pool and creating the present 700,000 million Olarians. This probably ought to not be a topic for us right now, but we do need to realize there are eight of us on a planet with 17 billion-odd non-telepaths. We might need to consider our position on this. The Olarians do not have our narrow time-limited perspective and many Olarian women would love to bear children sired by the four men in this room and many Olarian men would willingly and lovingly and happily sire children with the women in our group.

I burst out loud laughing at the expressions on their faces.

Please, I am not suggesting any such orgy as you are all imagining with horror. Please! I know we need time to think and feel this one through and I am simply putting it on the table so our Olarian hosts can understand how this idea impacts us at this moment. I am hoping in time you will all feel less horrified and disturbed by this idea.

The Olarians have built their world on the understanding that their gene pool needs to expand. I am totally committed to helping them and I seriously hope you will also all come to be. I hope you will not feel horror and discomfort that they have this hope, this expectation. Januti, I hope you will see this. None of you needs to feel the obligation I feel. I hope you will come to believe that the child Olaria and I have conceived is not simply some kind of genetic experiment. I do not want to feel insulted by that thought, this is not a 'Midwich Cuckoo' scenario. We are genetically interesting, not only on this planet.

Januti, who had been holding my hand, let go and it took her a full minute to study me very, very carefully before she put her hand back in mine and rested her beautiful head on my shoulder, whispering, finally, *It's okay, Zed, I do understand.*

It was Natalya who spoke for the rest of the group.

Sh—, Zed, that was some bombshell to drop on us. But I've been probing you very carefully and I know this is not some nightmare and I want to thank you for the courage I know it must have taken to put that out here and now. I get it, I really do, and I must say, I want time to adjust to it. When you finished, I knew Peter needed time to adjust, and now I see all of us do. And I want to apologize to our hosts, because I know this is a matter of enormous importance to you. Please give us a little time. This is a big thing for a short-lived human life. I believe we will all come around once we are able to think this through and realize that we are not being pressured here.

We could all feel the sadness of the 16 Olarians and felt them deeply probing our thinking and our feelings, then slowly assimilating and then accepting without the slightest trace of negativity the feelings and experience of the women and then the men in our group.

Esan spoke for them all.

I know you don't need me to say this, but thank you all, Natalya, and especially you, Zed, for raising this. I can see that was typically courageous and we will certainly be happy to wait to see if you become available to assist us. In the meantime, millions of us are watching Rozari and the other seven yet to be born.

Esan's comment brought the subject of our future interaction to a close, and we decided to break into our couples to assimilate some of what had been discussed and experienced before resuming what was our last day on the *Energystreamer*. Januti asked me to spend the night in her apartment. *Please take us there now, Zed.* Such was the depth of her desire, I could not refuse.

◘

There are not necessarily words for everything. Some experiences remain in a domain of their own. My brief time with Olaria was one. After my first intimate and passionate connection with Januti, I wondered if our explosive encounter had been just a consequence of our brief yet disturbing history, but that night I spent with Januti felt so much more again. Whatever had been extraordinary about my connection to Olaria, this one with Januti was landing me squarely in Jard and Leiti territory! After we had held each other in a hungry possessive moment, I again had that eerie out-of-body sensation that left me feeling I was not actually in charge of my life, that I was connected to... something else.

The sex was astonishing but it was not only about the sex. It was the quality of our intimacy and connection and the indescribable depth of our satisfaction in being together. Certainly it involved the mutual giving of pleasure and delight. There have been moments while playing my harp that the piece of music has been transcendental and I have had the sense of being at one with it when I have been lost in the beauty of the composition. What we gave each other during that night existed in this realm and it was dense with quality and connection. Truly indescribable. An experience of unconstrained intimacy and unearthly delight such as Olaria had shared with me. Yet none of these was right for the night Januti and I first truly loved one another in her apartment. She wanted me to remember it forever; she wanted me to know she was mine, to have as I wanted, feeling the pleasure as an incredibly generous gift, one being to another, totally free of constraints or conditions. Now that was something.

Last time had been deeply intimate; this night was unearthly. There is something a woman can give to a man if he is willing and genuinely respectful, something he will understand is not merely memorable but unforgettable, a very special gift. Memorable does it no justice whatsoever. Januti assured me it was not a one-sided experience, and so I would fully understand, she told me explicitly how she felt about me and how she felt as we gave each other sensual pleasures.

It had begun as we sat in her tub, she leaning back between my legs, me softly massaging her as we kissed long and gently. We talked silently, sharing the sexual things we each desired, but in the end we knew that none of these would be the thing that bound us together. Olaria had made me feel things I could not even describe but Januti belonged with me, absolutely, and I was totally aware that I belonged with her.

My lowly skill with words does not enable me to adequately encompass how we took one another beyond ourselves. I awoke in the morning to find us a tangle of arms and legs, her breasts pressed against me and her soft pure-black hair spread across the delicate blue of her sheets; I was in heaven. I took a picture of us in my mind. I truly wanted time to just stand still and a strange indescribable wave of energy slid through me. It was so eerie my conscious mind surfaced to fully wake me up.

This was the second time in my life where my deeply intimate relationship with a very particular woman left me bewitched in an experience that had taken me beyond any sense of myself I could possibly have imagined. It had transformed my understanding, stretched and gone beyond a boundary of which I had been blissfully unaware. Opened a door to the question unstated and almost unimaginable: if these two experiences could occur, then what else could I not even presently conceive?

Without warning I became aware of a need for Januti, Olaria and Rozari to meet, and in that instant we were in Olaria's sitting room and Olaria walked in with Rozari. The three of us adults were aware that Rozari had somehow willed our presence. It simply should not have been possible, yet we all knew we were here because she had needed us to be.

Olaria was looking at me, her head tilted just a little to one side, a tiny smile on her lips and a question in her beautiful green eyes. I looked at her. She smiled warmly at Januti and I heard her say, *We haven't actually met, but I first saw you some months ago. I am truly delighted he found you.*

Then, turning to me, Olaria asked, *Do you know how, Zed?*

I looked at Rozari, then I felt again the weakest, clearest, gentle call – my daughter had called me from across who knows how many galaxies.

Olaria picked it up *How could she?*

There was no real question that it had been her. Then Januti and an instant later Olaria heard it – the smallest, weakest signal from an infant had reached out across what seemed to be the furthest reaches of space/time to find her father with just the tiniest of questions. The choice and actions had been mine, the voice had been hers. I had responded because I had no idea what I had heard; how could I? And I suddenly knew I could have just reached out from home and given her the reassurance she had been seeking.

Olaria sat down and Rozari, now completely at peace, began to feed.

I apologized to Olaria for our unexpected intrusion, but she simply smiled as Januti and I realized we were entirely naked! Olaria was clearly delighted at what had transpired and at us being together with her in her home.

Listen.

Januti and I became aware of an indescribably huge audience who were present at this meeting and the astonished delight at what had just occurred and I realized only Januti and I were feeling embarrassed. As people welcomed Januti and expressed their delight and as she slowly assimilated what had just taken place, Olaria clothed us, more for our unprepared astonishment than for any Olarian reason.

What I needed was an even clearer understanding of what had just taken place. Rozari had not brought us – I had done that – but I had been responding to her faint but nonetheless clear call! I needed to remember and not let this happen again. The consequences could have been, could be, disastrous.

She did not want to feed this evening, Olaria said. *I think your absence was disturbing her and she reached out to you, but you were not near and without having any idea at all at what she was doing, she just reached out further to find you, except she reached out into the universe and she found you. She did not bring you here but you felt her and automatically responded because you have not yet fully integrated your simultaneity into your life. She has, I am certain, no notion whatsoever about what just occurred and could not have caused it directly even if she did. Her brain has, as we hoped, a tiny bit more complexity even than your own and it seems she can contact you wherever you are, which is wonderful and needs monitoring. It would be helpful if you did not feel the need to leap across the universe at her whims! Or, more specifically, at the whims of any of your other seven children.*

I agreed. However, all of us were aware of the excitement our little adventure was causing across the Olarian world. Januti looked at me. She had not heard Rozari but she was delighted that I had and that I had responded. She was, I realized, thinking about our children and their safety into the future.

We said goodbye to Olaria, Rozari and our audience, and I left Rozari with a feeling of love and safety. Holding Januti's hand, I took us back to her apartment. Januti had watched Olaria make our clothes. She had already learned to create them from Serra but observed that Olaria used an entirely different technique. She remade a set completely from her memory exactly as she had seen Olaria do. The process worked; the clothes were perfect. She smiled with satisfaction. I shook my head. I knew I had missed something but was not sure what exactly.

The others were all buzzing with questions, however, after we dressed we were not quite ready to return to *Energystreamer* and the others were happy to have another few hours together before we returned. We knew there were some curious and excited people, human and Olarian, and we followed some of what was happening for the others, knowing they would share more when we were together in a few hours' time. A very human pattern and one I knew from my experiences on OlarCret we would soon come to change.

One more piece of the last 12 hours clung to me. It was not a piece I had ever known before, not really. I could feel the quality of connection and the strength of feeling that my existence in her life, especially in our moments of intense intimacy, gave to Januti. I think until now I had never allowed myself to feel or understand the quality of relationship a woman could feel about a man. I hoped I could always bring that to us and I felt a heretofore unknown sense of completion.

CHAPTER 9

Januti & Zed

Not yet ready to return to the others, Januti and I sat together on the shaded private balcony of her apartment. The day was warming up and as we ate breakfast she reminded me of the journey she had taken us on yesterday aboard the *Energystreamer*. This time it wasn't about where she had grown up but how. Her parents had been part of the middle class that had grown quickly in Japan. Her mother was Japanese but her father was an American who, she had been told, had been recalled to the USA when Januti was only eight years old. She and her mother had lived very comfortably and her parents, well educated themselves, had been insistent that Januti also be.

They had succeeded in keeping her silent about whatever she knew about others and, like most of us, they had forbidden any discussion that might have led to a realization of the potential that lay locked inside her. She had studied Japanese history then global and big history and politics, philosophy and literature, and a strange convoluted collection of units in the anthropology streams. She was very quick to learn and found study easy, however, because of her parents' anxieties, she made few friends.

Her parents' almost paranoid concern that she not get too involved with other people had finally led her to her first sexual experience aged 18 with a teacher. He had been a gentle soul, and she had let him lead her toward their first encounter in his rooms when she had learned that she could not only sense what he wanted and what he was thinking but how to influence him to feel satisfied with her and let her control him sufficiently for her to feel powerful. It was the first time she had allowed herself to feel in control of any relationship she had. However, he had not been very satisfying for her and she had had two more violent and not really pleasant relationships – Jenko had been the second of these. She had wanted to believe there was someone out there waiting for her and, until I had shown up, had no idea what such a man might be like. She had never felt relevant to the men in her life until the night I appeared.

She had known immediately we met there was a connection, had lost the thread but recaptured it when I had returned. She knew, then, I was the one she had been waiting for. Once we reconnected, she began to allow herself to experience the world in a completely new light, and, as she looked at me over the small balcony coffee table, I understood how single-minded she was capable of being. She had thought through my relationship with Olaria, sorted it and been ready to accept me and move on.

She had a deep and quiet intensity, a focus, a sharp awareness of everything around her and now, feeling free, she was allowing the inner powerhouse that was her mind to open and expand. I realized she felt she needed me to keep her grounded as her potential slowly opened up. It was another extraordinary experience to feel her energy as we sat in the early-morning sun, the brilliant white of Mt Fuji in the distance, and she brought us together from several feet away, cocooning us in an emotional blanket that allowed her to speak freely about the experiences of her life.

There was an issue for me that I had not so far aired and now felt like the moment. So I turned to her and said, *There is something I want from you.*

She looked at me, trying to read what was in my mind, but I was holding it closed. By thinking of the question only in separate pieces, I stopped her from getting a fix on what I wanted to say. So she gently raised her beautiful eyebrows and enhanced herself so she knew I would be almost uncontrollably hungry for her.

I shook my head and smiled. *Januti, I need for you to agree to teach me about how to please you in every way. Everything you desire, each sensuous preference, how to give you pleasure and for other things about which I might not automatically seek to understand you and what would please you. And I want to know that you want to learn these things about me, deeply, genuinely and not just because I raise the issues.*

I sat very still and waited. What I knew was, without being with a partner who understood the need for this seemingly unusual request, intimacy could be a very hit-and-miss affair and might not develop as well as it might. I had seen enough of that on Earth. On OlarCret I had seen the Living Library memories of some failed relationships and came to feel the significance of what I was asking.

She did not immediately respond. I watched her and waited. For me this was not a throwaway or frivolous request.

For a start our hunger for one another will safely carry us to mutual loving and mutual satisfaction. That will be supported in our early days by our energy, novelty and raw passion. But as we move on in our lives, the things that give us deeply satisfying pleasure will almost certainly begin to change. I believe that behind them are the possibly more subtle experiences a lover, a partner, can give you, ones that are unique and capable of extending the richness and specificity unnecessary in the heat of early passion. I want to learn and come to fully understand these things about you, Januti, and I want to know that you not only understand but that you also have that desire to find them in me!

I stopped, realizing that this may well come across as a human male seeking knowledge an Olarian could find by merely desiring it! But I wondered, was this knowledge easily retrievable as time passed?

I watched her carefully as she took the information in and processed it. I felt her surround my words, if you can say that. She looked at me with more than love; she looked at me with total joy that one of my conditions for our relationship should be that she teach me how to take care of her as if I was a student as well as a skilled and attentive lover and a person who liked and enjoyed her. And now I also knew she was definitely delighted to be with a man who could and would unhesitatingly leap across the universe to be with his child because she had unwittingly called to him! I could see it as a killer quality on my resume.

Januti smiled. *I promise to take your request very seriously. I have never been asked for that and I have never thought about how to do that. However, I love it that you want that, and you have my word I will find ways to give you this and seek it from you.*

And that pretty much was it for me.

Januti was ready to burst open with joy and excitement and I realized we were going to need some big projects if she was to remain safe and satisfied. I looked at her and into her with joy and warmth and amazement; there was power and potential I could only barely apprehend. I thought, *I've got a tiger by the tail*, and she burst into laughter that was a mind-warming experience. It was a sound like no music I had ever heard; ripples of delight were running through me and it had a subtle rich flavor; it was a complete and fulfilling experience. I thought, birthdays, Christmas and New Year all wrapped in one package, and I could feel her joy and satisfaction as I grasped the energy she was using and fed it back to her from the joy inside me. What the hell we were going to do with all that energy I was unable to even imagine at the moment. She was so beautiful and loving and open with me, and with that I knew that words simply would not do it.

She wanted me to tell her my story again and go even further into some bits than I had the previous day, and I used the model I had seen work so well with the Olarians. I remembered using the images, starting with my childhood. She watched and listened and felt the movie of my life. An hour passed and I came into the present with her. She was totally delighted and absorbed but I could feel her sadness at my years in boarding school and her fascination at my holidays and long study periods in Japan in an almost unknown but prestigious martial arts schools. Today's journey had repeated some of yesterday's but had taken other pieces even further and I knew we would continue sharing like this. We had both seen some of the others also doing it, as though the pattern we had begun needed to be expanded even more.

What she found most difficult to understand was the shadow of disbelief that sat like a solitary cowled monk on my left shoulder, reminding me that I was a fraud. For a moment she even tried to persuade me to disbelieve it, but I simply did not possess the belief that I was the progenitor of my successes. This shadow self rarely left me for long. I could not resist asking her to consider how she thought we might have come into possession of the powers that we had all clearly been given. And I added, *I think the cowled figure is a reflection of my shadow self and must play some important role in my life.*

To which she said, *How can you be the success you are, have the power you possess, and yet feel so uncertain about yourself? How is that possible?*

However, at the level of our connection, we were coming to a better understanding of one another. I then had her take me on the same journey with her life and I was wonderfully engaged with some of the beauty her Japanese lifestyle – its elegance and subtlety and patience – had created for her. I followed her school and university career deeper than before and realized again she had a hunger for knowledge and understanding and an ability to manage complexity that was marvelous to see. I knew we would have many things to brawl about and discuss and with which to stimulate one another.

I wanted to have her and was deliciously pleased to feel the strength of her hunger for me, that it was at least as great as mine for her. I took her hand and led her toward the bedroom. She followed without a murmur, finally submitting to my hunger willingly and actively so she could give me what I wanted and get the pleasures she was seeking. I moved very close to her and slid her kimono from her shoulders and drew in my breath as I saw how exquisite she looked, her long black hair brushing her breast just above beautiful large hard nipples on generous breasts. She was a beautiful sensual delight and she was making it abundantly clear that she was mine.

She glided toward me, undoing the belt on my kimono and putting her arms around my neck and pulling me into a soft kiss, first with her lips then her tongue, and we did intimate and satisfying oral connecting with licks and kisses that were hugely sensuously delicious. I gently lowered her onto the bed, began to kiss, lick and softly stroke her body from her neck across each of her breasts, drawing deeply on her nipples and feeling her respond with a rapidly growing arousal, down her smooth, soft but firm belly to her clitoris, where I gently circled the sensitive head encouraged by her moans of pleasure and by a softly spoken series of instructions about what she wanted me to do, and how, and where, and I just followed them and learned.

It was easy, because with each instruction softly issued and each response from me, I could hear and feel the totality of her pleasure and delight and satisfaction build until she could no longer think with any clarity. Then she demanded that I be inside her. I first slid a finger inside her to find she was deliciously wet. I kissed her clitoris then ran my tongue around it as she moaned and moved up to me, begging me to get inside her, but I made her wait as I licked the edges of the lips of her vagina and enjoyed the flavor of her and totally enjoyed her moans of pleasure as she rose up to meet me. *Please be inside me,* and I did as she asked, and in an instant I had filled her and she was moaning, making delicious sounds of pleasure until we came together slowly, then with increasing passion and finally a moment of total ecstasy. The power of her orgasm ignited mine and kept reigniting me as it went on and on and finally I slumped beside her, pulling her with me so we were still coupled together, and we kissed and hugged and shared the pleasure of our bodies.

I had had a very small number of intimate engagements with attractive women in my life before OlarCret, but I knew that what had just happened with Januti was not just a very special encounter. She had willingly surrendered to me and I knew from the strong and gentle movements of her body she was not finished with me. I had looked after her carefully. I knew she wanted to give me more as she very gently disconnected and slid down my body until she reached my penis, which she took slowly into her mouth, causing it to grow again. She enquired gently what exactly I would like. And in some subterranean area of my brain I knew, felt, understood, how seductive it was to have a partner explore me simply to ensure they could enhance my pleasure even more.

'No,' I said, but she was clear my 'no' was an automated response, not wanting her to feel uncomfortable, but not my desire. And she was right, and I explained slowly to her what I would actually like and she engaged with that with a warmth and honest enthusiasm that undid me.

I'm going to make you come till you beg me to stop, and she did. She took me deep into her throat and slid me out again until I came. Her sounds of pleasure and delight flowed over me and when she was finished with me she slid her hands over me, kissed me on the slowly sinking shaft and, murmuring with pleasure, crawled up my body until we kissed again, sharing our most intimate juices with one another. As my arms reached around her to pull her close, she nestled totally connectedly up against me and we rested, sated.

Before we got up to face the day she pulled my face into her breasts and made soft murmuring sounds of pleasure and desire and joy. It was really not until this moment that I realized how well Olaria and the Olarians had taught me, and I felt several of them murmuring pleasured thoughts in my mind and I knew they were also connected to Januti and for the very first time I felt at home, loved and cared for in a new and entirely different way. My life had changed and Januti was a part of that change. She knew and snuggled closer, making sounds that were delicious and satisfying and resonated through my body. For a moment she acknowledged the others who had been with us.

Finally, we returned to the *Energystreamer*, where the eight of us drifted back into the meeting room. It was clear everyone had begun to build a relationship with their partner. What was even more satisfying, everyone had been able to make the small simultaneity jump to get here, and I was aware of the continuing surprise of the Olarians about the rate at which we were learning.

I have no idea how I managed the days that followed. I do know that I listened carefully to the connecting that went on between our couples and I knew I had created some sort of milieu in which the reality of our relationships might be worked out and was astonished later that evening to find that the three couples had agreed to share this complex entanglement and the women all agreed they would, in the years ahead, bear children for each other's partners and for the Olarians.

The stimulus for this shift had been the awareness that as they had each explored a relationship with their partners, using the experience of the Olarians from the Living Library memories, they had known the Olarians were there with them and it was all right. The total lack of negative judgements was a new and very powerful positive experience for them. Januti and I had been aware, during the night, that others had been occasionally with us. There had also been times we had been for a while with one or other of them and had felt uncritically connected to them.

It all started out feeling complicated, but it ended up, many hours later as our first meeting came finally to a close, being simple, but not in the manner anyone had imagined. I still did not know how much had been manipulated by the Olarians and how much by others, and I was of course thinking of the Seeders. But I knew as we ate with the Olarians that it was not only Januti and I that were joined.

Over the next 24 hours, with the help of the Olarians, each of our group had a personal tutor and the rate of their learning affirmed for the Olarians that as a group the human telepaths were genetically more advanced than most Olarians and the desire for our genes heightened. By the end of the time on board *Energystreamer* each of the group was able to make the simultaneity jump to and from their homes and – and this was the big one – to and from places to which they had never been. The others were not yet able to make the intergalactic jump and I still did not understand how the first of these for me had been instigated.

The Olarians had learned to make the simultaneity jumps through the pattern established when the first one had done it. But when Olaria, Jald and Esan had been able to make the jumps into space without their bodies traveling with them, a whole new learning had needed to occur. It was limited but not bounded.

When I had made the intergalactic jump, no-one was prepared for it, least of all me. So it had taken time for Olaria to follow how I had made my jumps. There were unknown elements and as yet not a clear grasp of what exactly we were doing when the jump was made.

Then I remembered: my first unusual jump had occurred immediately after Olaria had adjusted my age. I had not at that time made the connection. I first imagined I needed to think of where I wanted to be, yet I had the feeling that there was a way I could travel to a place I had not known but did not yet know what that extra something was. Olaria had been certain my brain would pick it up as I continued this journey and I would gain fuller control of the process.

◘

On the final night of our three day 'timeout', Januti and I were in her apartment. Her voice in my mind was soft and warm and surrounded me. She held me and sometime during the evening we made love and it was beautiful and I slept a sleep as deep as any I had ever slept. Exhausted, safe, comforted and relieved.

At the end of our last day, Donna had said, *Zed, have you given any thought to how we will be able to manage the eight of us being together?*

I had looked around the group.

I am imagining that everyone has given some serious thought to the future. I know some of you have. We need to do this as a group.

Donna had picked up the thread.

If I said I was about as loaded intellectually and emotionally as I can manage, would I be the only one who feels like this?

Within seconds she knew and everyone had acknowledged most were in this space. However, I did not want them to leave without having sorted our next step. Probably a bit anal, given we could easily have talked telepathically from wherever we were living, but it felt important to me that we be together for it, but for no reason I knew.

I know you are all overloaded. I do really appreciate that. I had more time to adjust than you have had, and I was on another planet so I did not have to worry too much about those around me because the crew were pretty much in as tricky an emotional space, not quite like mine but not too distant. But I fear we are in a particularly difficult and vulnerable space and I feel responsible for putting you all in this place. I am not seeking sympathy, just, I don't want anyone to be harmed as a result of my actions. I want us to be okay.

I apologize for being so untidy but I want us to leave here with some kind of a mutual understanding about at least the next steps for us and some feeling of equilibrium about carrying on our lives, to a reasonable degree, as they were before my intrusion.

Peter and Ai both began to speak at the same moment and Peter slid back to allow Ai to take the lead.

Zed, I will speak for myself and I think each of us needs to do that. I'm certain you know nothing in my life has been as momentous as meeting you and then meeting the rest of us. Nothing comes anywhere near. I doubt anything ever will, but... well... we'll see. I know that you want each of us to speak about how we imagine returning to our other lives and not causing ourselves or the others problems we certainly do not need right now. Some of you know, because you were with us when we talked, that Ajit and I have decided to try to spend time at each other's place as much as possible but to check before one of us makes the jump to ensure we have taken care of our holo message locations, our visibility and the security of our apartments.

Ajit has shown me how to manage our holo locations so the sats believe we are where we should be, and Ajit will help anyone who needs help with that before we leave here. I also know that Zed is more than capable of managing that. We talked a lot about how to manage people at work and our families. We are, I think, pretty clear about how we will do that. The thing we both discussed more than anything else, however, was how we would ensure our new awareness of how people around us are thinking does not trap us. We practiced a few scenarios to make sure we were clear about that. The thing we did not discuss was where we go to next and we thought that you probably needed to be the one to talk with us about that. But we know we want very soon to be living together.

It turned out that Natalya had been listening in and had spoken to the others and they had had the same discussion and I wondered why we hadn't been there.

Natalya was following me and said, *I'm really sorry, Zed, I think of you as up there, knowing everything that's going on, and it never occurred to me.*

Or to any of us, the others chimed in.

Hey guys, this includes me, you know, Januti chimed in. *I'm not any superwoman.*

The way she said it caused everyone to laugh. I realized yet again that I was the odd man out. It had always been so, for me, and I felt a deep twinge of sadness and a murmur from the cowled figure sitting quietly on my shoulder.

The group were listening to me and they were feeling guilty. I picked up their concerns.

Look, I know I am the oldest of us and I know I am the one who somehow got to be the one who brought us together, but I'm definitely not the leader and I'm definitely not in charge I'm just the one who got to find out first and I had some pretty potent help. Without the Olarians, I would probably never have known any of you existed. I really am just one of us.

The group was silent, looking at me and listening in to my emotional response. Januti and I were sitting together on an energy seat we had shaped to be a kind of two-seater couch. She slid closer to me so our bodies were in contact. I was silent and sad. These were the people most like me on Earth; they were all about eight or 10 years younger and already they were not thinking of me as one of them.

I was okay with responsibility, but isolation, not so good. They were all trying to think what to say and Januti was holding her finger on the emotional pause button. Like the others, she was monitoring my emotions. I did not attempt to control them and soon the group was clear that I was sad, a bit down and a bit sulky! Sorry for myself! I felt the range of emotions slide across my awareness without interrupting them.

It was Peter who broke the silence. *That's not okay, Zed. I feel more obligated to you than any other person in my entire life. I do not want to feel in any minute way responsible for causing you to feel excluded from us. You are, like it or not, our leader, at least for the foreseeable future, and I am totally satisfied with that. But I do not want you to feel sad or excluded and I will remember from here on.*

Without hesitation all seven spoke almost together, their message much the same.

It was Ai who said, *I'm really sad to see how you are feeling. I have been so into my own crap and trying to adjust to Ajit and truth is, I think of you as our leader because for now you really are and I think you need to be.*

I realized several of them wanted to come across and hug me but they were watching Januti very carefully. She was acting like a tigress with a threatened cub! Instinctively she had quietly put up a nearly impenetrable emotional shield about us. I turned to look at her; she smiled, laughed out loud and removed it.

God, I'm sorry everyone, that was so unlike me! But I feel so possessive of him. We met when he definitely saved me from lord knows what kind of frightening horrendous life. He is not just my lover, he's my hero; he's so precious, I'm sorry.

Everyone was smiling. They were delighted. She had taken possession of me and I was hers and that was now established beyond any reasonable doubt. That was making the group very happy. I smiled, delighted, comforted and genuinely feeling pleased. Her response had been totally automatic and it was not a response I had ever experienced apart from only slightly similar early memories associated with my mother's anxieties about me.

I smiled, lifting my attention to the *Energystreamer* crew who were paying attention to us.

I said to them with only a touch of irony, *This is all your fault!*

Then I laughed and shook my head and realized the incredible turmoil that had been roiling inside me since Olaria had first spoken to me on *Sunstreamer* more than a year ago. Esan and Serra were smiling at me.

Okay. For the first time I smiled a smile that came from a peaceful place. *We do need to tidy up our re-entry to our old lives and make a plan for our next physical get-together.*

The energy in the room was strongly focused on beginning our new lives, but we all knew we could not just cease to exist in our present worlds. We needed to keep our identities stable while we figured out how to become our new, preferably less-visible, selves. This could not exclude me. After another long discussion we decided to meet again in two weeks after everyone had looked at their work schedules and the time differences. With a little juggling it was determined we could do this again on board *Energystreamer* if we kept our meeting to just one day. And that became our plan. In the meantime everyone was going to spend most of their off hours practicing and developing their abilities while trying to imagine a way for us to become a community. Everyone realized that practicing meant never being in reach of the Global Satellite Scanning System.

Without almost any involvement with me the group decided that Canberra in Australia would be a good place for all of us to live. I was genuinely pleased but felt a stream of low-level anxiety at the idea of us all being in the one town. I believe I was thinking of the Midwich Cuckoos, yet it made a kind of sense; we did not need to be in the same place to travel to meet, yet the advantage of us all becoming residents of the one town, especially my town, did feel good.

We said temporary farewells to each other and the crew and each of us made the jump home.

The group had known the Olarians were still in discussion with Miyuki and the 20-odd people calling themselves the Global World Assembly about how to use the year they were to remain here and I wondered if we needed to somehow be a part of that set of conversations.

However, that would also mean the *Energystreamer* would need to return to OlarCret with the discussion team to bring back a specialized team to engage with the final problem selected and I was anxious about losing the incredible support the Olarians were giving us.

I arrived home to find an urgent message from Miyuki: 'Zed, I am in need of your services for a couple of days and I promise to add them on to your present leave. Would you please come to my office on Moon Base One as soon as you get this message. Your reply will activate a high-speed shuttle request.'

She wasn't kidding. No sooner had I affirmed that I was available than I was informed a shuttle would be at my apartment in three minutes. I changed and went to meet it after letting Januti know.

CHAPTER 10

Miyuki's Crisis

Miyuki's crisis was, as I realized when I scanned her en route to Moon Base One, the Global Assembly responsible for the formulation of the issue on which the Olarians would work for the human world over the coming year.

The arrangement was based on a clear 12-month period. The first part of this project involved a group of eight very senior Olarians familiar with the administration of their system whose job it was, in concert with the Assembly, to identify one substantive project on which they could expect to be helpful to us. The Olarian group had been sitting now for a week with the specially convened Assembly. The 20-person human group had been meeting for four weeks with not a single indication of progress! A list of projects culled from a complex collection of possibilities from all over the world had been identified, pretty much without surprises.

1. Rubbish on land
2. Rubbish in the oceans and managing fish stocks
3. Repair of the damaged ozone layer

4. Power generation and transmission (in the hope of finding something entirely new that connected human and Olarian power concepts)
5. Children, care and education (in the hope of learning something important from the Olarian experience)
6. Weather management (in the hope of finding a human equivalent of the Olarian power and control system)
7. Health of the human race
8. Food production and equitable distribution
9. Control of violent crime and property theft (really about creating safety for people in a heavily weaponized world)
10. Population management
11. Managing the consequences of conflict between different religions
12. The world's top physicist/mathematician believed there was one underlying area that really made sense to pursue, and that was the relationship between the Olarian ability to see and utilize energy and the human processes, a purely theoretical domain in which the two worlds might constructively engage. The issue had originally been put up by a global meeting of the world's scientific community and linked in some non-explicit way to the fact that the Olarians had been able to construct *Energystreamer* from the schematics of *Sunstreamer*.

While all the issues were real problems, only 2 and 12 had managed to get through the two weeks of wrangling. What was clear was that the 20 human representatives simply would not agree which of these projects the Olarians should be asked to help with. Also, the representatives were unable to agree on what kind of assistance they wanted from the Olarians.

The group was divided in two camps. One wanted the Olarians to actually solve the problem, which of course would be a one-off activity, so for example, if they cleaned the ocean it would almost certainly become contaminated again in a reasonably short period of time. The second group thought the appropriate way to use the assistance of the Olarians was to align them with scientists with whom they could work the problem, coming up with a solution that would enable human science and technology to be able to engage with it, so not a telepathically or telekinetically based solution.

An additional obstacle to a resolution was that the Olarians had been clear with Miyuki that the choice of the issue on which they worked could not be theirs – it had to be human selected. So they had sat with the group listening to the arguments swirl around the room, endlessly returning to a reiteration of the importance of each of the issues. Thing was, they knew who was blocking a resolution and why. However, they did not think it was appropriate for them to interfere in this strange and dysfunctional human problem-solving ritual.

Finally, in desperation, Miyuki had called a temporary halt to the proceedings. The group seemed to be no nearer a decision than when it began, although many aspects of the issues were now much clearer to the Olarians. Miyuki suggested the group return home for three days to speak with their various constituencies and the Olarians would now also consider what they had learned. It was when the group broke up that Miyuki had summoned me.

I was a little surprised that it was me that Miyuki had summoned, but further exploration of her thinking revealed that she wanted the entire SFC executive to help her sort out the dilemma, and she wanted us to do this with the Olarians!

It was a pleasant day on Moon Base One when I arrived and made my way to Miyuki's office. I was cleared through security with no hitches and found myself alone with her. She had organized for me to be the first to arrive. The others had been summoned only after I had arrived at Moon Base One. She greeted me warmly then, once we were seated in one of the cozier niches in her office, launched into business.

'Zed, I feel embarrassed. The Olarians have been extraordinarily patient with us, however, this group is divisive and apparently completely insensitive to the impact of their relentless bickering on our visitors and I am at a loss as to how to proceed. I do not have the authority to override this group so I need to find a political solution before the Olarians just give up on us. We have for more than a century been teaching our people to *work the problem.* This is really just another problem I am hoping you and I can explore. I wanted you to be here before the others because you know the Olarians and might be able to see some way through this.'

I looked at her, uncertain about the path we were pursuing. 'Have you asked the Olarians why they think the group is reaching no conclusions?'

She looked at me with gentle frown-lines showing on her forehead.

'They made it clear at the outset they felt obliged to allow us to decide what it was we wanted of them for the year ahead. They did not think it appropriate to be involved in that decision.'

I looked at her with some surprise and concern. 'Well, while they cannot be asked to help choose a project, they can be asked who in the group is blocking a solution and why. Surely that is not inappropriate?'

She shook her head and I could see that she was berating herself for not taking so obvious and simple a path. Then I realized she was not accustomed to having around her people who could simply know what was going on in other people's minds.

'Oh crap, and so obvious a solution. I wonder if they might be willing to speak with us.'

I already knew they would, and suggested Miyuki contact them in the way she usually did.

Sure enough, in the shortest time the eight of them materialised in Miyuki's office.

We did not understand why you had not asked us. It never occurred to us that you did not know, so it was not the kind of help we imagined you needed.

The spokesperson for the group asked me telepathically and I answered, *Yes, she wants you to tell her.*

Dr Khan, the group is being blocked by the five members who are in some way involved with ore and mining. They decided, among themselves before you ever met, to make certain no decision could be reached. Their objective is to discredit us in any way they can unless we can be made to agree to their mining on our planet. They are somewhat child-like, extraordinarily vicious and intensely greedy. They appear to have no interest whatsoever in a solution to your planetary problems and we have been wondering why they have not been challenged.

Miyuki shook her head. Two of the five were members of the SFC Board. Miyuki was not stupid; she had been aware that her two mining board members were undermining the process, but had been unaware of the extent of their duplicity and planned obstruction. She was hoping that, without damage to my position and because I had a strong relationship with the Olarians, I might be able to help her solve the problem they posed.

The Olarian way always relies on transparency. In this case that would involve bringing the little destructive enclave out of the dark and shining a light on them and their position. But how? I thought about making the next session of the panel one that would be transmitted to the entire world as a starter.

It was an acceptable option for this forum and its task, and Miyuki had access to the facility and we could ensure it remained an open channel. This could be supported by Elaine's worldwide media connections. The Olarian awareness of the five could be held in reserve if more straightforward and transparent processes failed. We had access to the recorded holo clips for the decision making of the group for each of the options. These showed only that more than five of the 20 were opposed to each and every one of the options.

The numbers were important, because the group had made one undisputed agreement: there should be 80 percent support for the chosen project. This decision stood out for two reasons: all subsequent decisions had failed to reach 80 percent , i.e., 16 people supporting the proposal. The mining group was comprised of five people – four men and one woman – and the voting was always done by secret ballot. The record did not, therefore, show which members voted for or against a proposal, only the final numbers.

When the group returned, they would be expected to make a decision not on each project but to vote for one and give it the green light. All votes were electronic and did not identify any specific voter. Nevertheless, we knew that no single project had received more than 50 percent of the votes. Each was rejected by several members of the group, however, we also knew that five of the rejecting votes were the same five individuals each and every time. This had been known only to the Olarians, but now Miyuki and I also knew. We also knew, now, as a result of a vote taken before the break, that there were two projects that had not been ruled out of contention, mainly to not block the intentions of the five: Projects 2 and 12.

So the plan seemed simple. With the whole world watching, the group would vote on which project would be the one we would ask the Olarians to work on with us. While the group had decided at its first meeting that 80 percent support would need to be achieved for any decision to be accepted, what the group did not realize was that the five mining executives were responsible for ensuring that every decision was blocked by their negative vote.

We knew, because of the Olarians, that if people supported their first choice there was now no chance of an agreement – five 'No' votes would ensure there was never an 80 percent vote. And we also knew that the five miners could block any choice whatsoever, even if all the rest supported it.

So here was the bind. Without being visible, the five miners could block any outcome, even now when there were really only two active options remaining.

Miyuki had a contingency. If the group rejected both of the remaining projects, which we knew they would, Miyuki would put forward a proposition the Olarians would support – the Olarians were willing to undertake both Project 12, which was a purely theoretical project, and 2, which was an entirely practical program. The mining group were not aware of the agreement.

Miyuki looked at me.

'Zed, how will my proposal that we run two projects solve our problem if we have the mining group blocking us from getting a new agreement?'

'Well,' I said, 'imagine the amount of global anger and disbelief if these five got their way and the Olarians left without a program that will help humanity.'

She looked at me, smiling.

'You were cut out for politics, Zed, although you despise the whole process. But these five are not going to go down without a fight. They have a great deal of wealth and ego tied up in this venture on which they have embarked. It is also very unlikely they are operating alone. So, even with the Olarian agreement to work on two projects, they might still find a way to not agree we should pursue this option that we have been given.'

'I know, yet the question we need to answer is, what will it take to make sure they are not willing to face off against the rest of the world? Or, maybe, what resources do they have in place to outmaneuver us that we can sabotage? We need some help before we go to this meeting. We need some intelligence on how these five are operating and what kind of support system they have in place. If you have no objection, I will discuss this with the Olarians, engage in any enquiries that need to be made and report back to you. This will be a last-ditch stand and it would be good to know they cannot sabotage it.'

I left Miyuki and moved to my new office. I met my new personal assistant and promised her I would have a long and detailed discussion when I returned from leave. I knew she had enough catch-up work to do to fill her time more than adequately. I contacted my other seven and the eight Olarians, summarized and clarified the present situation and asked if the Olarians could provide any further information of the wider support system being used by the five mining executives. They had been keeping a watch on the five and now could give us a playback of the response to our enquiries about how the mining enclave were certain they were not on anyone's radar.

The biggest surprise was their naivety – the five believed the Olarians simply did not have the resources to track their network. So they had no idea the Olarians would know who had voted against every proposal. They naively assumed they had been invisible, firstly because they had arranged to have the software underneath the voting rigged to show the wrong individuals voting against each proposal, and perhaps more importantly because they believed they could point the finger at Miyuki for the action. What was interesting was, while the voting was secret, who voted in each vote and how they voted was actually known to the computing system. It was this data that the five had managed to sabotage.

This meant our first job was to get the votes on the system showing the correct responses. This was necessary because the software had been re-established to its original state after the false readings had been set up.

It took only an hour or so for the human telepaths, with Ajit's help, to locate who had done the tampering and how the software had been tampered with. The culprit was a senior programmer who had been bought by the mining consortium for a substantial sum. His accounts and the details of the software manipulations were put in Miyuki's hands and she dealt with the programmer, promising him that his entire involvement with the mining lobby group would become public record if he ever spoke of this to anyone.

If he agreed not to, his activity would be erased from the record and his account would be zeroed out, leaving him with a job, a clean record and an unblemished financial record. But he would henceforth be under expanded security observation and if he wished to continue working he needed to keep in mind the consequences of any future breach of SFC electronic security. She also gave him assurances that the mining syndicate would not be aware of his change of situation. In the end that was only slightly more difficult.

Miyuki believed these plans would pretty much neutralise the mining group. She came to my office, enquired if I was satisfied with it and my PA, and then asked, 'Are you willing to chair this meeting if I get the Executive on side?'

'This will be my first act as a member of our Executive. I already have some kind of issue with Julian Kared with which I have not yet engaged. Are you confident you will be able to manage it?'

She smiled the smile of the tiger!

'Well, I will make it clear that you are the only one of us with appropriate knowledge of and experience with the Olarians. I will frame it as an appropriate challenge for you as a now senior member of the organization and ask if anyone has either any better idea or any objection to you undertaking this task.'

'Okay, but you need to ensure the Olarians understand what you are up to. And I want to raise a somewhat larger issue, probably more central to our problem.'

She looked at me in that intense way she had and I knew she was both anxious and hopeful that I might come up with a somewhat devious yet apt solution.

'Miyuki, please correct me if I have this wrong, but would you agree that voting by secret ballot is a way for the *villains* to remain in the dark on issues that affect the whole world? And would you ask yourself by what right all of the human planning group have been permitted to hide, not their machinations, but their decision-making from the world that put them in this place to work in all our interests?'

She looked at me and a smile spread slowly over her face.

'Oh, you beautiful man!'

I could see her reviewing how she had been manipulated into accepting that process and realizing that it had been just plain wrong. She had known from the beginning without being able to see the hidden impropriety of it. Transparency, she reflected, was what we thought we were getting; how had she been so easily duped into agreeing to the secret ballot?

As soon as the full implication of the process into which she had so easily been drawn was clear to her she just shook her head and smiled contentedly. I had done precisely what she had hoped I might be able to do – cut to the chase and identify the nature of the problem that actually needed to be solved: giving the world the transparency it deserved. As a final thrust I asked her if I was incorrect in assuming that by putting me in the firing line she was taking the heat off herself.

She looked at me and I watched her thinking about how much truth there was in my conjecture and what was the most appropriate way for her to respond to me. I saw her reject dishonesty and finally decide she did actually have to be straight with me.

'Zed, I am just a little embarrassed to realize you are right. I have been trying to get out of the line of fire. It's sort of what I have learned I need to do. And it is true that in putting you there I was taking care of my political interests. However, in my defense, I did believe that you would achieve something that I might not be willing to engage. And I think you have proved me right. So, if you think I am feeding you to the lions, I will take the role back, but if you stay with it, you have my word I will support you publicly 100 percent .'

I looked at and into her, saw immediately she was speaking the truth and that now she had a clear shot at solving her problem she was no longer seeking political cover. I was still a little concerned about the actual process of her fitting me into the role as the chairperson and her handling of the almost certain backlash from the powerful mining lobby. However, she made it clear she was on top of that.

'I propose to let the mining lobby hoist itself on its own petard. Once they agree with my concern for public scrutiny of the committee's process, they will call for the votes to be made public, thinking the information will support their case, not knowing their deceit has become known to us. I will, reluctantly, agree, if the rest of the committee agree. I can see no reason they would object. At that point the five miners will become visible and their plan to have us shown up will be rendered dead or, if necessary, we will make the details of our knowledge of their behavior known to them along with our willingness to "out" them to the world. They then have to either accept that or make some statement about the software being rigged and that will open up an interesting new engagement we believe we can now manage. We will also inform them we know and can show their voting deception and their actual intent, if that is what they wish.'

So far as Miyuki was concerned, that was settled.

The 14 members of the executive arrived within a few minutes of one another and were all seated in the executive meeting room by the time Miyuki arrived with me. There were several warm welcomes from individuals on the SFC executive team and an official welcome from Miyuki. After giving a succinct and clear summary of the time so far spent with the Assembly, she told them what she wanted.

Several members wondered why she thought it more appropriate to use me, a new and untried member of the executive team, however, it was only Julian who was strongly against using me, even when Miyuki had explained why I was the most appropriate person to do this task. Interestingly, his basic objection was that I was the member most closely aligned with the Olarians and most likely to support their needs and their position rather than giving appropriate weight to ours – the polar opposite of the logic Miyuki had used to insert me into the process!

I closely followed his thinking and his emotional state and found that not only did he not trust me, which at first I thought was an astonishing piece of information, but he was very angry that I had sussed his bug in my apartment and had his staff member remove it. He was convinced that I had used the Olarians to find the bug and he had built up a very corrosive story about me in his mind. He was not a good person to have as an enemy and I decided Miyuki and I needed to defuse whatever it was that was pissing him off with me.

There was a robust discussion about the meetings with the Assembly and with the blocking behavior that was being carried out in the World Group, but what was most informative was that there were three members of the Executive who were essentially bonded to the members of the Board with whom Miyuki was most concerned.

I was interested to see that the three with the deepest vested interest in the outcome of this discussion were unwilling to show their hand openly, merely satisfying themselves with putting as many obstacles in the way as possible, but in the end, faced with Miyuki's very strong insistence on people putting the full detail of their concerns on the table here and now, they backed off and supported her request rather than the primary interests of their Board members. Crossing swords with Miyuki was clearly not a safe strategy, and they knew it.

As the meeting closed Miyuki called to Julian and asked him if he would come with her and me to her office. I realized he was both uncomfortable and angry to be called to account here and now with me present but Miyuki was not open to discussion; she made it clear this was an instruction and Julian immediately let go.

When we sat in one of the nooks in her office she began without hesitation. 'Julian, whatever it is that is making you hostile to Zed, put it out on the table for discussion now. We are not leaving here until I am satisfied that I understand what is going on between you two.'

Julian looked at her, saw the tell-tale lines of determined intent around her eyes and mouth and in his mind cursed me and the situation into which he was being painted. Then I caught it. He was in the pocket of General Genarus, who oversaw the military domain of SFC and was fiercely hostile to the Olarians and their pacifistic position and deeply resented their being invited to Earth, afraid they might successfully erode his power base and his militaristic ambitions and was anxious to minimize their impact and find some way to best them.

Wow! I could feel Julian's frustration and his feeling of being cornered. He tried several avenues to avoid dealing with the affair of the *bug* but finally was forced to admit he was not convinced of my loyalty to either SFC or the human race!

Miyuki and I looked at him in stunned amazement.

'Excuse me!' I said. 'Where do you get off determining my status as some kind of alien spy? What wasp crawled up your ass? Who the hell do you think you are?'

It was clear I was beyond angry with him.

'What gives you the right to make assumptions about me without a shred of evidence to back up your absurd and totally unacceptable bigotry? Get that look off your face, mate. I know you don't have any evidence because there could not possibly be any unless you planted it.'

Miyuki studied the two of us, holding in her incredulity. Then, without flinching, she said, 'Julian, it seems to me that you are choosing to either put your position in this organization or Zed's on the line here. This meeting will end when I am totally certain I fully understand exactly on what basis you make these claims, that the evidence is irrefutable, at which time it seems to me likely that one of you will probably be suspended pending a full SFC enquiry. Either that or you will be making at least a formal apology. I am saying this to you, Julian, because if you have any information supporting your claims about Zed you had a responsibility to inform me immediately.'

This meeting was not proceeding along the lines Julian had hoped. He clearly had no idea how strongly Miyuki felt toward me or how thoroughly she had vetted me and he was feeling badly rattled. Miyuki was simply looking at him, eyebrows raised, head tilted to one side, a question mark waiting for a response.

I was following him very carefully, then I picked up the source of his hostility. He had been edged out of his position overseeing the crew debriefings by my new procedure, one which had Miyuki's seal of approval. He had been so angry at this loss that he had had his staff go over hundreds of hours of *Sunstreamer*'s records and found what he believed were instances of me inappropriately blanking them, which was of course when we had engaged with the Olarians telepathically and so no record had been made – a position I was empowered to take.

He had decided, because the general wanted him to, that I had to have been the instigator of illegal and inappropriate record erasures, and then he had proceeded to pursue every lead that suggested I had behaved improperly in favor of the Olarians rather than the crew, and on and on he had pursued this line of thought. He had multiple images of me clearly not speaking out loud with Olaria or other members of the Olarian Council, whereas nearly every other member of the crew, even when they communicated telepathically, often also spoke out loud, although mainly during the early stages of our engagement with telepathic communication.

I had become his obsession, and General Genarus, to whom he had some, so far unidentified obligation, had been pushing him very hard to tie the loose ends together and get me out of SFC. Finally he acknowledged he was following an instruction from the general to identify the traitor from the *Sunstreamer* crew and deliver him into the general's hands and out of SFC.

It was becoming clear that Julian had got himself in water that was way too deep for him. The general had him over some sort of a barrel and he was now attempting unsuccessfully to serve two masters.

'Before I rule on this matter,' Miyuki said, 'I want to hear what you have to say, Zed.'

I studied Julian very, very carefully, probing as deeply as I could go, looking for each little marker that would tell me more about what was going on beneath the surface here. I found it finally. Julian was thinking about that moment when he had lost control of his life. The general, then a bird colonel, had given the then MP Sergeant Julian Kared a 'get out of jail free card' when he had shot and killed what appeared to perhaps have been an unarmed military escapee who had been AWOL and illegally hiding out in a high-security zone. The then colonel had made it clear to Sergeant Kared that he would not be made to account for the absence of a weapon the escapee had supposedly used to threaten Kared, so long as Kared remembered clearly the nature of the obligation this rescue placed on him. The holo images of the event had been taken out and kept by the now General Genarus.

Without moving or changing my expression, I contacted Esan. Without hesitation he was willing to help in whatever way he was able.

'Esan, please speak to Dr Khan and tell her that her best move at this time would be to allow me to speak alone very quietly with Julian beneath the reach of the sound recorders in her office.'

Miyuki was at first taken aback, then when Esan explained that I may have a way of defusing the situation with Julian, she apologized to us, saying she needed to use the ladies room, and left.

I moved my chair closer to Julian and then I whispered to him, 'I have received some information that I need to share with you very quietly, for your sake, not mine. I have learned that you are fundamentally a decent and honorable man in a very difficult, embarrassing and compromised position.'

He made to move away but I told him, 'No, Julian, sit still, please.' My voice carried a certain persuasive authority to which I knew he would respond.

'With some help I have located the holo the general is using to blackmail you. It is stored in a personal safe in his private quarters. You will never be able to reach it. However, I want you to know that you do not need to try. I have been able to get it played. It shows your escapee was actually armed with a high-intensity hand laser. It does not show, as you have been led to believe, an unarmed man at whom you fired. You have been held to ransom with a lie.

'Like you, I am very thorough at checking people out and after our rather sad misunderstanding at my apartment I did a thorough search on you. I believe you are basically a man of honor at this moment on the verge of irreparably and needlessly damaging your career. The general, I am sorry to say, is not.

'I can guarantee you will never be faced with the general's threat. I can get appropriate help to manage the general. You will know I have been successful when he resigns from the SFC Board, which he will do in the next 24 hours. At this time I require you to withdraw your talons from your current attempts to damage my reputation and as soon as the general resigns please call me in order for us to have an honest and mutually supportive discussion. You will have your integrity back and I will have a colleague with whom I can work.'

He looked at me with a kind of dazed bewilderment. He was used to being the manager of people, not the one being managed.

Dr Khan returned to the room, looking carefully at each of us, her eyebrows raised questioningly.

So I looked at Julian, who said, 'If what you say is true you have my word, and for the present I apologize and withdraw my preposterous accusations and ask permission of Dr Khan to allow me to check that I have indeed been misled. Please. I do not enjoy the position in which I have been put and would like both of you to allow me to re-validate my source.'

Miyuki looked at me, one eyebrow raised and clearly hugely dissatisfied. I looked at her directly, and said, 'Dr Khan, if Julian is able to validate his information to both our satisfaction I will simply resign or accept whatever outcome the situation demands. If, on the other hand, Julian is not able to validate his source, I would like you to be present when he apologizes profusely for the accusation, withdraws the statements he has made and agrees that we should work together co-operatively.'

I thought she would swallow her tongue. She looked at me with incredulity written over her whole body.

'I know this looks absurd, but I suspect that Julian may have been led seriously astray by parties not inclined to like either your actions or mine with respect to the Olarians.'

She looked at both of us with an intensity that was almost willing us to spill the beans when Esan spoke into her mind.

Dr Khan, my apologies for intruding here but might I suggest that you accept Zed's suggestion. He is in this, as in most things I have ever seen, to be trusted, which I feel certain you know.

So the meeting ended on an impasse with the assurance that it would reconvene in 24 hours.

At 7pm that day a worldwide holo report confirmed that due to overwhelming military obligations General Genarus had found it necessary to step down from his position on the SFC Board, effective immediately.

Miyuki was delighted, I was relieved and Julian Kared was as good as his word. He knew he had his integrity back and that he owed me, and I knew I had a new friend on the Executive. We met with Miyuki and the entire matter was settled very amicably and afterwards he met with me as promised and we spoke for more than an hour. It was like engaging with a totally different person. We sorted some of his issue with the new debriefings and I promised we would discuss further modifications to meet some of his concerns. I left the meeting very relieved and sent Esan a very big thank you for his help.

Now the task of managing the Assembly was on my plate, I needed a conversation with the Olarians. It was an easy and comfortable one. They basically agreed, given their experience of the past week, that my suggestion was the way they would prefer to go. They believed they could work constructively on the basic underlying issue if the appropriate scientists could be brought together. And they agreed that probably some of the issues might be worked on by others as a result of the work they would do but that constructive work would probably come from the theoretical work the group would undertake.

It was at this point that Esan mentioned the Olarian desire to engage with one practical project and they had a preference for the ocean cleaning and the rejuvenation of fish stocks. The Olarians had had a scare during the life of the Originals when it had been found that one species of fish was slowly wiping out the entire ocean fish stocks. It took them nearly 10 years to fix the problem and they had been since very conscious of maintaining a supervisory eye over the state of various fish stocks in their oceans.

To relieve my anxiety about my seven charges, Esan assured me that the crew of the *Energystreamer* were monitoring all of us and, apart from having occasional risky adventures, all was well for the moment.

The next day the Global Assembly of 20 met with the Olarians and Miyuki introduced me and informed the group I would be chairing the meeting and explained why. With one or two exceptions the response to my taking over the role was positive. The mining group were outed in the first session and the outcomes that would work for our world – the theoretical energy challenge and work on clean oceans and fish stocks – both were safely established for the coming year.

CHAPTER 11

Zed's Group Reforms

When I returned to the world outside SFC, I found our group in various stages of transformational activities. For the 24 hours or so after they returned to their homes, most of the group had been juggling their work schedules. Natalya and Januti were the first to act. Natalya let her clientele know she had decided to leave the business she was in and make a new life for herself. It took her a week and she used all her talents to keep her clients happy about her decision, and she spent her time packing and putting her unit on the market. With no real difficulty she obtained the necessary permits and visas and arranged for all her worldly possessions to go into storage. She then arranged a holiday in Britain where she planned with Peter to meet and publicly fall in love and become a couple. She had three girlfriends she was sad to leave, but the opportunities ahead were pulling and although she was sad, she was seriously looking forward to a completely new life.

Natalya's Rocket Leaper ended its 20-minute jump from Moscow to London and Peter was with her telepathically as she negotiated Customs and crossed into the high-speed rail shuttle to Tavistock, another short ride, and when she stepped out of the shuttle Peter led her to the hotel where he was having a solo lunch.

She checked in, put her luggage in her room and wandered into the cafe. She walked nonchalantly in the direction of his table and smiled seductively at him as she moved toward him. To the observing security system a genuinely accidental meeting was about to take place. A waitress placing his drink on the table heard him ask, 'Are you alone?'

Heard the reply, 'Why yes.'

Saw him stand and invite Natalya to sit opposite at his table and heard her say, 'Thank you, and your name is?'

Heard him reply and heard her say her name before the waitress took Natalya's drink order and headed back toward the bar.

This casual meeting was one she would be asked, several times in the future, to replay for various people. But she would be crystal clear about the pick-up she had witnessed.

Peter smiled at Natalya and they became engrossed in a conversation that would not be able to be heard later on the holo security tapes, however, the waitress returning with Natalya's drink would report hearing Peter asking his beautiful new companion if she would like to spend some of the afternoon sightseeing his beloved city, and hearing her express what seemed to the waitress warm delight as she accepted his offer. And so it was done. Natalya had met Peter and their lightning affair had begun. Natalya would spend the night with Peter in her hotel room and then check out of her hotel the next day and move in with him. Fast, surprising, but not really that unusual.

Januti had witnessed the scene and the whole group got a blow-by-blow replay over the next 24 hours. The Olarians remained puzzled at the behavior and it was left to Ai to explain the subtleties of the event. There was nothing to connect either of them to any of the others and from my point of view and both Peter and Natalya's, it had been a smooth and satisfying day.

Within two days, Januti had given notice and the owners of her nightclub very sadly accepted her resignation and agreed to her offer to spend the following week replacing herself with a university friend who had nightclub hostess experience, was looking for a job and was totally delighted to take the opportunity. An agreement to have her friend replace her by the end of the week was surprising to the owners but acceptable because Januti had guaranteed her friend's abilities, and as she was of the same age as Januti and beautiful, no grit was put in the works. When Januti had put in her resignation, the owners, being Kyoshi-san's Yakuza enterprise, had notified Kyoshi, who had instructed that whatever she wanted to do she be allowed to do without impediment and that she be given a generous departure bonus. His gratitude to me for the discharge of my obligation was strong in Kyoshi's mind and he was certain his benefactor would appreciate his actions should any future transactions become possible.

Januti was delighted. She bought a round-the-world ticket by Rocket Leaper.

(The Rocket Leapers were initially a kind of joke name but it stuck. Rocket Leapers replaced traditional fixed-wing aircraft around 2055; they launched into a rocket trajectory basically going up and then down using rocket power. Their most noticeable characteristic was a somewhat strange stubby appearance: they had short fat wings).

She said her goodbyes to her mother whose anxiety for her was as great today as when she had first gone to school; she promised to stay in touch. Little did her mother know how easy this would be for Januti. She had two girlfriends who were truly sad to see her go but both were now engaged and for the moment Januti was in truth less important in their lives.

Within two days Januti was on her way to San Francisco where she spent a day sightseeing. Next day she spent in New York also sightseeing and the following day she arrived in London where her itinerary showed that she had planned to spend two days before traveling on to Paris then Holland, the Middle East, Australia and then back home two months later. She was, of course, never going to get back home.

When she reached Australia, she landed in Sydney and took a guided tour to Canberra. In Canberra she went to a symphony concert and there found herself sitting next to me. We made ourselves a little conspicuous by flirting and joking out loud and tipping too generously at the very upmarket bar! Several people heard our conversations and the security holomonitors would, should they ever be consulted, support the string of events. In front of the doorman at the high-speed transit ramp we were engaged in a seductive play, to which she finally capitulated in front of the maître d' and agreed to go back to my place if I promised to escort her back to her hotel later. Which of course I did. And so Januti and I were comfortably shacked up in my digs.

Surprisingly, for a Space Fleet medic, Donna was a homebody with a close connection to the children of two of her friends, and Darcy had to spend quite a lot of energy and encouragement to get her to agree to move soon, although he would have accepted any conditions she decided to apply to her move.

'I want to go back to school,' he said. 'I don't want to work unless I must. I have more than adequate funds for the next few years and I want to begin a lifetime of serious education.'

Donna smiled and stroked his face and felt delighted to have someone to care for, for whom she felt total trust and with whom she felt deeply connected and genuinely safe. They just had to find a story that brought them together.

What they found was a global conference on 'significant health issues in off-world environments' that was due to begin in a week. The organizers had already sought her out, however, at the time she had turned them down. The conference was multicultural and a number of human translators were required. It took Donna no more than a few hours to organize herself and Darcy to be re-invited to attend and it came to be the venue at which they were seen to become lovers. She had organized at the request of the conference organizers to have a multilingual human translator and so had set up her legitimate contact with him. It turned out to be simple to be seen getting closer together and finally be seen by her girlfriends to be right over the top. In fact be seen falling hopelessly in love. Darcy returned home, closed up his unit and caught a Leaper to New York, where Donna almost consumed him as he stepped out of the luggage claim area.

Donna had five close friends and she knew that leaving them was going to be hard. She had relied on them for several years and they had known one another since university. They met and all fell in love with Darcy and were truly delighted for Donna. When the time came for her to leave it was hardest for her.

Ai and Ajit had a slightly trickier scenario to work out. Ai had been waiting patiently for a long time to find us, so when she did and when she realized that Ajit was the man she wanted to be with, knowing how possessive she felt, it was easy for her to plan to be with him. She did not feel committed to life in China, really had no close friends there. Ajit was totally unconcerned about where he lived; his environment was not one of his highest priorities and he had been a loner for many years except online where he had numerous respectful connections.

So Ai and Ajit separately planned holidays in Australia. They met in a bar in Perth and, following a Rapid Surface Transit trip to a resort on the Margaret River, fell in love in clear public view and spent the rest of their two weeks traveling Australia together before ending up in Canberra. They were heard discussing the beauty of the city and agreeing to meet there so they could be together in two weeks' time, and that was all the time it took for them to obtain the necessary visas and reorganize their lives.

So four of us were in Canberra, two in the UK and two in the USA. It took me only a few days to find a position for Peter in Canberra and have him apply and be accepted, four more weeks for him to finish up at the Tavistock clinic and for him and Natalya to settle in Canberra. Donna and Darcy were the last to maneuver themselves into work in Canberra and that arrangement took them until the end of Donna's final space trip for the year; the battlecruiser on which she was to serve had security responsibilities to ore carriers from one of the mining asteroids.

Within eight weeks the entire cohort was established in Canberra. Meanwhile I had taken up my new position in SFC and had got my executive team organized and we were building a relationally more comfortable team, due in no small measure to my ability to insist on honest, open communication that I could now accurately monitor.

◘

Our next meeting took place on *Energystreamer* rather than in one of our apartments; *Energystreamer* seemed 'right'! We were all aware that this would probably be the last time we would use the Olarian spaceship but I suspected our decision to meet there had something to do with the fact that this was where we had first met as a group. All of us preferred face-to-face contact, which, given our life experiences, did not really surprise me. And although we could easily meet in one of our apartments, we did actually need more space and to be able to move around.

After greeting the crew, we set about checking in on each other, and it was soon clear Ai was wanting to get into an issue about which she was seriously uneasy.

She looked at me intently. *Why exactly did you come and find us and wake us up? I can understand why Olaria would come looking and, having found us, would tell you. But I am wondering, Zed, whether you had thought about the consequences of meeting each of us. What was in your mind when you came to find us and open our minds?*

I'm not meaning to be critical in any way as I'm certain you know I'm feeling uncomfortable, uneasy, curious. I don't fully know why I'm asking. I feel a bit stupid asking and I think it's because I have known for a while I was sort of telepathic and I knew there were others but I never tried to find them. And I think I'm feeling a bit guilty or just uneasy that I didn't and I want to feel okay.

Her words stopped me in my tracks.

Well, it never occurred to me not to come and find you. I don't think there was ever any doubt that that was what I had to do! And before I explore what lay underneath that, is there anyone of you who, having just found out that there were seven more like you in the world, would not have gone searching for them? Oh, yes, I know I was in possession of abilities I had not known and assumed that would probably be true for you and I felt an obligation. I mean, how would I have felt inside, if, knowing you were out there, I had done nothing to find you and help you develop your abilities as Olaria and the Olarians had helped me develop mine?

I looked around the group. Each of them was asking themselves the question and one by one each nodded an affirmation that they would almost certainly have felt that was the thing to do. So I asked Ai, *As I tell you what I imagine lay underneath my decision, will you help me understand what you would have done and why you are asking?*

She nodded and for just a moment I wondered if I was as clear about my motives as I had initially imagined.

I was lonely, I said. *I wanted a group to which I could safely belong. I wanted there to be other people like me. I wanted to find a way to make a difference to a world managed and controlled by people who seem to me basically self-centered, self-interested, essentially greedy and fundamentally hungry for power, often near-psychotic loners or less than completely adequate members of very powerful families whose interests spread everywhere like evil tentacles.*

I paused, collecting my thoughts, then carried on.

Individuals viciously defensive of their positions rather than concerned about the long-term interests of the people for whom they had accepted some real responsibility, often disturbingly unkind. I wanted to be with some people who were not like that and who might be willing to be my friends and confidants and might be capable of not being snowed and railroaded by people I have come to despise. My only friend and companion until now, Raille, could tell you that. Also, I wanted to be with some people who would perhaps be in a position to change the world, if that seemed possible and an appropriate way to use the extraordinary resources we have been given.

But at the moment I was starting to make contact with you I don't think any of that was actually in my head. I never had an instant's thought that I would do anything except make contact with you. Before I set out, I had not given the consequences any thought. That I think is my best answer to your question, Ai.

Well, said Ajit, *correct me if I have this wrong, but that would seem to indicate that at heart you are a do-gooder.*

I burst out laughing and said, *Yes, Ajit, I believe I might well be. However, unlike many do-gooders before me, I think I might have the power and resources to actually make a difference to the lives of people around me.*

Everyone in the room was looking at me. Darcy raised his eyebrows and said, *Is that like Don Quixote?*

I just laughed and laughed and finally I said, *Well, it's not my thing to tilt at too many windmills, but I have a lot of energy for getting people to face their fears, stupidity and destructive behaviors. I don't know if that really fits the bill. And, and this is a very incomplete thought, but it seemed to me that somewhere deep in the unplumbed reaches of my mind there might be bigger purpose and intelligence at work here. Not a god, but an intelligence far more complex and capable than mine. And I thought, if there was, I surely had some greater responsibility than to myself alone.*

I don't think there was anything complicated in coming to find you. I believe I never for a second thought about whether I would do it. But when I was about to visit Januti for the first time I know I briefly thought about the consequences and remembered the feeling I had when I was able to really make a difference helping a group of damaged off-world combat soldiers. Doing something genuinely helpful and impactful was a buzz and I briefly imagined having that feeling again.

It was just a brief memory that flashed through my mind – a moment when I had been effective and felt successful, and knowing how good that felt. I had always hoped I would be able to find or create that feeling again. I believe that moment was somewhere in the midst of my thinking after Olaria had spoken to me when I thought about making contact with you.

They wanted me to tell them, and suddenly I felt quite embarrassed, so I told them the story of the off-world group who had returned with PTSD.

I suppose it's sort of obvious when I think about it. The year on OlarCret changed absolutely everything for me. And, even the thought of returning to Earth was disturbing. I felt lonely.

And for a few moments I felt the warmth and caring from the group, and not for the first time I wondered if I would come to feel okay about what I had done here.

CHAPTER 12

Meeting of the Visitors to OlarCret

Miyuki and her 11 fellow visitors to OlarCret, their journey now nearly eight months ago, came together in Miyuki's meeting room. With them were a small number of Olarians, including some of the crew of the *Energystreamer*, which had returned with the team who would work on the theoretical physics and with the scientists on cleaning up the oceans and the fish stocks. I was present as were the crew of *Sunstreamer* and the entire crew of *Lightning*.

Thirty-six people milling, talking, hugging, smiling, sharing their time since... it was a big group. The Olarians, only some familiar to the crew or the visitors, did not hang together. As the group mixed they felt a harmony unlike their experiences with people in the World Council group and others with whom they had mixed. They felt the lives of these people and felt more at home than any other experience they had had with other humans on Earth. The human telepaths were, of course, a very different experience; while an almost Olarian experience, they were still transitioning from feeling and living an ordinary human life, much like myself. None had been brought up in the Olarian culture with its deeply co-operative values and none had thought it appropriate to be present at the meeting in person.

When all those present had said their hellos and caught up with one another, I suggested they find a seat. I was pleased to tell them that all the seats in the circle were energy seats supplied by the Olarians. As people settled I asked if each of the members of the group would share how they were feeling at the moment and one thing they would like to discuss. I added, this was a get-together without a specific agenda, but as there was a common reality for all of them, it seemed possible that there were things that such a group might want to discuss. In a very short time I was proven not to be wrong.

The first to speak was Jelice. I remembered her, 'just an ordinary woman', she had said, '35 years old from Central Asia, two children, no-one of significance!' Again I was reminded of the awesome power of seemingly ordinary people, not people who ran the world, but decent, sensible people who lived in it. And here she was again, getting the ball rolling.

'I feel a bit embarrassed being first but I am bursting a bit after watching the World Council group meetings. I became increasingly angry as I watched the opportunity to use the Olarian knowledge and skill be treated with such ill-manners and stupidity until Zed ever so satisfyingly sledge-hammered the corrupt miners and the group came to a decision to work on the really significant theoretical problem of energy, which I truly barely understand. And I was delighted when the Olarians wanted to work on ocean waste and our fish stocks after which, I must admit, I felt a great sense of relief.

'However, apart from being truly delighted to renew my acquaintance with you and meet some more Olarians, which is always a comforting and satisfying experience, I felt, watching the World Council group, there must be some things we could do about some of the other issues to improve the world we live in. It doesn't seem right that we should be relying on our Olarian guests to be the sole source of constructive work on our problems. Although I am not all that smart or well informed, I believe we can do better, that there is something pathetic about being dependent on the goodwill of another civilization to fix our mess. I don't ask some other woman to come and clean my house or my toilet! I know I am responsible for that. I don't know how, but the ability of this collection of people here gives me hope and confidence in the future more than any other group of people on our planet.'

Pierre Bizet, CEO of Euro World Foods, spoke next.

'Thank you, Jelice. As always you are a joy to have around and you have said some things I think would be pretty much shared in this room.' There were lots of nods. 'As you all know, until I traveled to OlarCret I thought I knew what I needed to know, I had made it to the top. I had needed to damage quite a few people to get there, and as most of you will probably remember, I learned that my journey to the top had made me someone I no longer knew and no longer liked.

'It was some of you people who pulled my feet to the ground. So I would like to say some things to you, Jelice. You are right, and today, as we sit here, Euro World Foods has taken responsibility for all the food that is not required for our products and is building a global transport network to get it to countries where food is not plentiful. We cannot solve the problem of food distribution alone, so we are today in conversation with almost all of the other major world food manipulators in a real effort to have them join us.

'Much has to be negotiated, many are unwilling and believe us to be so soft and stupid. But we have begun, because of people like you and others in this room.

'When I returned I had my executive team meet for several days and, with just the smallest amount of help from Zed, I had them agree to fully support my effort to involve our entire enterprise in caring for more of our business and bringing our industry into an agreement with anyone who would help to construct a worldwide food maintenance chain. This included some very powerful families, including yours, Miyuki. Your grandfather was extraordinarily supportive and I am sure helped move your family and so two of the other significant families to support our efforts. This has made possible some solutions we could never have managed on our own.

'The extent of hostility and unpleasantness from my competitors and others in my business was a long way further than disturbing. But I have noticed the hostiles are decreasing as their support base lowers and those working with us increases. Suppliers, staff, customers, investors, communities, creditors and governments are all beginning to understand that their profitability and the strength of their businesses and their successes all ride along with and improve with ours.

'Mutual support and care are profitable activities and they are learning this along with us. It astonishes me we have never fully understood this before. So, little by little we are beginning to reduce hunger and starvation around our world. Perhaps the biggest challenge is from our competitors who have so far been reluctant to believe we are also interested in helping them. We are making a start thanks to you.'

I could feel the ambience in the room had changed again and I reached out to the other human telepaths to make certain they were listening in. I need not have been concerned. Januti whispered to me, *Oh Zed, these people are beautiful and perhaps they are offering us a possibility we have not yet considered.*

I smiled. We had only just begun. I was surprised when the next person to speak was *Lightning*'s navigator, Miu.

'Zed, I don't know if it is appropriate for me to speak, but I am again being moved by these people.'

I interrupted her to say, 'Miu, everyone here is welcome to speak and I thank you for doing so. Please say whatever you wish.'

'Thank you, Zed. Every crew member in SFC is relieved and delighted that you are our head of Psych. Your changes to our debriefings have improved the morale of many hundreds of space crew in what we feel was so smart and simple a way, so you can be sure of support from us. I cannot speak for my fellow crew members, or for the rest of us, but for myself I would like everyone in this room to know that I would be both honored and excited to be able to participate in some venture that was intended to make our search for new habitable planets less urgent and less insane. As I said, I can speak only for myself. I really do not know how the others feel.'

Their captain, Dieter Alexey Sen Mil, smiled at Miu, whom he trusted and admired.

'I was not left untouched by the events on OlarCret, and in case there is any need, I would like to say to my crew, I will fully support any moves you wish to make that are intended to make our world a better place to live for all of us.

'John Washington and I have spoken to the flight crew captains on every available craft that has come home or been in repair bays since we returned. All like your innovations, Zed, and appreciate that Dr Khan has approved them. Not all are willing to go much further than that but some are, and we have been discussing what we have learned. I think you can expect considerable support for any project in which we can help and which is intended to make our world more responsible and self-sufficient and self-managing. I hope I have not said too much or overstepped the mark.'

Miyuki responded, saying, 'Dieter, I am delighted to hear what you have said. I don't know why I have trusted Zed, but I have and I do and I have absolutely no regrets; he gets little praise, yet he has been strong and effective and perhaps my best decision for promotion yet. I will be pleased to hear from anyone of our crew members, and I can assure you, I have taken extreme steps to ensure nothing is being recorded here, except in your memories. At some point before we leave the day after tomorrow, I will ask the group of you to put together a report you believe best summarizes this meeting. It will be a report everyone agrees is appropriate and acceptable to present to the world.'

She smiled.

'Before I met Zed, you would never have heard those words come out of my mouth!'

I felt embarrassed and uncomfortable. 'Hm... You know, I am just the facilitator here, really, you people are the engine room. I feel very fortunate to be asked to do these things. The Olarians have shown me that more is possible than I ever imagined. So let's keep trying to be useful.'

Eira Lin, our now 18-year-old Chinese schoolgirl, smiled knowingly at me.

'Zed, since we returned, Cadrin has flown me to the USA twice. He has shown me how a worldwide mining corporation works, has insisted on supporting my education and offered to help me get the job of my dreams. Cadrin!'

She turned to the Diggers Mining CEO sitting beside her,

'I am sorry to embarrass you, but they really don't know you like I do. You have been kind to me and more important, you have agreed with me when I've talked about somehow building a better world here on Earth. You know that's my passion and you have, to my amazement, nurtured and supported it. In our talks together and our weekly holos we have tried to think about what this means and what part I might one day be able to play. I think all these people need to know this.'

Cadrin was embarrassed but clearly pleased, I think proud would really be the word, but his feet were firmly planted on the ground.

Eira was neither overawed nor confused about the world. Cadrin had clearly worked hard to keep her solidly grounded, as a good miner would. This was obvious when she went on.

'I know that, alone, I have little chance of making a difference, but with Cadrin's help I might be able to reach positions from which I can make a bigger difference. However, I think I have learned from watching Zed manage us that I have to learn a lot about people and how to gain their support. So my time since OlarCret has been exciting, challenging and left me feeling better about myself than I would have believed possible. Cadrin's kindness has been a big factor in this. And for those of you who are right now asking what Cadrin gets out of this, well, that was my first question when he flew me to the USA, and I will, with his permission, repeat what he said.'

She looked at him, eyebrows raised.

He smiled indulgently, shook his head and said, 'Of course'.

'And what he said I remember word for word. "When I met you, Eira Lin, I was at the bottom of my well. I was angry at the world and everyone around me. Unlike any person I had ever experienced in my life, you cut through all the crap and the anger, you got to me like no-one ever had before – you, a kid, a girl kid! However, before I left OlarCret I had begun to feel like a human being again, not a useless angry man. Meeting you did this: your direct honesty, seeking nothing, having nothing to gain. You opened a door for me to life and I will love you for that until I die. In the meantime, I want to be in some way responsible for you getting the best opportunities you can. That's it".'

Eira was looking at him with warmth and affection.

'I think sometimes I have wavered, thinking he must want more from me than that, but I truly believe he doesn't. Then I have thought, "I'm not really worthy of this, I should stop it". And he forced me to face some of my demons and master them! He told me a story, one that had made a difference for him.

'I'm sure Zed and some of you will know it, but I would like to tell it as he told it to me.'

The group was nodding and supporting her to continue.

'Okay, thank you. This is the story of a man who left his house to go to a monastery to learn to become a monk. When he finally achieved his goal, he left the monastery to return home. While he was away demons took over his house. When he opened his front door, small demons snarled and screamed and threatened him. He brushed them aside and they disappeared. As he moved into the house, bigger demons threatened him. "Begone," he shouted at them, and they too disappeared. When he got to the large living area in the center of the house, a huge demon, the mother of all demons, was awaiting him. She opened her mouth and snarled a ferocious snarl and the man knelt down and put his head in her mouth and she too disappeared".

'The message I took away from this was simple: there is nothing to fear but fear itself and I do not have to feel it. I can stop and take another path any time I choose. Cadrin has no investment in my following a path devised by him, so I genuinely feel free! And it is great. I don't know if a kid like me can help but I hope some of you will think so and find a way to let me in.'

The group spontaneously clapped; I found myself clapping and I knew she was feeling embarrassed but also proud!

I could feel Januti and the others beginning to get an idea, just the germ of an idea, before I cut them off to pay attention to the group.

As each person spoke, whether crew, a visitor to OlarCret or one of the Olarians, I found myself thinking, *There are probably people all over the world who would resonate to what was being said here.* At the back of my mind I was thinking of an author, a great favorite of mine from the middle of the twentieth century, a radical community worker named Saul Alinsky, and my mind began to shift toward some different purpose for our group, but I baulked at the idea of being known and the risk to our children, and again I brought my attention back to the group.

Every item on the World Council agenda was raised during the three days and the report at the end accurately reflected a core idea that struck me during the group discussions. While it was true that the powerful families and the massive enterprises, a couple of whom were represented in our group and notably through Miyuki, were in control of almost every aspect of world government policy, usually through their huge financial leverage and their ability to support extensive lobbyists, the idea of a non-violent movement of ordinary people, people who were relatively safe from oppressive threats, hung around in my mind. A seed of an idea had been planted and was being nurtured.

When the session ended, Miyuki invited me back to her office.

'I don't know exactly what it is about you, Zed, but all kinds of strange people are drawn to you, including me. You did great work in there and you have never let me down. Flight crews from every part of the system affirm you. Are you satisfied here?'

I looked at her in surprise and then I looked deeply into her, and I saw she was getting a lot of flak from the senior members of her family about me.

'Miyuki, your family are probably not too pleased with me and so I'm guessing they're not too pleased with you, am I right?'

She looked at me. 'Would you by any chance be reading my mind or using your Olarian friends to do that?'

'Miyuki, it's not rocket science; it's kind of obvious I would have thought.'

She nodded.

'Do you want me to resign?' I asked.

She nearly leapt out of her chair.

'My lord, no! Don't even think about it! You are one of the most trustworthy, intelligent and effective senior executives on my staff. I apologize for the grilling, but I know you understand what families like mine expect. Even renegades like me have to meet some family obligations. I just don't know how.'

'Miyuki, which senior members of your family are the most difficult for you to manage? Is it okay for me to ask this? I am wondering if I might not be able to be just a little help here.'

She looked at me askance and for a second I thought I might have crossed a line. However, that was not what I was seeing; she was trying to imagine how I might be useful with the really tricky ones, and so I got a look at all the key players as she thought my question through.

'I have to think about that, Zed. It puts me on a track to disloyalty and I have never gone there.'

'Of course, but if you decide you can trust me and are not crossing loyalty lines, feel free to talk to me.'

She looked at me, eyebrows furrowed but desperately wanting to trust me. Wanting to have someone who could support her. She knew I was probably the only person outside her family she just might trust.

When I got back to our apartment, Januti was waiting for me and the next half hour disappeared in a blur of pleasure and intimacy and loving. I looked at her head resting on a pillow, her long, soft, straight black hair like a rainbow around her face, some resting just over the nipples of her large and beautiful breasts, and she was looking at me with a look for which I would return to her forever. One of just heart-wrenching pleasure and love.

Want to talk it through? she asked and I knew I did. But I thought it through, she followed me and then she watched as I honed in on the one thing I thought might work. She agreed. I kissed her lovingly and so I quickly dressed and made a simultaneity jump to the office of Miyuki's grandfather, Kenyato. He was sitting behind his massive synthetic American oak desk, which was packed with electronics. I settled in his lounge chair and very, very gently entered his mind: *Think about Miyuki,* almost a background whisper. I saw him look around, realize he was alone, assume he was thinking the thought himself and switch to reflecting on the family issues that were affecting Miyuki. She was one of his favorites, but she was unruly, hard to manage. As he thought about her I waited until he was having strong positive thoughts about her and whispered even more softly: *She needs your support.* Then, as though he had realized something, he touched his coded holo communicator and connected to her line. She answered with warmth and affection and he smiled contentedly to himself.

'Mi, I'm sorry if we have been harassing you. Please remember, I will always have your back.'

Without hesitation she replied, 'Thank you, Grandfather. I have always trusted you to take care of me.'

The smiling image of her grandfather nodded, smiled affectionately and disconnected the line.

I waited until I saw Miyuki settle back in her seat and relax a little, then returned to her grandfather's office.

Kenyato sat back in his chair and I fed him a deep sense of a job well done and support for his strong feeling of affection for her. I watched for a few more minutes while he processed what seemed to be his strong feeling about her before he moved on.

I returned to Januti and pulled her closer. I needed the feel of her skin under my hands, the warmth of her as I drew her closer to me, the connectedness of her as I found her lips and we kissed gently but with warmth and love and desire. I pulled her closer still, feeling as much of her body pressed against me as I could manage. Then my whole being hummed as she stroked me and kissed me in all kinds of sensitive places and we wound ourselves around one another in exquisite delight, her arms holding me close to her. And in these moments of peace and fulfillment my mind began to formulate an idea.

I think I might just have a ball park notion of what we might do.

She searched my mind but could not find it.

You're hiding it from me.

I smiled. *No Januti, I'm just holding on to a very drifty notion about something that may be possible. You were with me over the last few days with that group, so you saw what went on. There's a deep wellspring of energy under the surface to get our own problems solved by us. If the two spaceship crews and the travelers to OlarCret can feel it, then we ought to be able to sell it. Get and build support for a world that decides to solve its own problems and does in fact solve them.*

Our part would need to be the encouragement behind and under and around each of the issues. Blocking the bad guys, giving helpful information to the good guys, supporting and getting support from the right people when it was needed, helping outmaneuver the bad guys when they plan to get stuck into our good guys. We also will always have the support of Elaine O'Leary.

You get my drift. We help get a social movement set up, somehow, and we undermine the covert destructive tactics of the bad guys, wherever possible protecting our team from the violence, the vicious games and nastiness of the organizational greed that presently undermines everyone. We just might have the ability to do something about that. Unlike any change program in history, we probably have the means. What do you think?

She looked at me.

Don Quixote!

CHAPTER 13

The Biggie

Our four couples were seated in our lounge room, a truly unlikely collection. I was a few inches from Januti, elbows on knees, head in my hands. I knew from the silence in the room and the quiet in my mind they were waiting, knowing there was something weighing on my mind.

There are questions you know to ask and questions you know, if you ask, may have no real answers. It's one of the latter that is disturbing me now. I think most of you are aware I have been mulling over it but it needs putting out for our serious consideration, though I expect to find no answers at this point. Partly, I believe, because we are not fully developed yet. Some aspects of our telepathic and telekinetic brain have not yet revealed themselves to us and I am unsure why or how this might happen or to whom. However, I believe, on the basis of my first journey with simultaneity from OlarCret to my apartment, that use of a faculty encourages our brains to extend their capability.

So the question: what makes sense and feels right to do with our lives? It's one of those questions that is too gross and too all-encompassing to be answered. However, at some level, I know it is The Question and probably the one to ask first, and this assumes that we wish to act together. I am hoping that I may not be the only one hoping we will stay together.

If we do, are we going to be superheroes fighting however many individual causes we can manage? That seems to me at best inefficient and essentially not practical, like 20th century Superman and Superwoman. I also have a strong feeling we were intended – I suppose by the Seeders – to move beyond the current limitations of the human world on which we find ourselves, and this seems distastefully arrogant and somehow just wrong, but it may nevertheless be correct.

It is of course possible to just ignore the question and proceed with our lives until circumstances dictate a new strategy. That feels uncreative and unwise. So, to be strictly honest, I am already beginning to see us as not quite human, really, and that is disturbing and I wonder how the rest of you are feeling about my ramblings. We are not Olarians and we know they are not humans, so I have to ask: who or what exactly are we? Are we really human? Or are we like the Midwich Cuckoos, and will people eventually want to deal with us as they decided to deal with them... extinction?

I could feel the level of distress and confusion.

Hold on.

It was not the first time I had used the John Wyndham reference, but this was the first occasion I was realizing that they seemed not to know what I was talking about.

How many of you have never read The Midwich Cuckoos *or seen the movie version,* Village of the Damned*?*

Everyone except me!

Okay, I can pull up a holo copy. Are you all willing to watch it tonight?

They were. So we got some goodies and some drinks and sat down and watched it.

It was Ajit, as the credits faded, who said, *Are you seriously suggesting we could be cuckoos?*

I am seriously suggesting that, with the possible exception of how we were conceived, and I have no certainty about that either. We are, to all intents and purposes, like those children. Every now and then over the past year when I have been thinking about us, I have wondered if John Wyndham had the first bite of the cherry and we are the improvement that was consequential of the failure of the first group. For heaven's sake, don't take me too literally, perhaps except that we feel ourselves to be human. Truth be told, when I had been on OlarCret for nearly a year, I felt as Olarian as I felt human! Now, I don't know what I am or how I would know what I am, but I am damned certain if you knocked on my next door neighbor's door and told them what we know about ourselves, they might not be too welcoming and might not see us as one of them. Does that seem too improbable to anyone?

In a very quiet telepathic voice, with no sound, Januti began to speak. Something about the way she began led all of us to stop whatever line of thought we were on and tune in to her. It might have been the way she began, it might have been the gentle tone in the telepathic space, whatever, we all began to listen to what she was saying.

We are not quite right. Any of us. We are not what we seem to the world in which we live. We are a very strange and almost certainly unacceptable anomaly to the human world into which we have been born.

She paused. We were very still and I felt a kind of creeping disturbance that seemed to have no source and no destination. She had slid right through the stuff we were thinking deeper into that disturbing space. It was quite evident all of us were waiting.

We are, in a not very deviant way, like the Midwich Cuckoos. And, having watched that film, I am coming to think we do not belong here. We are not like them: our friends, our neighbors, the rest of this world. All of our parents seemed to know. If we had been born on OlarCret we would be seen as 'normal', but we were not. I've been asking myself, very quietly, how did Zed happen to get to OlarCret just when he needed to be there? And how did Olaria get to be brought back here to find and identify us for him to awaken us?

I am wondering if we are being pointed in the right direction. Zed is my marker for this. There is a place in my thinking that simply stops dead at the idea that he can, at will, cross an incomprehensibly enormous distance to other worlds in an instant in a way no ordinary human being could comprehend or seriously imagine or possibly even believe. And I feel confident we will all shortly be able to do the same. He is, I believe, our point man, our lead, the one to whom whatever or whoever is involved with us is in some kind of direct contact. And he's the oldest of us.

I am beginning to feel very, very strange. I am in some indescribable way ceasing to feel properly connected to the world outside of us! I also do not understand how we can conceivably belong here! I am starting to imagine that we have been created here to give the human race some kind of kick-start toward behaving like a survivable society, however, the minute I say it I feel disloyal and outrageously self-important.

I'm sorry if I'm freaking some of you out, but I really do not think we ought to continue to think of ourselves as human any more than an Olarian could think of themselves as human. We might look human but not for a second would any person we have ever known think that of us, especially as we acknowledge what we are becoming. I can't believe I am the only one with these thoughts, although I have not heard any of you discussing that particular thought?

It is impossible to say how we were in that moment. Deathly silent, very, very still, and we could hear the Olarians: not a murmur, not a sound other than breathing. My mind began to engage again. Was she right? Everything she had said felt true. I looked at her – a beautiful member of our species – that's what I was thinking in that moment. The seconds ticked by. Very slowly we all turned to look at her. She had just actually put some unspoken moments out there for all of us to hear and to think about.

She looked pale in the low light of the room, and slowly, as the implication of all she had said seeped in, we became deeply reflective. I stretched my mind out into the cosmos, as far as I could take it without giving a thought to any direction, but in those moments, when I could feel the others watching where I went, there was nothing except a strange awareness of distant worlds but no contact, no connection, and I quietly returned and wondered who I was.

A second later the babble of telepathic voices was deafening, and one by one people stopped talking and began to listen. It was, unsurprisingly, Natalya whose voice remained.

This is not easy to believe, but, Januti, I am feeling disturbingly confident you may be right. The worst part is that I have no idea what we need to do about it.

Then, one by one the others nodded and we all just sat in silence, looking at one another. Everything she had said, fit. Somewhere inside each of us the idea seemed to have been sitting. As we each chewed over the idea we all knew this was some kind of defining moment. It was not clear how to move on from Januti's articulation of a kind of fear I think we might have all been actually avoiding.

Does anyone have an idea how we might take this further?

I looked around the group, listened in to everyone, realized we were all, for the moment, in the same blind space.

So I believe we probably need to continue as we planned. It seems unlikely we were planted here by any kind of chance.

Then I recalled, as I had with Olaria on an earlier occasion, the argument of a 19th century mathematician whose name I could no longer recall. 'There is no such thing as Chance,' he had suggested. 'Chance was merely our inability to see pattern or order.'

And that, I am beginning to feel confident, is a truth about us. I am seeing us as an anomaly, but it's more likely we are part of a pattern we cannot presently recognize.

I am feeling some degree of confidence that we are supposed to do something here among the people we think of as our human family, people who we have until now thought of as others of our species. Am I alone in this or do the rest of you feel similarly?

Again it was Natalya who first surfaced.

Zed, this is more than I can manage! Januti, what you are saying makes a disturbing amount of sense, but I cannot begin to think about what to decide about it or how to deal with it. At the moment, I can't begin to imagine how I will make up my mind about whether I could believe such an idea, and if I do, then my first and strongest feeling is to ask: who exactly am I, how did I get here, what am I supposed to do? And, if I cannot get answers to those questions, is there anything I might actually do to enhance the likelihood I will find out? Or ought I simply get on with the process Zed is leading us through? Januti, do you think there is anything else we ought to do to clarify our status? Or do you feel satisfied for now to just follow his lead?

She stopped and we all knew all of us were thinking through the implications of Januti's idea and were reaching toward Natalya's solution. I was seriously concerned about what she had said, but I could find no genuine flaw in it. Nor at this point could I see what difference it should make so far as our actions were concerned, and I said as much to the group. Their response was not really surprising. No-one had any new direction in which to go.

So the question I wanted to ask, which still seems to be the question to ask, is Socrates' and Plato's basic ethical question: "What ought one do?" And so, "What ought we do?" I am thinking of this as not just a philosophic or ethical question but a seriously pragmatic one.

It goes to the heart of who we really are and what we are intended to actually do. When will we know what our other abilities are and what the significance of them is? For the moment I feel the need to stretch my abilities to their limit to find what those limits are. I have a strong need for us to all maintain our human, normalized lives while we learn as fast and extensively as we can. I want us to have children, ours and each other's, and I want us to become comfortable with having children with the Olarians. And most of all, I need to know how deeply every one of you is with me and Januti, who I want to believe is totally committed and connected to my craziness.

I was aware of some of the feelings and ideas that were bubbling up around the group. It was Ajit who articulated another aspect of the issue.

If we are to stay on Earth, we have to consider how we and others could possibly manage a slowly growing group of telekinetic telepaths secretly living among normal people and I think that could easily be a potential nightmare. I mean, most human groups have trouble managing harmoniously with each other, let alone a group of seriously powerful freaks... us.

The group were following and experiencing similar fears. They were all looking at me so I added to Ajit's thinking.

I am also wondering, am I thinking of abandoning ordinary people like Raille and Jessiqana and their children and Marlette. Where else can we go? Would the Olarians really want a colony of human telepaths among them unless we interbred, to which of course we have already committed. Or should we consider finding a new planet?

Then I heard myself. I was talking as though I was discussing moving to another state or another country, except, I was talking of another planet!

I felt the others stirring, a little confused and concerned, and feeling the beginnings of the anxiety and uncertainty that were leading me in this novel but disturbing direction. I also knew the very articulation of the idea that we actually had the choice to go find another planet on which to live must seem almost absurd, insane, yet, for us, apparently, quite realistic!

It's entirely up to us. No-one can tell us what to do. We just need to decide if we all want things for ourselves that fit together and what they might be. I am aware that it is also a possibility for us to live our separate lives. My heart sinks as I say those words but I know that any one of us surely has that right.

It was Donna who picked up that baton.

I really, really, don't want that to happen to us. I feel as though I might have found my family and I don't want to lose any of you, please.

Turned out she was not alone. One by one everyone supported what she had said. A disquieting silence settled over us and I began to realize something that was absurd: that I was feeling somehow responsible for all this.

Without conscious intent, the eight of us drew our chairs together into a circle and closer to our new partners. We had done that purely through telekinesis. We were looking at and into each other in a kind of fearful fright; surely we would not choose to be separate before we had become real couples and a real team. I could feel the intake of breath from the Olarians on *Energystreamer* and in other places; all were following us very carefully. The Olarians had watched *The Village of the Damned* with us and were horrified at the conclusion.

Why, Zed? Esan and Serra had asked, almost together.

Well, the idea of being controlled by creatures like themselves but pretty much certainly another species, an alien species infinitely more mysteriously powerful and not manageable, would, I believe, frighten people more than almost anything else. People in our world do not feel secure; they feel vulnerable to any sources of power over which they have no control. They do not like the body politic, they are rarely self-sufficient, so feel they cannot influence ordinary people, much less people with extraordinary powers.

I expanded my answer to make sure my seven were also involved and saw they had been following.

This sense of impotence, is, I believe, a significant contributor to the enormous amount of human violence, now and in the past. And it seems likely to be impeding the involvement of the Olarians in human planetary problems as we are seeing. To boost themselves the general populace would probably feel the need to bring us down. For the moment, I believe we are safe as the only people who know anything are Raille and Jessiqana and I intuitively feel safe with them. I have never had even a moment of doubt about their integrity and positive feelings toward me, and I feel confident that will be the same for the rest of you as they come to know you.

I would like you all to be involved with Raille and Jess and their children. I have a hunch this may have to do with all our safety in time to come, especially if I need to take them to visit Jess's family on OlarCret. This might be possible on Energystreamer *but I'm not sure SFC will easily come to the party. I may be wrong. Look, I know this sounds like some kind of almost incoherent rant; please trust me, it really isn't. I know something, but I actually don't know what I know. Sorry all.*

I felt the others, human and Olarian alike, bolster me with their caring and understanding. We were all on strange ground here, and the movie had exacerbated that.

In The Midwich Cuckoos *there were in play a few things that are not really in play here. Yet. The children born to the humans were all together in groups in identifiable places. They were quickly known to all the humans around them and none of them realized until virtually too late that there were other groups.*

They were feared by all the people around them and were not powerful or well-enough informed or mature enough to take care of themselves. We are, I suspect, in some ways, vulnerable. We are no longer the age or with the limited experience of the cuckoos. Additionally, their birth to ordinary women was known to all around them. We are, for the moment, free of that, and we are pretty capable of caring for ourselves without harming others. Also, we can leave the planet, or at least I believe very shortly we will all be able to do that. And do not forget we have the help of the Olarians – a society that not only does not have a culture that would harm us but that wants to share our genetic reality, mixing it with theirs. So we are not in any direct situational way like the Midwich cuckoos.

It's as if the Olarians were there for us to find, as if developed for our assistance! Look, I'm way out on a limb here, but if you are following me, you will know there is a lot of solid sense in this otherwise bizarre-sounding idea.

Although he was for a moment ominously silent, Esan finally quietly agreed and we could hear the other Olarians, now also involving the second eight who were the connectors to the World Group, agree. Esan reminded us of another way we were not like the cuckoos.

There had been a night about four weeks before when Januti and I had been in the tub when I had become instantly aware of a cry for help from Raille. Without hesitation I had been able to freeze everyone in their apartment until I could get there. It took me nearly three minutes to get out of the tub, dry, dress and arrive there. Two men, heavily armed and with legitimate security IDs, had the family in their lounge and were in the process of grabbing Jess and the two children. I freed Raille and Jess and the children, and Raille and I disarmed the frozen men. We examined their credentials while Jess got the children settled. Their IDs appeared to be genuine. Without disturbing the pair I asked who had sent them and watched them, confused but alert, think of the instructions they had received from General Genarus. Raille and I looked at one another. I spoke to Raille telepathically.

Raille, they have been instructed to get Jess and the children as hostages. They are trying to manipulate Miyuki. And I can tell you, these two are seriously disgusting pieces of work. I am checking the security tapes. They have managed somehow to disable them and so do not appear entering the building or coming to your apartment. So I am going to transport them to the alley in which their transport is parked and leave them on the street confused and without their weapons or their IDs and believing they must return immediately to the general. If you are agreeable I would like to ask Ajit, who is a specialist in electronic issues, to protect your apartment from similar intrusions.

Raille nodded. 'Sounds good to me, but now what?'

I thought for a moment.

'Jess, are you and the children okay?'

She looked at Raille and me. 'Yes, but after this I would like to be armed with my spinners. Are you okay with this?'

'The non-lethal ones?' Raille asked.

She nodded. 'Just the tranquilizers. And yes, I am able to make the whole weapon and the darts. It was one of the things required of us even as children!'

Raille and I immediately agreed. Jess looked relieved and disturbed simultaneously.

'Jess, I am going to take Raille with me for a few moments. We need to deal with the General permanently.'

She looked at me and the expression on my face clearly reassured her.

'I promise there will be no repeat of this.' I looked at Raille. 'Remember the drill?'

He nodded.

I transported us to General Genarus's office where he was awaiting his thugs' return.

I sealed his office from all his protective electronics and a surprising array of weapons and security devices. Raille and I were not visible to him when I spoke.

General, please sit still. Every device in this office has been disabled. You are unable to move from your seat. You have sent two incompetent operatives to the apartment of two of SFC's key operatives about which you have been fed completely misleading information. Your actions are not only unacceptable, they are going to cost you dearly. Not only will the world get an uncensored version of your attempt to blackmail Julian Kared, but your other blackmail acts – the tools you have been using to maintain your position on several global boards – will be revealed in detail, transparently and with holographic evidence in the world press.

Raille and I watched him review the events that could seriously embarrass him, failing to realize he was giving us the information we actually needed.

We are not Olarians. We are simple operatives with access to drugs you have never heard of. Our non-governmental organization does not like you or your behavior and we will use what we have should any untoward activity of the sort you initiated tonight occur again. I emphasize – any *similar activity. We will also release the images we hold of several inappropriate threatening manipulations by some of your staff. You know the ones to which I am referring.*

I showed him several segments of his sexual sadism, primarily by telling him to remember them so he would have no clear awareness of the telepathic nature of our activity.

You will see a document on your desk in which in your drugged state you yourself described seven of those incidents in detail. If you sign that document, which we will take with us, we will leave you alone unless you repeat any of the behaviors that have drawn our attention. Do you understand? We have friends, you do not. People who are afraid of you will never take care of you, so, as was the case tonight, we will always be warned when you are planning yet another of your disgusting activities. You need to think very clearly about your future.

There was a long silence. He was fuming. He was also trying desperately to figure out how we could have collected and collated the data in front of him, how he could possibly have been lured into providing it without any memory of it. He also was trying to find a way around this situation. With no obvious enemy and no access outside his office, he felt cornered. Finally he signed and agreed. He had a back door in mind and as I closed that one in his face, he blanched.

The next mistake you make, General, you will get absolutely no warning from us whatsoever. You will simply find yourself all over the world press and the sats.

When we were about 85 percent certain we had him contained, we left.

Back in Raille and Jessiqana's apartment, we reviewed the entire event. Raille and Jess were satisfied this episode was contained and this foe disabled for the moment. However, I was still concerned about the security for Jess and the children. We spoke long into the night with Januti joining us and the others all tuned in. In the end, we believed the children were okay, Jess was fine, Raille was quite calm and in control. With both Jess and Raille's agreement, Ajit had planted a tiny super-clever safety device that would give any of us automatic monitoring of any serious emotional disturbance in the apartment and a microscopic subcutaneous tracker behind the ear of Jess and each of the children.

After some thank you's and warm, connected goodnights ,we returned to our homes, relieved and disturbed. It had also been necessary to introduce the eight of us to Raille and Jess and, although I felt safe with them, this added an extra dimension to our growing world of complex problems to be managed. We had also decided to have SFC security bring Raille and Jess and their children into the security rostering system and we were certain Miyuki would issue the necessary orders.

Now, back in the living room with the eight of us and our Olarian friends watching on, I looked around the group, and I thought about Jard and Leiti and what they had faced, the eight of them, in a hostile world. We had the Olarians to help us, and they had been truly magnificent, and as yet no hostile world to brave, but then our world was 17 billion-odd people. I knew we were carrying more covert stress than was good for us and I felt a strong need to rest and to travel to OlarCret where I knew we would get some of the help we needed.

◘

Everyone continuously worked carefully but assiduously at developing their telepathic and telekinetic knowledge and skills, and this included me. We learned quickly from each other because our learning only had to occur with one of us for the entire group to get it. Some activities had to be practiced in very tiny forms that everyone could understand, however, no-one else could yet make the simultaneity jump to OlarCret so the group could meet *officially* with the Olarian world. Esan was strongly of the opinion it would happen. And it did, though in a convoluted way, thanks to his intervention.

We have replayed one of your early conversations with Olaria, he said. *She watched your first jumps to Earth and then back home. It was just a hunch until you spoke with her from* Energystreamer: *there might be a connection between the longevity changes and the bigger simultaneity jump. Can you make contact with her again and ask her to get the Living Library to look at the early learning about simultaneity jumps, to check how closely they followed our own and your age adjustment?*

I knew he asked because the Olarians were still able to hold only very brief conversations with OlarCret and neither they nor any of us could understand why.

But Esan was right. The original jumps, for Olarians, were only possible for people who had had their longevity modified, and Esan thought it possible that the aging management process needed to be established before the bigger simultaneity jumps might become possible for us. A somewhat spooky thought became clear. Whoever or whatever had created us seemed to have deliberately connected the length of our lives with our simultaneity abilities.

It did make a kind of sense. If you wanted a sentient being to explore the universe, you probably did not want it to live so short a time it would be preoccupied with other things! So with everyone's agreement I modified each member of the group so their age was now being controlled but allowed each to continue their aging until it would be slowed and stopped at around 38 years. Esan and Olaria had been right – once that was done, each of the group could follow my track to OlarCret.

I was aware that we would need a few weeks before we could all organize to be available to 'disappear', now that all of us could make the jump. Those of us with regular jobs needed to organize absolutely credible reasons to take leave. Januti, Ajit, Darcy and Natalya were clear. Ai could easily negotiate herself the time, Donna said she was okay to take the leave, and I was pretty sure I could be constructively involved with that if it proved necessary.

Peter knew he could negotiate special leave and I was confident I could manage Miyuki, so a date was set for seven days ahead and we made the necessary plans to protect our apartments and disguise our disappearance. The Olarians had been using Esan and Olaria's connection to get messages to and from home but were delighted to give us a much bigger load of messages, which we promised to take with us and bring back responses.

As we met in Natalya and Peter's apartment with two days to go, we felt the tension and the expectation. It was in this context that Januti looked at me and asked, seemingly out of the blue, *Why did you first contact me rather than someone else?*

Caught on the hop, I wondered for a moment if I had known why and where the question was coming from. Though I probably did have the answers at some unconscious level, I could not put them into words at that moment.

Januti, I don't think I know. When I first made the jump to your apartment I simply felt there was something I had to do. You were in my time zone, and you felt as though you needed me, except I could never have articulated that at the time. As I reflect on it, it feels as though, and this sounds absurd, but it felt as though you were calling me!

I shook my head. She was looking at me with surprise and the others were also staring at me.

Well, I don't know what words to use. But you asked, and it feels as though I was hearing you call me!

It seemed she was satisfied with my answer for the moment. I could not add anything to the thought. But she was not finished with questions. I could sense her unfinished feeling and so continued.

When I met you, without words or discussion I knew you needed help and I managed that for you because I felt an overwhelming desire to do so. At that point I realized you were trusting me, something new for you. Then I knew, without any window dressing, you seemed to want me, an experience I had then only had once before. I don't know that I really believed the feeling. Olaria had wanted me to be in a romantic relationship and when you and I got together I believed I was responding to your feelings toward me, ones I found a little difficult to trust.

Januti was asking for more and I was not sure I knew what she wanted. Then I realized it felt like a question, 'why me?' So I asked, *Is that right?*

She nodded, but I could see that was not quite enough, not quite right, and she expanded on that.

It's not just 'why me', it's also 'how'? How did you experience me needing you? I'm sorry, Zed, but no-one has ever wanted me in that way, wanted to help me, wanted to just be there for me. It's still hard to really believe. Being attractive to men has never proved wholesome for me. I never felt it was about me, but mainly just how I look, but with you, well, there was none of that, and in some crazy part of my mind it seems just too good to be true.

I could see how torn she was: 'me, too good to be true!'

Can you explore how you experienced me needing you? she asked.

I stretched my mind back to that first moment before I made the jump to her apartment. But nothing... well, almost nothing. A faint sense of being in contact with... what? Some unarticulated vague feeling, hunch, subtle sense of... something. Then I just had to let it go.

Not really...

She slid her body against mine. I could feel the warmth and the extreme delight and the hunger. There was a stillness in the group and I could feel each person asking themselves if my reality applied to them. Januti was just looking at me. She was no longer stroking my arm or trying to manipulate me. But she was deeply engaged in testing her desire to be mine and to have me be hers. I could feel she wanted to believe me, desperately now, but there was this tiny feeling of uncertainty, disbelief. She was just looking at me, willing something, then it was as if she picked up some intangible sense of confirmation and she burst into tears.

How will this all work when you are sleeping with Natalya?

Ah, I finally got it. Thought to myself, 'Slow-witted Zed'.

For that night I will love whoever I am with and give her the pleasures she likes and the things she and her partner share that give her pleasure as you will undoubtedly give the man with whom you are sleeping and whose child you will be carrying for nine months. I will know that, as will you and everyone else. But I will not be her creature as I will be yours, if that is what happens between us. I will be a good and satisfying lover but she will not possess me as you will. I would expect the same to be true for you with Peter or Darcy or Ajit.

I knew I absolutely needed closure; my own level of stress and tension was high.

Now, Januti, cast your cards. This is not now, or ever will be, a game for the fainthearted. And this is just the beginning of the issues we may need to face if we decide to stay together and on Earth. Be mine, choose someone else or choose to be a loner. Every option is truly open to you. But have absolutely no doubt about my preference.

At that moment it would be true to say all the options now sat on the table. So far we had leapt to link up but these ties were young and needed to grow to maturity from a solid base. Januti simply stared at me; she was piecing together the scenario I had painted for her and was in no doubt what I was offering and expecting. She was working hard under the radar.

It was Ai Shen, our very lovely Chinese veterinarian, who acted with clarity and firm conviction.

I met Ajit when the rest of you met him. I chose him instantly and without reservation. I really don't know why. We have all learned something of the Olarian way of love and sex and sensuous connection. I too am feeling the need for reassurance. However, make no mistake: my choice was right, I want him and I want him to want and need me in the ways you have expressed, Zed. Nothing less.

She turned to Ajit,

Ajit, if it is your wish to be my man, my partner in this new life, you must tell me clearly that you understand Zed's expectations. They are clearer than I have heard before but I know they are exactly right for me, so tell me and genuinely share which of them is right with respect to me. I think we have talked this through enough to fully understand what we need.

Ajit smiled and nodded and Ai went on.

Sometimes I will be your woman as Januti will be his but sometimes it will be the other way round – you will be mine. I believe that who is in control will change between us as we need it to. I promise to always keep the boundaries between us clear.

She became silent and watched him inside and out. He beamed, his inner strength and harmony slid over her, its promise absolutely clear, and the two moved closer together and we heard her whisper, *You know how good I feel being with you.*

There was no question this was an exchange between equals and they became in that moment a little more entangled with one another.

Darcy Rey smiled as Donna turned her head and looked directly at him. There was no doubt Donna and Darcy had settled into their groove.

Natalya looked at me while laying her hand on Peter.

When I met Peter, something much more gentle and much more right for me happened between us. I knew he was mine and everything you said about intimate relationships fits us to a tee for me and I don't have to ask to know he will be my man in deeply intimate ways for however much of our lives that is what we need. So, more than anything else, thank you for the framework. Although it is never the way I would describe our relationship, I am the dominant one in our relationship and Peter is willingly compliant and submissive.

She looked at him with a genuine query in her eyes and, watching and listening in to them, we all knew he was in total agreement. I think we were all a little surprised but within seconds we all knew she was right and that was exactly how it needed to be for them.

And it was back to Januti and she was looking steadily at me.

Zed, when I first met you I would have had you in my bed in a flash. You could have had me any way you wanted me. No man had ever taken such care of me or been so openly powerful as you were. I would willingly have become your loving and emotional slave. I know this would have been a very limiting relationship but wonderful in its way.

Right now, Zed, it would seem you are all that is left, my only choice for a telepathic partner!

Everyone was staring at her in amazement, unable to get a handle on whether she was really serious or not.

The truth is, and you know it, that would be absolutely fine with me. Since I met you I have had not a single moment's doubt that I wanted to be your partner. And it wasn't that you had almost certainly saved me from an awful life. I have never been willing, never wanted, to give myself to a man before I met you. But from that moment I have not wanted to be with any other man, and I believe, at least as I speak with you now, I never will. You are not only a magnificent bundle of powerful superheroes wrapped up in one desirable package, but you have taken care of me with absolutely no expectation of a consequence from me.

Every moment we have spent together has cemented my feeling of hunger for you and pleasure at our connection. I am, to my surprise, extremely jealous and I want no-one to have any part of you, and I know that is both unreasonable and impossible. Both of us are going to have to deal with that if you feel the same way toward me, which my experiences with you suggest is true. I believe we will be asked to take some testing journeys, but I don't believe they will cloud my love for you or my total trust in you.

The group let out a deep sigh of relief and so, in a short afternoon, we had become four more solid and genuine couples. The Olarians were delighted and I was fully satisfied.

Now I knew we had to face some new challenges, especially the unanswered question 'what ought we do?', the ethical question with which Plato and Socrates struggled thousands of years ago and which we had so far managed to avoid.

CHAPTER 14

Parents

Ajit looked around the group.

Since we are beginning to know something about who we are, I don't believe we have the choice our parents made. They were able to pretend we were normal while we know that by human standards we are not. But, in fact, I don't think my parents had any idea who I am now finding myself to be.

Everyone was agreeing with him as he continued.

Many of our parents are alive, so my question is: should we find out if any of them are actually like us?

A heavy silence fell on the group. We all looked at one another; none of us had taken that simple step. We looked around the group. My parents were both dead. Januti's mother was alive in Tokyo; she didn't know whether her father was alive in the USA or not. She had not spoken to him for more than 10 years. Natalya had no idea whether her parents were alive or dead; she had not spoken to them for seven or eight years. Donna's father had died in a construction accident but her mother was alive. Darcy had had no contact with his parents for several years but believed both were alive and well.

Ai's parents were both alive and well and she was occasionally in contact with them. Ajit had lost contact with his parents six or seven years ago and had no idea whether they were still alive. Peter's mother was still alive; his father had died from exposure in a mountain climbing accident three years ago. None of us, it turned out, had any siblings from our two probably telepathic parents, and, as we sat here now, none of us was certain they were our biological parents and, since everyone had watched the *Village of the Damned*, no-one was sure they wanted to know. I wondered why Olaria had said nothing about our parents and I realized I had simply never taken the obvious step of asking.

Esan gently interrupted our speculation.

I am really sorry I have not spoken to you about your parents. It never occurred to me you had not checked. Olaria found all of your parents. They are all telepathic, however, none of them are telekinetic, and she had no idea why. That is only true for the seven of you she found. Donna, I checked when Zed found you, and your mother is telepathic but not telekinetic. There are a number of other telepaths around your world with varying degrees of telepathic capability, but none of them are anywhere close to you. What surprised and interested Olaria was that none of your parents had more than one child who was both telepathic and telekinetic and all had only one child with their telepathic partner.

Many of the other telepaths are married to other telepaths but none of their children are also telekinetic and none have a great deal of telepathic capability and we don't know why. You did not find them, Zed, because you were searching for the vastly stronger signal that the eight of you generate and most Olarians have. But if you lower the intensity of your search you will see them, faintly.

I smiled at Esan. At some level it should have been obvious to me. So with all the others following me, I made the sweeps as I had when I found our seven. As we swept each major land mass we saw the faint signals – we guessed maybe a thousand or more. When we had finished we all sat there thinking about what we had found. It was Januti who decided she needed to test the connection for herself and she reached for her mother telepathically. She got a faint anxiety response. When she spoke to her, she could not get her mother to believe she was hearing Januti. I asked Januti if I could try; she nodded and I spoke to her mother, introducing myself in the way a Japanese man would do.

Her mother stood still and asked, *How are you talking to me, Dr Eko?*

Mrs Makie, you have always known your daughter was telepathic. I am her new partner and I also am telepathic. It was indeed her you heard before. I am going to ask her to talk to you again and this time you should know it really is her.

They had a short but quiet, moving conversation and as Mrs Makie said goodbye she finished by warning Januti not to ever let anyone know she could do this, telling her that this telepathy was the reason her father had left them. Januti was stunned and promised to talk with her again soon. Then she sat back and looked at me, put her arms around my neck so I could hold her and cried deep racking sobs. She had brought the past and the present together and was overwhelmed by what she had done.

I'm thinking that those of you with a parent somewhere might like to search for them and decide if you want to converse with them telepathically. I have a small and uncomfortable feeling that it might not be a great idea, but Januti's connection with her mother does not seem to have raised any risky issues. The idea leaves me feeling uncomfortable but it is clearly not my decision.

The group discussed the pros and cons for nearly half an hour and collectively decided not to make contact as Januti had done and had to reassure her that no-one was thinking it had been a bad idea. However, now they had talked it over, it seemed an unnecessary risk at this stage of our development. So each of them decided to search out and find their various parents and simply check whether they could communicate back with a simple one-word check.

They all found their parent or parents and established without connection that each of them was capable of communicating back to them. At this point all decided not to follow this piece of string and the conversation was put aside for the moment, each first dealing with the anxiety and emotions that had been brought to the surface. We did, however, have a discussion about needing to protect our parents if we were ever found out. That was an excruciatingly difficult conversation. However, everyone knew they would need to protect them if the issue arose and I added Raille and his family as my personal responsibility.

CHAPTER 15

Humans, Cuckoos or ?

Ajit had been talking to Ai. He was uncomfortable about having an intimate relationship with the Olarian women, not because they were not interesting or attractive, but because he wanted an exclusive intimate relationship with Ai whom he clearly adored. As we listened to him air his concerns, his distress and his recognition of his responsibilities and the needs of all involved, I knew that each of us had much the same concerns.

He stopped speaking but we knew he had not said all that was on his mind, which became clear when we reconnected after a 30-minute break. Januti and I, and we had checked the others, were also struggling with the idea of taking breaks. What they really amounted to was sliding out of the consciousness of the others for a brief time; it was a very human response to our feeling of the need for privacy.

When we reconvened, Ajit continued.

Every time some issue comes to mind and we deal with it, something else comes up. I feel uncomfortable being the one who keeps disturbing our harmony but I can't let go of all the anomalies.

Ai looked at him and said, *Ajit, we need to deal with all the things that are in your head. Bring them out.*

Well, he said, *let me make a list. It's only a short one and I don't think there is anything new on it. I am still uncomfortable about spending a night having sex with one of the Olarian women. I do understand why it matters, but even that's not as disturbing as the idea that I have to spend a night with Donna and Natalya and Januti, all of whom are beautiful and desirable women. I think I must be more prudish than the rest of you and am really wanting to be exclusively with Ai.*

But that's not the worst part. The idea of Zed and Peter and Darcy having a night with Ai and her carrying their child... I don't know, it disturbs me, and I did take in what you said the other day, Zed, that this is really a big part of our building deeply trusting relationships that we are going to need for our survival. I can see that we need to build a community of ourselves. There is, too, the issue we have broached only once before. Will our children be telepathic and telekinetic like us?

Everyone looked at him and then each of us nodded slowly. It was a possibility they would not be.

Then there is the question of us meeting and coming together as a group. I mean, first I thought, why did Zed awaken us and bring us together? Would I have done that if I had been in his position and what would each of you have done if you had been in his position?

Then I come to our earlier problem: what the hell are we going to do forever or for however long we live, now Zed has prolonged our lives? Not that I am regretting that decision. And as you all know, finding my parents was not a pleasant experience, and having found them I was just glad to leave them uncontacted.

So you don't think I am dumping this on you unconsidered, I am still quite certain I would have come and found you. I would not have been able to contain myself and I know the logic of our situation and our debt to the Olarians and, yes, I will find a way to be with the women in our world.

Finally, there is what Zed refers to sort of jokingly as the Biggie: are we human? That question we all are beginning to feel is somehow answered from our discussion the other night. Probably not! As we clearly are in some ways, we clearly are not in others.

I'm still mulling over the early sci-fi Zed showed us the other night where John Wyndham raised this issue: are we cuckoos? I know we talked this over after we watched the film but I just can't seem to let it go. The cuckoos were all killed as children because they so frightened their human carers. Does this mean we need to help humans understand us? I draw some comfort from Zed's friends Raille and Jessiqana.

He stopped and searched anxiously through our minds, starting with Ai about whom he was deeply anxious, but without need, it quickly became evident.

She simply said, *We ought not need to rehash this. If Olaria had told any of the rest of us what she told Zed, which of us would not have felt an obligation to find and tell the others? What kind of self-indulgence would have allowed any of us to feel that this knowledge, given to us freely, was really ours to choose to use selectively? I think it is sad but interesting that we all know we would have sought out the others but we are also having difficulty somehow putting the question to rest. Why is that, I wonder?*

She paused and examined everyone's thinking. Within a few moments each person made a clear statement to the group: everyone would have felt obliged. Ajit agreed he had no right to dump his awareness of our future difficulties on me. I had not created us, I was merely the messenger.

So, as each of the group thought about the issues Ajit had pulled out for our reconsideration, I wondered yet again whether anyone felt their most desirable course of action was to go it alone, that this might be a safer plan. But it took not a lot of time for everyone and each couple to go there again and come out feeling clearly opposed to that course of action, even when I made clear they would not really lose any of the information that became known to any of the group.

Finally, after a lengthy discussion, the consensus was clear: for reasons beyond our knowledge, we may well have a new and different role to play in the universe's drive for better-quality intelligent life – whatever that actually meant. At some level it was clear to each of us that it did not seem as though we were just a genetic anomaly. The Olarian eight and our eight seemed an unlikely coincidence.

There was consensus that we needed to do our best to maximize our individual and collective capabilities. The lid was not going to be put back on Pandora's Box and we were clearly hoping an optimal or more appropriate role for ourselves would become clear to us. It seemed likely we were going to have to figure it out for ourselves, especially if our understanding of how we came to be able to make the simultaneity jumps across the galaxy was a guide. And we knew from the Olarian observation of our brains, a process I could now manage and the others were getting on top of, we had undeveloped capabilities. Problem was, we had no idea what they were or how to activate them. I suspected Rozari might turn out to be some kind of key to this.

A few bad jokes about Batman and Robin, Superman and Superwoman, and a whole host of superheroes were made, and we slowly managed to get a better perspective on ourselves and cleared a path to temporary normality. Which, absurdly, seemed to be some kind of a relief.

CHAPTER 16

First Group Journey to OlarCret

The day we arrived on OlarCret was a surprise, for we arrived in Olaria's house stark naked. I had somehow managed not to think about the fact that, unlike the small jumps when our clothes traveled with us, on the intergalactic jump, they did not. So, suddenly in Olaria's home there were eight naked people! It didn't matter; the Olarians were not in the slightest uncomfortable and within seconds had us in Olarian clothing. That took the four women out of the conversation for nearly 10 minutes as they yet again explored the making of more interesting energy garments.

It seemed that there was no end to the variations Olarians used in creating their energy garments and no end to the interest and curiosity of our women about them. Although each of the four of us males could quickly make an adequate energy garment, none of us was particularly good at it or particularly interested in the refinements that the women enjoyed so much. There was a time we would have been called sexist, was the thought that settled in my mind. However, the truth remains, I and the other three really enjoyed what the women did with their clothes every time they began a cycle of innovation, and they always ended up creating very novel and often quite extraordinarily interesting clothes for us!

When we arrived in Olaria's house, she was surprised but delighted. She looked carefully at Januti.

I know there is a proper human way to do this and that it is different from our way. I think I should leave it up to you as to which way I should greet Zed when you arrive so you feel comfortable and my behavior does not disrupt our relationship. You do understand that this is not a concern an Olarian would have but we learned with the Sunstreamer *crew that the human responses are quite different.*

Januti looked deeply and carefully into both of us, then smiled happily and freely. There were no covert innuendos here, no hidden barbs, no deceit. She just smiled happily and with her ever-present delight said to Olaria, *The Olarian way is and will always be most welcome to me.*

And Olaria took me in her arms and we kissed and hugged. Then in one smooth shift she took Januti and hugged her, pouring enjoyment and delight at meeting her into their connection. She finished by reminding Januti she had been quite unprepared to find her and the others, and had not had then and still did not have any idea of the significance of the existence of the eight of us. She made it clear she was genuinely happy to see us together. The beauty of this was there was nothing dishonest or deceptive in it.

We were all conscious of the amazing skill and subtlety Olaria used to meld Januti and me into a gentle and loving connection with her. It took only the shortest additional time for a real connection to be made between us. In the small time that elapsed the entire group of us were focused on her and we were all learning at our usual rate from her process of managing us. When she was done, all of us had an additional insight into how and why the Olarian society worked so well.

We had skillfully been made to feel unconditionally welcome in a traditional Olarian way and Olaria knew we would all now be able to do that when we needed. I was watching closely. While no human would be able to do what Olaria had just done, the underlying pattern could be reproduced for a non-telepathic connection.

The Olarian world was delighted we had arrived. We had all kinds of human difficulties in managing their welcome to us, such was their excitement at our presence and their hopes for their world now we were known to exist. Finally we were all able to move on.

We knew we had only one day on this visit but the Olarians definitely intended to make it count. Each of the other seven spent their first session with our Olarian health team and made plans for the future. Ai and Donna both sought to understand whether they might learn to become capable of looking after us on Earth and it seemed certain they could be part of the process, however, there were not yet enough of us to create a workable health team using the Olarian model.

We met many people, we talked for hours. I had seen Rozari only when she was being born and once since for a brief visit. So I was delighted to be able to spend an hour with her, bonding and playing and enjoying her, as did all the women in our group. The three other men in our little group were generous in expressing their interest and I immediately understood how the gender difference impacted our relationship with young children. It was a momentous day. It ended with a wonderful meal and an assurance from the Olarian world that any and all of us would be welcome members of the Olarian community should we ever wish it. It was an overwhelming moment, hundreds of thousands of voices affirming the council's offer and an explicit offer for us to be here to develop our abilities in a safe environment.

I spoke with the Cretian change group and spent an hour going over the activities going on in Cretia, and then spent some time with Januti, who was trying to keep up with what was going on. I made the jump to Seliqana to give her a message from her sister and asked her if I should give her the physical hug that Jess had asked me to give her.

She was very gracious with Januti and they spoke for several minutes. She looked at me with surprise as I replayed the message Jess had given me with the images of her and Raille and their two children and Jess's telling me to make sure I gave Seliqana a hug, adding that she knew Sel would not be pleased with her. With surprise and sad delight, Seliqana came up to me, having checked that it was all right with Januti, and hugged me and kissed me on the cheek. A very big step between us. Piquant joined us, looking much older than I remembered but formal as always, just a little softer now. Seliqana thanked me, gave me a quite complex message for Jess that I promised to deliver, then Januti and I made the jump back to the group. Januti was truly delighted I had included her and was amazed at the stunning beauty of the tall, slender, elegant Cretian sisters.

When it came time to leave, I asked the council members if they would take us back to Human Haven in their drifters from where we would make the jump back to our apartment. They were delighted; our group was enthralled. The three other men in the group imagined making drifters back home!

Then we were home.

After we retrieved our clothes and dressed, everyone sat down and stared at one another. OlarCret was a comfortable known for me; it would be some time before this was not an entirely amazing adventure for the others.

I excused us while Januti and I visited with Jess and Raille after I sent Raille our coded holo message. He replied and I gave him a few minutes to disable the security devices around their unit. Then Januti and I made the jump. They and the children were delighted to see us. The children were never allowed to be aware of how we arrived, although I did not imagine at their young age they would have understood the issue. They had just been put to bed so Januti and I went in to say goodnight and give them hugs. Januti and I were always delighted to feel the joy in the children, which was satisfying for them, because we knew exactly how they were feeling and could always fill them with joy and satisfaction when we were with them, even at so young an age.

When we returned to the lounge Januti gave Jess a replay of our meeting with Seliqana while I caught up with Raille. Jess was delighted and I caught them both up on the change program and how it was progressing.

They gave us the latest about their education program on the intergalactic realities of Earth and OlarCret, with popular lectures blending the two. Once a month they gave a public presentation at ANU on intergalactic culture issues in the main hall, the biggest space available at ANU, with every seat filled and every aisle step taken. They were the only two individuals who knew there were eight human telekinetic telepaths and that we could travel to OlarCret with a simultaneity jump.

When we left two hours later it was too soon but we needed to return to the group. We also had to be very careful not to have Jess and Raille know things they could not really know without risking them. That was a tricky one because they already knew a great deal about us and our concern was for them more than ourselves. And, because we now knew we could, Januti and I felt a desire to transport Jess and Raille for a visit back to the GeGhan home. We could not immediately sort what concerns we needed to take into account but planned to do this soon if we could not safely organize for them to travel either during a *Sunstreamer* or an *Energystreamer* trip.

Everyone had by now actually met Raille and Jessiqana and their two beautiful children, Selma and Reggie, the couple's compromise for names that needed to span two universes and three strangely different languages. The names could be made to work in English, Cretian or Olarian.

◘

At this point I had returned to work, so nearly every regular weekday I was on Moon Base One, a 25-minute trip each way from Canberra's space port. Ai Shen, Donna, Natalya and Januti spent a little time each day grooming me on the subtle feminine patterns of emotional shapeshifting that enriched my ability to influence people in meetings. All the others joined in these sessions, wherever they were, which always occurred after my morning meditation. They were becoming creatively talented at using and extending this helpful range of manipulative tools. Januti and Natalya had a favorite activity they undertook once each week. This involved visiting a sidewalk cafe and be addressed as Sir by the waiter or waitress. They had to choose their clothes carefully for this to work as both were slim and had generous figures that would otherwise have given them away.

One evening, with my help, Esan was able to make a prolonged connection to Olaria on OlarCret from moon orbit. It happened just before I had finished getting an extended briefing from Esan on the longevity processes. I was describing to Esan, as clearly as I could, what I thought he needed to do to extend his connection with Olaria across the galaxies. Esan was able to make the prolonged connection, almost two minutes. Olaria was delighted that she could now contact Esan for long enough to feel they had a real connection.

Januti and I then made a full simultaneity jump to OlarCret. Olaria was wildly excited and embraced me and we shared a moment of deep intimacy and then, with all the sizzling awareness of her and Januti, she was able to smile and they simply held one another till she took me to visit Rozari who, infant that she was, knew her father immediately and threw her tiny arms around my neck. I knew she was being my daughter and I loved it and felt a deep and satisfying love for her. We played together for nearly half an hour before Olaria reminded me that we needed a further talk with the Living Library. We also needed to speak with the health specialist groups about our routine health check-ups and some more complex issues around my management of our group's age control.

I knew she was right. My Earth schedule meant this must be a brief visit. Along the way thousands of people were sending me greetings to which Olaria's assistants were responding. I stayed with the Living Library special team for more than an hour learning everything I could about the tiny puff of sub-atomic cellular energy rearrangement that guided longevity. I also realized I needed a heap of chemistry, biology, biochemistry and cellular biology and some other specialties to have a human understanding of this process. I had a suspicion if a complex-enough understanding could be achieved, non-telepathic individuals may be able to make some kind of use of it.

I needed now the best judgement of the group on whether there were any potentially negative consequences to the age-controlling process I had initiated because of the ages of our human telepaths. No-one had wanted me to take the risks but no-one could offer any reason the process should not be perfectly safe. In the end, even the most conservative agreed to support my decision and were willing to help if there were consequences down the track.

There was a promise that when the group visited again the two most expert groups on the age-extending process would check up on the eight of us. However, at Olaria's behest, 16 of their top 'cellular analysts' had examined me cell by cell to assess whether any changes had occurred as a result of the intergalactic jumps. At the end of their hour, they could find no change of any kind right down to what I would think of as the sub-atomic level, an amazing process I was beginning to enjoy following and learning about. I always found this comforting and expressed my gratitude for their work. They were delighted to have had the opportunity and offered to do a similar assessment when any of our women were pregnant, there being a standing concern about the health of a foetus.

Olaria and Januti went with me to another meeting of the Cretian change team. We had timed our visit to coincide with the meeting, which was convenient as it was a Saturday back on our patch on Earth. Seliqana was there and I gave her a long follow-up message from Jessiqana about her life and their children, and to my amazement she got up from her seat and came over with tears in her eyes and hugged me again, the second sign of emotional contact I had ever received from her.

She said, *When you fill her in on what's happening here, give this to Jess and her children for me please, Zed.*

Then she returned to her seat. The group were astonished. This was the first occasion Seliqana had touched anyone in the group.

I learned that the women's group was growing in strength and slowly gaining the right to make decisions about the life of the clans. Piquant remained the titular head but without the battles, he and the other clan heads had little interest in the activities of the women's group. New structures were beginning to emerge in the clans, some now run by the women, some shared between the women and the men. No open conflicts had occurred for several months and the education system was being developed with a heavy Olarian content, which the women's group was finding encouraging. A first meeting between the two educational systems, comprised mostly of women from the Cretian side and 50/50 male/female from the Olarian, had taken place a month ago, just after our previous visit. There were signs that future meetings might lead to a genuine shift in the focus of the Cretians and some substantive development in the interpersonal sensitivities of both the men and the women.

I was a little agitated, knowing I needed to leave. Olaria looked at me with the warmth and love I knew would always be between us, then she responded to my question about the other seven children for which I had been responsible.

She took Januti and me to each family and I found that I could enjoy the mothers and their partners without any feelings of guilt or jealousy on my part, theirs or Januti's. This proved more than pretty special to me. None of the children had yet been born but all were close to full term. Each of the women was loving and delighted to see me and to meet Januti, as were their male partners. It was a beautiful experience and each asked if Januti and I would try to be available for the birth of the children and I said I would if I possibly could and Olaria promised to keep me informed.

Each of the male partners was warm and genuinely friendly and very desirous of Januti and I being at the birth of the children. I returned to Olaria's home almost in tears and feeling overwhelmed at the generosity of the men and the love of the women, something I had not expected. Olaria smiled at me, and Januti and Olaria took me in their arms and held me while I managed my disturbed emotional state.

Zed, you were beautiful with those women, you were generous and kind and honest and willing. They and their partners genuinely love you, care about you and want you to play whatever part you can in the lives of their child, your child and their relationship. You are a part of them now, forever, and because you are deeply in love with Januti, they want you too, Januti. You are definitely a part of each of their lives now and the lives of the children they will rear. You are becoming welcome and treasured intergalactic members of our world, all of you.

She turned and looked directly at Januti. And both of us knew it was true and as always I felt embarrassed and I imagined hearing a grunt from the cowled figure I always felt was sitting patiently on my left shoulder, then I shook my head.

I thanked them, felt the weight of their messages and felt humbled by the quantum of genuine warmth and connectedness. When I had finally managed my feelings to all of them and was being held by Januti and Olaria, I realized I was becoming more than myself. A new itch had arisen and I had an intuition that I was on the verge of another change, however, it was time to return to Earth.

Before I departed, I shared with Olaria an idea that I believed might solidify for her and Esan the process of making the auditory jump so they could communicate more easily between Earth and OlarCret. Januti and I reached out to Earth and to a connection with the others. It took only seconds and we both spent several minutes in conversation with the others. Then we said goodbye for the moment and returned our attention to OlarCret. Finally, satisfied we had grasped the essence of the intergalactic communication pattern Olaria and Esan needed, we made certain Olaria had mapped the pattern we were using and could replicate it.

This time before we said goodbye, Olaria, Januti and I held each another and kissed

Then...

Januti and I made the jump to our unit. She was still feeling my connection to Olaria, knew I would not reconnect sexually with her, but she was a jealous woman and she collected me as we emerged naked in our apartment. In the instant of our arrival she had dressed in the sketchiest of clothing and during the next two hours made certain I knew where

I should be spending my time. When I refocused, after she had almost thrown herself at me, I felt a special feeling of satisfaction and belonging, a feeling of being loved I knew I would never want to lose. The result was extremely pleasant and satisfying.

We knew how well we fit together. My power guaranteed I was capable of caring for her, and she was beginning to put to rest that jealous, fearful, suppressed part of her that had been alive and active for years. She could trust herself with me. I knew she would give me, without conditions, the emotional intensity I craved. She would allow me to have her and she would want me with all the intensity of her being, knowing she had nothing to fear from me. My strength was enough to constrain her wilfulness and I was able to take her on journeys almost beyond imagination and ones that could help her grow and develop and I knew that was all part of her loving me.

Our lovemaking, sometimes long and gentle, other times explosive and passionate, satisfied both of us and it seemed to always include the things we were constantly learning about carnal pleasure. My understanding of the entirely feminine parts of her body, her sexual core, I never ignored any more. The effect on her was deliciously satisfying to both of us and she never failed to use what she had learned about men to please me in ways that were extraordinarily enriching. Why, she wondered, had she not known all these things a long time ago when she was growing up? As I heard her thoughts, I realized they exactly mirrored my own.

I again needed to contact Raille and arranged for Januti and me to go over for dinner. Since we had returned on the *Sunstreamer,* Raille and I had made a date for one day each fortnight to have a martial arts session together during which I had agreed not to exercise any telepathic abilities. I was also teaching him dozens of subtle new ways to pay attention to solitary or multiple combatants and was increasing both our jiu jitsu and ninja techniques, something I had only been able to do over the past months. The moves were so flowing, essentially simple, potent and effective, that both our martial arts skills expanded at a fierce rate. After, we would have a coffee, talk long into the afternoon and then spend time with Raille and Jess's children and have dinner together.

Jessiqana and I were strongly connected and Januti and Jess were forming a strong and mutually satisfying connection. Raille grounded me and was one of my strongest reasons for not wanting our group to resettle on OlarCret, now that was a real possibility, or on any other planet. There was, however, an additional factor. The group wanted to study and increase the breadth and depth of their knowledge base. They now had access to whatever they needed, could sit in on lectures of any kind anywhere in the world, could read and study whatever they wanted or needed. This aspect of their new lives had, at this stage, hardly begun to be explored but was high on everyone's agenda. Biology and biochemistry, nanotechnology and high-level mathematics and physics and high-order programming were areas several of us were finding exciting, difficult and satisfying. Mapping and merging our growing understanding with our other abilities was, we could see, something that might come to serve us well.

CHAPTER 17

Time Travel

I spent many non-working moments exploring my simultaneity and finding new ways to use it. I was more than vaguely considering how we could have our children brought up on OlarCret. It seemed an absurd notion, but I was very conscious of Rozari now nearly six months old and already able to connect to me in a very simple way even when I was on Earth. I missed her, and none of them knew why she did not need the age-management process to be able to manage auditory simultaneity. Januti was also able to hear her and was building a relationship with her, much to Olaria's delight. Januti was also becoming increasingly invested in the idea of us starting a family of our own. However, like the others, she felt we needed to wait till we had sorted out the tangle our abilities and our situation was currently placing all of us in.

Now they had all agreed to allow me to make the tiny change that would prolong their lives indefinitely, to which I would make a final alteration when they turned 33, their ability to connect to their higher-order simultaneity was coming into its own. Shortly they believed they would all be capable of making other even more interesting inter-planetary jumps across galaxies, once they could figure out how to make blind jumps to unknown destinations. Fortunately for my sanity, no-one was planning that anytime soon.

The Olarian women, especially those on *Sunstreamer*, were bursting with desire to become pregnant to the four human telepathic men. It was on a night a few months after our initial get-together that the women in our group agreed to have another discussion, one which might, not without some anxiety, result in an agreement for their men to spend a night with the Olarian women on *Energystreamer*. At this point all eight of us had finally agreed to have a child with the four Olarian women on *Energystreamer*. This had not occurred without a great deal of emotionally complicated discussion between ourselves, our partners and the Olarians!

It was a delicate scenario. Our partners could now both understand and emotionally relate to the Olarian culture values. Because there was no deception, duplicity or guile, and absolutely no covert pressure from them, the four women were able to see the significance of the genetic enhancement that was being sought. Over the next millennium most of the present generation of Olarians believed they would need to die to allow their more developed children to replace them. It is hard to describe how significant, how impactful, this insight was to the eight of us.

Each of our four women wanted their partner to start a baby with them first. However, they all knew this might be risky in our present circumstances. The level of self-sacrifice involved in the actions of the Olarian women had woven its way into all of us. On the night the women chose to discuss the issue *again* all eight of us were at Ajit and Ai Shen's apartment. The security was, as always, deaf and blind when we sat down to one of Ajit's delicious Indian meals, made this evening by Ai Shen – further evidence, if it was needed, about the extent to which our basic skill, knowledge and ability base had exploded exponentially.

There were interesting limits, some based on prior knowledge and practice, some on cognitive structure, some on willingness to obtain the complexity-management necessary and often just on interest alone. However, we were all gaining a brand new range of flexible skills. Also, a great deal of very covert telekinetic practice was taking place outside the visibility of the satellites, which, fortunately, could not cover every square mile of the Earth's or moon's surface. These were areas which all of us could use. The satellites also could not see us on OlarCret. In addition, with Ajit's assistance, any of us could now disable a particular satellite and could free an area on the ground where we could practice.

When we had finished all the social chatter and complimented Ajit and Ai on the delicious meal, we sat together in the lounge room and they all looked at me.

Oh no, why me? Any of you could begin this discussion and at its very heart are you four women.

No-one spoke.

Oh all right! We do need to decide how to deal with the jealousy felt by our partners and the guilt and discomfort felt by the men in our group in respect of our having, in a human context, an inappropriate engagement with the Olarian women on Energystreamer.

That set the cat among the pigeons. It was not the tack the women had expected me to take nor one they wanted. It was Januti, smiling and nodding, who picked up the ball.

I should have guessed it would be a mistake to put this into your hands. The trouble is, I know that in part you are right. It is our jealousy that is sitting in the midst of this issue. But it is not just that, is it, Zed? The truth is we are all just a little uncertain, perhaps read that as totally ignorant, about how we are going to manage children in this society if we are to bring them up in a healthy, open way. Especially a way that is unlike the way our parents dealt with us, and that is having an impact on our feelings about our partners helping other women have children with them.

We have been here before. Our options appear to be: ask the Olarians if we can live on OlarCret and become some part of their community; find our own planet and start again; and then the most tendentious, the most complex, the most difficult... find a way to live here and bring them up here safely. That of course is very like the original Olarian telepaths, and we know how they finally sorted their relationship with the original non-telepathic Olarians. And, oh, there's also the option of waiting for a decade or so until whatever we decide to do here is done and we choose to move on and then have our first children on OlarCret. If there is another alternative that anyone can conceive, now's the time.

As she said the words an idea began very, very quietly to emerge in my mind and I felt a transformation begin and for moments I sat still and waited. The group had stilled and everyone was looking at me and tracking the strange development that was activating a previously quiescent area of my brain. There was also a stillness on *Energystreamer* and the entire telepathic group was watching and waiting.

Then I was on OlarCret and Rozari was being born – not a memory; I was pretty certain this was not a memory, I was actually there. Next I was at Human Haven and it was the occasion of our first meeting with the Olarian telepaths. I moved my seat sideways telekinetically, something I could never have done when I was there. Then I was back in the room with the group and as I opened my eyes their astonishment and disbelief were evident. To them it appeared I had not moved, yet they all knew where I had just been, as did the Olarians! I retraced my memory of the first meeting with the Olarians and I knew I had two memories – one with and one without the moving of my seat.

The Olarians were as intensely focused as our little group. There was little doubt in my mind a new reality had just been opened up in my mind and all but one area in my brain was now, finally, active! I sat very still. No sound in the room, the group quiet.

Hold hands please, I found myself asking the group. They did. *Do not let go, please.*

Then in a way I could not immediately describe I focused on the moment of Rozari's birth – eight of us were there! Then we were back in the apartment and it was today as it had been when we came for dinner, and according to the watching Olarians we had not moved!

Esan, will you please make an auditory jump to Olaria and ask her who was present at Rozari's birth? A few moments later he came back to us. His voice as he spoke was tinged with tension. *She says she cannot remember for certain, but believes the eight of you may have been there. And she sounded very shaky because she feels strongly that the eight of you could not possibly have been there and at the same time has a sense that the eight of you were. Zed, what just happened?*

For several moments I sat very still. I could feel the turmoil in the room and on *Energystreamer*, but more disturbing I could feel Olaria's disturbance and wondered if I had gone too far. Then I realized this was not the result of my intervention. I had done nothing to deliberately open up this aspect of my brain. Whoever or whatever had been responsible for us was activating this nearly final feature of my ability in this time and in this place; it certainly had not been any conscious act of mine. I looked around the group.

All of you have this structure. How I came to be the first and the oldest, none of us know. I wish what was happening to me was happening to you. I do not want to be alone with this. I do not, it seems, as yet, have clear and definite power to control it. In any case, I will very carefully experiment and you will all learn, in case I make any kind of fatal or serious mistake.

Januti moved beside me, up close, her body touching mine all the way down my left side and her arm around my shoulder. It was clear. Whatever happened next, she wanted to be with me. There are no words to describe the depth of pleasure and satisfaction that tiny act created in me. I was, for the moment, yet again, way out of my depth. I needed time and space, and I was intuitively certain I had to experiment with this ability if it was not to become a source of fear.

They all got it, and for the next few moments we sat in silence. Who or what was controlling us? I had never felt so much like a puppet. At first I searched around for a who – some personage or creature of mind that was controlling me. Then, slowly, I came to suspect I was wrong. There might not immediately be someone or some gigantic mind controlling me, puppet-like. Who I was, what I had been at birth, might just be emerging as whoever or whatever was the designer had intended, way out of my ability to conceive. Darcy, Peter and Ajit almost simultaneously asked if I had any sense about how they might help. It was a strange and deeply satisfying moment as I realized they were genuinely concerned for me and wanted to be there for me. I was deeply touched, and another feeling I could not quite describe found its way into my conscious mind.

And then, no warning: the four of us men were one mind. It was a terrifying moment, and we... leapt?... to a place only I had been – the fighting room deep in Piquant's house in Cretia on OlarCret. Piquant

moving toward us/me, my actual body with the four of our minds in it (can I say that?), and as he hurled himself and the weapons in both hands at what was my body the four of us, with no sense of concern whatsoever, quietly brought him to a standstill and with my voice said to him, *Lord Piquant, you are so far out of your depth you should retire from this engagement now.*

Then, without a second's hesitation, disbelief etching every line on his face, he surrendered. Seliqana, about to rush to him, seemed to know in that moment not to move, and it was over and we were back in Canberra and we all sat back in our chairs and looked at one another. The shared tension slowly eased from the four of us, the four women staring each at her partner and questions coming from each of them.

We were there, Natalya said, *but we were also here. We saw you leave, we were taken with you, outside of you. Only you were actually there, Zed, that is, it was only you we could see. Yet when Seliqana lost control, something I think you either did not see or were unaware of, when she tried to move to help Piquant, we stopped her!*

Of the Olarians, Serra spoke first.

Zed, we heard your conversation, but you need to know we saw you, the eight of you, sitting in your chairs through that entire time. We got a fuzzy image of the fighting room in Lord Piquant GeGhan's home then that was gone and you were still all sitting here!

It was Januti who spoke first.

Zed, I think you just took the eight of us on a time-traveling journey to a moment of your past, but, and this is a big but, we seemed to be active in the events of that room. The four of us – the women in that room – stopped Seliqana from rushing to Piquant and dispatching streams of deadly spinners at you, Zed. And I think – she looked at the other three women – *I think none of the spinners would have touched you. So we did not save you, yet we were somehow involved. Zed, I am in no doubt you took us back in time to that room, a place none of us had ever seen before. You involved all eight of us in an engagement to which we could never originally have been a part! I think! Yet... I knew everything that was going through your mind during those moments we were there and of course we also knew what was going through Seliqana and Piquant's minds!*

We all sat, quietly, the others looking at me. Almost as one voice they said, *You did that, Zed, and somehow you involved all of us. Your actions activated one of the quiescent areas of our brain. All of us can now use it. It is no longer quiescent; it has come alive for us, jointly.*

They were right. I had just been made responsible for lighting up one of the previously quiescent areas of our brains. Now only one small part remained.

Everyone was looking at me still.

What?

Well, you have done it again. You have taken the next step and engaged all of us with you!

And while that was absolutely true, something else was demanding my attention.

Esan, would you please open up a channel to Olaria and simply ask her just one question. Would you please ask her again to tell you who was present with her the night she gave birth to Rozari? Please do not say more. I need you to just ask the question and await her reply, in spite of all you have seen and heard here tonight. Will you do that please?

Esan looked into me but I was shielding my thoughts for the moment and asked him to trust me to do this until he had heard from Olaria. And because he trusted me completely, he did what I asked.

Olaria replied, *Only the team and Zed, yet at the edge of my memory is a vague and ill-defined sense that there may have been others, but I think not. That is a very strange question, Esan, to ask from so far away. Is Zed up to something new?*

Esan replied, *I think so, Grandmother, I think so. I will let you know.*

Esan replayed the conversation for me word for word although we had all heard it. And then added, *I could have told you there was no-one else there, Zed.*

I nodded. *You could have done, Esan, but now I must tell you something new. However, first I need to ask the others, and I would like you to listen carefully to what they say.*

Esan nodded, I could feel it.

Then I turned to the others. *Can any of you tell me whether you were at Rozari's birth?*

They looked at me strangely. Then one by one they each replied, *Yes.*

Again I had to say, *I have a distinct impression that all of us were there, however, all of you know that is not actually possible, because at that time none of you had met me and none of you could possibly have made the simultaneity jump to OlarCret even if you had known where I would be at that time, so...*

I was silent for a moment.

I think we can move through time and I think others may well be aware of us for a short period, then their memory of the event seems to return to what they remember experiencing of it before we intervened. At this time I believe we probably cannot change what went on, although that may yet turn out to be incorrect. We will need to devise a totally non-consequential experiment to find out. I suspect we may not be able to actually influence past events but I'm not sure yet; we can certainly visit them. I am wondering about future events, but right now I do not want to find out.

I could almost feel the breath of relief from the group.

Esan, I don't know where this latest discovery will take us, but I think we are going to have to treat it very, very cautiously. Please let Olaria know what happened here tonight. I should add that I had a feeling, a very brief one, that had I wished I could have held time still!

And with that I felt as though I had, for the moment, come to the end of a long piece of string.

CHAPTER 18

The Intergalactic Education Centre

One evening a short while later, having spoken with the group about the Original Olarians and how they built their society, I realized we might have an opportunity to build ours without moving, at least until we knew what we were supposed to do. Even couching our future options in those terms felt irresponsible. The others were crawling through my mind trying to find the idea I was trying to formulate but I was not quite there yet.

The group were all looking at me, their expressions puzzled, astonished, excited, uncertain... I realized I could run off quite a list.

We are all waiting, you know that. It was Januti, encouraging, not really impatient but hopeful. I looked around at each of them and re-organized the thought sitting just at the edge of my consciousness.

I think I might have stumbled across a solution to several problems all at once. In my mind it has a name – the Intergalactic Education Centre – and it would need to exist on OlarCret and be run by the Olarians, with help and support from Cretian, human and Olarian educators. It might enable us to begin our families right away.

There was quiet and an unexpressed sense of excitement.

It would need very clear guidelines and responsibilities. Essentially it would be an Olarian initiative and there would need to be a clear and indisputable understanding that the Olarians would always have the final say in all matters to do with the running and management of the center. It would need several separate venues. And it would probably need the four women in our little group to be able to travel safely when pregnant and for our babies and children to be able to travel with us safely. This will need, at this stage in our development, thorough assessment from the Olarian health teams. I have a feeling we will come to be able to do these assessments for ourselves at some future time, not too distant – just a hunch but to be trusted.

The room was still and it was as if every sound was multiplied many times, yet I could feel the interest of the Olarians on *Energystreamer* and knew everyone was feeling some of the buzz of excitement that felt a little like warming up the strings on my little harp.

If our children could be educated on OlarCret essentially by the Olarians, in eights with some of the children we have sired with Olarian women and some of the children sired by Olarian men with our four partners, they would be out of sight of the human world. And we could visit them every night and be back home here on Earth in the morning if we had the Olarian site situated so that 5pm here was 5pm there. That is the beginning of this thought.

Now in addition, suppose we could persuade the powers that be of the advantage to the human world of learning the values and the deeply understood cultural behavior maps of the Olarians. Suppose we could persuade the Olarians to build an educational center on OlarCret where children would be raised totally in the Olarian way, and include human children from Earth and from Second Earth, some Cretian children, Raille and Jess's two children and our children, both those who are born to us and those who are born to us and Olarians. So I'm thinking of it quite literally as an Intergalactic Education Centre. So to tidy it up, here is my first bite at a rough list:

(1) Eight Cretians, probably from eight clans, with eight ordinary Olarians

(2) Eight Earth humans, probably from power families, with eight ordinary Olarians

(3) Eight Second Earth human children from families that will probably provide future leaders, with eight ordinary Olarians

(4) Eight of our TT children, if we can manage twins, with eight TT/Olarian children with four TT men and four or eight Olarian mothers

(5) Two groups of eight TT/Olarian children with eight ordinary Olarian children?

(6) Two human/Cretian children from Raille and Jess, who decide where they want them to be, with six other ordinary human children selected from around the planet and eight Olarian children.

My thinking is no more than speculation at this moment, froth, but I am thinking several not strongly connected thoughts.

As I say this I am wondering if it might not be more constructive to mix some of the Cretian children with some of the human children, but whichever way the groups were mixed, I think we would need to keep our children separate and in a different location from the human and Cretian children if we want to keep our existence secret from the Cretian and human worlds.

You need to keep in mind that I am still just getting the shell of an idea. But the initial impetus for these thoughts was a way for us to be able to start our families now and have our children educated in the Olarian way. Then as I thought about the possibility of them being educated on OlarCret I was also thinking about them being mixed up with other intergalactic groups. Then, of course, I realized we really might not need the other groups to shield them. As I thought further into it I realized the Olarians have the capability of helping both the Cretian and human children to become far better citizens of their worlds.

Suppose we could persuade the powerful families on Earth to have some of the next generation educated with Olarians and other galactic groups. Having these families come to support this idea and plan to ensure their education need lose nothing of their traditional sophistication, but could instead add to it an entire layer of behavioral excellence and emotional and intellectual understanding that would make them superior managers and leaders of the future. This would result in them having a cohort of powerful Olarians who would be part of their lifelong resources, or possibly a group of our children who may wish to be involved with the Olarians.

Now this world would have an enormous investment in them all because the educational center would offer incredible opportunity to the human students, possibly making them ideal future administrators of Second Earth and maybe, just maybe, ideal future leaders of this world. This would meet almost all our needs for a human society and we could start having children immediately. All we really need is the support of the Olarians. I believe we could easily manipulate the powerful Earth families. This might well open a door to as yet inconceivable constructive options for the future.

There are a swathe of details that need to be considered and negotiations that need to be undertaken. Also, I don't know if anyone has any thoughts on when we would want the program to begin.

We could give ourselves three or four years to prepare and set up the entire operation or we might find a way to simply have our children join their part of it later. We could start our families immediately and we could organize it so the Olarians and our children could grow up educated in the Olarian way on OlarCret and we could have our children invisible to the other groups, their existence hidden by being part of an otherwise ordinary Olarian group.

The Olarians should be in complete charge of the processes used and the Olarian way should be the controlling way in this process and they would need to decide what ought not to be on the table for discussion. Because only the Olarians, of all the groups, know how to manage this very complex process and have millennia of experience in building and shaping it. The thing I am uncertain about is the telepathy.

My excitement was huge, my sense being that we might be coming up with a solution that would be detrimental to no-one. Hm... it would, in fact, have an impact on all kinds of children and adults who were not part of this new Olarian/human/Cretian experience. I particularly liked the idea of a cohort of eight Cretian children. I could feel the palpable heavy silence from the group listening in – had I gone too far? But Serra, Esan, Ai Shen and Peter breathed a deep quiet breath and simultaneously thought something like, *Zed, that is very frightening in its conception and at the same time brilliant.*

Peter held Natalya close for support and said to her, *Do you fully support Zed's idea? I know it is just a kind of brush stroke at this moment but I need to know absolutely how you feel about it. I don't think there is any room for indecision and uncertainty if we are to move forward with such an extraordinarily exciting idea.*

He need not have worried. Natalya was shaking her head in deep, deep admiration for the bare-faced simplicity of it, the seeming impossibility, the nerve in the midst of the convoluted complexity of the plan. Our problem lived in a complex unordered domain, a place where there were no known solutions, but where creating some elegant and unlikely experiments might well bring together solutions to several aspects of the problems at the heart of nearly everyone involved: Olarians, Cretians, humans and us, the eight *human* telekinetic telepaths, the 12 visitors to OlarCret, the two spaceship crews, and at the edges, the connections between several worlds – Earth, OlarCret, Second Earth – and the various groups linked through them all.

Everyone was looking at everyone else. The Olarians had taken an almost simultaneous breath. I was just humming with delight at the idea that something so seemingly simple, albeit enormously complex to establish, might turn out to be the solution to several apparently intransigent problems.

I wondered about the synchronicity of our experience of time travel and my idea about a way we could start our families now, and I could not help wondering about the significance of the two realities arriving at almost the same time.

A thought edged into my mind. Suppose we could make this work! As I had this thought all the elements seemed to be in motion in my mind.

At that point I had to stop, my brain nearly pickled, but the idea still out there for everyone to mull over.

Another thought sitting somewhere in my mind was about the Olarians. They would need to be willing to use the same process with all these non-telepathic children as they had used with the *Sunstreamer* crew, enabling the experience of telepathic reality in its actual absence. Then I wondered if it was possible and if it was something the Olarians would want, how demanding it might be of the Olarians' resources. I suddenly felt as though I had taken us way out on a limb and maybe way beyond anything the Olarians would be willing to consider. So I paused. The Cretian part at least might offer some real value to the Olarians in their engagement with the Cretians. I have to say, I was already feeling I might have stepped over some very serious boundaries. I had not for a moment considered the extraordinary demands this might make on the Olarians and I felt a little ashamed to have even considered putting them in this position.

I slid my mind into contact with Olaria and let her collect all the pieces of this crazy notion and then waited for her to assimilate and evaluate the ideas. I could feel her joyful smile from across the galaxies. She dealt first with my primary anxiety: I did not know how the Olarians had managed to keep the *Sunstreamer* crew in telepathic space when they were not physically present. She showed me the process they had used to give us the telepathic experience and maintain the crew's telepathic state. It was not that difficult but they had had to conceive it then test it in real time with us! Now she passed on to me the process they had used. I immediately saw how they had managed and realized we could easily learn to do it and thanked her.

Zed, what you are imagining is truly brilliant. It just might make possible a future none of us can immediately imagine, a connection between our worlds that might begin to remove the dark and damaging attitudes and behaviors that have become part of the pastiche of Cretian and human life.

I knew we were opening up a very new and unpredictable engagement. Only the future would tell, and suddenly I realized I might be able to visit that future and find out. And at that point we said our farewells.

CHAPTER 19

Next Steps, Pregnancy, Families

Pregnancy and having a baby came up next. I think I understand why. It was certainly connected to the agreement that the four men of our group would sire an Olarian child. I listened to the four women talk. Donna and Ai were 31, Januti and Natalya were 28, and the discussion they had was simple – they did not want their men to sire a child for someone else before they were themselves pregnant with their partner's child. More intriguing was the discussion about whose child should be born first and in the end they agreed to try to have their babies on the same day.

It was really not something about which any kind of argument was appropriate; the feelings were strong and the discussions about how we would look after them in the future were just that – discussions. However, the Intergalactic Education Centre was an idea no-one could let go of. Everyone knew Esan had had several brief conversations with Olaria and the idea was being discussed on OlarCret. But I knew I could not proceed without Esan's willingness to support us. It was a strange situation: the Olarians would help us in any way they could, however, this was a project of such significance we could make no assumptions about it. So I asked him if he had any objection to Januti and me going to OlarCret and talking to Olaria.

He had none, of course. However, he asked if Januti and I would take him and Serra with us on the jump. This was not something anyone had asked of us so far. Januti and I were immediately willing. The others, cognizant of the unclear complexity of this situation, were supportive without hesitation. So, after Esan had had a brief conversation with Olaria, we made the jump. In the time between these events, Olaria had sought and obtained the approval of the council to have Januti and I and Serra and Esan meet with them. Within a few moments of our arrival and with welcomes managed we all made a jump to the meeting space of the Council of Eight. It was a very unusual occasion. The greetings of the council to me were strong, warm and immediate. Januti was formally welcomed by everyone, warmly and caringly. Esan, his father Jald and his grandmother Olaria all hugged and connected and then Serra was also warmly welcomed by everyone.

They all knew why I had come. The Intergalactic Education Centre had been discussed by them and by millions of Olarians since Esan had first spoken to Olaria of the idea. There was overwhelming support for the idea but a great deal of uncertainty as to how the project would actually work. I was clear the purpose of our visit was to lay out the issues for the Olarian community to consider.

I would like to tell you all the bits of thinking and our hopes and concerns around the Intergalactic Education Centre. I think that is probably the most useful way to begin.

I could feel the settling around the group and knew this was indeed the way to proceed.

This idea began when the eight of us were talking about having children. Our women wanted us to start a child with them before we started children with you. I think this is probably a human thing; I believe it is not how an Olarian would think. But it was this issue that started me thinking. How could we raise children on Earth and yet give them the kind of education you give your children? I knew we could not do it on Earth.

Now the reality is, I don't know which concern led me to the next step. I thought: if there were children from Earth being educated using the very constructive processes you use here, we could maybe hide our children in the mix. Then I thought, maybe this idea will open a doorway to helping the next generation of leaders on our world and in the Cretian world to behave more constructively and usefully than they presently are going to learn. And I thought, your Olarian education system gives children a really constructive and positive way to begin their community life.

So maybe finding a place our children could have the education we want for them and engaging with a solution to improving the future generation of leaders in Cretia and on Earth and on Second Earth could be another benefit and cover for our children. Then I began to realize that everything I was thinking could also be done without educating anyone but our children and at that point my thinking briefly stopped.

I think this was because there were many things that could conceivably go wrong – something could give us away. I then realized our four women could probably hide their pregnancy by using some of the shapeshifting tactics we have all been practicing. Then there was the question of how we could rear our children for four or five years on Earth in plain sight then account for their complete disappearance. And it was at this point, as you all know, we suddenly found a new part of our brains activated. We could travel through time and seemed to be able to manipulate it in some as yet unexplained or unexplored ways.

Now, we don't know how well we can actually change people's memories or on what scale, but I began to think this ability might allow us more flexibility. We don't know yet; we are going to have to experiment to find the boundaries to this ability. However, it was also at this point that I thought, if I was thinking of sending our children to OlarCret that we could be sending them to other countries to be educated and no-one need know where, especially if we did not discuss this with anyone. And we can now manipulate the sats so their records show what we want them to show rather than what is actually happening.

So I thought, okay, we could send them here to be educated with you. We can visit them every night so long as their education location was in the same time zone on OlarCret as Canberra is on Earth. We checked that and as all of you know that is not a problem.

They could be educated with some of the children who are a mixture of us and you: my eight – seven of whom are due to be born soon – and the children from the four men on Earth. Or, if you thought it more desirable, with your own normal Olarian children.

So there you have the idea, a little messy but in its essential pieces. We started out looking for some way to have our own children and we ended up with an idea that might have benefits to all of us on both our worlds and Second Earth.

All the above assumes that you see the situation somewhat as I do.

However, I realize that I am presuming a great deal about what you might consider was in your interest as opposed to what we are thinking. Then it got kind of complicated and I gave up and decided I would just outline as much of the idea as I could and wait to see if this was an idea that found sympathy with you. Hence coming to see you to lay it out.

I fell silent, listened in to the Olarian world. But there was only more silence. It seemed everyone was thinking about what I had just laid out. It was Olaria, looking at Esan, her grandson, who smiled and, nodding, said, *So that was what your little fishing expedition was about?*

I replied, *Yes, we seem to have acquired some kind of ability to travel through time. At this point we do not really know what the boundaries are, however, we will explore and keep you updated. This is why we believe it might be optimal if we could educate our children with those from your world that might also have these capabilities. Overwhelmingly, we would like to think we could enhance the capabilities of the future leaders of our world, Second Earth and Cretia.*

So now you are pretty much up to date on our educational thoughts, of course, heavily dependent on how you think and feel about them. We need to know how your world feels about this idea and if you can come up with any ways to change and/or enhance this very bare proposal, if it interests you, and obviously we hope it will.

However, it is a first thought and we have not explored it in any depth. Any thoughts you have on it will be welcome, I feel certain you know that.

Then I realized there were a few other things that needed thinking about.

I should also say that this idea would only work in the way I am thinking about it if you were willing and able to do for the human and Cretian children what you did for the Sunstreamer *crew: keep them telepathically connected to each other and your own children. I can only see this working if they spend the majority of their educational experience as though they were telepathic, so that your value system would be their value system.*

Also, I have no idea whether this is feasible, whether you think it would be worthwhile, and how they could be weaned away from the telepathic reality when they left school.

So I need to repeat, this is just the bare bones of an idea, and it all came about because we really desire some way to raise our children inside the value and belief system that is entirely Olarian.

One other thing: I realize it was only a very short time ago that Olaria explained to me how you gave the crew telepathic capability when they were not wired for it and what was involved, and we have, as yet, not explored this in any depth.

The Olarians needed time to assimilate this, so we thanked them for their time and left.

When we returned home the issue of pregnancies was again being discussed, I think because of the subject we had taken to OlarCret. There was a great deal of careful searching of each of the partners until I quite rudely stepped in again.

Please, you all know that for now your relationship is solid. You also know you are free to openly discuss every aspect of your needs and feelings. We all know how you enjoy your intimate times together. We genuinely are no longer like other people on Earth. In some ways we are more Olarian than human and this is definitely one of them.

We also know, and this is even freakier to say, but in 20 or 30 years, if our relationships do not continue, we know how to end them harmoniously. We know there will be other men and women in our community with whom we will be able to create new relationships, men and women from among our children and from among the Olarian world. If that happens we are going to have to learn to deal with that.

For a moment they all looked at me as though I had grown another head. I realized that my year on OlarCret had really rewritten my emotional value system. So I did something I had never done – I took them on my journey through love and sex and intimacy on OlarCret during my year there with Olaria. What the journey had shown me of many, many deeply intimate and satisfying relationships was that it was not uncommon for them to break up some years later when original needs were no longer being met.

I realized I had left some uncomfortable loose ends. *In answer to your concern about our future potential relationships with our children and their children, I am thinking that if any of us actually decide to separate, imagine it was Januti and I, then any of the children of our group who were not genetically connected to Januti and I, for example Peter and Natalya's children or any of the rest of you would be possible partners if the issue arose.* And I could see the feathers smooth.

It was then a matter of a few weeks and the loose ends were respectfully sorted and resolved and unfinished business was finished. This always happened, even though on some few occasions the couple decide to stay together.

Within just under an hour our deepest values were being explored. Some hours later, everyone was comfortably settled and four couples were cuddled together in our living room and ready to take the next steps.

I knew this would not be the end of it, but the door was now open to a different set of working values and a willingness to not dismiss them. We were not Olarians, but we were all absolutely clear that we wanted their value system for our survival, and everyone did genuinely get that.

I watched Donna shake her head and say to Darcy, *I feel very possessive about you, Darcy, is that okay?*

He looked at her with love, smiled, nodded and, looking deeply into her eyes, said, *Do you really need to ask?*

We knew they were planning to leave, but I asked if we could work on one or two associated issues first. They were willing.

Well, everyone needs two weeks on OlarCret to have their health patterns learned by the health group and especially this will be important for the four of you who will shortly be pregnant. It is also important for us that Donna and Ai are able to learn as much as possible about the process the Olarians use to understand and manage our health.

What we learned about pregnancy and child birth from the Olarians resulted in Ghia and Gerard having their child on OlarCret and they were delighted. Ghia wanted to know if SFC would allow her to fly there when she had her next child! It was only partly in jest. If there turns out to be any problem with that I would like to find a way to make certain she can have her next child there.

Esan entered our conversation.

Please let me sound a warning. We do not yet know how safe it will be to make the intergalactic simultaneity jumps when you are pregnant. We have no certainty and we do not understand the process, but we have had some problems with pregnancies where a pregnant woman has made a large number of simultaneity jumps on OlarCret during her pregnancy.

Can I ask you to please hold off becoming pregnant long enough to complete the trips to and from OlarCret to consult with the groups exploring this issue?

Also, we have several groups who have spent centuries exploring pregnancy and between them you may be able to gain the insights you need for decisions about pregnancy and intergalactic jumps. I had a long conversation with Olaria last night and she and I cannot tell you how many other Olarians are delighted that you are participating actively in our world.

Each of you will have two weeks to begin to explore whatever aspects of our world will interest you most and you will be most welcome. I cannot begin to thank you for opening up our intergalactic communication. It has made a real difference to how we are feeling about being away from home. I just wish all the crew could do it and we are exploring that and might need your help as we progress. He immediately knew we would.

I thanked Esan. As he and the other Olarians left, I heard Natalya ask them, *Would you have been okay for tonight to be the night?*

They all responded together, *Yes,* and again to her next question.

Are you really comfortable to put it off for a few weeks while we use that time to make sure we can all go to OlarCret, set up our medical care-taking arrangements and return home?

It was Donna who asked the obvious question.

Is it possible that the Olarian Energystreamer *or* Energystreamer 2 *could transport us to OlarCret to have our babies?*

There was a strong positive response from the Olarian crew, however, we all knew we were going to have to be exceptionally careful about how we managed this and we decided to keep this option open as we explored it over the coming months. One last thought hung around in my mind and I finally brought it to the fore.

I wonder if it might become possible for us to get pregnant and reach nearly full term, time travel back to before any of the four of you were pregnant, make a simultaneity jump to OlarCret, time travel forward to where everyone was on Earth and have our children on OlarCret without actually traveling while any of you were pregnant?

The idea, seemingly bizarre, did have a kind of sense about it, however, we knew so little about this ability we had no way to even guess whether it would work and, if so, if it would be safe. So for the moment we suspended that conversation.

It was still not clear when we would be able to start our families or when we should have our connection with the Olarian women on *Energystreamer*. What was evident, and what we were very conflicted over, was in what order we ought to start our families and start children with the *Energystreamer* women. We knew the *Energystreamer* Olarian women were very happy with any time we were ready.

The next day Donna enrolled in the professional child-care program that would update her qualifications to run the unit we would need during the first years of our children's lives.

We also scheduled some regular times to discuss what this might mean and make certain we were all comfortable with the simultaneity jumps to OlarCret. Donna was planning to spend some time on OlarCret and was clear she wanted Darcy to travel with her. Ai and Ajit planned to travel with them so that, as far as possible, they could all learn together as the women worked with Kyuto, who had been so helpful for Ghia. The two men would also learn something of the Olarian process of education.

Interestingly enough, it was Jessiqana who came to Donna's aid. Jess had studied the Olarian education system for her job with ANU and to help the Cretian educators should they come searching for ways to merge the cultures. So it turned out she was a font of knowledge and insights that Donna and the rest of us would be able to make use of. She was genuinely delighted and excited to be able to help. Also, because of the deep connection between Raille and me, it had become necessary for Raille and Jess to know more about our group. No-one felt vulnerable about this but it was an additional concern that was always present, if only gently, in the background.

We were all in our separate apartments when each of us became aware of the Olarians quietly being with us. They had been studying us and our lovemaking behaviors, it turned out, since we had got together. They were as familiar with our intimate behaviors as our partners. There was nothing unusual about this; often we were aware we were not alone and we were all slowly becoming comfortable with this arrangement. We had made certain between us that we all spent some time with the Olarians experiencing their relationship behaviors so that our level of comfort with this process steadily increased. It was not easy for us, and we remembered the problems that Jald and Leiti and the Eight had had when they knew they needed to increase their 'breeding stock'!

No one had accepted the need easily, however, they had succeeded in building an entire society this way. And we knew from the Living Library recordings that it had taken them more than three years to feel totally comfortable and relaxed about it. So we gave ourselves permission to do the same.

But it was much more than this. The Olarians were trying to understand a whole raft of other behaviors that were not part of their cultural world. We were excellent guinea pigs for that and we were all happy to be studied. They always ended up asking us questions that led us to new insights into ourselves and more understanding of Olarian ways.

It took all of two weeks to organize for everyone to be away together for two weeks. My absence had been the most difficult to arrange and I had had to inveigle Raille and Jess and their children into a holiday in a busy and obscure remote area and then, on day one while they were doing fun family things, I simply disappeared. The security system in my part of town simply went on the fritz and would take the appropriate authorities weeks to get back online; Ajit had done a brilliant job. We had timed our jump during the busiest weeks of school and kindergarten holidays to increase our participation in the global travel chaos.

On the allotted day we all made the jump to Olaria's home and we prepared ourselves to begin our families and give the Olarians the genetic gift we had promised them.

◘

For just a moment I felt how lovely it might be to find a new planet and struggle to settle it. At the back of my mind, I was also keeping alive my idea about a group of humans being educated by the Olarians who would go on to take charge of Second Earth.

Before we had proceeded far with the planning, the issue of our children was again raised and this time everyone agreed we would begin our families and find out how to cope later. All of us knew that would be a special night, and it was. So that problem disappeared and all of the women in our group got pregnant. When I looked at Januti a week after we had all conceived, I knew she was just a bit anxious, not for herself but for our children. I knew I would move heaven and earth for her. We looked together at our 10-day-old in utero... children! Twins!

Januti looked at me, smiling, willing me to move closer and hold her, touch her in any way I desired, so I snuggled up to her pillow and, side by side, we placed our hands on her belly and we both took our minds down to that tiny fertilized egg and examined it as I had done with Olaria when she was pregnant with Rozari and as we had seen the Olarians do. There were no words to cover that experience but we were aware that all of us had begun a process that would again totally change our lives.

The following night the now pregnant mothers agreed that we should ask the Olarian women to choose one of us with whom they would conceive. This turned out to be one of the exceptionally interesting journeys we would take. First of all, it was clear that the Olarian women had been discussing us and we had not been monitoring their discussions! I don't know why none of us had considered doing this. Probably a uniquely human and not an Olarian thing to do! We had agreed that each Olarian woman should decide with whom she would mate. All four of us found them all extremely attractive and each of them did indeed select one of us!

All of us knew these pregnancies might well be involved in changing the future of Olarian society and our reality. The Olarian women were not only all beautiful; they were also very skilled lovers and an extraordinary night of pleasure and procreation took place with our partners looking on. I could describe in detail the experiences of that beautiful night, however, the most significant outcome was not that the Olarian women, the mothers to be of our children, were able to use all that they had learned from the relationships between us and our partners, but that from that learning they gave us new behaviors that would enhance our relationships, and our observing partners watched and learned.

It was probably one of the most complex relational cross-cultural activities we were ever going to experience.

The Olarians were delighted and the negativity that might have been a residual consequence was washed away through the discussions we had with our partners and with the joy of the Olarian women and our partners when all of us got together on *Energystreamer* and the excitement of the Olarian women as experiences were shared and plans for the future discussed. The edge of jealousy and possessiveness got whittled away. The total lack of negativity of the Olarian women impacted strongly on our four women as did the loving contact between the groups of four and the sharing of what this might mean for them back home and for all of us in the future.

The thing is, each of our partners had been present so there was no deceit, no lies, no misunderstanding about what had gone on. This was a novel experience for all the members of our group.

Meanwhile, we had been exploring our ability to manage time. We were beginning to get a handle on what was and was not possible. We could create a place where time stood still, the other side of which we could be active...

CHAPTER 20

Lord Piquant GeGhan

A week had passed since we had returned from *Energystreamer* and our lives were beginning to settle down. I had just completed my morning meditation ritual when Esan appeared on my balcony. The expression on his face was almost comical but I could feel his agitation.

Zed, the Cretian change group have just found out that Lord Piquant GeGhan is suffering from extreme radiation poisoning and if left untreated he will certainly die. According to Olaria he will allow no-one to say he is ill and refuses any offers of treatment. We had not been maintaining a close surveillance on Cretia since you left except to run a monthly check on any weapons manufacture that may have started up. There have been only two, by the way, and both were terminated with a minimum amount of disturbance.

However, in response to the sudden information we received via Seliqana at a Cretian change committee meeting, we immediately began a detailed survey of the entire country. We have found seven of the biggest clans are experimenting with non-weapons grade uranium, and all have senior clan leaders and others with uranium poisoning. They clearly did not listen to your warnings and the distress and disturbance this has caused is having a very grim impact on Cretian life and has brought the development plans of the women's group to a halt. The Council of Eight want to know if there is any way you might be able to help.

Januti had joined us and was waiting for my response. I was trying to work the problem. Could this, I wondered, be made to be an SFC response? I had only a few minutes before my shuttle would arrive to take me to Moon Base One where I was expected at a meeting in less than an hour.

Januti looked at me intently. *I know you always say, work the problem, but we do not have time for that. Unless...*

I knew what she was thinking. But could I make this work? We had made one or two new steps in our abilities to manage time, preferring to sort out our families and our obligations to the Olarian women on

Energystreamer. Now this barely understood skill was needed. The others all turned up at our apartment, sat quietly, watching me and listening. I simply sat there trying to think this situation through. I could think of no known way to do this. So finally I looked at them.

It would be good if you all kept an eye on me. I don't know if you are going to be able to help me if I get into difficulties, but I can't think of another way. I think I need Jess and Raille. I need to go now and get them and make sure the two children are okay and in the next four minutes try to explain more about us, if you agree. Jess needs to come with me to OlarCret, if I can explain, if she accepts my explanation, if you all agree. I would like it if you could stay with me on this.

I stopped and searched them all. I wasn't panicked, but I was stretched to the limit. *Go!* from everyone.

And so began a new week and an entirely new chapter in many people's lives. I contacted Raille, who with Jess was preparing to open their front door and hand their children over to their day carer.

Raille, please shut down your watch-and-listen systems quickly. I need to make an urgent visit, now, before your babysitter comes into your unit.

Raille did not need me to explain anything. If I was needing him now, he knew exactly how to deal with the situation. Less than one minute later, the listening and watching devices now managed, I arrived in his living room.

Raille, Jess, I need your help. I need it now and I need to engage you with some stuff that will be mind-boggling but I cannot wait to explain. We have to leave for OlarCret in the next few minutes, but, and this is a big but, we have to do it so that we do not disturb anything here.

They looked at me, Raille head tilted to one side.

'Can you be a tiny bit more explicit?'

Okay, I want you to begin to let the babysitter in, then before she sees or does anything, each of you take one of my hands. I will then take us on a jump to my apartment where the others are awaiting us. But before we leave here I am going to freeze time in your apartment. Okay?

I really had not needed to ask. Both of them trusted me implicitly and it just felt so good. The babysitter arrived, then before they actually let her in, before she had actually seen anyone, I had both their hands and I froze the time in their apartment and made the jump to mine.

Januti! But she already had Jess's hand.

Jess, Raille, we have only seconds. I am taking you on a jump to Olaria on OlarCret, is that okay?

They both nodded.

We will lose our clothes on the jump and arrive naked, please do not feel distressed.

Then without any further explanation I made the jump and we arrived in Olaria's home and I could feel the others were with us – in my head, I suppose, because I knew they were with me but not really how! Raille and Jess were magnificent. We arrived stark naked and within seconds Olaria had us all clothed and was making her usual greetings. She hugged Jess and Raille, who she knew well, and they both hugged her back warmly, especially given the shocks they must have had so far during this hardly begun day. Then we sat down to talk.

I'm sorry, you two, I said, *I had no idea if we could pull this off so let me now explain. Since I last saw you something has changed for us. The eight of us can now manage time, in a fashion. Trouble is, I'm not sure how long we can keep time frozen in your apartment with you here on OlarCret. However, we had to try. Piquant is seriously ill. He has radiation poisoning as do seven other clan leaders and a number of others. They ignored our warnings and experimented with nuclear material without the appropriate protection. None of them will let the Olarians treat them, and without treatment, they will all die. So, Jess, I brought you in the hope that we might be able to resolve this issue today.*

Jess and Raille were just looking at me. Stunned expressions were simply inadequate to begin to tell the story of their immediate experience. Raille slid across to Jess and took her hand. My anxiety was near the roof when Raille burst into guffaws of deeply amused laughter.

'I should have known... from the day I saw you move that entire education center. You're way beyond that now, aren't you?'

I looked at him, my best and only real friend for my adult life. And I realized he didn't care; he really cared for me and knew it was reciprocated.

Yes.

And that was all I needed to say.

Jess was looking at him and immediately she knew he was absolutely trusting me. She just turned to me with her stunning smile, eyes alight, and said, 'Zed, I have trusted you since I decided to leave home to be with Raille. If he trusts you, you know that I also absolutely trust you.'

And really that was all it took. We all turned to Olaria. She was smiling with delight. Januti was holding my hand firmly and seemed unwilling to let go and I understood why. She was uncertain what would happen to our time warp if she did. And then I realized the other three women of our group were also with her!

Raille, I think we should go immediately to the GeGhan home. Jess?

I knew before I had finished speaking she was agreeable.

Jess, in our present state we are traveling while time back on Earth is standing still for us. We need to be here for the shortest possible time. We do not yet know what has or will happen to time when we leave here. It is far too complex for us to understand at this time, so my recommendation is we take you there and you and Seliqana and Piquant have the conversation you need to have to persuade him to let me bring him to a place Olaria will show me. If we can get him there soon the Olarians may be able to save him. Immediately we have been successful we need to visit the other seven leaders and get them to the same location as fast as we can.

I knew immediately Olaria would set the Olarian location up.

Jessiqana looked at me. 'Are you telling me that you need me to identify the place we will find the other seven clan leaders?'

I won't know until we get there but I thought you would probably like to be here and you might be critical to this venture. I don't know how much help, if any, I will need, but you are the only resource I could think of in this situation. Olaria has the Olarian map for the location of the others.

'Zed, you want me to visualize the location of the others as soon as you have transported Piquant, is that right?'

Absolutely, Jess, and it is possible I may need your help with Piquant. Are you two ready?

So with a nod I took us to the main room in the GeGhan mansion. Seliqana came into the room, saw Jess and let out a cry that was heartrending. Then Raille let her go and the two sisters ran together and embraced, tears, chatter in Cretian that we were just able to follow telepathically with Raille looking on and smiling. Then he spoke to the sisters in Cretian.

'Jess, please explain to Seliqana as briefly as you can what we need, and let us know, can the two of you persuade Piquant or do you need Zed's help or our help?'

The two beautiful young women were speaking together very fast and within a few moments it was clear that Seliqana did not know what would influence Piquant, however, she knew he was not listening to her. She thought I would probably have the most influence. I found Piquant in his 'study' and asked the group to please wait here for me. I made the jump to Lord Piquant's room.

Standing a few feet away, I let my image shimmer and I spoke in fast and impactful tones in ways I knew would cut through his emotional blocking. He did indeed stop, look at first alarmed, then went quiet while I spoke, explaining what I had told him nearly a year ago. I berated him for failing to follow my instructions about the dangers of nuclear material and made it clear his behavior had made it necessary for me to travel across the cosmos to help him and I expected him to allow me to transport him to a place where I assured him he would be made well, and in moments we had reached a clear and unconditional agreement. He would allow me to transport him and the other seven clan heads.

Lord Piquant, please picture in your mind now each of these men and their probable location.

With the help of Jess, the observing Olarians and Piquant's description,

I was able to find them all.

Lord Piquant, I am going to use your voice to tell these men to prepare to be taken to a place where their illnesses will be dealt with and that they should heed the instructions I will give them.

It was clear their plight was understood by all of them and they did not object. They knew the power Piquant had brought to bear a year ago and that it was clear that power was back. That was really all that was needed to get the men to the necessary help.

The sisters were beside themselves with delight that they could be together, having feared they might never see one another again. I promised them when Piquant and the others were recovered I would find a less disturbing time to bring them together again. The depth of their delight and hope was painful to observe and I knew I would find a time soon to do that. I could feel Raille's joy.

Then we were back in Olaria's home and I checked with her that the Cretians would be okay and she was able to reassure us that they had been brought to help in time. Now I had to see if I could get us home and back in time. We had no guides to follow; I was truly flying blind.

During all this time I had been aware the three other men of our group had been with me and the three other women with Januti. Now there was a collective tension as I said goodbye to Olaria and, with the four of us holding hands, I made the jump back to our home. I waited only long enough to dress us and then, taking Januti, Raille and Jess, jumped straight into their unit and with one shrug shook us back into time and left with Januti as the babysitter turned toward Jess and Raille.

Sixteen Olarians were with us and Esan was clearly stressed in a fashion I had never seen before. *Oh Zed, that was unnerving even for us.*

I looked at Esan and Serra standing together, clearly shaken. I considered this might be because Serra had chosen me as her partner for her children.

Zed, Serra said. *Zed, you were gone for only a few seconds! It was the way the others merged with you and then you all disappeared. I have never really felt terrified before, but I thought we had lost you, all of you, then before I really got my breath back, you returned! What did you actually do?*

I looked at them, then I smiled and shook my head.

Serra, I'm not sure I know, so let's all find out. Esan, would you ask your grandmother if she recently had visitors and how the Cretian clan chiefs are faring?

Esan looked at me, shook his head, smiled, and reached out into the cosmos to speak with Olaria.

CHAPTER 21

The Time Travelers

I settled back in my seat. The Olarians were with us and were all seated in our apartment where their relief was evident. According to Esan, we had been gone only a few seconds, however, by my calculations, based on my memory of what had transpired, we had been gone almost an hour. So the eight of us – Januti and I, Natalya and Peter, Ajit and Ai, Donna and Darcy – had returned, it seemed, undamaged from our first major slide through time.

When I contacted Raille I learned Raille and Jess believed they had been to OlarCret and had the same memories of the hour there as mine. Their babysitter, however, was quite certain she was on time and had not been disturbed. She was also quite certain about the time, as she always arrived at exactly the same time, which, according to Raille, meant that the hour they remembered spending on OlarCret had not existed for her!

Raille said, 'The time before you arrived, Zed, and after you returned us, for her it was no time at all. We would appear to have been out of our apartment, for all intents and purposes, for, at most, a few seconds! The time was accurate for the babysitter's experience but not for mine, and she, of course, saw nothing.'

I thought: *Nor was it accurate for Jess, myself or the others.*

I turned to Esan who was definite about their experience. The eight of us had disappeared and within a few seconds of our departing, not without a major momentary sense of terror from Esan and Serra, all eight of us were back in our seats. The date and time in Canberra now were exactly the same as when we had vanished a few seconds ago.

Esan was still a little on edge.

It was the way you disappeared that was so disturbing for us. The women seemed to vanish into Januti and the men seemed to vanish into you then you all left but not at all as you would normally vanish when you make a simultaneity jump. Serra was really frightened we had lost you. You all seemed to be sitting in your seats but we knew immediately you were actually gone. All we had were images sitting there. Then before we could engage with our fears, you were all back!

Esan connected to Olaria on OlarCret and asked my question. He listened for more than a minute, promised he would get back to her and rejoined the group.

Zed, Grandmother assures me you and Januti spent the last hour on OlarCret with Raille and Jess, salvaging Lord Piquant GeGhan and several other seriously poisoned Cretians. You helped get them to one of our health groups who are dealing with their radiation sickness, and because of you and Jess they will be all right! Could you please tell us what just happened?

With just the edges of a quizzical smile I promised to try.

So far as I can determine, the eight of us with Raille and Jess went to OlarCret and spent an hour there persuading Piquant to allow us to take him for treatment of his radiation sickness. Before we did that, and while we were at Raille and Jess's apartment, I froze time.

When we got to OlarCret we got Piquant to one of your health groups where he could receive treatment. We used his influence to help us get the other seven clan leaders and other personnel who had also been exposed to come with us to the Olarian health clinic where they are all now being treated. Arrangements have also been made to treat a not insignificant number of other workers in the nuclear facilities.

We managed to get the clan leaders to the facility in time because of Olaria's ability to get Seliqana's message to us through you.

When I say 'us', only Januti and I would have been visible to your grandmother and the others. However, Januti traveled with the consciousness of Ai, Donna and Natalya, and I traveled with the consciousness of Darcy, Ajit and Peter! At the moment, none of us yet understand what happens, how it happens, or why. My guess is that this mode of travel might increase our ability to get things done! At the edge of my consciousness I have a feeling this might be what it is about but it's a wild guess right now.

The eight of us had met at our place seconds before I needed to leave for work, I think it must have been because of Olaria's request, which they seemed to have known about. I haven't sorted that one yet. Now we were, I think, all just a little shell-shocked and in need of some quiet alone time to reset before we got back to more mundane issues. Well, no sooner was that thought spoken than all of us were wondering about the significance of the strange new way we traveled together. Then I realized I needed to catch a rapid transit arriving outside our apartment as I was speaking. So I said goodbye to Januti and the others and planned a quiet and thoughtful run to Moon Base One.

Today was already not just another day.

PART 4

ADVENTURES OF THE NEW MIND TRAVELERS

A Final Journey

'To fear death, my friends, is only to think ourselves wise, without being wise: for it is to think that we know what we do not know. For anything that men can tell, death may be the greatest good that can happen to them: but they fear it as if they knew quite well that it was the greatest of evils.'

SOCRATES

CHAPTER 22

SFC Managing Down

My rapid transit unit released me into the Moon Base One entry port, then took itself off and docked in my spot in the executive-level parking bay. I let go the reflections that had stayed with me through the journey. In spite of having only recently been appointed, I was wondering if my days in SFC might be numbered. However, I did not know exactly how long I could remain and did not want to ever need to feel I was leaving Miyuki in the lurch.

My early-morning meeting was with two senior psychotherapists who were exploring methodologies, some just now emerging and some a century or more old. All of us who spent our lives rooting around in human behavior were assisted by a continuously increasing understanding of the chemistry and biochemistry of the brain, as well as explorations of the nature of the complex functions in each different area of the brain and their interactivity. Both my psychotherapists were smart, senior and, as I found out when they came into my office, very anxious.

'Why,' I asked, 'are you two so anxious about our meeting this morning?'

They looked at one another. Xiandra and Parnite had been with SFC for five years. They preferred working together whenever possible and although they both undertook the annual space runs, their work was mainly with the problems involving SFC operational staff. Each was responsible for several intervention teams, including the professional and administrative duties of those teams.

They did not answer my question. Then I realized they were a couple; they lived together, they were in love!

Why had I failed to notice that before? So, okay, not a problem, but why were they anxious? Then I got the edge of it. They were a little telepathic; that was, in part, why they were so successful. However, they were afraid if anyone found out, they would be sacked or split up and were concerned this was the reason I had asked for the meeting.

Ironical!

I actually wanted them to take on more responsibility, but first we had to deal with their fears. But how to approach this? Carefully, I thought, thinking about this morning's activities so far, then I discarded that thought for a more practical one.

'Will the two of you please stop fretting and awfulizing? If I had asked you here for some unfriendly engagement I would definitely have let you know in advance. You both know me and know my style; you have both been heavily involved in the new debriefing program. To me, your telepathy is as plain as the nose on your faces.'

I watched and listened in and waited. Pretty much the second I finished they looked quickly into one another, did a quick read of each other's emotional state, confirmed their concern and then looked askance at me. They did not immediately speak. I knew that most of what I had just seen and understood would not have been noticed by a non-telepathic observer.

I continued.

'Why are you looking shell-shocked? You think you have been able to hide your ability to understand what is going on between you? That it is not reasonably obvious that you know more about your colleagues and clients than you ought to be able to know?'

Now anxiety and fear and distress! I wondered when they would simply 'fess up and let us get down to business. But not yet, it seemed!

'Look, ladies, there is nothing about your telepathy that does not favour our organization. Nothing that is not advantageous to your engagement with your clients and staff. What exactly is it you are so anxious about?'

This time I had them. Both immediately made it clear they believed being telepathic was neither unprofessional nor cheating nor inappropriate for a psychotherapist!

I looked at them with amazement and smiled. 'Whatever skills and abilities you have that enable you do your job more effectively are an organizational and professional asset. Now will you stop acting so inappropriately and let us get down to a seriously useful conversation?'

I thought they would rush over and hug me, their release from an oppressive anxiety was so strong. However, they still seemed tongue-tied. Their biggest concern was that they had been found out by their boss and had expected they would be dismissed. Instead, they had been praised!

Then Parnite nodded and for the first time, she spoke.

'Zed, if you are aware we are telepathic you too must be and right now you are successfully blocking me. How is that possible?'

'Parnite, my telepathy is probably more developed than yours, I have had the advantage of help from the Olarians. I will stop blocking you once we understand one another and you begin to engage with me. Is that clear enough?'

It evidently was.

'I need our two major intervention programs to be run by, and managed by, people capable of taking us into the twenty-second century, not back to the nineteenth. I want to know if the two of you would consider taking on those responsibilities. *But*, I obviously would not want leaders who are tongue-tied and not able to cope with their reality and organizational stresses. If anyone understands this, you two ought to. Nor do I want leaders who think that the theories and technologies of the past should be ignored instead of studied and enhanced where appropriate – read for that, effective and useful.'

I waited. These two were certainly capable of supervising the entire range of technical psychotherapeutic interventions the units would require. However, they needed the administrative and leadership qualities to renew, develop and manage the entire organization including the senior flight crews and the powerful politic of the administrative system.

The pair looked at one another. Then I picked up the pattern they used to manage potentially hostile environments.

Xiandra looked at me with a tight smile. 'Why am I unable to pick up your thoughts?' The words slid out, quietly but no longer with anxiety. Parnite watched, monitoring both of us. They did make a neat team!

'Because, Xiandra, your telepathy is not quite strong enough.'

I stopped closing her off and waited to see how far she could go. It was not very far. She could pick up my mood, my primary emotional state and could just get a sense of what I wanted to talk about with her. Her level of comfort picked up. She had been trying for most of the time we had been together to search my mind to get a feel for my emotional state and my thoughts; she simply did not have anything like the power to do so.

'Many people who are talented in our field are to some degree telepathic. It often goes with the territory. You two must know that.'

The expressions on their faces told the story. They both relaxed and finally we began the conversation that I needed us to have. I watched them slowly slip into the roles they played when working and being together. They were good. If I had not been telepathic they would have fooled me. I appreciated the amount of work and practice they must have put into working this well together. Okay, they did not need to know any more about me. They knew how to manage me, that was becoming clear, and that was all I actually needed to know. They had the professional qualifications, skill sets and abilities. They just needed a bit more information.

'I intend to merge all the psychotherapeutic intervention units into a single entity, run by the pair of you. I am fully aware that there has been a great deal of resistance to using multi-person senior leadership positions and that the organization likes for new positions to be applied for. I do not. I want the two of you to make it work as a single leadership couple. I plan to send you to a five-day program whose purpose is exclusively to familiarize you with the entire administrative process pattern of SFC, or for that matter most very large organizational systems. I am going to take you offline for 30 days after I announce your appointment and the new structure, assuming you are interested in taking the positions.'

I paused. They were still with me.

'During that time I want you to become familiar with each of the units, their personnel and their current practices and responsibilities. I also want you to be fully familiar with their success rates and their weaknesses in both managing people and professional practice, as well as the intervention models they are using and especially the gaps. Then I expect you to pick up the reins and begin to recreate your new system. While you are offline, each unit will manage itself and you will have an opportunity to see the individuals at work and assess their strengths and weaknesses before you pick up the reins. You should also observe carefully the leadership style of the unit managers. Is that clear?'

Only a moment's silence, then Xiandra gave me a clear and strong affirmation of their interest.

I needed these two to get engaged. They would report directly to me and, as they got control of the routines in the system and the developmental needs of the therapeutic, evaluation and debriefing teams, I would have more time to spend with the senior executive team, Miyuki and my non-organizational responsibilities. I hoped in time they would be able to run the entire unit and take over my role as well.

It was clear that they could not actually speak to one another telepathically, however, their telepathic intuition was excellent. They knew what each was thinking and feeling and when I stopped blocking them, they were immediately able to understand what I was wanting and could let me know. They were, however, unaware that I had no need of their ability to do this. I could easily read them both. It took very little time before they were fully and comfortably engaged with me.

It is very hard to describe how it feels to be free of constraints that have dogged you your entire life. I fully understood and at some level they both knew this. They were alive with hope and optimism, something quite new for them. We had established an understanding that would, I believed, pay off handsomely for them, for SFC and for me.

CHAPTER 23

Early Days for the Time Travelers

When my shuttle dropped me off and I reached our front door I was immediately aware the other seven of us, Esan and Serra and several other Olarians were here and we had enough take-away to feed us for a week! Which was good because I was seriously hungry. Which, of course, they already knew. The mood in the apartment was almost identical to the mood when I had left this morning.

Januti captured me as I entered the front door and it was several moments before I could breathe, which was also okay because she was oozing love, warmth and satisfaction at my return. Her eyes, as she looked at me, glowed with excitement, desire and energy; her passion energized, filled and delighted me. She was... perfect. My whole being lit up just looking at her. Her behavior was totally okay because if there was one thing I thought I really needed right now, it was to be distracted from the fact that we were playing with 'time' and none of us could yet untangle Einstein's mathematics, and we needed knowledge we simply did not yet possess.

But! I could stop time; I knew that because I had done that this morning. We could travel backwards in time to specific events and leave a trace of our presence there if we wished. Could we move forward in time? I suspected so, but here were no guides, no book of instructions, no people who could play the role of the Olarians... or were there?

I stopped at the door of the living area and asked, *Does anyone feel like they can make contact with any other time travelers?*

The group was in the process of plating up the food – the smell was delicious – but my question put a halt to all that. The Olarians, who had come to really enjoy our food fads, were delighted to be with us but my question stopped them too.

Well, all of you lot can do what I did this morning. Unless we move on we are going to feel trapped.

Looking at the Olarians, I said, *You helped me find myself but I know you cannot take me or us on the next step. We need to take responsibility for that unless we can find a society that already travels through time! Regardless of what the next step turns out to be, we will always keep you updated as to what we are learning. None of us knows what other help we will be able to offer you, but, whatever it is, you know we will always offer it.*

Everyone was looking at me and they fell silent. My whole body was vibrating and the air in our apartment had taken on a silent life of its own. Then, without any of us doing anything specific, what appeared to be projections of the eight of us were standing at the end of the living room looking back at us. They shimmered (can I say that?) – they were us watching us! Then my shimmering self spoke telepathically to us, but only to the eight of us; the Olarians were not seeing them!

We are, but not at this instant only, 1000 of your years away from you. You need to remember everything I am about to tell you, precisely, accurately. You opened a portal this morning when you shut down time. You must never, ever, do that when there are any other people around, ever again. We have been able to repair the tear in time that you created. It is okay, the Cretians will be repaired and will live but no-one except you and Rozari and Olaria will ever know anything about how you actually managed it; no-one except us, the eight of us, will remember the whole of it again.

Raille and Jess will have fragments of that memory, which you will want to update and fill out for them and them only! But I was really proud of us! The two worlds that were involved were running in separate time zones because of your/ our actions, my actions! Our actions... I remember us doing that but now I need to speak to you from beyond that experience.

I felt sure it would not be possible for anyone who was not here to believe the scene I was experiencing. However, as I looked around I realized there seemed to be no Olarians in the living room now! Then my shimmering image spoke again.

My apologies to them, you will have to repair this when we leave. You can get help, but not from us, ever again. There are, however, others to whom you can get access. In time you will understand why we cannot help you really. And, you must not involve the Olarians in your time journeys. Eventually you will understand and then you will need to teach our new children. I also need to tell you that this meeting can never have happened, is, according to everything we have learned, theoretically impossible. You will need to make up your own minds about this.

Then my shimmering image turned to look at the other seven with me, and without any warning the others all seemed to be shimmering; only Januti and my images remained solid! However, the others had not merged with us. My shimmering image's voice changed slightly.

I have almost no time left; the rest of you are helping us. That's what the merging does: it enhances your power management in time. Integrates us. Januti, take his hand – my hand – in your time; get the others, quickly!

In a flash there were just the two of us facing the two shimmering versions of us who were talking to us! The shimmering images began to fade. The shimmering images of Januti and I held hands and for an instant their images stabilized.

Find the Heral, find the Heral, go forward. Probably you won't be able to move beyond 70 years ahead, then backward around 70 years and more. They will expect you. You will be all right and you will get here. We, you, need you to grow and you need to find them. Rozari will get you started.

The images became unstable and before they could speak further, vanished. A moment passed and then another and suddenly the eight of us were solid, separate but still in our apartment. They were all looking at Januti and me.

I am not the leader here, I said.

Natalia replied. *Zed, don't be ridiculous. Without question, you and Januti are the leaders here. I really have no doubt our management of time is orchestrated through you. You need to stop fighting it and we need you to help us, to lead here and to learn for us, with us and take us with you each step of the way. I think I got what you, 1000 years from now, came back to tell us.*

Apparently, having two versions of you active at one time is not only impossible, and I am guessing here, but is also in some way not permitted. Which you obviously ignored to help us. Just thinking about what you did and what just happened almost bends my mind. However, typical, you just set us on our next journey!

Januti looked at me. She had become a part of this and she knew the other women gave her strength as the men were giving it to me. Everyone remembered, word for word, what my 1000-year-old self had said.

It seems we are to meet another sentient society! But not tonight. I'm hungry. Can we get our Olarian friends back here?

And within seconds they were. But they were not aware they had been here before, in fact they were quite adamant they had not been here until we called for them just now. All of us ceased the food preparation and looked at them, then at each other, and then we knew.

Esan, Serra, all of you, something has happened to us that I don't really know how to share. Can you pick it up?

But, for the first time in our experience, in my experience, the Olarians could not get a handle on what was bothering me.

I am feeling more than a little bit lost and excruciatingly uncomfortable, something I have never felt with you before, I said. *And I need it to stop. It just feels wrong.*

The others were looking at me askance! I looked at them; my whole being was one big frown!

Do you really want me not to share with the Olarians everything that has and is happening to us?

I could see/feel the ambivalence, the dilemma written all over their faces and in their minds.

Really? I studied all of them. *No. I can't do this.*

Even Januti was frowning.

Look, I really do not think I can go down this road.

Natalya spoke. *Zed, you spoke to us from 1000 years away. You were explicit: do not share this with the Olarians was the message I got.*

Natalya, what I said from down that timeline was not to involve the Olarians in the time journeys, *but that surely does not mean we should not share our knowledge with them? Listen, all of you, I don't think I can do this. I know what I seem to have said, but I really cannot cease to be me. I am yours but I must be able to feel okay. I know I have no right to put us at risk, but surely I have to be true to myself here? I have an obligation to the Olarians that I really cannot ignore. I am going to take what I said literally: do not involve the Olarians in the time journeys.*

I am as certain as I can be that means, in the journeys, and I am as certain as I can be that is for their safety, and I have to say to all of you, I cannot not share what I know with them. Some of our children with them will almost certainly travel with us. We need the Olarians, I need the Olarians, and I need you.

One by one the men turned to their partners. Ajit first spoke to Ai. *Ai, I want you to be with me, but I am with Zed on this. After everything we have come to understand, I could not, without damaging my integrity, turn my back on the Olarians in any way.*

Peter looked at Natalya. *I believe he is right, Nat. I want to support Olarian involvement in every way we can. We all share our family with them. They will be important members of our family and our community; they already are for us and they will come to be for you. You will bear their/our children.*

Finally Darcy turned to Donna. *I feel the same way. Please stay with me in this, Donna.*

The room was silent and still.

Januti looked at me. *You know I will go wherever you ask; I am not able to refuse you anything. I truly feel as though I belong with you no matter what. And I do feel they are our family. They gave us you.*

I could feel the tension as my mind wrestled with the new complexity of the world we seemed to be moving inexorably forward into. *I believe my warning was given to protect the Olarians, that is the only framework I can accept, and I feel the need to apologize for the way I seem to have said what I said.*

They were all looking at me. *What?*

Natalya gently cleared her throat. *Januti, the three of us need you, I am quite certain of that. Zed, no-one can possibly know better than you what message you brought us. I do understand your loyalty toward the Olarians and I will absolutely never turn my back on you. So I am accepting, without reservation, your description of your message from our future. I am overwhelmingly pleased that it seems we will all be with you then. We are all here with you now. If we do not trust you absolutely, we will, I believe, be lost.*

At which moment I told the Olarians, in detail, of our experience. Their looks of astonishment and finally relief were something all eight of us would recall for a long time. Then for a while food assumed pride of place in our attention.

CHAPTER 24

SFC Steps Up: The OlarCret Travelers & the Spaceship Crews Engage in Change

After the next SFC executive meeting, Miyuki asked if I would care to share a coffee with her and we retired to her office. She had something on her mind involving the Olarians and was going to seek my assistance.

'Zed, I am staying in contact with our visitors to OlarCret. Nearly all are involved in projects designed to engage with problems that appear to have become intransigent. I have asked the crew members from *Sunstreamer* and *Lightning* if they would like to be SFC's connection to these projects and most of the members of both crews have become involved. Some of the projects are really exciting and will, I believe, change some seriously dysfunctional social behaviors.

'However, they are also reporting to me instances where some vested interests believe their interests are not being supported. These seem to be drawing on support from other disaffected elements to cause unhelpful blockages to some of the projects.

'I am wondering whether we could ask the Olarians to help out and, if they are willing, whether you would be willing to act as a consultant for them as they utilize our process of "working the problem" in dealing with these unpleasantries.'

A swarm of things went through my mind and I promised Miyuki I would look into the possibilities and let her know.

It turned out Januti, Ajit, Natalya and Darcy were all up for being available to help with obstructive nastiness and they nominated themselves the Project Protection Committee! I was delighted.

I put that aside for the moment. Januti and the others were more than capable of engaging with the issues that would arise. I needed to talk with Olaria so I could arrange for Jess and Raille to spend a few days with them.

◘

A lightly armed Lightning Transit Security Unit glided along 30 yards behind Raille and Jess as they walked toward the ANU. Since the attempted kidnapping of Jess and the children, and without knowing the full story, Miyuki was taking absolutely no chances on any untoward events affecting the family. The toddlers, Selma and Reggie, had their own two-person team and were today at their childcare center. Although they were still too young for any formal learning activities, their rate of developmental learning was high, and they were living with parents who could not help but enhance their development.

Today was the day of the monthly lecture Raille and Jess gave on intergalactic cultures and events. Miyuki always made sure they had the latest intelligence from SFC's activities and that always included information from Second Earth, which both were studying and now occasionally offering suggestions with respect to its development. Today, however, they had access to other information and were presently discussing, quietly, in Cretian, as they walked, what if anything of the events of this morning they could possibly include in what was already a heady and intriguing collage of significant intergalactic cross-cultural issues. It was far more than rare to be transported instantaneously to a planet unknown numbers of galaxies away.

It was also more than rare to be party to events that would not be known for days or weeks from such a distance. Both Jess and Raille were keen to find out exactly what the Cretian women's group had been up to and how they were reshaping Olarian society.

This morning's events were exciting and far from insignificant in the life of the Cretian world. My, Raille and the Olarians' help had almost certainly swung the flow of life in Jess's native land. However, without visiting again for at least a few days, Jess and Raille would be guessing at what was happening in Cretia and that was not satisfactory for the pair. However, I had promised to take them back to OlarCret as soon as they were ready, and I could ensure they were cared for, and that would be in the next few weeks if they could arrange their schedules.

The memory of the events of the morning were still present for Raille and Jess. However, if I correctly understood my future self with regard to the time we had spent on OlarCret, there may well come to be no memory of the hour we believed we had spent there, or perhaps that hour would remain known there but there would be no Earthly knowledge that some seconds in a part of Canberra had appeared to be lost.

What in fact turned out to be the case was that Raille and Jess did not have a full and complete memory of the events I had been involved in managing, but did have a memory of the events on OlarCret where the events appeared to be remaining known!

It seemed on careful inspection that their memories were slowly thinning and bits were entirely missing and unless I deliberately filled them in would eventually disappear, to be returned as reported information from me rather than any experience of theirs. And, I wondered, what would happen when they went to OlarCret and were told of their part in the events? Hm. I would have to wait and see, but I had already decided to keep their memory accurate.

What later events would show was that the Cretian warlords had been treated for radiation poisoning, however, no-one from Earth who we would later talk with about this was aware of any of us having had any part in it, with the exception of our eight.

However, on questioning as to how the Cretians had got to the treatment facility, there would appear to be a blank! The Olarians who had been with us on Earth would know nothing except what we had told them! But the Olarians, including Olaria, on OlarCret, would.

A phrase from one of my mother's friends popped into my mind. 'Heavens to Betsy' she would say, and that was exactly what I was thinking now.

CHAPTER 25

Tanzin & Jald Re-ignite

Meanwhile, there was another issue that was going to stretch my flexibility yet again. I had received a holo message from Tanzin requesting a meeting over coffee on Moon Base One where *Sunstreamer* was presently settling into orbit for one of its routine maintenance programs. It would be non-operational for nearly 21 days. Before she returned to her home in northern Spain many miles from her family, with whom she no longer had contact, Tanzin wanted to spend a little time with me, sorting a dilemma she did not want to describe except face to face.

I would never have refused Tanzin any request. Not only did I find her a very lovely companion, a brilliant professional, but she was also a stunningly honest and intense individual I had come to genuinely admire. If she wanted any sort of assistance, I would certainly do whatever was in my power to see she got it.

As *Sunstreamer* settled into her orbit over the moon base maintenance system, I reached up to check on Tanzin's state of mind. She had completed her navigational duties on board and was thinking about our meeting, now only 20 minutes away, which is what I had hoped. I settled back in the chair in my office, a brilliantly designed piece of furniture, not only comfortable but capable of maintaining flexibility and tension reduction without any human intervention! I just loved it.

All right, down to business. Then I stopped, almost held my breath. Tanzin had fallen passionately in love with Jald, Olaria's son, during the year we had spent on OlarCret when he had been her host. Their parting had been deeply touching and sad for both of them but particularly for Tanzin for whom this had been *the* relationship of her life. The love affair of her life. Since she returned, nothing, absolutely nothing, had in any way dulled her ardor. She had only a month previously, before *Sunstreamer* had departed for its last mission, won the coveted Global Award for Intergalactic Navigational Excellence: the most coveted award available to any astronavigator. She had been offered a prestigious position as a senior fellow at the Astronavigational Training Institute. However, that had only acted to trigger what was her actual reason for wanting to talk with me.

I watched her think about Jald and realized this was definitely going to be a real challenge.

I stretched my mind across the galaxies to OlarCret and sought out Jald. He was preparing for a meeting with Olaria and Darl, who was presently reorganizing the Living Library group.

Jald.

He stopped and turned his head to one side as if to check on something he had just heard.

It's me, Zed. I'm reaching out to you from my office on Earth's moon.

I felt him smile, shake his head and sit quietly down.

I wonder, Zed, if I will ever get used to the idea that you can do this. I am, as always, delighted to talk with you, but I suspect if you have gone to this much trouble, something significant is concerning you.

There was a considerable limitation on how much information he could pick up from me when we were connecting this way.

He was of course correct. *It concerns Tanzin.*

I gave him a few moments to collect himself and immediately knew, whatever was concerning her with him was not one-sided.

Not a day goes by I do not think of that beautiful and exciting young woman. I have not felt like this for centuries. I berate myself, remind myself how stupid it is of me to keep her image and my memories of our time together in the forefront of my mind. But they are precious memories and never cease to surprise me. What exactly is it you are wanting to speak about?

I really do not know yet, but when I see her shortly I am aware that it is about you and her, so I thought it wise to find out how you are feeling about her at the moment.

I could almost feel his delight that she wanted to meet with me about him and the uncertainty he was still feeling months since they had seen one another. I told him about her most recent achievement and felt his surge of delight and... pride! Wowee, I really had not realized how much he was connected to her.

Sooo. I let the word drag out for clarity. *Would you want to meet with her again? Would you want to have me bring you here, maybe to* Energystreamer1, *which, as you know, is in moon orbit as we speak?*

I could feel him radiating anxiety, desire and concern all wrapped up together. When they had parted, on *Sunstreamer*'s last day over OlarCret, their parting had been exquisitely painful, sad, but over and above this, unfinished, was the thought that lingered in my mind. And Jald picked it up.

You are right, Zed. Unfinished is exactly how it was, and I am surprised to hear myself say it, but for me it is still unsatisfactorily ended. I would really like to spend some more time with her and try to find some kind of resolution for my feelings – feelings I probably don't need to tell you are, I think, inappropriate, but nevertheless they are the ones I have!

Well, Jald, she is about to go on a month's leave after our meeting. If my reading of her is correct, what would you have me do?

There followed a quite prolonged pause.

Zed, you know I cannot get a reading from you when we communicate this way, although I have a feeling you are better able to get an emotional reading than I in these circumstances.

I confirmed he was correct.

Okay, I will make my arrangements here. If you are right in what you think she wants, and you feel confident that your suggestion is appropriate, I would appreciate you taking me to Energystreamer1 *and arranging for someone, maybe Esan, to bring her up from Moon Base One. Would that be appropriate?*

Well yes. The security system has become accepting of the simultaneity capability of Olarians, so you could easily get away with that. They will check with me for sure, so I will clear that from our end if that is the decision the two of you want to take.

I could almost feel tangibly his anticipatory excitement and hoped desperately my reading of Tanzin's issue was right as I said adieu to Jald. A short time later I walked into the moon base cafeteria and headed for the far distant table at which I could see Tanzin's stunning red hair. Then I realized she had chosen the location because she knew where the security system was least likely to be able to easily hear a conversation!

When she saw me she jumped up and almost ran into my arms! Gave me a strong affectionate hug then stepped back, concerned that she had overstepped the mark, but I shook my head, smiled, and sent her a very carefully modulated feeling of warmth and pleasure at seeing her. She settled immediately and walked to one of the serving points, selected a drink then returned to our table. I did the same.

She held the warm container in both hands, elbows resting on the table as she leant toward me. I followed suit so we were close enough to hold a conversation that would not be heard by any part of the security system. She looked at me intently, trying very hard to read what she could see, but without the aid of either the Olarian telepathic help or mine she could not reach into me at all. So she just looked at me, willing me to guess correctly what she wanted to discuss. Within seconds I had confirmed my initial reading of her was correct: she wanted to know if I had heard from Jald and how he was.

I stared into a pair of deep-blue eyes framed in the face of a petite and immensely intelligent Spanish genius-level astronavigator, knowing exactly what she wanted of me. So, because I knew she was absolutely trustworthy and that we had a tight, affectionate and trusting relationship, I did not beat about the bush.

'I think I know what you want.' Then I paused as she thought about Jald. 'Jald is well.'

She relaxed and her face radiated pleasure and satisfaction. I had got it in one. I could feel her joy that she had been right to trust me and that I had indeed understood immediately what was on her mind.

'Zed, not one moment has passed I have not been thinking about him. I almost crashed out of that astronav challenge because I could feel him in my body. Tell me how he is. Do you know what he is doing? Do you think he feels anything like me? Is there any way I could see him again, do you think? I know you have access to them that is somehow beyond the capabilities of our systems.'

I let some seconds pass and sipped my drink. I had to think about how to broach this very tricky engagement, finally deciding that with Tanzin I should simply be direct and explicit while maintaining our boundaries for all the watching eyes.

'Tanzin, he is almost as hopeless as you. He misses you, knows how inappropriate that is but did get a message to me when I had the Olarians contact him. He would like to see you again if that was something you actually wished.'

She looked at me as though I had two heads. 'Zed, do you really need to ask? I would give away that last award for just a few minutes with him.'

I looked at her over the rim of my mug. 'Tanzin, get control of your facial expression. It would be best if you did not overreact to what I am going to tell you.'

She schooled her face and her body. She really knew how not to give herself away. Top astronavigators needed this capability; they were often watched carefully by their crew as they engaged with what were, not infrequently, life-threatening problems.

'Jald will meet you on board *Energystreamer1* if that is what you desire.' She did not leap out of her chair but emotionally that is pretty much what I saw and felt.

'Okay, in a few minutes, when we have finished our drinks, Esan, Jald's son who you know, will make a simultaneity jump to be beside you here in the cafeteria.'

I checked with Esan that that was his intention and he assured me it was.

'The security system will see and will observe you disappear as he takes you to *Energystreamer1*, which is in moon orbit. They will get Jald on board *Energystreamer1* – best you do not ask how but you can guess. A very few individuals can now make simultaneity jumps from OlarCret to Earth or an orbiting spacecraft.'

Her eyebrows shot up but that was the only sign of surprise she gave. The smile on her face would have lit up the entire cafeteria. Then I stood up. She followed and I stepped to her, gave her a caring hug, whispered 'Have a great time', and stepped back as Esan appeared beside her, smiled at her, took her arm and they disappeared.

I walked to the toilet block, the one place free of the intrusive security systems. I made the jump to OlarCret, picked up Jald, made the jump to one of the meeting rooms on *Energystreamer1*, left Jald with a huge smile on his face and returned to the toilet block and walked out and back to my office. Phew, so much for phase one.

Seconds later an urgent holo message arrived from Miyuki. 'Zed, we are having a minor security scare. The system has lost connection with Tanzin and it is presently radiating anxiety. I am speaking to you because you seem to have been the last person with whom she was seen in the moon base cafeteria. Would you please call?'

I touched my link with her and a moment later she appeared on my screen.

'Hello Miyuki, Tanzin is fine. The Olarians wanted to have contact with her and they have jumped her to *Energystreamer1*. She told me she was on leave and will be back online in four weeks unless someone urgently needs her. I told her I thought she should just go and relax and enjoy herself. Is there a problem?'

I slid into Miyuki's mind. Found no problem, just a mild concern that was now put to rest.

'Thanks, Zed, no problem. The system is still edgy about the Olarian ability to do simultaneity jumps.'

She disconnected. So, all well, so far.

I felt a concern for Tanzin and slid my mind up to the Olarian spaceship to see how things were going for Tanzin and Jald. They were clearly two lovebirds now in their element. I watched for a while, delighted to see not only how full of joy and delight Tanzin was but how totally absorbed Jald was with Tanzin. Whatever the outcome of this connection, these two were definitely meant to be together. Just watching them and feeling the chemistry was a delight and very satisfying.

Jald was holding her close against his chest, his nose in her hair, and he was filled with delight and satisfaction. Tanzin was holding him and absorbing the feeling of security and intimacy and safety she felt being in his arms. I knew that this degree of intimacy was not going to find hugging satisfactory for long and I was pleased to see them head for the living quarters on the spacecraft.

I could easily have watched them for much longer. I was delighted for them but also just a little anxious about what was going to happen when they had to decide what to do with all this energy. Separating on OlarCret just before we departed at the end of our year there, they appeared to have been ready to move on. Well, I could plainly see that was definitely an opinion to be binned. They were even more intensely connected now than they had been then.

I put them aside for the moment and returned to some more mundane matters that needed to be dealt with. While I did that, a new reality was beginning to be created while I was actively involved elsewhere.

Tanzin and Jald stepped into one of the sleeping units on *Energystreamer1* where Jald created a bed to suit the two of them and the next hour of their lives vanished in a feast of deeply passionate sex and sensuality. When they felt sated and deeply and satisfactorily connected, they were able to talk. Jald had re-established Tanzin's telepathic connection with him and they no longer needed to speak out loud. She gave him some navigational co-ordinates and within a few seconds he was showing her the exclusive and beautiful coastal resort to which she had pointed him.

It took no more than a few moments of her time for Tanzin to book their accommodation for the next three weeks and they dressed and picked a secluded spot to emerge. Carrying minimal luggage, they walked the short distance to the resort, checked in and were shown to a beautiful suite.

They spent a great deal of every day and night walking, swimming, making love and just satisfying themselves with one another. Then, when they felt totally connected, they began the most complex and tricky conversation either had ever had in their lives – and Jald's life had been long and convoluted. However, it was a conversation in which he knew they had to fully share everything that was in both their minds, something he was, in this situation, unhesitatingly delighted to do.

She wanted him to know that she loved him with a passion that had remained undiminished since they had been together on OlarCret. She apologized for the fact that she wanted more than anything else she could imagine to have at least one child with him and for them to be able to bring it up together. She also made clear to him that she realized all the potential problems she was creating for him and them, however, she made it equally clear that she would live anywhere he wished, just so long as they could be together and raise a family. *Please tell me if I am alone in this.*

She had thought through much that was likely to be involved. She realized she would age and die while he remained young and vital. She was willing for him to cease being with her whenever he needed. She knew it was possible she would bear a telepathic child and was prepared for their child to be educated in whatever way Jald wished and if necessary on OlarCret. She knew that both of them would need to be involved in appropriate and intellectually satisfying and challenging activities.

She knew she was being irrational, that she might also be being seriously unrealistic and possibly inappropriately selfish, but she did not want to live her life without him and a child they would have together.

It was a breathtaking exposé. Jald looked at her and knew he wanted to be with her. He was fully aware of how inappropriate he was being. He had never in his long life had any experience with which to compare this situation and nor did he have any Olarian experience that would conceivably match it. In addition he was not unaware of the fact that Tanzin was a massively significant figure in the human astronavigational world, probably one of the most famous, talented astronavigators in human history. In this he recognized in her an ability far greater than his own. And he felt only pleasure for her about it.

Tanzin looked at him and because she was telepathically connected to him was fully aware of his emotional state, the thoughts running through his mind, and immediately felt bad about her behavior. It had been, she began to think, inappropriate, selfish, and inconsiderate. She did not, however, feel that it had been an inaccurate appraisal of how she was feeling. She wanted to be with him, but did she want to give up her career, her newly offered position, to be a mother, a wife? She really did not know, but she was quite certain she wanted to be with Jald.

He was quite certain he would like to have an intimate, loving relationship with Tanzin, but was also cognizant of the range of reasons why that might be a very bad idea.

Both of them thought, 'Is this just a final fling?'

But neither actually felt this accurately described either their feelings or their desires and did not adequately encompass what was happening between them. However, sex and loving and mutually joyous experiences apart, they knew the future would not look after itself. At the edge of her mind an idea was taking shape and Jald picked it up, smiled and decided he ought to be responsible for following it. He knew it fit the rubric of the SFC problem-solving pattern he had seen me use several times with great effect.

Okay, he said, *I think I see the problem and the dilemma we need to resolve. I am right, am I not, that you do not have a circle of family or close friends here on Earth?*

She acknowledged that was correct.

So you could live on OlarCret with me if you could find something to do that fit your life?

Again she nodded.

So tell me again what exactly it is that the Astronavigational Institute want of you?

They want me to take charge of the senior class of students and be responsible for bringing them up to fully operational speed. This means they will be able to take their place on routine space flights, at first on routine mining and observation cruisers and shuttles but developing their capability to enable them to work on explorer vessels and battlecruisers.

There are in any year only three or four students who might reach the level necessary, though right now there are five who are showing the potential that might allow them to become top flight operational SFC astronavigators.

Training them takes a minimum of two or three years. They must be able to solve, on the run, with and without the quantum computers with whom they must be able to interface smoothly, the most complex navigational problems that could face them in operationally critical situations without fumbling or baulking.

Like, for instance, the situation you saw on OlarCret, when I needed to get Sunstreamer *out of the way of Cretian missiles and rearrange its orbit to avoid sight-lines to Cretia in an operationally short space of time. That is an example of a reasonably simple astronavigational problem they need to be fully capable of managing.*

Furthermore, they must be able to engage with operational calculations for any vessel traveling at near light speed that must undertake route changes and course adjustments in an unknown solar system.

Essentially, when they can manage all the routine requirements, they then need to be able to solve problems that involve travel across solar systems. This includes unknown systems in which they have not previously been active. There is a whole lot of stuff like that which involves a significant understanding of the ship and engine capabilities, including hull and engine stress factors, directional and speed management, and a whole lot of other fancy stuff.

She smiled at him, but he was following her.

So there is really no reason that could not be done on OlarCret, if you had the necessary computing equipment?

She finally saw the direction in which he was heading and looked at him with her large, smiling blue eyes, almost glowing with anticipation of what was implicit in his question.

No.

In fact, he continued, *there is really no actual reason you could not set up an astronavigational graduate-level unit on OlarCret? And further mapping of our own and adjacent solar systems would be a valuable activity for us and for SFC?*

She stopped, following the track he was taking, and began a reflection of the implications. No, she thought, there was no reason she could not work on OlarCret if SFC were interested and be with him for her short life.

They could have children who she knew would be looked after even if they were not initially telepathic. She knew there had been some non-telepathic children born on OlarCret. But how would the Olarian world feel about such an arrangement? She knew it was not a world that was enamored with change, although she knew her knowledge and skill sets could be of real value to them.

They looked deeply into one another. They felt a kind of smug delight. They might have just created a possible world for themselves. She looked at Jald. Love and pleasure and every form of delight radiated from her. She could feel his excitement and anticipation and... was it love from her Olarian man? She knew it would be very special if the Olarian and human worlds and SFC would allow this dream to be brought to fruition.

She looked at Jald with a question: *How do you imagine going about solving this problem we are going to create when we first broach our desire?*

But Jald had no question in his mind about how this needed to be done. However, he had to think carefully about how to do this without placing me at risk of discovery, and he was clear about this.

Tanzin, I think I might know a way to go about this, but I need to ask you to trust me to engage in some secret activities that would be both impossible and unnecessary at home. Here on Earth I can get some assistance that will carry some risks I need help to assess. Will you trust me to take the next steps, which I absolutely need to keep secret from you until I have sought the help we need?

She looked at him, very carefully exploring his feelings and thoughts, but he was screening her out. He needed her absolute trust and then, without hesitation, she stopped searching and gave it.

Tanzin, I am going to close you out of my mind and go and have some very tricky but very important conversations. Are you okay with that?

She let him know that she really was, if also enormously curious and of course beginning to guess at the direction his mind might be taking him. He smiled, acknowledged that he understood and then she lost telepathic contact with him. She sat, contentedly, looking at him with love and trust and hope.

◘

I had just finished a meeting when I knew that Jald was seeking a conversation and I let him know I would be free in a few minutes. When I reached my office, I told my PA to keep people away for the next little while and connected to Jald. I could feel his excitement. Then his proposal, request, plan, almost took my breath away, and yet, the more I thought about it, the more I could see where it was going, the more I began to think it just might fly. Not exclusively but very probably because it was Tanzin who was the centerpiece. She was a global phenomenon; her manner of winning the prestigious award had been inconceivable to the examining panel. The complexity of the pattern she had created to solve the problem and the speed at which she had implemented it was greater than the capability of the quantum computer that had helped generate the most extraordinarily difficult, supposedly human-insoluble problem in celestial navigational history, a complex Gordian knot she had cut through and unravelled.

So, Jald, are you telling me that the two of you want to live together – what we would consider getting married? That she is willing to live on OlarCret with you and that she would like to be able to run the elite senior class in an astronav school set up on OlarCret? And am I accurately perceiving that you want to have children?

I watched as he thought through all that had gone on between them and where they were at! Wow! I almost held my breath.

How long do you have before you return to OlarCret and Tanzin returns to duty?

Jald gave me the details. A week!

Leave it with me. I will get back to you as soon as I can but before the end of the week.

Jald thanked me and went back to Tanzin.

I sat quietly in my chair, just a little dazed perhaps, shell-shocked. The idea was typically Tanzin, improbable but yet do-able. As I thought it through I realized it was another thread in the connection between the worlds of Earth and OlarCret and another link in my plans for the Intergalactic Learning Centre on OlarCret to which their children and ours could go.

It was getting more interesting and complicated but not less do-able! So I connected to Miyuki's PA and sought an appointment, at which time I learned something very interesting. Miyuki had left an instruction with her PA that should I seek an appointment with her I was to get priority over any routine appointments. I raised my eyebrows and shook my head. That was unexpected. She could fit me in, an hour before my usual shuttle lift-off. I took the appointment.

Miyuki smiled warmly at me as I walked into her office. 'This is the first appointment you have sought since you arrived. It must be something significant for you to seek it and I am intensely curious.'

I smiled, wondering how she would feel when I had outlined what was on my mind.

'Well, Miyuki, I will quickly satisfy your curiosity and yes, I would say it was significant.'

Now I definitely had her full attention.

'First, I would like to ask a question and I am wanting a brutally honest answer, although I would normally not add that with you. But I am asking an entirely non-frivolous question. How big a loss would it be if Tanzin did not take up duties in our astronav school?'

I watched, listened inside and monitored her emotional state. She was seriously disturbed by my question, felt very strongly it would be an enormous loss if Tanzin was neither in the operational system nor teaching the senior group in the Astronav Institute. Talent of her quality was almost non-existent.

As a start, that seemed good.

'Zed, I am assuming there is nothing frivolous about this enquiry so I will cut to the chase. It would be nearly catastrophic and an indescribably serious loss. Please tell me we are not going to lose her.'

'I cannot absolutely guarantee that, however, it depends a little on what you might be willing to do to keep her. And please be absolutely clear, there is no threat or slippery manipulation going on here. Tanzin is hopelessly in love with Jald as a result of their relationship on OlarCret last year. Jald, I was actually very surprised to find out, fully reciprocates her feelings!

'I was not quite as astonished as I can see are you, but their really serious attempt to sever and end their relationship by Jald sending his son Esan as navigator on *Energystreamer1* and Tanzin ceasing any connection to Jald simply failed to take account of how strongly she felt. The couple have been together for the last three weeks of Tanzin's leave. She and Jald have talked extensively about how they could become a couple. How she could live her life with him, have children and still continue with her work. I am certain you know how important Tanzin's work is for her.'

I stopped and waited to see where Miyuki would go,

'Zed, are you telling me we are going to lose her unless we can meet a very tricky condition?'

'Yes. However, I think the tricky condition might appeal to you almost as much as it appeals to me. It is a very, very clever possible solution to the alternative probability of losing her talent. Because, we ought to make no mistake, this couple is fully determined to live together and have at least one child and I cannot see a way that can work with Jald living on Earth, so she will necessarily need to live on OlarCret.'

I paused again to watch where she would go with this. I knew Miyuki was not open to any form of blackmail or being held to ransom. Saw that she was looking at me in that way of hers and read the emotion. She trusted me and did not believe I would pull any kind of fast one with her. When I was sure she had thought that through and was genuinely interested in hearing what option might be on the table, I told her.

She looked at me at first with incredulity written all over her face, then, slowly, as she assimilated the cleverness of Tanzin's possible solution, she began to smile. A smile that grew and grew and finally made it into a happy and delicious laugh.

'She is really a stunner! If almost anyone else had come up with such a hare-brained scheme I would have thrown them out on their ear. But Tanzin, I would never throw her out before I had tried every alternative I could conjure up. She is one of the rarest commodities in our entire Space Fleet system. And because you are putting this to me and I trust you more than almost any person I have ever met, I'm going to take this home with me and think it through. My god, Zed, you are the most extraordinary man. They trusted this task to you, didn't they? And you would not have brought it to me if you did not think it was workable and desirable, and it makes me wonder what else you are connecting this extraordinary request to.'

I remained silent for several moments while I watched her emotional state traverse several shifts and finally settle on pleasure at being able to be working with such likable and resourceful people. Okay, take a punt.

'I do have another very unusual idea that the Olarians are considering at the moment. It is not directly connected to my role here, but they trust me, much as you trust me, so I am involved with them in an idea which is no more than an idea at this point. However, if you feel able to give me your word that this will be a discussion that will go no further than this room and we will have below the level of your recording devices, I will outline it for you. I make this condition because there are many people involved who would not like it discussed yet and because I too trust you implicitly and know, when I have outlined it, you will fully understand.'

I stopped again.

This time she was looking at me through narrowed eyes, but the thought going through her mind was a surprise. *Why could I not have found this man 20 years ago? I would have married him in a flash!*

Now that one got to me.

She continued looking at me with what I would have described as a deeply thoughtful expression.

'Tell me, Zed.'

She slid her chair forward and bent down so we were only inches apart.

I was surprised I could feel her attraction to me even more strongly. I told her my version for the intergalactic education/learning center on OlarCret. When I had finished she smiled at me, one of those beautiful smiles that says it is promising whatever you are hoping for. I knew exactly what it was promising. She was deeply excited and pleased she had me with her, not sexually, just satisfied that the level of excitement I was bringing into her life and SFC was overwhelmingly fulfilling.

'Oh Zed,' she murmured. 'That is truly brilliant.'

Then she slipped Tanzin and Jald's proposition in alongside and I knew we were home and hosed. She could hardly contain herself. However, true to her word, she slowly sat back up, smiling and nodding quietly.

'Zed, you are the best investment in staff I have ever made. However, I am feeling confident that I will not have you for as long as I would wish. You are very ingenious and creative. That was your idea, yes?'

'In a manner of speaking.'

'I don't have to take this home. You can tell that amazing young woman and her lover I will find a way to make this happen so she will be the first senior fellow of the ATI to hold a position on OlarCret. Before you leave me, I would like you to give me an honest answer to a hunch I have been nursing.'

I raised my eyes, smiled and told her if I could I would. She leaned forward again and our faces were only a few inches apart.

'Over the last few weeks I have begun to believe that the Olarians have found a way to communicate across the cosmos, that they can now speak to one another from OlarCret.'

I smiled into her eyes and sent a warm and friendly trusting emotional feeling to her.

'Please do not put this information out into the system yet, but yes.'

We sat back up and she was smiling.

'Zed, as soon as you leave, I am going to erase this meeting and the backup of it as well. And thank you.'

I took my leave with minutes to spare until my shuttle would be ready to leave.

As I moved toward it, Januti joined me. 'She can't have you; just as well she knows that.'

I smiled. I was delighted as always to feel Januti's possessiveness and jealousy. It was like a warm energy blanket. She smiled and left me with a delicious feeling that made me wish I could simply make a simultaneity jump home, however, I restrained myself. One final task, I thought, and I spoke to Jald. He had been with us at the meeting, knew the outcome and was ecstatic, an unusual emotional experience for an Olarian, but his pleasure was nothing compared to Tanzin's who was almost jumping out of her skin with delight. Tonight would be a pretty good night in Spain, I thought, then settled back in my seat. It had been a big day.

CHAPTER 26

Jess & Raille Visit Cretia

Following another outstandingly successful presentation by Raille and Jess at the ANU monthly intergalactic cross-cultural affairs information session, Miyuki had accepted an invitation to dine with the couple. The meal was delicious. Jess had prepared Cretian dishes that had been modified for Raille's taste and human food varieties. After the meal, the three had a long discussion about work, and finally Jess and Raille informed Miyuki they wished to take a 10-day study leave. The Olarians had offered them a trip home and they believed this would be an excellent opportunity to catch up on Olarian/Cretian developments.

Miyuki was pleased; she knew SFC could easily have made such an offer, however, she was also aware that this was a significant budget saving for her, but more importantly, an opportunity for the ever-enthusiastic Olarian space travelers. So the couple set a date that began on a Saturday, knowing I would be pleased to transport them that weekend, at which time the Olarians would simply engage in an initial launch, then cloak *Energystreamer2*, return to moon orbit and leave it invisible for the 10 days I would take Raille and Jess to OlarCret, making an appropriate return appearance as required. Since the Earth/space scanners had found a way to detect *Sunstreamer* a year or so back, the Olarians had found a way to improve their cloaking of the Energystreamers.

There had been an extraordinary volume of traffic around whether Selma and Reggie ought to be taken on the intergalactic simultaneity jump. No-one wanted there to be any serious risk to their health.

However, after a week of discussion on OlarCret, the consensus was the jump should not have a negative impact on them. After each jump the Olarians had examined all the travelers for any change whatsoever, right down to what we would call the molecular level, but no impact of any kind was visible. They were 99 percent confident that the children would suffer no negative impact from the trip, and they promised to check the children the minute we arrived. At that point, Jess and Raille were willing to take them, Jess knowing her family would be ecstatic. So the decision was made, and on the following Saturday, after I had sent a message to Piquant and Seliqana, who were genuinely delighted, Seliqana more like ecstatic, Jess, Raille, Selma and Reggie, Januti and I made the jump to Olaria's home. At this stage it was hoped the children would not really know they had made a simultaneity jump to OlarCret so could not blow our cover.

Olaria was delighted when we arrived, had all of us dressed in an instant, then gave Raille and his family over to the Olarian health group for nearly 30 minutes. The group could find no evidence of any changes about which anyone ought to be concerned, which was a great relief to all of us. I spoke to Olaria quietly while the others were arranging the return trip with Januti. I wanted to be sure that one of the Olarians would be monitoring Raille and his family the whole time they were in Cretia. I knew I was being a little paranoid, however, I could not stay with them and I was stressed, probably unnecessarily, about their safety. Olaria gave me the reassurance I needed.

So, pleasantries managed, their health checked and their security assured, Januti and I told Olaria we would be back shortly and transported the Korzyst/GeGhan family to the GeGhan home. After nearly 10 minutes of absolute chaos, which gave us some idea of the warmth of their welcome and the delight created by their visit, Seliqana and Piquant ensured we were very properly thanked and we, in our turn, were surprised at the delight Piquant showed at the visit of his nephew and niece. This was a side of him none of us had seen before. On top of our Olarian security, I realized, I could be quite confident that Piquant would allow nothing to happen to any of them.

We said our goodbyes and promised we would see them all in 10 days. Then we made the jump back to Olaria's home. Her pleasure at having us for the day was always reassuring and satisfying. Today, however, was something else. Olaria told us that the Council of Eight, along with millions of Olarians, were genuinely delighted to begin to create the plans for the intergalactic education program and the Intergalactic Learning Centre. Our health group wanted an hour with Januti to examine her pregnancy. That visit confirmed again that we were having twins, a boy and a girl, and that they were both in excellent health! We were delighted with their confirmation. Januti could not stop smiling. We spent several hours with Rozari and Olaria and then I took Januti to some of the places I had visited while I had been on OlarCret for my year, and finally I asked Olaria if she was comfortable taking us to see Tall Trees Valley.

She smiled at me and said, *Zed, I am unreservedly happy for you to take Januti anywhere you and I went together. What we had involved deeply satisfying intimacy, and that is what you two have together now, and that is how it should be. You were very generous with me and the other women who you allowed to give new life for our society: new life and new developments. Januti will carry that deep connection on. My gift to you was given in what you refer to as love.*

I believe you will pass it to her when the time is right. For now, my debt is not a debt of gratitude as I have seen humans do; my gift to you was simple. We will never cease to be connected for my entire life, yet this will never disturb the beauty of your connection to her or the rightness of it. I just feel right about us and about you, Januti, you and him. I think all of us are connected in some ways none of us fully understand, at least, not yet. And, Januti, I believe you probably understand this even more deeply than Zed, who we both would agree is someone very special.

I was holding Rozari as Olaria spoke and as she finished the air around us wavered and became in an indescribable way unsettled and then with my daughter holding tightly to my neck we disappeared from OlarCret and emerged in what I knew, somehow, to be the world of the Heral. Nothing was stable here but we were met by what seemed to be a couple. They were a very attractive couple, and I could not tell their age. The instant they were connected to me, Rozari and I were transported through my life. One year at a time. We were just observers. We went at the pace of the woman who was holding both my hand and the hand of the man who was with her. She never spoke, but when she came to the present where Rozari and I were in Olaria's home, she and her companion left us. The air around us ceased to shimmer and we returned to solid ground. Olaria and Januti looked at us, their faces one huge question mark.

I don't know, was all I could say. *I just don't know, but if I was to guess, I would say Rozari and I were just introduced to the Heral. The couple with whom we had connection took us, quite literally and substantively, one year at a time through my life. We traveled from one significant and identifiable event to the next, one for each year, then they left us back here with you!*

I don't know any more than that really. Strangely enough, it felt quite easy and comfortable, but they have left me a marker that I think will connect me again to them when we are ready. They said nothing, they made no other connection than the journey, which was clearly through time! We quite literally visited my life, a key moment each single year. My mother and father and step-father and many others including you, Olaria, and then you, Januti, and now here together, us!

What was perhaps the most intriguing aspect of our journey was our sense of how long we were traveling. At the time it felt as though we were with the Heral for many days, yet when we returned here, it now feels as though it was but a moment.

Kyuto joined Olaria and they examined Rozari and myself. The element of our brain that allowed us to travel in and through time was clearly increasing in complexity and activity. There remained one unopened area. However, unlike Januti and myself, all areas of Rozari's brain were alive and active, including the area still lying dormant for us!

In the same way as there was no stress for us in the intergalactic jumps, there was absolutely no stress in the time travel. My life appeared to be transforming at a rather astonishing rate, and I had a strong urge to connect with the others and bring them up to speed. So we said goodbye to Olaria, Kyuto and Rozari and made the jump back to our apartment, where we found the others awaiting us.

It was Ajit who responded.

We just knew you would return here, now, and that you wanted us to be here. And all of us wanted to be here to meet you when you arrived.

I related my adventure with the Heral. They all looked at me with a question mark.

Okay, my 1000-year-old self said 70 years past and future, so although I now understand that travel back into the past is somehow permitted, sanctioned, I am feeling also, even encouraged, to not take seriously the traveling back marker. However, I am clear that embedded in my message from the future was a strange warning: 'Go back if you wish, but be careful not to meddle in our life'. I am feeling the urge to do that, using the marker they left with me.

If I join hands with Januti, can you join us?

And with smiles all of them nodded. So I turned, took Januti's hand and, using the marker the Heral had left, I focused on 70 years in the past. Now, I don't really know what exactly I did when I say I focused, but I know how it felt, and Januti squeezed my hand and I followed the Heral marker in my mind. And we were in Canberra. The first thing we noticed was we were outside a shopping center, everyone was dressed differently, so Januti remade our clothes to more closely resemble those around us. Then, in an instant, I knew we were not alone. The man who had been with Rozari and me was with me now, not visibly, but inside me, somehow, and Januti let me know his wife was with her.

Then the man who was with me spoke.

My wife and I are with you. My name is Albor and my wife is called Felarv. When you travel this way, they – he waved at the people around us – *cannot see you, so your clothes do not matter unless you plan to interfere with the stream of time. That is a very risky act. Once you have adjusted to your present state I will explain to you. Do you understand?*

I told him I did, and Januti nodded, so we were all connected.

We need you to understand something of great importance. You can seek out and find yourselves when you travel, but you must never, ever, please, engage in any form of interaction with any of your selves through time. We know that you have done this when you were around 1000 years old. We do not know how you managed it without destroying yourself and your group.

Something that we do not understand is special about you, something of which we have not been appraised. Nevertheless, I must impress on you, please do not interfere with the flow of events in time when you are traveling. This will result in some staggeringly large disruptions in the life of others, apart from yourselves. Should you ever choose to do it – and we are aware that unlike any other travelers that you will be able to – please be careful and circumspect.

We suspect that is why your future self suggested 70 years. Remember, when you go back that far in the past, this is not a time you were alive. However, when you take the slide through time that will take you to 70 years into your future, into the 22nd century, you must not meet yourselves or you risk dying in that time and in your own base time. You will likely kill all eight of you, do you understand?

Let me say one final time: we know, Zed, that when you reach a 1000 years old in the time line in which you are presently traveling, you will find a situation you decide requires your breaking one of the cardinal rules of our world. Somehow you will pull that off and we know that none of us will ever understand how you will do that. It must have to do with some ability you possess, one which we do not understand, or perhaps something about who you are. Not even your parents are here in Canberra today. None of your parents are yet alive. I think that is why your 1000-year-old self chose 70 years when he gave you parameters for your first journey. You can, we suspect, in spite of the warnings, visit your 1000-year-old self, but, beware, please, *do not interfere with the flow by attempting to speak with him, I beg you,* please.

He was so urgently insistent that I gave him my word, hoping almost desperately that that was the thing to do.

So you are free to see whatever you desire. Once Felarv and I have shown you how to travel in this time and through time, we will leave you to your own devices.

With that they both began to speak to us, sort of like an instruction manual, Felarv to Januti, Albor to me, and I could feel his words, none of which I understood, being filtered in some strange way in my mind. Then, when I assume some time had passed, they said goodbye and before I could call them, they were gone. I looked at Januti.

I get it, Zed, take my hand, and she said or did something and in a rush my mind opened up, and I understood exactly what needed to be done to move up or down in time. I was aware of the strangest learning experience so far, and I now realized I was able to grasp each new experience so long as Januti or, I suspected, Rozari, was involved!

We looked at one another, knowing the others also understood, and we went to a shopping mall we knew had been around in this time and wandered through it, avoiding people contact; although I felt as if we could have contacted them, we were at present unwilling. We looked at one another, then with a shrug Januti squeezed my hand tight and took us home.

The scene in our living room was not something I could easily describe. There were the eight of us and 14 Olarians; only the lone watchers on board the two Energystreamers were not here. There was not a lot of spare space, and I just burst out laughing.

I knew immediately they were bursting to find out what the time travel was like and to know if it was possible for us to take them with us. But our instructions from my 1000-year-old self and from the Heral had been explicit. If we attempted to transport anyone through time they would die, and I did not feel willing, certainly not at this time, to risk the life of our Olarian friends. They understood, and I promised them, if we could find a way, we would. We were able to show them what we had seen and they were genuinely satisfied with that.

◘

It was early Monday morning on the tenth day of Raille and Jess's visit to OlarCret when Januti and I made the jump to Olaria's home. She was so excited to see us; she held both of us close, our heads all nestling on each other's shoulder, and she asked us to tell her, ourselves, about our time trip, and we did, and she was delighted and full of satisfaction that we were expanding into the cosmos in new and exciting ways.

We made the jump to the GeGhan home and found Raille, Jess and the two young children waiting for us with Piquant and Seliqana. Their visit had been hugely successful. They were bursting to tell us, but we knew that would have to wait till dinner tonight when they would come to our place, and Ajit had promised to cook some of the delicacies he knew Jess really liked. She and Ajit had clicked the moment they began to talk about food, and Jess was pleased to be able to have the kind of discussions only serious foodies could have. The rest of us, including Raille, who, to give him his due, had tried to engage, left them to it. We knew that after dinner we would hear all the excitement of the Cretian visit.

Also, before they left, I had quietly shared with Raille and Jess some of my fantasies about the Intergalactic Learning Centre. It had been my hope that Jess might find a way to sound out some of the very senior Cretians regarding the possibility of children from the leading clan families being a part of the first group. It turned out she had. While they had been cautious, mainly because it would be inappropriate to show enthusiasm over something that was not primarily Cretian, they were quietly excited. She believed it was probably at the prospect of some of their children being part of something so vast and powerful, and their opportunistic selves had been primed.

I smiled. Jess was a very clever and astute negotiator. She had known exactly which angles would tweak their excitement and draw them in to the proposal. Olaria had also left her and Raille fully telepathic during their visit and that had been extraordinarily helpful for them. So, one small step at a time, the possibility of the Intergalactic Learning Centre was being brought into being.

CHAPTER 27

Tanzin, Jald & the Eight of Us

Once it had been established that Tanzin and Jald were definitely going to be a couple, Jald had done something totally un-Olarian: he had decided he would propose to Tanzin the way a human partner would. We showed him a range of examples of how people might propose, and he found a process that he felt would honor the human tradition yet suit Olarian behavior. Then he had arranged for Januti to show him different kinds of engagement rings, and all of our partners helped him find a design they believed would suit Tanzin. Then we all watched him create it from pure energy. It was not outrageous and it was beautiful.

I had quietly slipped into the future a year ahead on OlarCret and found Jald and Tanzin *married!* In spite of what the Heral had told us, I could remember what I had seen during time travel! I had found Tanzin living in Jald's home with a baby, so, their home. Okay, that had done it for me. I asked Januti if she thought there was any downside to bringing Tanzin into our reality. Jald would be unable to lie about us, and Tanzin was bound to be curious about a lot of things to do with Jald, and I was willing to bring her into our fold if everyone agreed; with no hesitation they all did.

Okay. So the next step was to invite Tanzin and Jald for dinner, which we decided to do the day Miyuki signed off on Tanzin's new job on OlarCret and authorized the quantum computers and other necessary human gear to be transported to OlarCret. Miyuki had decided to transport everything on *Sunstreamer*, which was just large enough, and to use the original crew including Tanzin just for this trip. Raille had agreed to crew, especially because *Sunstreamer* would remain on OlarCret for two days, allowing the crew to reconnect with their hosts and for all the gear to be unloaded into the new complex and be set up, Olarian style.

There had been no discussion of the unloading of *Sunstreamer* as Jald had assured Miyuki he would personally supervise it. He also had learned enough about electricity to be able to assure Miyuki the Olarians would be able to establish a stable power source for the computers, and having had several clarifying discussions with Gerard and John, he was fully cognizant of the computers' requirements. Jald also had had a discussion that totally fascinated him with Yuri, John's computer. At this point, Tanzin had still not been appraised of all the things she needed to know.

So a few nights before Tanzin and Jald were to leave with *Sunstreamer* to travel to OlarCret with all the gear for the new OlarCret Astronavigational Training Centre, I invited the couple to dinner with Raille and Jess.

Tanzin was excited, Jald a little less so, being more than a little anxious. I reassured him that he need not be worried; I believed Tanzin would have forgiven me just about anything at this point in her life, and I already knew from my brief journey through time that their future as a happily married couple was certain.

The dinner was something Tanzin would never forget. When she arrived she was welcomed by Januti, who introduced herself as my partner.

'Of course,' she said. 'I ought to have realized he would have someone as totally gorgeous as you, and I am so pleased for both of you. He totally deserves the best.'

Jald was smiling. Tanzin gave me a huge hug. She explained to Januti that I had made everything between her and Jald and their future possible, even though she was not, at this point, exactly sure how I had managed it.

Raille and Jess said how pleased they were to invite Tanzin to one of their social occasions.

Dinner went well and Januti and Tanzin clearly hit it off and she and Raille and Jess were already comfortable with one another. However, as dinner progressed Tanzin's intuition that all was not necessarily as it seemed began to bother her. So, with Jald's anxiety remarkably high for an Olarian, now seemed the moment to do the deed. It was my task. So I began.

'Tanzin, I am going to ask Jald to keep you telepathic as he will do, in all probability, for the rest of your life.'

She smiled, frowned and narrowed her eyes, getting that canny look that everyone who worked with her knew well. She was getting a hunch, a very big hunch, and she was watching me and Jald like a hawk. Jald had activated her telepathy as he did whenever they were together, so I continued.

It is not only Jald who is telepathic here. Januti and I are also fully telepathic and telekinetic and Raille and Jess already know this.

She smiled. *Okay, Zed, but you must know I am really not surprised. Some of the things you did and pulled off for us on OlarCret, I more or less thought that might be true.*

Well, Tanzin, first you probably ought to know that it was not until I met the Olarians and during the first few days on OlarCret that I discovered my telepathic and telekinetic capabilities. As you know, you are buying into a telepathic and telekinetic world and we are a strongly connected part of that world. But you should be prepared to adjust to quite a lot. Januti and I are not only fully telepathic and telekinetic, we are able to do some other stuff as well, and we are not alone. There were eight of us born on Earth. We think of ourselves as human – this is our world too – but we suspect we may be a lot more than that.

I watched her, looked into her and accepted that she could, now, as easily look into me and Januti.

Well, she said, *I plan to keep this man within reach until he cannot tolerate me any further, so I had better get adjusted to whatever other things you are going to tell me.*

I smiled. So Tanzin. So open, honest and direct. So I continued.

Okay, Jald did not get onto Energystreamer *by magic. I made a simultaneity jump to OlarCret to bring him back with me. Januti and I and the other six who we would like you to meet tonight, if you are willing, can all do that. So I made the jump to OlarCret and then brought him to* Energystreamer *while Esan, his son, who you know from OlarCret, was bringing you up to it. How are we going so far?*

Tanzin looked at me. *I think you should just keep bringing on the surprises until you run out, then perhaps give me a little time to talk my feelings over with Jald and begin to adjust to an amazing and exciting and improbable new world. No wonder you were able to persuade Miyuki to buy into your incredible idea. Does she know?*

Good lord no. She has absolutely no idea. If she had, I would know and I might not have a job.

Tanzin nodded, smiled and shook her head.

Okay, Tanzin. The eight of us are also able to travel through time and, if needed, we can freeze time. There are probably some other things we can do with time that we do not as yet know. And, finally, we have some other capabilities which we do not yet know. These are related to areas of our brains that have not yet developed. However, in the process of developing our ability to move through time, we have met yet another society about whom we do not as yet know a great deal. We are still learning. And that, Tanzin, is pretty much the lot.

I stopped and we were all watching her inside and out and she turned to Jald and said, after a few moments, *You have some very interesting friends.*

He looked at her and into her.

And so, my beautiful astronavigator, do you now. And they are nearly as pleased for you as I am and you already know how pleased that is.

He smiled at and into her. And she just looked at him with love and satisfaction.

Wow, did I bite off more than I knew! Before I take him off and we spend a little time discussing my feelings, which I realize you will all hear, perhaps I should meet the rest of you.

I nodded and the others all appeared in time for the dessert, which I knew all of them loved. With no more than a nod from Jess, Januti extended the table, laid the other six places, created the chairs and one after another the three couples introduced themselves. Tanzin was smiling, almost hugging herself and clearly filled with sheer delight.

God, you're all so beautiful. Before I partake of this dessert, which is clearly worth waiting for, I should ask if there are any more surprises for which I should be prepared.

Yes, I replied, *there is just one. Raille is a part of our family, along with Jess and their two children, Selma and Reggie.*

She turned and looked at them. *Are you...?*

Jess replied for them.

No. We are not telepathic or anything except what you already know about us, but we know about these amazing people and they are an important part of our extended family. And I am certain you already know we are truly delighted to welcome you.

With that Januti served the dessert, and when the babble of telepathic conversation stopped for a few moments, Tanzin asked if, absurd as she realized it was, we minded if she took Jald outside and beat his brains out for not warning her what exactly she was getting into. We smiled. Jald looked a little sheepish and with our blessing she took him onto our little seating nook outside the lounge, where we were all delighted to hear her say out loud in English, 'Holy fucking hell, Jald, but they are such beautiful and wonderful people, what a fantastic gift to bring me into. I just love them and I could not be more excited and certain I have made the best decision of my entire life. Especially, I think, because I have been anxious that I was either putting you in an invidious position or wondering how lonely it might be for someone like me in your society. And yes, I know they live here on Earth, but they seem to me to be like a kind of extended family.

'And, as we were leaving the dining room, I wonder did you catch Januti? She said, and I truly love her for this, "You don't need to feel alone on OlarCret; one of us can easily come and get you, maybe each month and bring you down to socialize with us. Raille and Jess will often be part of that, now they have become connected to all of us".

'It was thoughtful and kind and I just love them, whoever they are. They have been more inclusive and generous than anyone I have ever known. They have the same generous nature that all your people seem to possess.'

Jald smiled at her. *You just may find yourself busier than you think. Try to remember what your social life was like for the year we were together.*

Tanzin grinned at him. *Funny, you know, that year I have always thought of as work and that all the socializing was because we were strangers and interesting.*

Jald just shook his head. *For us, it was just part of our life. And although a lot of people were very curious, in future there will still be the curiosity, but there will also come to be the friendships. You will be a part of our community, it will also be your community. I assure you, work aside, you will never be lonely or bored while you are with us. You will become part of our world and you will always be healthy.*

And so the first stirrings of her future bubbled and fizzed inside and Tanzin began to feel her life being rearranged and felt happier than she could remember.

◘

The next day after I had spoken to Raille, and Raille and Jess had talked it over and agreed they would like to be at Jald and Tanzin's wedding, I made another appointment to talk with Miyuki. Miyuki looked at me as I entered her office. She really did like me and was pleased that I had reason to spend time with her. As I picked up the feeling, I smiled to myself. Having her positive connection was definitely helpful. Today I had a somewhat tricky arrangement to negotiate.

'Good morning, Zed. I am pleased you have reason for us to meet. You know I find you a very reassuring presence. What can I do for you this morning?'

I looked at her and into her. It seemed she was getting a kind of comfort when she was with me, and I realized it was because I was feeding her the emotional warmth that mostly did not exist inside the operational organization of Space Fleet Command. I was, in a not unhelpful way, a pleasant diversion for her.

'I would like to discuss the transporting of the quantum computers and gear and Tanzin and Jald to OlarCret.'

She raised her eyebrows. 'A little out of your domain, isn't it?'

There were no barbs in the comment, just a curiosity.

'Well, yes and no. Think of this as a psychological well-being discussion about some of your staff.'

She chuckled. 'Well, stretching my imagination, I can certainly do that for you. Go ahead.'

'Jald and Tanzin plan to live together on OlarCret, but, and this was as big a surprise to me as it will probably be to you, they want to get married!'

Miyuki smiled at me and I could feel that she was both surprised and pleased.

'Okay, and so?'

'I would like to be able to offer them be married on *Sunstreamer* on the journey to OlarCret, Married by John, as he is enabled to, once they are in space, and I was hoping you would crew *Sunstreamer* with the original crew, and yes, Raille is willing. I of course am willing and Tanzin is happy to crew as the astronav both ways and the Olarians will get her back to OlarCret.

'Knowing you as I do, I anticipated the possibility you might want to make a holo recording that could be beamed to the world as an example of the closeness of our civilizations. With that model in mind, I imagined you might be pleased to allow Raille to take his beautiful partner and their two children, so showing the world that the cosmos may well be populated with people who may not be so different as they might appear.'

She was smiling from ear to ear. 'Zed, I am going to say this once and only once and I know you will not misconstrue it in any way, being who you are. I would have liked to have met you a decade or more ago, then I would have fallen hopelessly in love with you. You are one of the smartest, most generous, most attractive and capable men I have ever met.'

She smiled at me, knowing I did genuinely understand her but not exactly how or why.

'Okay, I will cut the orders exactly as you have asked. Will it be okay with Jess and her children?'

I nodded. 'It will. And I was wondering if perhaps you would agree to be on *Sunstreamer* for this trip. A short return journey to OlarCret to renew your relationships, see the computers set up in their new home at the Olarian Astronavigational Unit. Tanzin's family barely recognize her existence and have not responded to her successes. So she has asked me to "give her away", as it were, and subject to your approval, I have agreed. If you give this the go-ahead, the wedding would take place after *Sunstreamer* entered the Olarian system, probably once we were in orbit over OlarCret, and we would be joined physically by Olaria, who as you know is Jald's mother, and his father, and, in absentia, several million Olarians.

She looked at me carefully, nodded and smiled.

'You know I would not miss this for the world. I am also taking the liberty of guessing you would have in mind contacting everyone as soon as my orders are cut, which will be by close of business today.'

Again I acknowledged that was what I had been hoping she would say. She looked at me again with that wistful look to which I was becoming accustomed.

'I take it our business is done?'

'Not quite.' I smiled at her and sent her again a warm and reassuring bundle of energy. 'For a while now, Raille and Jess have been discussing the possibility of their getting married but each time the idea stalls because of the absence of any of Jess's family. Now you need to know that I have not broached this with either of them. But, from orbit over OlarCret the Olarians could bring Piquant and Seliqana on board, if – and only if – you were comfortable with that idea and if the Olarians and Jess were also. I can, of course, get the Olarians to test that out long before we arrive. In fact, before we leave.'

She looked at me. 'Is that all?'

'Well, no, I would also really like to bring my partner along. She and Jald and Tanzin and Jess and Raille all get on well!'

This time she shook her head and smiled.

'I really don't know you, do I? I did not even know. Would you like to have a drink with me?'

My turn to smile and acknowledge her. I knew she kept a delicious Australian red, which was my favorite. I said 'yes please' and thanked her for everything.

◘

When I left Miyuki's office I was aware that I was no wedding planner. We had all been present the evening we had introduced Tanzin to our group and we had all witnessed Jald's proposal to Tanzin and her delight at him giving her a ring. But now we had two weddings to plan and they needed to take place on *Sunstreamer* when we arrived at OlarCret. Our group of eight wanted to be present so I would let them know as we approached OlarCret orbit, allowing them to make the jump to *Sunstreamer.* They would do some rather strong shapeshifting to appear as Olarian relatives, which they would show Tanzin, Raille and Jess so they would know who they were. All this assumed that Raille and Jess would like it.

My next task was simple enough: check with Raille and Jess if they wanted to do this. I need not have been concerned. As soon as Jess realized that Seliqana and Piquant could be brought on board for the ceremony and Jess's few really close relatives and friends be brought to the post-wedding festivities, she was delighted. The couple were more than pleased to have the assistance and organizing skill of the rest of the female crew. I was not unhappy about being considered responsible for them being married on *Sunstreamer*.

I had a long discussion with Jess about how to approach Piquant and Seliqana, plus the small group of really close friends and relatives. Once I was clear on this I made the jump to OlarCret to Olaria's home. We quickly caught up and I explained what I was planning. She promised an appropriate audience and what she decided to call a genuine Olarian and Cretian and human wedding breakfast. Once she understood the intricacies of these ceremonies, she could blend them together, then check with each group their feelings about the final product.

Next I made the jump to Piquant's home and with very little difficulty made the arrangements for them to be present at the wedding and the breakfast. Promising them that I would personally transport them to our spacecraft, I could feel Piquant's excitement, not at the wedding, of which he did actually approve, but of the opportunity to see the spacecraft. Not insignificantly, because I had promised him a tour of *Sunstreamer* before we took them to the wedding breakfast.

Finally I did a brief check with Raille. I knew he would not be wanting to involve his parents and I was right about that. It was something we had talked about many times. They could not believe he had established an intimate relationship with a Cretian and had never wanted to meet her or see their grandchildren. I knew somewhere in the depths of his mind Raille was deeply sad about this but, by now, reconciled.

In the end it turned out to be relatively straightforward. I think. Peta, Ghia and Elise were absolutely delighted to be responsible for Tanzin and Raille's on-board weddings. Our four were able to be involved without anyone being aware of them, but in the background they followed all the planning of the crew and were involved in ways that kept them busy but out of sight.

Jess was excited at the thought of her and Raille getting married and it was with absolutely no difficulty that the women on the crew included Jess and Raille's wedding in the arrangements and the details were thrashed out by the crew under the watchful eye of the skipper. I should probably add that John was as pleased as he could possibly be that he would be conducting the marriage of two of his crew.

Bringing the Olarians on board was easy. Seliqana and Piquant were both impressed with the simultaneity jump I made with them, and once on board *Sunstreamer* Piquant was overjoyed at the opportunity to see the machinery about which he had only heard discussions. John met him and Seliqana formally, introduced him to the crew, our visitors, and then offered to take him on an inspection tour of the spacecraft while Seliqana was delighted to be able to help Jess. By the time Piquant came back to the flight deck, which was now set up for the weddings, he was filled with admiration at the human capabilities. John had answered all his questions and he realized just how advanced was the technology of these humans. He was more than pleased to have been invited to play his part in Jessiqana's wedding to Raille who he respected and, in his uniquely Cretian way, liked.

The weddings went off well. The wedding breakfast was held in the center the Olarians had built for the visitors the year previously, which was a perfect venue, and 30 people celebrated with Jald and Tanzin and Jess and Raille in what must have been, to the Olarians and the Cretians, the most amazing ritual they had seen. Tanzin was happier than she had ever imagined she would be, and Jess, as the crowd dispersed late in the evening, turned to Raille and said, in our hearing, 'This really caps off a fantastic year. Meeting humans was the most astonishing thing to ever happen to me because they gave me you.'

Raille, at six feet tall and with his longish brown curly hair and his neatly clipped beard, could not hide his blushing. For a moment Jess thought she may have said the wrong thing, but, typically for him, his first response was not his final response and he just picked her up as though she was a leaf, held her close and whispered, loud enough so we all actually heard: 'I love you, Jess. You are the most magical thing to ever enter my life, and I am delighted that you agreed to marry me.'

Laughing and crying at the same time, she said yes she did know, and everyone clapped, and Tanzin went up to him and diminutive as she was gave him a huge hug and he bent down and she kissed his cheek, overflowing with happiness for him.

The weddings, with people present from three cultures on two worlds, would, Miyuki knew, be seen by millions, quite probably billions of people back on Earth, and it would not fail to enhance the status of her organization. As she looked across the small crowd at me, she felt certain she had somehow underestimated just how important I was. I happened to turn at that moment and Januti, standing beside me, murmured telepathically, *You need to be cautious, Zed. She is getting a very strong hunch about you.*

Without any visible sign I whispered back, *You know I'm yours, and I am aware of her. She is very bright. We may one day need to bring her into our family and our world.*

Januti just nodded.

CHAPTER 28

Astronav OlarCret

One of the things Miyuki had enjoyed during her two weeks on OlarCret had been watching the things the Olarians could do, such as lifting huge weights with no effort at all. The quantum computers were not small but were in some ways quite delicate, however, they were a very considerable weight. No human would have considered moving one without heavy-lifting machinery; the eight or nine people that could have got around the perimeter could not have lifted one no matter how strong they were.

So when the outer hatch on *Sunstreamer* had been opened in space where two men could easily manage one and it was loaded piggy-back onto one of the shuttles, she found it an impressive sight. When the shuttle landed in a very gentle vertical descent she had been on board. Tanzin had brought the shuttle down and now the two of them and Jald stood by outside as two of the crew released the cradle supports and holding arms, which could be safely done because Jald had encased the computer in an energy bubble and planned to walk it the mile or so to its new home.

Jald with absolutely no apparent effort had the first of the quantum computers in the air ahead of them as if it was weightless and Miyuki watched the couple as they walked hand in hand toward the new Astronav Centre. The center was identical in shape and appearance to the center on Earth, just much smaller, needing really only to house the equipment and a maximum of a dozen people at any one time. The center was self-contained and the students could, if they wished, live there. However, a not inconsiderable number of Olarian families had offered to house them, should that be something they wished.

Because of the way the center had been set up, it was possible to run the whole operation with just one or two administrative staff, and while the Olarians had offered to be trained to undertake the job, and Miyuki had immediately assured them she would organize that, there had been no shortage of volunteers from within the astronavigational training community. In the end a married couple had been selected to spend the first period on OlarCret, and the Olarians were delighted.

Once the unit was operational it was planned to begin the training of one or two couples of Olarians so they were familiar with the management of the facility and could, when the need arose and during leave of the managing couple, take over the running of the center.

The couple had not come up with *Sunstreamer*, by their choice, but would come up in a week's time on a slower supply shuttle. Both were longstanding members of the SFC Astronav Unit administrative staff and could easily run the center between them. After a great deal of discussion, they had been allowed to know that the Olarians had a method of communicating across the galaxies between OlarCret and Earth should any emergency or significant incident or resupply become necessary.

Miyuki had watched the supply pods be taken to the center and now she was happy to see the last of the equipment put in place. It was such an interesting process. When they arrived at the center, a section of the outer shell had been opened and moved aside so the last computer could be installed in its final home, at which point the building was fully reconstituted and no sign that it had ever looked like a damaged shell could be seen.

The center was, in effect, one huge solar panel, in human terms. It absorbed and stored energy from the sun and supplied an unbroken stream of the electrical energy required by the computers and the other facilities in the center. There would never be, in the normal course of events, any interruption to the supply.

Then, without any warning, the ground began to move, deep rumbling sounds increasing in volume and intensity. Three Olarians were keeping the astronav center off the ground and I realized there was no time to waste. Januti and I made a jump with Miyuki to the shuttle. The Olarians had got Jald and Tanzin and the entire crew in the shuttle and before Tanzin had the engines established the Olarians had the shuttle off the ground. Two of the Olarians were paying full attention to the motion of the tectonic plates and describing the motion to others on the ground.

Within seconds Tanzin had the little shuttle under control and heading for *Sunstreamer*. As soon as the shuttle was housed, the crew wasted no time making their way to their stations. The computers were informing the crew of the events on the ground but making clear that the surface disturbance was not being transmitted to the upper atmosphere and their geostationary orbit was stable.

On deck were the crew, all at their stations, with Miyuki and the rest of the human telekinetic telepaths, who in appearance and dress might easily be seen as Olarians. Jald stood beside my station, keeping an eye on Tanzin and feeding information to the crew as to the state of activity on the ground. The computers were running simultaneous scans and feeding almost identical data to the crew. The Olarians were managing the disturbance, the astronav center was in safe hands and the shifting tectonic plates were settling with, it turned out, more than a little assistance from nearly 100 million Olarians.

The computers were also relaying information visually on the three holo screens with their auditory comments about the status of the sub-surface instability and then about the slowly stabilizing and settling of the deep sub-surface plates. Less than a minute later the situation had stabilized, the plates had settled into their new locations and the Olarians were comfortable that the situation was now fully under control.

Miyuki, however, was looking at me with a frown.

Januti and I simultaneously spoke to Miyuki telepathically, *Later, please.*

She looked at us, but particularly at me. She was nodding her head very slowly and had a glint in her eye that was not a result of the quake that had disturbed our day. I knew what she was thinking and I also knew here and now was not the time for the disclosure she was about to instigate. She got it in one. With the hint of a smile, she mouthed the words, 'Later, Zed!'

There was nothing threatening in the tone. It was somewhere between delight and bubbling awareness.

The computers were giving us stable readings on the sub-surface activity, and the sub-surface management group of Olarians were sharing with Jald the final assessment of the impact of the quake and assuring him the astronav center was safe and now resettled, which he passed on to Tanzin, Miyuki and the crew.

Jald had not missed the interchange between Miyuki, Januti and I, understood what we had asked her and was relieved that she had agreed to await a more suitable moment for the conversation she had in mind. It turned out that she would need to wait until we arrived at Jald's, now Jald and Tanzin's, home, where the couple were having a dinner for the entire crew, Jess and Miyuki, Olaria and the rest of the TTs, who were still in appearance Olarians and in usual Olarian dress.

When the dinner was over and people were settling in small groups chatting happily, Miyuki found her moment and took Januti and me outside. She looked at us meaningfully and we were able to read her unspoken question. She was quite clear that we were not what we seemed.

'Tell me, Zed, you two are not like me, are you?'

I looked at Januti and smiled. *No.*

And with the others, including Tanzin and Jald and Jess and Raille able to leave the five crew chatting with Olaria, we told Miyuki everything. It was not certain, at this point, that we knew exactly what Miyuki's response would be. So when the entire tale was told she looked at me with a smile settling on her lips, realized that all of us were waiting on her response but with the telepathic help that Jess and Raille and Tanzin were also getting, we knew. She was not astonished, not even really very surprised, but, it seemed, she was delighted!

Then, now connected to us telepathically, she said, *All my life I have wanted to be connected to people who were kind and loving and very smart. It feels I have finally found you. It was the feeling I had with Olaria when she first visited me. I really do not have the words right now to tell you how good it feels that you have brought me into your little group – no, that is not right is it? –your family.*

And, I am really quite cognizant about your need for secrecy and privacy and you can absolutely rely on me for the rest of my life. There are absolutely no words that can describe how good I am feeling at this moment as I am certain you all know.

And we did. The eight of us helped Miyuki understand the kind of shapeshifting adjustments we had all learned to make to be invisible in plain sight. She loved it, understood immediately how we had traveled as Olarians and understood also how we would get back home. This part quite shook her, and when she understood that we could transport someone with us she made me promise that we would at least once in the near future bring her here with us and take her home the same way. So now, although the risk was spreading wider, we did at least have a more substantive network. Miyuki was pleased when she realized who was supporting the OlarCret travelers in dealing with obnoxious behaviors.

She spent most of the day before she departed on *Sunstreamer* visiting Olarian education centers and became more conscious of the potential value of the Intergalactic Learning Centre, which she totally supported. The final thing she did before she said goodbye to the other six of us who were going to make a jump back to Canberra was to watch the sexual behavior experiences of the Olarians, so she would know what had never found its way into the debrief but would also give her something very special for herself. Then, an interesting smile on her face, she almost reluctantly climbed aboard the shuttle to begin the three-day journey home.

We had decided while we were on OlarCret, when we were all together with Jald and Tanzin, we would host a dinner each month at our apartment, because Miyuki could be seen to visit with no suspicious overtones, as could Raille and Jess. Tanzin and Jald could be brought by one of us making the jump to and from OlarCret and Olaria had asked if she could be part of these soirees at least once or if acceptable several times a year and everyone was delighted to have her and gave their unhesitating agreement.

So a new intergalactic social network bloomed into life and for the moment remained invisible to the rest of the world. To keep appearances balanced, Januti and I planned to visit Raille and Jess at their place one Sunday every month or so. A new step had been taken, but it was by no means certain where it would lead us.

In addition, I had found that I could create an energy field only millimeters thick around our bodies, so when Raille and I were engaged in combat practice we could use maximum force, as we would do with a genuine opponent, and, apart from some jarring experiences, remain entirely unharmed and fully combative with and without weapons. We both found this made our practice many times more effective and satisfying, no holds barred, so long as I used no telepathic or telekinetic processes.

It interested me that I was continuing with my martial arts practice, now not only quite unnecessary for my safety but the violence was also anathema to my beliefs. The thing was, martial arts were not, for me, about violence! I realized I was for some reason wanting to maintain a connection with my past and with Raille. I also found myself still practicing my miniature harp at least three nights a week and realized my mother was still managing some pieces of my life from beyond the grave!

Then it hit me. I could see her again! I realized that the Heral had never stopped at any point when my mother or father were present when they had taken me with Rozari back through my life! I wondered why and realized I needed more information but guessed they had correctly imagined I would want to meet and talk with them. Then I also knew I had to be very, very careful and disciplined about this.

CHAPTER 29

The Intergalactic Learning Centre

I woke up one Saturday morning deciding that today was the day I would begin the process of bringing the Intergalactic Learning Centre into being. When I had completed my morning meditation I decided to begin with a discussion with Jess and Raille that would enrich my limited understanding of Cretian and Olarian culture and education.

Januti was awake and wanted to be involved. Good. So I made a holo call to Raille. They were about to go shopping but he and Jess would be delighted to see us that afternoon and have a serious discussion about the two cultures and the ILC. I thanked him and nominated 2pm if that was okay and we would jump a fast transit. It was, and the arrangements were made.

Januti smiled at me. *Using fast transit vehicles seems to increasingly be neither our most common nor our most comfortable travel pattern even while we are in Canberra. Sometimes I wonder when I first felt this way. We are becoming less well integrated into our human culture, don't you think?*

I looked at her, realized she was thinking about a future we all believed we would need to have. The eight of us had talked many times about the future and had kind of decided that while Jesse, Raille, Tanzin and Miyuki were alive we would try to remain on Earth.

We knew that Reggie and Selma would need to be somehow involved in our decisions about the future, however, as yet we did not know how. They would grow up knowing something of a normal human life but would spend much of their first 20 years in a telepathic world. None of us could foresee where their future would lead them unless we decided to track them through time and for some reason this was a journey we were all reluctant to make!

It was a decision that appeared to make no sense and each of us had asked the question: why were we so reluctant to undertake so obviously useful a journey? Interestingly, every one of us was as uncomfortable and confused about this as the others and we had clearly decided that, for the moment, we would not make that journey.

One almost overwhelming aspect of our logic appeared to be that, if during our travel we found something had happened to one or both of them, would we decide to intervene to change any negative aspect of our discovery? In the face of the warnings we had received from the Heral, we might be biting off more than we could chew. So for the moment, we sat pat.

We had, however, assured Jess and Raille we would not abandon them, and that had been all they needed to know to begin thinking about the ILC as the educational starting point for their children. However, we all knew the future of graduates from that center was really no more than vaguely conceived. That had to change, however, how future decisions would be made was anyone's guess.

I contacted the others and told them of our plans and all decided they would listen in. The Olarians had confirmed our four partners were all having twins: a boy and a girl! None of us believed this was in any way coincidental. The ILC would be the education facility for our children. A week previously Jald had let us know that Tanzin was pregnant with their first child, a girl. Another month and Olaria had let us know that my other seven children were doing fine. The four women on *Energystreamer* were all carrying twins – a boy and a girl! In times past I might have said... spooky... but now I knew there actually were forces at work I simply did not yet understand.

Januti and I arrived at Raille and Jess's like a normal couple: stepped off a fast transit and took the rapid elevator up to their apartment. It felt just a little odd and I realized, in light of our earlier conversation, it was neither our preferred nor our most frequent way of getting around! Once we had established ourselves around their dining table we shut down the watch-and-listen capabilities in their apartment, making the usual arrangements to ensure total privacy. The security facilities were actually not intended or, in most cases, able to hear what we said or see what we were doing. However, our precautions were now automatic, because they could be used to spy. We simply ensured they could not.

Jess and Raille waited, coffee in hand.

I began. 'Since we started to think about having children, we have, as you know, been concerned about the future here on Earth for our children. So the ILC came up as a notion. In the beginning I thought of it as somewhere our children could hide in plain sight and be educated in a value system that we loved, one that the Olarians offered their children.

'At first I thought if we had human children, Cretian children, Second Earth children and your children, and now Tanzin and Jald's children and our children and the children we are having with the Olarians, then a range of children from different cultural situations would be educated in the best value system we have ever seen.

'This, however, has some assumptions and some problems. First, I am not clear how, or even if, we need to give our children and your children and some of the children of powerful families the kind of subject information they would get on Earth and the appropriate human-centric technological information and skills. I would really like to hear both your opinions about this. However, I feel pretty confident we will need something of this kind of education somewhere in their educational journey.

'But I also need to know something more about Cretian education and values. I'm looking in part at possible future powerful leaders because, if we could give them a moral, relational, values-based education, we might be able to influence the future in a constructive way. I don't know how to do this precisely, but I have some weird ideas that I need to float past you two. You probably have more understanding about our problems than anyone and I really do not know who else we could possibly safely discuss this with.

'Because there are so many bits to juggle I wanted to talk with you who probably have the best knowledge in the universe on Olarian and Cretian and human learning and educational systems. Now I have laid out as much of our problem as I think I know and would love to hear your thoughts. Oh, yes, now Miyuki is involved I thought she would have some idea about the involvement of the children of the powerful families, given she is a member of one of them.'

I looked at them. Jess just burst out laughing.

Raille shook his head and said, 'Oh, is that all. I thought you had a complicated problem you wanted to discuss with us!'

Januti and I laughed.

'You realize we only have a couple of hours, don't you?' Jess asked. 'Kids have a way of redefining your time! As you will shortly find out.'

'I think I probably need to add a few bits, including, you both know I am not expecting anything resembling some sort of solution,' I said. 'I want to see if the thoughts I am having are supported by things you know that I do not. Especially, I am genuinely afraid for our children if they were to stay on Earth and be part of any educational scenario I have ever heard about. I am not afraid for us, but if someone hurt any of our children I am afraid of what the consequences might be if one of us lost their temper. And that is one scenario where one of us conceivably might.'

Jess and Raille looked at each other. They knew how powerful each of us was and for perhaps the first time both became aware this was a very serious issue for us. Perhaps even a survival-on-Earth scenario. And now they frowned and settled down to a quite complex conversation.

Neither Januti nor I interrupted Jess and Raille as they described the Cretian education system, then the Olarian system, then mapped these against the human system.

'Some of the others would like to ask some questions. Would you rather they asked them through us or came over?'

The couple smiled. Jess said they would be delighted to have the mob come over. The other six arrived and, with Natalya asking Jess's permission and getting an unconditional affirmation, she extended the table and added the chairs, thanking Raille and Jess for their generosity and their open, caring willingness to help us.

Raille held up his hand.

'Please, I need all of you to understand something I have probably never said to any of you before. Zed has been my one and only friend on Earth. He could be my brother. I would never use this word to him,' he said, smiling warmly at me. 'But the truth is, I do love him. We have been through a lot together. I might not ever have met Jess or negotiated our relationship without him. I do not want him or any of you, who I now number among my family, to have to leave Earth.'

He had now spoken the unspeakable – the elephant in the room – and all of us knew this was the alternative scenario to pulling off the Intergalactic Learning Centre. It was clear he and Jess could feel the waves of caring, warmth and affection that were genuinely pouring over them. Everyone in this room wanted – needed – the ILC to work. This was not an inconsequential discussion. It was the beginning of some tangled issues we had to sort out.

I looked at Raille, smiled and nodded an affirmation. I wanted him to know that I had fully heard his message and I wanted him to know he was to me exactly what I was to him, no matter what else I was also turning out to be. I knew immediately he was aware that our connection was equally important to me.

'We could really use Miyuki to help sort some aspects of this issue,' Raille said.

His observation was definitely right. Question was, could we get her here?

'Give me a moment,' I said. 'Let me try to find her and see if it is safe to contact her.'

The group went quiet and I sought her out and I was aware most of them were following me. She was at home sitting at her desk working on some administrative issues she needed to take to work on Monday. I gently entered her mind.

Miyuki, this is Zed. With the words I sent feelings of warmth and connection and I saw her stop, frown, then smile knowingly and warmly.

What can I do for you, Zed?

We are meeting at Raille and Jess's apartment, discussing the Intergalactic Learning Centre, and we could use your knowledge and help.

I stopped. I did not want to press her in any way. However, I need not have been concerned. She was delighted at my contact and more than willing to shelve the administrivia for connection to us, an important element of her new family. So I told her I would come and get her, if that was acceptable.

Our conversation had been necessarily carried out telepathically and she warned me that her security would know the moment she ceased to be in her apartment. We had a short and focused discussion, with Ajit sliding in to let her know he would deal with that if she wished. She thanked him, let him know that would be welcome and so, Ajit having managed the security, I made the jump to her apartment and brought her to Raille and Jess's home.

She was excited, delighted and genuinely happy to be with us and be a part of our, to her, astonishing family. We took a brief break for some of the group to help Jess get some drinks and snacks while I filled in Miyuki. At the end of that, which took about 10 minutes, Miyuki was nodding and we could see she was thinking her way through some of the complexity of the issues our discussion had raised.

Raille and Jess had raised the big one: how could the parents of the human children from Earth or Second Earth get to the education centers for dinner and evening activities? My thinking jolted to a halt. The only workable bit seemed to be Raille and Jess, who were crystal clear they wanted their children brought up with ours. They would arrange to be able to travel with us to OlarCret every evening, there being no more than a dozen nights in a year when they were definitely going to be unable to make that trip. As Januti and I were unhesitatingly willing to do this, that element was managed. But what about all the human and Second Earthers?

The Olarians had told us they could and would willingly manage the Cretians. So we were for the moment stuck, unable to find an answer for humans and Second Earthers, all of whom were members of the seven families who controlled most of the economic and, indirectly, military world. How were we going to deal with the issue of bringing parents to children every day, or could we see a way to make the system work without doing that?

We knew, because of the structure of the political, economic, governmental and business world that all the children who would be educated at the ILC would be children of the seven families, the ones who controlled a huge portion of senior governmental and organizational positions in the world. For the moment this would be a necessity if we were to gain any traction for our center.

CHAPTER 30

Twists and Turns in the Intergalactic Learning Centre

'I think,' Miyuki began, 'you might not be surprised to learn that I believe none of the seven families with senior women currently about to become new parents would want to spend time with their children every day. In many ways, the majority of them are not unlike the English monarchy of a century or more ago. Their children, both genders, would automatically be sent off to boarding school. I am thinking of the current generation who are presently pregnant among the most senior ranks of those families.

'There are one or two families about whom I am uncertain. Some would not want to spend any time with their children, especially when they are very young. They would be planning to send them to one of the approved boarding schools they have been using for decades.

'I think you might find that having some Olarian surrogate parents might work better for the children and the world than having the actual parents. I hardly know my parents; they have been not in contact with me for most of my adult life and almost none of my early life. I see them less than half a dozen times a year. I would have to say, in all honesty, I hardly know them. My only real family contact is, ironically, my grandfather and grandmother, both of whom I love and who love me. I have far more contact with them than my parents.

'Several senior women of the current seven families are pregnant. You need to remember, I really do not know all of them that well any more. However, I believe most would be very happy to have their child brought up at any exclusive school, and given the way this entity is shaping up in your mind, I suspect they would be keen to have the newest of their children brought up that way.

'And have no fear: they would not, under any circumstances, want to be part of their children's education. Most of us learned this about our parents before we were four or five years old. They would want them to be home only for Christmas and once or twice for special occasions, like a grandparent's birthday, a wedding, things like that.'

The rest of us were looking maybe a little surprised as we tried to fit this lifestyle information into our picture of life at the top.

'My recommendation would be that each of you take one family. I will give you a really clear briefing about each of them and the key stakeholders, then you spend a little time getting to know them. You might be surprised what you learn. You could easily do this without being observed?'

I nodded to her. This put a very different slant on our problem. In fact, it might well offer a solution to our problem for these families, leaving us only the Second Earthers! All of us sat there metaphorically shaking our heads and mulling over Miyuki's information. I was considering our options and decided to leave the problem of the Second Earthers until we had sorted out the seven key families. But, as Miyuki continued, it turned out there was yet another twist about which none of us had any idea.

It appeared there had been a struggle going on for some years after Second Earth was found. One of the families wanted controlling rights to the new planet. None of the seven families wanted to go there but all wanted a piece of the action. And so, in the face of much grumbling and potentially catastrophic disagreements, a blended family involving three of the others, and with extraordinary risk to all of the individuals concerned, had been created by mutual agreement, and two generations of this new amalgamated family went to Second Earth.

All but four of the members were less than 30 years old and they had concocted an agreement of sorts that gave the new blended family rights to control of the political structures of the new planet. This disturbing pattern was supported by all seven of the dynastic families. They were 18 individuals in all: seven young couples and four mature members from two of the families. These had a working relationship that avoided any conflict of their political or economic interests. They lived in a single compound on Second Earth, more or less in each other's pockets.

Miyuki's point was, the seven couples were having eight children between them, and a great deal of angst had been generated while they were trying to decide on educational arrangements for them. As none of the children had yet been born, the possibility might still be open to making them a group for the ILC.

It almost seemed the cosmos was working with us to create the possibility our fantasy of the ILC might be made to work. Then, as I was sitting there, the room began to waver! I do not know how to describe these moments, like the one I had with Rozari in Olaria's home. Then very quietly I heard Rozari's three-and-a-half year old voice. *You need me, Daddy. Please.*

The tone was not pleading; it was clear and strong.

Whatever we were involved in had some connection to Rozari and some aspect of our lives; she somehow knew I needed to involve her! The air around me was now wavering in complex patterns and the group later told me I was slowly becoming invisible. I reached out across the cosmos to find Rozari and we met in her room in Olaria's home and then we were joined and she was with me in Jess and Raille's home and the eight of us became enmeshed! Rozari's arms were around my neck, her head on my shoulder, and then everyone in the room was enveloped in this quite indescribable miasma.

Jess and Raille and Miyuki were also gently enveloped in this wavering energy and then we all could see what appeared to be a map of the cosmos, the strangest multi-dimensional map we had ever seen, with innumerable tiny spots of light and I immediately knew we were looking at some kind of schematic of cosmic life. At least millions of live planets in millions and millions of galaxies among billions of solar systems. It was totally awesome.

Societies of every kind, some unimaginable and indescribably odd, others not. I could not even begin to describe how we knew all this. We were getting flashes of them and I became aware that without her knowledge or understanding, Rozari was the key. Her brain was alight and she was without intention activating a very strange cosmic geography of life and for the eight of us the last area of our brains was coming to life. Then, without intention and right out of our control, images of learning were being fed at very high speed to us and then they ceased. It was a bit like being in a three-dimensional theatre.

Rozari said, *Can you take me home now, please, Daddy?*

She said goodbye to me with a beautiful child's version of a kiss and cuddle and I took her home to Olaria, promising I would catch up with her later, and then I returned to Jess and Raille's and the room settled back to being and feeling like an ordinary room and everyone was looking, as usual, at me!

No, no, no, all of you were involved in that.

But my eight were shaking their heads and Miyuki, Jess and Raille were also blinking and shaking their heads.

It was Raille who spoke.

'Zed, you and Rozari were the only thing I was certain were with me. You and Rozari took us, as far as I could tell, on a journey. I don't know if it was like anything you've done before, but you and Rozari were like tour guides. I don't think I even understand where you took us!'

Jess and Miyuki were nodding.

Januti was looking at me in that way she had.

Ai picked up the thread. *I will tell you what I believe I know. You had one of those moments we have seen before. The final part of our brains, that part we all have, that has been dormant is no longer dormant! In one of those moments we have now had several times with you, the last inactive element of our brain came to light the instant Rozari was on your lap. It was as if she held the key to what had to happen next. I saw that part of her brain alight and she held you tight, then that element of your brain came to life and within seconds, it seemed, that element of our brains also came to life.*

Through all this Miyuki, Jess and Raille were in a kind of soft pink cloud. The air around us was clear but with that extraordinary wavering instability we saw when you took us to the Heral and we slid through time with you.

This time you took us to a map of what I presume included among an extraordinary number of others, our universe in which there are evidently thousands of life forms, separated, I assume, by billions of light years but connected by a species who manage the creation and operation of the wormholes through which entities and space vehicles can travel.

For some reason, we do not need these to travel these extraordinary distances. You seemed to be showing us learning going on in all these places, some of which we could just kind of understand, and then they were gone!

The environment of the room was settling and everyone was still looking at me and then at Ai. However, it was Raille who again took up the thread.

'It was not like that for me. It seemed like only an instant, but I saw life like I have never imagined, in flashes, doing something, and then it was gone.'

Jess was nodding. *They were all learning! I don't even know how I got to that!*

Miyuki was nodding.

But Ai had not finished yet.

Here is my best guess at what we have just experienced. The non-telepathic members of our family were dragged into a moment of our learning. They got what might have seemed like an image of the civilizations, the living societies in the cosmos. We were connected to a three- dimensional movie, which we will now, it seems, be able to activate when we are ready, and it feels to me as though we will be able to... visit them! All this because we were trying to plan the kind of learning we will need to be able to produce for the ILC!

Esan spoke to us. *Can we join you?*

Januti asked Jess, *Would it be all right if the 14 Olarians joined us?*

Raille and Miyuki looked at Jess, and, although at this moment she looked more than a little bewildered, she smiled with a warmth and delight all of us felt and said, *Of course.*

And they were with us and with Jess's non-verbal agreement the table disappeared and we were all in comfortable energy seats all over the lounge.

I looked at Raille and Jess. *This seems like a considerable imposition, I'm sorry.*

But both were shaking their heads.

'Nothing would be further from our minds than that you should not be here. We are absolutely entranced with what we have just experienced and neither of us want to miss a second of it. Please. This is beyond exciting.'

Miyuki was just nodding her complete agreement.

I was about to move us back to our conversation when Januti had one of her a-ha experiences. She moved closer to me and took my head in her hands. That was all it took. Immediately everything that had just happened became clear to me. A whole range of options had just been opened up for us to see and I had been left another marker that would allow us to see into the educational world of something like six or seven cosmic societies whose educational realities were in some way material to what we needed for the ILC. I knew I would need to feed the experiences that were being offered to Jess, Raille, Miyuki and the Olarians.

What I had already learned, first from Ghia and then Kyuto about the Olarian value system that lay beneath and wound through Olarian education, was connecting my insights and understandings. This was creating new knowledge about education systems, and it was clear that the rest of our eight were getting the connections. I could see that the Olarian system did indeed fit in some complex but significant ways into the learning processes of several cosmic communities. Also, I realized I was going to need to feed the entire experience through Kyuto for him to translate it for us and see how it fitted into the Olarian learning system. I could now lay the pattern of learning, values and emotional enmeshing together. I also knew that later was when I would need to engage with this huge dump of new insights.

I reached out to OlarCret again and found Kyuto and asked if he would join us. He was delighted. When everyone was settled I outlined what I believed were learning pieces that the Olarians might be able to weave into their educational process. Kyuto agreed and as I unwound my insights he translated and rearranged them to mesh into the Olarian logic that lay beneath their educational process.

We talked over what these seemed to be, essentially a combination of structural and process ideas that Kyuto assured me once fully thought through would fit into Olarian learning very neatly but would require considerable collective discussion among the group who formulated ideas for their learning centers.

I was happy to leave the discussion with him but Jess and Raille asked if he would include them in the whole engagement. Kyuto asked whether I would be willing to ferry Jess and Raille to the meetings. Instantly all eight of us assured Kyuto, Raille and Jess we definitely would. Although it was getting late, everyone wanted to stay until we had completed our discussion and everyone was totally delighted to be involved. Jess and Raille had a quite absurdly large volume of assistance in bathing the children, entertaining them, feeding them and putting them to bed. Finally Raille finished reading to them and they were settled down to sleep and the entire group reformed. They were looking at me again, and so I just shook my head and moved on.

I moved back to our logistical problem with parents of the seven family groups.

Miyuki, how do you imagine your family members on Second Earth would relate to the idea of having surrogate Olarian parents who would be responsible for their children while they were at school on OlarCret?

I don't actually know, Zed, but I imagine they would be delighted, seeing this as a way of ensuring their child was properly looked after! While I cannot actually help you with having a look at these people, I can introduce one of you to the pregnant wife of one of my brothers. I have five of them; I am the only girl, the oldest. Sjyen is 24 and has just announced to the family that she is pregnant. Because of the way these things have been negotiated, her son or daughter will be the next generation's senior member of our entire family.

Everyone around the table was looking at everyone else with a mixture of satisfaction, disbelief and incredulity. With the introduction of Miyuki with her unique knowledge, an apparently insoluble problem appeared as if it might have a workable solution.

Now that we had reached a point from which a solution might indeed be possible, the question on everyone's mind was simple enough: what did we need to do to make certain everyone with an interest got what they needed? In the background was the thought, why had this latest awakening of our brains happened now? What was the significance of the timing of this extraordinary event?

Miyuki was shaking her head. We were all looking at her when she said, 'There seems to be thousands of societies out there with lives we might one day be able to share.'

I let the flood of insights that we had been given filter through everyone's awareness and immediately I knew the Olarians could have access to knowledge that was different in kind and substance and in its very nature to what we considered knowledge to be learned. The education on OlarCret at the ILC would be of a different order to any knowledge we currently possessed.

We became aware that Esan was speaking with his father on OlarCret and Jald as always nowadays was keeping Tanzin connected with the conversation. Their excitement was almost palpable enough to be felt by those of us in the very crowded lounge room.

Esan and Serra looked at me.

Of course.

But Januti shook her head. *Stay there, Zed, I'll get them.*

And she was gone. Seconds later she returned with Jald and Tanzin and in only a couple more seconds they were dressed and sitting with us, but not before Tanzin had given Januti and then me a huge and excited hug. And then another surprising moment in our lives occurred.

Tanzin, who had briefly said hello to Miyuki at their home on OlarCret when she had been, herself, pretty overwhelmed, now for the first time saw Miyuki in our social context and beamed, moving swiftly toward her, then, before she did what she clearly had in mind, she stopped. Miyuki smiled at her and the delight and warmth and connectedness between the two women could be felt by everyone in the room and then without a pause, Miyuki hugged Tanzin and was hugged in return and a very touching and deeply satisfying moment flooded everyone. Tanzin had always really liked and admired Miyuki and the feeling was more than fully shared and a new connection – one that had never been allowed to do more than flicker in the background – now lit up the couple, one of mutual respect, satisfaction, appreciation and warmth. Then, to my surprise, the girls were all clapping with delight and the couple separated, smiling and genuinely flooded with the realization that in this extraordinary environment, 'love was (really) everywhere'.

A week later Donna accompanied by Darcy visited Second Earth where they found and met with Sjyen. The couple had a very satisfactory talk and Sjyen was more than enthusiastic about the possibility that a place such as the ILC could be a suitable place for her child's education.

CHAPTER 31

Time, Rozari & the Heral

During the following year, we finally met the Heral in what I thought of as a genuine meeting. It happened, fortuitously, but not, I realized, accidentally, during a visit the eight of us were making to OlarCret. We had taken Raille, Jess and their two children and were at Olaria's home. Rozari was four. I had picked her up and she had her arms around my neck when she spoke to me telepathically.

Can we visit the Heral now, Dad?

I paused in the conversation I was having with Olaria and Donna. Everyone had heard her and everyone was looking at her, eyebrows raised.

How do you know the Heral, darling? I asked.

Since we first visited them, they have often come and talked to me.

Olaria and I and the rest of us were all staring at her.

When you say they have come and talked to you, Rozari, what exactly do you mean?

She smiled that secretive smile she often did with me. *They know all about you. They often visit and tell me stories about you! They know I can't see you often, so they tell me stories after Mum has put me to bed. If you and Janu bring the others, we can go and see them. Please?*

I paused for a moment. Everyone was looking at us and I shook my head, raised my eyebrows, tilted my head to one side and looked at everyone. Olaria smiled. She knew she could not be involved with these journeys but was very keen for Rozari and me to be. So, when the others all smiled and nodded, Januti curled her fingers around Rozari's hands, the others slid into us and we vanished from Olaria's home.

The journey to the Heral, with the Heral – I do not know how to refer to it – was something else. First, Albor and Felarv met us and they took us to their home. They introduced us to several of the Heral who had come to meet us. They had all known we were coming! They were delighted to hear how Rozari had got us here; that was one part of the story they did not appear to already know! We became engaged in a conversation about themselves and their world.

They were, it turned out, a species not entirely unlike us, and were engaged with a number of other societies in different areas of the cosmos. However, they had a specific role to play in helping only a few of these to move easily through time. We, obviously, were one of them. Why us? I asked the question but realized I was probably not going to get a real answer; they were no more privy to the larger plan than were we. They lived and worked inside quite tight parameters. Their children were, as they grew up, educated in the finer points of travel through time and learned that their role was to work with people who, they were given to understand, needed to learn to do the things that were natural to them.

They were a small society of some ten million individuals and they could not tell us how long they lived, in part because of the time reality in which they lived. However, they had only a small number of children and, again, they did not know how many! Some members of their society ceased to be with them periodically but they apparently did not think of themselves as alive or of those who ceased to be with them as dying or being dead!

Okay, no concept of death, and so no real concept of life! They could only barely comprehend our notion of living and dying even with our best attempts at description and illustration. So, we realized, our framework for thinking about existence and the cosmos was... wrong? Or merely a limiting perspective?

Our experience on Earth and on OlarCret was in itself limiting, our very language led us to closed loops. We all realized we needed either another language and or another set of reference frames if we were to get away from our life-and-death model. In a way, we realized the Olarians might more easily do this, but what variety of thinking, what conceptual framework, would be needed to lose the notion of death and replace it with something qualitatively different?

Okay so far. They had no more awareness than did we about who made the decisions, communicated them or managed the boundaries around who they could assist. But Rozari knew something she could not yet tell us. She tried a couple of times but her grasp of reality was too small and uninformed. However, we knew she possessed something that would, in time, help us understand. For now we learned what we could from the Heral.

They showed us many things. How to more easily freeze and unfreeze time, something we had managed to figure out for ourselves but nowhere near as simply or effectively as they were able to show us. How to control the flow of time and the locations in time where we wished to be. How to speed up and slow down our journeys through time. They taught us the rules about safety in time travel. They could visit a small number of other societies but could not help us to do this. I came to believe that this would happen when Rozari was old enough to open that door and I have no idea why I thought that.

They showed us why we must never again travel through time with others. They did not understand how we and the others had not simply ceased to be, but knew we should never do that again. We accepted that advice, for the sake of others, and I was thinking of Raille and Jess.

It was on this particular day with Rozari that I learned she already knew everything that the Heral had told us. She knew, we came to understand, without being told! Fortunately, at this time in her life she could not go travel to the Heral by herself, which was a relief to us, but I could not help wondering, for how long? Then I would squash that and defer thoughts about it to another time.

There were so many other lessons we had to learn, and this was the first of many visits. During these, it was always Felarv communicating to Januti and Albor sharing with me. It was not until they left and Januti spoke to me or touched me that the floodgates seemed to open and I suddenly understood everything Albor had been saying!

It was during one of these journeys to the Heral that we learned that not only Rozari but my other seven children on OlarCret also spoke with and had connections to the Heral.

◘

I remember the evening Miyuki asked about time travel and we told her about the Heral. She was fascinated, asked some very penetrating questions, only some of which we could answer. Then she made one of those insightful statements that almost take your breath away.

She said, quite innocently, 'So time travel is as if you go to some place and then turn reality through 90 degrees and travel in this other dimension.'

It had been at one of our dinners and at first I thought of it as a clever throwaway remark but later, as I reflected on it, I realized what she had said seemed... right.

And she had continued.

'Can you go forward in time, see events that will happen, and return and discuss them? And if for some reason they make you unhappy, can you return to them or to any other moment in time and influence them so they do not occur as you first saw? And how about going back and changing something?'

I was able to describe how devastatingly consequential changing even a single aspect of the past might turn out to be. However, the big surprise for us had been when the Heral had informed us that of all the groups for which they had responsibility, we were their greatest concern, because we were the only ones who could actually enter time and render changes, and this terrified them. More to the point, they were totally unable to understand how and why we alone could do this.

I can't say this was the first time we had been involved with the ideas that floated around in this domain. We had, when it first came up, visited with the Heral and asked Albor and Felarv. However, they had declined to enter into a discussion of this aspect of their reality. Unlike us, they could not substantively enter any time they visited. They were always ethereal. We, however, were not, and this aspect always concerned them. It turned out, after much questioning, when they returned to their present from any journey with any 'others' they had no memory of what had occurred except with whom they had been and that they had seen something, taken someone somewhere, explained something to someone. We, they assured us again, were the only creatures with whom they were required to engage who remembered what they had seen or heard.

Usually they had no memory! All of which left me wondering if, as they progressed, they may come to be able to do more and remember more of what they did. Felarv was unequivocal about this. The Heral had no plans to learn these things. This knowledge was out of bounds so far as they were concerned. It was not a direction their development was taking them! It was becoming clear to us that there were rules and guidelines, but not who made them or enforced them. Immediately that thought had taken shape all of us knew it was wrong in some particular way. The human perspectives of good and bad, carrot and stick, were in themselves limiting. The emotional valence attached to them was simply inappropriate for the cosmic world, and this was true in a way none of us could yet articulate!

In this regard they could take us no further, however, while we were in Olaria's home discussing one of these adventures, Rozari tugged at my hand and looked intensely at me and said, 'It's okay, Daddy, I will be able to help you when I am older.'

When I asked her what she meant and how she knew, she had no idea. It was just something she knew would be true!

What the Heral had been able to tell us was, outside of time, there were always multiple optional pathways and each had different consequences, but we still could not get a grasp on whether we could influence a future time and if so whether we would know exactly how to do so and what that would ultimately mean. However, the Heral were crystal clear: this was a path to potential cosmic disaster and we should treat our journeys through time with great respect. Failing to do this, they explained, would mean that what was to be would no longer come to be, instead, something else would. And although they did occasionally think of this outcome it did not concern them in the same way it definitely concerned us. It was as though we were exploring our own history and substantive reality.

Well, we did know that interfering in time was something we probably ought to avoid, however, it was more difficult to get a firm grasp on how to think about this. Whatever the future held was of no consequence to the Heral, yet, at the same time, it was!

So, after chewing over Miyuki's question and trying to think about some of the implications of answers to it, we rested that topic. It would be some time before we would be forced to return to it to make a decision that would be anything but inconsequential.

◘

It turned November and it had been decided the Intergalactic Learning Centre would commence its first year during what would be January for us. It happened that at this moment, a pocket battlecruiser, *Genardi*, was making a routine journey to Second Earth ferrying some critical medical supplies when it simply disappeared. This was not known for nearly two weeks until its return schedule was passed and a search and rescue mission was instigated. The fully armed and crewed advanced battlecruiser *Plaxia* was sent to find the *Genardi*.

It was given seven days to undertake the journey. It was using the new Reclin light speed engines and ought to have been able to locate the pocket battlecruiser within two or at most three days and return with its crew, unless they had somehow been destroyed. On day eight SFC was in a near-panic state and Miyuki asked me if I could help.

We communicated in telepathic space so the two of us simply looked as if we were viewing the moonscape beyond Miyuki's office.

Zed, I must apologize for this, but we have just apparently lost two battlecruisers somewhere between here and Second Earth. I have no idea what has happened and the Ultimate Scenario Rescue Plan is the next step, but I am not confident even that will help if we have lost these ships in one of the instantaneous transit zones. I have absolutely no right to ask you to use your incredible capabilities to try to help here, but I do not have an alternative plan. So I thought I would just ask and make clear to you that I will feel no differently toward you if you feel unwilling or unable to help here.

She stopped, embarrassed at having made the request but unsure there was any other possible solution. I looked at her. I knew how difficult this had been for her and how uncomfortable she was in making the request.

Miyuki, Januti is here with us and you will be able to hear her.

At which point Januti's voice joined the conversation. *Miyuki, all of us understand what has happened here. We have agreed unconditionally to help if we can.* She sent a warm and reassuring bundle of energy to Miyuki who acknowledged her and the rest of the eight.

I made my offer. *This is my proposal. It is fraught with uncertainty and unknown risk, nevertheless, if the others agree, we will give it a go. However, the choice must be yours. We could, in a moment, leave you. We would go to my office. We need to be in a room that is not as security sensitive as your office and Ajit and I have heavily modified the security in my office. From there we could visit the Heral from whom we would seek advice. Depending on what they told us, we would decide on the best course of action.*

Miyuki said she would appreciate whatever help we felt able to offer. I told Miyuki that unless something seriously untoward occurred, it was likely we would be back in what, for her, would probably only be a few seconds, and we said au revoir. The security system would see me walking back to my office. Then security would see and hear nothing until I reactivated it, hopefully with less than a second or two of error in the time clocks. If the Heral could find a way to search the wormholes that ought to have been used by the two battlecruisers, we decided we would ask for their help.

Everyone agreed that if the Heral could not or would not help us, we would seek other help in the cosmos. Our biggest concern involved messing with events with the high probability of doing serious damage to life on our and possibly some other planets.

Felarv and Albor listened attentively while I outlined our problem. It turned out they were seriously disturbed by what we were telling them, because they were responsible for the clear tracks through the wormholes that had been created by entities they had never met but who had passed the maintenance task to the Heral. So space, we were beginning to understand, was not some vacant lot. It was inhabited by a variety of species with varying responsibilities toward aspects of its maintenance and organization!

The Heral appeared to have knowledge about what may have caused our problem and asked us if we would please remain at their home while they investigated. We did just that. We think a period of time elapsed before Albor and Felarv and several other Heral returned.

'Your space vehicles are presently trapped in a cylindrical time warp because they were traversing a wormhole that was in the process of being managed, probably reorganized, by the race responsible for their development and non-routine maintenance. We cannot communicate with them and they will not communicate with us, we do not know why. Your two vessels were blocked from exiting the wormholes as they would normally have been able to do by a kind of reorganization that ought not to have been being done if the race responsible had observed the likely traffic inside the wormhole.

'We are not permitted to alter the shape of events through time, however, you are not prohibited. Nevertheless, to repair this situation, you will need to bring both vessels back to moments before the first would have entered the wormhole and ensure the first enters 60 seconds before its return fail-safe date/time. In this case the second will not be trapped, however, given what you will need to do, both vessels and your home base will have no explanation for what has transpired. Without being aware you have played with their timelines, they will simply have an unexplained anomaly. We have examined this situation from every angle and believe if you make this specific intervention, it is likely the only other consequences that will negatively impact the reality in which you will be operating will be associated with the knowledge that the two battlecruisers had been missing. It will, for everyone except Miyuki Khan, be an unexplained set of events.'

The Heral suggestion as we understood it ought to work. The suggestion was logical and seemed likely to enable us to manage the situation with a minimum of fuss and disturbance to events. However, it did make us realize that the *Genardi* crew would not really understand what had happened to them, that is, that they had been trapped in time in the wormhole for the exact number of days that would explain why *Plaxia* had been sent to rescue them. They would almost certainly be totally unaware they had been in a time loop.

This solution, while leaving *Genardi* with an inexplicable problem, might conceivably work to save the vessel and the crew, however, they would actually have no knowledge of the events in which they had been involved.

The plan would mean *Genardi* would exit the wormhole and show a date-time disparity of a number of days during which they ought have been to Second Earth and then returned to Earth, specifically, to Moon Base One. They would in fact have no explanation whatsoever that would account for the discrepancy, and their records – both computer and voice recordings – would not explain anything!

The eight of us knew we were seriously out of our depth, however, in concept, the idea might work to save the two crews and their vessels.

We decided to return to Miyuki. Only I would be visible and we would need to be very careful about the conversation we had and how it might be carried on.

We thanked the Heral, made the time shifts and returned to Miyuki's time and space. I returned to my office and went to visit Miyuki, walking back into her office very shortly after I had walked out and, but for her PA being in the bathroom at that moment, it might have been a bit awkward. I had gone and then come back and in the interim her electronics had gone briefly haywire then immediately I returned they came fully back online, thanks to an invisible Ajit.

Now, if we had done this well, Miyuki and I would actually be seen to be quietly drinking our coffee! It might look as though I had briefly used her bathroom. Unusual but not weird, unlike what was about to transpire. So I began a telepathic explanation to her of what I believed she was going to find out. She raised her eyebrows and in telepathic space she asked what we had done. Lord knows what any security staff looking at the tapes would make of us sitting silently sipping our coffee! However, I began an explanation, hoping she would be able to remember it in real time.

Her two battlecruisers would return shortly. They would have absolutely no idea what had resulted in *Genardi* arriving at Second Earth only seconds before her rescuer! Would have no idea she had lost days of time, and her on-board time and date records would totally fail to account for why she arrived at Second Earth days late with no indication of where she had been. Miyuki was going to have to decide what she would speculate might have happened after I explained what the Heral believed had actually occurred! She might decide to postulate a time warp!

She looked at me, no expression on her face, speaking slowly and telepathically, which she was beginning to really enjoy.

Zed, you, Januti and your friends will have saved the lives of 60 highly trained crew, saved us the unexplained loss of several billion dollars in advanced spacecraft, and saved us from the inexplicable and disruptive loss it would have been. You may well have saved us the possibility that we would need to disrupt all major long-distance space travel for an unknown period of time, and you are sitting with me drinking coffee after a rescue of mind-bending complexity with no expectation of any reward of any kind.

I know I keep telling you how invaluable and generous you and your little family continue to be and how totally delighted I am that you have been willing to include me in it, especially when there is nothing I can do to either compensate or reward you. I feel unfinished. You know I would personally or within the bounds of my organizational remit do anything you asked if I possibly could.

She looked at me with warmth and concern and, I realized, almost with love, not sexual, although I knew that was probably not too far beneath the surface, and I could feel Januti connect lovingly to me with a feeling of almost jealously but without the harsh negatives of that particular emotion. She knew she and I were safe together and she genuinely understood Miyuki's feeling.

Miyuki, you know there is no debt or obligation here. If we can help, we will. It is just the way we are learning to be, no longer solely from the Olarians. You are in no way in our debt or in my debt. Apart from relationships, we do not really need anything. We learned some interesting things from this adventure.

There is a race or a living community of some kind who create and do structural work on the wormholes, and the Heral, who are essentially time travelers, are responsible for the ongoing management of them. I think that actually means maintenance. It is their job. They are aware of users who travel the routes they 'maintain', and it was the accidental mistiming of some structural rearrangement work on the wormhole when Genardi *entered that created the situation. They seem to be unable or unwilling to engage in any kind of intervention with users of their wormholes. That at least is our understanding.*

They were willing to allow us to solve our problem by allowing us to manage time relating to Genardi*'s passage into and out of the wormhole. As you know, there is an astonishing number of intelligent species spotted all over the cosmos. We have only officially met the Heral. As yet we cannot actually contact others, however, we believe Rozari will, as she gets older, be able to help us do that. We have no idea how that will happen or where it might lead. It is certain that mankind is merely one sentient life and we feel strongly that we need to help improve it if we can. We have come to believe we will learn more about how the universe works as time passes.*

I studied the expression on her face. I knew what she was thinking and feeling and I tried to match them up! What we could do excited the hell out of her; she desperately wanted to let us know just how amazing and wonderful she thought us to be, but she also wished she could be part of what we could know and do. She was not jealous, but she was wistful and felt her connection to us to be deeply satisfying.

I smiled at her, nodded, acknowledged that I really did understand how she was feeling and took my leave after we had held a brief discussion about how she would manage this situation without halting future travel through the wormholes. We did manage to come up with a framework for her decision to allow flights to proceed as usual.

CHAPTER 32

The 15th Year of the Intergalactic Learning Centre

Life had settled down after the minor crisis with the *Genardi*. The ILC had begun that year, the year Rozari turned four. It had seemed a young age to send our children to school, which was how we thought of it. Nevertheless, by the time we had been involved in the establishment of the center, we already understood how powerful a force for good the Olarians had created with their learning centers. However, it was actually considerably more than that. The knowledge that Kyuto had gleaned from our experiences had created an entire additional framework of thought that had deepened and extended the Olarian learning system; it had also transformed their ability to engage others in telepathic experience that ensured the recipient remained telepathic, maybe for their lifetime.

Initially we had been afraid that our children would be at risk if they were seen to have abilities others did not and we were concerned about their future on Earth. Within a short time we realized Raille and Jess had a similar concern about Selma and Reggie. Tanzin and Jald had had two children, Jatty and Targe, and both were telepathic and had some telekinetic ability but not anywhere near the capability of the average Olarian child. How, they wondered, would they be able to fit into the world of the Olarians or the world of work in a human community? However, only a few discussions had been needed for the eight of us to realize the Cretians, the children from the seven families on Earth including those from Second Earth, and Raille and Jessiqana's, were all substantially in the same situation. They were not naturally telepathic and none of them were in any way telekinetic. Tanzin and Jald's were in a slightly different situation.

Only the Olarians, our children and the blended families (our term for the children who were partly ours and partly Olarian) were naturally telepathic and telekinetic and capable of the other journeys we had begun, which now seemed long ago. So how would all these children be able to spend their lives? We also now knew something else. There were concepts about the *use* of time that were quite a divergence from the human, Olarian and Cretian one, and even now we could not articulate them, merely recognize they exist.

What was of importance to the eight of us and to our entire 'family' was to know all our children from constant contact every day of their lives and now, as the years passed, we knew we had achieved that. We loved them all and they all related to us openly and honestly over almost everything. However, we knew they also had a more secret life among themselves in which both the Olarians and we did not interfere.

The one deep sadness I alone carried around was my half-sister Marlette. We had been great until she learned I was telepathic. It turned out she was a little telepathic but not at all telekinetic. However, immediately she realized, she closed off all contact with me. She was in her late twenties when she found out and immediately told me she wanted to have no more to do with me. I was clearly an abomination and she wanted me to stay out of her life entirely. She had found and married a man who worked in the State Library with her. He was a religious fundamentalist and they were planning to have a normal family and she was crystal clear: she would not speak of me to others and she wanted nothing more to do with me.

She had taken her husband's name and religious beliefs and wished to remain invisible, did not want to be known to be related to me in any way! And that was the end. She did not want to see me, meet my partner if I ever had one and, in case I should have children, she did not wish to be involved with them. This, she informed me by holo message, was to be the way ahead. She hoped I would respect her wishes and she hoped I would be all right! Several sorties to attempt to change this had brought strong clear responses and I finally realized I needed to respect her wishes! So, with sadness in my heart, I finally put Marlette out of my mind. It had taken some time for Januti and several of the others to get me to feel at peace with Marlette's choices. I suppose, fortunately, she actually had no idea what I had become.

The Olarians believed, from their study of all the children, that only the Cretian children and those of Raille and Jess and the seven families would not be able to live prolonged lives. However, something entirely unexpected had begun to emerge around the time these children reached 19 or 20. It was a completely unexpected phenomenon.

In the beginning the ILC had been constructed as a number of separate learning centers all in the same general geographic location on OlarCret covering a ground area of many thousands of acres in the rolling hills on the continent of Jeland – Jeland because of the need for time zones across the galaxies to suit mainly us Canberrans. During the early years the children – at first from the groups not naturally telepathic, then it spread over about a year through the telepathic and telekinetic children – created an unusual kind of bonding. It was so strong and pervasive by the time the average age at the ILC was around 12 years old that not a single child wanted to take holidays away from the center unless they knew the non-telepathic children were going to be with at least one telepathic friend!

Rozari, now 19, was deeply connected to Olaria, her natural mother; Januti who she referred to as her Earth Mum; and me, to whom she was bound not only because I was her natural father but through ties that none of us really understood. She knew, intuitively and as a result of trying stuff on her own, that her journeys of exploration needed to be done with me. Every new discovery of mine and so of the eight of us had come through her being with me and she had been unable to have more than one or two without me!

So it came as no real surprise that she took me aside one weekend shortly before her twentieth birthday to inform me that she was acting on behalf of the entire Intergalactic Learning Centre community of children and that for more than eight years now they had been discussing the future. It was a topic that had been initially raised by the adult learning staff – they still could not come at being called teachers – but had then been unobtrusively hijacked by the children, all of them! Without the knowledge or involvement of the adults, they had been quietly talking about their future, especially the members of their community who were not naturally telepathic but who now it seemed might conceivably be able to remain telepathic for the rest of their lives. This was still an unknown quantity.

There were 86 children aged between 16 and 20 years old participating in this discussion. The children who had come into the ILC four or five years after the first batch were allowed to participate but mainly were encouraged to listen to the older children unless they had something special to add, and they mostly trusted the 'Originals', which was what the original 86 called themselves!

No-one – none of the Olarians or any of our eight – could understand how they had managed this, but Rozari was telling me that she had organized it and that she had been since her eighth birthday able to screen their telepathic conversations from the rest of the telepathic world.

Wow! was my response on being told. I had not been totally unaware of this organizational arrangement but had simply left them alone, completely alone!

She told me that the only adults who would have been able to penetrate their discussions were me and my eight but given we had not known what to look for, we had not. And, she added, if we wished, we would in future be welcome, as would any Olarians who wished, now the children fully understood that we would never stand in their way. There was something wonderful about their power, openness and trust. Rozari told me it had taken more than a year for the non-telepathic children to trust all the adults enough to allow her to share this information with us.

It was essentially about the children who were not naturally telepathic that they were concerned. And then she told me what they had decided. Before they left the ILC every non-telepathic member of the ILC community would be in a lifelong deeply emotional and sexual partnership with a telepathic and telekinetic partner who would, should it be necessary, keep them telepathic, care for them and ensure they were safe and healthy for the whole of their natural lives.

Rozari, you know I would never try to stop you from doing anything unless I was concerned for your safety. However, you also know, because we have talked about this lots of times, I will always try to understand what you want to do or what you want me to do so that I can feel safe for you and for anyone else involved with us.

She acknowledged immediately what I was saying.

Daddy.

She paused, looked at me in a way she always had and I knew she wanted something important but was either being coy or anxious not to ask in the wrong way. She knew I knew that expression and she smiled at me. It was both loving and just a little puzzled and slightly uncomfortable.

Roze... Roze. You do know that I know you want to ask me something about which you are uncomfortable. I am also certain you know I have never been unhelpful toward you over anything. So this must be very personal?

She smiled at me. *Daddy, I would like to feel that it was comfortable for both of us for me to call you Zed!* She looked at me and into me with all her very considerable intensity, but I blocked her. I could still do that. She smiled. *Very clever, you don't want me to know what you are thinking about that. But why?*

Roze. I need you to talk with me about your thinking and feeling about this.

She looked at me in another way.

Yes Roze, you know you are always free to do that, to try it out, but I would like you to help me understand what is behind your request. I don't mind what you want to call me. You know that I love and cherish you and that I would almost never wish to block you unless I was concerned about your safety. This certainly does not come within that boundary, so what is it exactly that you are wanting to change between us? And yes, the feeling I am screening from you is something between sadness and disappointment that I might have failed to understand you or take care of you in some way.

She smiled and quietly shook her head, emanating concern and love. She had clearly not wished to upset me and was busy trying to find a way to have me understand that she loved and absolutely trusted me and that this was something very personal between us and it was not something she wished to get in between us in any way.

Sometimes I forget how direct, blunt and honest you are with everything, especially interpersonal things. She smiled a deeply satisfied smile. *I am not trying to be devious or clever, and I do not want to disturb the beautiful relationship that exists between us. You absolutely know how much I love you, and if my calling you Zed instead of Daddy was going to disturb rather than enhance our relationship I would not do it. But I feel as though I am wanting you to see me as a person in my own right as well as your little girl, which I will always be no matter how old I become. I think I want you to be okay with me using either so that I can have different kinds of conversation with you.*

I understood immediately and happily responded.

My beautiful girl, you call me what you need and I will understand and of course I will love you unconditionally no matter what.

She smiled, oozed love and satisfaction and threw her arms around my neck as she had done since she was a child, and I loved it and reciprocated as I always had and hoped I always would.

Daddy...

I smiled; the name had not changed but the tone of voice had, to what I'm sure she would have called the Zed voice.

We children have been having these conversations among ourselves for a long time. It has never been that we were wanting to exclude you, more that we wanted to have this conversation among ourselves so we could feel responsible for some part of our future. I think when you dreamed up this idea as a way of protecting our Earth family, you had not thought through all the implications that would exist down the track. Is that true?

I only had to think about that for a moment to know it was.

Yes, we were wanting to have children on Earth because we did not want to desert Raille and Jess and because we had not figured out, at that time, what we might be expected to do with the rest of our lives. We believed we ought to have some responsibility for the state of human life on Earth but we did not want our children born on Earth to be in danger, so, the ILC.

However, the truth is, we had not thought much further down the line at that point. What we were hoping was the non-telepathic members of the ILC would become high-quality leaders of human institutions. That they would influence life on Earth and Second Earth and Cretia in constructive ways.

As I am certain you know, we have been having conversations about how this might all play out ever since. We ought to have realized you would be doing the same. What we could never have planned is the solution you have created, which was, I should tell you, a version of our best fantasy!

Rozari smiled. *I am like you, aren't I?*

I nodded and she continued.

We have created a plan for all of our couples who will live together for the life of their non-telepathic partner. Since you opened the channels across the galaxies, we have been experimenting with what we could do and have found a way for all the telepaths to let someone know when they need help, no matter where they are.

We have also found a society who can modify the brains of our children in order for them to become telepathic, even if they were born of one non-telepathic parent, however, they cannot help us unless you let me introduce you to them so that you can open up the connection they will need with us.

I looked at my daughter, again thinking how alike we were in so many ways and yet how she was also so like her mother.

Have you talked with your mother about this?

No. I have talked to no-one outside our group, because you are the only person we know who will be able to meet this society, which the Heral have identified for me. I am able to see them, but without you and I being together I cannot open a channel between us to seek their help. And I know what you are asking and actually, I really do not know. I did not deliberately not ask you. I think I liked the idea that I might be able to do it on my own, but it seems certain, now, it is important that I do this with you. I think there may be hidden dangers of which I might be unaware.

And there it was.

Rozari, I would like us to pick up Januti and the others and talk this over with your mum. Are you okay with that?

Of course she was. Olaria was only a little surprised; she had suspected the children had found a way to have their own conversations free of the adults – nearly every group of Olarian children since the Originals had found some way to do that, she informed us! Then Rozari called in several of her friends and they were delighted to see us. We knew all of them and they were entirely unembarrassed and comfortable that Rozari had drawn us in. They had seen the Irawars but like Rozari could not communicate with them without my involvement and were delighted that I was now involved.

They had found what little they had been able to pick up from their journeys to the edge of their world very hard to understand. Also, although the others knew Rozari was in contact with the Heral, and that Felarv often communicated with her, and that the other Olarian and our mixed children could all participate, none of them could visit the Heral or travel through time. Rozari knew that this would not happen until they were ready to travel with me. She also knew there were safety concerns that hedged this kind of travel, concerns they could neither influence nor cross over. So I was their doorway, and they were without exception willing to await my judgment on what would be safe for them.

The next step did not occur in any expected way. Around mid-year Albor made a heretofore unexperienced connection with me and Januti.

It happened one evening at our apartment in Canberra. The moment he arrived the other six of us appeared. Albor was traveling with Felarv as a single entity and it seemed the consciousness of a member of the Irawars! He/they sat and told us they were here mostly at the instigation of the Irawars who were both present and not present and that was the extent of the ability of the Heral to give us information about them! Our children had been journeying to the edge of their ...lands... the boundary word had no equivalent in any of our languages. They knew the children were seeking help to modify the brains of the non-telepathic children in their school or of future children they might have. They were familiar with the center. They were sympathetic.

The Irawars would be able to communicate with them if we were present, however, they had examined all the children and realized that with the non-telepathic ones, they were not permitted to interfere. The most they were prepared to do was, for this generation of ILC graduates that were a couple, one of whom was fully naturally telepathic, guarantee the natural children of such a couple would be telepathic but not telekinetic. They wanted us to understand that should they attempt to go further, the child would die.

With my agreement they would take care of the partners of telekinetic telepaths who had been educated by the Olarians. That was the limit of their willingness and ability to meet Rozari's wishes. It turned out this was already at the extreme edge of what they were actually capable and permitted to do without harming the universe's 'Guide for the Management of Species'.

They either could not or would not explain further and that was as far as we could go. They did not believe they should involve us either in their lives or their history and for the moment bade us farewell and vanished – vanished in a fashion that made further access to them without the Heral seem to be impossible. I thought that may be true, yet I also felt, should I really desire it, the eight of us might be able to influence them. It was an itch that I felt we may be able to scratch!

The eight of us sat there and absorbed the information we had been given. Sometimes when we had an intellectually complex message like this I felt as though I had scrambled eggs for brains! We were being nudged and prodded, pushed and edged in a variety of ways by both our children and the communities of the cosmic world in a fashion we only vaguely comprehended.

What I now believed, on the basis of no more information than we presently had, was that we needed to help our ILC graduates to work with human limitations and to understand the nature of the human and Cretian economic cultures. At some point in this discussion we were told about the work that was actually already being done at the ILC to educate all students about the nature of economics. So, for the moment, I was satisfied to try to clean up our corner of the galaxy in whatever ways we could.

Humans were warlike and as such unacceptable to the galactic community. Until this quality no longer existed on Earth, humankind would be unable to make contact with any other species. I mulled this over a lot. Raille and I had dreamed up a method of disarming the Cretian world and it seemed not unlikely they would, at some time in the future, be possibly acceptable members of the galactic community, as it was now evident the next generation of Olarians would probably be. The Olarians had been not drawn into the wider cosmic community while the Cretians had been an armed and militaristic culture; it seemed that cohabiting on a planet with a violent race was an unshakeable impediment! Our intervention had begun to put an end to that! Raille and I had, with the Olarians, been responsible for that. However, I could not understand why I seemed to be being made the gatekeeper.

I had a hunch. It was seemingly nonsensical, but I was unable to let it go. So, while sitting in my office on Moon Base One, I stretched out to find Rozari. She found me in an instant and asked if I wanted her to come to my office. She knew that would frighten the security system. Initially I had planned to ask her to come to our apartment in Canberra with her seven siblings and the rest of our Olarian family, which was no small number. However, I realized after a second or so that the number was way too large for our living room so suggested she tell us where the best place for us to have a meeting might be.

She chose the ILC common area. I told her a little intergalactic travel was on my mind. I suggested she should invite anyone she thought appropriate. I explained that we might actually go traveling. She understood, hesitated for only a second, then said it was okay for the non-travelers to be with us. They were aware of their limitations and untroubled by them. I did actually understand what she was telling me. I knew the limitations that would always bother a normal human and, I guessed, a Cretian did not bother this generation from the ILC because those limitations were probably intertwined with the life they all had experienced at the ILC.

So we made a date for 7pm. I remembered to ask if she wanted everyone to eat before they arrived or did she want a kind of interesting eclectic meal for everyone? She laughed. I caught her thought, and I realized the eight of us had never thought to explore a method for bringing 'stuff' when we made intergalactic jumps, given that we always shed our clothes, but they had, and they had with help from the Heral learned a way to do that! I immediately collected the pattern; it was, in retrospect, obvious! Rozaria and her travelers brought Selma, Reggie, Jatty and Targe, even although those four would never be able to do the journeys. They had become, in some surprising but very satisfying way, an important and significant part of the intergalactic travelers' family.

Okay, I could live with that. This generation was making their own rules and none of the eight of us thought it appropriate for us to interfere with that. So when we had chatted, eaten and socialized, because we liked to keep our connections with them as rich as possible, they all looked at me. They knew I had an agenda, however, before I could say anything Rozari and one of her half-brothers asked me for help with a project they had been working on with the Heral for almost a year.

It was a project that could only be brought to a conclusion with my agreement, and they knew that meant the eight of us, and then my willing participation which would be necessary to make it actually possible. The other six of our eight were simply shaking their heads.

Rozari was the spokesperson.

Zed, the Heral, Albor and Felarv, have negotiated on our behalf with the Irawars for a once-only transformation for Selma, Reggie, Jatty and Targe. Now, before we outline what I believe we have negotiated, I am hoping you will be okay with one of us bringing Jald and Tanzin and Jessiqana and Raille to join us, if they are willing.

They were unmistakably excited and a little nervous, but they were quite definite about what they wanted. Did they want Miyuki? Without hesitation we got a yes. They had taken to Miyuki in a fashion we did not fully understand but with which we were delighted. We were almost as curious about what was going to unfold as they were hopeful that we would go along with them.

Given that none of us had ever done more than ensure they were safe and able to develop whatever they needed, they really had no cause for concern, yet they certainly did have on this occasion. I added Miyuki to Rozari's list and she was immediately willing. I also asked about the Second Earth and other human children from the seven families who I had not seen.

We are here, Zed.

I looked around through the mob and immediately saw them.

Okay, I was just missing you. My apologies.

In an instant they made it clear that none was needed. They knew we included them in the ILC mob and had never in any way excluded them from anything. They too absolutely trusted us, loved us and knew they were loved by us in return.

We said yes, of course, and two of the group disappeared, one with Selma and Reggie and the other with Jatty and Targe. A few minutes passed and Natalya had twigged as to how they were keeping us at bay and the eight of us realized immediately we could have bypassed the tricky maneuver they had created so that we would not know what they had in mind.

The eight of us could see their machinations, but outside their awareness, and we agreed not to interfere. Within a few more minutes the travelers returned, each with a set of parents who were immediately pleased to be with us and intrigued at the assemblage!

Tanzin spoke first, telepathically as was now her most common way.

If I have got this right, the ILC mob have hijacked the parental mob? Smiles and chuckles around the room. *So let me just say how pleased I am that we have been invited into this clearly very targeted soiree.*

The tone of her hello and the expression on her face made it clear that within a nanosecond of her arrival she had accurately assessed something of the essential nature of this gathering, as was her way. Surprising her was something very few people had ever been able to do. She might not have the subject matter, but she certainly had the nature of the meeting into which she had so willingly been inveigled, maybe just invited.

She was so obviously delighted she and Jald had been invited. Her smile almost set the room aglow and her children looked at her with love and pleasure. Raille and Jess were smiling and nodding. Both were connected fully telepathically into the group and they immediately understood what the eight of us had found, however, none of us was going to disturb our children or their plans. So, as Rozari seemed to have been nominated spokesperson, I looked questioningly at her.

Hm... I am intuiting that our plans and intentions may have been rumbled. At which point I burst out laughing. But Rozari was looking at me intensely. *You're blocking me, aren't you?* she asked. *We haven't actually outmaneuvered you at all. You know what we are meeting here for?*

I looked at her with sheer delight. *I love it that you have come within a hair's breadth of outmanoeuvring us. But all of you being so carefully cautious with what you were thinking kind of gave the game away. But we have all refrained from exploring what you have so far not told or asked us! So, as you intended, the floor is yours.*

They looked at me, then at the rest of us, then at each other, and I realized there was a tiny edge of anxiety, or perhaps concern was a better word, that there might be hazards attached to their plans that they did not know to look out for. Given what they were playing with, I thought they might well be right, however, we, as yet, did not know what hazards there might be, so we listened and Rozari continued.

We have found a way for the non-telepathic members of our little society to be safe for the rest of their lives. It involves a partnership arrangement that suits and protects them and will allow them to become engaged in resolving some problems that plague the non-telepathic world. And, for the course of their natural life, everyone will be able to be looked after as they engage with the kinds of change we know are needed.

The majority of us have a sound and, we believe, quite sophisticated grasp of economic theory and practice currently in use by the non-telepathic human and Cretian worlds. What concerns us is the possibility that some of our couples will want to have children. Also, some of those children could be born without telepathic capability, and as a result they will continue on in a tradition that may not be useful or satisfying for them.

As you know the Heral have introduced us to the Irawars who can ensure all children born to our non-telepathic couples will have telepathic ability, however, not telekinetic ability. We do not fully understand why, and they are unwilling to tell us why. The Heral have also assured us that all future generations of these couples will bear telepathic children!

I quietly checked around our little group of eight, then spoke.

We can tell you why.

Rozari looked at me, but this time I was deliberately blocking her. I let her know I thought it was best if I tried to take the next step my way. She immediately, willingly, gave me the floor.

This is a very big issue to the cosmic world. We have understood it for only a short while. So let me explain. At one level it is very straightforward. Every form of interpersonal violence is totally unacceptable to the cosmic world. No species that is violent in any way – permits violence or sanctions it in any form – may be connected with the cosmic community.

By a happy choice, Raille and I were involved in disarming Jess's society, and we have subsequently learned through the connections of the Heral this has meant the Cretian world, if it continues on this path and eschews violence, may at some time be invited into the cosmic community, as the Olarians now certainly will be through your generation. However, the human world, what the eight of us think of as our world, has, sadly, taken no steps whatsoever to deal with the issue of central concern to the cosmic community.

All communication with the cosmic community is premised on the absence of violence. It is for this reason that several members of the cosmic community are confused about the eight of us who ought to be ranged alongside the human world but clearly are not. The eight of us, and so many of you, our children, are somehow not connected to the human world from which we believe we came, and somehow Raille, Tanzin and Miyuki are seen as connected to the eight of us, as are Jald and Olaria and Jess, which until very recently we did not understand.

As soon as we realized we were being given access to the cosmic community, we realized there must be more things about ourselves we still do not know. In our few engagements with the cosmic world, we have found some unexpected and so far inexplicable things. We have been allowed to break some of the rules without the usual consequences. For example, we have taken Jess and Raille on one of our time trips and this is apparently totally prohibited.

My 1000-year-old self has been permitted to talk to my present-day self, also absolutely prohibited, yet we survived. There are some other examples. So we imagine that somewhere up the hierarchy of the management of species and societies, someone is looking out for us in some unusual way, because the Heral, whose job it is to manage and help other species manage time travel, cannot understand how we have been permitted to survive.

There was silence around the group. Everyone was looking at me. I felt as though I must have grown two heads. Finally Olaria, who Rozari had gone to get, spoke, looking directly at me.

I have somehow been told I can now say this. She looked both a little puzzled and somewhat surprised. *When your little probe arrived in our solar system many years ago now, we were told, and do not ask me how, because I really don't know, to look out for you, Zed. We were specifically told in some way I cannot even explain or fully comprehend. Somehow, it was communicated to us that we needed to look out for you and we had no idea who or what we were being told to look out for.*

It only became apparent to me, intuitively, that it was you I was supposed to look out for and I know it is true, because I was irresistibly drawn to you the moment I saw you on Sunstreamer, *and I have never known why. And don't get me wrong, and my apologies, Januti, but I did indeed find him irresistible, I believe as do you?*

In that instant it was definitely unambiguous; she looked at me and I knew what these two beautiful women were saying was true.

Rozari looked at me, smiling.

So, Zed, we wish you to take us, your eight and all your children, to the Heral, and then to the Irawars, and seek their agreement to have the children of all our mixed couples bear children who will all be telepathic. And do whatever else they are permitted to do with us regarding our telepathic abilities and whatever is needed to ensure everyone is enabled to bear telepathic children. We know that cannot include telekinetic abilities and we know the Irawars are either unwilling or unable to tell us why.

We believe this will free their telepathic and telekinetic parent when their partner finally dies – ceases to exist in this reality. We know there will be consequences in future generations but have decided we do not wish you to look into that future yet, please. Although we know we will be able to and you are able to actually do that, and the Heral have told us that you can cross that boundary should you think it wise and safe. We realize there must be significant risk in doing this and have agreed we will not do it without discussing any such plans with you first.

I beckoned to Rozari and she came over. I did not need to speak. She sat on my lap and put her arms around my neck. Then the room altered slightly and the representative of the Irawars arrived with Felarv and Albor and whispered in my ear and then vanished. The next moment Rozari was back in her seat and as usual they were all looking at me. This time, however, I did understand why. Januti took my hand and in a second my mind cleared and I knew.

The Irawars have agreed, this once, Rozari, as you suspected, apparently because I asked. Now, I say this in the way a human would say it. Trust me. This procedure has never, ever, been allowed before, and we are talking billions of our years! Way, way before even our solar system had been brought into existence. The Irawars have pleaded with me never to ask again and requested you do not seek such an arrangement ever again.

Our children were ecstatic, we were pleased, but the real message from the Irawars I found astonishing. It had been delivered directly to me in the tone of their response. It had been a form of plea, directly and explicitly to me! Januti and the others had got it, the children had not. The Irawars were desperately hoping I would not seek to do this again. They briefly explained that they were obliged to meet my requests, and I was content to let that rest for now.

CHAPTER 33

Rozari & Zed, Other Powerful Cosmic Entities & Issues

Some months passed as the eight of us slowly extended our capabilities and powers, and sometimes I would sit in my office on Moon Base One and wonder what we were doing. Coincidentally and not because anyone had asked, Raille and I knew during this period that either of us could easily have won the Mixed Martial Arts world title, however, neither of us really had any desire to be associated with the world of competitive martial arts! We both felt our practice was an exercise in physical, mental and spiritual ecology. Our partners were actually the only people who understood. They had watched us work out on several occasions and felt a sense of satisfaction in our way of going about our practice, both knowing it was not actually competitive in any real way but was essentially about relationship, art and ecology.

We were both asking one question: to what should I be paying attention? As I returned to this theme again and again I knew it seemed to have more significance than I was able to grasp. And then, in that moment I realized we continued in our practice because although it was, essentially, a violent activity that ought to have been totally unacceptable and at worst guaranteed us exclusion from the cosmic world communities, it was not that for us. And certainly, it was not being seen that way, we knew, because I was still acceptable to them!

The answer was, as was so often the case for us, counter-intuitive. We were actually non-combative. Our practice was an art form, but also a discipline and a personal management system. So it was about getting and managing self-control.

In the midst of one of these meanderings I became aware of Rozari seeking my attention. *Zed!*

I sat up and focused. This was not my daughter's usual manner of connecting to me.

Okay, Roze, you got my attention.

I would like to go traveling.

I slid my mind out to OlarCret where she was sitting alone high on a peak above Jald and Tanzin's home. The view was not unlike untouched parts of the Amazon forests.

Is there some significance in this beautiful and breathtaking view?

Immediately I knew there was.

Daddy! I don't know why, but, I do know that now is the moment!

I stopped what I was thinking and sought clarity on what was going on in her head, but for some inexplicable reason I could not.

Are you intentionally blocking me?

My question was, as always, couched in plain curiosity, no barbs, no hidden meanings. She smiled.

Oh fabulous, I have been practicing hard and I know you will be able to bypass me but I am pleased with myself.

I smiled, thinking almost nothing she could do would really distress me unless I thought she was in danger. I knew she was not.

Okay, if you are sure right now is important?

I hesitated. Was she just testing me or did she want/need to go traveling? She needed me to go with her – now! Puzzled, I realized there was only one way I could meet her request. Before I froze time in my office on Moon Base One, I was about to ask my PA to hold any calls, then realized how absurd that was! I mean, I would be gone for no more than one or two seconds!

So I froze time in my office and made the jump to Rozari. As always, she threw her arms around my neck and the world around us shimmered in a fashion to which I was now familiar. We went first to the home of Felarv and Albor, who, as always, were expecting us. They chatted with Rozari for a few moments, were friendly and welcoming to me, then looked expectantly at Rozari.

I don't know, was all she was able to say.

So they turned and looked at me. *It's not time through which you want to travel, is it?*

I really did not know, then I did. Felarv looked at me enquiringly and I in turn looked at Rozari.

Are you sure you do not want me to bring the others?

But Rozari shook her head and I wondered why specifically she wanted or needed to do this with me alone.

Felarv merged with her as I became aware that Albor joined me, then we were no longer on the world of the Heral.

Memory?

The voice was Albor's and I saw Rozari nod. Then we were somewhere else. I knew we were shifting in time and space, visiting worlds that had a vague sense of familiarity, six of them, and then we were back with the Heral, said goodbye to Felarv and Albor, and then I was sitting with Rozari above Tanzin and Jald's home. Rozari hugged me, kissed me lovingly on the cheek and promised she would see me tonight with our extended family due to meet at our place. She promised to bring Olaria, Miyuki, Tanzin and Jald, and we said goodbye.

Back in my office, I unfroze time and promised Januti I would tell all, when whatever all *that* was had caught up with me.

◘

That night, Raille and Jess were the last to arrive, but then Esan and Serra asked if it was all right if they came to dinner. They had picked up the human pattern and were using it with us, while we had adjusted to the Olarian pattern and assumed they would come to dinner if they felt comfortable doing that. For us, the Olarians were quite universally family. Whenever we met one we had not met before, they seemed to always know us and it never took more than a few moments for a deep, warm, intimate connection to be made.

Their courtesy and awareness around interpersonal space guaranteed they would never behave insensitively, would pretty well never fail to take cognizance of any situation into which they might be moving. However, I should not make this seem one-sided; whenever we did meet someone new we immediately felt welcoming and in an instant we were able to know who they were and we never really came to understand how that happened. We had always assumed it was an act of theirs, but Rozari pointed out to me that it was not; it was a deliberate act of ours, some kind of intuitive awareness that never failed to feel satisfying.

Again, it was in the first few moments after I arrived home when Januti took me in her arms and I had buried my face in the rich softness of her hair that the full meaning of my time with Rozari and the Heral tumbled into place. It left me smiling and wondering what part Rozari had played in my little adventure. In the few seconds that had been involved in my awareness catching up with me, Januti and the others had understood my journey.

We said hello to Miyuki, Jess and Raille, who all were immediately aware of their telepathic connection. The Olarians, any of the eight of us or Rozari could set up the non-telepaths with full access to telepathic reality instantly now we understood the mechanics of that process.

As we sat down to eat, the others realized something had occurred that was claiming the attention of the eight of us and Rozari. I felt the need to talk about it.

At 3.30pm today Rozari asked me to go on a journey with her. Neither of us actually knows the source of the urge. So I froze time in my office and joined her on the rise above your home.

I was looking at Tanzin and Jald.

She was sitting on that rock way above your delightful eyrie that allows an uninterrupted view of the forest that stretches in every direction. Her urge took us to the Heral where Felarv and Albor were, as usual, expecting us. They joined with us and took us on a journey to six planets in different solar systems spaced all over the cosmos, then brought us home to OlarCret, to your eyrie, and said goodbye. I did not at that time have any idea what I had just learned, nor apparently did Rozari, although we both knew it would become clear.

It did when Januti met me at the door to say hello; the entire experience fell into place.

It was precisely at that time I got it as well, Zed.

Everyone looked at Rozari, but Natalya, Ai and Donna all just smiled. I looked at them, remembered a very, very old film I had seen recently on holo that I had enjoyed again, *The Witches of Eastwick*.

I screwed up my face to look fiercely at the three of them. *That is definitely you.*

So, beware Zed, we are brewing our spells.

All three laughed. Rozari and Januti shook their heads and the others around the table looked from them to me for an explanation.

It is really not very complicated, I said. *Those three were just reminding me that often when we go on an entirely new learning journey, especially with*

Felarv and Albor, I only really find out what happened when Januti connects with me and at that moment the entire message or experience simply falls fully fashioned into my consciousness. As you know, this is not the first time.

This time I seem to be getting a very specific message. All six worlds I was taken to see, which I now know I can revisit at will, have had a sentient population whose behavior was responsible for their extinction, in some cases many thousands and in three cases many millions of our years ago.

I believe I was given some images that help me understand what went wrong. All these worlds died from some form of resource stripping. They all bred too many people, seemed unable and or unwilling to manage the number of people on their planet. Sound familiar? The populations used all their natural resources or failed to maintain the level of natural resources necessary for their survival, however, the significant thing was that none of them had developed space travel to the degree that would allow them to travel to other solar systems. The human world, our world, has succeeded in doing this and that distinguishes us from the six worlds I saw today.

However, today we are growing the trees that the planet needs to create the atmosphere, re-establishing the ice caps and re-establishing the ocean levels, cleaning CO2 and re-establishing the levels we require for our survival. Somewhere in the deep recesses of my mind, I believe I have the ability to find out how each of these worlds created this destructive pathway, but it is at present just out of my reach. The interesting thing about the human reality is that humans have solved the problem of interstellar travel and we have done it on our own, I think.

However, dealing with the greed and the violence and the lack of sensitivity to one another, specifically overcoming the violence that is so much a part of the underlying pattern of life on Earth, is not yet possible. At this point not even conceivable. Part of my real concern is that I feel as though being non-telepathic might have something to do with this, because without telepathy people do not know what others are thinking or feeling and this makes misunderstandings and relationships more difficult to manage.

I stopped, overwhelmed by a sense of frustration at my inability to see a way through. I added to myself, 'Yet'.

CHAPTER 34

Miyuki & the Original OlarCret Mob

Miyuki spoke briefly at one of our soirees about the projects her original cadre of OlarCret visitors had started on their return, one of which included re-afforestation and another a pilot project in southern Asia seeking a population reduction target of 1.5 children per family over 20 years.

They have reached their target! Right at the 20-year mark!

The re-afforestation project is still meeting road blocks, into which our Project Protection Committee has had to intervene in four countries. In each case the logging community has needed help to see that their activities would result in the demise of their own families. They have needed a considerably extensive aid program to enable them to finally become supporters of the project; at present, employment and income replacement programs are proving successful.

However, it seemed unlikely sufficient land would be reclaimed in a short enough period of time to repair the global damage. So the group sought help in finding other solutions from people in many countries, and very quickly a 'Re-afforestation in My Backyard' program began to bite with many millions of voluntary subscribers from every continent participating.

An ever-increasing funding base was established to help with the purchase of the necessary trees. And on every continent 'planting parties' are being held with the active support of social media. It has turned out that they have done and are still doing some amazing things to re-afforestate areas that have been denuded of trees. This includes many areas that were farmland and now are not needed as farms any longer. Many areas had to deal with the issue of bushfire and huge progress has been made in reducing the fires, but the biggest came when we were able to add some programming to several of the key layers of global sats so they now report any outbreaks and automatically activate suppression bombing of the fires.

The result has been that no bushfire has burned out a property or been responsible for loss of life for more than 10 years. And, because we can observe anyone deliberately starting a fire almost anywhere on the Earth's surface, the number of arson-related fires has dropped to less than 10 across the world in any single year.

An ingenious program was first trialed and then begun in earnest by a now cohesive collection of major food product suppliers managed by Pierre Bizet, CEO of Euro World Foods. This is now supported by a majority of food management organizations from around the world. Pierre, by the way, is still CEO, but is planning to step down when he has a replacement who will definitely continue his program!

In countries with high family numbers – five to nine per family – a guarantee of food stability was offered if their family, firstly, did not increase in size, and then their children gave an undertaking to have families that did not exceed three children.

Because of the amount of support and engagement they generated, and at first because we could actually monitor their family size and the community support being given by political and familial leaders, it looked as though it might work. Then it did, and those families were guaranteed economic and food survival if they met their family size targets.

Already population numbers in the major political and economic powerhouses are at historically low levels. One of the groups still being run by Cadrin, with Eira Lin supporting him – perhaps I should say that the other way around! – is looking at other economic incentives and new opportunities for their children in one or two of the highest population countries.

As a result, it seems pretty certain that the visitors to OlarCret returned full not just of good reports but of a real zeal to be actively involved in creating change. You might imagine the large families would readily cheat and have more children, believing, rightly, we would not remove their incentives, however, that is not what is actually happening. And it does seem the world population is almost static and will show a very slow decrease over the coming decades, which I will probably not live to see reach completion.

Well, that's the good news.

I spoke up.

We have an issue of our own which is about to require attention, at least for me. I am noticeably younger than I ought to look, so each day, as a part of getting ready for work, I do a minor shapeshift so my age and appearance look as they ought to; Januti usually actually manages that. So in the interests of maintaining our invisibility I have spoken to Miyuki and told her that I plan to leave SFC at the end of this year. I will pose it as an intent to follow some other interests.

Now I know I could continue to use the mild shapeshifting that has worked for me up to this point, but it is really a drag doing it each day. I would much prefer not to have to do it. So I think it feels right that my time with SFC is about up. It is also a threat that hangs around when I am home and not aged.

No-one was disagreeing and when I looked at Miyuki, she smiled her complete agreement. So I continued.

Miyuki herself is planning to resign during the next year. She has already been the head of SFC far longer than anyone ever imagined.

Raille and Jess, as well as Miyuki and Tanzin, are being assisted to almost perfect health by a team on OlarCret. I will call them our medical team. They assure me the four of them will live healthy lives for many decades to come. So they will remain in their positions probably for...?

I turned to look at them. It was Jess, with her beautiful smile, who answered.

Probably, Zed, about a decade will see us through this job. However, because of the help you give us, we are the best informed academics in the world over events on other planets. No-one wants us to cease. At least, not yet.

I should probably add, we have over the years had to fend off numerous attempts to have us reveal our sources regarding our interplanetary information. Early on, Raille found a delightfully evasive way of not responding to enquiries, but at the same time, people are intensely curious about Olarian and Cretian life. And there is continuously serious curiosity about the aspects of different societies that result in relationships between members of those societies being satisfying, especially sexual behavior. I don't think we have had a single session over the years where the subject of sexual pleasure and violence and the nature and quality of sexual life for societies on OlarCret have not been raised.

And so it was that our family meeting drifted on through more sharing and catch up until it was time for everyone to go home.

CHAPTER 35

The Cretians, the ILC, Violence & Economics

A few weeks later we were on Jeland at the request of the ILC senior group. They had invited the eight of us plus Miyuki, Tanzin and Jald, Raille and Jess, and their Olarian parents: in short, a pretty big mob.

Some of the senior ILC group were planning the next stage of their lives.

They had a pretty clear understanding about the eight of us and our involvement with them. Most of them, from all three planets, were preparing to move on from the ILC. Most were in their early twenties – young for an Olarian to be moving on from school, but not, it was turning out, for an ILC graduate. They all knew we were involved in an all-or-nothing game involving three planets whose populations might together join the cosmic community – *together* was the key word, otherwise none would be invited. We were pretty certain that was the situation we were all in. All or none. So in this room there was no misunderstanding of the stakes for all of us.

Zed.

I turned to look at the speaker. One of the older girls, Quianna. She was beautiful, one of the GeGhans, a lot like Jess. Willowy, strong and smart.

We all understand that the key issue is violence. We also believe, like you, that money, an economic reality, may be underlying or at least deeply connected with attitudes toward aggression. The question for all of us at the ILC is simply what contribution can we meaningfully make toward this end?

None of us have been able to figure out how to remove the economic reality of a world using money, although most of us now do really understand the Olarian way. However, we have not been able to figure out how to remove money from the human system. The Cretian system, perhaps because it is slowly becoming a female-run world, is beginning to undertake a conversion to an Olarian style of survival. And it seems likely the Cretian world might be an intermediate step in removing money and the trappings of a money-oriented, economically managed world! This seems to be being linked to the shift toward a genuinely matri-focal society.

I know you are not putting us down, Zed. I know you well; I have learned to trust you absolutely since I was a small child. I know you are genuinely loving and kind. I feel as though I am your daughter. Jess long ago helped me understand how you are seeking to get the three societies to a point where they will be acceptable to the cosmic community.

I do really want to help and I would like to lose the slight feeling of inferiority I feel as a result of my people being non-telepathic and needing help from one of your direct family or the Olarian contingent. Aunty Jess, I know that you and Sel have found a way to be at peace with our limitations, and we have been able to maintain our telepathic connection because of the generosity of other non-Cretian friends.

Zed, you know that Aziq and I are together and so I am now, really, your daughter-in-law by human thinking, and I do actually know that you are also someone else, more powerful than I can even imagine, and I know Aziq, who I truly adore, will stay with me for my short life. But I would like to feel independently useful while I am here, so I have asked Aziq if he would be willing for us to live together with Piquant and Sel close to the GeGhan compound. Both he and they have agreed.

We will work with them and the women of other clans toward finally doing away with money. The economic bits and pieces that we have seen are essentially not helpful in the life of our people. I believe you know that all of the Cretian mob, both genders, are pleased to see our world becoming matriarchal without any punitive or nasty anti-male overtones, and that other Cretian women who are part of our ILC mob have been crystal clear they want to join in. Want to work toward a truly violence-free and money-free Cretia. I just felt today I wanted to tell you, wanted you to know.

The feeling in the room was deeply satisfying and supportive. I don't really know why I was in the slightest surprised. I also knew that Aziq would turn out to have more abilities and power than he yet knew.

Quianna, I have known you since you were very young and I am pleased to hear you say the things you have said. I want to say some things to you, and to some of the others who must, at some level, feel a little down, knowing they will live short lives by comparison with the Olarians. You need to know that we have talked a lot about longevity, and we have spoken a lot about death and life – what it is, how long it lasts, what the consequences might be. So I have something to say to you and all those others of you from Earth and Cretia and Second Earth who must also have had such thoughts.

We do not know for certain, but it is now our belief that life and death may be a bit trickier than is obvious on the surface. First, we are pretty certain death is not an end – it is merely a transition from one state to another across the cosmic communities.

We believe death by violence disturbs the equanimity of the cosmic community and that this, among other things, is one of the reasons communities that are violent are unacceptable to the cosmic world.

Death is not more, really, than an ending of one situation before the beginning of another in the societies of the cosmic worlds. This is of course no more than an intuition, however, we have reason to believe it may not be an intuition that is actually awry. So, no matter how long or short a life, what you do with it may be the central issue.

Consequently, comparisons are probably unhelpful, especially invidious ones. Short or long, one may not be better than another, we don't know. We have come to believe that it is what you do – and we have thought this for ourselves, the eight of us – that really counts and that is what is worth focusing on. What really matters, we have thought many times, is the quality of everything you do, all the time. So everything is managed by perspective.

She and Aziq, who had caught my eye as I spoke, smiled, and I could feel the satisfaction that flowed smoothly between them and knew they understood.

So I felt free to move on.

What we have so far been unable to engage with has been the de-weaponising of Earth or Second Earth and managing a change in the warlike, intemperate and uncontrolled behavior, without which the human race will never be admitted into the family of cosmic communities. They will never move beyond contact with the Olarians and the Cretians and within a century or two they will be even more isolated as these two societies themselves seem likely to eventually be able to become members of the cosmic community. However, our hunch is they will be being held back by the human condition.

Thing is, as most of you know, we believe we are in some way responsible for ensuring that all three societies are ready to become members of the cosmic world together! We have intuited that it might be an all-or-nothing deal. I think that is why it has been set up with us, from Earth, being the initiators! We believe we need to get the human race up to the starting gates, quite possibly in everybody's interests.

Without us, they would have no way to understand that it is their unconstructive attraction to violence that is for all of us our Achilles heel. We can see how the process of removing weapons has begun to change the Cretian society. It is still not something humanity has learned. I believe it may be connected to, entwined even, with economics/money, something the Olarians have managed not to do. To the human observer this makes Olarian society beautiful and seductive but incomprehensible. So, Quianna, everyone who understands and works toward these ends is making a significant contribution toward all our futures.

It was at this point that the evening needed to come to an end, unfinished as it was, to enable everyone to be functional for work tomorrow, so we said goodnight. It had been a particularly interesting get-together and we knew it would almost certainly be the precursor of the next phase of change. We were also aware that many of the human members of our community were uncomfortable with much of what had been said.

◘

When the eight of us returned to our place in Canberra, everyone wanted to carry the discussion on a little further.

What if we could find a way to have the world choose to free itself from money and greed?

How?

Darcy was seriously curious. He had no solution in mind but did have some interesting ideas.

Suppose we were able to make the market, the economic world, globally dysfunctional? It nearly happens each time there is a major global pandemic. Each time, so far, the economic world has been pulled back from the edge by a series of fiscal measures, which have on each occasion involved the cancelling of debt and the refinancing of the small-business sector.

On the last occasion, the small-business sector was more than halved in size. The larger half was reconstituted by two of the seven families into a kind of interconnected market, free of all debt, and it was the cancelling of debt to the individual small businesses that made the whole thing viable. Now, the original small-business owners all own part of their business together with the conglomerate that supports them and manages their legal and financial structures, including their insurance, accounting, taxation and pensions.

It has stabilized a large portion of global small business, and we are both astonished and pleased to be able to report it has not become corrupt, nor has rampant greed torn it apart. At least, not to date! The truth is, they are actually no longer small businesses, but the language and the marketing have almost entirely hidden this.

We have also, because we find the sector so deceitful and grubby, found ways to slowly discredit the insurance sector and help individuals and groups who have been part of it find alternative options for their talents. We have, as a result, almost eradicated the entire industry and plan to continue the process we have begun until the sector disappears.

We estimate no more than four or five more years should see it disappear from the world and from Cretia. We have taken steps to care for the individuals who otherwise would have no work. No harm has been, or is being done, either to those who have been running the industry or those who have traditionally relied upon it.

I could see where he was going, but it was elsewhere that I was looking.

I said, *So, if we consider the resources we have, might we not find a possibility we are not discussing? Suppose we could transform the value system of the seven families? Do we not have at least one member of each family who has had an education at the ILC on OlarCret and do we not also have another eight members of the seven families who are in what will probably be their final year at the ILC?*

If these people and perhaps their partners were to make it their major project to change the operating value system of the seven families and all their governmental and business connections, might this not be the thing that opens the door to a different future? Might they actually be able to impact the values of their family?

All of them understand the Olarian way, and those 16 are really only the tip of the iceberg. We have managed to lure all children from the seven families into the ILC. Those who are members of those families know we have been taking care of them and their partners while we try to sort this difficult and sensitive situation. We are as fond of, as caring for them, as for every member of our educational community.

We were of course reflecting to ourselves what we knew.

But even as I said it I could see real historical and structural problems. I was also enamoured of the idea that we find another planet and make a Third Earth where we could start out with some of the seven families group from the ILC, and say 16 or more young Olarians, and maybe some of the older Olarians who wanted to be part of a new experiment with human children as well as their own. Maybe a number of ordinary human children. Trouble was, even as I said it out loud, I could see the difficulty when it involved their parents who were unlikely to support or possibly even actually understand what we were trying to do.

I felt like grinding my teeth in frustration. I could see the possibility of a new planet with ILC graduates and Olarians. They might be able to slowly create a human community without money or weapons and without violence. I was thinking this because I was beginning to realize how much difficulty we eight were having in shelving the economic side of our own lives. We could get any amount of money we needed, whenever we wanted to, yet we were still having some difficulty shedding the notion of money in our operating on Earth. And that was after more than 20 years!

The others slowly crunched over the idea. There was support for it in principle, but practically it seemed a little fraught. And so the next night we fed the idea to Jald and Tanzin, to Raille and Jess and to Miyuki. We asked for them to just think about it, explaining again our motivation and hesitatingly reminding them that time and lifespan were not really issues for us, and perhaps they could use our framework to think about it?

This had, after all, been the motivation that lay in part underneath the idea of attracting these children into the ILC. It had been effective in getting them there, and I wondered whether it might be effective in beginning the next steps. So for the first time I contacted Rozari and asked her if she was willing to ask the 16 members of the seven families, with their partners, to a meeting at the ILC with the eight of us and Olaria and anyone else she thought ought to be there. With no hesitation, Rozari said she would be really pleased to do that.

CHAPTER 36

Third Earth

It was not long after the meeting we had had on violence that the eight of us were sitting together with Raille and Jess. We had just replayed the discussion about violence, economics and space travel and were not yet getting ourselves settled around this as being simply one problem. We were all getting the feeling that if humanity was going to have a chance, it would need to metaphorically start again.

Not only would we need to remove money and weapons, we would need also to develop a generation free of violence caused by a mixture of ignorance about others and notions of ownership and power. All the characteristics we needed were present in the Olarian learning community and Olarian society. There were options, but not, we realized, on Second

Earth, which had begun with no telepathy, no non-violent policies, not weapons-free and with a fully established economy. I was coming to believe our thinking was a mess.

So, while we still seemed to not be thinking holistically, we decided what we needed might be a fresh start, a new planet, an Olarian education system, and a population of humans who would be educated by the Olarians so they would absorb and internalise the value system of the Olarians. We were no longer ambivalent about the necessity for telepathic communication. We all found it difficult to think about real trust without telepathic capability.

The reality was, the ILC worked because everyone had access to the telepathic world. The thing about the telepathic world that we realized was paramount was people always knew what you were thinking and feeling, so duplicity was impossible, but the other side of that coin was, if you were constantly paying attention to the feelings and thoughts of other people, this would probably inhibit your capacity to build the scientific world humans had built. Then the question would be, would they be traveling intergalactically, which is the characteristic that had made humanity interesting to the cosmic community in the first place?

The most penetrating question was, therefore, could a non-telepathic relationship contain the elements, intimacies and ethics of the telepathic world, and how exactly could it be managed so that the strengths of the telepathic world and the strengths of the non-telepathic world could be sustained?

We were toying with an answer, because all of us were feeling confident there either had to be a telepathic reality or we had to find a way to have a non-telepathic reality and simulate a telepathic one. This meant no covert emotions, especially emotions that people would have hidden or tried not to share, and a willingness on everybody's part to continue to work through a complex relationship issue no matter how uncomfortable or fraught.

I thought back to our first meeting with the Olarians and our first year with them. Wondered what we would need to do to create the optimal conditions for a violence-free world. We were cognizant of Aristotle's small commentary on death. We knew we had no real knowledge about death. We suspected, really we intuited, with some confidence, that death was not an end, merely a transition, however, we seemed unable to find an immediately obvious way to check this. Our primary feeling about a non-violent world was, if we created a new planet and began it with an ILC, and if it went the way the first had gone, then there might come a time when we would need to protect it from human violence generated from the other human worlds.

We struggled for quite a while with the question of why not simply destroy the entire human weapons stockpile. We knew we were capable of doing that; on Earth, the moon, the space fleet, Second Earth. It would take us a little time but it could be done. We were less certain we could find a process that would successfully persuade the human population of the world to do it themselves.

Absurd as it might seem, we felt, now that we knew something of what we were capable, that we ought not to. When we reviewed what Raille and I had managed with the Cretians it just seemed entirely something else, different! Raille pointed out we had actually been motivated by a concern for the survival of the OlarCret planet and had been acting on behalf of one of the species to whom the planet was home.

He asked me, *If they asked us now, today, given everything you now know and can do, would you de-weaponize the Cretian world?*

I had no immediate answer to that. Would it not be either more prudent or more practical and less invasive to simply find them a new planet? Even as we talked about it the conversation seemed absurd, even unreal, yet we knew it actually was not. I think I was unable as yet to take seriously the idea of moving an entire species off one planet and onto another. Then in a flash I knew we would almost certainly be prevented from doing it!

Prevented?

But that was the word I could not push away. In that moment I knew we were neither omniscient nor omnipotent. There were real limitations that applied to us and so some things we simply would not be permitted to do. I knew we had found an absolute boundary. How we knew and how we could be prevented continued to hound us.

Nevertheless, none of the eight of us was in doubt; I could hear my mother's voice, *sure as eggs is eggs* she would say. We explored if we would be enabled to move a population from one planet to another if their home planet was becoming inhospitable. We looked at one another and believed we knew that would be permitted. In that moment our feet were firmly returned to the ground. We were, it seemed, finally attempting to cross a line we were able neither to understand nor ignore! I did not even know where that feeling, understanding, belief, came from. But I did know it was not ambiguous. Somewhere, some entity had just drawn a line in the sand and we were not to ignore it!

So we returned to the idea of Third Earth. Possible, yes, we were certain. Permissible, no-one had any sense it would not be! So, do-able.

We decided we seriously wanted to try. We did not want to give up on the human world on Earth. However, for now, we seemed not able to imagine a pathway to non-violence. We were getting stuck on telepathy and knew we needed to move past it. However, while none of us felt a great deal of confidence in the idea that a new world might be our best next step, we knew we were grasping at straws and we seemed to be... stuck.

Another way to think about this, we concluded, was to imagine we were being led to explore some of our own boundaries. We had a further conversation with the ILC contingent after they had churned the idea over. They were unambiguous. They had talked this over among themselves many, many times. Now that too was a surprise to us. They could see no way to create a safe and genuine violence-free non-telepathic world. That was, in itself, really disturbing. We were not really surprised; it was just another option we needed to explore. We were in a complex and unordered reality; the rules pertaining to this reality were not unknown to us, so 'experiment'!

Everyone was in agreement that if we were going to try to do this, we needed a new world. Although we could travel to any one we found, we wondered if we would be blocked if we tried. However, I was not convinced I ought not to proceed to find out. So, as the others watched and waited, I reached out for Rozari and asked when she could be free for a journey with me.

Now, it turned out, was a good time. This phenomenon, her being free and available when I needed her, had at first surprised me. When she arrived a few seconds later, I asked her about it. She smiled, looked at me and shook her head. Her hair swung gently around her face and shoulders. She was very pretty even allowing for my prejudices. Her smile and gentle laugh floated through me and I had this unusual feeling, one I had had before. She knew something I ought to know, but I could not quite reach it.

Daddy, any time you want me, I will be free to come to you. You must know that's how it works. As to why, well, you need to be the one who answers that.

I noted what she said and decided to simply wait.

Rozari, we want to find another planet. My feeling is the Heral could help, the Irawars might be able to help, but we ought to be able to search by ourselves. I am uncertain how, and it seems to me if I have you with me, we may be able to simply do our own exploring.

She smiled that secret smile that I was now used to seeing and she simply sat on my lap, put her arms around my neck, rested her head on my shoulder and I thought, *Let us find a safe and ready world.*

I felt the others join me, felt Januti take my hand, felt us scanning! Knew Raille and Jess did not want to miss this journey so we added them to our connection. Then...

Although I could not see them I felt the same feeling I would have if I was flipping through a card index except it would be an index of available worlds! It was a strange and absurd notion, except the process slowed and then we were standing on a hill, all 11 of us, no... 12! Then I realized, somehow, Olaria had joined us, holding Rozari's hand, so there was connection between all of us, and I was pleased, realizing it must have been Rozari who had brought her. We were overlooking a green valley with a river flowing down into a lake of considerable size. We were all standing together as a group. I was holding Januti's hand and she was looking at me, smiling and slowly shaking her head. In almost no time she had us all clothed.

Zed, do you have the slightest notion what you just did? She stood there looking at me and impulsively put her arms around my neck and kissed me with a ridiculously large and joyful grin. *You continue to be amazing and extraordinary and you have done it again and you really don't know how, do you?*

No.

The other six were looking at me.

What? I don't know what I just did that got us here. I don't even know where exactly here is.

Zed, we may not need to know, but we need to transport people here and for them to be able to return to OlarCret, Earth or Second Earth. Although we actually do not know precisely where any of them are in relation to us, there is someone who might be able to map it.

I nodded. I had thought about bringing Tanzin, but I had spoken to her earlier and knew she was doing something with Jald and the children.

Januti and Rozari were shaking their heads.

I stood on the hill overlooking this attractive scene and asked no-one in particular, *How do we assess this world?*

Rozari looked at me. *Zed!* She just said my name with a huge exclamation in her voice.

I looked at her again. She wanted me to get something.

Daddy, stop being thick! Sit down, put your head in your hands and soak up this planet.

I don't think I had any idea what she was asking me to do, but the way she had asked was unusual and she seemed quite certain about what I ought to do. So I did. And, of course, she was right. My mind sprung into life. Everywhere, there was life. Insects, birds, animals, oceans and fish: a variety in every way unusual and significantly different from Earth. A botanist's, ichthyologist's and a zoologist's treasure house! But no animal form that resembled human or any sentience.

I looked at Rozari again.

Okay, so, how do I find out if there is a wormhole journey here by spaceship from Earth?

She looked at me again.

Daddy, don't be tedious! You definitely know how to answer that question. Ask Tanzin.

She stubbornly refused to say more. I was left with the feeling she needed me to find a way to stretch and I was yet again forced to recognize that she was only my daughter because of how she had been born. I mean, she was my daughter but she was also something else. I was having a lot of these experiences recently. I could not pinpoint what exactly they were, at least not at this moment. However, it must have been obvious because I knew they all knew.

I put my head in my hands and sought out Tanzin and Jald. Found them walking away from the astronav school. Their two children had gone off to stay with friends.

Can I borrow you for a little astronavigational exploration?

Tanzin knew I was asking her but knew I wanted them both. They both agreed. I connected to them fully and had them make the jump. And that was all it took; they had joined us.

You have developed that maneuver to an extraordinary degree, Jald said. *You don't even need to be with us to do it anymore. And you dressed us as we landed. That was very smooth!*

He smiled, shook his head and looked around.

So, you have found a new planet, which you want for...? Oh!

He shook his head and that was essentially all it took.

Okay Zed, what is the question? Tanzin asked.

I smiled. *Where are we in relation to OlarCret and Earth and Second Earth? That's the first question. Then the second question is, is there wormhole access to this planet from any or all of the other three?*

Tanzin looked at me and smiled.

You remember many years ago now, Zed, you took Jald and me to the edges of the universe in which OlarCret resides. From there we were able to map the entire Olarian/Cretian system. Then, if you recall, you took us to either entry/exit points of each of the wormholes that eventually allowed me to get us a kind of fix on our location in the cosmos.

So this time you need to do the same journey with us but you will need to do this in stages for me. First take Jald and me with you to the boundaries of this universe, then let me experience you stretching your mind back to OlarCret or any of the three.

Next you will need to go and talk with the Heral with the maps I know you will be able to lift from our minds. The two models will mesh. They have fit easily for several exercises Jald and I have undertaken while we were trying to find OlarCret's relation to Earth. It took us nearly a full year to solve that one, however, I think this time will turn out to be much quicker since we managed a partial map of this whole sector of cosmic space. Okay?

I nodded. I could see the maps the two of them were forming of our location and I could just make out the distant images of Earth, OlarCret and Second Earth, which they suddenly seemed able to see! I realized Jald had made some amazing leaps in his understanding of the structure of the cosmos as we were coming to know it.

Will you two be okay waiting? Or would you like to go back to your walk?

Come on, Zed, this is way too exciting for us to budge. What you are about to do is impossible. Inconceivable. No way am I moving until I see you back here with what I need.

I picked up Rozari and then Januti's hand and the nine of us went to the Heral. As usual, Felarv and Albor were expecting us. We spoke with them for a while until, reluctantly, they agreed to another difficult request. They knew we knew. They left and when, seconds later, they returned, they had had to spend more than a day undertaking their first actual connection to the Wheeir. They were also getting used to the idea that when I turned up with the eight I would probably make a request that would have been impossible for them to fulfil but which somehow would now be fulfilled. What they reported was beyond me, but they left the messages in my mind and Januti thanked them and yet again they asked, could we please try to stay within the bounds of our known abilities. Again I smiled, thanked them and promised we would try.

We returned to 'Third Earth' to Tanzin and Jald, Raille and Jess and Olaria, then Januti held my head in her hands and in seconds I knew what Albor had told me. I sat on the ground and showed Tanzin and Jald what I knew.

Zed, there are many days of work here, Tanzin said. *Take us back to our walk and Jald and I will contact you when we know where we are, and if I actually have just an inkling, then these Wheeir will have to build you some new wormholes, and you should know this will be the most incomprehensible mapping experience of anyone's life and by far the most exciting and amazing should you believe it will be possible to share with the astronav community.*

Whether we will be able to do this or not, this is the most astonishing and fascinating project anyone has ever given us, and it could only be possible because of the extraordinary person you are becoming and who you are. One day, I hope in my lifetime, you will know and be able to share with us.

I want to say this, although I know it will make you uncomfortable, but, anyway: you are the most beautiful and generous man and I can only reiterate what I have said before, with no need I am certain, 'Look after him, Januti, he is one of a kind and in our world far more than a living treasure, and especially because without him I would not be with Jald and even the thought of that nearly breaks my heart'.

We returned to OlarCret where we said goodbye to Olaria and Rozari and the rest of us returned home to Canberra. It had been an exciting and enlightening day.

I ought to probably report that the eight of us had now ceased to work. Not only were we easily able to obtain anything we wanted or needed, we were now easily able to manipulate the planetary security systems so we were, in a sense, invisible to them and when necessary manipulated the planetary systems to maintain our safety.

We were all involved in learning through the institutions of the world and on OlarCret and through our journeys, and we all knew that our rate of understanding was growing very rapidly. What we did not know was, toward what. Or, put another way, for what reason? It ought to have been a stupid question, however, the others told me it was time for me to retrieve the answer.

I looked, at first blankly, at them. Then it was as if the fog simply cleared from my mind, and I knew and it was quite simple: my responsibility related to helping mankind find a way to a non-violent existence and to bring all three societies to a place where they could get the invitation they needed to join the community of cosmic societies, and as the confusion cleared I realized it had become obvious to them. The seven of them smiled tolerantly at my bemused expression.

Natalya said, *This is a door you opened for us. But you never said it out loud, you were busy putting it all together. We just got the punchline!*

▫

I should divert here for a moment. We wanted to bring Miyuki in. Her way of thinking about large, complex issues was not merely valuable, she had spent most of her life managing precisely these realities. Managing, leading and negotiating the political, economic and military worlds that had an interest in SFC was a unique task and brought with it an extraordinary skill set.

Over the past two decades, Miyuki had sought and achieved agreement to find a sexual partner and companion from among the Olarian community. Interestingly, she had had no difficulty in attracting a number of very interesting Olarian men who were willing to share their lives with her for a time and after some experimentation she had fallen pretty heavily for Paldi, who was more than willing to spend this part of his life with her and provide her with a thoroughly delicious loving, emotional relationship that had for the past decade or more been wonderfully satisfying for both of them.

She had decided to retire a year after meeting him and I had known I needed to do the same. She had chosen to retire to OlarCret and live with Paldi not a great distance from Jald and Tanzin. As a child she had been drawn to the visual arts and had spent her spare time doing pencil sketches of everything and everyone around her. She had kept this propensity entirely out of the sight and awareness of her family with the exception of her grandparents, who always quietly and surreptitiously encouraged her but who were now both dead. She had also kept it entirely out of sight of her workplace. However, she had not stopped sketching during this period.

Now, with no empire to run, although she had been pressured by her family for a short while to consider learning to run the family enterprises, which she successfully discouraged, she was free to do as she wished and she wished to draw and to learn to paint. It had been easy to arrange for her to get the help she needed. She was very organized and one of us was always willing to ferry her to classes on Earth and bring her home or take her teachers to OlarCret where they could stay with her and where she could paint in the magnificent studio Paldi had created for her. Transporting an art teacher to OlarCret required a degree of manipulation, not the least of which meant one of us needed intense shapeshifting so they always were able to assume their transporter was Olarian. Miyuki and Paldi had slid into our family with not a hitch, Paldi being a very attractive and interesting man, as any of us would have expected from Miyuki.

So within a year she was simply another member of our intergalactic family and played her part in our social life and was appreciated in ways neither she nor any of us would have imagined while she was running SFC.

She was passionately attached to several things: her art, her garden, her man and cooking, though not in that order. Paldi, we knew, found her endlessly interesting, exciting and stimulating. He had studied her and learned myriad ways to please and engage with her. She followed his work and his interests to exactly the degree he needed. They were a beautiful and satisfying couple and all of us but especially Raille, Tanzin and I were deeply pleased that she had found a fulfilling life after SFC.

Before she had left she inducted her replacement – her deputy for the last three years of her tenure – to make certain the organization would be in a safe pair of hands. This pretty much assured its direction would be unlikely to be twisted away from where she had been taking it.

I had left at pretty much the same time and Xiandra and Parnite had easily slid into my job and together now had the confidence they needed to make every aspect of it work. They were also comfortably connected to Miyuki's replacement.

■

But I was diverted from the thoughts I had been having. I knew I wanted Olaria, Tanzin and Miyuki, their partners, and Raille and Jess and a handful of ILC children to be with us when we went exploring the new direction for our endeavours. I don't know why, but I was truly surprised and delighted that so many of the ILC mob also were intensely interested in Third Earth.

We met in the center that had been created for the first group of visitors to OlarCret. It was the right place to meet. We easily arranged to bring everyone and it was comfortable. I began with a kind of ramble. In essence:

We are all pretty clear that the human race, and so none of us, is not going to get itself into the cosmic community until some problems with which we are all familiar are solved. Violence is the most difficult. No discussion we have ever had over the past 20 or so years has led us to be able to imagine a non-violent human race on Earth or Second Earth, given how it was established.

So, I began to think we needed a new planet, however, I am aware that while this is proving interesting it cannot actually be a solution in the fashion we were originally thinking. We know this new planet we have found could be a kind of experiment. We have not as yet approached the Council of Eight to seek their approval and willingness to assist us to create another ILC on another planet. We feel optimistic that they will want to help us in this.

We have either learned or believe we have somehow been told that we cannot move a whole population or society to a new planet. We do not know how we have been informed, but we are confident we have. We think that such a planet can only be an addition to the human and other worlds. So that's fine.

We are hoping to create a model, based entirely on the Olarian model, of an optimal solution to a violence-free, economics-free and weapons-free society. We have been hoping it would then give us a firm direction for our efforts on Earth. And, as all of you are aware, we are not yet certain we understand how human life will work out in these circumstances.

We hope to have removed the military and the economy as possible ways to engage with a working life. However, the fact is even that might not guarantee our success. We have as a kind of ill-defined hope to create a more holistic religious model for people wanting strong religious directions, one that is without the competitive or combative focus of some religious orders. However, the leaders of most of the world's religions have made it pretty clear that we are simply failing to understand religious truths.

We have tried to keep in mind the strength of the conviction of many millions of people. We have been trying to not show up the logical flaws in the differing belief systems, but rather show how the things each of the major religions have been teaching are life-enhancing, not necessarily because of a god, but because they make social/survival sense. However, some of the beliefs come from a very long time ago in human history and are not life-enhancing as we have come to think about that concept. We are not really feeling optimistic about this.

When we have tried, carefully and slowly, to discourage some of the more primitive elements of religious systems, usually elements involved in hurting people and controlling them by supporting, perhaps unwittingly, behaviors and attitudes that cause interpersonal harm, we have been less than successful in our discussions.

This seems to have been a consequence of our focus on the purpose of life in the universe and of our growing belief that the universe has been created and managed by entities of extraordinary ability far beyond anything we are able to grasp.

We thought we had been successful to a small but not insignificant extent in offering a feasible alternative to religious and supernatural explanations for pretty much everything, including the creation of everything. However, we now believe we were wrong, and we have as yet found no other substantive explanation for creation. So... who knows? We still like Jard's idea of the Seeders.

We have found a planet, which we initially called Third Earth but which after some strong discussion we have come to call Crolea. Crolea is the acronym for CRetia/OLaria/EArth.

The one small snag is that as yet we do not know exactly where it is, nevertheless, we have also found another society, the Wheeir, who create and maintain the wormholes.

Tanzin and Jald will, we believe, be able to give us a location soon, and because we have found the cosmic society responsible for constructing wormholes and maintaining them, and have established communication with them, I believe access to the planet by space vehicle will shortly be possible.

We have not tried to engage the Wheeir in the location and navigational issues as they seemed either not able or not willing to communicate with us about these issues, or perhaps it would be fairer to say, we could not communicate with them except through the Heral, and this is not a connection we have yet been able to make work smoothly.

I looked around the room, becoming aware of the gob-smacking impact of this basic information, especially among the human contingent. Raille, Miyuki and Tanzin were just quietly shaking their heads.

It was Raille who said, out loud, 'You met the society that creates and maintains the wormholes and you are apparently confident they will create one to facilitate travel from Earth, Second Earth and OlarCret to CROLEA? Did I get that right?'

Yep!

The human contingent just stared at me.

Oh come on! I continued. *Once you recognize that the universe is not made up of just humans or Olarians or Cretians, then the rest kind of falls into place, doesn't it? I mean, there has to be organization, there has to be differentiation or specialisation, and just so long as there is some underlying order, as I said, the rest kind of falls into place.*

The absolute baseline for membership seems to be complete non-violence, and we suspect this might require an absence of economic motive as well as all forms of negativity. If you can maintain a boundary that will keep out any violent society, no matter what level of complexity is involved, then, again, the rest is more or less straightforward.

Let me take another step. Suppose death is actually not an end to anything except your current existence. That you put aside all the mystical religious hypotheses and stories, then what you call life is just the existence you experience at this moment. Then everyone in the connected world of entities merely cease, at some point, to exist in one society and their sentience takes its place in another.

Now, obviously, we don't know any of this for a fact. We are just spinning our wheels and reaching for explanations we can accept. Ones that seem to cover the facts as we are coming to know them. If we are right, and given what we are learning it is possible we are, then the most useful thing we can do with whatever existence we have is find ways to get humans and Cretians out of the violence business and into the peace business and see what happens.

So I was wanting to have a discussion about the possibility of starting to build a society on a fourth planet, on the planet we found/chose the other day. This would seem to involve managing the development of a Cretian, human and Olarian population. It ought to involve what we have learned from the capability developed by the Olarians. It would take advantage, in a mutually beneficial way, from what the Cretian world is learning. If we were successful, this would maximize the possibility of humanity also becoming acceptable to the cosmic community.

Nevertheless, I was uncomfortable. I was still quite certain we needed to create a human society totally violence-free. But, and it was a big but, once we had created a non-violent society with no economy but working effectively as did the Olarians, then there was the question of how to change the behavior on Earth and Second Earth so that the human race was in its entirety violence and weapons free. I was not seeing a track we might follow to get to that place. I knew all of us were feeling certain we would need to.

The group spoke for hours, but in the end we really were no closer to a solution we could accommodate, and for the moment we agreed to go our separate ways and keep thinking about it. There was also an understanding by the group that this new planet would be creating and building a society that consisted of the members of all three societies – human, Olarian and Cretian – and somehow that genuinely felt right.

CHAPTER 37

Januti & Zed: A Further Non-Telepathic Relationship Experiment

Januti and I sat on a high perch on our newly discovered planet looking over a pristine, beautiful vista. It had, we realized, not always been like this and to get a sense of it in its historical perspective we used our latest capability, allowing us to travel backward any amount of time. We traveled through burning heat and freezing cold through the massive geologic disturbances that had shaped the planet and brought the life forms into existence and watched them fight for their survival. We were surprised, but not as much as we had imagined, that we could travel, here, on this planet, millions of years back in time!

We were not naive. We knew the violence and death that were at the heart of species management and survival. When we returned to the present day it was with a feeling of confusion. If non-violence was the key to membership of the cosmic community, why was violence fundamental to the survival of species, certainly in every system for which we had information? Survival was bloody, tooth and claw! Was it that there came a time with every sentient species when violence was no longer required for survival and no longer desirable? If that was true, why was the gap between violence and peaceful reality so large?

Did every sentient species begin with violence? Or did some never pick up that strand? There were unanswered questions we had at the beginning and for some reason, our attempts to locate cosmic communities in which we could explore were being blocked without explanation. We guessed there was purpose to this! But what exactly was that purpose?

Were we going to be allowed, enabled, shown, more of the logic of this, or did we need to explore further, maybe much further? We were pretty confident that violence and unpleasantness of all kinds sprang from one or other form of ignorance and impotence and fear and survival anxiety... in other words, people feeling not good about themselves or their ability to look after themselves, their partners and/or their children, especially into the future.

For some reason, we knew we were being denied access to the history of the races and worlds of the cosmic community in order, I felt confident, to learn something, but I thought, repeating myself, what? It seemed as though we were being forced to do our own research on life but were being blocked from seeing beyond 70 years ahead, the time my future self had told us to explore. Seventy years ahead, but unlimited travel backward! Seventy years was nothing in the scheme of things and nothing of significance in the plans we needed to make. I had already met myself roughly 1000 years from now!

Non-violence seemed to be counter-intuitive. All survivors on Earth had been violent at some time in their past; it was how they had survived. Yet we were being made aware that for survival into the future, we had to move beyond it! I think we were also being told/shown that the primitive violent mechanisms associated with survival of non-sentient species needed to be reversed or shelved or totally denied for the survival and development of sentient species! Right now this made no sense. It appeared there were at least two sets of rules.

We had a hunch all of this was somehow connected to death, whatever that actually was, and so to life, whatever that actually was. And then we were just left sitting there with more questions and no sense of direction. Yet I felt the need to add in a quiet way to myself, yet again: 'just work the problem, Zed'.

Januti looked at me. *Do you have any idea at all as to what this is actually about?*

Not yet, but I feel as though I ought to. And, here's the thing. I was wondering if maybe you and I might take ourselves back to a time before we met and before either of us was knowingly telepathic. Just cease using our telepathy and spend some time in a non-telepathic space, seeing how we can manage our relationship. See if we can establish whether telepathic reality is an essential element of a non-violent and hence non-weaponized world.

Does that feel like something you would be willing to explore with me? I get the weapons thing, but I believe it may be – and this would be very sad – that telepathic connection may be necessary to deal with the violence, especially the interpersonal violence. So I am moved to return briefly to our non-telepathic state to see if we can learn the part telepathy plays in our dilemma.

Januti looked at me, shaking her head and smiling.

Zed, you must know I would do anything you asked without question. I totally trust and love you.

Okay, let's choose a start time when we are home together, set a boundary, and then begin?

Januti was totally willing, so we chose tonight after dinner, checked that the others knew what we were going to do and that they would not attempt to contact us telepathically for the next five days. We also passed the message on to our Olarian friends so they would also know. The others, all six of them, found it curious we would want to do it, but decided they would likewise explore and see what there was to learn in their reality during the time before they had met me.

Olaria had reached out to connect to remind me how it had been for them when we had first asked them to be non-telepathic, to have them begin to know what it was like for us, as humans, way back when we had first met on OlarCret, and I quizzed her for a short while, extracting what new learning I could from that experience.

After dinner we looked at one another, truthfully, with real pleasure, then we stepped away from our telepathic connection. The first few minutes we just sat there looking at one another, and I was wondering what we ought to do. It was so strange. Januti seemed to not really have any more idea than me! An observer might have imagined we were like the Olarians when we had first suggested this course of action to them. Yet this had been our normal until I had met the Olarians, only a flicker of time away.

'Zed, on top of all the feelings that have always been there for me with you, I now must add confusion. I have become so used to being intimately connected to all your thoughts and feelings that I am feeling quite bereft and more than a little confused. In addition, I feel as though my connection to you has been severed somehow. I have what feels like an irrational desire to re-connect to you telepathically immediately so I can lose this hollow, distressed, disconnected feeling.

'I think, for me, our intimacy is deeply maintained by my certainty about how you are feeling, especially about me, as well as what you are thinking at any moment we are connected. Knowing, not having to guess. Right now, I could be guessing wrong about how you are feeling. My confidence is slipping. Tell me yours is too.'

So I did.

I continued looking at Januti. I had always found her beautiful to look at. I had never ceased to feel real pleasure just looking at her. I had never had a relationship with her when I did not know exactly what she was thinking and feeling, so as I now sat at our kitchen bench looking across at her, I realized I felt quite isolated, uncomfortable, out of place, yet she was beautiful, and I knew that I loved her. But I actually could not even guess what she was thinking or feeling and had a strong urge to have her tell me, a kind of lower-grade replacement for the information I was now used to receiving from our continuous telepathic connection.

Even as I thought about it I realized the telepathic connection could not be replaced by her telling me how she was feeling or what she was thinking or what she desperately wanted to know. Even though I totally trusted her, my knowing because I could get the information and my knowing because she could give me the information were two entirely different things. I am uncertain what it was that was stopping me from simply telling her how I was feeling and what I was thinking and what I wanted to know. But because I couldn't really know what she would think, how she would respond, I held back. I felt unsure and I had never felt unsure with Januti before. It seemed as though knowing how she was feeling and what she was thinking was not – was definitely not – the same as asking and being told. I experimented. I asked her to tell me how she was specifically feeling. And she did. But that was still not okay, it was not the same!

'Wow, it is so long since this was my normal state I don't know what to do or say! You and I have never been together when I had no information about what was happening for you. I am aware that I am concerned I will say or do something that will upset you, might alienate you, might give you the wrong impression about me. I suspect that before telepathy I felt continuously inadequate.'

Januti shook her head and her hair swirled from side to side. I smiled. She noticed and her smile momentarily reassured me about our connection. I was imagining she was feeling pleased but was not quite sure, realized I did not really know, if I was guessing or just hoping. Perhaps, worse, my confidence was ebbing away! I felt hesitant asking for information about her feelings that might be a mismatch for my assumption or guess. In some part of my brain I knew this was beyond ridiculous.

What would I do if it turned out she did not actually like, desire, or admire me as much as I experienced these things with her? I was genuinely afraid she might not. Was our relationship based on a thin and fragile line? I noticed that without the validated information from Januti my sense of comfort was going down, my confidence was going down, and my willingness to try to obtain the information about her and her feelings seemed to be slipping out of reach. I did not want to risk getting a negative response to any of my questions, and so I was obtaining no information except my imaginings!

'This is more than a little frightening, Zed. I really don't like it. My comfort and quality of life have come to depend on you and I being in a mutually satisfying and loving place, all the time. I don't seem to feel that now! Let's go to bed.'

I felt my anxiety go up. If I didn't know what she wanted or what she was feeling, I might not be able to please her.

'No.'

I immediately saw her withdraw and frown and guessed she was feeling distressed. That had been a bad response to say out loud.

'My "no", Januti, did not mean no I don't want to have a deeply connected sexual relationship with you at this moment, it was a "no" spoken to myself about my stupid anxieties and unacknowledged fears that I might fail to satisfy you and so damage our relationship, possibly irretrievably.'

Good lord, everything was becoming so drawn out and ambiguous and difficult. In fact, I could not now imagine anything I might say that might not sound inappropriate or out of place in this non-telepathic space. I was beginning to feel this had been a very bad idea and was deciding I wanted to stop it. However, I was almost as afraid to suggest that as I was to keep on potentially making a fool of myself or hurting our connection.

So I decided to just talk.

'Januti, I love you. I think you are beautiful and desirable and I cannot imagine my life without you, but I am also anxious that you might not be feeling the same way toward me.'

She looked at me; surprise was the emotion I thought I was detecting.

'Zed, I am certain you know how much I love you, you are the light in my life. Since I met you I have not spent a second feeling uncertain about my choice to be your partner, your woman. There is absolutely no violence that hovers between us. You have never hurt or threatened me in any way. I have never felt so certain, so safe, so willing to be available to a man, so brimming with pleasure and ready to be excited and pleasured, or so filled with pleasure at the thought of finding one of the many ways I have learned you like me to speak with and touch you.'

I heard every word she said. I know how I felt about her, but the idea of taking her to bed without knowing everything that was going on between us was causing me to feel anxious. Would I satisfy her, would I be able to detect among all the things we liked to do the one she would want next from me? So I told her how I was feeling and she frowned. Usually I immediately would have known what the frown was about but now I didn't and I assumed the worst-case scenario: she was displeased that I was anxious and perhaps inattentive.

I could feel my anxiety blocking my sexual hunger for her. I had never had that experience before. I could not even reach out to get help. I began to believe that I understood why I had never had a seriously satisfying sexual relationship before Olaria: no deep and confirming feedback. How could anyone even begin to imagine themselves in a deeply satisfying sexual relationship? I would never know if I was giving her what she wanted or simply doing something that pleased me, in effect, equating that with pleasing her, and so just being selfish.

'Januti, I am feeling inadequate, yet I know that right now I can make a simultaneity jump to another planet. Nevertheless, I am full of anxiety that I will not be able to pay attention to exactly what you want. So I fear I will act selfishly to get pleasure for myself rather than doing something that fully pleases you. I cannot believe what a mess losing my telepathic ability is making for me. I know when I did not have it I was not this crazy. So it must be less that I don't know what to do and more that, having lost it, I am now aware of the value I was getting from it.'

Januti became silent, then she walked around the serving bar in the kitchen till she could reach my hand, pulled me off the seat and kissed me passionately, then when I was coming up for breath the second time she just said, 'Zed, take us to Crolea – now.'

And I did.

As we touched the ground I looked at her and slowly shook my head.

'No clothes, my beautiful woman?'

She stood in my arms, naked, and it was abundantly clear I was very horny, and as my hands clasped her beautiful, generous breasts, I could feel them swell just a little and her nipples swell and harden in my hands. I felt amazing and she was kissing me and reassuring me we were as loving and connected as we had always known we would be. I looked at her with love and lust, and then I turned just slightly so I could see the lake down below us, and in an instant I had us standing on the sands at its edge. I created a tent with a soft strong floor and I pulled her ever so gently down.

As we fell into our lakeside shelter she fell in front of me but with her back to me so we could both look at the lake and I pulled her close. I felt myself slide gently into the now wet lips of her vagina and I held her steady, not moving. My hands firmly holding her waist slid slowly and gently up to hold her breasts. I let my hands remind me just how breathtakingly strong and firm and soft and beautiful she was, and although I knew she wanted to move, I held her stationary. I could feel myself just inside the lips of her vagina. She and I were both pulsating to a rhythm I had never felt before. I could also feel her willing compliance, and I allowed myself to believe this was in no way connected to any sense of superiority or power I was exerting over her.

'Stay still with me, my beauty,' was all I said and she did not move. I held her firmly and slowly kissed her neck and, as the minutes slipped by, I began to feel her vibrate, the warm depths of her calling me. However, I patiently held her, just keeping her open as I began to feel her whole body vibrate. I felt her orgasm building and she was begging me to thrust inside. I knew to be patient and still. Then I felt her pulsing ever more strongly, and as I felt her on the edge of exploding I thrust myself inside and she came over and over and over again, and I had my own explosive orgasm and collapsed, pulling her, moaning with pleasure and joy, down against me.

We must have fallen asleep. She moved to disentangle herself from me and turn so she was facing me and kissing me and pulling me against her. I smiled to myself and with no effort of will I slid inside her again. She kissed, stroked and held me. Then for no reason I could conjure, I felt confident I knew what would please her. We gave each other pleasure until we were both again sated but in a different way. Then she rolled over, pulling me with her, pushing me down and kissing me down my belly and finally taking me in her mouth and making sure I came yet again. I thought the pleasure would finish me as she crawled up my body and we kissed with passion, tasting each other and feeling deeply satisfied.

As our energy slowly returned she took my hand, pulled me up and raced me to the edge of the lake and we went in together. When we finally left the water, having swum until we were puffing and satisfied, I felt her wet body in my arms and found myself kissing her again and then pulling her down into our shelter. I closed the front and, with her in my arms, I sealed an energy barrier over our little dwelling and we fell sleep.

We awoke; it must have been mid-morning. The sky was grey and rain clouds were scudding over us, rain pelting down on our shelter, but we were warm, comfortable and dry. Januti looked up at me from the crook of my arm and said, 'Do you have any doubts that we are deeply in love? That we do actually understand, in the absence of our telepathic selves, exactly how to look after one another? How joyful our connection is because we are meant to be together and do know how to do that, telepathic knowledge aside?'

I knew she was right.

I thought, *I seem to have learned to give and receive sexual pleasure*, and then I thought, *Actions speak louder than words*.

But I knew I had not properly plumbed the depths of what had taken place between us or what was still unexplored. The last two thoughts were mine and she did not know what I had thought and would not, unless I deliberately shared them. So I did. And her response was truly satisfying.

'What you did last night, that was a first for us, and it was *the* most incredible experience ever. Even with all the things we have learned to do for and with each other, that orgasm was the most complex and powerful I have ever felt. Where did that come from?'

I thought for a moment.

'Well, surprising as it may seem, that came from decades ago when I was a postgrad student! I was studying women's sexuality. I don't know why I suddenly remembered it. I was thinking back to things I had learned about women and their physiology for some paper I had to write for a subject we called Social Biology and I remembered how complex a neural network was a woman's vagina. I had read quite a lot on how it worked. In the years that followed there must never have been an occasion to use the knowledge, so it must have just sat there until I needed to draw on what

I knew and not on what you and the Olarians had shown or taught me!'

She looked at me with a gentle smile on her lips and a slow shake of her head and I loved her all over again, the way her hair would softly and sensuously follow the slow shake she made.

'Well, I would like you to know that anytime you want you can repeat that. It was fabulous, the slow build-up from inside until every nerve ending inside me was vibrating and screaming with pleasure and begging me to get you to slide inside me and come. I can still feel it as I remember it and tell you about it. The others will not know because no-one is being telepathic at present, so how will they get to know? Unless we intentionally tell them?'

Why had I not remembered, given all the sexual information and education I had had with the Olarians? How, I wondered, would they take to the information we would share with them when we returned to our telepathic reality? I imagined they would be first surprised, then when they had experimented, delighted.

So we had managed the sexual connection pretty well. We could engage in that without our telepathic reality and could very definitely give each other mutual satisfaction. There was no question we could and did feel loving, caring, loved and cared for, and without any negative spin-off of which we were aware.

But had we learned anything about how humans could operate successfully, non-violently in a non-telepathic world? Human hostility, violence, aggression, anger and rage had no part in our intimate connection. So I was not sure how convincing ourselves we could be loving and share pleasure took us any further down the road toward the absence of violence between people. It had opened the door to the fact we could be loving without our telepathic connection. However, unless my brain had become unhinged, I already knew and had confirmed the link between mutual care-taking, pleasure and non-violence.

But I'm not sure I could see how humanity would be free of weapons and free of any impulse for violence toward others – any others. This was what we needed for entry into the cosmic community and for me, now, it seemed to be as far away as ever. I shook my head. It was an acknowledgment of my frustration.

Then I began to wonder why had we chosen sex and intimacy as our very first port of call after moving away from out telepathic contact?

Certainly it was not in dispute that people who felt emotionally satisfied in their relationships were unlikely to feel hostile and violent toward others. And the opposite was true: people who were unsatisfied and could not express their needs or pay attention to others appropriately might well slide toward violence. So not knowing how to ask for what they wanted or needed, and if they were unable or unwilling to ask, then the failure to make a good connection to another human being might well be incentive to act violently, antisocially. I let that thought take me further.

If I was rejected or felt deprived, I might feel angry. If I felt angry, I might want to lash out, strike or hurt another, be violent, responding inappropriately to my inadequacy, incompetence, weakness. Also, if I could see others who had things or money or wealth that I did not, might I not also feel competitive, angry, and act to do something that would, I might believe, make me feel better?

Then there was the issue of violence on a very large scale: war, a form of state-sanctioned violence based on locally held values and a degree of homogeneity perhaps, and undoubtedly underpinned by the motivation of people in positions of power. Other strands of violence lay with feelings of weakness or anxiety/fear – a desire to feel powerful, or one powered by a belief system that insisted on, or created, a feeling of righteousness in destroying others who were simply different and did not believe the same things; people who simply looked different, were of a different color, believed different things, had a different history.

At its core, it seemed probable that growing up feeling not okay about yourself, about whole- of-country self-depreciation, schoolyard bad experiences, home-based bad experiences, if not dealt with when they needed to be, might well become the wellspring of negativity and hostility that led to violence, something that was unlikely to emerge among people who took care of one another.

In a similar vein, people whose education had been minimal, who did not have a wider perspective or knowledge and understanding about the more complex belief and value systems outside their own, might also be led toward violence in the absence of that larger perspective. I included in this melange someone, usually male, who was minimally intellectually in a place to allow them to understand how to deal with others whose behavior made them feel small; often men, but sometimes women, who took out their frustrations and expressed their inadequacies through actions against others in small or large scale.

I could see the two strands that needed managing. Weapons needed to go, but without managing personal fears, inadequacies and a full range of emotions, people were not going to be non-violent. It was so much easier to be non-violent when everyone always knew what others were thinking and feeling. Especially if those thoughts and feelings were caring, loving and co-operative, and where homogeneity left little room for hostility toward others, especially outsiders.

The week came to a close. The eight of us sat around our dining room table looking at one another, knowing there was an hour or two to go before we would return to our telepathic reality. We had agreed to do this, and I imagined that I was not the only one wondering 'where is it leading us?'

In telepathic space, I totally trusted and felt safe and comfortable with these seven people. In non-telepathic space, I had no idea what was going through their minds or how they were feeling about anything, especially about me. As I thought about that, I wondered why in heaven's name I was questioning everything, especially these people, with whom I felt closer than any other people in my entire life. But not knowing what they were thinking and feeling was seriously disturbing my ability to sit here and be comfortable, to engage with any meaningful conversation, except one that cleared up this uncertainty so we could move on to getting things done!

'Okay, I'm going to have a crack at dealing with this in a non-telepathic way. To each of you I need to say, in the absence of telepathic certainty, I feel as though I cannot trust you absolutely, yet the moment these words are out of my mouth, I am appalled that I have said them.'

And so I realized I was not necessarily behaving in my head in the way I would have behaved before I became actively telepathic. Nevertheless, bit by bit I was coming to see the obstruction that a non-telepathic reality actually was. I think I was assimilating the reality that, without a continuous telepathic connection, trust, mutual understanding and caring were very considerably more difficult commodities to possess and experience. It was only a small step away from this point where uncertainty, mistrust, then anxiety, fear and violence were lurking.

I knew that if I had to live without the knowledge of others that a telepathic reality made possible, I would need, and would want to spend time, *doing* something that felt useful; something as mundane as earning money to live or engaging in something that I could believe to be creative or constructive. Doing this would probably compensate me for inadequate connection to others Yet some people I had met were not violent. Some of the women especially were not violent, ever; they were essentially nurturing, which seemed to be a fundamentally non-violent position.

I looked around the table and smiled.

'Is there any one of us who is not feeling uncomfortable and uncertain about what everyone else is thinking and feeling?'

I laid out what had been going through my mind. It was as if my simply saying all this stuff opened the floodgates and there was a babble of conversation and I burst out laughing.

'Just listen to us. Imagine having watched us for the last 15 minutes. It's horrifying! The longer we drag ourselves through this seriously limiting reality, one that was the norm for us until we learned about our telepathic capabilities, the more difficult it is becoming to move forward with confidence, to be collectively creative, confident and comfortable.

'And yet, I feel as though we might be missing the point.'

I turned to Januti.

'I would like for us to talk together in a way we might have talked if we had not met when I was telepathic. Will you give this a try?'

She smiled at me. It was a knowing smile, not one to which I could properly connect. 'Of course,' she replied.

And then I realized...

'Januti, when I asked, you smiled, and I felt your smile, and the feeling was that you knew stuff that I did not. Have I got that much right?'

She looked at me, just a little differently.

'Yes,' she replied.

So I raised my right eyebrow and tilted my head to the other side, a question mark hanging between us.

'Zed, you must know. I'm a woman; my automatic response to people who do not threaten me is nurturing. If I feel threatened, because as a normal human woman I am not powerful, I become sad or fearful and am likely to cry or behave in some other either submissive or indirectly aggressive way. If you understand this and you do not want to harm me, and I know that is true for you, then we can talk about how we might deal with disagreements so they do not need to result in violence. However, if I was smarter than you, I might be able to say things to you or about you that would further strip your sense of being in control, then you would probably become even more angry, which would be your way of hiding your feelings of inadequacy toward me. Is this not clear to you?'

I looked at her and thought about what she was saying to me. I knew she was right. But... and I was thinking about why this did not happen at the ILC or in any ordinary Olarian education situation. I realized that on OlarCret there was clear intention to take care of others, especially children, and in the early stages of their education they all learned constructive behavior.

Understanding other people's discomfort was always associated with helping them understand and know they were being taken care of. Every interaction in their learning centers was premised on the clear intention to care for others first, then establish understanding, and never attempt to move to any form of violence or interpersonal damage. I knew this was not the way these situations were managed on Earth or Second Earth in homes or educational organizations, or almost anywhere...

As I thought about this, I remembered Ghia's intuition, way back after our first contact with the Olarians. 'If we spent our time managing interpersonal situations like the Olarians, we would never have developed our science and technology, and so never have been able to design and build *Sunstreamer*, so we would never have got here. Maybe that's why the Olarians have not. The rest of the crew could not do their job on *Sunstreamer* if they had to pay attention to how everyone was feeling and had to make sure everyone was feeling all right.'

She had indeed captured a central issue in this dilemma. We had had to choose between people or things. The telepathic and telekinetic Olarians had chosen people and non-telepathic humans had chosen things.

I realized we might have achieved what we had set out to do and suggested we return to our new normal.

There was a quiet in the room as everyone re-established their connections. Then came a flood of relief and satisfaction and an extraordinary amount of exploration by everyone of each of the others, but especially of their partners, before our usual chatter, banter and awareness re-established, and we all were feeling the sense of relief that now attached to it.

Then a discussion began in earnest that reflected the level of disturbance and concern everyone was feeling. There was no longer any lack of clarity about the consequences attached to the absence of telepathic awareness. Everyone agreed it was huge, that they had simply lost sight of their pre-telepathic experience. It took almost no time for us to agree that to make a non-violent, sensitive world might well require a level of openness and honesty, a level of determined intent and education, that was simply unlikely to ever occur universally in a normal human population unless there was an almost uninterrupted and nearly unimaginable information flow about thoughts and feelings.

On top of that, to erase the tension, anger and interpersonal hostility associated with the extreme range of differences between cultural groups, language groups, geographic groups, religious groups, skin-color groups and physical-appearance groups... meant teaching everyone to do... what exactly?

I felt depressed. None of the others were feeling optimistic. CROLEA might seem to be the obvious starting point but even with the re-afforestation work on Earth, and with the beginning signs of population management, we were not going to manage the violence, the weapons or the almost continuous outbreak of small wars. Disarming the human world seemed a seriously incomplete but essential strategy. All of us were thinking, 'might it also be true that they all need to be telepathic as well?'

So we looked at one another and shook our collective heads.

The reason we were all struggling with the weapons, violence and money was that the money economy made everything have a monetary value, which meant everything could be bought. But you can't buy integrity, honesty, and the important things in societies that tend to get lost in the soft twilight. So, money, greed, power and status quickly replaced softer, gentler values. Money and power alongside building 'stuff', even stuff like spaceships and sophisticated navigational systems, became what mattered. But if you look carefully, as we did on our first visit to OlarCret, the Olarians do not get trapped in the impersonal.

So, in the end, we thought money had to go and the weapons had to go, yet we knew the violence would not go with them. It would be no more than a beginning. Probably the best start we were presently able to imagine.

CHAPTER 38

An Uninvited Intervention

We sat and looked at one another. The eight of us certainly believed we were supposed to do something about helping the three worlds in which we had become involved reach a position from which they could receive an invitation – from somewhere, some entity perhaps – to join the cosmic community. With that in mind, I found myself wanting to talk about what we had done to de-weaponize Cretia. Then I began again to think about some of the other people we could benefit from having present in this conversation. All the non-telepaths, now aging but all in good health, had remained our friends.

So, Jess and Raille, Olaria, Tanzin and Jald, Miyuki and of course Paldi and any of the Olarians who wanted to participate. Realising we needed only a small number of actual physical bodies, we added the Olarian Council of Eight and that was as far as I could go without risking our visibility, except for members of the ILC cohort who were wanting to participate.

Paldi and the ILC contingent excepted, all of the others had been involved in some way with de-weaponising Cretia, and of all of them, I believed, Jess might have the strongest feelings. All were happy to come and three of us went off to get them. An hour later we had all settled down. Not surprisingly, more than 40 members of the ILC community had chosen to participate and this naturally included Rozari. In every case they came with their partners. I looked at Jess and realized I had invited none of the non-telepathic Cretians. I immediately felt bad about that, and I asked Jess if she thought there were members of her world who ought to be here. She spoke to Rozari's Cretian partner, Atrick, telepathically so we could all hear. They both believed that, for the moment, it would be best not to risk jeopardising our visibility!

With that decided, I began.

I have to say that I do not really know how, or perhaps more accurately, where, to begin. Over recent years we have met three different cosmic societies: the Heral, the Wheeir and the Irawar. For reasons that do not appear to be known to any of them, the eight of us are somehow involved in the introduction of the Olarians, the Cretians and the human worlds into the cosmic constellation of species. That is pretty highfalutin, arrogant-sounding stuff, but we think it is probably true.

We also believe we are somehow required to be involved in solving the problem of how to get everybody into the cosmic community. This may sound a bit bloody pompous, but we have just spent a few days without our telepathic capabilities and it has helped us confirm this belief.

This is a not insignificant step away from how we were thinking a few years ago. We were wondering what we ought to be doing, as though this was something we needed to examine ourselves about. Then it began to occur to us that we were not here to fulfill our personal agendas. We were here to undertake a task that may not have been of our choosing. That has changed our thinking.

I suspect we are, in fact, not human, but that we are indeed travelers from somewhere in the cosmic community. That we are here to help, somehow, to support the changes that will result in these three worlds moving onward and upward into the cosmic world. From a human perspective: arrogant. From another: meaningful? But whatever is the reality, we are here, alive, we feel human, we want to act intelligently and we want to be a meaningful part of this existence.

We have spent a not inconsiderable amount of time talking about ourselves! Thinking that it is, in some way, as I said, pretty certain we are not human, even though we look human and feel human and most of our early lives were lived as humans. But we are in a number of ways enhanced! Seems a strange word to use, but we are able, as are our children, to travel to worlds none of the three societies with whom we primarily connect are, as yet, able to do.

And, more significantly, we seem able – permitted – to undertake some activities in the cosmos that are usually not permitted, and this seems to be information we ought not to ignore.

I stopped for a moment to let that thought seep into our minds.

We have tried to find an explanation for our existence here and been unsuccessful. So we are guessing we are here to do something that cannot be done by any of the three societies with whom we now interact and with whom we have numerous deep and satisfying relationships.

The other thing we have learned, primarily from the Heral, is that a genuine and absolute absence of violence of any kind is a non-negotiable prerequisite for entry into the cosmic community. Our best analysis is there are in all three societies issues involving violence that are unresolved.

I really don't know how we seem to have come to believe we are expected to do something about this, however, right now we feel the need. So for no other reason than that we know all of you and do not feel it would be safe to include any other members of the human or Cretian worlds yet, we have asked you to help us. Or if you disagree with our belief, please say so and help us take it out of our way.

I ought to add, we have allowed ourselves, or at least Januti and I have allowed ourselves, to be seen and known by the Cretian world but not by the human world. That feels quite strange, although I do understand how that happened. For the moment, if I actually understand Jess, that does not seem to be a concern. If I am wrong, or one of you thinks differently, please say now.

No-one did, so I went on.

We had one other thought but do not at present know quite what to do with it – maybe we ought to find a way to begin discussions among and between all three communities. One of the issues here is that we are not clear what exactly people would be discussing! We think it might be about having Cretian and human societies made telepathic. We would also like to hear people's opinions on that and also anybody's opinion about maintaining, as far as possible, our invisibility.

It had been a clumsy introduction, however, it had taken us into the issue with which we believed we were engaged. It fit into the rubric of 'what were the eight of us doing here?' So I listened to the groups and waited. The others were with me in agreeing that this did seem to be our issue.

Tanzin was the first to pick up the challenge.

Zed, I know I have said this before in other situations and it may sound repetitious and so a bit unlike my usual self, but, you have been single-handedly responsible for making my life genuinely satisfying. I cannot tell you how many times I have been deeply grateful I was on Sunstreamer *with you when we first visited what was then, to us, an uninhabited planet designated Omega5Z3.*

I have also said this before: if you want help of any kind that I can offer, you can rest assured it is yours for the asking. It no longer surprises me to find you and your group at the heart of something astonishing; it has simply become the norm. So, for mine, just lead on, and in whatever way I can I will help you.

I was watching Jald as she spoke, and I was absolutely delighted to see the way he looked at her and to feel the depth of pleasure and satisfaction that they had got together after thinking they ought to stay apart. He turned away from his feelings of pleasure as he looked at her and focused for a moment on me and the others.

Zed, you know you were expected when Sunstreamer *slid into orbit over our beautiful planet. Mother had somehow been warned to expect you, unbeknown to you. I don't know how she knew* – he was looking at Olaria – *but from wherever that awareness came, it was a very great thing for all of us. Just count me in.*

As he finished, he smiled, because he had learned that phrase from

Tanzin and had become very attached to it. 'Just count me in.' I smiled. We were lucky to have people who had come to love us. Over the next 15 minutes every person in the room spoke quietly and warmly. That included every one of the members of the ILC community. No-one sitting in this space on OlarCret really knew where to next. I was filled with satisfaction to find that everyone, including Jess, was open to exploring with us the dilemma we had brought here. So after looking at Januti and the others I knew I was expected to make the running.

All right, here is my summary, please correct it or take it on if you can. The closest to an entirely violence-free society in act and intention is the Olarian world. They have supplied the rest of us with education and understanding about co-operation and non-violence. However, we and they know that an unresolved issue is that there have been no natural enemies who would or could challenge them and put to the test their non-violent value system. This is true because Olaria's father and his Originals removed access to their enemies. He hid the Cretians behind an energy wall and destroyed the early non-telepathic community who had been fighting them.

In retrospect, it was an incredibly deeply insightful act but also abhorrent in its way from where we sit today. But it is truly difficult to imagine what else Jard might have done given what he knew and his prior experience at that moment in their history. However, history and events are not isolated elements of reality. What was real in the value system of one time does not necessarily fit appropriately into the value system of a later or different time. It is easy to miss the significance of this idea, and the consequences may not always be constructive, helpful, or appropriate. Making retrospective judgments may well be an act of arrogance and clouded thinking.

However, what we do not know is, if there should be a threat of destruction or annihilation, would the Olarian world turn violent and defend themselves in the most powerful way they could, or, with no other choice but to retaliate, choose instead to die? And what we also do not know is whether this is even the right question.

I'll go on, then someone needs to help us take a new step.

The Cretian world has seemingly been violent and militaristic since its very early days. We traveled back nearly 4000 years to see what had been the reality near its beginning. We found that it too had become militaristic to protect itself from a very aggressive warlike society who had been oppressing them for hundreds of years. Their militaristic fervor was a direct result of working to ensure their survival in a hostile world.

They successfully destroyed their oppressors but maintained and developed their warlike stance; its purpose, to ensure such oppression would never happen again. When it became clear there were no other hostile societies around them, they turned to more structured hostilities among themselves. It was this society that Jard and his Originals confronted 3000 years ago. And, since we made the journey, Jess and Raille have been working to fit Cretian history into a wider perspective, comparative to human and Olarian realities.

In 2096 Earth time, our spaceship, Sunstreamer, *arrived and settled into orbit over this planet, which we knew only as Omega5Z3.* Sunstreamer *arrived over OlarCret with a human crew including Raille, Tanzin and myself aboard. We had been sent by Miyuki, who was running SFC at the time. Perhaps the most significant event was that the Cretians attacked us at the same time they exploded a nuclear bomb against the energy wall. Subsequently we learned they thought we were Olarians who had decided to intrude into their airspace.*

Thus alerted, we were able to see the danger to the entire planet posed by their nuclear developments. Then, at the behest of the Olarians, who had had for 3000 years no substantive contact with any non-Olarian society, we engaged in a social change program that began with de-weaponising the Cretian world. This was done in the interests of both their future survival and that of the Olarians. Not forgetting the survival of the planet.

Now this turns out to be one of the strange twists in this story, because had we not been involved, it is not unlikely the Cretian world would have developed like the human world. Assuming they did not wipe out their own society with nuclear fallout, they might have finally got over the wall and confronted the Olarians. That might have sparked a violent response from the Olarians, or it might have sparked simply another blocking response, a great deal depending on whether the planet remained free from devastating nuclear fallout.

So reality at this point posed a conundrum. But it was essentially the concern that the future for the planet might include a nuclear disaster, brought about inadvertently by the Cretian experiments with nuclear weapons, that got us involved.

Have I stated anything inaccurately or inappropriately so far from your perspective, Jess?

I could feel her crawling through my reality, my intentions, my feelings, my judgments and finally settling back in her seat and smiling warmly at me.

Zed, I don't know why I still feel as though I have to check that you are not putting us Cretians down, but again, having checked you out with the tools you have given me, I know that there is absolutely no put-down, no malice and no negativity in your presentation of what you, I believe, accurately see as the facts. So no, I have no discomfort whatsoever about your analysis. I believe it to be very likely as close to the truth as it could possibly be.

I smiled at her and into her; she was not only beautiful on the outside, she was a beautiful creature inside as well, and I could see and feel Raille smiling at me.

Okay, that being the case, the Cretian world is now free of weapons and is slowly moving toward a non-violent culture. It seems probable that its move toward a matriarchy, or perhaps a matri-focal society, is helping it move away from violence as an acceptable social process.

Human society is less unclear. It is fully weaponized and extremely violent. There is no doubt that while it is so extensively weaponized and economically controlled, it is very unlikely to become less violent. And that would appear to be a kind of low-level and simplistic broad brushstroke of the state of violence across our three societies. Anyone wanting to improve on that will be very welcome. Anyone wanting to propose measures they can imagine that might work toward the removal of any attributes of violence will be even more welcome.

With that I shut up and looked around. No-one spoke but Rozari leant over to Atrick and gently kissed him. It was just so satisfying to see him almost glow with delight. She whispered to him and he nodded slowly and quietly and she left her seat beside him and came and sat on my lap, put her hands around my neck and rested her head on my shoulder.

In about 15 seconds, two wraith-like figures slipped into our space and settled either side of Januti and me. Both smiled at Rozari and they greeted each other. Felarv slipped inside Januti and Albor did the same with me. Then Albor spoke to me, and I could understand.

You need to tell everyone except your eight and your children that we are here. They will have seen nothing, and even though you have summoned us, they will still not be able to see or hear.

I paused for only a moment to look at Januti. She smiled, slid closer and took my hand. So I addressed the room.

It seems, although I was not aware, I have asked two friends to visit. To all of you who can neither see nor hear them, Felarv is with Januti and Albor is with me and they are our contacts from the Heral. If I understand correctly they will have a message for us from among the societies of the cosmic world.

Moments passed. I had no idea how much time was involved before I was aware that Felarv and Albor were speaking to us. Then each slid out of us and Albor spoke to me.

You must know by now, if you need us, we will always come. However, we would ask that it be only in a situation of dire distress or, as in this situation, pressing need. You know we must come if you seek us, but would ask you, in so far as possible, not to, please.

Both disappeared.

I looked at Januti. She smiled and rested her head on my other shoulder and in an instant I fully understood all that Albor had shared with me. Rozari returned to sit beside Atrick, took his hand and moved as close to him as she could. His contentment, as well as hers, was unmistakeable.

I smiled at them and then began to relay the information that had been shared with us.

In more billions of years than anyone of us can count, no act of violence or any act of hostility has ever occurred in the cosmic world community. In the course of time, in solar systems in many places, many millions of sentient societies have come and gone, unable to even meet the cosmic community world.

Several things are true. The Olarians have found a path toward absolute non-violence. They have managed to help the Cretian world de-weaponize and move toward a genuine non-violent future. The human world has found a way to move beyond the limitations of life inside their original solar system. These qualities mean all three of these societies might, in the future, be able to join the cosmic community. However, each has a different challenge with which to deal. It is likely the fate of each will be tied up with the others, for reasons we do not fully understand.

Each life form is around the same age. Because all three societies have met, an interesting yet unusual situation, it is feasible all three might join the cosmic community, but only if all three can work together– Albor and Felarv stressed this – to solve the issue of absolute non-violence. All three are now, though not truly knowingly, bound together.

That was the message from the Heral.

Natalya was looking directly at me, and Peter, who was sitting beside her, was looking at her. He knew what she was about to say, was just slightly uncomfortable about it. Then, before speaking to us, she spoke quietly to him.

Peter, it is okay. Truly, please trust me on this. I have been quietly mulling it over since I picked up the vibe in the room. We have some diverse but not hostile differences here with which to deal.

He continued looking at her, studying her, finally acknowledging she might be right. So she began.

Zed, everyone. I can feel the discomfort that is lying at a low level among many of you and especially among the human contingent, more especially our children with human partners. However, I feel obliged to put my cards on the table in all our interests.

I feel quite certain our first and most pressing concern is to remove the weapons of war and hostility from the human world community. I am equally certain this will never be done voluntarily by them. So I believe we ought to simply do it, even given the extraordinary rift this will make in our engagement with them should they find out who we are.

She paused.

So for us to continue to be useful we will need to remain out of sight, in much the way Zed originally did with Kiyoshi some 30 or so years ago, even though this did not seem to be necessary with the Cretian world. Although Jess has reminded me, more than once, the only Cretians who actually know who we are are her family and the members of the ILC. In total, a very small number!

There was an almost silent kind of hiss of surprise, almost disbelief, from many places through the group, however, after only a short silence the message being thought was most strongly one of agreement. So Natalya continued.

It would be my thought that we ought to proceed in some orderly fashion to simply remove every weapon from every location we can find, which should be 99 percent of them, and then pick up the odd one we miss later. My feeling is, we ought to begin this by engaging with the absolute power brokers and those who might have the information we need. The Cretian world were reluctant supporters, however, they had political and social structures that could work for rather than against them. The human world, so far as I can see, does not.

The group was holding in a lot of tension, and I was not entirely certain I had picked up the major source of it. Then I slowly got it. It was coming, in different forms, from every group in the room. It was not that the idea was not fully supportable; it was that it seemed to be a very intrusive and imperious act, one which ignored the possible interests of the human society, and it appeared a huge and unmanageable job to them. So I picked up the theme.

If you break it down, surely it is only time. From the office of most of the heads of state every ICBM, every space weapons system, every manufacturer of every kind of weapon, every individual weapon and all ammunition, every weapon on an aircraft or a boat, in a police station or a military locale can be identified and reduced to dust with ease by any one of us. The truth is we could denude the planet of weapons and remove all weapons on any spacecraft in all probability in less than a week.

With the expressions of surprise, there were nods of understanding followed by agreement. So Natalya continued.

We could then seek out and destroy all the ones we had missed in the week following, and we could in the following weeks identify everything else that we had missed: all holdings and manufacturing and storage everywhere. We would need to wait only for the space weapons systems of spacecraft out of our solar system, and these could be identified and picked up as they returned. We would have to make it crystal clear we were not Olarian so they were not inappropriately being held responsible. We would have to make similar sweeps on Second Earth. But, essentially, these days, there is nothing either difficult or complicated about such an intervention for any of the eight of us or, in all probability, our children.

However, like Zed and Raille with your people, Jess, there has to be a follow-up. We know, as Zed described in the early days, creating the disturbance that heralds change is the easy part. Finding the pathways that will enable the change to have its desired consequences is by far the more difficult thing to do. In time that will lead to a new normal, however, we do not want the new normal to be either violent or unpleasant, and our only point of reference for how this ought to be done is the Olarian way. In addition, we ought to consider the time frame. It does not have to be done in a few years, a few decades or even a few centuries, nevertheless it does need to be begun.

Natalya looked around the room.

And that was as simple as it could be. Everyone in the room turned out to be in agreement. Everyone wanted the human world to have a reasonable chance to pull itself into the framework needed for the cosmic communities because, it seemed certain, we were operating in an all-or-nothing environment. Most of us realized we were probably talking many years, maybe even many centuries.

So during the following two weeks, using a map similar to the one I had first used with Kiyoshi-san of the Yakuza all those years ago and the map Raille and I had used with the Cretian world, pretty well every weapon connected with the human world was destroyed, but not yet every single one. Slowly over the following week, with the help of our children and the ILC Olarian contingent, the specific exceptions were located and the eight of us destroyed them. This was intrusive; it did not involve the actions of the human world, however, we rationalized this by looking at the extent and volume of weapons, weapons systems, ammunition and on and on.

No-one believed the problem of violence was in any way resolved by the removal of weapons from every place. It took not a week but more than five years to weed out every single one and to manage the almost continuous attempts to create new weapons factories. But in the end, after almost a decade had passed, there had been a full year with no attempts to create weapons. As with the Cretians, a limited system of old-fashioned, small hand-held weapons were made available to farmers and hunters all over the world, but with a very, very well organized and monitored licensing system. In addition, extensive discussions and communications, all of which kept us out of sight, had to be held to manage police and security systems. However, we remained firm: no exceptions, no weapons.

During this time Miyuki, Raille and Jess and Tanzin were aging and we knew that our ageless appearance did act as a more or less constant reminder that they would eventually die and leave us. To be honest, I am not certain we were prepared for the loss this would be for us. Sometimes when the eight of us were alone together, we would share our thoughts and feelings about this, and I realized during one of these discussions, really, I was the only one who had been emotionally connected to them. Yet the other seven did feel deeply connected, and so the sadness was going to be genuinely shared among us.

It was not until the absence of weapons was finally real to all of us that we felt we could begin to deal with the issues that increasingly large numbers of people from every society were beginning to consider. Our most disconcerting act was to finally, 35 years after we had found ourselves, inform the human world that among them, and totally out of their ability to find, there existed a small community of telekinetic telepaths, and that it was us who had made the decision to remove weapons from the human world.

It is hard to encapsulate in words, or in this brief space, the extraordinary range of emotions and responses this act and this information spawned. Everything from rage and frustration to fear, and in other quarters, hope and satisfaction. The webs – the network of online discussions and sites that discussed everything – exuded anger, rage and frustration and demanded we immediately return everything to the state it had been in before weapons were removed. In place of all the sophisticated weapons we had destroyed, sticks, stones and knives and the like had quickly become the weapons of choice.

The entire original group present at the time of The Decision believed it was necessary to inform the human world not only what was being done and by whom, but why. This had proved a very complex task, because many of those involved were not hostile to the process but were hostile to the idea of being manipulated by some unknown outside force.

As had always been the case, the 'virtue signallers' – those who appeared to want to be seen as concerned over the moral status of the world but were actually simply frightened and deeply prejudiced and emotionally unsatisfied, and sometimes very angry people – could quite easily be seen for what they were: people with little real courage, people who wanted power but could see no honest way to get it except by bad-mouthing people who were not like them and who were not interested in their disingenuous goodness.

In similar fashion to the experience in Cretia, removing the weapons did not impact significantly on the violence people wanted to inflict on one another. Fewer people were being killed, that is true, however, every day huge numbers of people were being hurt. It was evident as we began to follow the violence that it was in homes where mostly men were feeling under attack from the society around them, but also from many of their female partners. Our observations supported what we had come to believe: frustration, a degree of insensitivity, a feeling of limited ability to manage their relational lives, and similar factors provided the backdrop for violence and were a vehicle for managing interpersonal relationships and beliefs of all kinds, of which almost none supported a non-violent world.

There was still, of course, the covert racism, domestic violence, classroom violence, workplace racial and country-against-country violence to which we now needed to add civilization-to-civilization tensions.

Humans and Cretians had always felt comfort from associating with people like themselves. And, in spite of the extraordinarily successful multi-cultural life that had been developed all over the Earth, humans remained often deeply connected to those who were like themselves, if not in skin color or place of birth, then religion and like-mindedness. This was not actually difficult to understand, and it permeated every domain of human society. Difference, it turned out, did not only influence and impact less well-educated members of society.

Religion and the inculcating of religious beliefs in children were extraordinarily potent elements. A small number of religions had a colossal number of followers, and the efforts of these groups to find us and undo what we were doing consumed the energy of many. Olarian society was the unique exception. It seemed very likely being telepathic accounted for that.

We wanted to ensure that, like the Olarians, every person grew up with positive and self-affirming experiences with more loving and caring in their education. We also wanted people to grow up understanding that verbal and emotional violence was at least as toxic and destructive as physical violence. But where the hell were we going to begin? Was it even vaguely conceivable that we could ask the Olarians to become responsible for human and Cretian education? But then, they might benefit from this as much as the other societies would do.

In the end we met with the telepathic world and asked one question: how could we help the intense – to us, fanatical – religious groups consider changing their early teachings and their need to hold so tight a grip on their young adherents? And ought we? If we could just persuade them to accept pacifistic beliefs and principles and build these into their early teachings, might this be enough? And we wondered: what might the effect/impact be on their children if they were to become telepathic? We felt confident that without the Olarian value system, telepathy might not be as helpful as we would like to imagine.

CHAPTER 39

Baby Steps

As time passed, the various groups in our three worlds just got on with their lives. It seemed as though not a lot was happening, then something would stir up a new direction. About two years after our last engagement, a group of eight people decided they wanted some action. They wanted first to sit together and talk about options. The group comprised an Olarian couple; one of our children and her partner; a Cretian girl, Quianna, and her partner, one of my sons, Aziq; a human man from one of the seven families with his Olarian partner; and a human man from one of the seven families from Second Earth and his partner, who was one of Peter's daughters. They asked Januti and me to join them. This was an entirely ILC contingent, and it was Quianna who began.

I am choosing to begin because I have probably been one of the loudest voices in this discussion. I want to say first, I do not believe any possibility exists for the deletion of violence from my parents' world until or unless every Cretian is telepathic. I know that my educational experience is in no way similar to that of any of my family or their friends, and I do mean any *of their friends.*

Aziq and I have been, during the long break from ILC, living with my family in Cretia. We have told them from the moment we became a couple that Aziq had agreed to keep me telepathic for the entirety of my life with him. Immediately the majority of my family ceased to be loving and caring toward me, became afraid, distrustful and barely communicative. Even my mother and father, both of whom should have known better. It was just awful.

I desperately wanted to cease being telepathic and at my insistence Aziq stopped the telepathic process and I went back to being an ordinary Cretian with them. However, this made no difference. The damage had been done. Nothing I could say or do would unpick this destructive knot that had been tied.

After only three days, I gave up and had Aziq return my telepathic ability. In this condition I could better deal with my family and after nearly three weeks they relented and agreed to keep me connected within the family. They decided they would accept – accept, not welcome – Aziq. I don't know if I was more hurt, angry or frustrated.

I should add, the days when I was not telepathic could easily have done extraordinary harm to my relationship with Aziq because in that short period of time I had felt uncertain about how he really felt about me and I had no idea what he was thinking. It was appalling. I never want to spend another second of my life being anything except telepathic.

Now I will briefly speak for every genetically non-telepathic partner in this room, welcoming anyone to contradict me. We felt the power and value of our telepathic state when each of us gave it up for just a day, which everyone did after my experience.

Deceit, duplicity, lies, misunderstandings, fear, uncertainty, lowering of confidence... I could go on and on... these were the minimal dysfunctions we all found might occur in a non-telepathic state, even though we knew this was not the way any of our partners or our friends would ever behave. Knowing this made no difference. We have come to rely absolutely on the constant accurate awareness of others' thoughts and feelings.

This is why we did what Zed originally persuaded Olaria's Council of Eight to do when Sunstreamer *first arrived here. We and our telepathic partners ceased being telepathic for just three days. Like your eight, Zed, we found it horrible, potentially destructive, damaging to us as a couple, and we all returned to our telepathic world with some new understandings but without having really sorted it all out.*

These experiences have brought us to a very clear position. We believe we need to ask you, your eight and your children, acting together, to arrange with societies in the cosmic world to biologically engineer telepathy into our world. We need to find ways to ensure that every child over the coming centuries will be helped to be and remain telepathic from very early in their lives. We believe they will need to remain that way through an Olarian-constructed education until they die. We think this is the only hope for the human and Cretian worlds.

We have worked as carefully as possible to understand what might work. We know Cretians and humans have both learned to operate co-operatively in some aspects of their culture, have learned to work co-operatively on many really complex tasks, for example in the building and operating of everything including interstellar spaceships.

So it seems likely they will be able to learn to not tolerate any form of violence in the same way the Olarians have done. However, we are certain they will be unable to do this in the absence of telepathic capabilities or in the absence of an Olarian education such as we were able to have.

We suspect, based on our limited experience and on the Living Library's records of Zed's group, that both human and Cretian development of ever bigger and more complex projects may be based, as Zed suggested way back then, in the attention to things in these projects. Attention that moves the mind away from the interpersonal and allows it to rest and operate in the logical and impersonal world of mathematics, complex logical concepts and things. This ensures that only a limited degree of energy and attention needs to be paid to others. Rules built inside a hierarchy are put in place to allow the operation of 'things' and the system, and so no energy needs to be wasted in the exploration of interpersonal emotional concerns.

Aziq, who had been studying very ancient human history, suggested that the relationships inside the late British monarchy may well have been based on a similar framework. He suggested they put in place extraordinary levels of protocol to maintain their public front and so cover up their interpersonal distress. They even went so far as to block marriages based on love if they would be outside the rules of protocol that had been established, as though these were actually more important than the living emotions of the members of the family! If you study what they managed to achieve and maintain for centuries, in some ways perhaps they were correct!

At which point she stopped and all of us just looked at her.

At ILC we all learned how to operate without an economy, without money and everything connected to it. We have talked this over numerous times. None of us ever want to be involved with money and with the behaviors and values of an economically managed world, but we cannot see how this will be possible if we have to live on Earth or Second Earth or Cretia.

It is the slow grasp of greed that seems to take hold of some, and for others it's the urge for possessions, especially possessions of great magnitude. This urge seems to just creep up on them. I think they somehow bypass relationships and come to see themselves – and want others to see them – as larger than life or smarter than others. So many destructive, negative emotions seem to be elicited by the behaviors surrounding the operation of a moneyed economy.

She paused for a moment.

The very existence of a financially operated world is disturbing to us. We feel trapped by it. We know that our telepathic capabilities and our telekinetic skills, which exist for one partner in every couple, could ensure we had all the money we needed, but we would have to cheat to achieve this. An economic world seems to almost demand greed and cheating as its drivers. I have come to feel that greed, avarice, and their associated emotions and states are not far away from cheating and several close forms of dishonesty.

A large percentage of people appear to want more money than they need in order to feel secure. They also generally want more 'things' than they need, often because other people have these better, bigger, more beautiful 'things'. So our question is to you, Zed. How are we to survive and achieve the outcomes you and your group have espoused for us and the three wildly diverse cultures? I am asking, what will replace the economic aspirations of the majority of people who survive in an economically managed world? What purposes, aspirations, ambitions, hopes and fears can realistically and practically become the basis of people's lives?

The rest of our eight had joined us. We looked at one another and I realized what each of us was actually thinking and that we were probably right. Firstly, we could not solve this problem. The ILC children, the first cohort of which were now young adults, needed to lead the way, and all of us knew this problem could almost certainly not be managed in one generation.

We had early on come to believe that knowledge and enhancing relationships were primary Olarian goals, though certainly not primary ones for a large percentage of the human population. The appropriate question to ask might be, how ought we to begin, and how ought we to progress? Recognizing our task would be to begin a process that might take any time up to or even beyond a single century, a different mindset and time frame were needed. The strategy ought to be thought through, as far as seemed possible and practical, before beginning the process, and we all knew we could not extend the lives of the non-telekinetic members of our worlds.

Furthermore, a new awareness had arisen for the eight of us. We could not travel more than 70 years into the future, and journeys into the future did not allow us to return with knowledge of what we had seen and heard. Every attempt to do so failed; we were simply being blocked from traveling further on or bringing back memories. Not only could we not travel further ahead but when we asked the Heral to make the journey for us, while they reported they could and would be willing to do this, they could not bring back any information about what they had seen. They never had any recall of their journeys; we were the only group they had ever encountered who were able to recall what they had seen and heard in their travels into the future! And this had been extraordinarily limited and then only to Zed and Januti and only twice before it ceased to be possible.

So, 70 years ahead was our limit, set by whom we did not know, and we could only guess at why. So we could not easily establish the long-term consequences of any action we might take or be involved with. Then there was the final straw in utilising this capability: if we did travel 70 years ahead and did not like the consequences of a decision, would we dare to interrupt and make a change that would impact history? No matter how we sliced and diced this, the answer always came back to us the same: until or unless we could know in advance how changing events in time might play out through future history, we simply did not dare!

We made one last attempt to pass this boundary when we asked the Heral to take us to 100 years ahead, which they very, very reluctantly did. However, on our return we could recall nothing of our experiences beyond the 70-year point and had no residual feelings onto which we might have been able to attach meaning. We were definitely being blocked. We knew there was something in this for us to learn but we could not yet fathom it. So this was not a method to make judgments about what we should do next. We were clearly intended to take this next step on our own!

We scanned back through what we had done and decided we needed to examine what specifically we had learned when we had disconnected our telepathic reality.

I was looking at Quianna. She was Cretian and she could have been a younger version of Jess or Seliqana. She also was quite stunningly beautiful and I could easily see how Aziq was drawn to her. Then I remembered she was Seliqana's niece. An instant later I realized this was not a one-sided love affair or a simple infatuation; she adored him and wanted to have a child with him but was accepting, reluctantly, for the moment, that she needed to wait. I searched but could not find the specific reason that was holding them back and wondered what I was missing.

I was focused on her because she was looking at me, then Jess, and then Raille. She wanted to say something but was having difficulty formulating it, then I began to pick it up.

Quianna, you seem to be wanting something but feeling very ambivalent about asking for it. Is that right?

She looked at me. She knew I had picked up her uncertainty and was really hoping I would get the rest of her concern and follow it. Then I got it.

You want me to bring the ILC group together with their partners with no telepathic communication and facilitate a discussion between you that will show what happens when you lose your telepathic connection? Much the way we did a little while ago for ourselves, and as we did when we first met the Olarian world, also the way you did with your family for a day when you took Aziq to meet with them? You have seen the Living Library memory of our visitors from Earth?

She nodded and then replied to my question.

Yes please, Zed. You know my mother and her sisters. They trust you, but even they could not adjust.

I nodded, looked at Januti and the others. They were nodding.

It was Olaria who added, *When you did this with us, and when you facilitated – that is your word if I remember correctly – the visitors who Miyuki brought to OlarCret that first year, you were not being telepathic and we were all astonished at what happened with them as a result.*

I nodded, looked at the members of the ILC group and asked, *Is that something you all would like to do?*

A rapid dialogue began with several asking Quianna what she hoped would be the outcome of this experience. She looked at them, people she absolutely trusted.

I want to really understand, just a little, what my life might be like if you lot did not keep me telepathic. What you are doing for us is not just generous, it is, I know, life-changing, and I want to appreciate it fully, and I totally trust Zed to help us.

They looked at her and into her, exploring the unspoken nuance in her request and then, one by one, they nodded and with no further hesitation agreed. So, as soon as I was confident we had 100 percent agreement, I asked, *Why don't the 16 of you come across here to make a circle with me?*

They did and I watched all the partners shut down their partners' and their own telepathic connections. I could immediately see the level of anxiety and uncertainty rise; the demeanour of the group changed almost instantaneously. I nodded. I also stopped using my telepathic awareness, choosing to rely on my pre-telepathic perceptions.

Why don't we go around the group and ask each of you to make just a brief statement about how you are feeling now your telepathic connection has been broken and what you most fear as a result?

Quianna was on my left and beside her Aziq, so it was Quianna who began.

'My anxiety has gone through the roof. As soon as Aziq withdrew my telepathic awareness I became afraid – afraid he will no longer love me, no longer desire me, no longer find me interesting. He is so beautiful and powerful, he could choose almost anyone he wanted.'

She turned toward him.

'You could, Aziq. You could choose from any of the beautiful women in our group and they would have you in a moment. I could lose you just like that.'

She snapped her fingers.

'It is my greatest fear that I will become uninteresting to you, dull, and that you will cease to really desire to be with me. Although I have learned that I am a loveable and attractive woman, those are not the qualities that will last a lifelong relationship. I don't think I am as smart as you.'

She was looking at him, talking to him but also talking to the group.

'I feel ridiculous saying these things because you have never given me any grounds for feeling this way, but, and it is a big but, I still remember my first four non-telepathic years. I think I wanted this experience because I knew the moment I was not being kept telepathic my confidence would plummet. You make me special, but it is your ability, not any quality of mine.'

She looked at him with love and sadness. I could feel, at the edge of my awareness, Jess almost getting out of her seat, wanting to help and support Quianna. I looked up at her and Raille and very gently shook my head. Jess frowned but Raille took her hand, and, as she turned to look at him, he too gently shook his head and I saw him mouth, 'Trust him'. She looked again at me very carefully, found whatever it was she needed and, still with an anxious frown, settled back in her seat.

Quianna and Aziq had been entirely unaware of the transaction between us; they were deeply absorbed with what was happening between them. I could see they were feeling very vulnerable, very exposed, mainly I was sure because they could no longer check their feelings or their perceptions. I waited.

Tears were rolling down Quianna's beautiful face and most of the group were exhibiting anxiety. Two or three started to speak and I looked at them, gently shaking my head. Probably because they knew me so well and knew I would never sanction physical or emotional harm to any of them, they accepted my request and sat back, upset but accepting that they were actually getting something that Quianna had been seeking.

One of my daughters in the group opened her mouth to speak, but before she could, I looked at her with love and caring and very gently shook my head, repeated Raille's words to Jess with just my lips moving and she sat back, trusting, and I nodded very slightly, very gently to her.

We had begun only moments ago. Only Quianna had said anything, yet the group was full of tension, anxiety and uncertainty. This was for them an intense and disturbing experience. Another young Cretian woman and one of the young women I recognized as one of the Second Earth group left their seats and sat beside Quianna on the floor. Each took a hand. She demonstrably appreciated their support and after just a few moments they went back to sit beside their partners.

Wow, was the thought in my mind. I would never have imagined there was so much angst lying underneath the surface that none of us has really seen or understood!

'Quianna, is there anything else you would like to say at this point?'

In the quietest of voices, she said, 'Yes please, Zed. I don't think I have ever said this out loud, but being short-lived by comparison to Aziq also has had the effect of leaving me feeling inferior.

'From the beginning of our learning at the ILC, when the Olarian adults, who were always kind, understanding, open and fair, told us as often as we needed to hear it that the length of a life was not a basis for judging the quality of a life, I have felt, in a manner I could not until now articulate, that there was an implicit put-down in that idea.

'I do not for a moment believe they would have thought that thought or felt those feelings, but to some of us for whom it was true, it has left a near invisible mark. So, today, when I am closer to my unenhanced self, I am most aware of my natural limitations in my relationship with my beautiful man, and I am desperately relieved that I have been able to say what I have felt almost outside my awareness.'

Aziq had tears in his eyes. He was looking at Quianna in a way I recognized; it was the way I often looked at Januti. I could quite literally feel the depth of the love and passion he felt for her.

I smiled. There was no time when each of us did not have something to learn. Quianna was for the moment being deeply introspective but she was also thinking about her present feelings. I could see her confusion and her desire to master it. Then she nodded, recognized she had fulfilled my request and became silent, reaching over to briefly touch Aziq who responded with a brief look of love and understanding. I knew he was in pain. Then he too spoke.

'Zed, I love that you have always treated all of us with indistinguishably equal love and caring. I did not think this was a great idea when Quianna proposed it, but I had no idea what depth of angst was present in our little group! Especially as I am certain every one of us would unhesitatingly do anything necessary to look after one another in the way you and your eight undoubtedly would.'

Then he stopped and for a few moments was quiet and I could see that he was seeking to identify exactly how he was feeling.

'When I first came to the ILC I was allocated an eight to which I would be connected for the rest of my life. I was just a little kid; I had no idea what that would ultimately mean. Then I saw this beautiful girl, little like me, smiling at me, and at that moment my concerns simply disappeared. I was quite literally basking in the warmth of her smile and I knew it was directed at me. I have no idea why, but I could not stop looking at her. I was four, nearly five, and I have never stopped looking at that smile and feeling incredibly good now nearly two decades later.

'I am not aware of anything that I fear. All of you and all the adults in my life have contributed to that. But the thought that Quianna might not smile at me, might not desire me as strongly as I desire her, comes as close to leaving me in fear as anything I could imagine. We have known each other, it feels like, forever. I know we can't have that, but...'

He stopped speaking, was looking at her with an expression of love and intent that was beyond... moving. Then he continued.

'I am feeling so many things now as I reflect on what you asked us to say. I thought we knew everything about each other, yet it is evident I was wrong! So I am looking inside at what I am feeling that I have not shared and do not share with the others. And I am just beginning to realize I take for granted that they all care about me and feel cared about in return. I am now, without my usual telepathic awareness, feeling anxious about how everyone is actually feeling toward me!

'I am also quite sure that if I stay disconnected like this for long I will lose my confidence and will begin to doubt what I know of their feelings and will become anxious and begin to behave in ways that will be unhelpful and will almost certainly be based on my fears and not on the reality we actually have.'

I worked my way around the group. Quianna and Aziq quickly learned their experience was not unique. The group talked for nearly three hours. Things were said that had never been said before. The rich resources of telepathic connection had masked many uncertainties and fears. As these were brought out, aired and then put away, the group settled and a new level of insight was born.

When they had all returned to a telepathic reality there was no longer any uncertainty about what needed to occur. Without telepathic connections based inside a genuinely Olarian value system, the efforts of all three worlds to reach a new level of connection and a potential to join the cosmic community were not going to happen. The challenge was simple, in its way: build an intergalactic education profile that the Olarians would monitor and manage. Get the help needed to create and bear only telepathic children, or partner every telepathic child with a non-telepathic child, preferably for the whole of their lives. That was the only direction we could see the future creating the reality which the cosmos required.

◘

The epiphany provided by the ILC children helped we eight to finally know why we did not belong here. We still felt welcome. Our children did love us, especially Rozari, who I had come to believe was a member of my original home world brought to help me on this journey.

It was just that we were not part of their lives or their world but something else. The eight of us were not, as we had indeed come to fully understand only over two centuries, what we seemed.

The eight of us were more! We *really* did not belong here. When we reached the thousand-year marker we realized, especially after the day I realized I needed to go back and help myself 1000 years before, we had spent 1000 human years and finally achieved what seemed to be a place in the cosmic community for what had originally been the human race, the Cretians and the Olarians.

They would not have recognized their 21st century ancestors, or more especially their ancestors from the first thousands of years of their existence. They were today a beautiful society, entirely free of violence, had had no weapons of any kind for more than 800 years and had been totally free of violence for nearly 700 years. They had developed extraordinarily sophisticated transport machines, which most acknowledged were actually quite unnecessary for their lives but fulfilled a deep and often unacknowledged desire to remain connected to a past now getting more distant and more disconnected from their present. They did not know they were on the edge of breakthroughs that would change who they were. And we, their parents, needed to return to our world after the flicker of time it had taken to visit Earth and the fledgling human society.

EPILOGUE FOR PARTS 1 TO 4

WHO IS ZED?

Zed is a being from what would be, in human terms, a far distant future and from a society way up in the cosmic community – an incredibly powerful and significant figure in the cosmic community's (we will call it) bureaucracy or organization. He, together with seven other entities of his world, chose to appear to become members of the human community because, with no interference from any other society, humanity had already solved the problem of interstellar space travel and was able to continue its species' survival on new planets in new solar systems.

Many societies have developed over the millennia. Some have grown very sophisticated but have been unable to get their species off their dying planet. Because humans had made this step, Zed decided, from his position way up in the cosmic food chain, to temporarily become a member of the human community and to go there without knowledge of who he actually was.

He also decided he would have help from eight, not seven, other beings of his world, and with their help he would slowly be assisted to become aware of who he was through being able to do more and more in his attempt to assist humanity to reach a point where it might be acceptable as a member of the cosmic communities.

Rozari turned to him. She smiled a smile he knew and loved – his alter ego, his special cowled figure. She laid her head on his shoulder and immediately transformed into that tiny cowled monk!

In the beginning he had no idea because he had arranged it that way. However, as he became more and more involved in helping the human world develop and interact with more of the cosmic realities, he began to have at first a vague and then slowly more substantive developing awareness about who and what he might actually be. Even at the end of this story, he had not fully reacquired his original persona.

It is Rozari's job to bring him home, and she slowly commences what sounds like a deep tantric chant that resonates through his being and slowly transforms into a form of meaning he immediately understands. Then his transformation back into his original form begins.

PART 5

HISTORY OF THE ORIGINAL MIND TRAVELERS

A Short History of the Original Olarian Telepaths

JARD & LEITI

CHAPTER 40

Jard

'Stop cheating!'

An angry voice from across the clearing, easily heard by everyone playing the game.

Jard sighed. Now almost 17, he had heard this accusation for years. Cera and his small cohort of thugs from the village never ceased their efforts to get him, always accused him of cheating. Now, for the most part, he no longer played in their games.

Here we go again, he thought as he turned to face his accuser.

'I don't cheat, Cera. It's just that you and your huddle of dillberries are too thick to get it. I'm just better than you at this.'

'You're a cheat, Jard.'

The words were issued in a sneering tone as Cera and his two buddies advanced.

'You always win, and the only way you could manage that has to be by cheating.'

If only you knew the truth, Jard thought. They never thought to ask him how come he won; they simply accused him, then tried to vent their frustration by beating him up. This was the first time for months he had engaged in one of their competitive games.

'Admit it,' Cera said, scowling as he came toward him. 'Admit you're a cheat, Jard.'

Jard swept his sandy hair out of his deep-brown eyes and glanced at his cousin Irah who stood to one side watching the confrontation. This would not be a good time for the truth to come out.

In fact, no time would be a good time.

People who were different in this village were not treated well; in fact, being different could result in more than just severe punishment.

'Just admit it,' Cera said again as he and his two friends continued their advance. 'Everyone's sick of you cheating, Jard.'

Jard stared at him. For the past eight years he'd managed to keep his secret; he needed it to stay that way.

'I'll tell you for the last time, Cera,' Jard said. 'I wasn't cheating; I never cheat and I'm sick of hearing your pathetic accusations. They just cover your incompetence.'

Cera's dark eyes were fixed on Jard. 'You're a cheat and we're gonna teach you a lesson, Jard. By the time we're finished with you, you'll never even think about cheating again!'

'Yeah,' one of the other boys said as the three of them spread out to surround him.

Jard suppressed a sigh. *Are they*, he wondered, *actually incapable of learning?* The game always ended in a fight with these three. Jard always won, but it didn't stop them.

'Fine,' he said. 'Come on then. Teach me a lesson.'

'Jard,' Irah said, her eyes flicking nervously over the three boys surrounding her cousin. 'I don't think you should do this.'

'Just stay back, Irah,' Jard said, his eyes on Cera. 'Don't worry about me. I'll be just fine.'

Cera's angry thoughts entered Jard's mind, telling him Cera was going to charge first, try to kick him and get him on the ground, then the other two would enter the fight and help Cera give him a good kicking. Cera's thoughts also told Jard that Cera had intended this even before the game began.

'You going to face me, Cera?' he asked.

The boy hesitated; it was as if some sixth sense suddenly told him this wasn't a good idea. 'Perhaps your normal cowardly nature has reasserted itself yet again eh?'

Cera roared in fury and charged. As he reached Jard, his leg snapped up in an attempt to catch Jard in the chest. Jard grabbed Cera's foot before it made contact. He twisted. Cera cried out in pain and hit the ground.

Jard turned as the second boy came at him. He sidestepped the blow from the meaty fist meant to catch him in the face. The boy's momentum took him past Jard. He tripped. Jard heard Cera gasp for breath as the weight of the second boy knocked it out of him. The third came at Jard, screaming something about how he'd make Jard 'sorry for that'.

'Peabrain!' Jard yelled at him as he sidestepped the boy's wild blows. Jard waited as the boy turned and came a second time, his snarling face bright red with anger. Jard's fist connected with the boy's chin, stopping him in his tracks. A moment later, Jard's foot snapped up and slammed into the boy's chest, knocking him back so he fell on the other two.

For the second time, Jard heard Cera's breath whoosh out with the sudden additional weight. Casting them a look of contempt, he went to Irah and took her hand.

'Let's get out of here,' he said.

Irah's eyes went to the tangle of arms, legs and bodies on the ground. 'They'll make you pay for that, Jard,' she said softly.

'Don't worry about them,' he said, giving her hand a squeeze. 'They won't come after me.'

He grinned.

'This isn't anything new, Irah. This game always ends with them trying to beat me up. They accuse me of cheating; we fight; I win. That's the end of it until the next time we play. It just seems new to you because this is the first time you've visited when I decided to play this game with them. I think the only reason they asked was to have the opportunity to beat me up in front of you. Come on.'

Ignoring the curses and threats that followed them, Jard led Irah toward the low hills on the eastern side of the village.

'Why do you always win, Jard?' Irah asked.

'What do you mean?'

'That boy, Cera, said you always win the game, and you said you always win the fight. How is it you do that?'

Jard glanced at her as they walked. She was his mother's sister's daughter and his favorite cousin. A year younger than him, they shared the same sandy hair and brown eyes, but the family resemblance ended there. He was tall and rangy, with handsome chiseled features and a toned, fit body from spending his life hunting in the forests; she was petite with her long hair framing pixie-like features.

'Jard?' Irah said.

Jard glanced at her again as he silently debated how to answer. *I trust her enough to tell her the truth,* he thought.

Of everyone I know, she's the one I trust the most. Unlike others, she doesn't treat me as some kind of outcast. It doesn't make a difference that she lives in the next village, because even if she lived here, I still don't think she'd treat me like everyone else does. Can I tell her the truth when I barely understand what that 'truth' is myself?

If I tell her, it'll put her in danger. People who are... 'different' aren't accepted in her village any more than they are in mine. I know she'd never tell anyone what I said to her, but if my... ability becomes known and any of the Elders of this village finds out she knew, they'd tell the Elders of her village. She'll get in all sorts of trouble for not revealing me.

'Please answer me, Jard,' Irah said, a touch of impatience tingeing her tone.

Jard came to a decision. She was too special to him to put in any kind of danger.

'I always win the fights because I'm fit and can move quick. Besides,' he added, grinning at her. 'Those three fools are easy to read. They always try the same thing every time we end up in a fight. They never learn.'

Jard let go of her hand and put his arm around her shoulders. Irah leaned into him.

'Are you sure they won't come after you?' she asked.

'Yes.'

'What about me? They know I'm your cousin and we're close. What if they come after me to hurt you? I won't be able to fight them, Jard.'

Jard's arm tightened around her. 'They won't come after you, Irah,' he said. 'I promise. Despite their bravado, Cera and his friends are bullies and like all bullies they're ultimately cowards. I'll never let them hurt you.'

Besides, he thought. *I hear their thoughts just like I hear the thoughts of everyone else. I know what they intend to do before they do it, so if Cera and his friends try to harm her in order to hurt me, I'll know about it. I'll also make sure they regret it for the rest of their lives.*

'You're my favorite cousin, Jard, you know that, don't you?' Irah said.

'Yes,' he said with a chuckle. 'You're *my* favorite as well. We really should visit each other more often.'

The pair continued walking as a comfortable silence drifted over them. Jard looked around. It really was a nice village. Low hills to east and west created a sort of valley in which the village was tucked, protected from the worst of the cold season.

Unlike some of the others in the area, his village was not considered a poor one. The wood and thatch-roofed houses were strong, stable and well maintained, as were the shelters for the animals. A large nearby river running from north to south made this a fertile area with rich dark soil. The village's yearly crops were always abundant, as was milk from the animals who were well fed and cared for. To the south and west the forests gave them good hunting. Jard had always liked living here; he enjoyed getting up each morning and looking over the green land, cultivated crops and tree-covered hills.

If only life was as good as it sounded.

He suppressed his sigh, not wanting Irah to hear it and ask what was wrong. He'd told her he always won the games and fights because of his hunting skills. In small part, that was the truth. But it wasn't the *whole* truth.

Jard was eight years old when he discovered his ability to hear the thoughts of others wasn't, as he'd always thought, *normal,* in the sense that everyone possessed this ability.

His mother and father had explained it to him. He'd started talking aloud about it, thinking it was something everyone knew about. They'd told him only *he* had the ability. They weren't sure where it had come from, but it was certainly there.

Jard remembered how he'd asked them why they'd not said anything about it before. His mother had replied that they wanted to be sure of their suspicions. That he'd often unconsciously repeated aloud the thoughts in their heads had told them there was no doubt about his ability.

They'd also told him he must never speak to anyone about it. When

Jard asked why, his father said, 'People like you wouldn't be welcome in the village.'

While no one past or present had ever displayed the ability to read other people's thoughts like Jard, there had been other people with... unusual abilities. Those unfortunates lost their lives quickly through hanging or other less pleasant, more painful and drawn-out means.

The Elders saw unusual abilities as evil; anyone possessing them must also be evil and therefore removed before they could 'infect' others. Anyone found to have had knowledge of someone with unusual abilities but who had not reported the person also faced death. What the Elders believed, the people they governed also believed.

Jard recalled how his parents had hammered into him the importance of never speaking about his ability. Jard had obeyed them, fearful of what would happen if he was discovered.

But the people in this village, they know there's something not quite right about me, he thought as they continued walking.

I can read it in their thoughts. They look at me and think 'what is it about that one? He's a strange one for sure'. I've never been truly accepted here. The other boys let me join in some of their games but their thoughts tell me they really don't want me around. The adults are polite to me but I can hear the coldness in their voices and read their hostile thoughts. They don't understand what it is about me, but they do know there's something that's not right, and they don't like it.

Our villagers, like the others in the area, are insular. They welcome people from the other villages when they visit but don't like strangers, and they don't like people who are different. The families living in this and the other villages have done so for generations. Sons and daughters marry within their respective villages except for the odd occasion when someone will leave to marry another in a nearby village. When their sons and daughters are marrying age, they marry within their villages as well. I'm surprised we're not all inbred but then again, perhaps we are. Why am I so different though? Where did I get the ability to read everyone's thoughts? I wish I understood what it was about.

Jard scowled as he thought about it. Other than that 'talk' they'd had with him when he was eight years old, his parents had never spoken of his ability again. When he tried to bring it up, they would change the subject. Their thoughts told him even they were uncomfortable around him. He'd given up trying to talk to them about it when their thoughts had made it clear they'd never speak of it again.

They wanted to pretend it wasn't there, that Jard was just like the other boys in their village. They hoped if they ignored it long enough the problem would just go away.

Jard felt pretty certain it would not.

To some extent, his ability made even him uncomfortable, and it certainly made his life difficult. Despite his handsome looks and his ability as a hunter, none of the girls in the village wanted him to court them. Even if they had, Jard suspected any relationships he entered would be short-lived, given his ability to read any girlfriend's thoughts would most likely put a real dampener on a relationship. Even being able to read the thoughts of his own parents strained that relationship, probably because they knew he was doing it.

Jard's scowl deepened. It wasn't as if he deliberately read the thoughts of his parents and everyone else. He didn't. The thoughts simply came to him, and he had no idea how to stop it happening.

'What's wrong, Jard?' Irah asked. 'Why are you scowling so ferociously?'

'Am I?' Jard asked, making a conscious attempt to turn the scowl into a smile. 'Sorry. I didn't realize I was doing it. There's nothing wrong. I was just thinking of Cera and those other two idiots.

'Irah, do you think you'll ever leave your village? Do you even want to?'

'Sometimes I wish I could, Jard,' Irah said. 'Sometimes I wonder about what else is out there to see and experience.

'But no,' she said after a moment. 'No, I doubt I'll ever leave it. That kind of thing just isn't done. We're born in our villages, we grow up, marry someone from a local family, have our own children and work to plant and provide food for them. We grow old, we die and we're buried in our village. That's the life we've been given.'

'You're right,' he said with a smile as her thoughts warned him not to argue with that. 'This is our life, and I like my village.'

'But no one here likes you, do they, Jard?'

Jard's eyebrows shot up before he could stop them as he realized his cousin was far more perceptive than he'd imagined. 'What makes you say that?'

'It's just a feeling I get. I've been here for a week and every time you're near someone I get the sense they want you to go away. I don't think it's only Cera and his friends who don't like you. I don't think the other boys here like you either. There's something about you.'

'Is there?' Jard asked carefully. 'What do you think it is, Irah?'

'I don't know,' she said. 'I only know there's something that makes you... not like the others here. You're not even like your parents or mine or the rest of our family. You're not like me.'

'Does that bother you?'

'No,' she said without hesitation. 'I don't understand what it is and I don't really care either. I still love you. I just don't like seeing you treated as some kind of outcast. I'm scared that one day things will come to a head and the Elders will make you leave – or worse.'

'They won't do that,' Jard said with more confidence than he felt as

Irah's words hit home. 'I mean, yes, I think that people do believe there's something... different about me, but I don't know why. I'm tolerated here, Irah, but that's all. I think the only reason they do tolerate me is because I'm the best hunter in the village. I'm the one who brings back the most game for the village and the best of that game.'

He looked at her as he felt the unease in her thoughts. It was not because she wasn't comfortable with him; rather, she was afraid for him.

'I think they're all just jealous because I'm such a good hunter,' he told her.

'You might be right,' Irah said, her arm going around his waist and tightening.

'I am,' Jard said even as he heard her thoughts.

'I don't believe that's the reason. I think there's something more to you, Jard, something special, but the Elders won't see it like that, will they? I also think you know what it is and it's got very little to do with your ability as a hunter. I wish you'd tell me. I want to help you.'

'We had better be getting back,' Jard said rather than continue the conversation. 'It's nearly dusk. Mother and Father won't be worried about me, but they will be about you. They promised your parents they'd look after you while you're here.'

Irah smiled at him. 'I'd rather it was you who looks after me, Jard. I think you're the best at it. You're a wonderful cousin and friend.'

'As are you, Irah,' Jard said as they fell into a comfortable silence again. *I just wish other people saw me as you did, little cousin,* Jard thought. *Even knowing there's something that's not right about me, you just accept me. I wish others could do that.*

As Jard thought about it, he realized that would never happen. He'd never be fully accepted, not here.

◘

Jard watched the group of hunters leaving the village as the sun peeked over the horizon, slowly replacing the cool blanket of the night with ever-increasing warmth.

They'd not asked him to join them. Jard pushed down the sudden bitterness, surprised at the strength of it. Irah had gone home three weeks ago, yet their conversation had stayed with him.

He wished it hadn't, because what it brought was slowly increasing bitterness and resentment against the people in his village. Irah's words had made him realize just how much of an outcast he was in this place, *his home*! He'd always known it, always felt a sense of alienation, but since that conversation with her he'd felt it more keenly than ever.

'Why didn't you go with the others, Jard?' his father asked as Jard entered the kitchen and announced he was going hunting. 'Why go alone? It's dangerous.'

You already know why, Father, Jard thought as he sat down to a breakfast of hot bread, honey and a good tea made from an infusion of local herbs. *The real reason you're asking me is you're trying to find out how I'm getting on with people. You and Mother are worried; you know I'm becoming more isolated here.*

'I prefer to hunt alone, Father,' Jard said aloud. 'Most of the other hunters are clumsy and noisy and they usually only end up frightening the game away.'

'Will you be out all day?'

'Depends on what I find,' Jard said. 'I might be back by midday if I get something early, but don't worry about me unless I'm not back by dark.'

His father nodded.

Jard hastily ate his breakfast and swallowed the last of his tea. He picked up his bow and arrows and his spear and took the small bag of food his mother handed him.

'Just be careful, Jard.'

'I will, Father,' Jard said and kissed his mother's cheek.

Jard went south; the other hunters had gone north, and he had no desire to meet up with them. Within minutes of entering the forest, Jard's sharp eyes picked up fresh tracks. He crouched. The five-toed prints showed long claw marks, telling him the animal was a boar-like creature common to the area. The creatures were dangerous, more predator than prey, but worth the work of bringing down.

Jard decided to go after it and set about following the tracks, noting slight depressions or broken twigs here and there that told him the animal's path through the forest.

As he walked, his thoughts drifted back to the problem of his ability. It *was* a problem. That he could read the thoughts of others meant he knew all about them, what they were doing, where they went, and the lies they told with their lips as their minds thought the opposite.

Just last night, he'd listened in to the Elders' weekly boasting session. The lies they told to each other in order to impress grew more outrageous each time. Jard knew that very little of what they'd said aloud was actually true. They all needed to be seen as more capable or more in control of their lives than most of them felt.

I wish I could control what I hear, he thought as he continued on. *I wish I understood this ability, but I don't, and there's no one I can ask. I think one of the reasons my parents are so uncomfortable about it is they don't understand it either.*

He wondered if there was someone out there who did.

Surely, I can't be the only person in the world with the ability to read other minds? If there was just someone who could tell me what it's about, and explain why I have it, and how to control it. If I understood it, knew its name, I'd feel so much more comfortable with it. Right now, I don't feel that way. I just feel alienated from everyone...

A thought chased itself across his mind. This was not the first time he had felt... known... imagined there were eight of him, whatever that meant. The thought had popped into his mind before, always when he was concerned about being an isolated man in a village where he seemed not to belong. This idea just turned up and he wondered how it had got there.

Jard's thoughts broke off as crashing and squealing shattered the silence. A large animal with a brown hide, wiry hair and two very sharp and dangerous teeth protruding over its upper pig-like jaw burst out of the undergrowth.

It came straight for him, its red eyes fixed on him. Jard dropped everything but the spear and tried to leap aside as the creature neared. It moved quicker than he had anticipated. Jard managed to wound it but cried out in pain as the animal's teeth caught him on the side. Blood poured from the wound but Jard couldn't think about it right then. The creature turned and came for him again, the wound Jard had made with the spear only seeming to make it angrier.

Jard again leapt out of its way, rolled and came to his hands and knees. Desperately, he crawled away into the thicker brush. He dropped to his stomach, barely daring to breathe as he heard the creature snuffling around, seeking him. Jard stayed where he was, his mind willing the animal to be unaware of him as the creature's rooting around finally ceased. The crashing through the brush eventually became more distant, then faded completely.

He groaned as the adrenalin stopped pumping through him, replaced by the fiery pain in his side. Jard sat up and pulled off his tunic, examining the gash over his ribs, wincing at the depth of it. He pulled the hunting knife at his waist, using it to cut up his tunic to make a pad and a makeshift bandage. After tying the bandage around his torso as tight as he could, he pressed his hand over the wound, applying as much pressure as possible to stop the bleeding.

He was going to need stitches if he could make it home, though Jard wasn't sure he could do even that. His head swam and he began to feel weak. As he continued to press down waiting for the bleeding to stop, he repeatedly cursed himself.

Idiot! he thought in utter disgust. *What did you think you were doing, thinking about other issues while tracking a dangerous animal? If you'd had your mind on the task instead of other things, you'd have realized the creature was close by! You were lucky you weren't killed, you bloody fool.*

Thinking like this was not helping. The animal was now the least of his problems. He could barely move without the fear he would further open the wound.

Damn, he thought, *this bleeding has to stop or I'll likely die here.*

The pain was affecting his ability to think clearly. There was no help available here. The throbbing of the wound and the loss of blood were combining to make him delirious. He began to imagine if he thought hard enough he could stop the bleeding and maybe heal his own wounds. He had little sense of time passing as he lay there, hoping he would stop bleeding, willing his body to co-operate, drifting in and out of consciousness.

In one of the periods of clarity, he realized the bleeding seemed to have eased. He dared not lift the bandage to find out but slid back into his delirious state, imagining he was sewing up the wounds, which of course he was not. Yet he had some sense that the wounds were healing. In a lucid period he knew that was his imagination looking after him, and then he drifted off again.

The day slowly progressed with little conscious awareness for Jard, then when the sun was setting, he felt certain the bleeding had stopped. The stain on his tunic had ceased to spread, he was drying, and he began to feel cold. He looked around and noticed he was in a very small clearing, a rock behind him, the bushes several feet away.

He was getting cold. He wished he had the makings of a fire, though he had no idea how he would light one. All his gear was gone. The pain was dulling his thinking. His desire for warmth grew. As dusk settled a fire seemed to burst into life a few feet from him.

'Oh how I wish that was true,' he muttered in his delirious state. However, this fire he was imagining seemed to continue burning while he watched it, and he thought how amazing that was and he was pleased that he was imagining he was beginning to feel warm. Then he got to thinking he really was warm, and the presence of the fire began to both warm and disturb him.

Jard knew he must be really delirious if he thought the imaginary fire was warming him. Perhaps he was dying. His wound was throbbing; the pain was sending waves of nausea through him. Finally he fell asleep.

He awoke and it was dark. His fire was gone and he was cold and shivering. In his weary and dazed state, he imagined himself wrapped in warm furry skins protected from the cold and the elements and safe from the animals. He drifted back to sleep.

It was mid-morning and the sun was well up when he next awoke, warm, cosy, wrapped in warm soft furs, except... he wasn't. There was nothing around him, yet he was, so far as he could tell, suspended above the ground and lying on... nothing!

He lay very still, puzzled and confused. Who had trapped him? What was happening to him? He focused his attention on unravelling the puzzle. He had been wounded, bleeding, in pain, cold, and now he was suspended in the air and feeling warm and... okay?

He became aware more that the sunlight was playing on him. Flashes of color and... something he could not name were creating this feeling of being wrapped in skins, comfortable and warm.

His immediate concern was how to get out of this cosy trap. He could feel his anxiety rising. Had someone he could not see somehow imprisoned him?

Maybe I'm going crazy; maybe my wound has become too badly infected.

However, looking down at his now unwrapped wound, he could see no sign of it, nothing...

Nothing? I must be imagining all this.

His distress was growing when suddenly he dropped to the ground. The drop was small, the ground not too rocky, and he did himself no harm. He sat up, his mind replaying all that he could remember. Slowly, reluctantly, he began to realize that, if he was really alive, he was probably the author of these events in some way he did not understand.

Sitting there on the ground, mostly naked, he felt puzzled, not displeased, and filled with a disturbing curiosity and an enormous sense of relief. Now he only needed some covering, his weapons and kit. Within a short time he was sufficiently recovered to look for and find his gear. He had lost only his spear. He headed back to his irate and distressed parents.

As the weeks passed and no further odd events occurred to disturb him, he began to think perhaps he had just imagined it and his mind was not quite okay.

That at least might account for his complete lack of any wound, but not the loss of his spear. It was neither a comforting nor quite believable thought, but then, what explanation was?

I arrive home with no credible explanation for my lost spear, lost clothes, blood on what I am wearing, and no wounds. My mother understandably upset and angry, and my apology adds nothing to my parents' understanding and certainly doesn't deal with their distress. I'm as confused now as I was then, and there is no one I can even share it with.

Jard was sitting outside the house when some of the other young men of the village happened by.

'Your magical tracking skills not so hot eh?' Ceil jeered as he sauntered by with his friends. 'You should know, hot shot, we fed the entire village with our kill. Perhaps you could learn something from hunting with us?'

'I thought I'd give you the opportunity to be useful for once in your stupid lives.' Jard was feeling tired of their endless putdowns. He watched them saunter off and again found himself confronted with the inexplicable events of that day. He thought briefly of Irah, but knew if he spoke with her he would be compromising her and reluctantly decided yet again to keep his own counsel.

He sat, feeling the warm afternoon sun on his skin, watching some of the women working in the fields, and found himself listening in to a conversation between his father's sister and brother. It was indicative of the life around him, which added to his feeling of alienation. Without exception the members of his family were disingenuous and somehow disrespectful of one another. His aunt and uncle were involved in one of their regular spats. As Jard listened he was thinking, *I ought to be used to this by now.*

However, these little interchanges never failed to distress him. He remembered when he was younger wanting to rush into the middle of one of these and shout at them to tell the truth.

Fortunately for him, he had resisted the urge. Now he was listening to his aunt saying in one of her most telling voices, 'Best you think about that, Grie. If you want me to look after your needs, best you look after mine.'

Jard knew what that meant and so did his uncle; most of the men in the village would understand that phrase. The conversation between them died away, but Jard could feel his uncle's angry compliance. He intended to do what she wanted – he did not want that threat hanging over his head – but he was also thinking how he would make her pay for it. It was a common threat from the women in the village, though they rarely carried through with it. Jard felt disgust and knew it was just this kind of unpleasantness that he was finding hardest to tolerate. He shut them out.

His mind went again to the strange weavings of light and the flashes of inner sight that plagued him and added to his feeling of estrangement from everyone else in the village. He knew this problem was a lot more than disruptive. At this point his mother approached.

'Are you ever going hunting again?' she asked, irritation, frustration and anxiety clinging to every word.

'Maybe.' He almost spat the word out. She was looking at him with frustration and annoyance but also something else; he could read the fear. No girlfriend, no real friends... without his hunting he would become a target. She knew if he did not change his ways, it was likely his days were numbered, and she didn't know what to do or say.

Jard looked at her, reading her thoughts. He was wondering if there had been others like him and if so what had happened to them. She didn't seem to know.

Clouds boiled up over the western hills and the sky grew dark as the deteriorating conditions promised rain, a not unwelcome sight for the time of year. Jard could feel the haunting awareness of things he could not fathom, could not reach. He also felt the jangled anxiety of his parents and the way it so easily turned to anger.

There was nothing they could say or do to make him right. He felt it all and hated it, but for the moment he was able not to hate himself. Frustrated by the situation, he wished the strange power behind it all would leave him alone.

It would, of course, never do that.

CHAPTER 41

Leiti, Daria & Repin

As she looked up, Leiti felt as though the sky was just hanging there. Small tufts of white cloud skimmed the nearby hills, the fields were swept by gusts of wind, and the crops seemed to be doing a dance conducted just for her. It was the neat rows she admired, how the farmers managed to get the seeds in such straight lines. They would have food throughout the winter. Olarian winters were cold and in the past there had been winters when they went hungry. The entire community was fewer than 300 people, if you didn't count the smaller village of Little Epinaria, less than a mile down the track that connected them with several other villages of Greater Epinaria, together in a very defensible valley.

Leiti knew the men were out hunting and the women were about to go and search out berries to supplement the crops and the vegetable garden. This garden was a new venture for them, the idea having come from a casual traveler. If successful, the women would spend less time scouring the countryside.

It was early morning and Leiti was looking for Daria. She wanted to play. At 13 years old, she was not expected to interfere in any way in adult things. She would be chastised if she did. The village was quiet today. There had been no battles over land or hunting territory for more than a year, and had there been any serious squabbles between the communities or over partners, everyone who had ears would know. Squabbles usually got out of hand pretty quickly, because tempers flared and patience thinned rapidly in small communities where people always felt vulnerable about something.

'I want to go find the others,' Leiti told Daria when she found her coming from her family's end of their long hut. They held hands and hurtled down to the area where different groups of kids were playing, expecting to find Repin, but he was not there. Some of the others had seen him go off toward the cliffs, so the girls played together until late in the afternoon.

They arrived home to find groups of adults standing around. Repin had not returned home, which had alarmed family. His young sister had been killed by a wild animal only six months before, and when he had not returned for lunch or to do his chores in the afternoon, the anxious parents had gone out to look for him. Now, late in the day, their anxiety was high. They had sent out small parties of older children and adults to look for him. To Leiti and Daria everyone seemed unnecessarily distraught. Small groups were talking loudly and every now and then a few would break off to go search a particular area.

Leiti and Daria sat down to think about where Repin might have gone. Daria looked at Leiti and asked, 'Did you hear that?'

Leiti nodded. 'Is that Repin talking to us?'

'But he's not here!' Leiti was puzzled.

Can you hear me? This time Repin's voice was clear.

'Of course we can hear you!' Leiti replied, feeling stupid and embarrassed at the absurdity of talking to someone who was not there.

'Where are you?' Leiti looked at Daria, raised her eyebrows and shook her head in disbelief. *What am I doing, talking to thin air?* 'Repin, where are you? Everyone is out looking for you.'

I'm down the shale bank, where the two rocks sit on top of the ledge. I fell down the crevice. I'm stuck and my leg hurts.

It was clear both from his tone of voice, and the girls' experience, that he was in pain. Leiti and Daria looked at one another, not knowing how to tell about this, then they ran to Daria's mother, shouting. When Daria's mother had calmed them down they told her where they thought he was and she did not seem pleased! For Leiti, the expression on Daria's mother's face was a bit unnerving.

Something was not right, and she guessed it might be to do with how they seemed to know where Repin was. She was clearly concerned about why they had not said something earlier. She told the girls to sit still in the hut and went out to get one of the older kids. She gave him the message about where to tell the searchers to look for Repin, then came inside and waited.

As soon as she heard the news of Repin being found she faced them, demanding to know how they had known where to look. She clearly expected an answer from Daria. When Leiti saw the look on Daria's face, her stomach tightened, then, all innocence and surprise, Daria said, 'We heard him say that he was going to play there.'

Leiti's heart was in her mouth.

Daria continued, 'So when we remembered, we thought that would probably be where he was.'

The words seemed to slide out of her mouth, her expression surprised and distressed so that her mother simply hugged them, said they had been very good, and suggested that Leiti should go home.

Next morning Leiti and Daria talked.

'What happened yesterday?'

Daria had no answer.

'Well, listen, Daria, we heard him from miles away. How can that be?'

And although that was a pretty scary thought, it did not compare with another thought that was hammering for attention. What if their mothers knew or even guessed how they had known?

'Angry would not begin to cover it,' Daria said.

They were both distressed and in need of answers, but there seemed to be none.

'We both heard Repin,' said Leiti, 'and we were a long way away. We could not have heard him from there, the others would have heard as well. He was able to speak into our minds. But people can't do that.'

'Well, maybe they can't,' said Daria, 'but he actually did. We both heard.'

The girls were sure they had heard Repin and had known he had hurt his leg. But how?

When finally they got to see him, he held up his finger to shush them. 'Wait till we are on our own.' He walked out of the hut toward the edge of the village, the girls following.

'I was in pain, and the only thing I could think of was to call to you for help.'

'But how could you know we would hear?' Leiti asked.

'I didn't,' he replied. 'But suddenly, while I was shouting, I sort of knew that you were there. Not nearby but somehow in reach of my thoughts. It was strange, yet not as strange as when I say it now.'

They looked at one another.

'We have to find out more,' Repin said. 'We need to see if we can talk to one another – all three of us – find out if it is only when something bad is happening or if something is wrong with us.'

Repin, without speaking out loud, thought, *Ask me about yesterday.*

Daria and Leiti looked at one another.

Without speaking, Daria replied, *I heard you ask us.*

Leiti, eyebrows raised, said, *I heard both of you!*

'We can,' they shouted out loud together. Then the realization of what this might mean hit them.

They looked at one another in discomfort, awe, excitement, then anxiety and fear. They did not live in a village that appreciated change and innovation or deviant behavior in any form.

Leiti's voice was full of concern. 'We need to keep this to ourselves. No-one else can know or we could be in an awful lot of trouble.'

They all nodded.

Repin added, 'No-one we know likes things that are different or strange. Look how many months it took to even try out the vegetable garden idea.'

The three were all conscious that there were severe sanctions against people who broke taboos of almost any kind or did things that were definitely not allowed. The thing they had done would certainly fit this category of behavior. But the girls were becoming aware that Repin was holding something back.

Leiti pressed him. 'Tell us.'

'All right. Do you remember Haen?'

Neither of the girls did.

'Haen was supposed to be a dangerous weird kid. He was four years older than us, 17 when they killed him. No-one will talk about him.'

'Then how do you know about him?' asked Leiti.

'He was my cousin. He knew they were coming for him. It was just after dawn. He took his bow and arrows and tried to slip out into the bush. I don't know how they did it, but two of them were waiting for him at the edge of the common. He killed one but the other got him. An arrow in the leg. Then they stripped him and tied him to a tree, shouting all the time. They shot arrows into him for a long time, keeping him in agony. All the while they questioned him about being in league with the dark gods. He didn't know what they were talking about, and between screams he tried to tell them, but they wouldn't listen. I think they only wanted to convince themselves about him being *wrong*. In the end he died. It was horrible. After that no-one would speak of him, not even my mum who always talked to me about most things. And I know because...' He paused. 'Because when he was dying, there was a moment he somehow left a picture in my head of what was happening to him. To this day I can't get rid of it.'

'Why are you telling us this dreadful stuff?' Daria shouted.

Leiti was looking at him with horror written all over her face. 'You mean, he was like us? How do you know?'

'Because once when I was a little kid, he was desperate to find out if he was the only one who could hear what everyone else was actually thinking and not the rubbish they were saying. He asked me, and he knew I could, and then suddenly he realized I didn't understand and told me to keep my mouth tight shut. I was so scared I did, till yesterday. Then I realized that he was probably like us and they killed him because they were afraid of him, and if they find out about us they'll probably kill us too.'

The three just sat there in seriously frightened silence, all suddenly totally aware of each other's awful thoughts.

So two years passed before any of the trio dared raise the subject again, and Leiti only broke their taboo because she could bear it no longer.

'Daria, have you been having unusual things happen to you lately?'

Daria looked at her. The stream beside which they were walking bubbled and splashed its way to a small waterfall near the base of the valley, a good half day's walk from the village.

'What exactly are you asking?' was Daria's evasive reply. Before she could say any more Leiti was in her mind. Daria leapt away.

Leiti stayed where she was. The growing noise of the small waterfall would in any case make conversation difficult.

Come on, Daria, this is what I mean. I know you haven't been free of it.

Daria glanced nervously around. She tried to smile, but it was more a grimace. *Why, Leiti?*

You know why, Daria. You must be hearing the sort of stuff I'm hearing?

The expression on Daria's face and the thoughts she was recalling supported Leiti's comment and sent a shiver of relief through her.

'Why don't you want to talk about it? I know we said we wouldn't but that was a long time ago and a lot has been happening to me during the last couple of years. I need to know that I am not going crazy.'

Daria stopped and looked at her. Again without speaking, she said, *I'm scared, Leiti; even thinking about all the stuff I've been hearing is distressing me.*

'Well, Daria, it won't go away by pretending it isn't happening. We need to talk about it – the three of us.'

This time Daria didn't argue. 'I know.'

And so, sitting by the stream, they talked until sunset. The lives and behaviors, the thoughts, loves, arguments of their families and the villagers. Repin joined in during the afternoon from his room and added his thoughts, and they were all realizing they had a problem for which they could see no solution. They just heard too much of the private thoughts of everyone.

Have either of you found a way to be free of them?

None of them had.

You know, Daria, he said at last, *the question that has haunted me to this day is why was your mother so anxious that day?*

I thought you would have figured it out, she said. *I have never been able to ask, but my guess has always been that she has something like what we have, but perhaps not as developed, and whenever I have tried to listen in to her I have had the feeling that she's hiding whatever it is.*

Repin and Leiti agreed.

Two weeks passed and they had several more conversations, but none led them any further.

One day early in spring Repin was out on his first garzen hunt with the Elders. The garzen was a gigantic four-legged shaggy creature hunted for its meat, skin and tusks. Repin's uncle was responsible for his hunting education as was the custom in Epinaria, and he believed Repin's hunting skills needed further development by joining the village Elders.

Although Repin would not be permitted to participate in the actual hunt, he would be able to carry weapons, listen to the planning, watch the kill and help with the meat. The men were stalking the largest garzen Repin had ever seen. He crouched behind a tree, watching his uncle take some of the most experienced hunters along the side of an escarpment where the herd had been grazing.

Suddenly, Repin saw that his uncle was going to be trapped between the biggest male garzen and the cliff if the beast did not fall into the pit dug for its capture. It was too late. The garzen charged, trumpeting, across the narrow strip of land, avoiding the pit but not the party of men trying to shepherd the beast into it.

Before anyone could warn his uncle, the garzen, frightened and crazy, stomped him to death. Repin was distraught, and Daria and Leiti heard him cry out. At the time they were not together, and both were asking Repin what was the matter, and he was telling them, and they had a conversation at a considerable distance. Almost as soon as it was over, they again became aware of the significance of their experience.

They agreed that after the funeral they should meet and talk, though at the time, and later, they often wondered why they needed to meet; their physical proximity seemed to be important. The trio sat down some distance down the creek but short of the waterfall. Their voices would be drowned out should there be passers-by.

Leiti began. 'Thing is, whenever stuff goes on in our house, the sex, the arguments, the incredible lies, I hear it as though I am in their heads. It doesn't happen all the time, but as soon as there is any reasonably strong emotion, I'm there.'

The expression on everyone's face was a study in relief and uncertainty.

'So,' said Repin, 'we know that we all have it, but what exactly do we have? The first thing we need to keep in mind is that whatever it is, no-one else is likely to understand, and no-one is going to approve in any way. Do either of you think I'm wrong?'

No-one did. No-one could get Repin's story of Haen out of their mind.

'That's all very well,' said Leiti, 'but it's not as though we have any choice in this, is it?'

Daria said, 'Well, when I tried to talk to my mother it was almost a disaster. I got a lecture about what rubbish I was saying and reminded that people do not talk to each other except by speaking. With the exception of the priest, and any other suggestion was blasphemous, and a whole lot of other words I did not understand. Worse, she was very clear: I was not only mistaken but also must *never* even suggest such a thing, and I should go to my room and think about that and never speak of it again. I must say, I thought that made our position pretty clear.'

'Well, I didn't get that far with my mum,' Repin said. 'I was lovingly and unceremoniously shushed up and told "there, there, not to worry", and sent off with several silly explanations.'

Leiti's version was much the same. 'I knew not to mention it. My mother would do more than throw a fit. My father is the only member of the community allowed to speak with the spirits, so anything I said would be seen as me involved in a seriously taboo activity.'

'Listen,' said Daria. 'This is not okay, Leiti, nor is your mum's warning. But we have been warned and it's not as though we really didn't know, is it?'

The three looked guilty and then began a conversation about some of the other odd things they had been experiencing.

'You know, Daria, about the stuff you've been hearing,' Repin said. 'Well, I think we all know that is not all, don't we?'

They looked at one another, trying to test the waters.

Leiti burst out laughing. 'You mean do we know you want to have sex with Daria?'

Repin blushed in just about every part of him that they could see.

Daria also burst out laughing. 'Of course I knew, all of us know, and we know you find Leiti attractive but only as a friend. Why are we all being so cute about this?'

The depth of relief was clearly reflected in the laughter and the collective release of tension that followed.

'I thought at first that I was the only one who had these feelings, until I began to listen in to them...'›

'You mean the other boys,' said Daria.

'Yes, but some of the stuff they were thinking was mind-boggling! The girls too, planning how to get noticed and entrap a particular guy.'

Daria became outraged and Repin turned and looked directly at her. 'Come on, Daria, you know this is not just the men.'

The ensuing conversation opened the door to the most frank and open discussion of their lives. It also made them aware of the danger that surrounded them. Speaking openly about what was actually happening around them, especially inside people's private thoughts, was not only something no-one in this community would ever think to talk about but was not something anyone would consider appropriate to discuss. In fact, no-one in their world would think that was okay. It would not be a subject of any conversation they could ever have. This included all the lies, games, deceits, and yes the loving and the caring, but that was not so disturbing. What they were learning was going to make them outcasts and they all knew it. In fact they knew that actually they were already outcasts, just not yet known to the rest.

'Look.' Repin's voice was rough and full of concern. 'We can't pretend this is not happening to us. We know more about everybody than any of us would like, including each other! What are we going to do about it? What control do we actually have over this... ability?'

Leiti looked at them. 'Ability! This is beginning to feel more like a scourge.' She lapsed into silence and they just looked at one another, pleased to have the reassuring sound of the water in the background.

The silence lasted for some time, each lost in their thoughts, until Leiti spoke the thought they could not avoid. 'We have to decide how we deal with this or we are likely to get trapped and we could easily be in real trouble or a lot worse.'

They didn't solve the problem that day, nor did it go away. It was brought to a head over Daria's sixteenth birthday when her parents informed her they had decided she should mate with one of the more eligible of the hunters in the village. Daria was aghast. The only man she wanted to be mated with was Repin, but for reasons more to do with the economics and politics of the village, it was not going to happen.

Daria was beside herself. Not only did she find her soon-to-be husband not even pleasant but she knew, as did they all, a great deal about his activities in the village, especially that he was an unsavoury and violent bully.

It was Repin who spoke. 'No matter that we all think this arrangement is wrong and Daria will be harmed by it, we have no power in this community to do anything about it, we are just kids.'

As Daria's sixteenth birthday approached the group spent more and more time traveling outside the community, sometimes hunting and picking berries, whatever legitimate activities they could manufacture. However, time was getting short. It was becoming clearer to them that a big issue was going to be their ability to manage their feelings toward one another.

Leiti one morning threw her hands into the air. 'Surely you two don't imagine my first sexual experience should be through you two making passionate love? The way you ooh and ah at one another and the dirty thoughts you share with me! Well, of course I have seen a lot of sex over the last couple of years, but with you two I could hardly escape, could I?'

'Well, get out of our heads.' Repin's advice was easier to give than to take.

They were all experimenting with how to give one another privacy, but as their abilities grew, they were less and less able to do this, especially where any strong feelings were involved. Leiti was clearly disturbed, and although the three of them laughed long and loudly, it was a genuinely complicated situation.

After this, the three began to explore in more detail the sexual life of their community. Daria was the most vocal. 'Last night the goings on in our hut were diabolical. I can't believe that these people ever claimed to care for one another. The selfishness and insensitivities and the duplicity...'

She then described in detail one of the young couple's sexual encounter, but Leiti had also been an observer so there was little to say.

'What I don't understand is why they don't try to understand how to take care of each other,' Daria said. 'You'd think they would see that was the way to get what they each want, but they don't! Why is that?'

Daria was looking at the others, seeking an explanation.

Leiti looked at Repin. 'Could it be that they are afraid of what they want, afraid that if they say it they will be ridiculed and be more vulnerable to ridicule?

'The boys and the men all seem unwilling to ask what their women want, what would really please them, and as they cannot see their thoughts you would think they would have the sense to ask, but they don't. I have heard none of them ask, have either of you?'

They had not.

'So the girls do not know really what would please their men most, and the men have no idea what would really please and delight their women partners! Great moon-magic, no wonder they all spend so much time dissatisfied and increasingly angry with one another after the first excitement is over.'

Leiti's curiosity for the moment satisfied, the conversation dropped. It was, however, Leiti who finally framed the question they all seemed to be avoiding.

'How long can we survive here, and what are we going to do about Daria's birthday next week?'

Leiti put the finishing touch on their concerns. 'We don't seem to actually belong with these people, which I find myself having a hard time believing. I mean, they are our parents and relatives, but we don't really seem to be one of them. And if we stay, what is happening to Daria will happen to me shortly after, and I don't think you, Repin, will have a lot of choice either. Surely we can't be the only Olarians with this problem?'

'Okay.' Repin's voice was full of stress. 'What about us? How well have we been able to take care of one another really? We can't hide our feelings, and we know bugger-all about how to behave differently from our families and friends. If we plan to leave together as a group, we are going to have to do much better than we have so far managed, aren't we? And I don't know how. Do either of you?'

It was clear they were sandwiched between disturbing alternatives. But Leiti put her foot down. 'On the day before Daria is forced into this horrible relationship, I want us to leave, together, and face the truth that we all know. We are going to have to brawl and struggle to find out how to do this better than they can. Somehow, and I don't really know how, we have to agree to sort out every bad thing that happens between us. We have to be willing to live with our discomfort or we will destroy ourselves.'

No-one disagreed, yet beyond the idea was the very solid fact that they were going to be really isolated and would have to deal with their own problems.

And so, the day before Daria's sixteenth birthday, they left the village at first light, fully laden with whatever they felt justified in taking with them. They left their old lives forever, heading south, feeling excited, fearful, but resolved. They were pretty sure this would be the last any of them would see of their village, their relatives, or their lives as they had been up to now. Tomorrow was really going to be *another day!*

CHAPTER 42

Jard & Leiti

Jard knew that with his father's untimely and unlikely death, some of the men in his village were planning his demise. At 17 he should have a mate and a child on the way. He ought not to be contemplating early death. People usually lived to around 50. Both his sheer size and by far the sharpest mind in the village made him a force to be reckoned with, but neither of these qualities accounted for his survival so far. His safety, amidst the turbulent political animosities in the small village, had been dictated primarily by his father.

Jard was the tallest and the most powerfully built man the village had ever seen. He radiated energy. He had been a big child and now stood at six foot two. At 17 an Olarian male was considered a man. However, when his father, who had been the village spirit leader, died suddenly and mysteriously one night at age 40, Jard knew it was time to leave the village. Not because he was afraid – he was not – but because to win the fight that would take place tomorrow would force him to play a hand he could not afford to expose.

Jard was an anomaly to them, even to his family, but worst of all to himself. He was isolated and deeply angry. Not unreasonably. Not by choice. He had been protected until yesterday by his father, who, because he was the community's spirit leader, was someone who could not safely be challenged or crossed. Jard knew his father's death was at the hand of someone with courage and powerful friends. Jard felt some guilt that he had not detected the plot. Immediately his father had been properly buried, Jard collected his hunting gear, and, having established there was no immediate danger in the village, he left in the night.

He knew that come first light several people would be seeking to send him to join his father in the world of the spirits. He intended not to be there for that send-off. He also knew, had he stayed, he would have survived their efforts, but several of them would not have. However, this was not his way.

The moon was waning as he sat high up on the northern end of the hills running along the eastern side of the valley. This might be his last glimpse of the place in which he had lived his entire life. In the moonlight, the wood and thatched huts looked a little eerie and untidily arranged. Built above the highest flood line, they followed the east side of the river that ran through the center of the valley.

The west side was a steep, rocky escarpment. No-one ever built there; rock falls discouraged building. The eastern hills were easy to climb, well timbered, and in times long past had been rich in game. The village had grown, and over the past hundred years the country within 10 miles had been reduced to providing only sparse hunting except when the grazers migrated during autumn.

The things his father had actually known about the world of the spirits were, Jard believed, few, though not in his father's imagination. Jard stretched his telepathic mind across the entire village until he picked up the three conspirators talking quietly in one of the cooking spaces. He was angry about his father, but not enough to avenge him! Which surprised him. But then, there was so much disingenuous venality that constituted the managing of families and governing the small community, he got a headache listening to the lies and self-deceptions that kept their little community politic active and alive. He was in no position to manage a coup. They were afraid he might try and, worse, might succeed. But sitting high above them in his eyrie, he was simply pleased to be no longer enmeshed in it all.

Now, finally alone, he had to make a decision about his future. He had been born with some important differences from everyone else. His parents guessed or somehow knew, but they would never discuss it, nor would they allow him to raise the subject. Nevertheless, by age three his telepathy was already very strong, and his father, who partly understood, believed it was due to his own communion with the spirit world.

He thought Jard was *special* because he was the son of the spirit leader, which perhaps, in a way, may have contained a grain of truth – just not in the way his father thought. His father had taught him to hide it, and inside the umbrella of his own special relationship with the spirits persuaded his son never to reveal what he knew to anyone and never to speak of it, even to him!

So Jard became a very special kind of recluse. He knew pretty well everything about everybody; he generally despised all of them and kept to himself. It was the only way to stay safe. He inevitably won the few fights he had ever been pushed into. Hunting and other skills had come easily and made him unintentionally considerably superior to those around his age. Whatever other abilities he might possess, he had successfully hidden, even from himself, his way of protecting himself from those around him. So now, high above the village, alone, really alone, he needed to try to find others like himself.

He had since early childhood believed there were seven other children like himself, all his age, somewhere. He had no idea where or whether this was any more than wishful thinking, but the feeling had hung around him since he was about five years old, and it felt right. He hoped very strongly it was not just a wishful dream. His plan now was to search for them. Picking up his gear, he moved out of sight of his village. He was determined to visit every Olarian settlement he could find, though at this moment he had no idea how many there might be or where.

He was hampered by a lack of information and by a lifetime of needing to hide and so not use, extend, or develop whatever the power was that he had. He felt that maybe that was just as well. He was not emotionally very mature, and for all his rangy height and strength and his latent abilities, he had no idea how to manage girls. His exemplars among the other young men in his village were shockers, with at best the barest minimum of sensibility and subtlety. He had not assumed their crude relationship skills should be a model for him, and at best he understood he had a lot to learn.

Two days passed before he became aware of a trio of hunters about half a mile ahead of him. They were moving toward him. He heard one of them warn the others: *We've got company.*

He stopped. He should have been invisible to them at this distance; he was being careful. Who were they? The three began a conversation; he listened in. They were speaking a dialect he did not understand but he could follow their thoughts. He picked up some anxiety but no immediate threat, no hostility. Without thinking, he asked, *Who are you?*

The trio stopped. It was not the most elegant question, but clearly he had to start somewhere.

We are hunters, travelers.

They were telepaths, he knew immediately. Just one problem: he had no plan. And that was how Daria, soft, blonde curly hair down to her shoulders, met him. She was the talker. She was strong. He could feel her; she was undaunted by the situation. *Can we approach you?*

Of course. He really didn't know what else to say.

The trio moved toward him and he continued toward them. Ten feet apart they eyed one another and made basic introductions. Repin was the male. He had short dark hair, a strong barrel chest, wide shoulders, about five foot ten, not tall like Jard or the very beautiful third member of their party. Leiti had long straight brown hair, was tall, just not as tall as Jard, was quiet but alight with energy; his heart jumped at the sight of her.

He felt their caution, instinctively knew they were all about the same age. They were some of the eight he believed were out there, well, out here! He could feel them seeking his thoughts and feelings as he sought theirs. The feeling was odd; he had never felt it before. These were people like him. He knew it, and so did they.

By silent agreement they sat, dropping their hunting and travel gear. Leiti had a metal pot not unlike his own, and she was carrying herbs. She sat and focused on the space between them. He saw colors play on the ground then fire. He immediately knew what she had done and smiled inside. She collected wood and arranged it on the fire, then set her pot down to boil water. Their containers were not unlike his own. Their drinking mugs also.

She responded to his thought.

We have got so used to using wood in case others see us, but you are correct; it is not needed.

He understood. His experience a year ago with the injured wild animal had taught him some things about himself he still did not understand, but he knew, somehow, he had access to energy that could be used in times of crisis.

The energy she used to light the fire was from the sun and from usually invisible bands that were everywhere. The fire would stay alight while she needed it, then it would simply cease to be and, because she had used wood, leave a charred spot on the ground. They drank the hot delicious infusion. Looking at one another. Just as well the conversation was not going to rely on him.

Daria realized that Jard was unlikely to begin this conversation. She decided to be her usual blunt and friendly self.

Jard, I want to start by saying we are really pleased we found each other. We did not know if we were the only telepaths in Olaria but we desperately hoped we were not alone. So, it feels likely, if there are four of us, there will be more.

Daria, I think there are eight of us.

The other three were silent and more than a little puzzled.

It was Leiti who picked up the thread. *You know this?*

Jard nodded but raised his eyebrows, pulling them in together, a sight that caused both the girls to smile. He had thought no thought so they had to wait.

Sorry, he said, *but since I was very young, I have had the idea there are eight of us.*

Repin joined in. *Did someone tell you?*

No, Jard replied, *it was just a feeling I had, have always had. I have no idea where it came from or whether it is just my fantasy.*

Well, Daria continued, *let's hope your fantasy is right, because four is a very small number to begin a community.*

Jard raised his eyebrows, which seemed to be one of the ways he liked to communicate. More chuckles. Repin smiled.

Daria was not finished. *We need to get to know you, Jard, and you us. We have the advantage of growing up together in one of the larger villages in a place called Epinaria. Do you know of it?* Jard shook his head. *It means we have known each other forever, and if we are to be together, we all need to know each other really well, don't you think?*

Jard felt himself pulling away from so much intimacy. His minimal people skills, his lack of confidence with others, were strong and disturbing. Finally he became aware of Leiti looking deeply into him. He could feel her very strong attraction; she was feeling that he was the most interesting and exciting man she had ever laid eyes on. He was aware of her feelings, quite overwhelmed by them and her closeness and the intimate thoughts she was having about him.

She burst out laughing and he was briefly startled.

Jard, you clearly know how we are feeling. Surely you are aware we know what you are thinking and feeling also.

But Jard was not. *I have never had anyone who was able to know what I was feeling and thinking. Until now my thoughts have always been private. This is very strange and disturbing, and truth is, I never thought about what it would be like to be with others like me.*

They talked about themselves, shared bits of their childhood, their growing up, their parents and their relatives and as much of what they had learned as they could. When the day was gone, they ate, put up their shelters and slept. It was not an easy sleep for Jard or for Leiti, in part because Repin and Daria were lovers. Jard found himself and, he became aware, Leiti, watching and listening and feeling the depth of their loving and the pleasure of their sex. Jard finally slept, his mind filled with disturbing understandings about what he had found his way into contact with.

The next day the four sat and talked. Jard shared his isolated childhood and his loneliness. The three sat looking at him in disbelief. Probably the most powerful man they had ever seen, and certainly, seriously good looking, lonely?

Repin, Daria and Leiti told Jard how they had discovered their telepathy and decided to leave their village. Leiti laughed as she explained to Jard how they had studied the sexual behavior of most of their village and felt very uneasy about what they had learned. However, when Daria and Repin had first become lovers, it was nothing like what they or Leiti, who was watching, had ever expected.

Leiti turned to Jard and said, *Don't worry, they will watch us when we become lovers.* The stunned and shocked silence from Jard seemed to convey it all, and Leiti had nowhere to go as Jard's blush grew everywhere he was visible, and it took several serious apologies and no small amount of backtracking for some sort of equilibrium to be regained.

The feeling between Jard and Leiti was intense, not unlike that between Daria and Repin, and that excitement and hungry desire made for a powerful bond. However, it also had a quality of brittleness that often haunts young love. The first rift between them happened over a seemingly insignificant discussion before they had actually become lovers.

As they were settling on a camp site for the night, Daria said, *We should give gifts to the gods for our good fortune.*

Jard tensed. *Whatever do you mean?* His voice was full of challenge, his face tight, his hands clenched by his sides.

Repin was quick to respond. *The gods have played an important part in our lives! What's wrong with you?*

Jard's face reflected his incredulity. *Oh, come on Repin.* Jard rolled his eyes. *You must know as well as I do that that god stuff is complete rubbish.*

A shift in mood settled over the group. Leiti stepped away from Jard, her eyes widening. Repin's face tightened as it darkened. Daria could only stare in astonishment, and the three Epinarians faced off seemingly against him.

There was surprise, distress, anger and serious misunderstanding all mashed together in the space between them. Jard, large bushy eyebrows raised and pulled in at the sides, his forehead furrowed, shook his head slowly as he tried to sort his shifting feelings.

What on Olar just happened?

Jard made frantic efforts to grasp the appalling discord that suddenly sat around them. *We don't share beliefs about the gods,* he thought. *They actually believe in them!*

He said desperately, *I apologize if I've offended you all. I had no idea you felt so strongly about the gods. In my village one Elder in each generation spoke to and for the gods. The last one in our village was my father. The thing is, what he claimed the gods had told him was often wise, but also sometimes he would claim the gods were insisting on vicious and sadistic punishments and they often disgusted me. Then I came to know what was going on in his mind and realized he spoke with two tongues, neither of which came from any god.*

Sometimes I could see him think through what he had to gain before issuing his judgment or pronouncement from his god. He was not being given words from any gods, he was often merely looking out for his own interests. So I came to distrust what he claimed his gods had told him.

I learned he was afraid of me and for me, because he thought I might somehow usurp him! I think he might have been a little bit telepathic, but not like us. I believe he feared I might somehow ultimately undo his powerful position. At least, that was what it seemed when I studied him. So, I concluded, he used his so-called gods to simply support his powerful position in the community.

The only other person he seemed afraid to confront was the village healer. Without his gods he would have been nothing in the village. His underlying nastiness and anger repelled me, and so, in the end, I simply did not believe any of his nonsense about what the gods wanted or demanded. It was not a good way to feel about your own father.

Repin said coldly, *You have no right to speak against the gods just because they never spoke through you.* He glared at Jard. His hands tightened around his drinking cup in an effort to control the trembling brought on by his rising anger. *How could you know the gods were not shaping his words to support their wishes?*

His voice was strong but full of tension, his emotions clearly confusing him, and Jard recognized this but was determined to get to the bottom of their strong disagreement. That Leiti had moved physically a little away from him had made an enormous impact, and he was busy also steadying his feelings.

The air shimmered with the tension between them. The power of the Elder, who in his village was his father, who spoke with the gods – who said he spoke with the gods but mostly said he received the word of the gods – had been unquestionable, and Jard could see the Epinarian Elders held the same power. What should he do or say? Nothing. He had crossed a line; it had been like this at home.

Jard got up. He was drawn back to his village and how unacceptable he had been. Now he had offended even Leiti and was responsible for disturbing what had seemed to be an extraordinarily positive relationship. This was a repeat of exactly the situation he thought he had escaped in his own village. Now he was the cause of losing his new friends and a special woman, one he considered might be a truly satisfying partner for whom he was beginning to feel strongly.

I'm really sorry, he said as he began to pack his gear. *I'll just leave. I didn't mean to cause you such distress. I'm just not good with people, as you can plainly see. Always opening my mouth and getting into strife. I thought I had learned to be silent till we met, then I thought that speaking my mind was actually going to be all right finally. Now I realize it's never going to be all right and I have to find a life perhaps without people.*

Years of keeping his feelings and thoughts to himself crowded in on him. He had been too outspoken, too desperate. It had been a mistake; in an instant of hubris he had alienated the first people who had ever seemed likely to become genuinely close to his real self.

Sadness clung to him like a dark cloud, and it spread over the four of them as he tied the last of his things together.

Leiti was shaking her head. *No, Jard.* Almost a whisper, yet clear and distinct in his mind over the other soft late-afternoon noises of the forest.

Jard looked at her, knew she could feel his deep sadness. He'd withdrawn, years of practice that had kept him safe returning to help him regain control of his life. Years of discipline he had carelessly thrown away here in the belief that things would be different with this group he now saw to have been false. Wanting a thing to be so did not make it so.

He had been careless, and it had hurt his chances with the first real friends he might have had. The pain and distress were blocking him from them and them from him. Had he been a little less trapped in himself, he would have heard them, but for now escape was uppermost in his mind and he was deaf to their voices. Then he was gone.

Leiti, determined to go after him, had her stuff repacked in moments. Daria begged her to reconsider but she had already become hopelessly obsessed with Jard. As she was about to leave she said, *Please wait for me. We cannot let him go. He is the only one we have found so far, and I don't want to lose him, and you both know I have never felt like this before. I'm going to bring him back. This is a ridiculous misunderstanding. Please.*

She left, following his easily identified and already deeply known energy trail. Her words lingered in their minds as she pursued him. Some part of her knew what had happened was bizarre, and another part knew what she was doing was both stupid and dangerous; she neither knew these woods nor was she a real hunter, however, she was not really in control of her actions; none of them actually were.

I've never felt this way about anyone in my life. The thought/feeling ran through her mind. *I can't just let him go.*

Another part of her knew if she lost him now, if they lost him, they were unlikely ever to build a new life for themselves.

Back at their campsite, Daria and Repin were still angry and distressed but did not want Leiti to leave. Jard's sudden departure and Leiti's had broken the train of the exchanges that had created this unholy mess. They looked at one another, feelings chasing themselves in a kaleidoscope through them, no clarity, no boundaries.

Finally it was Repin who got focused. *Daria, we need to stay right here. We can keep track of Leiti and in contact with her if we work together. If we feel she is moving out of our reach we will move after her. Pack quickly. Are you okay with this?*

He realized that his being dogmatic and inflexible had been partly responsible for getting them into this situation. He looked at Daria, who took his anxious and strained face in her hands, kissed him gently and said, *Of course.*

She could feel how the sense of responsibility for this disaster was weighing heavily on him.

They became aware at that moment that Jard had stopped, and moments later Leiti was able to let them know he was sitting in a clearing and she had caught up with him.

He was sitting on the ground, his gear beside him, head in hands, radiating distress and frustrated confusion. She fell down beside him, throwing caution to the winds and her arms around him, cradling his head like a child.

Daria and Repin could read nothing except the intense distress from both of them, and so sat anxiously with their gear. He was in no rational state, and neither was Leiti. Daria and Repin could only monitor them and stay out of the way.

Jard did not respond to her, so Leiti stopped touching him and moved to sit in front of him, and she now took charge in a way that surprised her. She seemed to understand Jard's intense and unrelenting pain. After no movement from either of them for several minutes, the pair forming a strange tableau in the clearing, Leiti spoke to Jard.

You cannot leave us, no matter how much this hurts, no matter how bad this feels, we... I need you to deal with me. Please do not run away here. I absolutely refuse to let you do this.

He looked at her, shocked and without real comprehension.

How can you bear to be with me?

Leiti heard what he said but knew it was not really a question.

Her tone was angry as she loudly responded to him in his mind.

You have no right! The words punctuated his distress and brought him abruptly into the present moment.

What do you mean I have no right? What sort of a statement is that supposed to be?

She repeated it.

He focused his attention on her. *No right to what?*

To feel free to walk out on us, especially me, just because we had a disagreement.

How can you say that? I just made all of you angry at me because I spoke my mind, and you were so offended you moved away from me.

She looked at him in amazement. *Have you never had a disagreement with any of your family or close friends before?*

He felt as though he wasn't hearing right.

She continued. *When Daria, Repin and I were growing up, we disagreed violently with one another lots of times. Sometimes we didn't speak to each other for days, but then that blew over and we just got on with our lives and went on with our friendship. We still don't agree on everything. How come you don't get it?*

Without any intention, I have fallen hopelessly in love with you. We are certainly not going to agree on everything in our lives. Do you plan to walk out every time I disagree with you? What kind of a relationship will that be? I'm sorry, Jard, but you do know that I am hopelessly in love with you, even though as yet you have been unwilling to acknowledge that you have similar feelings for me. Nevertheless, I feel it is wrong for you to feel free to walk out on me because we don't agree on something, anything! Surely you can see that?

Then, looking at him fully and intensely, she could see he really didn't get it. She was appalled then desperately sad for him as she grasped the depth of his aloneness, but she was not finished. She had no idea how this was going to turn out with this beautiful, strong but lonely man. She became aware that Daria and Repin were listening but brushed it aside. She needed to be totally here with Jard.

They were sitting a few paces apart and he was staring at her in disbelief. Angry and distressed as he was, he felt himself slowly drowned by her intensity. For whatever reason, it was making him feel even more totally in love with her while simultaneously his mind was telling him not to be stupid. He must, it insisted, be misunderstanding her somehow. But slowly he came to see he was not mishearing her; she was angry and it made her even more beautiful. Then suddenly his confusion collapsed and he found himself in tears. Sobbing quietly, hands over his face as he had not sobbed since he was a young child.

Leiti, torn between her desire to comfort him and to hold her distance, kept her boundaries sharp and clear so as to not lose the import of the moment, the need for him to confront whatever demons were within him.

Again, *Jard, I've never felt this way before. It's a feeling I know Daria has for Repin, but I love you, you know I do. You have to face whatever is at war inside you, please!*

She sat there watching and waiting, hoping he would talk to her, get through this moment of pain and anguish and, she was sure now, embarrassment.

Then it was Repin, no longer able to contain his emotions, who burst in to the conversation between them.

Jard, I'm sorry! We have lived life only in our village, and I never dreamt of doing what you have done, never would have had the courage. I know our Elders did not have kindly and caring thoughts for others, and I felt bad when I realized I was taking my naivety and fear of them being wrong out on you.

He paused.

Jard was trying to take it in. This experience was still too new for him. He was feeling really bad about his outburst, his anger, not at these new friends but at the intense abuse of the adults in his village. The others were following his thoughts as he reflected on his experiences back there, back then, not really so long ago, though right now they seemed a long time ago and a long way away.

Leiti was being magnificent. Daria knew how desperate she was to hold Jard and how much discipline she was exerting to hold herself back. She intuitively understood he needed to get his confusion sorted, get his anger and distress under control. He needed to find some clarity in everyone's part in this early but monstrous disagreement or misunderstanding, but that was yet to be sorted.

Perhaps more than the others, she recognized their need to deal with the range of very real differences between them, differences that needed to be discussed without breaking them apart if they were to have any hope for the future.

Repin seemed to be recognizing their problem as his part in it was becoming clearer. Daria was always going to be the peacemaker and would bow to Repin unless she thought he was going too far and knew she could always make him slow down and listen. Leiti had always been the smartest people person in the group, however, none of the three knew enough about Jard.

Leiti was in the process of finding out. Time seemed to pass slowly while they were waiting, quickly when they were engaged, and at present they were all fully engaged with Jard and the issue that had triggered the whole confusing event.

Leiti and Jard were silent. Jard had become quiet. Now he looked at Leiti, still feeling deep sadness, mainly for himself, but also for the pain and angst he had stirred up.

You actually still want me? His question was directed at all of them but addressed to Leiti. Repin and Daria were silent; they knew their relationship with Jard hung in the balance, and perhaps they were also feeling the possibility of a new communal life, though this did not seem so probable a thing right now.

Leiti was quiet, looking intently at Jard as she heard his question. *I think I need to know if you want me, us, because it was you who left.*

The air between the two and between the two couples was still but crackled with tension. Jard could feel his world hanging in the balance. He had behaved badly but in his mind with good reason. Nevertheless, he was looking at Leiti and was sure he would be willing to make a very big sacrifice to have her in his arms, but what did he need to do or say that would enable him to stay with her – with them – now?

He could not accept the hypocrisy and the self-righteousness of the god thing, but he knew he had no right to deny them their beliefs, even if he thought them absurd and dangerous.

He knew he must communicate with her soon. He knew that talking about himself and intimate things was, at least for him, scary stuff. But he could see no outs here. So he began.

You already know something of my life back in my family's village. The people there were, in their way, okay, but the truth is I didn't fit in and I was never going to. I am really just over it – over a life lived with lies, deceits, half-truths and misdirection. I clearly do not know how to play well with others. However, I know what's true, just not what's necessarily right. If I am going to be okay with you, and you seem to know how I actually feel about you though I have been too anxious and inept to show it, then I need you to give me room to be wrong and stupid.

He paused, wondering should he go on. Then he realized she expected him to.

I know I am not going to be an overnight success, but there has to be room for my opinions. I realize I have to make room for yours. However, I will only be all right if you agree to talk without judgment or reservation about stuff over which we might have seriously big differences of opinion. Maybe I can learn to be a bit less touchy, but please remember, until now no-one, not one person except perhaps my young cousin Irah, has ever believed me or been able to understand or share with me. You at least have had each other, so some chance at sanity and mutual support. I hardly can begin to know what that is like.

Without further hesitation Leiti moved closer him and took his face in her hands and, with love and care oozing from her, she said, *Jard, I will always listen to anything you say. I reserve the right to totally disagree with you, but I will never stop loving you, and I will never walk away. I need you to solemnly promise me, if you can, you will never again walk away from me without fully and genuinely engaging with me first. Let us agree to genuine mutual commitment here. I really want to know, need to know, are you up for this?*

She stopped, looking deeply into him as he struggled with himself until finally he said, a bubble of confused feelings tumbling over one another, *Leiti, I absolutely do!* And they were holding, hugging, kissing and touching each other with a sense of relief that nearly swamped Daria and Repin's voices that now came through their tears of relief and confirmation.

We are not always going to be in there with you, but we want some kind of understanding like this between us all.

When Jard and Leiti returned to the campsite, all four hugged, cried, laughed and felt a sense of relief that was both deep and satisfying.

Repin was looking at the others, his brows pulled in, and when he spoke it was in a voice just a little not his own.

I truly never thought to look inside the Elder who spoke to his god. It never occurred to me; it would have seemed just wrong, and yet, hearing what you did and what you saw, raises issues I have never even thought about. The very idea that he was making this stuff up to control us, control everyone in the village, it just seems... I don't know... wrong. No, I don't mean what you did was wrong, Jard, it was courageous in a way... risky, gutsy, and in the end... bloody obvious.

So now I am thinking, do I, did I, really believe all that stuff? To be truthful I am going to have to think long and hard about that. I mean, some of the stuff he said his god had told him to do was appalling, mean and vicious. But I never thought to question it or to go look when I could have. Even when he was responsible for the most horrendous cruelty I ever saw.

Repin was beginning to think through all the years he had simply taken for granted the truths of the Elders. It was slowly sinking into his mind that they were going to need beliefs, but maybe they would not be the beliefs they had brought with them. This was not a thought he had ever had.

This would not be the end, but it might just be a good beginning, because it was the night Leiti and Jard finally slept together, becoming officially lovers and a couple. To say Leiti was ecstatic would be an elegant understatement; to say Jard was delighted and very uncomfortable would definitely be true also.

They awoke the next morning knowing they needed a plan. They started a fire, boiled water for tea, chewed some of the grains and fruits they had picked during the previous day and looked at one another with fresh eyes. Everyone was feeling a bit touchy, but it was Leiti to whom the task seemed to have fallen to take the next step. She wasn't sure why but knew they had to talk more about yesterday and tomorrow.

We had a close call yesterday, she began.

She saw Repin immediately begin to raise an objection.

No! she said, looking directly at him. *I know yesterday was uncomfortable and we would all like to not raise the discomfort of those events, but we are beginning a new life, a new village community if you like. We cannot afford to leave unfinished emotions swirling around between us. We have to take responsibility for everything that happens and not slip into the ways of our parents or pretend we are children and that someone will make the bad things go away, because there are no somebodies here, just us. We have to do the hard things ourselves, otherwise we are done for before we really begin.*

They were looking at one another with something like the guilty expression children get when they've been caught out.

Daria laughed and the others joined in, easing the tension for a moment.

You are definitely right about that, she said, *but what is it exactly you think we should do?*

It was clear no-one had an answer. But Jard had been thinking seriously for much of the night about what had happened to him yesterday, as the delight in his connection to Leiti started to sink in, and they too began to settle as a couple. So it was he who picked up the thread.

All right, he said. *You started my train of thought yesterday, Leiti, when you came and found me in the clearing. You said it was not okay for me or any of us to walk away from unfinished issues. Now I can see your point. If we don't deal with something that has happened to upset us, any of us, we will carry it as I have been carrying stuff from my early life in the village.*

I don't think it is all going to be cleared up in one go. But it seems to me every time any of us has an issue that brings up bad stuff from our past, we need to discuss it, find a way to stop carrying it around. Did I get the drift of your message yesterday?

Leiti looked at him with just a touch of amused admiration and surprise. *Better than I could have said it,* she replied. *Especially for someone who doesn't do well with people.*

So they looked at one another in a slightly confused silence. What was it they needed to say that would free them from whatever residual angst remained from the disturbing events of yesterday?

With a slight frown on her forehead, Leiti took the next step. *Suppose we just tell one another about yesterday? How we experienced it, what we were thinking about and where that has left us feeling now, today, about ourselves and each other.*

She was looking around and scanning the group.

You all know we are feeling anxious and unfinished. I am certain, as I know you are, that we are not finished with that stuff yesterday. It opened up a can of worms for us, isn't that right?

Jard, who seemed to recognize that his actions the previous day had been precipitous, hesitatingly began.

Well, for me it was when you spoke of the gods, I just saw red. All the humiliating lies and twisted behaviors of our god-owning Elder – my father – got dragged up for me. I suddenly thought I was going to be in the midst of a whole lot of trouble because of what I thought about gods and the lies of the Elders.

I just lost it. It wasn't you, Repin, or you, Daria, it was them – the really quite unpleasant dishonest people who seemed to have had control of my life and everyone else's. I know my father was simply willing to lie to maintain his position in the community.

When I think about it now, after yesterday, I believe he and his cohorts simply knew no better. Could not think about how to have a different or better world, so they used what they knew. But we don't know much, and as yet we have built no fixed ways to be or to do things or to explain things. I think we need to find a process that allows us to talk to one another about things that are emotionally uncomfortable.

We need to do this without getting ourselves so involved with the negative emotions that we cannot think clearly. We need to be able to find the best way for us to be together with whatever the issue is. I believe this will be especially true because we can't really deceive one another, even by omission. Do you think that's right?

Jard felt his way around the group, watching and waiting. Interestingly, neither of the couples was in physical contact with their partner. It was as though each knew they had to maintain a clear boundary around their feelings and their thinking, not sit together in a way that would contaminate their ability to be clear with their emotional connections to one another. It felt just a little odd yet uncomfortably appropriate.

It was Daria who commented on it.

Why, I am wondering, am I resisting my strong urge to snuggle up to Repin while this conversation is happening? I think it's because I know the moment I touch him, my love for him and my pleasure with him will immediately cloud my ability to be my separate self in some really primitive way. I will have begun to merge with him. As a result I will be unable to be objective. I won't be able to be just myself. That contact is so comforting, so reassuring and warm, I know that sometimes and for some things it clouds my judgment.

Jard picked up Daria's piece. *I agree with that.* He looked at Leiti. *I know that if I move over and put my arm around you, I will no longer be able to think clearly about this issue you have raised, and while that is an added discomfort, it seems to be adding significantly to my ability to think with clarity.*

They were looking at one another in a different way, and this conversation was both a little stilted and uncomfortable, yet each clearly sensed its importance.

Leiti spoke again. *All right, I get that, and I think we should learn from how we behave what works and remember it for future conversations, but it shouldn't stop us having the difficult conversation I suggested. How are each of us feeling about yesterday? Because I asked the question I will take responsibility for answering first. Is that okay with all of you?*

Although filled with discomfort and anxiety, they all nodded.

All right. When Daria first suggested appreciating what our gods were doing for us I thought, these gods I have always felt obliged to respect, they seem to have thought it was good to hurt people who disagreed with them. We have seen and heard stories about this in our village. We know about occasions where agony was inflicted on naysayers for their disloyalty, which I always found horrible. They have seen fit to make us outcasts from our own village, to allow Daria's parents to promise to partner her to a man she dislikes, one who would have abused her violently. We knew this for a fact, based on his previous behavior with his girlfriends. So I asked myself, what have I got to thank this god for? And I could only guess, making us outcasts was a good thing for us.

Next I tried to think, who then was responsible for giving us the idea that we should go? Was it these gods who only spoke through one old man? And although all this confused me somewhat, I felt pretty certain I did not want to feel obligated to ideas coming to one old man. Especially from an unknown source, one that often suggested repulsive though sometimes beautiful ideas.

So, I thought, why would I not think for myself about what is good and bad, ignorant as I am? Could I not learn to create a world more pleasant to Olarians and other creatures than the gods, and there were several, so we were told, who spoke to our Elder? And my unequivocal, if arrogant answer, was yes. And so that's where I am now. I don't know any truth but I want to build my own with help from all of you.

She looked into the others.

They were staring at her in awe. Repin knew he would never, ever, have allowed himself to voice such thoughts, even if he had been able to have them, but his uncomfortable admiration for Leiti in doing so was immense.

Daria was smiling at her friend. *Wow, you really are amazing. In 10 lifetimes I would never have guessed you could have been so free of them. But I just love what you said, and though it scares the living daylights out of me, it does feel good!*

But it was Jard whose response she most needed. She was looking at him, into him, with the fiercest intensity any of them had ever seen. Whatever his response, she felt as though her life was for the moment suspended, and what he thought and shared next would determine the entire rest of her life.

She was holding her breath, eyes wide, willing him to be with her. He stared at her without moving, his mind racing to catch up with his feelings. By now, all of them were totally focused on him. When he spoke they could hear the silence of their clearing as a tangible part of their world.

I think, he said, *in my entire life I have never heard my unspoken and unclearly thought ideas put with more beautiful clarity and with more conviction. I just love you, Leiti; your mind and your feelings are truly beautiful and I feel nothing but total relief.*

Tears of joy and relief took over the entire space. They hugged and in the silence of the little clearing their tears of relief seemed to cleanse them somewhat.

Jard continued. *There is so much we do not know or understand, I realize that, and of course we could be wrong about all the god stuff. But, for myself, as a result of all the unpleasant experiences I have had with the gods, I would like to try to start our lives with a clean slate. Try to understand, to think through what are the things that would make our lives meaningful and satisfying. Keep those bits of the past that seem to make sense to us now and get rid of those bits that do not seem to fit with the world we are going to have to create.*

We live for a bit, we learn some things, we raise children, learn a bit more, somehow stay alive, find food, do some things that improve the lives of ourselves and those around us, then we die. If we are lucky we pass on to the next generation some things we learned that our parents did not know. Maybe there is more to it, but so far, I have not found it.

The others were looking at him, each wondering what they might be missing.

It was Daria who added an important idea.

Well, that may be true, or it may not be. But until we get some new knowledge or one of us gets to know something new, so long as we do not close ourselves off by thinking we know everything and that we are right, I can live with that. But we need to agree to tell each other should this ever change, that is, assuming we won't actually know anyway because we are telepathic and seem not able to hide things

Has that not been true for the three of us over the past years? And is that not something our parents did not, and perhaps, could not do? We seem particularly well equipped to do it because we know so much more about what is going on for each other all the time.

We have already learned to do some things together that we did not know we could do. Who knows how much more we will be able to learn to do?

And so they left that conversation for the moment and the two couples did some of the lovely things young couples who are exploring like to do, and a short while later sitting comfortably together Jard raised the issue of their future.

CHAPTER 43

The Emergence

Well? It was Leiti, a look of concern and understanding etched into her face. They had returned to Jard's home village so he could have one last look at his village before they moved right away.

Is it really okay? She wanted it to be. Only days since they had met, she had never felt so strongly drawn to someone as she was to Jard, but she did not want for him to feel any regrets. She knew regrets from the day they had left Epinaria, but she also felt strongly that it was the best decision and she wanted to know this move was right for him.

In a final bitter-sweet moment, Jard looked down on his village from the hills, and for perhaps the last time tuned in to his mother and her brother who were now living together. They were engaged in a lively dialogue about him! He turned to Leiti and smiled ruefully but without doubt.

Yes. Then, *I know a good fishing spot which is also a good camp site about two hours' walk from here.*

Because he could not speak their language, nor they his, there was only one way for them all to communicate and that was telepathically. At first he thought this might prove tiring, but it didn't. As he led them toward the site, Leiti began to ask him about his life. He could feel the caution in her quest to understand him and the strong urge to know him better. It was an unusual feeling for him but far from unpleasant.

He was aware that Daria and Repin were listening in and felt the intrusion as mildly uncomfortable yet not oppressive. They needed to know him and he them if this arrangement was to work. Nevertheless, it felt a little strange. To quiet his discomfort, he asked whether tonight after they had eaten they would share some of their experiences and history with him and this was willingly offered, which left him feeling a little easier.

Ah yes. Repin's murmur of approval covered the camp site and the fishing hole. They dumped their gear and followed Jard to the water where he unpacked a handwoven net, a couple of weights and two poles. Jard threw the net attached at one end to one of the poles and allowed it to sink into the water; the other end he held attached to a second pole. The net sank and Jard held the top of the net just above the level of the water. He then sat down to wait. The others, equally curious, sat with him in silence.

Within minutes it was possible to see fish swimming up to the net but prevented by it from continuing their journey. Jard slowly pulled the furthest stick toward himself, causing the fish to move toward the bank. It was then a simple act to bring the corners of the net together and pull the several trapped fish to shore. It was not a technique the other three had ever seen and as they prepared the fish for dinner, Repin studied the intricate knots and spaces of Jard's fish trap, and, as he would always do, considered how it might be improved, even how it might be adapted for use in the sea.

Repin was at heart a designer of things. The three were delighted with the new process and shared with Jard their own fishing methods. The conversation went on until the fish were cooked. The vegetables and berries the group were carrying were prepared and the four sat down to a satisfying, filling and tasty meal.

Jard looked at his new companions and asked himself, *Why have I so easily left my entire life and joined up with these strangers?*

For a moment an eerie sensation washed through him.

We are only a little more than children and we are alone. The thought hung around as he looked at his new companions.

Why did I so easily leave my village and my family?

But as soon as the thought had emerged, he turned over in his mind the moment of their meeting. There had been a powerful surge of belonging! That had been a totally new experience for him. He could not forget the hardly credible grab he had felt in his heart as he looked for the first time at Leiti.

Then he realized they were all watching and listening to his thoughts. For an instant he felt excruciating embarrassment, then, with a new kind of certainty, knew they were looking at him with warmth and honest concern. He realized they were, and probably would always be, able to follow his thoughts, and the feeling was not frightening but reassuring, a feeling of 'coming home'!

He had broken their fear of being the 'only' ones and had felt, and still was feeling, their warmth and welcome, an honesty and directness that had been missing from his life. For more time than he could know, the feeling of this very instant would return to him, give him comfort and conviction of the rightness of his decision.

We need to talk about our lives till you know us and we you, Daria said. *I think this is what you were asking this afternoon?*

It was, Jard replied.

So Daria began the conversation that was to go on even during the days of their search for others. A storytelling like no other, for these were the earliest moments in the creation of some kind of new life, and although none of them really knew just how momentous these events would turn out to be, each felt a strong need for this process of sharing to begin. They had all done the unthinkable: left the safety and certainty of their village lives to find others with whom they could feel deeply connected. People in their villages did not engage deeply with one another and never with honesty.

The three shared the events of their lives, the moments that had defined them, and finally had led each to move on. Listening with rapt attention, Jard wondered how his life might have been if he had had others. It seemed not to have materially helped his new companions. He told his story, but when it was over the girls wanted him to finish by telling them about his girlfriends. But on this matter, Jard initially baulked!

He had had only two. One was an older woman who he had known was sexually very hungry for him. That had been his initiation. Even remembering it now he squirmed with discomfort. The other had been a brief and unsatisfactory relationship with a young woman who he realized, unfortunately, was being with him from curiosity because of his reputation for being odd; she had been egged on by her friends and this, not unexpectedly, had not ended well. He had felt unable to escape her very confusing thoughts about him.

The girls laughed but not with any harshness or malice, just genuine kindly amusement. Repin merely raised his right eyebrow when their eyes met and smiled gently, knowingly, and Jard felt at ease with him. His connection was gentle and absolutely free from judgment or criticism, an experience for which Jard was really not prepared.

This led them to a discussion about openness, honesty and freely shared information. Jard, unlike his companions, had never been able to share his world with anyone; his new companions had been sharing intimacies for some years. There came a moment when a bridge was needed. Leiti broke the ice with one of her blatant, honest statements, which widened Jard's eyes and nearly took his breath away.

I had my first orgasm when Daria and Repin were having their first sex. So you can understand that the early awakenings we had to our special reality were disturbing and often confusing, not to mention sometimes frightening. And I recall this memory because once we had reached some kind of adult-like maturity, there was actually no privacy between us anymore. To our surprise at the time, there simply could not be!

It took the three of us several months to get used to this. Now you and I have become lovers – Jard was blushing, even in places that did not show – *Daria and Repin are already a part of our sexual intimacy, as we are already a part of theirs. You do realize this was inevitable, don't you, Jard?*

She looked at Jard with warmth, desire and one of those expressions of honesty and connection that destroyed any semblance of the duplicity with which he might have preferred to engage.

I mean, it's not that we cannot stay out of one another's minds, but as we are all now aware, whenever any of us experiences any kind of stress or disturbance, the rest of us know immediately. When, and if, there get to be many of us and children, this will somehow have to change, but I don't quite understand how.

This thought would grow and come to permeate more of their lives than they could yet imagine. Leiti was thinking, *When there are, say, 150 of us, all known intimately to all of us, how will we manage our uniqueness, our self?* But without the actual experience it remained just a question.

For the rest of his life Jard would remember this moment, not just the shocking and disturbing information, but the caring and the way Leiti looked at him. It melted him, reduced him to a single emotion: joy. However, his mind remained in turmoil.

I, we – he paused – *have some huge things to understand, accept and manage.*

When he was unable to continue, Repin stepped into the fray.

We really do. If we all know pretty well all the thoughts and feelings of each of us whenever we are in contact, this is a lot to manage. What we don't know about each other is really primarily those things we don't know about ourselves, and if we were to agree to never try to lie and never judge one another, and be as open as we can to everything, then it seems to me we should be able to build a safe community.

At this point none of them could really imagine the four of them becoming a community. Repin was thinking without intentionally speaking to them.

Even as I say these things I know how ridiculous they sound. I think about our village and what went on there. And I wonder if we are being absurd to imagine we can achieve this. But, unlike our families, we actually know what they always thought of as private stuff.

I am thinking that probably none of us has any real idea about how to go about this. We just believe, having talked and talked about this, we are probably pretty right about needing some deeply held value, some kind of deep fair and unshakeable ethical something. We all seem to know we have never been encouraged to think about ourselves or to study or understand ourselves in any way, and what it means is not really clear to me.

I mean... we know very little about ourselves really. Sometimes when we have spoken of these things we have wondered how we would learn. When we were ill our magic woman would work spells and use herbs and potions. We know nothing of these, so we are incredibly vulnerable should one of us be injured. And that is probably the least of our areas of ignorance, wouldn't you think?

While Repin was speaking, the others had seemed to be in clear agreement. Jard put up his hand. *Wait! What you are saying may not be entirely true! No, it's not a criticism! I need to tell you an event that happened to me.*

He related the story of the animal that attacked him and how when he focused on repairing his wound it healed, and about the fire and the sleeping container! The others were staring at him, mouths agape, eyes wide open, brows drawn.

Repin sucked in his breath. *That's astonishing. We've never thought about it, but when I was trapped between some rocks and the girls got me rescued, my leg was originally more damaged than I had thought, but while they were preparing to get me out I focused on it, just willing it to feel less painful, and although I did not think any more about it at the time, it did!*

The four were looking at one another all feeling just a little odd.

Perhaps, said Leiti, *we can do much more than summon and use the lights?*

Jard suggested they should try to do something together with the 'lights' that none of them had ever tried before. The air around them felt as though it was crackling; the trees and the stream noises faded away as they sat looking uncertainly at one another. The tension, the anticipation, seemed to have a substance of its own. Finally they settled on a task, something simple but significant: move the rock on which they had all been sitting. It was a pretty big rock.

Okay, said Jard, *let us move a few feet from it, sit on the ground in front of it like we did to make the fire, and all at the same time think rolling the rock one revolution?*

They sat down in front of the rock and on the count of three thought, like they had thought about the fire, 'Roll'. Nothing happened. Leiti and Jard held hands, Repin and Daria did the same, Daria and Leiti joined hands and then with their entire focus and concentration they thought 'roll over'. It did.

They all drew a deep breath, feeling the effects of the effort they had used in concentrating but realizing there had been no effort in the actual moving of the rock!

We did it! The atmosphere was electric.

Repin said, *I'm having trouble believing we did that.*

This was the moment that the four realized they possessed something beyond simply their telepathy. It was the moment the concept of 'telekinetic telepaths' came into their existence. They were excited, they were disturbed, they were filled with feelings that as yet had no name.

They realized they may well possess more powers than they had ever imagined. What was now becoming clear to them was that they might have had more difficulties in their home villages than they could have imagined. But now there seemed to be possibilities far beyond anything they had, or could, conceive. They were truly beginning a new life.

CHAPTER 44

Searching for the Eight

I think, said Jard, *we need to make a more coherent plan than simply moving down the coastline looking for villages and hopefully more people like us. And I have a very strong urge to think about what we might learn about what we can do together, things that may well help us stay safe and healthy.*

There was no disagreement on that score. But it was a shift in thinking none of them really knew quite how to arrange.

They remained at their camp site that day and talked, thought, rested and ate. The weather was still pleasant, a long way short of winter.

After their evening meal, Jard decided to try again.

Perhaps the biggest question in my mind is what exactly we need to learn and how we go about learning it. I think about my village and the people who were powerful, who controlled what was allowed and what was not, who usually decided what was right and true and what was not.

Often I thought their judgments were silly, or nasty, or destructive, and I never understood why people accepted them. Now, here, there are four of us, we seem to have been able to learn something new, to reach a mutually agreeable, peaceful and acceptable solution, at least to our first significant disagreement.

Leiti was tucked under his arm with her head on his shoulder. He was feeling more warmth and contentment than at any time in his life. A part of him did not want to disturb the ambience of this moment; it was a moment to be savoured unlike any he had known. Leiti not only felt 'right' to him, but she too was in a blissful state. They both knew it might not last, and they also knew there were some hard decisions to be made.

Leiti said, *I think that is definitely a big one, but there is still the question of whether we are the only energy telepaths. To resolve that question means continuing to travel.*

Daria agreed. *There is also the question of where we will live, and I don't know if I am alone in this, but what about children and creating a future generation of ourselves? I always assumed that we would produce children with our abilities, but the truth is we really don't know, do we?*

Jard frowned. He had not really considered that. The girls each looked at their men and the men looked at each other. *Now that is a question! I am having some real difficulty in even thinking about it right now.*

Leiti snuggled closer to Jard.

Daria continued. *Since Repin and I have been together, I have not come to be with child. I believe I know why.*

All three were listening intently; even Repin had a look of surprise and uncertainty.

Well, she went on, *I knew if I got pregnant when we were in the village I would be in terrible trouble, so each time we were together I prayed not to get pregnant. But when we moved away from the village, and now, as I realize I am deciding I do not believe in the gods, I am thinking about the fact that my time of the month had come and I was not pregnant. I thought that perhaps my prayers were simply me wanting not to be with child, and given what Jard has told us, that actually might have caused me not to be. So I am now thinking that perhaps I am actually controlling my fertility, which seems odd but feels true.*

Leiti smiled. *I feel pleased you said that, Daria, because I had decided, not really consciously, when Jard and I got together, I was not ready for a child yet. I know I am not with child and I feel confident that I will not be until I am ready, and as I say it I feel a bit silly. Yet...*

Across the space of the small cooking fire the four looked at one another. All held questions in their eyes; there was so much they did not know. They were comfortably paired, with little or actually no privacy, and they were still experimenting with ways to feel comfortable and at ease with the very public nature of their lives.

Jard added another issue to the ones still unanswered. *What if we are attacked by a hostile party of warriors, either Olarian or as we have heard from our villages, Cretians on the warpath for women and food?*

The Cretians were a warlike nation known to the Olarians over hundreds of years. Periodically a Cretian war party of men would reach Olarian shores in strange craft they had constructed. They would plunder, rape and kill for sometimes weeks until a concerted retaliation by several villages drove them away. None of the four had ever seen one of these Cretians, but in the Epinarian valley there were stories.

So, along with trying to create a new community, if that's what they were doing, there was the question of how to defend themselves against hostile attack. Jard reminded them of his close call with the injured predator.

I am wondering, he said, *whether we may be able to think aggressors away.*

The others looked at him, at first with amusement but then slowly with genuine curiosity.

How are you thinking that might work? asked Repin.

Well, he replied, *remember what we did the other night with the rock? Suppose we can use this ability to influence people or even animals. And then there is the question of distance. We need to learn about the limits to our abilities.*

Repin was intrigued but all of them were tired. He said, *Okay, my mind right now is overloaded. I don't know about the rest of you but I would like to rest and begin again in the morning.*

Everyone agreed. Repin and Daria moved toward their rough shelter, but Jard turned to Leiti and said, *Would you like to explore with me the process of creating a warm and protected sleeping place with our minds, like the one I somehow created that night I was injured?*

Daria and Repin paused to follow the conversation. Leiti looked up into Jard's eyes. She would have done for him anything he asked, and this odd request intrigued her. Jard explained what he had done and suggested that they do it together, keeping their thoughts simple and general.

We will think of being warm and snug together, safely protected in our own cocoon. You can think the thought with me but still weave the lights in the way that you do.

She nodded, smiling.

All right, he said. *Now.*

Repin and Daria watched as the seconds passed and the lights were spiralling around the two bodies. Then suddenly they were only partly visible inside a kind of cocoon, the boundary a kind of swirling cloud inside which the two were lying together in each other's arms.

Daria and Repin smiled with delight. *I think,* Daria said, *they will be just fine tonight, and I will be happy to be with you in our skins in our shelter, but tomorrow I think we may be up for more surprises.*

For the next several days the group continued their search, still traveling south, hunting when the opportunity presented itself, but always on the lookout for new communities.

It was during one of these sorties that Repin said to Jard, *I believe I can tell when there are animals around. I seem to be able to locate them from quite some distance if I am intentionally seeking them.*

Jard said, *You have me wondering now whether my reputation back in the village as a hunter was perhaps in part driven by a similar sense of their presence.*

Their capabilities, many seeming to have lain dormant when not attended to, were slowly emerging under the impact of need and curiosity.

On the fifth week of their travels they came to another village. The group sat down about 500 yards from it, a vantage point from which they could not be seen yet one from which they could tune in to the life of the village. Again they sought out any telepaths. It was a valuable exploration. They stayed for many hours learning how the village worked and who the people were. They were beginning to be familiar with different patterns of life that seemed to exist in the Olarian villages.

They left soon after the midday meal in the village, all feeling a little sullied by their experience. They had witnessed some tender and distressing moments: a funeral, the feast afterward, the intense emotions of some of the villagers, the usual deceit and dissembling and petty power plays, but no-one with telepathic capabilities. They were sad but glad to move on.

They traveled further south along the broad coastal strip sheltered by the range of mountains that ran down this coastline about 10 miles inland, realizing as they better studied the terrain that there were likely to be a number of villages on both sides of the range.

The issues raised by their discussions over these weeks were weighing heavily on their minds. They were not only learning more about themselves but also beginning to grasp more about the nature of their strange abilities. The mood of the group was quieter and more considered, and there were continuous discussions going on between the four of them.

The success of the cocoon building by Jard and Leiti was discussed over and over again until they felt they understood enough to know how to do it whenever they wanted shelter. The following night the four had worked together to create a bigger cocoon inside which they would all be comfortable, and it had delighted them. Weather considerations aside, it meant they needed to carry less as they traveled .

While traveling they had become aware of game nearby. As they approached, Leiti asked the others if she might try to immobilize the animal. As it came into sight she wove the lights around it, effectively stunning and freezing it so the men could easily approach and painlessly kill it. Again they were recognizing more about the way their lives had led them to accept the limitations on their abilities and their understanding, which in its turn allowed them to give the appearance of fitting into their communities.

The mountain range came to an end and they could see in the distance where it seemed to turn westward and meet the ocean. The clouds were massing over the ranges and they knew there would be storms before the day ended.

The four had reached the southernmost extreme of the western half of Olaria. So far, no more telepaths. Their choices limited, the weather now cooling as autumn took over from the warmth of summer, they decided to climb into the mountains that separated east and west Olaria. The climb took them nearly five days before they found themselves on the upper slopes of a vast valley deep in the mountains.

A river had carved the valley many centuries earlier and now ran down the center of it, flowing from east to west. On the northern side were steep cliffs, essentially unclimbable; on the southern side stretched a forest of huge trees the entire length of the valley as it climbed toward a very distant rocky escarpment. Rich pastures lined both sides of the river, and hills climbed steadily toward the higher reaches on the northern side. The only access was to the west and east.

The four travelers looked down at this breathtaking and amazing scene. They were unlikely to find a more perfect site; there was clearly enough food here for them to stock up for the winter and wait it out.

'Tall Trees Valley,' said Leiti under her breath, and the other three just nodded.

For the next six months the small group lived in a luxurious energy shelter, sleeping in super-comfortable, energy-based constructions. They quickly figured out they could construct a weatherproof energy garment that hugged their body shape and essentially protected them from the weather, the cold and, it turned out, wild animals and falling branches. The energy outer garment acted like an impenetrable shell. A great deal of their time outdoors was involved in learning how to use their discovery in new and more practical ways.

It seemed no time before spring, when the snows were replaced by sun and warmth, and massive plant life burst forth. It seemed as though life in all its forms was returning to the valley, and the group decided it was time to continue across the mountains down to the eastern half of the continent.

There was little doubt in any of their minds they would return here before the next winter, and all thought this might be the place to settle and establish their small community, hopefully eight souls by autumn's end, if Jard's hunch was correct.

They worked their way down the north/south range to the eastern coastal strip of the Clarian continent. After three days they could clearly see the ocean. A day later they were standing on its shores.

They moved northward up the coast, wondering if there would actually be any villages on this side of the mountains. There were. The first they encountered consisted of only nine huts, constructed to contain, they estimated, about three families each, so approximately 200 to 300 people. They settled down several hundred yards away from the village to listen in and watch. No telepaths. That became clear quite quickly. Then the pattern of life began to unfold and it seemed to pretty much follow the village life they had either experienced or seen on their travels. As they carefully circumnavigated the village, they suddenly became aware of a voice informing them they had found another telepath.

It was a man's voice, and it spoke not to them but to another, saying, *Pron, we are being observed,* and was answered, apparently by Pron, saying, *Dornal, look up to the southwest. I can't see them but I know they are there.*

Daria challenged them. *Can you see us or are you simply hearing us and know we are here?*

There was, for a moment, complete silence, then the voice of Pron came back to them. *We are two brothers, hunting with our village hunting party. Who are you and what are your intentions? You are clearly telepaths like us.*

Jard replied. *Are your people all telepaths? We are a party of four and have been seeking others like ourselves.*

Pron and Dornal looked at one another as they shared a thought that had been with them for several years. There were other people like themselves! The brothers were twins but no-one would ever have imagined this to be true. Pron was tall, just on 5'11"; he was rangy and slim, laconic, and just a little impulsive. Dornal was 5'8", built a little like Repin, barrel-chested, strong and solid, steady and careful. They seemed to bear no relation to one another, yet were as close and deeply connected as they could possibly be.

Right now they were looking at one another with surprise, delight and caution. There were eight men in their hunting group and like other places in this land, had any of their companions known they were telepathic the pair would have been dead in a very short time. Apart from their telepathy, they had no more idea as to what their abilities might be than Jard had had. How to slip out from their hunting group at this point they could not yet imagine. They were neither liked nor trusted, and always when they were included in a hunting party, someone was surreptitiously made responsible for keeping an eye on them.

Now, while wildly excited on the inside, nothing of their inner turmoil or excitement showed on the outside, and so their watcher remained unaware that a small party of telepaths was keeping a close eye on them.

Daria began a conversation with them in an effort to find out what their situation was and what their intentions might be. After several minutes the small party of telepaths understood Pron and Dornal's predicament, it being not greatly different from their own, and she briefly conveyed this message to the brothers.

The four then held a brief discussion about the best way to assist. Jard's suggestion was the simplest. The four would move closer to the hunting party, carefully monitoring them until they could be immobilized, which would allow Pron and Dornal to slip away.

Is this something that would suit you?

Immobilise them? It was Dornal trying to get a handle on what exactly the four intended and how they were going to do this.

Daria explained some of what they had learned, which made this possible. The brothers were fascinated and agreed, warning the four of the possible predicament they would be in if the process did not work.

The four moved carefully and very quietly toward the hunting party, guided in part by the brothers. The procedure worked, and Pron and Dornal joined the four who moved a considerable distance from the remaining hunting party before releasing them. Now well away from the hunting party and safe from it, the six telepaths listened in to the confusion. When they realized Pron and Dornal had slipped away: anger. However, carefully monitoring the hunters, the six telepaths continued north and away from them.

It turned out they had collected two more unlikely travelers, delighted to find themselves no longer isolated from the majority of their village. They belonged to a large tribal group who had no time for strangers or for odd and incomprehensible attitudes and behaviors. It seemed the most common attitude of ordinary Olarians toward those who were different in any way was hostility and violence.

They became aware of a significantly large community in the direction they were traveling. Moving toward them at a reasonable pace was a woman, who, on sighting them, swerved away to the west, heading for the hills, clearly in order to avoid them. They hailed her telepathically in case she was one of them and were rewarded with an immediate response.

Her name was Enita and she was headed away from her village as fast as she could manage. She was entirely without supplies or weapons. She told them she was glad to be with them, so long as the group were traveling. She was so scared she was hardly able to express any appreciation of her possible rescue, nor did she initially grasp that she was being rescued by a group of telepaths uncannily like herself.

As long as you are going anywhere my people cannot find me, she said. It would be some time before the group would get to hear Enita's distressing and disturbing story. It would also be a considerable time before she understood they were all telepaths and in no way similar to the people in her village.

The group, now seven strong, continued their journey up the east coast, with villages becoming sparse. Jard's belief seemed to be shaping up as true.

Some weeks later, the seven were sitting on a sheltered rise scanning a village when they were disturbed by a hunting party of six men who came silently up behind them.

'Who are you?' The challenge was full of menace and threat.

The group turned slowly around to find themselves half-cordoned off by some unfriendly faces and some very nasty spears pointed at them.

Jard spoke silently into the minds of the other six. *Let's not take any risks here, these men neither look nor sound friendly, and I'm not keen on the way they are looking at our women.*

A few seconds later, he added, *Nor what they are thinking.*

There was instant agreement.

Leiti, do you think together we could immobilize them quickly?

Jard, Repin, Pron and Dornal were considering alternative strategies. They could not speak to the men as they did not understand the language, and if they spoke telepathically, there was a good chance they would be attacked.

I think we should try it, Leiti said. *Before this gets out of hand.*

Jard spoke quietly to the other three men. *If Leiti and I cannot quickly disable them, you need to be ready to fight.*

Enita, clearly afraid, stood behind the others.

There was immediate and complete agreement. Leiti and Jard smiled at the men then projected their intentions to freeze the warriors. The effect was immediate. The six men stood like statues.

A rapid discussion began between the telepaths.

How are we going to get out of this without finding ourselves exposed? asked Repin.

No-one had an immediate answer. It was Daria, thinking of some of their childhood experiences, who came up with a novel suggestion.

Suppose we try to plant in their minds the suggestion that their god requires them to treat these special strangers with respect? Jard, it needs to be a man's voice to issue the instruction.

Jard heard the others agree that in the situation anything was worth a try.

However, it would be nice if before you did that, we were not standing right in the line of their spears! Daria added.

Okay, here goes. Jard, still smiling, spoke in the voice his family had known as the voice of the god. *Put down your spears. These are special people who should be treated with respect. They visit from afar and will not harm you if you cease to threaten them.*

The telepaths held their collective breaths. As one the men put down their spears, Leiti and Jard released them.

Return to your village and do not speak of this to others.

Jard's final instruction seemed to have reached its mark. With a respectful genuflection, the hunters retrieved their spears and slipped away, murmuring respectful words as they quickly retreated toward the village. When they were nearly out of sight of the telepaths, they began a frightened and rapid conversation about the enormity of their good fortune. The travelers breathed a huge sigh of relief, quickly retrieved their possessions and moved away.

Two weeks later Karina, walking slowly as she examined plants with deep attention, found herself confronting the group of seven. She was clearly frightened, but it quickly turned out was telepathic and desperately hoping she would not have to return to her village in which, they quickly realized, she was a barely acceptable outcast. She willingly and joyfully joined the group, another victim of the prejudices of her community.

So, as summer came to an end, they had become a band of eight. It took a not inconsiderable time for the two brothers and the two very uncomfortable women to begin to have any but a minimal connection. Nor was it clear by the time the strange band reached the furthest northerly point of Olaria whether these four would become couples. The two men were inseparable and the two women extremely cautious, untrusting and very isolated.

The group found only two more communities, however, no more telepaths. It was getting steadily colder, and the group kept warm and safe by building energy shelters. Getting to know one another had really only begun when they realized they needed to head back to Tall Trees Valley if they were to winter there. It was not as though even that decision was simple.

It took days before Jard, Leiti, Daria and Repin realized they could show the others their images of the valley, now firmly stored in memory. It was their willingness to describe and show the four still skittish new members of their little community their experience of the valley as images stored in their minds and the willingness of the four to not impose their desires on them that finally led the four newcomers to be willing to move to Tall Trees Valley with them.

However, the telepathic band of eight kept as close to the eastern edge of the mountains as was comfortable in order to stay clear of any further contact with any of the Olarian communities. Within a few days, the group had reached the southern tip of the mountains and were ready to begin their climb to Tall Trees Valley.

CHAPTER 45

Tall Trees Valley

The four original members of the group spent a great deal of time talking with the two brothers and the still very nervous women, who were still reluctant to create too close a connection. The original four were clear that they would like to make the valley their home, but the decision would need to be agreeable to everybody, and at this point they became a loosely connected group of eight with a destination on which they were all more or less agreed.

As a group they decided to cease searching for more telepaths. Their decision was influenced by the length of time the original four had been searching, their belief that they had indeed met nearly the entire population of the country, and the approaching onset of winter.

When Jard woke on the final day of their quest, everyone else was still sleeping. He touched Leiti on the shoulder. She turned over and snuggled into him. The warmth and the pleasure of her filled him with the same sense of delight it had done since she first made it clear to him that he belonged with her. She had been right then, and he knew it was right now.

Why do the others always ask me about the things we are planning to do? he asked.

She looked at him, an experience she found filled her with satisfaction. She studied his thinking carefully. *You really don't understand, do you?* she said with a touch of surprise.

No. His reply was typical, and she looked again at his expression. His hair was, as always, a bit tousled; his eyebrows looked bushier today and his big eyes and his even bigger smile filled her with delight.

You have by far the strongest telepathic capability of any of us. You must know that by now. He looked at her, his brows drawn together, forehead wrinkled, and with a shake of his head he said, *It seems ridiculous. How could I be any different from the rest of you?*

She smiled softly and shook her head.

It was true. Jard had become the leader of the group. At first it was not clear why. But during their time together he had come to be seen by everyone as the most powerful telepathically. But it was really his natural caring and good humor, as well as his capacity to sort out problems, help everyone get to decisions, and especially to never harm anyone in the process, that had sealed it for all of them.

He was gentle, sensitive, and always conscious of the life of the whole group. Without any action on his part, the role had fallen to him, and he had slipped the mantle on without a murmur. Everyone seemed content with this. Now, Leiti realized, he really did not even know it had happened. She patiently explained it to him. He was in turn surprised and a little embarrassed

But I didn't choose this, he said. *I have only ever done what the others have asked!*

He acted like a magnet for her and she responded inside with a powerful desire to crawl into his skin and snuggle up. He was a genuinely beautiful man and she was feeling that fate, or whatever it was, had been incredibly kind to her. But she needed him to understand.

You may not have deliberately chosen this for yourself, Jard, but it is simply who you are. It's not only that we all trust you implicitly, but you have never done a mean or spiteful or hurtful act to anyone in our little community. It's okay for you to feel a little uncomfortable about being seen this way, but good values, kindness and intelligence are qualities we are going to need in abundance before our time is up. Things will not always be smooth and easy for us.

He nodded, knowing this would be so. But he still felt just a little bemused; his status in this group did not seem to match his experience of his life in his family's village. Leiti, however, reminded him of their first nearly disastrous disagreement about the gods. How she had been able to help them find a new way, and how he had seemed to grasp what she had done without hesitation as though he had needed only to experience it. His ability to learn and innovate was extraordinary. A little self-consciously he acknowledged what she was saying.

It was a long climb up out of the coastal plain, through the north-south range and across to the range in which their valley lay. Several days of hard travel were involved. When they arrived in the valley, the autumn leaves with their colorful hues were coming to an end and the air was cold but not yet freezing.

Clouds slid majestically across the landscape, making shade shapes over the green grassland, and it was now quite evident how the river, which wound itself around the center of the valley, had once been responsible for cutting the valley out of the landscape. The group stopped to take in the beauty and power of the place.

As they dropped their weapons and all their gear, Jard asked, *Does everyone feel satisfied with the idea of constructing our collective shelter together? The ones we have been trying out each night might be the basis for us to take a step further and create a grander shelter that will be our collective home for the near future?*

There was complete agreement.

What exactly did you have in mind regarding the grandness? asked Enita.

There were smiles from the others.

Well. It was Repin who had become the designer of their energy shelters. He had really taken to the idea of making them more interesting rather than just functional. His voice carried his enthusiasm. *I like the idea, and if everyone says what they want, we could construct a bigger and more complex structure than we have ever attempted. It could have sitting areas and perhaps it could also contain our own internal cooking space!*

The shelters, which had begun as Jard's cocoon, had grown and grown, taken different forms, and finally they had been able to create shapes, colors and textures – Leiti and Repin's contribution – which gave them the feeling of substance, as though they were created from solid materials.

After Repin had assembled ideas and shaped them into a single design, the group sat down together to create their first really large communal dwelling. They had already been successful in maintaining their design shapes, which they believed would be permanent. That had taken time. Some of Leiti's color strands seemed stable and rooted, drawing their energy at a constant rate, the core source being the sun. This held constant during the night and was fully replenished during the day. Now they built a quite huge building. They designed and made all the separate shapes inside, including those that acted as furniture – beds, tables, chairs and an ever increasing array of useful and functional artifacts.

The group took personal objects they had made during their travels into their shelter. This energy creativity was fast becoming a feature of their burgeoning cultural story. The addition of color had been Repin's idea and Leiti's talent. Energy-built objects did not necessarily have clearly visible boundaries.

So that we know the location of everything and its dimensions we can put a color into our weavings, he said. *It works easily. I have tried it. Look.*

He produced a small bench with a distinct color clearly outlining its boundaries. Everyone was impressed, and it was so obvious that they wondered why they had not been doing it all along. Although everyone in the group could see the energy shapes, the colors really added to their clarity.

It was the brothers who first raised the issue of the management of their fledgling community.

We have had many discussions about how we were going to live together since we found one another, but now we actually have to make some concrete decisions.

Everyone was aware the group would need some form of organization, but the only thing they had total agreement about was that everyone's opinion or desires should be taken into account.

Pron said, *We have several things we have identified as essential for our survival: shelter, which we seem to be solving, at least for the moment; food, which is one of the things we cannot manage by our mental powers alone; and safety, which although we can manage somewhat through our combined abilities, still really requires a plan and some mutual agreement. We do not want to be surprised by marauders.*

Everyone was in full agreement.

We also need to manage our health and deal with injuries. So far, we have been able to manage the injuries we have sustained through our own individual abilities. That is okay while we have had no children to look after, no serious illnesses and no babies to deliver.

Dornal added, *Winter is coming. We need food supplies for ourselves, but not for children, at least for this winter.*

And, Jard added, *we need to figure out how to spend our time during the long cold. Now we have the beginnings of our community, we are no longer searching and moving around. We can build a stable life here. Things we could take for granted in our home villages no longer exist here. We have many times discussed our different gods and beliefs that clearly cannot all be true, and I think we are fortunate that the most common experiences we have had of the gods have been unpleasant and have turned most of us away from the beliefs inherent in most of the faiths in our land. We have an opportunity here; we can use our discussions to bring together a way of life we all would like. One that does not harbor the serious dangers and unpleasant experiences we now understand inhabit almost all Olarian communities.*

There was a collective silence.

We should not allow ourselves to feel overwhelmed by the task ahead. We don't have to solve all the problems at once. We can deal with the survival ones first and work our way toward a lifestyle that makes sense and meets our needs. Our opportunity here is truly incredible.

Everyone shared their agreement and relief at the thought that it did not all have to be done at once.

So, Jard continued, *let's deal with the key ones: shelter is for now taken care of, but we do need to organize food for the winter and think about our health and our safety.*

He looked over the group, and as he scanned the thoughts of the group he realized, not for the first time, they were seriously short on experience in the management of community life. Several members of the group caught the thought and added their agreement.

A couple of nights later, Karina brought up the issue of safety, and Jard realized she had never been part of any of their warlike experiences.

How will we be able to protect ourselves in this valley from marauders, whether Olarian or Cretian?

They looked at Jard who raised his eyebrows, shrugged his shoulders and looked at Leiti. *This involves you and maybe it ought to involve everyone.*

There was no indication from anyone that they agreed or disagreed, so he continued. *Suppose we use the process that enabled us to create this very substantial dwelling of ours to build an energy wall around us? We could make it as much as four people high. It would need only to be thick enough to maintain the power that we want it to have and encircle ourselves about 20 yards out from the building. And, as with our shelter, we can give it permanence and stability by using the solar energy that feeds our structures so long as the sun rises each day. The cloud cover does not inhibit it. So we are, for all practical purposes, secure.*

He listened to the thinking of the group.

There is no reason we could not sink it a foot or so into the ground as we have done with our dwelling.

This simple but seemingly effective solution raised another possibility.

Why might we not fence off a section of the valley to corral a number of the grazers that we use for meat? Pron suggested. *We could then have them within easy reach during the winter months.*

Sounds like an idea, but they would starve to death if we kept them here, said Dornal. *There's just not enough feed through the winter for more than about six or so, but even so, they would likely freeze to death without shelter.*

Shelter is not really a problem, is it? Dornal was on a roll. *Couldn't we just create an energy shelter and give it some color and warmth so that it was clearly visible, like our dwelling?*

Before long, with the exception of plants, most of the immediate problems of the winter were sorted. The idea of a vegetable garden, like the ones in most villages, became a focus. Repin and Daria agreed to build and establish one, but, for this first year, it would not grow enough vegetables to carry them through the winter. So the group divided its time between hunting – gathering meat and protein for the winter – and collecting grains and other starchy foods from the valley and the lands beyond.

They worked together to build the energy walls, and it was clear that they would discourage both animal and plant predators. The group was easily able to open the walls without harming them in any way and they could seal them as easily. As a group they were becoming more than confident of their ability to manage their physical environment.

The winter came and toward the end of it the first babies for the group were conceived. During the early months, Karina decided that Pron would be her mate, a decision that pleased and surprised him. It was almost inevitable then that Enita would attach herself to Dornal, and this turned out to be true in more ways than they had expected. Her early life had been diabolically lonely and painful. Dornal was a gentle, phlegmatic and non-judgmental man, and he had from the start been drawn to her. It took only her first expressions of interest to ensure the relationship would flourish and nourish them both. By late spring, all four women were heavily pregnant.

The winter nights were times when the entire little community could sit warmly together and talk about anything and everything. To make certain the range of topics of significance to their lives was covered, they tended to organize each week to tackle one particular aspect of their lives.

Everyone participated in the cooking and in the essential discussions about themselves, their experiences, and their hopes and fears for the future. They shared some of the ways they wanted to explore their abilities, knowing this was going to necessarily be a significant aspect of the way the community organized itself.

Everything that had been canvassed when Jard had joined the original three was also made a topic of the discussion of the now larger group, and much of what had been shared by the original four was shared again with the new members of their little community.

When the first winter drew to a close, each member of the community had identified the plans they had for the coming spring and summer months. The vegetable garden was designed so they could grow vegetables all year round, and an exciting aspect of this venture was the creation of a system for giving the garden a covering for the winter that they could use to contain heat.

This meant they were able to continue to grow vegetables that were not actually in season. It also involved some creative and unusual watering systems. There was so much to occupy them during their first spring and summer there were almost no times when they were together during the evenings.

However, evenings were the time discussions could take place. Discussions that did not have to do with the multitude of programs they were running to create a stable community. Everything was new, so it often took days or weeks to sort out how to solve a particular problem and how to organize themselves to get things done.

By the next winter there was a daughter to Enita and Dornal, a son to Karina and Pron, a daughter to Daria and Repin, and a son to Leiti and Jard.

However, the autumn months produced a great deal more than this. Jard had decided he wanted to understand the energy they used to do things and Leiti was content to be a part of that enterprise. A part of Jard's curiosity was understanding how the energies they seemed able to trap worked in their bodies.

He particularly wanted to understand where the processes they were using in their lives came from. This energy research was, in Jard's mind, linked to their ability to heal themselves. Only Karina was as curious, but her attention was directed to the medicinal qualities of the plants in the environment around them and she spent many hours studying their energy signals.

It was a few weeks into their second winter. The group had been managing well when Enita posed a question they had been skirting around for some time, but predominantly since the four women in the group had become pregnant.

What if one or several or even all of our children are not telepathic? I mean, to start with, how will we find out? Some of us did not find out until we were as old as 10.

With the children now joined into the community, it was a very real issue. As usual, all eyes turned to Jard and Leiti.

Jard looked at Leiti and then around the group.

I can only speak for myself and I'd like everybody to do the same. Any child Leiti and I have will be given love and caring for all of its life. Our telepathic quality has seen us separated from our families and our villages, mainly through the prejudices and closed-mindedness of the communities in which we were born.

I would hate to think that I had brought that closed-minded world with us to this beautiful place. I would like to think we are together as a result of community values that we each in our separate ways found repressive, inflexible, close-minded.

I genuinely hope we will build a community with values we would like to have experienced ourselves. I don't know what they will be specifically, but now is undoubtedly a good time to think about them. I believe, because of the experiences we have had in using and developing our telepathic abilities, we may well be able to tell very early about our children. If we cannot, we will know that, and I plan to be patient and find out as our children grow up. Regardless, I will love them without reservation.

He paused and Leiti just smiled her beautiful smile and said, *There is no way I could have voiced my feelings better.*

Around the group the thoughts were all of a like mind, except Enita, whose face was streaming with tears and who was clearly distressed. Dornal moved closer to her but she could not be consoled. Everyone was asking her what was wrong. She was wringing her hands and almost whimpering, a sound so distressing that Dornal looked to the group for help, his face pulled in with tension, his brows furrowed, his body held still, even as he held Enita close. She had her head on his chest and was sobbing. The room was still, everyone attempting to locate the source of her distress.

Finally, as she began to slowly relax a little, Dornal said, *In the first few weeks when Enita realized she too was pregnant, she shared with me some of her story. It was a mistake that I was not able to persuade her to share it with you all. However, I am coming to believe that we are genuinely building our lives around open, honest communication, and I am sure you have been aware that she has been unhappy.*

There was complete assent.

So, slowly as her tears were beginning to subside, Enita told her story.

First, she said, *I want you all to be clear, I am not crying because of what Jard has just said, but it was his beautiful words that started me off. I want for our child – children – exactly what he said. But in my family they knew from a young age that I was somehow different and the Elders did not like it. They blamed me for being essentially bad and for about seven years I was punished unmercifully nearly every day. When finally it stopped I was pitied and do not remember a day when I was treated with love or genuine concern. I knew from the first that my ability to know what they were thinking was the problem, even though they were themselves not aware that I could do this. They did know that I seemed able to understand what they were thinking. Too well!*

When I finally got it, at about seven, I ceased to allow them to know anything at all about what I was thinking or what I knew of their horrid thoughts about each other and about me. When I was 16 they decided that one of the Elders could have me to use for sex, to train me to be obedient and perhaps have a late child for him. It was the week before I was due to be presented to him that I ran away and you found me. If Dornal had not been so beautiful a man and treated me with such warmth and caring and respect, I would have taken my life. I know it. So, to hear you, Jard, say how you wanted our life to be here for our children is an unspeakable relief.

By now she was almost calm and the group had relaxed and one by one, first the women, then the men, moved over to her to give her a hug and say something warm and reassuring. After her revelation the group was silent for a long time.

Pron and Dornal were looking at one another with a knowing look but they were sharing a moment the others could not share. They were not needing to consciously think for their mutual affection and realization to be a palpable experience in the group.

We have all shared some of our lives with everyone, Pron said. *We agreed to that when we came together. But there are things which, of course, we did not share. I think it is time* – he looked intently at Dornal – *that we told you a little more about us.*

The two young men were looking at one another with an unreadable intensity, but they were clearly in agreement about the story they now felt the desire to share.

When we were about five or six, I think it was, Dornal and I had our first telepathic experience, at least the first of which we were consciously aware. Our mother was having a sexual relationship, which we did not actually understand, with our uncle, and our father did not know. We knew because we could feel the intensity of desire that flowed between them. We could not believe our father did not know, yet it was clear he did not. One afternoon he came home earlier than expected. There had been some kind of incident on the hunt and one of the men had been injured and brought home. My mother was needed to help the medicine woman.

When my father came home and found our mother with his brother an incredible argument broke out and a violent fight ensued. As a result of his injuries, our uncle died.

My mother went to help the medicine woman, not knowing about the consequences of the fight. When she returned home, it was all over. Our father beat her horribly then demanded to know why we had not told him. We were terrified and did not know what to say. We were spanked almost senseless and sent to bed without dinner. No-one spoke to us for several days, and we were sent to live with our grandmother in the next village.

We never saw our mother or father again. We believe from snippets we gleaned during the occasional visits from relatives, when they were speaking with our grandparents, that our father beat our mother every night for a week after we were sent away, and at the end, she died. We were blamed for not having spoken to him about what he believed, correctly, we knew, and he would have nothing more to do with us.

Although most of the other kids were okay with us, some believed that we were responsible for some of what had happened, and it was only because we were good fighters and looked out for one another that our lives were not horrible. Our grandfather made sure we were taught the hunting skills necessary to survive. And, like Enita, we were unbelievably relieved to hear what you had to say about values, Jard.

He lapsed into silence and the two brothers stood up and came together to hold one another and nod. The messages from every member of the group were warm and supportive and the group decided to break up for the night and get some sleep.

Conversations occurred every evening and went on often late into the night. Jard finally suggested, from the experiences that had been related to the group, some precepts that seemed to best offer a way for the little community to no longer carry on the traditions from which they had all emerged.

It was about the gods that some of the more difficult conversations took place. There were discussions about whether there were any gods. There were discussions about which of the gods were genuine and which were not. There were discussions about how the Olarian species had been created, by whom, and who created energy telepaths to be different. These conversations were carried out under Jard's rules because that seemed the only way for them to not become hopelessly acrimonious, and he had stated these rules pretty persuasively.

He had said, *If we are to have discussions about things of great importance to us, and I believe we must do that, we have to be able to do that without causing harm to ourselves. Besides, we are actually unable to have disagreements that we can keep to ourselves, unlike the people in the places from which we came. For the most part it is true that we actually can't really keep secrets.*

So, if we don't wish to allow our different ideas to become leverage for the destruction of our little community, we must allow just about any differences to be acceptable. I don't know how people can possibly get along if their ideas are different and they are inflexible. It must be okay for us to believe different things without those differences coming between us.

We have all seen how destructive inflexibility is. I, myself, cannot conceive of any god who would presumably be a lot wiser – a gigantic amount wiser – than us, some entity who could build societies in which the horrible things we have all seen and experienced would be okay. That would have to be some sort of unpalatable god.

So, for me, I figure I am just here, and I have to learn whatever I can learn about and need to understand. Then I will die, and if my time here is to have any meaning at all, I will be responsible for creating that meaning for myself. If others believe different, then we just need to talk about it and see that the consequence of our differences does not lead to anyone being harmed.

Daria agreed and put in the next piece.

I don't know if there are gods or not. I think I can live with Jard's notion, at least until something more convincing comes along. For me, I want someone to love and someone to love me and Repin fulfils that role for me well. I hope I do that for him and we continue like that, wanting to take care of each other, no matter what, until we die, as we most certainly will.

Karina spoke quietly into their minds. She was the group's medicine flower girl, a name the group had given her. What she said resonated with the group.

I want to feel useful. For me, what matters is that I have something to do that fills in my time and which results in me feeling glad to be alive, useful to those with whom I live.

There were nods around the group and they could hear and feel each other thinking about how these guides applied to themselves.

It was Enita who added the next piece of wisdom that captured their collective struggle with life.

What I need is simple. I need to feel 'hope', to have something to look forward to, whether it is dinner tonight or something that will take me a long time, but which I really want. I have to have something to look forward to, because for so long I had nothing.

The conversations went on, more and more topics were discussed, a multitude of ideas were floated and explored, and this desire to keep themselves talking and thinking became, of itself, a piece of the life of the community.

Not all the group shared the interests, but everyone got heard. And what came through was again summarized by Leiti one night as the winter was drawing to a close, and they all knew that the next babies were begun.

If we agree to stay open to opinions that do not trap us in certainty, I will feel a bit happier, and also if we always continue to put out our concerns and hard thoughts so that we can all share in them. I think if we can keep our minds open and not feel the need to shut other people and their ideas out we have a chance here to take care of ourselves and our future in ways that will be more nourishing than most of us experienced in our families as children. I for one want to be sure there will always be room here in our new community for voices of dissent. I know that almost everything we know about ourselves has come from qualities with which we were born.

Every time we think – unless the others are asleep – our minds are open to all of us. But we also know and are learning fast how to hear one another's quiet thoughts. Our mutual respect will be our last resort in the times when we are angry or upset or unhappy, and our willingness to be caring, no matter what, will be our strength. This will prevent us becoming like them.

It was on this note, with so many exciting and life-affirming ideas afloat, that winter drew to a close, the first buds of spring could be seen and the sun came back. Everyone was enjoying the cries of babies and the hollering of parents as the group discussed the plans for hunting and farming. They knew that before the next winter, caring for the children would take over more of the life of the group. But what seemed idyllic, and wonderful now, would turn out to have a darker underside.

CHAPTER 46

New Lives & New Explorations

The next year passed quickly in Tall Trees Valley. The population rose to 21. Jard and Leiti were able to test the telepathic potential of all the children more simply than anyone had imagined. Not surprisingly, all the children were telepaths. In the process of seeking ways to confirm this, Jard and Leiti had begun a new project. Its purpose was to help them understand how they were able to manage energies, both within themselves and from sources outside themselves. Jard reasoned that it had to be important because it was one of the group's distinctive qualities.

They were identifying energies in the land itself – in the vegetation, the sun, the clouds – and some sources that left them puzzled. Slowly they began to explore and understand a little more about the nature of what they were calling 'energy'. Inside their bodies every function was both drawing energy and emitting it. There were incalculable numbers of sources from which energy was drawn and to which energy was being sent.

Karina was collecting medicinal plants. Jard and Leiti sometimes took a break and worked with her, identifying the kinds of energies plants produced and some of the ways that energy became available when the plant was eaten or applied to the skin. While in their original villages the women looked after the babies, in this foundling community the task was being shared in some new ways.

All eight adults were engaged in caring for the children. No-one was entirely clear why, but that was the choice they were making. Tasks like growing vegetables, cooking and maintaining a continuous watch for strangers, especially potentially hostile strangers, were undertaken by them all, but hunting still fell to the men. Gender seemed to be playing only a minor role in the division of labor. Jard sometimes wondered if this might be to do with their being no positions of power or hierarchy in the group.

When they were all in residence, they engaged in catch-up, but rarely during the warmer months did they become involved in deeper discussions. Everyone had jobs that focused their attention. But when winter came, and in the evenings, and sometimes through the days, they discussed the big issues of their lives.

It had been a cold day, the children were asleep and the group was sitting in their comfortable sitting room. Enita began the conversation. She was the pixie of the group. She stood only 5'3" tall, had brownish hair she kept short, always fuzzy and a wee bit disheveled. After being with the group for only a short time she had become deeply connected to Dornal and now smiled a lot, an action that totally changed her otherwise stern appearance. Her eyes were a strange but entrancing deeper shade of green with soft lilac flecks. What she said quickly captured everyone's attention.

I have noticed that when we sat here last year we were very dependent on our telepathy and I hardly ever listened to people speak out loud, mainly because I could not understand anyone. I communicated by thought, but I too spoke out loud, though I knew no-one could understand my words. By the end of the winter I found I could listen to the sounds of everyone and understand, and I can now speak out loud each language. Am I doing it right?

The group burst into laughter, because she had been speaking in first one language, then another, and although there were some odd phrases, she was right. Everyone looked at one another, smiling, and then everyone spoke a sentence in every language. The group were delighted with themselves. The game went on for an hour or more with people correcting one another, adjusting colloquial speech, laughing and enjoying the game. In the end, Repin, tears of laughter rolling down his cheeks at a quirky phrase from Pron, took the conversation in a new direction.

We are doing well here with language, Repin said. *But I am having a problem I would like to raise. I am having some trouble with long distances. I was hunting two valleys away when Daria was having difficulty with the children, but I could only catch pieces of her thoughts. I could sort of push my mind to see her but not well enough, and I couldn't make her understand what I was thinking. I never have the same difficulty with you, Jard. Am I the only one, and does anyone have any suggestions about how to improve my ability to speak or see over greater distances?*

Everyone looked at one another and finally then at Jard.

Well, he said. *We use different energies for speaking and seeing and when we move objects. Leiti and Karina and I have been exploring some of these. I am sorry that I am not good at sharing what I am doing, but Leiti seems able to do that.*

I focus on the energy to picture what is happening in a particular direction and I can slowly bring everything in that direction into focus. It takes me a few moments, but so long as I stay focused there seems to be no restrictions as to how far I can travel. But if you asked me to speak when I was first stretching my vision I wouldn't have been able to do that as well.

However, that first time, I stayed focused, and it was only moments before I began to hear the sounds from wherever I looked. After that first time, whenever I stretched my vision I was immediately able to hear the sounds. If it was one of you, I was able to hear what you were thinking and the sounds if you were speaking out loud.

Leiti had a suggestion that would change the group and the energy telepaths for their entire future.

I have found that when I want to see further than I can see myself, like three or four valleys away, I begin to lose focus. But Jard has let me show him where I want to observe and he will focus and let me travel with him. After I have done that a couple of times, I can do it by myself. So I guess my question is whether Jard is willing for us to travel with him and have him take us to different distant places until we develop the capability ourselves.

Everyone looked at Jard, who appeared embarrassed.

If you think I can help and you would like to try it, I am certainly willing.

So began a journey that excited everyone. Jard took them to distant places, each day a little further until all the others in the group could travel those distances alone. Then he would take them further until one night Karina shouted with joy and the group looked at her askance.

I have just got back to the village where I was born! she cried. The expression on her face went through a panoply of shifts – first astonishment then delight and finally a mixture of anger and fear intermingled.

I'm with you, Karina. It was Jard's quiet confidence that calmed her; she was able to see her family, then realized that she wanted to hear them but couldn't.

For the entire winter this new development took precedence over everything else. They traveled over distances that were greater than any of them, including Jard, had ever gone. Then one day Leiti and Jard took them back to Leiti's village, and she watched her mother and father engaged in some kind of dispute. They suddenly heard the speech. Later, Jard said it must have been the intensity of her desire to know what they were saying or her urgent need to hear their voices. Whatever the reason, it changed everything, and within a week they were all able to do it.

The excitement was so great their dwelling seemed to vibrate with their energy. Then one morning Jard made a suggestion.

If we could pick up the energy threads we use to move things, not just the creative threads but the actual power threads that seem to be all around us, and more strongly from the sun, weak as it is this time of year, we might be able to move objects that are at a distance from us. We would then be able to protect ourselves better should the need arise, as I feel certain it will.

Everyone was focused on his thoughts. Breakfast was over and they were sitting playing with the children. Jard had just picked up a toy with his mind and was twirling it around the children's grabbing hands when the thought had struck him. Together the eight adults joined Jard's adventure with the toy, sweeping it around the children's heads but just out of reach.

They were all looking at him when he spoke, the toy dropped to the floor and the children began to squeal with delight and demand more. The eight of them picked up the toy and made it dance, then do gymnastics, all the while laughing and feeling a growing excitement. When the children went down for their nap that morning, the sun was shining, there was abundant energy around, and they decided to try.

At first Jard picked up a small rock a few yards from their dwelling and carried it up to hover over the energy fence. The others joined him, following his process until they were all connected to the rock. Then together they collected more and more small rocks until there were dozens of rocks suspended above the energy wall. Jard focused their attention on a very large boulder a hundred yards away and together they sent the storm of small rocks straight at it. The stones struck it and bounced and jumbled themselves all over the nearby landscape, but the point had been made. They could do it.

By the end of the winter they could fell small trees one or two valleys away. The problem was, after they had performed each of these feats, the entire group was exhausted. The group, in consequence of their new learning process and their increasing capabilities, spent a taxing but rewarding year.

When they first learned some new telekinetic action, the learning drained them, but subsequently the action itself proved not to be tiring. Very quickly the tiredness disappeared, then each was able to do more and more without it. They talked a lot about this experience and quickly came to realize that the energy they used was in the learning. The actual energy management was, of itself, not tiring at all. It was as if they were simply the managers of it.

None of them could have lifted a rock or a tree if they had needed to be physically strong enough; the tasks would simply have been beyond them. However, using their ability to manipulate energy, they could lift astronomically huge loads. The energy came from elsewhere, frequently the sun, but when it was night, there were energies from many other sources on which they could draw.

At the beginning of the next winter a new concern became the focus of attention. Each couple now had two or three children. The issue concerning the group was ensuring some diversity in their community and a very difficult discussion took place over two entire weeks about how to resolve this issue. It was Karina with her studies of plants and Pron with his interest in the animals who were the instigators of the discussion. However, neither was keen on the seemingly obvious solution. Karina named the issue late in the first week of winter.

Most of us have been thinking about increasing our family by having another child or children. I know, as do all of you, we have been deliberately putting off our third pregnancy to give ourselves a break from pregnancy and babies. But we know that we need to build the diversity of our community. There will only be four pregnancies at any time for the next 15 or so years. I think, she said, speaking to the other three women, *I think we need to have at least one or two babies with each of the men.*

There was a breath-holding silence. The tension and disturbance in the group could be felt like an invisible dark wraith.

It was Daria who broke the disturbed silence.

Since Karina started to discuss this with Pron we have all been following them, and I have been intrigued that none of us has taken this up with our own partners. But now it has been said, perhaps we should.

We know there have been no infidelities in our group, but we have avoided openly considering the issue. Does anyone seriously think we should not have a clear, open, if a somewhat embarrassing exploration of this? I mean, it's not as though we don't know everyone's sexual preferences, likes and dislikes, fantasies. Most of us have had fantasies about sex with other partners, have we not?

Everyone was nodding.

I have no idea what will happen to our relationships if we do this, but I think the prudish and punitive experiences from our villages have surely given us some important lessons.

No-one was interested in interrupting Daria's brave exploration. Everyone was waiting, almost trying not to think about the other men or women in the group, but of course it was a process certain to fail when everyone's lives were more or less an open book.

I propose that we put out in the open, together, our feelings toward each other and each other's partners. Say out loud and for all of us to hear exactly how we feel, how sexually interesting each other's partners are to us. See, the thing is, we all know but have been – are being – reluctant to be open and honest about it. And we do, I believe, need to be.

A whisper of wind through the room would have created a deafening roar at that moment. Everyone was searching for a way forward, a way that would not result in horrible revelations, embarrassment and perhaps permanently damaged relationships, which they could ill afford.

However, Daria's courage and determination that so much that would previously have been unthinkable or at least undiscussable could and should be discussed drove them on.

What once might have been irretrievably damaging was now a necessary option. Every couple had in a quiet and private way been observed having sex, trying new things, new feelings. All the men had learned from the women and vice versa, things their village relatives had never had the will to explore and understand. Daria was just making it explicit in the interests of the entire community.

We know from our experiences, all of us, that the infidelities and sexual adventures of our communities were primarily because no-one ever learned anything about sex from anyone else. I could not even list all the things I have learned from you all as well as all the things I have learned about what was not good from my village.

Except when they were young and inexperienced and over-anxious, Epinarian men never seem to have been even interested in what their women wanted, needed, liked. Similarly, the women never thought to ask, they just assumed what the men wanted was just the sex!

I think there would have been much less hanky-panky if there had been more genuine curiosity and sharing of real information. But here we have been teaching each other about how to be together with mutual concerns and satisfactions about which they never had a clue.

I know, as do all of you, that Pron and Dornal find me sexually interesting, and that I am fascinated with them! That takes nothing from my intense and deep feelings for Repin who has been my love and I believe will be until I die.

We have to have this discussion out in the open and put to rest the bad attitudes and emotions, and particularly the fears that make sex and intimacy feelings taboo or almost undiscussable. And we have to allow ourselves to have lusts and desires and intimate thoughts about each other and our partners without them being destructive or in any way bad.

She stopped, almost not daring to allow herself to slip into their minds. But, slowly, almost painfully, each spoke openly to everyone about the silent thoughts and feelings they harbored about each other. Instead of the cataclysm they feared, there emerged a deeper and more honest understanding of what it really meant to be open and honest about their usually most secret thoughts.

But, of course, that was not enough! They would have to make a decision and live with all the consequences.

Daria was not finished.

While I still have the courage, I want to make a suggestion. Each of us should speak directly to every member of our little community about their feelings for and about that person, he or she respond, and we should do this until everything we can put into the open has been put there. We should finish off this process by an intimate discussion with our partner for everyone to hear.

It was Enita in her quiet but clear and determined way who put the group's feelings into words.

Daria, you've got guts! Everyone knows I have had feelings toward Repin and Jard but I would never have had the courage to put those thoughts openly to everyone. And I know you are right about this, even though it makes my skin come up in goose bumps.

So it was that the community began a process of open declarations and intimate disclosures that contributed yet another strong bond to what it meant for them to be fully functioning telepaths. It wasn't that very much got said that was not already at least partly known, but in the process of explicitly putting it out into the community, it acquired a new dimension, more depth and substantive reality. It also took away the hidden fear and shame or anxiety about having the feeling, and that in itself improved the person's emotional harmony.

This cleansing process led Daria to make one further point.

The thing that became clearer to me as we talked was about feelings I think some of you have felt me having. They are not good, but then they are not real in a way. I don't know how this is going to come out, but again I feel confident at some level that putting it out will help me find some more meaning in it, and it would be lovely if I wasn't the only one who felt this way.

She looked around and saw and felt nothing but support and curiosity.

Okay, here goes. I am aware that sometimes out of what seems to be my unconscious thoughts, a feeling or an idea comes up about which I feel ashamed or guilty or sometimes even sort of disgusted, yet that doesn't stop them coming!

She paused, feeling around the minds in the group. *Can anyone resonate with this or am I really alone?*

A murmur through her mind told her that at least a few of the group were quite clear about what she was saying and understood through their own experience.

Whew, thank goodness, she said.

There was laughter around the group, so she continued.

I am curious about my unconscious. Sometimes it seems as though it is really either not a part of me or a part of me with which I am somehow not properly acquainted! I know this sounds ridiculous, but recently, because I have become a bit obsessed with it, I notice it seems to be the part of me that actually does the work of my thinking. My mind, that is, the part of my mind that I think of myself as being me, seems to be getting its conclusions from somewhere else!

Things said by my parents or other adults that I was supposed to believe and follow seem to have become stuck to ideas I am thinking today, and feelings from those people seem to get attached to the thought. All hardly conscious. But as soon as I realize and can make my own adult decision about what I think or feel, it becomes a lot clearer, then I feel cleaner.

There is all this stuff stuck just outside the reach of my consciousness, but sometimes I can get to some of it, and when I do, if I can think and feel it through, I feel more myself, if that makes any sense.

She looked around again, confirming that the group were still connecting. There was no doubt; everyone was concentrating on her thoughts, and several were deciding they too could make use of these insights.

I know this sounds weird, but I have come to think that a part of my mind, which I don't seem able to control, does its work quickly, and I really don't know what it is doing. It seems to take all the bits of the problem, then dredge up whatever else it needs to make decisions and stuff. I only know the conclusion, not the how of my getting there.

She paused again, the thoughts so many-sided that she needed to be certain she was not just talking to herself. She need not have been concerned; most were confirming their familiarity with the experience she was describing.

Now I am sharing this because we all know what each other thinks about just about everything. But I want to know if anybody ever knows how the not-conscious part of their own or someone else's mind is working?

What I am asking may be absurd, because perhaps you would not know that I was unaware of my unconscious, say, sorting out a problem. I have tried to watch some of you think about a situation, but I only am aware of what you tell me, not how you made the decision. Am I still making sense?

There was cautious affirmation. Jard and Karina seemed about to share something and Karina asked Jard to go ahead while she sorted some thought.

As you know, Leiti and I have been sorting energy strands from obvious ones to ones so subtle that without help a person would hardly notice they existed. When we were working with Karina the other day I was watching Leiti follow a single strand of energy between two organs when she suddenly told us how it worked.

Karina and I were puzzled. We had been following her but had seen no evidence that she had figured out what was going on. When we asked her she said, much like Daria has said, she had no idea where the connection she had just made had come from. I think that is exactly what you are saying, but this time about emotional stuff instead of logical stuff.

Karina said, *That is a much clearer way of saying what I was just thinking.*

There was a deep quiet among the group. The implications of the idea were beginning to sink in. The group knew only the conscious thoughts that each was having but not the process by which these thoughts arrived. There was more here to be explored, but for the moment the group was content to chew over this sufficiently complex piece.

The next year, Leiti had had a son with Repin and Jard's new daughter to Enita had been born. Everyone was aware of the unfinished business of the partner swapping. A small swirling of incompletely explored emotions was present in everyone's mind.

Then Leiti started the ball rolling one evening after they had all gone to bed.

You are asking me to tell you what it was like when I slept with Enita? Jard's tone was a bit puzzled. *You want to know how it was for me, exactly, but Leiti, you know, you were there with us for some of the journey. I could feel you sometimes, even though I knew you were doing your best to be unobtrusive.*

Leiti looked a bit uncomfortable, but persisted.

I... I want to hear you tell me about it. I know we agreed not to do this, but I can't let go of it, Jard. And after Daria started that discussion about unconscious processes, I knew, to be honest with you, I had to bring it up and deal with it.

Jard was paying close attention to her and realized that she was not in any way being critical or punitive, but felt in some way disturbed by sharing him with another woman, and wanted – needed – to talk about it. He realized in a flash of insight that he needed this as well, and he needed to hear about her and Repin in spite of the fact that he had watched them too with some strong feelings of unacknowledged distress. Was it jealousy?

You know that I think Enita is beautiful and loving and wonderfully attentive. She let me look after her and she looked after me wonderfully. I would be being dishonest if I did not acknowledge that. But you know the difference between any woman and you, for me, Jard said.

She knew what I liked and I knew what she liked. We both enjoyed the physicality and the raw sexual loving, the passionate emotional desire for one another, the excitement of someone new and different, the use of all the sensuous playful things that you and I have taught each other. You know I used those with her and she loved them.

The oral sex she enjoyed giving me and receiving, the way she has seen you giving to me and me giving you, so often... it was a bit shallow for me, because it was not you, but it was delicious and pleasant and nourishing.

But what you want me to say is that it wasn't you, and that is absolutely true, and you know that, and this will probably always be so. So it was better than all right, but we do not belong together and I know you have checked that out, but now I am saying it to you because you ask. Does that put this episode to rest?

She looked at him with love and that deep internal warm, almost smug, feeling she always felt when she snuggled up with him and they held one another, full of the delight of their intimacy.

Okay, now I need to hear you tell me about Repin.

For a second Leiti looked alarmed, then looking deeply into his warm dark eyes, knew that he too had his doubts and uncertainties and that she must give him what she had asked from him.

Of course, she said. *Repin was beautiful. We have been friends for so long that at first I was not sure I could do it. But he has watched you handle me so much, and I have seen him with Daria from the day of their first lovemaking, that I quickly slid into a loving state with him. The sex was beautiful. He has seen you please me so often he knew exactly how to seduce me, and I was fully willing for him to do that. And I knew, quite certainly, everything that he needed to feel at his loving and sexually energetic best.*

He loved me giving him the sort of oral sex Daria has been giving him, and he willingly followed my pattern of desire. The sex was wonderful, the caring and affection were a delight, and the evening one of positive pleasure.

However, and you know this, but I am going to tell you so you hear it from my mind and know it to be so, I do not love him as I love you. We two do not belong together. And even though it was a truly exciting and wonderful sexual and emotional experience, it was not you. As I was back with you and you pulled me into your arms, we both knew that this is where I belong. I am absolutely your creature.

She smiled fully into his mind,

You can have me anytime, anywhere, anyhow, whatever you wish, you know that. I am totally your woman, Jard, no matter with whom I have sex and babies. You are aware, aren't you, that we have had a quite large audience?

Jard nodded and, slipping into a slightly different mode, said, *To the rest of you, I think what we just did was the best thing I have ever done to tidy up a loose end, and to you children, it is all right that you don't really understand what you have heard. The time will come when you will get it. Go back to sleep. As a kind of addition to all that, I am becoming clearer about what kind of stuff seems to be going on in my unconscious that I don't actually think about, and I am beginning to see that many of my confused emotions arise from thoughts that are not generated consciously and which I therefore cannot fully manage.*

Jard and Leiti continued thinking about this and they smiled as there were some murmurs from the others and the children mumbled and went back to sleep. Jard and Leiti did not immediately drift off to sleep. They needed to make love, long, gently and passionately. It was a night they would remember. It somehow gave the affirmation that the words and the assurances could never quite achieve.

However, that too was not all. Jard needed to understand how he and Leiti felt bound together. How they could be deeply loving and emotional with others yet feel absolutely clear about each other. They had seen the cheating and the sexual duplicity of their families and the dreadful harm it had done. It was of significance that they understood that they were not traveling in that direction.

Leiti looked at Jard. Her eyes filled with satisfaction, pleasure and love.

My feelings for you, she said, *are not only about sensual and sexual pleasure, but in ways I cannot yet speak clearly about. You are known to me, I can anticipate your moods and the direction of your thoughts though you have not shared them explicitly with me. I know you from inside. Experiences that you have shared have under them feelings and meanings that are, I believe, known to me alone. Our intimacy seems to be created from unspoken and perhaps unknown things about ourselves. I know these things of you and when we make love they flow out through our actions. Is it not so for you?*

Jard lay still, feeling his way through Leiti's thoughts and ideas, finally finding his way into the subtle nuance she was describing.

Yes, he said, *it is the things I know about you, things that are actually not known by others, perhaps unable to be known by others with whom you do not share things, of which we cannot actually speak. Yet they are there to know but outside the conscious explicit things we say to one another. I think, because our parents did not share deeply enough or explore their needs deeply enough, that they were somehow afraid to permit themselves to be so fully known to one another, so the misunderstandings and the destructive silences of which we saw so much ate away at their connection.*

Leiti lay quietly, feeling simple delight. Yet her mind was seeking the threads of this mélange.

What we do, Jard, is seek out with each other each occasion when a feeling is subtly wrong or off and demand of one another that we explore honestly what that is about. Sometimes we have found that hard, but I think, because we have been willing to do that, to really explore every seeming discord, we have wound together bonds that are so very strong.

They lay together, thinking through each of the other couples, knowing that none of the others had fallen asleep, that the whole dwelling was listening in to them sensitively and very carefully and were even now beginning to seek those connections in their own togetherness. It was another night none of them would ever forget. It seemed as though things that had been passed over were being drawn up and gently and sensitively understood by each of them.

In the end the consequence of the breeding program deepened both the bonds of each of the couples and their understanding of the complexities and nuances of their intimacy in ways their families would never be able to do. There was some sadness about that. However, it opened a door to feelings that seemed to have no known roots, to issues and discomforts that did not lie in anything known. It meant there were truths and realities that could not be reached by simple enquiry, not even by honest exploration. This truth had implications for their lives that were, as yet, merely vaguely troubling feelings.

CHAPTER 47

The Cretians

New babies were born to the community each year. For the next five years partners were swapped every second year, though never for more than the actual night necessary to ensure that a pregnancy had begun. The pattern had become part of the culture of the community and would stand it in good stead in the future.

The winter discussions were a very significant element in the development of the culture and there was never a winter when some significant issues were not canvassed. On the seventh year in the Valley, Jard began the discussions on a subject of serious collective concern.

The Cretians have come within 50 miles of our valley in their last incursion into Olaria. Probably because of the unpleasant stories we have heard of their aggression against Olarian villages, and because we have been busy getting ourselves established here, we have chosen not to visit the Cretian lands.

As you know I was able to discourage their last war party by instilling a sense of fear about traveling further toward us. But I'm not sure how well that will work again. We need to understand them better. Do you agree or do you think this is merely an irrational anxiety of mine?

There was full agreement about Jard's concern.

I propose that two of us visit Cretia this winter, that the rest stay connected and we will then have some specific information on which to base our plans for managing them. We can use the same energies we use for surveying the Olarian villages, but it may be a little more difficult knowing what is being said.

When we explored the last party to arrive here, we found they use some concepts we could only partly understand. While we will probably be able to listen in to no more than three or four groups before we will need to return, that may be sufficient to give us some understandings, otherwise we will have to make several trips.

Daria voiced a concern.

We have traveled long distances this way only a few times. We have never gone this far or into such a hostile place. I am unsure what might happen if whoever goes becomes exhausted or very stressed or distressed while they are away.

I would be happier if we did our first exploration without traveling over water, although I don't know why that seems so big a thing. Suppose they went, say, to the extreme edge of Olaria, stayed for an hour and then returned. If anything happened we might be able to solve the problem in friendly territory. This may not even be rational; it may just be my apprehension speaking.

They all knew this was an irrational anxiety but an understandable one. The group already knew they could generally understand the Cretians although they could not speak their language; this had been tested with some of their war parties. The threat posed by the Cretians was an unpleasant one. They were uninterested in trade and came to fight, rape, damage and destroy.

They were not a society with whom the telepaths had any inclination to engage. Nevertheless, they did pose a threat to the safety and security of the little community and understanding them better might prove sound security behavior. So it was decided that after this winter Jard and perhaps Daria would physically travel to the closest point on Olarian soil before making a mind trip to Cretia to attempt to gain some better understanding of the Cretians.

In the meantime there was an increasing interest in the community about the work that Jard, Leiti and Karina were doing in trying to understand more about the energy that formed so crucial a part of their lives. It was their telepathy and their ability to experience and consciously use the energy they were able to perceive around them that had separated them from their original families and communities.

Jard was by far the most obsessed. He seemed driven to understand, explore and push the boundaries of their understanding. He needed the input and often extensive support of the others, not only because he could not bring off what he was imagining without their help, but because he wanted their involvement. They all constantly used his help in projects they were pursuing to improve the quality of their lives, and he always gave whatever was asked for, but he felt uncomfortable being in the spotlight.

When Leiti looked at his untidy sandy hair and his large, deep, warm, soft brown eyes, she felt the strength of him still growing steadily every year. One day she asked him, *If you feel so uncomfortable when the others ask you for help, why do you always give it so willingly?*

Jard knew they had a genuinely interested and concerned audience at that moment, and, as always, he answered with honesty and clarity.

I don't feel there is a choice for me, Leiti. When I had no-one to speak with I knew what loneliness meant. When I met you that changed completely. I can never refuse someone who wants or needs my help. Especially because, until I met all of you, I never thought anyone would ever really find me useful or want to share their world with me.

She just loved his open generous nature; she hugged him, knowing he would always delight her. Whatever came next would be yet another adventure.

The energy studies that Jard had instigated covered nearly every part of their lives. The flows in and around the women when they were pregnant and when they were feeding their babies were amazing; the patterns inside the body every day showed many thousands of flows, from and to every organ and piece of tissue in the body. There were different energies everywhere.

Meanwhile, Pron and Dornal had been playing with extending the speed and range of their weapons. They could now collect energy similar to that used for building their dwellings, roll it into balls, and propel these energy balls at amazing speeds and over considerable distances with sufficient force to flatten trees and logs and almost anything in their path.

Jard and Daria had explored energy lines around the entire planet, identified the energies from the sun, the moon and undefined areas of space as well as from the planet itself running into and out of every living thing. It was a time of extraordinary learning and experimenting. When they talked of this during the winter, they realized they would die long before they had learned all there was to learn.

One morning Daria and Jard were following energy lines flowing around the planet that originated from different sources. They found they could see for miles if they allowed their energy to stay connected to the flows. It was these flows that allowed them to visit places around the planet while their bodies remained in Tall Trees Valley.

At first they traveled only a few miles, but the distances grew. Each time, the trick had been to stay with a flow line that brought them back close to where they began. Days had gone by with them traveling small distances, then down vertical flows to the ground again and back to their bodies.

The sun had been a help with the vertical flows. There was excitement and anxiety attached to some of these journeys. But as energy travelers they had no power; they could see and hear, but that was it. Energy travel seemed to be about information; it seemed incapable of being connected to substantial action.

They knew, as each month went by, their ability to use energy and understand how to harness and utilize what they needed was increasing almost exponentially. It was as if the action of using a particular energy somehow fueled their ability to extend that ability, opened a door to a new element previously unknown to them. Do something, get a new insight or ability; it was as if intent and action were what fed learning and new options. Sometimes it felt a little unnerving, but it was also exciting and enormously satisfying.

Everything one of them learned was immediately available to anyone else, but although the eight had come to manage their information sharing with relative ease, the inclusion of curious children was requiring some adjustments, and not all of the eight shared identical abilities. After several days of sharing energy understandings, Jard again raised the issue of the Cretians.

I know we have talked about doing this after the winter, but we all continue to feel anxious about the Cretians. I have an uneasy sense of urgency. I really want to know more about them. I think if we are caught unawares, we risk being harmed or killed, or we will have to seriously injure or kill them. I'm not sure everyone is going to feel okay about this or even necessarily be willing and able to do it.

The four women were a little uncertain what their reaction might be if they were threatened. Unlike the men, they had not been trained as hunters even though in this new community almost all the tasks were shared.

Enita spoke up. *If anyone, especially any unknown male, tries to use me or harm my children, any child, I will, without hesitation, kill them. I know I will be able to do that!*

Within seconds the four senior women were able to understand her intensity and acknowledge they felt certain they would be willing to respond in a similar way. They were, however, not certain as to whether they could take another life.

Otherwise, Leiti said, thinking out loud, *I know I can immobilize them, just as we do with game when we want to kill without pain or suffering.*

In the end the group decided to take a risk and have Jard and Daria use the atmospheric energy flows to visit Cretia before the winter ended. The group would stay telepathically connected with them and be available to help if needed. It was an uncertain venture, but the consequences for their tiny community of being caught unawares was also pretty frightening.

The day of the first journey arrived. It was decided that the pair should attempt to locate one or more sites in Cretia. This would enable them to get within connection distance of a group of Cretians and then return to make a listening journey the following day.

The first journey was nearly a disaster. The couple returned barely able to communicate. The amount of energy they had needed to hold themselves in energy flows that would take them to their targets and then allow them to return after engaging with their task was far greater than either had imagined. It was the manipulating to control their movements that provided the greatest energy drain, and they knew intuitively they were doing something unnecessary but not what.

It was two days before they were able to fully discuss their experience. No-one knew what the consequence would be of exhausting themselves while traveling, and no-one was keen to find out. There was a feeling, expressed by Dornal, that if they exhausted themselves while traveling, they might die. Daria was breast feeding at this time and she realized that she needed not to take another journey in this condition. Pron agreed to take her place.

For the second journey they targeted a village of about 20 huts and managed to listen in to about 15 minutes of conversation that was totally uninformative and of no strategic value whatsoever. They needed more power and more development if they were to take this further. These experiences persuaded them of the need for more practice and more development of their traveling skills.

CHAPTER 48

Increasing Cretian Hostilities

The next 10 years passed with relative ease. The power and learning of the original eight, now referred to by the whole community as the Council of Eight, had increased way beyond their early expectations. The little community had grown to 60. The Big House had been extended and extended and finally an entirely new one had been constructed. Then a third, so the three formed an interlinked circle surrounded by an energy wall. In the center there were vegetable gardens and flower beds and beyond the wall were two very large and protected vegetable and fruit gardens and a protected area for their wintering animals.

When they had begun their little community, none of the Eight had really thought much about the future. Now the future was always a substantive element of the conversations each winter.

In spite of their earlier concerns and their decision to put their concern with the Cretians on hold, it had been years since anyone had seen Cretians, and no Olarians from the old villages ever traveled as far as Tall Trees Valley. However, that changed quite suddenly. Year 17 turned out to be a dark year for the little community, one that would shake its foundations and create some irreversible changes in their lives.

Enita and Daria were about 10 miles beyond the extreme end of their valley with a group of children – once a child passed their twelfth birthday, they were expected to take their share of responsibility for the survival of the community – when they became aware of a war party of Cretians a few miles away. They contacted the men who were working on a project to increase the water storage in the high valley. There was no way for the men to reach the party quickly, and although Enita and Daria thought they could easily manage the war party, there was a small sense of doubt. No-one wanted to take any risks, so two of the men agreed to take responsibility for dealing with the intruders.

Working with the two women, they managed to spread undifferentiated fear into the Cretians. Then, while they were in this emotionally vulnerable state, the four of them brought down two large trees in front of the war party. The effect on the Cretians, who they knew from earlier experiences to be superstitious, was to scare them away. The two women and the children rapidly made their way home.

The event caused a serious discussion among the group that evening.

Enita opened the discussion.

Today was very scary. At first I was afraid for the children, then I realized I was also afraid for Daria and I. I have been thinking about why. Although I believe Daria and I could fairly easily have killed or discouraged the Cretian war party – there were only about 12 of them – I found myself feeling that I needed one or more of our men to aid us. Since we have been together I have hunted and killed wild animals, but always with one of the men, and I have never fought other people. I felt ill-prepared. It seems absurd but that's how I felt.

I felt the same way. Daria added, *even though it seems absurd and somehow inappropriate.*

The feeling was shared by the four women. Everyone was concerned that they had been in so unpleasant and potentially hazardous a situation. Repin and Dornal were sitting with their arms around their partners. The mood of the group was disturbed and uncertain. None of the older teenagers had been with the party, however, several of them joined the conversation. Garten and Denne spoke of their growing ability to use force to build objects; they felt confident that their hunting skills were now such that they could manage a group of Cretians if the need arose. They were aware of the extra issue of fighting with genuinely nasty opposition – people were clearly very different propositions to creatures – however both believed they could have protected the group and dealt with the Cretians. Jard and Pron agreed that was probably true. However, combat with armed and experienced hostiles was not a recommended way for a young man to engage in his first real battle.

Unless they were surprised, any of the eight adults had the power to easily deal with a group of armed hostiles, probably of even several times the size of this party, but that was not the issue. Long-established habits had emerged, and the woman had been frightened as much for the children as for themselves. They had not been mentally ready for such an event. The children without the two adults would have been utterly defenseless.

The Cretians had been armed with spears, clubs, some kind of throwing sticks and slingshots. At best the two oldest boys in the group, aged twelve, might have been able to propel fist-sized rocks at reasonably high speed at the Cretians. However, they did not yet have the presence of mind to be able to manage their emotions and control their interactions, nor could they understand what the Cretians were saying or recognize their intentions. Everyone was certain this was not the last war party the little community would encounter. For some reason the Cretians were again finding their way a long distance from the coast toward Tall Trees Valley.

The group were also aware that over the past two years some of the Olarian villages had apparently become curious about them. The story of their disappearance from several villages had somehow found its way to nearly every part of Olaria. So far there had been no overt signs of hostility from the Olarians. However, the small community was feeling vulnerable. Jard had listened without comment to recent events and he was far from calm. His special concern was for the children who, had they been alone, might easily have been in very grave danger.

It seems to me we need to take precautions not to be caught unawares again.

No-one disagreed. The group had learned they could create energy lines that, when breached, gave them an auditory warning, however, it was not known which part of the line had been tripped. With a little work they figured out how to build their warning system in sections and receive a different auditory warning signal from each section.

I suggest, Jard went on, *we build a warning line about 15 miles out from our valley in five segments. Under most circumstances I can envisage, this would give us adequate warning of any approaching groups of people. There really are only five approaches anyone on foot can take.*

The energy from the sun boosted the system by day and enabled it to stay live during the night.

Tall Trees Valley was in a very remote section of the central mountainous core of Olaria, in an area that saw them remaining free from further incidents for some time. The first children were pairing up and planning to start their own families. Repin and Daria's daughter and Pron and Karina's son had their first infant in the community's eighteenth year, and it was the cause for major celebrations.

The couple decided they wanted to set up their own farmlet two valleys away. This would be right at the boundary of the warning system, but as there had been no real threats for years and they had chosen a beautiful spot with year-round water from a strongly running creek, well sheltered from the prevailing winds, they expected no objections.

Every member of the Eight was opposed.

Denne, Pron's 18-year-old son, was adamant, a lot like his father.

I have listened to the stories of our community for many years now, and I understand that we do not impose our will on one another. Am I mistaken?

This was near the end of the eighteenth winter. The group were in one of the sitting areas in one of the Big Houses. Jard looked around the group, his eyebrows raised over such strong eyes, a quirky smile playing on his lips.

Well, do we believe this is an issue for the young couple, their parents, or all of us?

Jedina was sitting beside Denne and she was feeding their baby, Greaa. Most of the group, and that included about 30 of the 60-odd members of the community, turned to look at the young couple. But everyone was also scanning the now officially named Council of Eight – their parents.

It was a crucial moment for the fledgling society. Not that there had been no challenges to authority; there had been plenty. However, these had generally been managed well. Big issues had been the subject of many shouting matches, though many of the children spoke out loud only occasionally, and a not inconsequential number of tantrums by the children. In the end the principles they had set down for living together in harmony and with equity had stood them in good stead.

Well? Jedina asked, with all minds and all eyes focused on the Eight. *We have said what we would like. We have always stayed within the bounds set for us, if only because we know the boundaries have always been set up primarily for the safety of us all.*

Leiti agreed. *Question is, is there any reason not to allow these very capable young people to live where they wish? They are within reach of our caring capabilities, which would not have been the case 10 years ago. So I am wondering what arguments we can advance that might encourage Denne and Jedina to stay in the Valley with us, apart from the obvious fact that we would like them to be around. There is certainly plenty of space for an independent unit for them in our valley, and I'm certain we would all be willing to help create it.*

There was no disagreement at all about that.

It was one of those moments when everyone was wanting to do the right thing, yet no-one was quite sure why they were hesitating about supporting the couple.

It was Jard who put the words to their unspoken concerns.

I think Jedina is entitled to an answer. She and Denne are strong and competent to care for themselves and contribute to our growing community. Here is my concern. We have been free of marauders for a long time. As a result of everyone who travels outside the warning line always letting us know when they are going and where, we have come to feel safe. However, some of us remember past experiences that suggest this may be blinding us to real dangers.

There was strong support for this from the Eight, however, the young couple and a few of the older children argued their right to not be overprotected. In the end there was agreement they could choose their home, and many offers of help to construct and stabilize their home and set up perimeter warning boundaries were made. So the couple got their way and a new principle had been established for future young couples, about which the Eight were unhappy.

The young couple were fiercely independent and they had drawn a line in the sand.

No more smothering.

The four parents acquiesced, not without complaint and admonitions about safety and care. Nevertheless, they watched from the Valley every day. Over the next year there were occasional reports of Cretian hunting and war parties coming close to one or other of the little community's hunting or work groups. The group were noticing the increase in Cretian incursions and believed it likely they would get more of these and that they might become more adventurous. However, no-one was prepared for what happened next.

It was late one night in late autumn. Denne and Jedina had been visiting their parents in the Big House and were returning home. It was a pleasant two-hour journey and they were content and unwary. Without warning, a Cretian war party who had been waiting about 100 yards from their house broke through the warning lines and speared Denne, who in his pain could not defend himself. The warriors grabbed Greaa and made it clear that either the parents co-operated or the child would die.

The Cretians had been watching the telepaths for some time and were to some extent aware of their power – not exactly what they could do, but that they were dangerous. Holding the infant at spear point, they beat Denne in front of his wife until he died, then raped and finally killed her.

The alarm from the warning system and then the screaming child's terror were picked up by Pron who had been sleeping. He saw too late what had occurred. In rage and pain Pron killed the entire war party. It was an act of energy control and management greater than would have been possible a decade earlier.

In just over an hour the four senior males were on the spot. They retrieved Pron's grandson but were too late to do anything but express their anger and distress at the death of Denne and Jedina. It was days before they could discuss the event after burying their first dead, an entirely unexpected and awful death.

Pron and Repin tracked the war party's energy trail back to their watercraft, a primitive outrigger moored at least three or four days' walk away. Pron was for traveling immediately to Cretia and meting out retribution. He had in mind wiping out at least an entire village. He did not care how many Cretians that might involve.

Karina and Daria were the voices of reason. *We cannot get our children back.*

It was a flat and indisputable statement. Daria was wracked with grief. She did not want any more loss of lives from their little community, and there was no certainty that an attack on Cretian villages might not bring down further retribution, greater than they could manage. Her pain and her intensity put an end to the immediate pressure for action, but did not deal with the real issue.

This was an isolated incident, but there could be more, and the Cretians were unlikely to accept the loss of their war party without taking some action of their own. The Valley's warning system had been triggered too late to be of value. The couple had built too close to it and so had triggered it on numerous occasions. This, unfortunately, had left them unnecessarily vulnerable, the Eight being asleep, and the seeming security of their arrangements had made them careless.

It was not the end of it by any means for anyone in the community, especially the four parents involved. Leiti brought the situation up several nights after the awful event and after the funeral and send-off they gave to the young couple who had become so deeply integral to their little community. They had also burned the bodies of the Cretian warriors and retrieved their weapons. This cremation had not been a comfortable ceremony but one they knew was needed. No-one wanted to bury the Cretians in the Valley, so they were burned in the next valley.

Leiti's purpose was clear. The four parents as well as the brothers and sisters were traumatised to varying degrees. The infant Greaa was fortunate to know nothing really about what had happened to his parents. The group needed to find the emotional will to let these two go so that the community was not damaged irreparably by the loss.

The directly related members of the community were unwilling, in their pain, to speak about it. But Jard was adamant. Two weeks had passed and the four seniors were unable to fully participate in the life of the community, and in this small community this was serious. Everyone understood, but another event like this involving others would entirely cripple the life of the slowly developing community, and Jard knew it must not be allowed to happen.

He and Leiti shared a moment.

We might have lost more of us if Pron had not picked up the cries of his grandchild. We all had agreed, in the end, that we should not stop Denne and Jedina from building a life on their own. But we cannot afford to lose even one member, and we certainly cannot be at risk from violent marauders with no shred of decency, just anger and viciousness toward us. This will not be the end, and we are only a small group, and we need to be much smarter about protecting our own.

Jard was vehement, and everyone, including the small group of older children, agreed.

Leiti then said, *I know that feelings are high and that many of our children have strong opinions, to which we will listen in their turn.*

Everyone was with her.

I would like us each to say how we are feeling about our loss and what we feel like doing about it, without any holding back. We have to get this process understood and managed between us, otherwise, every time there is a loss we will become a bit disabled and we simply cannot afford to indulge ourselves in those feelings of self-pity.

Although there were some anxious and doubtful expressions around the group, there was no argument, and the children who had been permitted to participate in this meeting indicated their understanding.

One after another the members spoke to Pron, Karina, Daria and Repin. They shared their sadness, their appreciation of the lives of these two children. They included the brothers and sisters of the lost couple, and for two hours there were sharings of every kind about the lives these two had lived in the Tall Trees Valley community. When everyone had had their say and every last important memory had been shared, Jard spoke to the four parents.

We have learned some things about loss. We ourselves lost our families in our early lives. We dealt with our pain by reliving all the moments good and bad we could remember before we were able to move on. We all need you to do this with these children, and that includes the pain and anger you feel toward the Cretians who did this and the society that spawned them.

They knew this was right, and so for an hour the four spoke of their children, their love, their pain, their anger, their rage and their unwillingness to forgive. There were tears, shouting, hugging. In the end there was stillness and a kind of peace.

When the eight adults felt that there was no more that needed to be said to put the lost members' memories in safe keeping of the entire community, Jard said, *We have been not thorough enough about our safety. We all share in this; that is our agreement. I am not comfortable with my part in failing to ensure that our small community is safe from unnecessary invasions.*

His voice was harsh and rang through their minds in a way no-one had experienced before, and he spoke out loud as the Elders nearly always did when they were emotionally disturbed.

Since the event you will all be aware that Leiti and I have been focused on building our power to travel in some new ways. Some of you have also participated with us in managing physical objects. We have been studying for many years now the amazing array of energies on which we are able to draw.

Learning to use more of these, and with some streams of energy supporting others, you know we have achieved some significant increase in our resources. We have also been able, with Karina's help, to increase our ability to manage the health aspects of our internal energy streams.

You all also know I have been attempting to figure out a way to put a stop to these brutal incursions of the Cretians. They appear to have no natural kindness or care for others. I had thought about simply destroying their canoes, but they would just build more. I think we now possess the resources to handle easily a very large group of Cretians anywhere on our shores. I would like to be prepared for the next incursion, which I am sure will come, and see if we can put an end to these threats to our lives. If only they were respectful traders instead of violent hunters and killers.

Several of the children wanted to know what the non-telepathic Olarians did about the Cretians. It was a good question, but no-one knew the answer. Three or four of the Eight had heard stories of killing and rape and destroying crops, but no-one in the telepathic community 'knew'.

One of the 15-year-olds asked, *Why can't we keep watch for a Cretian landing near one of the Old People's villages? Then some of the Council, and perhaps one or two of us, could watch and maybe learn something that would help us?*

Jard sought opinions from the others but no-one could see a good reason not to follow this suggestion.

However, neither Jard nor any of the Eight had an answer to the question of what they would do if the Cretians began their killing and raping while they were observing.

It soon became clear from the discussion that none of them would be able to stand by and see that happen and so really could not be uninterested observers. However, they also knew that as ethereal observers they would be unable to physically intervene.

Nevertheless, the community's survival might be determined by what they knew and it was agreed they would watch, but, if killing and raping were going to happen, they would be bound to do something – just what, they could not figure out. They did not have the power to transport themselves from place to place. They had no experience with acting on physical reality when they were ethereal observers.

The sweeps proved uneventful for a month then two parties of Cretians were seen approaching Olaria. Jard and Daria then added Belden and Jaree to their scans, working each day to increase the level of skill and understanding of the two 15-year-olds.

Can we do more than just watch? Belden asked.

How would you imagine doing that? Jard asked.

Well, we could help the Olarians by using some of the power we have with objects, Belden replied.

Think about it, Jard said. *We are merely energy travelers here, we have no substantial form, our bodies are miles away. Ask yourself, Belden, what do you think you might be able to do?*

Belden tried a few of the things he knew only to quickly recognize Jard's point; they were ethereal observers and at the moment that was all they could be. As they watched, Jard and Daria felt Jaree's scream. The Cretians had approached the first Olarian village who were entirely unprepared, not even a lookout.

The carnage that followed was truly horrible to watch. Men and women were beaten unmercifully. The Cretians appeared to enjoy their power.

Women of all ages in the village were raped mercilessly and several young women were chased into the forest, tortured and killed. After a little more than 30 minutes Jard could stand it no longer and instructed the children to return with him and Daria to their home.

Jard was angry at the pointless violence the Cretians had used to get what they wanted. The children were silent, traumatised by what they had seen, and for several hours the adults worked with them, exploring their feelings about their adventure and pressing them to be very clear about what they had learned.

There was no excuse for what the Cretians did to the girls and the women, Jaree exclaimed. *It was disgusting. How could they do those things, so vicious and insensitive and pointless? There was no pleasure in any of it. They fed off the fear and their violence seemed to be full of anger and viciousness. Such inexplicable cruelty, and the pleasure they seemed to be getting from the harm they were doing!*

Belden asked, *What must their homes on Cretia be like?* But no-one could begin to answer that.

A day later, at Jard's insistence, the two children accompanied him and Daria to make a brief observation of the other raiding party. They were approaching a village that the four could see was aware of the approaching Cretians and was preparing to engage with them. This looked like a much more satisfactory situation. They were wrong. The Cretians seemed to be aware of the forward scouts, easily captured the three of them, tied them to a tree and beat them to death. It was disgusting.

Does anyone need to see any more? asked Jard in a clipped and angry voice. They did not and returned to the Valley in an even more distressed state than the previous day. The debriefing and discussions went on well into the night. No-one felt much like sleeping. If this was standard Cretian behavior, the community needed to make absolutely certain they were prepared. No further convincing was needed. The whole warning and fortification system was immediately at the forefront of their plans.

The entire community was involved in the next discussions. *They should not be allowed to do that stuff,* some of the younger children were heard to say. *They need to be stopped, they are disgusting.*

The vituperation didn't end there. Jard called a halt to the discussion to get the Eight to focus on what they needed to do. The children recognized that they needed to take a back seat and listen. They needed no encouraging. What they had seen through Belden and Jaree had been enough.

Jard took six of the Eight and, working all that day and the next, they strung an energy warning system along the entire beachfront covering the area that gave access to Tall Trees Valley. When the warning system was in place there was a feeling of increased safety.

Does anyone think what we have done is enough?

It was really a rhetorical question. Jard was still feeling angry at what he had witnessed of the Cretians with the Olarian villagers.

We need a strategy for dealing with any large-scale landing party, he added.

Pron had the most comprehensive suggestion. *When they come off the beach, pull the ground out from under them and bury them – all of them.*

The horror on the faces of the women, except for Karina, said it all – definitely not acceptable – and Pron had known it would not be. However, the discussion did raise the issue and identify the problem. Some of the children wanted a say.

Given what we saw when we visited your old villages, and what happened to Jedina and Denne, why is that not all right? The older children needed to be heard. *If we don't kill them, will they not kill us?*

The Eight thought about the implications of that one.

Leiti cut in. *Just because they do it doesn't mean we should do it. One bad act ought not to require another to balance it, surely, or do any of you think that one destructive act entitles another to do the same?*

There was, for a moment, silence among the children. Two children picked up this issue. Lenke, one of Enita's daughters said, *What is the most appropriate and moral way for us to deal with these Cretians, or any similarly aggressive Cretians, when they kill and rape and destroy our people because we are different from them?*

Garten, Jard's eldest son who had a budding relationship with Lenke, picked up the thread.

We could surround ourselves with defensive walls. But surely eventually we would need to go outside the wall and while we were protected they would be growing in numbers and strength. I can only imagine that the end of that would be a nasty conflict, probably of the kind we have seen and were revolted by?

The Eight were impressed with their children, but the question remained: how could this little community become a large and safely growing society if battles for survival were a constant aspect of their lives?

Would we not, Leiti asked, *end up spending a substantial amount of our energy on defense and weapons for defense and essentially killing? Would the issue of feeding everyone not become more difficult and finally force war and killing?*

Many people had their say that day. However, the possible solutions did not seem to encourage a constructive, healthy and exploratory style of learning or life.

No solution that did not involve war, killing and some form of isolation seemed available to the group. The anger at the vicious and horribly senseless harm and destruction that appeared to be an inevitable aspect of Cretian life did not seem to be controllable.

Jard, Leiti and Dornal spoke reasonable Cretian and by using only a few words and their telepathic abilities a seemingly normal conversation could be simulated, so it was decided that they would attempt to negotiate a treaty that would guarantee no more attacks. Of course such a treaty with a violent warlike people had its uncertainties.

In the event this could not be managed, the Cretians who came to kill and harm the little community would be drowned in their boats, a feat the telepathic community were now quite capable of managing. It was a shaky solution but at the time and in the circumstances, it did at least give the Cretians an escape, even though they would not give the telepaths a similar option. However, if successful, this would allow the telepaths to get on with their lives and learning.

The day came sooner than expected. Eleven days after the decision, the warning system informed them of intruders. Enita was monitoring and quickly established that nearly 30 heavily armed Cretians were landing at the beach near one of the tracks to their valley. The children were brought into the house and the energy barriers fully checked and sealed. Six adults traveled rapidly toward the advancing Cretians.

They met around midday of the second day at a pass approximately half way between the landing place and the Valley. Three sat together out of sight while Jard, Leiti and Dornal, now fully protected by an energy field that would prevent any harm from the Cretian weapons, advanced in plain sight with no weapons of any kind. The war party stopped, partly no doubt from surprise and partly from disbelief at the naivety and stupidity of three unarmed people walking confidently toward them.

Jard spoke.

Who is in charge here and what are your intentions? You are traveling fully armed across land that is not yours toward our village, and that is not the action of a friendly traveler.

The guffaw of laughter was full of confidence and bluster.

'I am the senior member of this war party and you will be our prisoners, and a delightful gift you bring.'

His eyes filled with Leiti.

What is your purpose here? Leiti asked, and the Cretians seemed unconscious still of the fact that these strangers were speaking their language.

With confidence in their strength, the two most senior speakers moved rapidly toward the telepaths.

I suggest you stop right there. Jard's voice was sharp. It held no fear or concern, and the two armed men stopped about 20 yards from the trio.

Either take your war party back to Cretia, now, and live, and return if you will with women as well as men and trading options, or you will never reach your home again.

The bluster of the Cretian leader grew stronger, and without any further hesitation he launched a stone from a sling straight at Jard, who picked up the stone in midflight and returned it, with considerable acceleration, at the thrower, killing him instantly.

You seem to think we are powerless, perhaps because your cowardly associates came here to kill and rape. Be certain that will happen no more.

There was now consternation among the Cretians, but their fear and anger blurred as they attacked Jard again, clearly still having unpleasant intentions toward Leiti. It was their final mistake. The six now literally buried the first 15 marauders in the ground beneath their feet, lifting it out and dumping it down over their heads.

Horror was the primary response from the remaining troops, who turned and fled. This was not an enemy they could understand. This was not warfare as they knew it. The six followed them to their boats and as soon as they were about half a mile from the shore drowned the entire group and remained long enough to ensure they were all dead.

The entire episode had been observed by all but the youngest members of the community. It was an unpleasant experience, and no sign of jubilation or pride in the victory was shown by anyone. The incident left a bad taste in the community; death was unapplauded, respect for life predominated with sadness at its loss. Even those who had lost children to the Cretians did not feel any lifting of their spirits at the demise of the war party. Life here was valued for itself. It was a value that stood them in good stead.

Among the six adults involved, the enormity of their actions was sinking in. They were filled with contrary emotions. The Eight sat together in their home in deep silence. They were respectfully being allowed to be alone. The chattering and sometimes the inappropriate boasting of the young children could be heard in the background.

Jard summed up their position. *At some point they are going to attempt to avenge this loss.*

The statement held a certainty; they all knew it was undoubtedly true.

This engagement with the Cretians must be brought to an end. They will return with more people and weapons, and we may not be so fortunate next time.

There was no disagreement.

Tomorrow, when we have recovered sufficiently, we need to visit Cretia and this time find out what they are planning. This will require some of the new resources we have developed. If two of us do the traveling and at least four of you support us, we ought to be able to stay the distance this time. We should be able to locate where they do their planning and listen in. This might be a long stint, so we might need to do it by one pair relieving the first, and so on.

There was no disagreement and the plans were made for the next day. After a night's sleep, Jard and Pron went first. The group followed their trails. It was a disturbing few hours until Jard and Pron returned.

It is clear, Jard said, *they are planning to attack us.*

Pron continued. *The array of weapons and men is very disturbing. There are literally hundreds of them.*

Pron's message carried a lot of stress, and it was unlike him. Everyone was focused.

As you would have seen, there were several collections of men with arms of many kinds we have never seen. Hundreds of men are collecting along their seafront. They have decided to come over here and deal with us once and for all. It felt scary.

The older children wanted to be heard. Jard recognized their right, and some of them began.

Will it be all right for us to kill them all? If we don't kill them all, some could come back and kill us when we are not looking out for them.

Without waiting for a response another of the teenagers, one of the older girls said, *I find these people scary and disgusting. They seem to want to hurt us women and seem to have no idea of sensitivities and good manners. If they ever get here, how should we look after ourselves?*

It was a question on everybody's mind.

There was a great deal of uncertainty, even among the Eight. The question was, were their resources sufficient to ensure they could protect themselves and their valley from an attack by a hundred or more marauders intent on inflicting pain, destruction and death?

The group knew they could manage a small force, but, it seemed likely the Cretians were massing a veritable army of soldiers from across Cretia. And while they knew it was possible they could handle one or two attacks, there were too few of them to manage constant violence from the Cretians. Their lives would be fully engaged in battles for survival and they were certain this would impact them very badly. It would change the direction of their activities, possibly forever. The Cretians needed to be managed permanently.

CHAPTER 49

The Cretian Solution

Leiti spoke first to Aurin, one of her daughters, now nearly 16, then, with her hand on Jard's shoulder, she addressed the children.

Children, there is no point in pretending this is not a serious and dangerous development, but it is yet not disastrous for us. We have to be allowed to think this through and come up with a solution acceptable to all of us. Killing everyone who does not get on with us is not an acceptable way to run our lives. I think you would agree with this.

There was no question about that.

So the Eight would like the opportunity to discuss this, and while you are all welcome to listen in, please do not interrupt until we have reached some decisions. Once we have done that, we will then invite you to offer your thoughts. Are you willing to let us proceed?

Aurin replied for the children. *Yes, Mother, I think that most of us are okay with that,* and the murmur from the children confirmed this.

When decisions are made we will talk with you about them and you can ask whatever questions you need answered, Leiti said.

The children respected the Council of Eight – their parents – as the decision makers. The adults were understandably responsible for the entire community and its survival, they were never imperious, and they were respected in a community where no child had ever been harmed by an adult and no abuse of any kind had ever happened, and this was known to all.

The Council of Eight sat together in their sitting room and reviewed their options.

If we do not take this battle to them, we could be fighting battles we might easily lose and that would probably be the end of us all. Who knows what they will do once they truly understand our capabilities.

I agree, Pron said. *But the question is, are we powerful enough to put a final end to this state of affairs? We would have to beat them so convincingly they would never be willing or able to attack us again. That is a big challenge.*

Leiti, Daria and Karina were determined that the men did not for a second imagine this was an event for the men. Enita was also quite certain she intended to be part of this. There was a moment's hesitation as Dornal, Pron and Repin looked to Jard.

You remember our last really big energy experiment? Jard asked. *We went together down to Einiga, the gorge where we were losing dozens of our herbivore breeding stock to the dangerous rock falls throughout the entire length of that gorge. Together we caused about 100 tons of overhang to break up and fall into the entrance to the gorge. It blocked any likelihood of animals entering or leaving by that path.*

We were able to do that with only a month of practice. It was one of the biggest and most tricky feats we have undertaken so far. It also took the eight of us. This is going to take more single-minded concentration and tenacity by far. The rocks were passive and the consequences did not include the likelihood we would kill many, many people.

Everyone knew what was being said. But they also knew the consequences of not engaging in the venture: probably the community's survival at some future time, plus the tension of waiting for that to happen and constantly preparing for an awful event. It was neither a healthy nor a pleasant prospect.

After an hour a decision was reached. The Eight would spend the next four weeks practicing a number of very straightforward but draining earthmoving and rock-transporting activities.

Then Jard came forward with the thought that had been foremost in his mind since their trip over the entire land of Cretia, a continent surrounded on all sides by sea.

As you know, Leiti and I have been working out what would be involved in closing them in! Locking their entire continent inside an energy wall that would have to be at least 100 feet high.

None of the others had been following their detailed discussions over the past few months, so this was an astonishing proposition. The alternative proposal that Dornal put forward was that they avoid the Cretians and build a wall around the Valley, but there were so many disadvantages to this proposal that he happily let it go.

So, Jard explained, *Leiti and I have figured the energy strands we would need to build this wall. They must be supported and boosted daily by the sun, it being the only source from which we know there is sufficient power to create the bonding needed, and because it rises every day it will renew the field of energy that would actually be the wall. We know it works because it is the source for the maintenance of all our homes and defenses, although on a smaller scale.*

In order to construct the wall we will need many thousands of energy sheets each linked or interlocked. It will take the entire power of the eight of us working together for about six to eight hours a day for maybe a year, a huge project. We will have to be selective about when we work at it and when we do other things, especially we will be unable to work through the winter. So we would have to begin by covering the most common sea lanes, then move further afield.

We figure that the energy drain on us will mean we will be able to work at it only every second day. This is particularly so because the energy required would be too much for Leiti and Repin, whose design and organizing knowledge will be required for each stage. It will also involve some of it being built from a boat, which will keep us at appropriate distances from the shores.

It was an astonishing concept they were proposing. Most of the children would have to be kept and cared for in the Valley and would need to be put under the charge of the eldest. The Eight would have to begin physically on the point of land nearest Cretia, about 200 miles from the Cretian shore, and would have to move each day to a new construction site.

Arrangements for food and other necessities, and sleep, needed to be made, and for some of this they would rely on the oldest children. The Olarian mainland was too far for the battle to be managed but not for the building of some of the wall.

There was one long pause when one of the children asked why the Eight did not just build the wall without any discussion with the Cretians. At first this proposition seemed to gain a great deal of support. But, little by little, the idea of locking them in without any warning or explanation seemed wrong. It was surprising, because it would avoid war, but it was too one-sided for the council, and in the end, after a very extended and intense discussion, it was considered somehow too wrong! And so the original plan to defeat the Cretians and extract a forever treaty prevailed.

So they built a craft after the style of the Cretian boats, larger and more stable but entirely of energy, using the same processes they had learned from building their land shelters. It was indeed a strange craft, but it worked extremely well, and they were able to use their energy capabilities to pilot it to wherever they chose. It was, when finished, invisible unless they colored it, and it was according to Garten when he first saw it 'an amazing floating monstrosity!' To which the Eight had to agree. They were nevertheless proud of their incredible achievement. Everyone acknowledged it to be an interesting way to travel their world.

The day of the confrontation drew near. The Eight took themselves outside the walls of the Cretians' largest military outpost, which seemed to be the rallying point for many different Cretian clans. They set themselves on a rise about a mile away. Jard and Pron went forward and issued the challenge. The Cretians ignored them. The group then smashed a hundred yards of the village's protective wall and waited.

This time they were not ignored. A force of some 30 fully armed men marched out of the village. Their leader still did not take them seriously. He had his men charge the two aggressors. The detail of 30 men was summarily destroyed. The Cretians withdrew and sent their commander out to negotiate. Jard and Pron made their proposition: cease all Cretian war parties to Olaria or face total annihilation.

The commanders withdrew and the Eight watched them planning a major assault on the group for the next morning, imagining that this must be the forward unit of a larger army that would be brought out when the assault began.

In the morning the Eight wiped out the hundred or so warriors who had been sent to destroy them. But the day had taken its toll on the group, and they needed time to rest and also to recover from the distress of what felt like senseless killing. It took four days before the Eight could see that warriors were being brought from all over the country, and clearly this was part of a plan that had been proceeding for a considerable time. The troops were led by a much better organized and militaristic chief.

The final negotiation between Jard, Pron and the two militaristic leaders resulted in a threat that tomorrow would be the last day on Cret – their name for the planet the Olarians called Olar – for the advance party and their entire army.

The huge armed force of Cretians came out ready to do battle. Jard and Pron put out for the last time their request for a treaty that would keep the Cretians off Olaria forever. The military leaders laughed and told the two to do their worst and say their goodbyes to their maker. The two returned to the Eight. They linked hands, smashed all the boats used to get the Cretians to the Olarian mainland and created a single force field that brought most of the trees and soil from the hillside down on the advancing troops.

No-one knew how many died that day. However, before midday, the head of the military of the Cretians surrendered unconditionally and a treaty meeting was arranged for the following day.

The meeting involved the Eight and four of the most important Cretians still living. The treaty was incomprehensible to the Cretians, however, in defeat they were ready to sign. It read, in simple language:

Since it is acknowledged that the Cretians have been defeated by the Olarian Council of Eight, the Cretians agree to accept the Council building a wall one mile out from the Cretian continent. This wall will prevent the Cretians ever again leaving their own land. No Olarian will in future ever enter Cretia to invade or spy on the Cretian people, however, to ensure the safety of their world, the two countries will arrange a meeting on the first day of every fiftieth year, eight members of each world to be present to speak of the safety of their part of the World of Olar, which the Cretians call Cret. On that day, the Olarian Council of Eight will construct a pathway to the wall and open a gate and provide a place in which all will meet, be fed, and share any matters that might affect the world on which we all live.

This agreement was duly signed by the four Cretians and the eight Olarians for whom it was a solemn pledge. It was clear the Cretians thought the telepaths were insane but dangerous; they clearly thought this treaty was worthless. In this the Olarians hoped they would be proved wrong. Then the Olarians left, feeling confident that this would for a substantial time to come be the end of hostilities. No-one, however, actually knew what the future might hold.

CHAPTER 50

Residue

The building of the most amazing sea wall imaginable, which took the Eight the most part of a year, was finally completed. A testament to determination, creativity and an indomitable will to survive. This fledgling society had, they believed, rid their world of the menace of the Cretians forever.

Back in Tall Trees Valley, the defeat of the Cretians was perhaps the most significant event in the life of the fledgling community so far. For the first time the group felt safe from attack from that source. Perhaps now, Jard and the council felt, the little community could expand and some of their cherished projects be rekindled.

This would have been ultimately satisfying but for some unfinished business of which they were unaware. Thirty Cretians, a war party engaged in hostilities with the Olarian communities, had been left stranded on the Olarian mainland. When they attempted to return home, they were prevented by the wall.

Days of futile confrontation left them frightened, angry and in the mood for retribution. They had no idea what had actually transpired but needed somewhere to live. This problem they solved by returning to three of the Olarian villages and totally defeating them, taking the women they wanted and forcing the villagers into service to them as the new masters. Over the next years they integrated the communities into their lifestyle, building militaristic structures and reducing the status of the Olarians to primitive serfdom. All Cretian efforts during that time were directed at gaining control and consolidating their position.

The Cretian/Olarian hybrid communities engaged in a few clashes with other village communities. It was soon clear that the new order contained the worst elements of both. It was nearly three years before the telepaths became aware of the changes during one of their visits to the Olarian communities.

Much might have passed unnoticed had the resentment of the Olarians not spilled over onto the telepaths and the subsequent determination of the Cretian remnant to even their imagined score with the telepathic community. They were not exactly sure what the background to their angst was but believed the telepaths to somehow be responsible for their unhappy situation and meant to teach them who was in control and, if necessary, put an end to them. They began to build their military strength to do just that.

The error of judgment they made was to decide to try to make things right. The Cretians had, unfortunately for them, made some very serious mistakes. They had taken over Jard's village, killed his uncle and forced his mother to be mistress of the senior Cretian's household. To make his point about who was in control, he regularly beat her in front of the others in the village. When Jard found out he went straight into action – no discussion. He took Pron with him and they walked five days to within visual sight of the village. He intended to be present and to actually see the situation for himself. He and Pron singled out each of the Cretians when they were alone and killed them by the simple expedient of stopping their hearts, a technique Leiti had developed for killing the animals they hunted. It was a huge relief for the village, but as Pron and Jard watched the village over the next two days, they realized that the harm done by the Cretians had become, in some ways, irreversible. The anger and violence had taken its toll and the village was unlike anything Jard had seen in his time in that place. However, Jard's now slowly aging mother was no longer being beaten. Jard made certain she was all right then, with a heavy heart, he and Pron returned home.

The militaristic frenzy that had driven the Cretians had somehow been injected into the Olarian culture; the fighting and regimentation did not cease with the death of the instigators. This development was not a promising one. The desire to find and eliminate the telepaths had become part of the purpose of life in the village and in the other two villages.

The group knew this threat would not go away and sometime soon they would have to face a new enemy: their own people.

CHAPTER 51

The Discovery

Since the horrible death of Pron and Karina's son and his wife, every young couple had been allowed to live in their own dwelling if they wished but always within easy walking distance of the Valley and always protected by energy walls and devices to ensure there would be no more 'situations'. While the safety of the small community seemed to be taken care of, at least for the moment, it remained a concern and hardly a day went by when one of the adults did not systematically scan an area of several hundred miles in every direction around the Valley. There seemed to be little threat to the telepaths, at least at the moment, but everyone suspected it was still not a peace that was going to last. It seemed to the small but rapidly growing community that everywhere outside the Tall Trees world wanted to solve their problems and take out their frustrations on others through violence and pain. It was anathema to the telepathic world that was being built and it was clear that it too would have consequences that would impact everyone.

However, the end of the Cretian War and the rather tense standoff with the *others* did not turn out to be the central issue in the lives of the newly established community. Another event overtook these in importance and significance as the eight original telepaths entered their late thirties.

Jard had, since they settled, been relentlessly pursuing his attempt to understand *energy,* the single most significant aspect of their uniqueness, as he and Leiti saw it. Every kind of energy they found they explored: where it originated, how it traveled , what impact it had on their world, the plants and animals, the very planet itself, but now especially themselves.

Finally he and Leiti had settled down to explore and understand those energies that entered and streamed around their bodies. This was no small task. There were many, many hundreds of internal energies, some created, it appeared, from those entering the body from the outside, and sometimes from energies being created and managed by the body itself. Some of these were seriously tiny.

Seeing the really tiny strands required an amplification of thousands of times, which was possible because of the strange arrangement of their energy 'sight'. Finding each and mapping its journeys was a time-consuming activity. They often swapped roles, first Jard studying Leiti, then when she could reproduce those learnings from Jard she would continue with him as the subject. Years had passed in this living learning laboratory they had set up. Karina was doing a similar journey with the plants of their world, although she would sometimes swap with them, and they regularly took time to compare their understandings, and often they had a quite large and more than interested audience in this.

Jard and Leiti were tracking a tiny single strand that had been the focus of their attention for some months. This journey had begun while they had been watching the repair to an injury Dornal had sustained. The activity of a tiny energy strand on the repair had caught their attention. They had watched for days with all three of them noting what it did to the cells being repaired.

They noticed that it traveled , apparently using absolutely every bodily transport system, fluids and fluid energies and a variety of mixed non-fluid energies, and it made this journey every single day. Finally they noticed that when it had left the cell, any cell, that cell suffered the tiniest deterioration or perhaps imperfection in its replication. This little energy flash was, seemingly, responsible for changing every cell in the body every day and Jard and Leiti began to believe it was aging the cell slightly! Or, more accurately, it was replicating the cell slightly inaccurately and deteriorating it!

The small energy element impacted the cells every day. The energy puff seemed to either inform the cells to replicate accurately following their instructions and make a correct and accurate copy of the structure of the cell and so of all its functions, or it did not accurately replicate the instructions for the rebuilding of the cells and so the cells began to deteriorate slightly, probably, they assumed, after a certain age.

Later they would learn, if during the late 30s and early 40s nothing was done, the cells would very slowly replicate every day just a little incorrectly and there was little doubt in their minds it was aging them! If, on the other hand, they changed the instructions carried by this initiating cell, what it passed on to the body was an instruction for each cell to replicate accurately, and in a fashion they did not understand this accurate replication seemed to also halt what they considered to be aging. So the person and their internal organs looked the same as they had the day before, and so the process appeared to effectively stabilize their age!

They chose one of the children and for a week ran the same exploration. They noticed that with the child the energy was of a minutely different valence and the cell did not age but *grew or replicated, producing more cells, so the individual was growing!* The change was so minute it was barely noticeable, but it was there. Then Jard had a flash of intuition, one that was to change the lives of this community forever. This infinitesimal energy was providing aging by growth in the youngest and aging by deterioration in the older members of the community. Aging meant replicating every cell in the body ever so slightly inaccurately.

They tried to track this energy strand back to its source, but always lost it in a primitive area of the brain. Nothing they could do, none of the help they could get, would take them any deeper, however, they could see the tiny flash begin and, as it were, pick up its instruction before heading off to do its work for the day. This then appeared to be an apparently unending stream of tiny inaccurate replications fed to every cell in the entire body once the individual was, they would later find out, over about 38 years old.

So the change after 38 included a minute deterioration: aging. They knew this was, of course, not quite right. The accurate and inaccurate reproduction of cells did not proceed in a simple linear fashion. It took them more than a year to understand how this replication happened throughout the body over different age groups and with different variations. But finally they could see the pattern and understand how cells were either deteriorated or enhanced.

It seemed as though it corrected the reproduction of the structure of the cell in the young but not in the older members of the community. In the older members of the community, and this was usually themselves, it did not correct flaws in the structure of each cell. It appeared to permit some cells to become ever so slightly more flawed!

They decided to see if they could change the valence of the tiny energy as it left its source in order to ensure it repaired each cell rather than allow it to ever so slightly deteriorate. They could, so they began to experiment with themselves. Every day they changed the valence in each other so that the message from the tiny source was the opposite from its original intent, so it was now replicating cells accurately, according to the original design of the cell. They found the instant the brain appeared to be making the decision and they adjusted it. After several days, they no longer had to make the change – the brain was doing it for them. This tiny adjustment caused every cell to be given a new message. With their explorations over the next month, they were able to adjust the energy so that its impact on the cells was to enhance and rebuild deteriorated cells and then to neither increase nor decrease their apparent age. Every cell was repaired and reinstated into its pristine form. They had, inadvertently, discovered a method of stabilizing their age and, it seemed, their physical health!

Leiti looked at Jard.

We can see where it starts, and then when it reaches a target cell it flashes a truly minute message to that cell, which then seems to pass it on to millions of adjacent cells in an increasingly large chain reaction. If we don't interfere, the impact is always exactly the same: the tiniest deterioration we have ever seen. Then, when we make that tiny adjustment at the source to a 'no change' message with totally accurate replication and no additional cells, there is no cell destruction! When we followed our teenager the valence was the tiniest bit different, all the cells reproduced and multiplied... grew!

Jard was smiling. They both got it. They might have found the manner in which the body aged and a way to halt it. They had also built their understanding of the variations and alterations that differentially modulated cells in different parts of their bodies. It was complex, but finally they believed they understood how to change the valence and to do this in a way that allowed the cells each day to move toward cell optimization and remain there.

Over the next weeks, with everyone feeling anticipation, they checked the pattern with every member of the community. It was the same. Up to a certain age, one valence, for the most part, exact replication and additions, then with some, almost no valence changes, then a shift to a new valence, inaccurate replications and so, aging began, differentially at first. They had no old people to explore so they chose half a dozen of their flock of grazers. After several months they knew they had got it. They worked with Karina to study some plants, but here they were puzzled; at first they could find no such strand.

It would be years before they would solve the nature of the cell reproduction in plants. However, for the moment they decided to monitor themselves and see if through the coming winter they were able to hold their age constant. They wanted to ensure they could manage, differentially, the repair and rejuvenation. If they could the next step would be to discuss with the entire community whether they should introduce this as an option for everyone.

They spent months during the winter continuing their attempts to locate the source of this energy strand. Many energies entered the body continuously from the world around, but even with the entire adult community working together, they were unable to isolate the source that fed this element in the brain. Too many incoming energies every day seemed to be involved.

They worked tirelessly throughout the entire winter. On the first day of spring the entire community knew Jard and Leiti had actually succeeded in finding a way to neutralize the aging process. The question being, could they hold age constant, using only this tiny adjustment to the even tinier signal from the brain to an energy stand that came from somewhere they could not track?

It seemed improbable, but they had been able to change the valence of the energy the strand delivered to the cell. Once the valence had been changed and the cell was replicated exactly so that it fit some apparently accurate pattern a small number of times, it appeared to pick up the new pattern as though it had learned it and then continued delivering the new correct cell pattern. What's more, the slightly more accurate cell replication appeared to also be slightly improving how they felt.

Finally Jard spoke to the entire community.

As you know, Leiti and I believe that we have a very primitive understanding of how our bodies are aged. And it does seem to be primarily by the activity of an energy strand that acts every day. It seems that if we get it to replicate cells accurately, it learns, and we appear to be stabilized at the age we began the process! So, by a little manipulation of this little energy puff, we can reduce, stabilize or increase our age and seemingly improve our overall health!

So it holds age constant. The tiny replicating energy puff does not change the cells in our bodies which seems to be its function and its only function. If we have grasped this correctly, growth is managed by accurate cell replication and the addition of new cells. It creates growth until we reach our thirties, mostly with accurate replication. Sometimes it seems to reproduce with small failures, beginning in our late thirties. At this point the replication fails just slightly but consistently, and this seems to be connected to the way new cells are added. So, aging! Failure of daily cell replication by just the minutest degree. At least, that is what we have found so far. And that is probably a really huge simplification of what this energy strand actually does.

However, on top of that, once this earlier accurate replication pattern is set up, the brain seems willing to continue it. For how long, we don't yet know. It allows the cells to regenerate but not age, that is, neither replicate incorrectly nor add or delete cells in that area! If we are not wrong about this, we may actually have found a way to halt our aging without damaging our bodies! Incidentally, if we have actually got this right, there appears no reason we may not, at some time in the future, be able to reduce age, but we need to wait and see.

Leiti continued.

If you are agreeable, we will monitor ourselves daily for the next few months. If nothing bad seems to be happening to us, and the rest of you will probably be able to tell, everyone can decide if they want to participate in our 'never get old' experiment. At this point we don't know what, if any, other consequences might be associated with this little entanglement with nature. Especially how long we will be able to make it last. So if you are willing to watch us, say, through to the end of summer, if we are still okay and you are satisfied, well, you might all wish to give it a go?

There were lots of questions and excitement. They also sought and found one of the 15-year-old girls who wanted to work with them and Karina, and they were delighted to include her in the team. Health issues were always needing someone's attention. Jedina was a daughter of Enita and Repin, named after Repin and Daria's daughter who had so tragically died, and her interests were caring for the children and understanding health. She would fit nicely into the little team and was to join them within a week.

In the villages, the education of the children had been somewhat haphazard. They used to play until they were around 11 or 12, performing some simple routine chores around their houses and then were slowly adapted into village life. Since the telepaths had been together, the children had been cared for a little more systematically, mainly because of the threat from outside and the small number of them. Because they were constantly within reach of adults, a lot of indirect learning took place. There were more systematic efforts to help them with their telepathic and telekinetic learning.

Every year the reach and powers of the senior telepaths grew and were frequently stretched by the need to solve problems. In a small community with few older strong people this meant they had developed the telepathic but especially the telekinetic energies that enabled them to do things that would otherwise have required many more people. An interesting example was the locating and taming of a species of small flightless birds they liked to eat. These hapless creatures were in constant danger of being eaten or lost in the wild. The couple who took their management in hand built very cleverly organized energy walls to not only manage their movements but to prevent them being the meal of larger predators. In doing this, they recognized the need to better understand the food chain. It seemed every learning or change in their capabilities had to be balanced by a range of new things to be understood. The idea of keeping their world in balance became a primary driver associated with all learning.

The children were now always in reach of adults, and so they were informally learning most of the tasks the adults needed to do. They often experimented when one or other of them had learned a new thing. As they aged, they attached themselves to one of the adults who was doing the things that most interested them, and so began the usual sort of apprenticeship common to the learning of the young in the villages in which their parents had been raised. During the winters, the adults told the children stories of their original homes and of the things that had happened to them during the period before they came to Tall Trees Valley and then of their lives since they arrived.

This particular winter there was a lot of interest expressed about what was or wasn't happening to Jard and Leiti regarding aging. However, until more time passed, speculation tended to be circular and finally Jard persuaded the group to wait and see what the year would tell them. There was, as always, a considerable focus on the children. There had been explorations other winters, but this year Karina and Daria particularly wanted the community's position clarified.

Karina posed the issue that was uppermost in her mind.

I have eight children and two grandchildren whom I love dearly. But I feel almost as possessive about half the children in our community. It's not like it was back where I grew up. There everyone knew to which family they belonged; here nearly everyone belongs in nearly every family. I know that is a slight exaggeration, but you all know what I mean.

Daria agreed. *I think I understand what you are getting at, Karina, but I am not sure where you are going with this.*

Karina stopped. She was also not sure where she wanted to take this.

We are not like the villages in which the eight of us grew up, Repin said. *Although Daria and Leiti and I were together a lot, we never felt part of each other's families.*

Jard agreed.

Karina had her teeth firmly fixed into the issue.

The thing is, she said, *we are almost one big mixed-up family, in a good way. I don't feel possessive of any particular child, I feel parental to everyone, and it seems to me we should somehow include this collective thing in the values that matter to us.*

We have several times agreed that we do not own our children. They are the future of our people. I don't know how to say it, but they are both part of all of us and uniquely themselves, and we need to think of them differently than as children. I mean, that sounds ridiculous, but they need to learn things, especially things we have learned since we came here, in a better way than we learned – in a more organized way.

Although the discussion went on late into the night and was carried on over several nights, it always returned to a similar point. All eight original parents had cared for every child in the group and been part of their learning, their emotional upheavals, their excitements and concerns; all children were lovingly managed by whichever adult was with them at the time. As a result, there was almost no sense of possessiveness developed by the parents or the children. Everyone fed whoever was with them that day, and food, shelter, love and a very large range of feelings and difficulties of all kinds were part of the developing culture of this community.

Only the original eight knew anything different. Everyone was happy to have children staying or sleeping with them, and sometimes the children chose to sleep together in the large children's wing in the big house. Everyone realized that a new pattern of living had developed and they really wanted, more than anything else, to acknowledge and affirm it. As this winter drew to a close there was not a lot of peace and quiet in the Big House. An entirely new strand had been added to the telepaths' world.

Leiti was looking thoughtfully at her man. Her long lithe body stretched out beside him and her hand resting softly on his thigh.

Do you ever wonder what your life might have been if you had not left your village and met us?

The question was new but the thought was not. Jard had wondered many times.

You must know I have thought about it often. I truly cannot imagine a life without you. But I think if I had stayed I might never have developed the knowledge and skill I have today. We do not live a normal life by the standards with which we were raised. My life would probably be just like my parents', but Leiti, you know our children have a very different view. We have seen it often. They have known nothing else and the stories of our lives until we left are just that for them, stories, like pretend. Why are you asking me this now?

Leiti smiled a shy warm and gentle smile. Jard's blood heated and his passion for this beautiful woman almost overwhelmed him, but her warm simple curiosity always trapped him, and he knew she was exploring something important. Lying beside him, looking at him with pleasure and satisfaction as she did every night and every morning, was something that, when he caught her, enriched immeasurably the quality of his life.

Because, she said, *if we are really going to live forever, that is a very long time, and I wonder if we were designed for this. Will I be lying here looking at you, loving you and feeling excited and delighted by you, a thousand years from now? And how many of us will there be?*

At which point they became aware that one by one the others had unobtrusively joined in, listening to their conversation.

Jard smiled. *When I think about it I think if we are not designed for such longevity we will probably not make it, but if we are, and if we have found a way, then I can only see one possibility: we must be designed to learn.*

Nothing else makes any sense to me at all. If I have understood what a fundamental part of our reality is, it is that each new extension to our abilities comes from our attempts to solve problems in new ways. To learn.

A long silence followed, not a word, not a whisper, not even the gentlest emotional vibration from outside the two of them. It felt as though the Big House had become deathly still. Leiti, her long hair lying elegantly on her headrest, her beautiful green eyes softly massaging her man, finally continued.

We have never been violent unless our lives and our future or that of our children or our friends have been threatened. I am hoping we will always be this way together, but lately I have been feeling how difficult others have chosen to make this for us. I am unable to help wondering how the people we grew up with in our villages would feel about us if they could know us, really, and our parents, would they like us? Would they approve of us?

Jard was looking closely into his beautiful partner, saw the deep emotion lying nearly hidden in the depths of her eyes.

It makes me sad to say this, my love, but I think not.

Then, one by one the others whispered into their conversation, *Nor mine.*

Leiti stretched her hands so they slid slowly down Jard's muscular body. He held her, softly stroking her gently, and they slept.

CHAPTER 107

Simultaneity

Soon after they were confident they could now prolong their lives, Jard became aware of a sense that he could do something he had never done. It was not unlike an experience he and Leiti had shared during the period when they were testing their ability to extend their lives into an unknown future. Initially he had no idea what it might be, however, this feeling that something was about to befall him was not entirely new. This time, however, even he was taken aback at the events that took place.

It was a day seemingly no different from any other during the autumn. However, today a possible crisis would establish yet another significant change for the Olarian telepathic and telekinetic community. It would be a day that would be remembered.

Several of the Eight were felling and clearing trees for some new works they planned.

A very large tree in a clearing in which Jard was working began to fall and he was directly in its path. Pron and Karina had been horrified as they realized the tree would certainly crush him, but neither attempted to stop it because they assumed he would – a feat easily within his capabilities. He turned to stop it and suddenly thought of the children who had come to watch the clearing work. As he realized they were safe he knew the tree was falling toward him and without any conscious thought found himself standing beside the children. He had no idea how he had got there.

He had looked toward the children and the two adults with them and in some part of his mind decided he wanted to be there with them. At the moment of that thought he had found himself there, standing beside them, as all of them watched the gigantic tree fall safely to the ground.

This was the first known occasion of such an experience anyone had ever seen. When the three talked it over, they realized at the moment when Jard had moved he had been feeling a desire to be with them and not standing in the path of the falling tree. Something had simply moved him to the spot on which he was now safely standing.

Leiti asked if he could do it again. Think of another place he wanted to be.

He looked at her strangely, but realized she was telling him of her hunch that the strength of his desire might have activated a capability of which he had heretofore been unaware. If that was true, might they all be able to do it? Whatever *it* was. He stood still, looking at her and seeking the experience he had had in the moments before he had seen the tree falling toward him.

He got it. In the instant before the tree would have certainly killed him, he had a powerful feeling he wanted to be with the others, and as he wished it, had found himself there, and he realized he knew what he had done.

He turned to Leiti.

Quickly, take my hand and feel what happens.

He immediately reproduced the feeling he had had in the moments before the tree fell. Except this time he thought of the space beyond the children. In an instant they were standing there, 50 feet from where they had been a moment ago.

Within seconds, Leiti was able to make the shift. Next he tried to reproduce the experience with Karina and then Pron, but to no avail, whereas normally in their learning both ought to have been able to make the shifts with no connection to Jard. However, they could not. When the three returned to the Big House in Tall Trees Valley, the others had all had a rerun of the event but could not duplicate it. Moments after their arrival the Eight held hands and tried to make the jump, but no-one except Leiti was able to. This was different from all other learning experiences they had had.

There was a lot of confusion in the group. Why could only the two make the jump? Hours were spent discussing the phenomenon before everyone went to bed. The couples continued discussing it, unable to sleep. After all had finally fallen asleep, Jard sat bolt upright in bed, shook his head and then settled himself down again.

In the morning he reported the thought that had woken him, that had been going through his mind when he went to sleep. Apart from age, a significant phenomenon that differentiated Jard and Leiti from the others was the adjustment of their aging process. It seemed possible that when they had taken the steps they needed to increase their life span they had opened the door to their ability to shift in space/time, to make a jump.

The only way this could be tested was to make the age adjustment with one of the Eight and see if that made any difference to their ability to make a similar jump. Karina, who had been most involved in the age-extending studies, immediately agreed to have them make the change with her. Immediately they had done so, she held hands with Jard and she made the jump with him. Immediately following she was able to make the jump herself. It seemed pretty certain that making the age adjustment opened a doorway to the ability to make a jump. It took no time at all for the others to agree to have their age adjustment made. Sure enough, within moments they were able to make the jump.

To solidify their conviction they decided to take one of the oldest children who still had some years before they would reach their late thirties when the age fixing would most likely be done. Belden, being a daughter of Jard and Daria, enthusiastically consented, so they set up her age adjustment. Within only a few minutes they were able to engage with her new ability to make a jump. It seemed their hunch had been correct. However, no-one could guess why.

The Eight had acquired a major new capability. It remained to explore its boundaries and find out what was involved in this startling new development. Once begun, Jard could not let it alone. He spent a not inconsiderable time each day making what they were all calling *jumps*, and each time he would extend the distance of the jump. Then one afternoon he decided to increase the distance from Tall Trees Valley to the next valley. For a moment he seemed unable to make the jump, then, after an almost imperceptible pause, he was in the next valley, but somehow not in the same way.

As he looked down at his body he realized something was not quite right. He feared he had done some permanent damage to himself. He was a shadow of himself. He looked the same but knew he was actually not quite the same. Then in the instant he knew his solid body was still standing in Tall Trees Valley. His conscious mind was not. His consciousness was in the valley into which he had just made his jump! He was confused and wanted to be back in Tall Trees Valley, and then he was!

Leiti and Pron had been watching when he made the jump. He *shifted* and was fully and substantially back in Tall Trees Valley. A gasp of relief burst from him, and Leiti grabbed a hold of him and hugged him. He was feeling more than a little disturbed and confused. He held Leiti firmly to him, but he was *seeing* into the next valley without being there, thinking about the difference between then and now. He realized both he and Leiti were actually in the valley. The couple looked at one another. Then, his anxiety still very high, he was back in their valley, and he let Leiti go.

He stared at the others. For the moment no-one seemed to know what to say. He stopped this disturbing experiment. He felt out of control. He sat on the ground, head in hands, and began to replay the experience, making sure he was willing himself to be here seated on the ground in Tall Trees Valley. Leiti sat beside him and they talked. Pron joined them, but not before he had tried to be both here and there in the next valley, and then back here! They were all feeling a bit *mad,* somehow not quite in control. By now the rest of the Eight were trying desperately to get Jard to tell them what had happened to him, what he had done.

They looked at each other in fright and excitement; confusion and anxiety hung over the three. What had just happened? Had they been in control? And how had they suddenly been able to do this...*jump?* Who was in control here? No-one else tried anything for the rest of that day. Then, that night after dinner, they sat down together. There was a great deal of anxiety hanging over them. At first the Eight thought, *People cannot do this.* But it was obviously untrue; they had done it, but what had they actually done?

Their talk went on into the night. Whatever had created their telepathy and their telekinesis must also have created this ability to make a jump. Why could they do it now? It was very, very late that night when the Eight finally went to bed and finally all did get to sleep.

However, no sooner was he awake than Jard was busy replaying each experience from yesterday. Leiti was awake almost immediately Jard woke and she accompanied him to their kitchen to boil water and create their morning steeped herbal brew. Then, sitting in their big room, Jard decided it was necessary for him to fully understand exactly what had occurred yesterday. What exactly was the nature of this phenomenon they were calling a *jump*?

So he began a series of jumps across the room. Sometimes a full jump and sometimes staying where he was and making the apparent jump. It took only a short while before he could understand the difference. In both modes he could see and hear everything at the place to which he had made the jump, but in both instances he could neither see nor hear anything at the place from which he had made the jump. The only version of himself that had the ability to move and act was the one at the location to which he had jumped.

In solid mode he could drink his morning brew; in the non-substantial mode, he could not, however, he could act: throw a cushion in the air and catch it, pick up a chair, use his telepathic and telekinetic capabilities. Little by little he began to understand the nature of this new phenomenon. Then he experimented with Leiti.

He could travel with her to his destination in both modes, however, when he went as a duplicate, which was his way of thinking about it, she traveled with him in the same form. Solid or duplicated. And in duplicated form his duplicate was unable to be harmed; a piece of wood simply passed through him and on return to his body no injury appeared to have been done.

Leiti and Jard played with this experience for nearly the entire day;

the other six adults watched and learned. By the end of the day they had established a significant number of the boundaries this new ability seemed to possess. Everyone thought the most unusual quality was the ability of the traveler to take one or two people with them with no apparent expenditure of energy! However, the whole experience was quite a disturbance to their sense of reality. From whence came this new power or ability?

They call Belden in. Could she also do this? The answer was yes. Within a minute of Jard showing her and taking her on the two journeys, she could travel by herself. None of the other children could. The ability of a person to control their age seemed to be a key to them being able to make the jumps. Belden was calling it a simultaneity jump, and within a few days that was the label they were giving it.

It took several weeks before they also learned the distance they could travel was directly related to the amount of practice they undertook. Within a month Jard could reach the coast, and at the end of another month he could reach their original villages. It was only a matter of time before all of them could do this, and the next step was clearly... could Jard visit Jeland? Within another week the answer was, yes, he could! Simultaneity could now be added to the range of behaviors in the panoply of telepathic life. During the first months of this new behavior, Jard, Leiti and Karina could see that a part of their brain previously dormant had now been activated.

CHAPTER 53

Cretians & Olarians, Back Again

At the very midpoint of the winter of their twenty-fourth year, during an evening exploration session around plans to extend the settlement the following summer, the group was suddenly interrupted by an alarm. The entire perimeter around the settlement was walled for the winter, and every wall was set up with energy alarms that triggered a warning to the Council of Eight. The group immediately followed the warning.

Outside the wall, 16 fully armed warriors clad for winter had thrown a hook over the wall to which was attached a rope ladder, and the first was preparing to climb it.

Jard, Pron and Enta lifted one of the piles of stones placed strategically around the perimeter and rained them down on the would-be intruders. Several were injured but not very seriously, and the intruders withdrew.

The next day the Council of Eight increased the walls to six people high and another foot into the ground.

Pron and Repin tracked the attackers back to their village. It was one of the villages now partly Cretian, partly Olarian. The raiders sent parties to several other Olarian settlements. It was clear that a concerted campaign against the telepaths was being mounted.

There was a sense of déjà vu. Were they to now return to the days of the Cretian threat, only now, the threat was from some of their own?

When they met to discuss the issue, Karina was beside herself.

We have only recently finished the most horrific war with a nation of insensitive, brutal savages. We have begun to expand our world and our activities. We have found ourselves in possession of some amazing new abilities. Now we are again confronted with people who are afraid of us, envious of us or just plain opposed to us. Some of them our own kin, although not ones we have ever known.

As a result of years of study and learning we seem to have found a part of the very process of life. We very well may be able to live forever, a thought some of us are still struggling to consider. Now, will we have to abandon or change our life again in order to exist on the same continent as our own ancestors?

It sounded like a question, it felt like a statement, and it was experienced by the Eight and most of the young adult children as an expression of utter exasperation.

We will never be able to keep our outside projects going if we have to be fighting these war parties off, constantly surveying the areas around each piece of work for possible hostiles, and either defending each project area or retreating to our valley every time they come. We simply don't have the resources. We would have to build masses of energy walls everywhere we wanted to work.

Pron was frustrated and Dornal was clearly supporting him.

The group was not divided, but it was frustrated and felt blocked.

Jard added his thoughts to the mix. *There seems to me to be several interconnected problems here. If we do nothing, we will have great difficulty in expanding our liveable land and we must do this to be able to survive and allow our little community to grow. We still have to feed everyone, especially through the winter. If we do not grow in numbers, eventually our hostile neighbors will be so numerous we may be trapped, defeated or have to kill many of them.*

We already know how traumatic that was, even with the Cretians, with whom we had no ties. I believe we are all agreed we do not want to have to kill them all; this would be a horrible and wrong thing on which to build a decent moral life. But we cannot do nothing, so we need another solution.

There was agreement with his logic, but that was not enough to deal with the problem.

Tentatively Leiti put forward a possible alternative.

Suppose we were to find one village that was willing to join with us, who would negotiate with us for a life without fighting and hostilities, in return for which we could offer to help them with solutions to some of their problems. If we were successful with them, we might be able to expand this arrangement to slowly involve the other villages.

Well, Enita said, *I think that is a great idea, however, there are not many of us. If we were obligated to help even a small village, say one of only a couple of hundred people, how would we be able to do that and still manage our own lives? And what would happen if some of the Cretian-controlled villages continue to wish to destroy us? Do we have the resources to deal with that?*

After only a short discussion it was obvious the community was still too small to manage such an agreement, even if the services they might be able to provide like health and hunting or even building dwellings was all that was involved. In addition, no-one could imagine how such a proposal could be made to sound acceptable to any village they knew.

It was becoming clearer a solution of a different kind was going to be needed. Negotiating with either one or several village groups was not going to work. What was now a worsening situation was made worse by the fact that the Cretians had infiltrated villages on the east coast that had not been involved with any hostilities against the telepathic community.

Jard was frustrated. *If we are not going to try to negotiate, and I happen to believe that would not be possible given our experience, then what kind of non-negotiated positions remain open to us?*

There were simply not enough of them yet to be able to keep the projects going and defend the Valley. The total telepathic community was still only 140 men, women and children. It was no easy task to have to keep protecting themselves from the unrelenting hostility from outside. It seemed certain that as things stood, they would be spending another summer protecting themselves from people who seemed to have nothing better to do than fight with them, essentially attempting to destroy them.

Pron and Dornal were seriously arguing for dealing with each war party by destroying them. They argued it was a fair and just behavior. They came to kill and harm, they would die and be cremated. Maybe, they argued, that would eventually put an end to this behavior.

Daria and Leiti disagreed. They argued that, as there were very considerably more outsiders than telepaths, it would mean years of defense and violence without any solution necessarily resulting. In addition, they argued, this process would slowly build up a warrior culture among themselves and that was surely the last thing they would want to do. With that there was absolutely no disagreement. The discussion continued for days. It was clear that some solution was needed, but what?

Repin was unhappy with the idea of fighting their own relatives and no-one really disagreed with him, however, these war parties were often a Cretian/Olarian affair. They had not had these problems with their own people before the Cretians had been trapped on Olarian territory. So this problem was essentially contributed to by their defeat and the sealing off of Cretia. In a manner of speaking, the carelessness of the telepathic community in allowing the 30-odd Cretians to take over Olarian villages was itself an aspect of the problem.

There were four more attempts to breach Tall Trees Valley before the winter was over, and another two attempts, with increasing numbers, over the summer. The community could not safely pursue many of its routine activities, at least not without endless military-like checks on the territory for many miles around where they wanted to hunt, gather plants or pursue other activities. The children had to be constantly supervised, and by the following winter the Valley had become a fortress. This was bad enough; no lives were lost or even put at risk through the diligent surveillance the community had established.

By the beginning of the next winter, Jard and Leiti had been able to safely inform the community that so far as they could tell, none of the Eight had in fact aged over the past year. As well, all of the Eight had been able to maintain the fixed age with no extra activity on their part. Once the tiny strand that modified the cells was given new instructions, it had entirely ceased to send change instructions to the other body cells, all of which continued to be rejuvenated. In other words, aging had, for all practical purposes, apparently ceased. And Jard and Leiti were feeling better than they could remember. The same was true for the others. Cells now replicated without flaws and this appeared to be improving everyone's health! They imagined, if this continued, they might live on for an unknown period, fixed at the age they had first interfered with the energy pattern of the strand. This was the simplified explanation of the years of work they had put into their project.

We all knew when we made the adjustment for us it was not unlikely we might all live forever! Jard said. *But we still don't have answers to the questions this raises.*

The group was hushed, everyone trying to imagine what this might mean. What did you do forever? Then the questions began again, including some new ones that had not come up the first time the group had discussed their novel situation.

Enita aired some pressing issues: *How do we manage how many children we should have? And for how much of our lives will we be able to have children? How old might we be when we should definitely stop?*

Daria wondered, *How many children can we have? Would our women want to go on having children when they are 100?*

Several of the women, especially the younger women, were horrified by the thought. The questions continued through that first night.

It was as if Jard and Leiti's experiment had opened up so great a can of worms it would take all the time in the world to answer. Yet this was only the beginning. Jard and Leiti were faced with one question they could not answer: where did this infinitesimally tiny energy strand originate in the brain, if that was where it originated, and what exactly was it?

Karina answered it out loud so everyone would understand. They simply did not know. Every attempt to locate the source from which it emerged to influence the cells led nowhere.

One night in his frustration at being unable to answer the question after all their explorations, Jard exclaimed, *The Seeders do not seem to want us to know yet!*

There was a somewhat stunned silence.

What do you mean? Enita asked.

Karina smiled. *Can I?*

Jard nodded. He was smiling his enigmatic smile.

I'm surprised none of you picked it up when he first came up with it. Jard has an idea, a seriously weird idea, but in the absence of any real information and in his hostility to the idea of gods, he proposes that Olarians and Cretians are the creation of a super race or species. They somehow travel the cosmos, seeding some places with life. He calls them the Seeders. And he thinks the Seeders must not have wanted us to find out about our extra abilities unless we had become smart enough!

There were several chuckles and raised eyebrows, but the idea somehow stuck. The group had never been able to get anywhere with the subject of who had created them, where had they come from, yet they did want something in which to believe, so it was this somewhat way-out notion that took hold. It got a toehold in the community that winter and stuck. It obliterated the need for a god or gods, and it satisfied the desire to have some seemingly reasonable explanation for their existence. 'Seeders'!

As the winter came to an end, decisions had still not been finalized about everyone managing their aging. That needed to be sorted, as the idea was still disturbing the community in numerous ways. Then, within a few days of winter's end, an event occurred that again cast them into the role of defensive survival. Four villages of Olarians attacked the settlement simultaneously. Fortunately the Council of Eight had organized a routine area survey for about 100 miles from any group. They did this each day. They had seen the attackers making for the Tall Trees Valley settlement and were pleased to observe that the attackers had not been prepared for the higher walls.

Two groups from the community, however, had already left the protected areas to hunt and one group with children had gone adventuring. Another group of Cretian/Olarian warriors came in behind the hunters. Two of the Eight fought a short and decisive engagement with the 20 marauders and left them with dead and wounded without harm to the telepaths' party. The children's group was not so fortunate. By the time the Elders got to deal with the marauders, one child had been seriously injured and another killed, and one of the two 17-year-old carers had been hurt. The marauders were all killed.

The injured were taken care of quickly and a funeral was arranged for the child who had been killed. The council were no longer in a mood to accept these vicious punitive expeditions against the community.

Jard was a great deal more than frustrated. *No sooner do we rid ourselves of the Cretian menace than their remnant visit massive destruction and unpleasantness on our old villages. They pervert the lives of the rest of our earliest families to create further disruption to our lives. They stop us from living in peace.*

Jard's next suggestion chilled the council and the rest of the community listening in.

It is unacceptable that we must live in a walled fortress and be constantly on guard against some of our own kinsmen who want to kill and destroy us. So I have a plan to put an end to this forever. In a year or two all of us will probably be living much longer lives, perhaps forever, we don't know. But what we do know is that we do not want to be living with this. So I want to put an end to the non-telepathic Olarians once and for all. This means our own families, so what I am about to suggest can only even be considered with total support. If even one member among us does not want to pursue this course of action, we should not proceed.

There were some raised eyebrows. He had their full attention.

Several years ago we tried to have discussions with them, including some of our own relatives. We spent several days having discussions about ways we could coexist amicably. These discussions, I am certain, no one has forgotten. They were very disturbing and unsatisfactory. Finally, you will recall we were told they wanted nothing to do with us, ever, under any circumstances – essentially to stay away from them. We were, their god had told them, an abomination. If they had really meant that we should stay away, they could have simply left us alone, but they clearly have not.

The influence of the Cretians has now spread to nearly every settlement we observe. The hatred of us has spread. I want to destroy them totally, every last one. But I have had enough violence and killing for my entire life. I really want to put an end to the need for such unpleasantness, such primitive and unthinking behavior.

I know I am not alone in wanting no more violence and killing. I know I am not alone in still having nightmares about our final battle with the Cretians. However, they can now live their lives without bringing their savagery to us. But yet they seem to have still managed to bring their disgusting ways to our own families. If I was a superstitious man I would say we were being tested.

He paused, settled himself down, and turned first to the other seven originals.

The rest of our community can have their say. But these include our relatives and families from the past. So each needs to speak all their thoughts and feelings about this issue before we invite the next generations to join our discussion. I am proposing we end the existence of these communities by terminating their ability to reproduce.

Although everyone was at their wit's end, the idea of genocide of their own kin was horrendous. There was a stillness across their little world.

The discussion that raged for a week was often heated but always acknowledged the need for an end to the hostilities. Finally, when every alternative they could conjure had been explored, the council acknowledged that Jard's proposal had merit and could be managed without any further loss of life.

Jard said, *We are not able to live in harmony with our own ancestors. Not because we are not willing but because the Cretians have taken control of their lives. If we systematically sterilize the men in every village community, in 40 or 50 years they will all be gone.*

The response was primarily incredulity, then for most, horror.

However, Jard was clear. *I don't like ending the lives of our own people. It feels really bad, no matter what they are doing. But I want to put an end to our own deaths. I want us to sterilize them! We know how and we have the capacity. Then, over the years, as they die out, we will look after them. It is a long-term solution, but we have a long time. We will kill no more, but we will allow no more killing of our own people. We will simply allow them to die out!*

It was a breathtakingly self-centered and destructive proposal. But the community had just buried another of their children, killed violently for no reason; were presently repairing another who had been seriously injured, and were still repairing other wounds and dealing with some very disturbed and frightened children. The entire community was being asked to remain within the walled valley, and everyone over the age of 14 was told of the council's intentions and asked for their response.

For the entire spring the group talked of almost nothing else. However, Jard was really intent on making the decision. While the community was engaging in the debate, several more attempts were made to breach their defenses. Every project they had been engaged in for the past 20 years outside the defended valley was damaged by one or other of the Olarian villages. This included villages that had been the birthplace of the Eight.

It was this final act of unremitting destructiveness and the absolute refusal of any of the village communities to have any engagement with the telepaths, except with the intention to kill, that swung the opinion of the majority. However, it was still not until every person of age had agreed that the council made their decision. They decided to begin immediately.

For the next six weeks two of the eight Elders visited every community and sterilized every male.

The marauding parties did not stop attempting to breach the defenses, which had to be strengthened continuously as ever more ingenious attacks were mounted. However, no further breaches of the wall occurred, and as the years passed, two events focused the telepathic community's attention.

The telepaths decided to minimize the number of children they would bear during the first 10 years of the ending of the Olarian communities. No-one quite knew why they had made this decision, but it stuck. In part it had to do with the amount of protection needed to get plants and animals for their larder, but in part it was a kind of acknowledging ritual connected to the decision they had made.

The other event was the final agreement of the Eight to change the status of the aging cell process for everyone over 38. The Eight had already made the adjustment, however, from now on, every adult approaching 38 would be offered this option.

It was more than 20 years before the attempts to attack the telepaths finally ended. Then it again became possible for the community to venture outside the walls of the Valley to reinstate projects. This included their dams. They were again able to look at allowing couples to build dwellings outside the Valley. Constant vigilance was still needed, but the effect of the birth rates dropping to zero was having a huge and quite disturbing impact on the life of the village communities.

The next stage of the plan was made possible by the developing simultaneity of the older members of the community. It was at this point that the telepathic community began to set up regular visits to each of the original villages, checking on health, and ensuring food was being grown or hunted. If it was not, the group would find ways to help. Help not always wanted or appreciated and sometimes not accepted by the aging communities.

The communities were dying out quickly under the impact of no new children. Finally it was deemed safe to remove the defensive walls around the settlement and the telepaths expanded across the country.

The still-beautiful 38-year-old Leiti had been born around 60 years ago. One evening as she and Jard lay in bed she said, *You realize, Jard, we will and yet will not really ever understand what it is like to grow old and deteriorate physically and mentally together. I am not sure still about how our brains are going to manage some of the transitions we will need to make. What we will never understand fully is the sense of deterioration and increasing dysfunction that seems to have been the way of everyone before us.*

Our children will probably never get it at all. But I believe we will replace that experience with one that may be even more difficult to confront. We must find meaning and purpose for our long lives, have things to do and things to learn that will make our existence meaningful.

He looked at her. *Yes,* he thought, *I really could look at you forever.*

The question was, how long would this forever really be?

CHAPTER 54

Djia, the Death of the Last Original

It was the winter following what they believed was the death of the last of the Old Olarians. Day one drew to a close. There were around 200 members of the telepathic community still living in Tall Trees Valley in the Big Houses. The emotional health of the community was not good. Success had not brought satisfaction. It seemed to have brought a pall that hung over the telepathic Olarian world, and not just Tall Trees Valley.

During the long years while life in the Old Villages was coming to an end, life for the new community seemed to stagnate. The birth rate had dropped to around 50 children a year and the entire population was only a few thousand. The winter discussions were desultory and the major projects were renewed but not expanded. With the withering of the Old Villages, the new telepaths were only marking time. It felt as though this society had been dying with the Old Olarians, as though it would not recover from its horrendous endeavors to ensure its survival!

◘

Djia and Grah were both in their mid-twenties. They had moved only two weeks ago with several other families to a new community on a promontory running from east to west on the southern coastal strip. There were 18 members of the little community, invited there by other young couples to whom they were related and with whom they had grown up.

They had not yet explored a great deal of the surrounding countryside. It was early autumn, and with two other couples, Djia and Grah decided to explore northward along the west coast, looking to extend their winter vegetable and meat supplies. Like most of their friends, they only occasionally spoke out loud.

Djia wanted to get moving and stirred up the other three.

Move it, you lot. We want to cover some reasonable distance today.

The others moved along. They were a hunting and exploring party. They had no weapons, no sleeping gear, no extra clothing. Each couple carried a small pack of supplies mainly for flavoring food, assorted eating implements and containers that had been unnecessarily fashioned from wood but often preferred by their generation, and water carriers. This generation was almost entirely energy dependent.

Within an hour of leaving their new communal site, they became aware they were approaching what appeared to be a village of the Originals. In their lifetime, none of the six had ever met any of their ancestors. They believed all were now dead and no-one had warned them of the existence of any remnant villages near their new communal home. Originals tended to live into their fifties, rarely beyond 60, and it was impossible for any alive to be less than in their late fifties.

It was indeed the remains of an ancient small village. One hut still stood, made of timber with a thatched roof. The three couples stopped some distance from the site. They sat together and without further discussion focused on the hut and the inhabitants within.

Two elderly men were sitting in a partially open room with three solid walls and a fourth wall that was demountable. The room appeared to be a cooking and eating place. A fire was burning in the cooking space. In the other large room were two couples. They were sleeping on beds constructed using a wooden skeleton covered with the same thatch material as the roof, over which were stretched skins. Softer well-worked skins covered them. The two men were talking and the telepaths listened in.

It had been decided that Djia, who was telepathically the most powerful of the six, would go into the village alone. The others would watch over her. The six knew the Originals were not keen to associate with the telepathic community. The group felt it was wisest and safest to let Djia have her way, only partly because she was the most sophisticated linguist among them. They also knew it would have been extremely foolhardy for any of them to try to talk her out of it once her mind was made up.

When Djia returned, she sat with Grah and he held her while she cried, tears streaming down her face, distress, anger, sadness and horror each taking their turn. There seemed to be no end to her tears. She looked at the others, confused and uncomprehending. She said, *How could we have done this?* But they had no answers.

When they visited the old Olarians at the end of winter it was to find them all dead, frozen in their hut. There was evidence of clear intent. Plenty of firewood remained, the additional food the young telepaths had delivered for them was uneaten. It seemed clear they had simply given up.

◘

On the first night of winter, an insistent request made by a young community taking its first winter in a new settlement away from Tall Trees Valley was the very first item for discussion.

A young woman by the name of Djia wanted the attention of the Eight. No-one had had any contact with her since she had left. Such occurrences were not uncommon at this time, so no-one thought it particularly strange. Her request was clearly from a very upset young woman.

Karina, to whom she was most closely related, asked her why.

Djia was overawed but unhesitant.

When we first came here in the autumn, we found, quite by accident, six of the Originals in a badly deteriorated hut, old, two of them unwell, poorly prepared for the winter during which they would surely have died. My generation was not born when it was decided to sterilize the entire male population of the Originals. None of my generation has ever been threatened by these poor old people.

Their appearance brings up a feeling that the very core values we have been taught to live by have been violated when we allow these people to be in the conditions in which we found them. They had no young people to care for them, their healer and their spirit leader had died several years ago, and there was no-one to take their place.

It felt just horrible. Surely it shames us and disgraces us, when we have been taught to show concern for the life of all things, especially people, yet these people who were our kin have been left in this awful condition by our acts.

These six people were all that remained of their village. Many apparently took their own lives rather than continue in their deteriorating state when they could not produce children. Many believed their gods were punishing them and they simply ceased to be involved in the life of their village. They stopped planting crops while others stopped hunting. Apparently, they never herded grazers. It was horrible to hear the stories and to know that we as a community were responsible.

I felt helpless as I listened to their tale of slow death and their desperate attempts to understand why their gods had deserted them and made their women barren. They did not know our people had been the cause, and worse, they blamed the women. They seemed at first pitifully grateful for our interest and our offers to help them, but rejected them nevertheless. We left feeling disgusted with ourselves, our community, our behavior, and this when we were only trying to help.

We desperately need to hear what you have to say to us. And, Great Mother Karina, I apologize if this seems disrespectful, but we have been very distressed by what we found. Perhaps I should add that, although we looked in on them during the winter to ensure they were all right, and indeed they did seem to be, when we returned at the end of the winter they were all dead. The fires had clearly not been lit for several weeks and their food supply was rotten.

A deep hush fell over the Eight and the listening community.

Jard said, *Djia, I really do not know right now how to respond appropriately to all that you have said and to the depth of feeling you have expressed. However, you have my assurance we will find a proper and appropriate response. Thank you for what you did and for bringing this to us.*

In response to your hurt, anger and distress, I and the other members of the Eight would like to offer you a journey back to the time when we made the decision to sterilize the entire population of Olaria. You would perhaps be better able to appreciate our decision were you fully cognizant of our circumstances at that time. Would you and your community be up for that?

A long silence followed Jard's invitation, then, one by one the entire community, not just Djia's but from every corner of their land, agreed. Their respect for the Eight was great enough to enable them to restrain their distress. The Eight replayed for them the month prior to the decision: the death of another child, their review of the endless and pointless savage harassment by their ancestor communities. They then replayed the discussions that resulted in 100 percent of the living telepathic community over 16 affirming their choice.

A deep and singularly disturbing silence followed the historical review of the circumstances of the lives of the telepathic world prior to the sterilization of the entire male community of the non-telepathic world. The silence extended over several minutes before Djia murmured quietly to the Eight her apologies. None of their community had ever enquired about or been told or shown the events leading up to the still horrendous decision.

This information dramatically impacted the entire youthful world of the telepaths. It changed the perspective with which they were viewing the recent events. Some of their implied criticism and concerns were noted, but it was made clear that repeated attempts to be of help had been made but had been brushed aside or even violently rejected.

Jard was clear that this did not absolve them from responsibility for the situation of the distressed and dying ancestors, however, he wished it understood nothing that Djia had described was unknown to them and they were not seeking to be making excuses for what the group had found.

Djia acknowledged that knowing the background circumstances made what they had experienced easier to understand and at some level accept.

CHAPTER 55

The Recreation of the New World

The Big House was still the center of their world. This was the evening of the first day of winter. Enita stood up and said out loud in their now common language, 'I need every one of us—' she was referring to the Original Eight '—to join me in our old room, to close the door, and ask the rest of our world to give us time with no interruptions!' She had everyone's attention. She was clearly determined. She had the right and the Council of Eight agreed without hesitation and the community, feeling the intensity in her demeanor, respectfully agreed to leave the Eight alone.

They sat in their accustomed places, then Enita 'closed the door' for only the second time in their history. The extraordinary gesture resulted in disturbed expressions. Enita spoke out loud and directly into their minds.

You all know how the first years of my life were spent. If I had not escaped and found you, I would right now have been dead a very long time. I would certainly not be looking at a future streaming into unimaginable time. I truly know the experience of being constantly depressed and in pain. I have been feeling, and watching us become as a group, and as a society, seriously depressed.

We, who have blessings no other creatures on this planet have probably ever imagined. We have just recently undertaken the destruction of the entire society that spawned us. We are now soul weary, appalled with our actions. We seem to have pretty well given up! I know some of you may feel I have no right to say this, but we are behaving inexcusably badly.

We made the decision to survive and thrive, and for this to happen we all agreed on the course of action we took. There was no dissent in the end. We chose life, for ourselves and our children. It was an appalling decision but it was our decision. So, unless we are choosing to have allowed our ancestors to perish for no purpose, we must get our heads out of the dark places to which we have taken them and move on. We have no right to have ended their world if we had no intention of building a better, healthier, sounder society. No right at all.

You taught me about everyone saying what they needed to say in order to end emotional crises. You showed me how to do the unthinkable, the almost unbelievable, to have babies with all the men and make it healthy and wholesome.

You helped me become someone who I could never have conceived. So now you have to stop this deathly behavior. You have to help me – help us – move on. We have generations of children for whom we alone have responsibilities. We need to pick ourselves up now and do something about them.

She sat down, and a deep silence settled in the room. Everyone knew Enita was right. The absolute quiet from the entire Olarian world, as it now was, seeped out into the frozen air of their world. Their room felt cold despite the heating.

Jard finally spoke.

Thank you, Enita. This is not the first time you have called our attention to the consequences of our actions. Ones we have not foreseen as clearly as we might. I feel as though I foisted the solution on you all. I feel shaken to my very core at what, in retrospect, has felt like an unspeakably morally wrong decision. I feel as though I persuaded you to help me destroy our childhood world. I know as I say it how arrogant and inappropriate that sounds, but I still feel it with every fibre of my being. In my heart I know they were never going to let us alone. But of course I can't really know that at all. And our solution ended any possibility I would ever be proven wrong.

One by one they spoke. One by one they unburdened themselves. One by one they claimed the guilt. The alternatives they might have tried were aired again and again, never without the unshakeable realization they had to live with their decision and slowly come to realize that nothing from the past could be undone except their response to it, their attitude toward it.

The past needed reconstructing and it needed responsibility for the reconstruction to be owned by them all. They came slowly to feel they had no right to damage the lives of their children through their own guilt. The thought arose from the Eight simultaneously: 'Should we end our own lives? We did this thing and it is our responsibility alone'.

From every dwelling on the Olarian world came back a reply, one leaving no room for any doubt. Thousands of voices shouted, *No, you have no right!*

They sat there, tears streaming down every face.

Then came a single voice, one of their first children. *You made a decision for life for all of us. You have an obligation to fulfill it for all of us, your children!*

The Eight were shaken to their core, first by their renewed awareness of the consequences of the decision they had made in the interests of the continued survival of their new society, and also by the reminder of the consequences for their ancestors.

One at a time each of the four couples climbed to their feet and left the room without a sound, without looking at one another and without a single conscious thought. It seemed that the planet held its breath all that night and all the next day and the next night. The following day, as if by unspoken agreement, they all came to the original Big House for breakfast.

After which, with snow falling steadily outside, they sat together again, this time knowing they had to find a way to move on. This winter they were not going to be alone. Every descendant of the Originals was listening in.

It was again Enita who took the lead.

I am deeply saddened, not only by what we have done, what we are clearly and fully responsible for doing, but also I am saddened because we did not know better what we might have done. So we have lost the opportunity to learn to live with others, others who are significantly different from us but who were nevertheless substantially family.

In my heart I feel we were wrong. Nevertheless, I supported what we did and Djia's words have left me feeling enormously guilty but certain it is our responsibility to find a right way to put it behind us. Because we cannot undo it. And, although I believe what we did was just plain wrong, right here and now I do not know of any other way we could have acted to take care of our children and ourselves. But we cannot afford to indulge ourselves, beating our breasts over it.

I know that ending my life was foremost on my mind when you found me. Well, continuing with my life is now foremost on my mind as I sit here with Dornal, who I adore, and with you, all of whom I love and cherish. That is also how I feel about you, our children, who even now are listening in on us, hoping we will shake the lethargy we have allowed the consequences of this event to throw over us.

One at a time the other three women spoke, supporting everything Enita had said, and made a commitment to put aside their angst. All admitted to having agreed to a proposition they had felt to be wrong but against which they had been unwilling to fight. The violence against their children had swayed them. They all agreed, even now, they were not certain the effects of the Cretians on their ancestors could have been undone, but felt there might have been a way and perhaps they should have tried.

Jard finally spoke. *I will no longer trawl over ground I have revisited every day for the last 50 years of my life if we are actually going to live forever!*

Jard could hardly believe he was saying the words.

We have to think differently about our lives and our future. We have to really extend our thinking about how to educate ourselves and our children. We have to find new and compelling reasons for our lives. Not short term or limited in any way. I do not expect we will do this with any speed. It may take us years, but we do need to make a start and continue working on these issues if we are not to be victims of our own cleverness and be trapped by our own limitations. If we fail to do this, I know our civilization will become shallow and we will damage ourselves.

It was not the kind of observation about which he was going to get any disagreement or procure any quick and easy solutions.

The other men spoke. It was always about the same thing. The energy telepaths must create a society in which learning to make optimal decisions and find optimal solutions was a primary responsibility of all. It had always been clear they needed to organize the education of their children. Now they felt an unshakeable commitment to their learning.

If they were going to move on, it would be because they were determined to use it as a guide to each decision they would need to make. How do you plan for an endless future? Years of intense and seemingly endless discussions had only ever turned up with one single answer about which there had been no disagreement. You learn.

◘

After more than 110 years, the still 38-year-old Enita informed the world that she and Dornal were planning another baby to be born in the summer. With the idea sown, each of the couples decided to join in. A new baby, a new life and a renewed commitment to life. And so a decision was made, and plans needed to be made for the future of their world.

An earlier decision had been made to remove the walls from around their dwellings. A warning system designed to discourage predators around the vegetable patches, crops and grazing herds was all that remained. Plans were laid for several habitable spaces to be created along the coastline and a fishing tradition be established to help extend their food resources.

Immediately these were done, the idea was floated to form working groups to study and expand the community's knowledge. This was closely followed by how what was learned could be saved and made available to anyone who wanted it. Project groups were formed and learning and working together became the focus. Olarians from every corner of their small world became engaged with the ideas and plans that were growing from the rejuvenated center of their world.

Winter was still the time they settled down to talk. However, as the knowledge, power and ever-extending capabilities of the community continued to grow, so did their ability to continue their special-interest explorations, weather conditions notwithstanding.

In the midst of one of the conversations about learning, 14-year-old Gelna asked, *If being eight worked so well for you, and as our Council of Eight is how we organize ourselves, would it not be helpful if we organized our learning in groups of eight: four girls and four boys?*

With that enquiry from one of their children an idea was born.

The Eight and many others joined in polishing and extending the idea. Eight was their number.

Jard and Leiti knew Gelna well. She lived in the Big House with her parents. Gelna's idea grew wings. Before the first month of winter was out, eight children and two adults became the signature model for learning groups of children. Then it was decided to make four of these groups an entity.

Next the discussion spread to the working groups. There were many of them. Some groups had been undertaking tasks and others had been studying energy activities. This winter the discussion took them in another direction. The activity groups and the studying groups linked up according to their particular shared area of interest. The community was seeking different ways to keep the balance between work and learning.

The fishing group was the first to take up the thread. They were interested in catching fish but wanted different and more efficient ways to do it. They also wanted to understand how fish life was organized and whether the fish were healthy. They set up several groups with four fishers and four learners. This trend began to spread during the winter, first to water and weather, then to herding food animals, to growing crops and vegetables, and then to travel and the nature of their world. And so it went on.

A map was set up. It was going to grow because it stimulated them and offered a healthy way to develop. The other new thing that was discussed all winter that year was how to preserve what they were learning. One of Karina's great-granddaughters began to assemble a knowledge storage group. They called themselves the Knowledge Holders. They began to think about how to put ideas together. They knew that this was an exploration into the very nature of their minds and how they could be managed, especially the conscious and unconscious connections and the patterning of their activity, so far minimally understood.

Before the following winter the Council of Eight were approached by one of their children who, while maintaining her 38-year-old appearance, was in her eightieth year. She proposed that each of the Eight somehow take responsibility for one or more of the working/learning groups. She suggested that each assemble an organized group of eight to support them and work together to be a kind of oversized village council. It took no more than a few weeks for this proposal to gather the support it needed from the Eight to enable it to move forward.

Then one day before the end of that winter 72 people sat in the biggest meeting room and the Administration Unit came into existence. They sat together, the snow falling gently outside so the whole of the landscape looked like fairyland and the only thing visible of the huge trees was the outline, long crystals of ice hanging below their branches. It was a wonderland they never tired of watching, as had every generation of children looking out on the breathtaking scene. Outside the Big House, no more defensive fences stood in the landscape and the world was tranquil.

Dinner over, Jard and Leiti, sitting side by side, invited the children on a snowland adventure. They had started this extraordinary journey when the need had been great. Over the past decades they had expanded it, made possible by Jard's extraordinary power. He took about 20 children aged six to 14 on his tour. As usual, before he began, over 100 young voices asked to go along, children from many miles away. He never turned anyone away; he picked them up as the journey began. He knew every valley, every crag, every tree and stream of their world. He connected all those who wanted to come to his mind and set off on his journey.

They visited his favorite places, saw streams and huge white animals, small furry ones and the sly and cunning predators of the winter creeping through the mountains. Then he took them through the valleys and down onto the coast, up past his old home, and to the place where he and Leiti and Repin and Daria had met. As he traveled he told them the story, which most had heard before but always wanted to hear again.

Finally he brought them home over crags and rocky country over which no Olarian had ever walked. It was a wonderful journey, and as he brought them back into the big sitting room, leaving others to return to their homes, they smiled and thanked him. Those in the Big House got up from all the places they had been sitting and lying around and headed off to other parts of the of the now gigantic living place that was the Big House. It now comprised many houses.

The Eight now met with an audience of 64 who made it their task to pass on the discussions of the Eight. Anyone could listen in, but their questions and opinions were now passed through the 64. It had taken nearly 10 years to sort through ways to make this work and it would continue to be an openly explored process.

The Eight wanted to talk about the issues that impacted on their world, and right now it was the community's underlying value system, their beliefs and, still, the Seeders. And so it seemed a new life had opened up for this unusual little community. Enita's voice had not gone unheard.

◘

It was the middle of the night near the end of winter. Jard sat up in bed fully awake and said, *Of course.*

What he saw with more clarity than at any time during this extraordinary and productive winter was simple. Everything depended on there being shared knowledge and shared values that would permeate every aspect of all their lives.

There must be no future occasions when a group like Djia's would be isolated. In the morning he contacted Djia and asked, *Will you and your community consider becoming responsible for ensuring that the values and the information known, learned and held in our world is never again lost to any member of our world? That no members of our telepathic community will ever be in the position in which you found yourselves? Connect yourselves to the Knowledge Holders?*

Djia simply said, *Yes, absolutely, and thank you.*

CHAPTER 56

What Do You Do for Eternity?

Everyone knew Enita had probably been the recipient of the most consistent antisocial behavior of any of the Eight. She was clear that she wanted to ensure her childhood experiences would never be a part of this new society.

She was adamant any issues had to be managed out in the open and involving every member of their world. She wanted to be certain the community could ensure everyone would begin life being safe and without any uncertainty that they would, short of uncontrollable circumstances, remain safe. She knew that most of the old communities, as well as the Cretians, used conflict as a way to stimulate action. She also believed this was not an essential aspect of life and that it should not be an aspect of their new lives.

Okay, she said, *let me start with deviance. Let me try to focus on what is concerning me. Some antisocial behavior that hurts someone or is uncontrolled and inappropriate cannot go unmanaged as it did in our parents' world. Things such as anger, jealousy, frustration, shame, severe confusion, feelings of gross inadequacy, envy, wanting something someone else has, desiring power or control over others or a particular project, wanting to hurt someone by damaging something of theirs that they treasure, perhaps going so far as to kill another.*

Enita was on a roll. Jard and the Eight were thinking about all the behaviors they had experienced in their villages, ones that had been considered punishable because they were not allowed, wrong, bad, harmful to the even flow of life in the village. Usually sanctioned or prohibited by the gods, which they all now agreed seemed to be a duplicitous and dishonest idea. They were also realizing that in all probability none of these experiences or this knowledge would ever be part of the world of their children. They wanted to ensure that resolving disputes by violence was unacceptable in this new society.

But what was the appropriate way to deal with any antisocial behaviors?

In their villages several very unpleasant methods had been used: flogging, isolating physically or socially or both, spearing or beating to death, and a number of such unpleasant, painful behaviors.

Almost always these had been based on the very strong punitive, power-based emotions of a single individual or collection of individuals. These had usually been men whose sense of themselves was twisted and inconsistent. None of the Eight had examples of healthy men meting out these punishments. There had been occasions when infidelities, winkled out by one or other member of a couple, had led to both men and women demanding violent and nasty retributive punishments, usually to make them feel a score had been settled, or perhaps to act to discourage themselves and others from following this course!

Enita continued.

We seem to have an edge that ought to make such antisocial behaviors less likely to occur here. Firstly, among the eight of us we can know, accurately, what everyone is thinking and feeling. This will be more difficult in our expanding community.

We must establish, and live, values that enhance life, eschew any violence, develop sound, open and healthy behaviors that we will all experience and explore. In our original villages, they had no idea how to do this. They knew nothing of how others were thinking or feeling; we do. We have the capacity to know. We can use our knowledge and abilities properly, by which I mean sensitively and helpfully.

While there were eight of us we managed well. Now when there are so many of us, this is only a little more difficult but not if we grow up with our eight.

Well, if we ask Djia and her group to accept the task of thinking through how to help each group of eight experience and learn fully the values we desire, maybe none of the disgusting experiences of some of our pasts will ever need to arise.

Suppose that we take ourselves as the basic case. We all are constantly a little curious about each other, about our sexual relationships and how we share aspects of our lives together and how we explore and change and add to and work to develop them. So although we all know a great deal about each other we are still curious when one of us thinks about or tries something new. None of us could really hide from the others – the only possible exception to that is you, Jard, because your energy is so strong you might be able to deceive us, at least for a short period.

Jard was about to lurch into a defense of himself when Leiti smiled into his mind and everyone in the group laughed. Jard smiled.

Well? Daria said. *Remember how Leiti believed that if she let you control her she would have stronger orgasms? You haven't forgotten that night, have you? We were all watching and listening and you tried to screen us all out because you thought it was wrong or bad or some stupid thing. You were concerned that we would think you were enjoying restraining her, but what you did was actually more than all right because being explicitly controlled was actually what she wanted. And you both knew that she could, at any time, cease being restrained. She was allowing you to restrain her for her own ends!*

Jard was embarrassed. *I found it very hard to think it was okay to restrain her, although I knew she could always escape.*

Yes, but you had a hunch that you would enjoy it if that was actually what she wanted you to do, and you knew that most men have forever wanted control of their women in some way, and you and Leiti have slid up to that barrier several times. All of us women have occasionally wanted to allow ourselves to be controlled/restrained if our man wants to control us and ensure we are safe and fully cared for.

I believe many women who have not been around male violence want those things. Surrender to someone who wants to take control of and care for you can be wonderfully fulfilling. We all know it. Then she asked you to take control so that her pleasure would be greater and you agreed, trying all the while to keep us out, unsuccessfully, though you nearly succeeded. You have to remember the talk between you. She said you had to want to control her and get pleasure from it or it would not work. You did eventually find that place and went there.

The pleasure the two of you got from that experiment has enabled all of us to try new things that balance pleasure and control in ways that have enhanced our sexual experiences immeasurably and that worked because there was love and desire to please and not the other seemingly distasteful feelings.

We learned how much it is about control of our lives. We realized that if the men who wanted control took it and guaranteed always to consider the needs of their woman, that relationship would be healthy and would work. True? And then, the biggest surprise of all was when we asked the four of you to be willing to try it in reverse. You would allow the four of us women to control you, restrain you. We sorted that out and for each of you we found a way for that to be seriously fulfilling. And the eight of us decided it worked for us because there was absolutely no oppression involved.

Jard had to admit he had tried to keep them out but had been actually unable to do it.

Enita looked at Jard and then at Dornal and everyone laughed. She had initially refused point blank to be involved. Then when she thought the others were asleep she had whispered to Dornal that she wanted to try it with him and she had enjoyed it. Unfortunately for her, several of the others had actually been awake!

All right, Enita said. *We have pretty strong evidence that if you cannot shield your thoughts from us under a very strong incentive to do so, it is unlikely that in normal circumstances hiding will be possible. So let's take that idea on into this discussion about what was considered criminal behavior in our villages. Let's apply our experience together as telepaths to our future. What if we make certain that all children born into our society live in groups of eight in which they grow up and in which they learn? Let's make sure we include every living Olarian and do the catch-up necessary for this to work.*

Sure, some people will want or need to change their groups for pairing and child rearing. But they should always connect to another group where they make up the eight and the system would be reorganized around them. In essence we make certain that no member of our society, now or ever, is not intimately connected to a group of eight within which mutual responsibility is an absolute requirement. And, if every group of eight is itself connected to another group of eight, we will build strong networks for all. Would that not establish a structure that might give everyone real continued safety?

There was a lot of thought going into this proposal. It was an interesting, unusual, and yet very persuasive piece of logic. What they realized was that this was already a little complicated because of the time that had passed and the expanding numbers in their world who had not been involved. Ways had to be found to connect everyone up to this pattern if it was made to be an unvarying and inflexible requirement for the security of the society.

It seemed modifications and adjustments would be needed, but they would have as their outcome the guarantee that the society would not fall into the barbaric ways of the villages from which the Eight had all escaped. There was overwhelming support for the idea.

A twist on the plan came from Jard. It involved their growing understanding about how their brains worked. Also, if through Jard and Leiti's explorations there came to be genuine understanding of the mechanisms by which imbalances and dysfunctions were created, it was probable they would be able to rebalance brain energy. This seemed to open the door to realistic solutions, but that would be in the future, as their understanding of the billions of energy signals and patterns was as yet too primitive for them to fully manage everything.

There was agreement among the Eight and the discussion then pursued by the vast majority of the population led to complete agreement. Djia's group was given a clear and focused mandate for her task.

So Djia and Grah and their friends took up these discussions about how to renew and build their society. They began to make the arrangements that would form more of the foundations of their renewed society. She was excited at the extraordinary challenge involved in building a society where everyone was safe, always informed, and where support and encouragement and a good life belonged to all.

Until now, the Olarians had lived on very limited areas of the Olarian continent. However, they knew that there were three major continents on their world. One was sealed and occupied by the Cretians. The third continent was larger than Olaria, and Jard's exploratory energy journeys had shown a continent unoccupied by sentient life but rich in every kind of resource.

Substantive oceans separated the continents, and while they could telepathically travel there, as yet they had no means to physically do so. Djia knew that Jeland, by far the largest continent, would one day need to be inhabited by Olarians. Today it was just a dream as she and Grah sat, warm, in a tiny energy shelter they had constructed on the shores of the Great Southern Ocean. They were considering the challenge Jard, the Eight, and especially Enita had given them.

The waves of the Great Southern Ocean broke against the rocks to the west and rushed up the sandy shores to the east. Djia and Grah watched them breaking all along the shoreline to the next headland. Hundreds of miles away in Tall Trees Valley another set of discussions was underway, and like more than a thousand others, they were riveted, watching and listening to the Eight, now filled with energy in a way many had never seen before, fully engaged in the reconstruction of their world.

Jard was using his extraordinary ability in sorting energies to find structures they could use to make everything fit together. It was the model Djia was going to need for her part in the task. Jard was using the structure of their brains with its billions of neurons. He was using the ways these each connected to thousands of others, forming seemingly endlessly rearranging patterns. This was to be his model for the way their world would need to be organized for them all to be safe and optimally connected together. She knew he had it right. Endlessly interconnected networks forming patterns connected the learning that began in infancy through the many expanding operations of each task group.

She was already at work with his basic concept, and Grah and their little group had joined her. Their attention was divided between the discussions in the Big House and their plans to make their agreed responsibilities workable. Gelna's idea was getting wings.

To manage the task elements, they started by thinking their way from the biggest bites first: the extreme outer cosmos beyond their solar system, then their solar system, its planets and moons, their world and its outer atmosphere down to the surface, and this included weather, the surface seas and lands and the myriad tasks connected to it, the sub-surface all the way to the core. Separating the surface into seas, waters and land, then the myriad tasks associated with the Olarians, the plants and animals, food and the huge set of energy connections. And so it went on. All over their continent groups were being formed, connections established, and Djia and Grah and their group watched and followed them one at a time. In less than a month their group grew to nearly 64.

Their attention was pulled away to the discussion in the Big House.

Jard was speaking.

I am holding onto the idea that we might live to an extraordinary age. I can't think of forever. We eight were not raised in a world where that was a concept we could have believed in. So I think our lives may differ from everyone else.

We know that the idea of living forever, whatever that actually means, seems to be open to us, but our generation, which of course means only eight people, did not grow up preparing ourselves for such a gigantic task, and no-one before us is available to provide knowledge or advice, so it is up to us. We don't even know if our minds are developed in such a way that we can even plan ahead for such a reality. It is, at least for me, unthinkable. So perhaps I need to ask how any of you are able to think constructively about our future.

People looked at Jard and at one another. The snow continued to fall, and from the children's space the sound of games being played could be heard.

Finally everyone was looking at Jard, slowly shaking their heads. It was an idea but no-one really had any reference points for it. A year, a decade, you could think about. Forever seemed too big a step.

Jard sat back and felt his way through the minds of the entire group. No-one ever tried to disturb his journey into their thoughts and feelings, the surface and the deeper, more subtle things. Jard had never harmed any member of his community, was trusted absolutely by even the youngest child. He wanted everybody to think deeply about how they were going to live their lives. They needed to be conscious of the implications of living until, perhaps, some would choose to cease living. He wanted everyone to think about what might be a way to feel stimulated and energized every day of their lives, which could possibly mean forever.

Dornal said, *I can't think about this. My mind simply cannot find a way to stretch to so vast an idea. You all know I have never been able to do this. I can really only live for now and plan for a short while ahead. But I do understand the need to do what you are saying.*

He looked at Pron, and Pron nodded.

I don't think it is unwillingness, Jard, Pron said, *it's just, we don't know how to stay with an idea that is so large and complex. It's not the way we are.*

Karina looked at Enita and their men. *I think,* she said, *we are going to need to find some different ways for each of us to be involved with this new world we are creating. We've made several pretty big shifts since we came together. I think this step will be bigger than even the Cretians, and I think of that as our biggest challenge, although not the most difficult, so far.*

She slid into silence, feeling her way around the group. Everyone was looking at them and the atmosphere felt somehow wrong.

Daria and Repin looked at one another.

Our world is expanding faster than we could have imagined, Daria said.

None of us could have begun to imagine what we have created here, mainly because of you, Jard. The horizons of our children are beyond what we, even as adults, could imagine. Do we still have a place in it? And if so how will each of us be a real contributor? You, Jard, will almost certainly be the most important link to every energy source we ever find. You were born with capabilities even you were unable to imagine. You will, because of this, we believe, eventually lead us out into the universe and off this planet of ours.

We have begun to imagine that we will in time become travelers to places more distant than anything about which we can now imagine. But the rest of us, we need to be happy with lesser abilities. The idea of using our group as a council, a reference source, an over-arching body for everyone, is perhaps a good idea, at least for a start. But we know that some of our children's children are even now more powerful and talented than some of us. It is just the way it is.

A quiet had spread over the Big House; these were not encouraging words. They spoke of a usefulness smaller than any could relish.

Leiti again said the unthinkable. *Are you suggesting we should die or perhaps take a quiet place as oldies?*

It was probably not the most encouraging thing they could have heard, but it needed to be said or asked.

I can hardly believe what I am hearing, Jard said. *We eight have dealt with a murderous society intent on killing, damaging and raping. We defeated them forever and sealed their land from access to us. We erased the remaining threat to our survival here among our own people. I know we do not feel very good about this, but we did our best and will no doubt find there is a price for our choice, one we cannot yet see.*

We have seemingly solved the problem of prolonging life for an unknown length of time. We have achieved things for our society that have never been achieved before. We have created a race that will survive. We have built a working society from our abysmal ignorance. We have learned about ourselves and managed ourselves without significant or lasting conflict for more than 100 years.

How can any of you think of yourselves as anything short of incredible? We are, at least for now, capable of caring for our developing society, at least as well as any other living one of our descendants. If, and/or when, the time comes for us to move away from our role as leaders of our society, we only need to make sure they know they are entitled to ask us to do so. However, I hope we have helped them get so good an education in values we have represented and they will help us find useful ways to use our abilities as we go on.

He stopped and from everywhere around their world a warm and satisfying affirmation reached them.

Please notice I did not say forever or eternity. These are immensely difficult ideas to hold onto for very long. One day you are mortal with a sense of the nature of the journey of your life; the next apparently immortal, with no idea whether there are transitions or what they might be. There are a certain number of practical things you must do to live. But then what? Do you just keep doing the same things?

It seemed unlikely to Jard this would work for long.

There will arise the question of population. How many people ought to be born and should we even feel we have the right to attempt to control this? Probably this is a decision in which everyone who wishes needs to participate.

He continued.

Without some renewal of the community how could the next species anomaly occur? We need to set signposts for how children ought to be raised and educated. We know what an energy telepath needs to do to learn new stuff. There are no end of questions but few answers.

Jard clearly wanted the group to think intensely about their society's lives, its future, how everyone could and would be together, bringing up their children and managing their affairs.

There was no disagreement.

That was the journey they would continue for the next three winters.

I hope, he said, *this activity will always be a critical activity of our telepathic community.*

His concern was that everyone in the entire society knew and understood what really decent behavior involved and never needed to engage in something else in order to feel satisfied.

This seemed a huge expectation. He knew it, and so did the others. He believed, for example, had they had the right values in place, they would have found an alternative solution to the genocide that haunted him intermittently. However, he was also aware that this very failure of judgment, on his part at least, was causing him to be more thorough and careful in his current decisions. He was learning to recognize that with every down there was an up. Learning to ride these seemed to be a critical element of life.

So he argued, with himself and others who were following him, making mistakes was a critically important aspect of learning. He knew they needed to be real mistakes in judgment, have real consequences, and yet be able to be managed without catastrophic effect.

This shared experience of the Eight, even as they thought it through and spoke, was being carefully unwound and built into the education system. It grew through projects and processes that teachers would be required to not only understand but to make into real experience, a part of the development of every child. A bit tricky to organize but it would be effective and they hoped successful. Indulging in failure was not an alternative.

The Eight were perhaps more deeply concerned with the education of their children and the teachers of their children than any other aspect of their society. This concern was rooted in a deep understanding of what had been present and missing for themselves in their early village life and when they had begun their life together.

So teachers had to understand specifically what a value represented in actual behavior and how to learn the bad and the good versions of it. This meant them being involved initially in every family with no sense of intrusion.

Having children put at risk, so they learned what risks were and what consequences were, had to be about real day-to-day activities. They could not be simulated or synthetic. However, they needed to design a process that would not actually risk the lives of their children as they learned. This would prove a very complex challenge. Every time they explored this with one group and worked it through, the Knowledge Holders picked up the data and others could then get engaged in the learning, and slowly the system developed.

The inevitable unpleasantness involved in this kind of learning came slowly to be understood and respected and could be resolved by comprehensive debriefs when each experience was over. In the beginning they were lucky no one was killed or damaged irreparably and no child was harmed in ways they could not redeem.

Some of the most powerful lessons were constructed around the central values of the system The core were based on the concept of never doing harm. The Eight realized that everyone – every child and teacher – needed to feel love for someone or something, needed to give and get it, and had to make sure real opportunities to have children experience being with and without it really happened. They learned that these lessons could not be implemented by people who did not understand or genuinely grasp the love and the not-love polarities.

This took many years and many near disasters to perfect. They learned how to train the adults who willingly took on these roles and found they needed to be developed through their experiences in working in the system. Real tasks meant creating situations where children actually felt abandoned and without direction, but were, to the maximum degree possible, nevertheless safe. There could be no cowardly evasions or avoidances if the society was to grow genuinely strong and healthy.

Every participant in child development was required to achieve a sense of what to do. They had to have real experience, even of pain, but without destructive consequences. It was certain these experiences had to be built into the learning system. Avoiding the discomfort was cowardly, costly and unmanageably destructive.

The most powerful message to give teachers and get them to give children was the message of hope. Everyone had to learn that no matter what their situation, there was always hope. There was always something to look forward to. Finding the range of things that could be included under this rubric was a great challenge. Enita helped everyone understand how important this had been for her.

So, finally, the education process was being thoroughly thrashed out in the living situations with children, and the process of building into it honesty and integrity was less difficult than the Eight and their helpers had imagined. In the end, every basic value, every rock-solid principle, could be learned and built into the process of producing a society that could manage itself with no harm to its fundamental core: its people.

◘

Of the Eight, only Jard and Leiti lived beyond the first thousand years. They lived to see changes so enormous and of such vast consequence they were sad not to have the other six with them. However, Repin and Daria chose to end their lives at 830 years, feeling they no longer wanted to adjust to the rate of change and complexity in the world around them. They were not keen to have any more children and were essentially weary of life. Pron and Dornal, with Enita and Karina, chose to depart together in their eight hundred and fortieth year. Their reasons were not dissimilar to those of Daria and Repin, they said.

We feel we have lived a good and productive life. When we agreed to the extension of our lives it seemed the right thing to do. It gave our little community unprecedented opportunities to survive and thrive. We have achieved a lot, but now we feel that it is time to leave our new world to others and future generations. So we have decided to say goodbye. Everything we have learned is now stored in our Knowledge Holder Group and that means we will always be with you. And we want to say to you Jard, 'incredibly well done'. The idea of building the structures of our minds into the operation of our lives we still find astounding.

It was a sad time, especially for Jard and Leiti who did not feel that way, and it left them as the last of the Original Eight. But they were parents to many children and their descendants. During this entire period only 2000 Olarians chose to not have their lives made fixed when they turned 38 and wished the society around them to watch their aging and learn from it. Another 52,000 either chose an early death or died before their six hundredth year due to the life-prolonging process not working effectively for them or to a state of mind that was not conducive to their continued harmonious existence.

The records tell that less than 10 of those were in any way unhappy about the outcome for them. No records after the year 200 in the telepathic calendar have been lost to this day thanks to the work of Jard and Leiti, and to Djia and her group, and the incredible sacrifices of the original Knowledge Holder groups.

One of the environment groups calculated that for the size of the planet, and for the two continents on which they now lived and the resources available to them, one billion Olarians was about the comfortable limit for the planet and that number would be reached about the year 4000, before which there would need to be a major discussion about the future of births and deaths. No-one had ever even raised the issue of the Cretians, how many there might be, or what consequence that may have on anything.

Every 50 years a meeting occurred, but they were so formal and ritualized they provided none of the information that might have been shared. Initially, the guilt from the Olarian hosts prevented any meaningful interactions.

When Jard and Leiti were 1250 years old they gave birth to a daughter they called Olaria. She was only the second child in their history with a genetic anomaly. It would take more than 200 years before the nature of the anomaly and its consequences for the telepathic world would become clear.

What characteristics would determine the possible or optimum life of an Olarian telepath were not yet known. When Olaria reached 200 years of age, Jard and Leiti informed the Olarian world that they felt their time had come. They wanted their world to know they had been born into a time-limited world. They were reasonably certain, from the experience of their lives, that for their generation eternity was probably not a feasible option, certainly not for them, and they wanted to die in their version of a time-limited world!

Managing the transition of time had indeed taken its toll on their personal resources and the loss of the rest of their friends had never really been resolved for them. So they informed their world on their thirteen hundred and fiftieth year they were planning to die in 30 years. Jard and

Leiti wanted to finish their journey with an adventure that connected them to their original village in an ironic way. They wanted to renew themselves before they left and together they had a plan.

Leiti said to Jard, *You can have anything at all you want of me for our last time together. What is it you would absolutely most like?*

Many of their friends and children were listening to this most intimate and personal conversation, a phenomenon with which they were now completely at ease.

Leiti, I remember how you were when we met, and the most amazing gift you could give to me would be to take your age back to 17 and stay at that age until we are ready to leave. Is that a possibility for you?

The smile on her face told how all right that was and delight flowed from her. She was ecstatic. A gift she could give him that would also fulfill her. She looked at him, so filled with life and desire. She crawled up into his arms and whispered in his ear.

My turn?

Of course, anything.

I want you to allow your age to climb to 70, maintaining your perfect health as we have always been able to do, and become the elderly powerful and beautiful man that I know you are. Nothing will be so magnificent a turn-on for me as to see the powerful mature man you are.

She looked at him, imagining him and feeling the pleasure he poured over her. And so it was agreed. They would play their game with time, sex and love until they were ready to leave.

From around their world there were innumerable gasps and wide-eyed looks of amazement and a multitude of deep curiosities, but delight that their plan would give everyone at least some more years with them and the pleasure of their mutual adventure. No-one could imagine where such a journey might lead, least of all Olaria, their latest and their last daughter.

Jard chose to allow his age to progress to 70 and Leiti allowed her life to return to 17. They had the most amazing and satisfying time as they continued doing their usual routines but now built within their wonderful game of make believe. It was exciting, and in plain sight of the entire Olarian world they played it out to the end without a single regret. When their birthdays had brought Jard to his seventieth year they said goodbye to their world and stopped their hearts beating.

A sadness so deep it could never be truly expressed descended over the thousands of their descendants. Their memories were now safe for future generations and on their final day they said their goodbyes and with Olaria and her many brothers and sisters and their children and the entire Olarian world in tears, they died. No funeral in the history of their world was quite like it.

Postscript

Fifteen hundred years after Jard and Leiti's death, a small object was observed entering their solar system. Olaria and her son Jald went to explore it. It seemed not to be sentient, to contain no sentient life and to be either unable or unwilling to communicate with them.

It was scanning on multiple wavelengths each of the planets in their solar system. When it turned its attention to Olar, Olaria blocked its ability to see their dwellings and any animal lifeforms on their planet. Numerous attempts were made to communicate with it but none was successful. Olaria and her son agreed it must necessarily have been constructed by a sophisticated and sentient species and so, as it was clearly searching for something, they would probably one day meet its creators.

THE END

Acknowledgments

Thank you to my wife, partner, lover over many decades, Madeleine, who has tolerated thousands of hours of me vanishing into my study to sit in front of a computer.

Second is to the nearly two thousand participants in my workshops and participants in individual and group therapy sessions who helped hone my skills and build many lasting and satisfying relationships.

Finally but not least, Kayla my Schnoodle who sat patiently under my desk waiting to be taken on her walk.

About the Author

Phill was born in Melbourne, Australia. He graduated in Social Work and Psychology from Melbourne University where he completed an honors MA. He began his working life as a Social Worker and Psychotherapist and ended as an Executive Educator at Melbourne Business School.

Phill has worked in solving problems and building better relationships with groups of workers on the shop floor to Senior Executive teams in multi-national corporations and in Commonwealth and State Government. During all those years he had also worked as a psychotherapist helping individuals, couples and groups to manage crises in their lives.

After finishing this career he decided to become an author and he wrote *The New Mind Travelers*, which sits on the margins of the Science Fiction and Fantasy and the Speculative Fiction genre, from which standpoint he believes he is better able to explore marginally unthinkable issues.

This deliciously fulfilling work is an interesting example of Utopian speculative fiction. After fourteen years he is delighted to have finished this fascinating story, which actually utilizes skills and knowledge built up over 50 years. He is confident readers from many walks of life will find this book deeply satisfying and thought-provoking, but especially an interesting story.

He now lives in Central Victoria with his wife.

CPSIA information can be obtained
at www.ICGtesting.com
Printed in the USA
LVHW030452061222
734629LV00006B/70

9 780648 942030